SPAR
BOOK ONE OF '

In a realm of fantasy a tale of dark dramatics unfolds

At the height of the reign of the Sect of Seven, a prophecy was brought forth that depicted an end to the way of life as people knew it – a land destined to be ruled by darkness. In their arrogance it was laughed at, cast aside, and soon forgotten.

Now, generations have passed since it was thought that the Nyte-Fyre prophecy had been laid to rest, but signs point to its resurgence. Destiny refuses to be manipulated.

Against all odds, the fate of Izandüre will fall to rest in the hands of two mismatched teenagers...

Fura: A girl who's played with fire all her life until it destroys the only home she's ever known. Thrown head first into a land she never knew existed, she must find the strength in herself to rekindle that fire and pull from the stories she grew up with that she never once dreamt were real in order to make sense of the devastation.

Kiyani: A self-exiled rebel who's resolved to living life in the shadows. Emerging into the light, he must dig deep within to realize that no matter how dark of a past may haunt you, there's always a future.

Brought together by fate, it's up to the two of them to put aside their differences and work together to restore Izandüre back to its glory. Will it be a new beginning or a brutal end?

Like the phoenix, she must pick up the pieces of her life and rise from the ashes.

Like the wolf, he must put aside his solitary ways and learn to lead the pack.

Nyte-Fyre Prophecy
Sparks and Shadows

KENDRICK VON SCHILLER

2nd Edition

ISBN: 1517182999
ISBN-13: 978-1517182991

DEDICATION

Being a writer is a long, lonely road of never-ending self-doubt and denial, but the shimmering light at the end of the tunnel makes it all worth it in the end. Riches and fame don't always await, but that glowing feeling of accomplishment is worth so much more. To look back at what you've done and to truly feel proud of yourself. That's what it means to be an author.

That being said, I would like to send a huge thanks to everyone that has encouraged me and stood by my side along the way. However, the biggest thanks are reserved for my parents, who gave me the freedom to chase an unconventional dream.

I would also like to recognize the musical genius of artists:

- Nox Arcana, Midnight Syndicate, Adrian von Ziegler, Peter Gundry, BrunuhVille, Wardruna, and so many more for continually providing the insanely great instrumental music that has become the soundtrack to my long writing days over the years. Dark and eerie, your music has not only allowed me to tune out reality as I dive into writing, it's also given me great inspiration at times when I couldn't quite figure out where the story was going.

And, also to Faun and Loreena McKennitt – though not instrumental – for always providing the musical pick me up needed when I've found myself in a writing slump. There hasn't been a dark mood yet that your music hasn't been able to fix.

Each one of you has proven, time and time again, that there truly is magic in this world, if only we take the time to acknowledge it.

For Stacy McClellan

CONTENTS

IZANDÜRE

N

W   E

S

Durmacial Mountains

ICE FLATS

RUZINMARE
PLAINS

Schizan

Numorez
Basin

Fae Rue
Keep

Drätin
Mts

Frieland

VERBOTEN
FOREST

Avantguard

PROLOGUE

September

Flashes of putrid green light slithered across the darkening evening sky in a demonic haze. Rising in theatrical tendrils, plumes of thick gray smoke wove its way throughout the cloud cover, staining the sky and the moon with the sickening colors.

Down below, the small, water-locked town of Augden lie in ruin.

Covered in a dense fog of blinding ash, the misty dust swirled among the ghastly wooden skeletons of what had once been homes and shops. Misshapen chunks of stone lay strewn across the cobbled streets for miles as if a bomb had been dropped on the generally quiet square. Flames the color of a rotten lime ate away voraciously at the splintered wood and crooked beams that stood askew in the wreckage.

It looked like a post-apocalyptic scene of war.

On the hazardous streets, littered with twisted metal, uprooted trees, and crushed rock, people rushed about like ants frantically trying to find their way through a collapsed hill. There was no order as they broke off into groups. A number of individuals simply ran, only looking for a way out of the green-stained hell they had been so rudely awoken to in the depth of the night. Meanwhile, a few of the brave and adrenaline-filled took up temporary positions of leadership. Working as teams, they dug through the rubble where the fires had fizzled out to a mere smolder. Some searched for survivors, others possessions lost. And in the strange light a few stood by themselves, their eyes glassy as if lost in another world as they watched their homes, their lives, turn to ash, knowing that once it drifted away on the breeze there would truly be nothing left.

The noise of chaos drifted through the town. Moans from those trapped beneath rubble mixed with the anguished wails of those who lay draped over the bodies of the unmoving, all fighting to be heard.

But it was the thunderous roar of the flames that overtook everything else as it rose higher and higher, engulfing the entire town in its ravaging, insatiable hunger. Like the rise of the sun brightening the day, its deafening maw only seemed to grow with each new piece of kindling it devoured.

1

Separated from the pandemonium, a heavily hooded figure stood on the edges of the surrounding forest. Situated high on a cliff that overlooked the town, it provided a perfect view of Augden's destruction. The folds of the long, dark fabric that made up his clothing trailed around him like broken wings in the breeze, giving him a wraith-like appearance. Unaffected by the morbidity of the scene below, he fed off the frenzied screams and howls wrought from the victims that had lost everything. The only thing visible in the deep cowl of the cloak he wore like a dark emblem was a twisted grin.

Even if he couldn't be heard over the commotion, the man shouted into the night with all his strength. "Let that remind you," he cackled maniacally, his arms rising to the sky as if framing it like some sick picture, "to never forget the past!"

TWENTY YEARS LATER

1

♦♦◇♦♦

THE MAGIC IN MYTH

Fate is a double-edged sword: casting us the most glorious of destinies or driving us to the lowest edges of the earth.

Yet, even if the mischievous woman of fate herself deals you the worst hand in the deck, one always has the ability to turn it around. It is all in how you play the cards.

Even those with the most dire of futures can make a name for themselves.

The woman at the front of the room smiled as she spoke with bravado, flourishing each and every word as she carefully read them from the page that sat open on her lap.

Running her hand across the gilded binding of the old tattered book, Miss Mayvel Surrei knew she didn't even need to glance at the print to tell the tale. It was one of her favorite stories, one that she could remember hearing in her own school days when she had been a mere child, and one that she knew by heart, deeply ingrained into her brain and the very fiber of her being.

"It was in this mindset that the fabled Sect of Seven came to power," she continued. "In a far away land, full of mystery and magic, seven individuals were elevated to a king-like status by an ancient and powerful council. But, this was no ordinary line of command. Chosen for their hearts, these seven were plucked from the citizens of the land, not much different than you and I, and granted great power for the promise that they would use these magics to make the land that had fallen into disarray at the hand of greedy kings a better place.

"Each of these seven were proclaimed a Lord of One and were brought to power by an ancient magic long since lost.

"In the statute it was deemed that there would be one Lord for one area, one minority – many of them echoing the natural elements they held so dearly. These individuals both complemented one another and served as a contrast, each of them created to remind the others of what had already transpired and what could be. If they moved forward in planned harmony, all would be well and the prosperity of the land would continue into eternity."

"How many times do we have to hear this load of crap?" a young boy suddenly shouted from the back of the small classroom, disrupting his teacher's intricate tale.

Miss Surrei peered up through the fringe of her mousy brown, side-swept bangs to the back of the classroom where she knew the challenge had originated. Slouched back in his seat, with arms crossed over his chest, sat the offender. The deep scowl that was etched in the set of his mouth told her the last thing he wanted was to be here.

"It's curriculum," the teacher reminded him.

"We already know it," the same boy shot back snottily, the glare of his eyes stealing through the shock of blond hair that fell over his face.

"Do you?" the teacher challenged.

"Like the back of my hand. Doesn't mean I believe it."

The teacher sighed. It felt like only yesterday that her role had been reversed and she had been the one on the opposite side of the room, sitting in the uncomfortable desk, hardly caring as she had been wide-eyed and immobilized, listening to her own teacher tell the tale of the Sect of Seven.

That feeling alone had been one of the reasons she had pursued teaching as her own career – wanting to be able to give children that spark of imagination to sweep them away with her into other worlds. Worlds of high fantasy where magic and heroics truly existed. Only now there was no amazement, no glitter in the eyes of the children as she swept her gaze across the classroom. The fifteen students were noticeably fidgety, itching to leave as they waited for the final bell of the day to release them from the stuffy room.

It was a sad realization as Miss Surrei knew that what they were craving wouldn't be found in the letters of a story scrawled across a page, but the mindless static of technology. The minute they left this room they would undeniably be pulling cell phones out of their bags and rushing home to the computer.

It was true that the Sect of Seven was nothing more than a fantastical fairy tale – even Miss Surrei couldn't deny that – but what was wrong with letting yourself believe in something magical, if only for a moment?

"So?" the boy cut in, taking the lengthening silence as contemplation, as her defeat. "Are we done?"

The words were rude and biting and Miss Surrei had to fight not to flinch at his tone. The crudeness of some of the kids nowadays was something she would never get used to. "Not so fast," she spoke firmly, reaffirming her authority over the room full of kids half her age. "Whether you think you know this or not there will still be a test on it come Monday. Now, if you just let me go over the basics we can call it a day." Miss Surrei took in a breath, peering across the room again. The spell of magic she had been under when she had started reading the book's fancifully illustrated pages was now long gone. It was the teacher in her that kept her moving ahead, dredging forward in what was becoming another tiring day. "So," she tried again, plastering a smile on her face, "who can name me one of the seven Lords?"

"The Shadowlord," the same boy who had been taunting her all class period smirked.

Miss Surrei had to fight a sigh of contempt. "Yes, but let's not start with the darkest of the subjects. Who can name me another?"

"The Firelord?" a girl from the front of the class piped up, so timidly that it came across as a question rather than an answer.

"Thank you, Katie," Miss Surrei smiled. This time it was genuine. "The Firelord, or the light-bringer, is what some may say is the polar opposite of the aforementioned Shadowlord. It was the job of this lord to keep the spirits of the people up, and to keep a light burning in the darkest of times. Living in a grand volcano, it might have been light that this Lord provided, but it was the dancing fires that were always close to his heart."

"Impossible," another boy challenged. "You can't live in a volcano. You'd be fried!"

Miss Surrei shook her head at the interruption, but continued forward without being drawn off track. "Overall, the Firelord was created as a sign of hope to all the people of the land that, even in the darkest of times, there would always be a light to guide them.

"Now, the Shadowlord, also morbidly known as the death-bringer, was just that. Probably the least sought after title of the seven individuals, he was, quite literally, a servant of the shadows. Living in the darkness, it was this Lord's job not only to ferry the dead to the other side but also to remind everyone that nothing, no matter how good it may have been, could last forever. The Shadowlord was never the friendliest nor the happiest person and probably the most susceptible to corruption."

When the teacher let the last sentence fall into remiss she was surprised to find the smallest glimmer of interest from the students present in their faces. No matter what year it was, it always seemed to be the Shadowlord that they all found the most intriguing. Somehow, that worried her.

"Come now," Miss Surrei pushed forward, glancing at the clock on the wall as it ticked down the last minutes of the class. "Who can name me another?" At least they were finally on track, if only by doing mere footnotes of the full subject.

A hand shot up and was followed by another answer. "The Earthlord!"

"Very good. The Earthlord, or the provider, was given the task of keeping the citizens well provisioned without stripping nature to its very husk, and it was no easy feat. As we all know, life and death is a very delicate balance. There were limitations, of course, but the Earthlord was called upon to keep the forests thriving, the wildlife abundant and happy, and the crops of the towns plentiful. If it was green and of the plant variety, it was in this Lord's nature to enact his skill-set to keep that balance of life in working order."

Miss Surrei took a pause, hoping that the children were retaining some of this information. "Can someone please tell me the name of a fourth Lord?"

"The Skylord."

"Absolutely! The Skylord was also known as the watcher, and it is fabled that he lived high among the clouds. It was his sole duty to keep a watchful eye over the land, and was often the first to alert the other six of the Sect to dangers and discrepancies that needed to be taken care of immediately."

"Couldn't he control the weather, too?" a girl piped up suddenly.

"No one knows for sure," Miss Surrei corrected, "but it's not to be completely ruled out. It has been said that he could call upon the wind, at least, to help in his duties."

By now, despite their inherent lack of interest in the subject of the mythical Sect of Seven, the classroom had awakened from its previous dormant silence and had erupted into a frenzy of hushed whispers.

The teacher only hoped that those words directed into one another's ears at such a low frequency she couldn't make them out were at least on topic. Clapping her hands, she did her best to quiet them down and regain their attention. "We're not done yet. Come now, give me another."

A student raised his hand. "The Waterlord."

Miss Surrei nodded in approval, not only of the boy's answer, but of the respect he had shown by that one small act. "The Waterlord," she repeated loudly over the rising voices. "Also known as the healer. What the kings those of the Sect were replacing had left behind was a land of darkness and disease. Now, it was his affiliation with water that this Lord was best known for, but he was also highly trained and skilled in the arts of healing."

"Could he heal those who were dying?" another student spouted from her desk.

"Just like all the Lords, there were limitations," the teacher softly reminded her.

The boy sitting in front of the girl turned around. "That would be the Shadowlord!"

"No, he would *raise* the dead!" someone else argued.

And just like that, things had gotten out of hand yet again. "Children!" Miss Surrei called out as she rubbed her temple with a petite hand. "Focus. We're nearly done. And this may be fantasy, but the dead stay dead. Now, come on, come on. Keep going!"

"The Icelord," the same timid girl who had given the first answer tried again.

"Thank you again, Katie." It was good to know that at least someone was at least halfway paying attention in the chaotic mess that was the sixth grade literature class. "The Icelord was also known as the purifier. Some may stake the claim that water and ice are actually the same element, only in different form. However, that makes no difference here. This is not science, so that discrepancy doesn't apply. Now, with the destruction of the caste system of the kings, many corrupted minds and factions were left in the wake. It was the Icelord's job to rid the land of these deceitful people and also to counteract the dark magics that stained the land."

Just as she was thinking it, the metallic ring of the bell echoed throughout the room and what little attention she had been able to grab from her students vanished. As if they had all been merely sitting there staring out the window, rather than deep in discussion, a flurry of bodies raced towards the door.

"Remember!" Miss Surrei shouted above the raucous hum of the hustle. "Read the chapters I assigned. You'll be tested on this whether you're interested in it or not!"

There was no indication that any of the students had heard her as the last long-limbed pre-teen slipped out into the hallway and raced towards the freedom of the outdoors. Sighing, the teacher discarded her daily façade of importance and let her posture slump. Still resting on the desk edge she closed her eyes and ran a tired hand over her face.

It was days such as this that she found herself questioning why she did what she did.

"And the Starlord," a definitively female voice continued faintly, though it was thunderous in the now empty room. "Who was not always affectionately known as the destiny keeper. As much as the Sect of Seven was created to be equals, it was clear that the Starlord had powers that reigned above the others. Awarded a home amongst an ebony backdrop, riddled with stars, the Starlord was assigned the most delicate and fatal of roles. Creator and controller of the destinies of all those on the planet, the Starlord was given the power of life and all the happenings in it."

"It's good to know that someone has listened over the years."

"I still believe," the voice came back, reassuring.

Miss Surrei raised her head and peered towards the doorway where the young voice had permeated her momentary silence. In the empty arch stood a familiar face. At seventeen the girl had long outgrown her sixth grade class and was on her way to graduating soon, but she had never stopped visiting with her former teacher.

"How are you, Fura?" Miss Surrei asked.

"Not nearly as frazzled as you look," the girl replied affectionately.

"If only every student was like you," Miss Surrei claimed as she studied the exuberant red-haired girl. She was no longer that gawky little girl that Mayvel remembered teaching, but fortunately she hadn't yet lost sight of the creative imagination that had graced her papers, and that Miss Surrei had begun to look forward to grading. "So, what brings you to my classroom after the bell?"

Fura walked across the room in a few steps, pulling a packet of papers from her shoulder bag. "Mr. Reskin wanted me to give you these."

Holding out her hand, the teacher reluctantly took the stack, knowing that it would only mean more work for her in a time when she just wanted to go home and relax and forget about this day.

"Don't let it bother you, Miss Surrei," Fura said brightly, seeming to pick up on her former teacher's thoughts. "Remember: It's not about the hand you're dealt, but how you choose to play the cards."

"I don't believe that's quite how it's worded."

"No," Fura smiled, "but it still holds the same meaning. Don't give up just because you got a group of students this semester who refuse to let their imaginations run wild."

"Do you really believe?" Miss Surrei asked.

The girl turned to her, not seeming to expect the continued conversation. Instead of irritation though, she only smiled. "We've all got to believe in something, right? Besides, I'd love to meet one of the Lords one day. Wouldn't you?" she asked brightly.

The teacher couldn't help but smile at the girl's infectious spirit. "Maybe one day you will."

2
♦♦✧♦♦
DEATH AND DESTRUCTION

Kill. Destroy. Vengeance.

The chilling tendrils of fall drifted through the air, sending leaves skittering across the pavement. Their dry and crumpled forms glittered in the ever changing moonlight as tufts of cloud moved across the deepening night sky. The world was awash in the ghostly gray pallor of the half light, casting the surrounding houses on the street in an eerie incandescence when the quarter moon decided to make an appearance.

It was a gorgeous night, but one likely to be forgotten by those whose minds focused on the hustle and bustle of their everyday lives.

However, one man sought to change that. If he had any say in the matter, this picture perfect, pristine night would soon be turned upon its end, marking itself as a date that no one in the small town of Barandor would soon forget.

It had been far too long since anything extraordinary had rocked the town to its core, and back during that fateful year it had still been known by its original given name of Augden.

Kill. Destroy. Vengeance.

Those three small, but powerful, words echoed through the man's subconscious as he stood surveying the darkness in the deep shadows of a wiry old willow. He rested against the gnarled trunk, listening to the creaking of the boughs above, plotting and restructuring his plan. Even with those dangerous words in his mind, he was never one to go about things half-assed.

Dressed in layers of black, he hardly seemed to notice, or care, that his long robes were distinctly out of place in the middle of the suburbs that lay beyond Barandor's main square. The thought had never once crossed his disturbingly morbid mind.

Even if he had decided to take caution in his dress to avoid attracting unwanted attention, it hardly mattered. Despite the fact that his clothing camouflaged him almost seamlessly into the night, it was actually attention he craved.

However, the streets were dark and silent. The only life he had borne witness to within the last half hour had been the mangy alley cat that had darted down the road as if it were possessed. Here and there lights flicked on and off periodically in house windows, but no one ever came out, as if they stayed locked behind closed doors, feeling the dark chill of desperation that was soon to close in on them.

Paying little attention to any of this, the man's determined focus remained on one house and one house alone. Long strands of his jet black hair drifted across his face, his stony blue eyes set on the house directly across the street, the little green reflective sign on the mailbox bearing the numbers 1934.

Normally, it was a pleasant street to live on, but after tonight those living there would curse their address being on Wixley Road. It was only this particular address the man was interested in, but the rest of the street would go down with it, if only by association.

Before he set forth his plan, the man surreptitiously scanned the block, taking it all in before it was laid to waste. For those who hadn't lived there all their lives it was almost hard to imagine that the pristine, symmetrical lines of the homes and the neatly manicured lawns had once, not all that long ago, been the base of tragedy.

Twenty an odd year had passed since that horrific day. It had never been forgotten, but it was also never spoken of. Even if the name of the town had since changed, and nary a scar was left on the landscape, the man could remember it like it had only been yesterday, the outline of the fires tracing the skyline imprinted in his mind.

The famed Augden murders had been plastered across the front of newspapers for weeks, even months, following the fatal event. Numerous witnesses had come forth in the aftermath, claiming to have known who had done it, telling authorities that they had seen more than they should have. One man had even been tried and now sat in the prison of the neighboring town, waiting for the end of his falsified and condemned life.

But the fact was that no one knew the true extent of what had transpired that day; not of what had caused the explosions, or of whom the real culprit was. For all the citizens of the town knew, the case was solved and closed, leaving it as nothing more than a horrific image staining their memories. For local police, all the grisly details that had been collected that day still sat in the back of the filing cabinet in a folder marked *unsolved*.

The dark-haired man knew this, and so much more. The mere thought of it brought a wicked smile to his face, contorting the sharp features into something far more sinister than usual.

He had been waiting near the tree for some time now, surveying and planning. The creaking willow stood on the very edge of a yard that was a few days past prime mowing time. Being careful not to give himself away too early in the day, the man had waited until dusk to make his move into the town, and had chosen this yard for its view of his intended target. Not only that, but it boasted a pleasant lack of life, as if its owners were on vacation. The static silence of emptiness drifted through the air, a muted haze that he could detect on his tongue. It was just the way he liked it.

Peering at the dark navy sky, the man waited until the thickening clouds drifted across the waning moon, blocking its light before deciding to finally move forward.

Bordering on late evening, the lights of many of the houses had been extinguished long ago, the people inside going to sleep at early hours despite being a Friday night. However, the lights of the house he moved towards had only just gone out. It mattered very little to the man. He could care less if he was seen, but what he had been waiting for was not the intense cover of darkness to mute his deeds, but the right moment in time to enact his wrath.

Fog had only just begun to drift in among the streets, rolling in the dim haze of the streetlights, while a chorus of frogs and crickets could be heard, echoing from the moors nearby. The desolate eeriness of it made him feel alive. An owl called from the twisting branches overhead, and the man looked up in time to watch it spread its powerful wings and take off. As the light from the moon flickered through the clouds again he knew it was time.

Pushing off the gnarled trunk, he moved out into the street, exhilaration pulsing through each and every fiber of his body. It had been far too long since he had caused such mass destruction.

Not even bothering to check to make sure the street was clear, the man strolled across the road, the dark fires of destruction burning in his eyes. Rubbing his hands together as he walked, leather boots clicking on the pavement, a greenish glow steadily grew from his palms, illuminating his spindly fingers and the distinct hills of his face.

With every step closer, the man's heart raced faster, the beat of it drumming in his ears as he lost himself in the pre-doom silence.

This was it. This was what he had been waiting for for years. The start of something wonderful would follow his actions tonight. His prize was so close he could nearly taste the delicious victory of it all. The world would soon be in his hands to do as he saw fit.

Losing a fraction of his focus, the man paused in the middle of the grassy expanse of yard. Though he had made no noise, he could hear something from within the house. The indistinct whine of a dog carried through the window and into the yard. Claws frantically tapped at the glass, indicating that he had been noticed, not by the family themselves, nor any of their neighbors, but the loyal family pet.

Where most would have taken this as an invitation to flee, the man only stood rooted in the center of the yard, posed like some towering, demonic tree.

Even when a light popped on, creating a shadowed silhouette of a sleepy form stumbling through the house, the man refused to budge. This was his night and no one would stop him.

"Let them come," he whispered to himself, the words whistling eerily through his teeth. It was always more fun to watch the fear on the victim's faces anyways, he thought. Besides, why waste such a dramatic display? Fireworks were no fun if there was no one present to witness them.

Eyes narrowing, he watched the doorway of the house, letting the fiery glow dance within his quivering palms as he waited.

As if on cue, the bronze doorknob began to turn. Pulling inwards, a sliver of florescent light filtered through the crack and gradually grew larger as a small boy, the age of eight, stepped out onto the porch. A raggedy brown bear crushed in his tiny arms, he gazed across the yard, his eyes searching the darkness before falling on the figure in the grass.

"Mom!" the little boy shouted, clutching the stuffed toy to his chest. "There's a man in the yard!"

"Evan!" a woman's voice cried from inside.

Immediately, the child was joined in the doorway by the woman who pulled him back inside and put herself before him, as if she could protect him with just her frail body.

The man nearly laughed at her foolishness. If only they knew what they were dealing with. No human body, acting as a shield, could stop him.

Seeming to pick up on the frantic fear in her voice, the dog who had been at the window came tearing out of the open door, nearly knocking her and the child to the ground.

"BARRY!! NO!" the woman screamed.

Even though the golden retriever ignored her words, driven by the raging passion to protect, he never made his target. In one swift, fluid movement the stranger pulled a dagger from within his cloak and embedded it in the thick ruff of the dog's neck. Barry let out a gurgling whine before falling silent.

A shocked shriek emanated from the woman on the porch as she fell down to block the boy's eyes from the violent sight, trying to hush his anguished cries.

Wiping the blade on the grass, the man rose from his crouch.

"Who are you?" the woman called out.

Not 'why are you here?' or 'why are you doing this?' the man noted. It was an unusual question to ask in such a threatening situation, but just as entertaining to answer.

"Why are you here?" she spoke again when he didn't answer right away.

There it was.

There was a tremble in the woman's voice that betrayed her true feelings, and the man knew that if he could see her eyes they would be frantic and dewy-eyed. She would've been among the ones who pleaded for her life, if only she knew it was going to end so soon.

"Who are you?" she cried again, his silence frightening her further.

"Your darkest fears made manifest!" the man purred wickedly, his heavily accented voice ringing through the night.

No longer finding a need to draw things out any further, the man's face pulled into a delighted sneer as a surge of raw energy coursed through him, the green fires of his creation growing into a rage of full-fledged flames. Sweeping one hand over the other, he created a roiling ball of fire that trembled in his hands, pulsing as it waited to be let loose.

The woman's face paled in the light as she pushed her son behind her, screaming, "Get back in the house!"

Succumbing to the energy's will, the man threw the ball towards the house, watching as it sailed through the air in a dazzling display of what felt like slow motion, though was only a matter of seconds.

The door to the house slammed shut and the man could hear the metal clicking of locks trying to be put in place.

None of it mattered as the green fires overtook the house the moment they made contact. Unlike most normal fires, this one erupted in a grand explosion that rocked the very ground on which the man stood. The house collapsed in a pile of stone and wood, the fire quickly devouring all it could. The shockwave that followed after the fall echoed with a great boom that traveled straight through the town, shattering windows and setting off car alarms.

If he had been indiscreet before, there was no such thing now.

But even then, the dark-haired stranger took a fleeting moment to admire his work, feeling the stormy breeze rise around him as the ashes that floated in the air circled him in the wind. With a wicked smile of contentment adorning his face, he turned and walked away, his lithe form a mere silhouette as the putrid fires raged behind him.

3

♦♦◇♦♦

FIRES IN THE NIGHT

Fire burned in the night sky; shades of orange and hues of golden yellow illuminating the faces below. Dancing in their eyes was bewilderment and awe, fear and elation.

It was each and every one of these emotions that the young woman on stage fed off of as her copper hair dazzled, blending seamlessly with the dancing flames of the torches she twirled effortlessly through the star-speckled night. The raging torrent of colors captivated her audience as it left lasting streaks of firelight suspended in the darkness. Each dip, bow, and catch of the sticks extracted a chorus of *ooohs* and *ahhs* from the spectators.

Lithe, seventeen-year-old Fura Feuer barely heard any of it. No matter how many times she found herself on the stone stage of the Fireswell Renaissance Festival she ended up lost in the performance. There was nothing but her and the intimate dance with the flames – something that most would proclaim dangerous, but to her was just a part of her day. The fires may not have engulfed her physically, but it consumed her emotionally, her senses all but lost in the warm glow, her mind, body, and soul at one with its addictive energies.

She couldn't remember the first time she had found herself drawn to the warm comfort of it, more fascinated by it than she should have been, but Fura could distinctly remember the first time she had been to Fireswell. Barandor's annual renaissance festival had always intrigued her, but it hadn't been until she had turned thirteen that her parents had finally caved in and taken her and her younger brother. The food. The music. The people. It had all instantly sucked her in. But it had been one show, and one show alone that had truly called to her.

Led by a man with hair so red that it rivaled her own, and put on by the Firedancer's guild, *Pyropheric* had been one of the most crowded shows of the day. Even so, Fura had been able to weasel her way up front to a spot where she could see, and had been blown away as she had watched the performers move with the flames without a care in the world. They had made it all look so devastatingly easy, the fires approachable and friendly. As the last torch had fallen gracefully into the hands of the performers a tremendous rumble of applause had broken out, a sound that Fura had been able to feel deep within her bones. It had been in that moment that Fura had known what she wanted to do with her life.

Now, as she danced with the glowing sticks, it was hard to imagine herself back at that age. This was only the second year she had been allowed to perform center stage during the twilight hours, but Fura couldn't imagine doing anything else. Sending one of the torches twirling high into the air, Fura returned her thoughts to the present before she caught it on its return, earning another round of applause that was dappled with a few hoots and hollers for more.

To the side of the stage, Fura could see her two best friends, waiting in the wings. They had already completed their acts, but they stayed put, there to cheer her on. The gorgeously exotic Kieli, with her waist-length, sleek black hair, and shimmering blue eyes had always reminded her of a mermaid. And then there was Tiyano. Even with an age difference of nearly twenty years, he had always felt like an older brother to her. He had a family whom she had dined with often, knowing she was always welcome. Older and more experienced in everything, Tiyano was just a friendly face Fura knew would always be there for her. Where Kieli was the one to initiate troublesome schemes to find new fun, Tiyano had often times been the shoulder to lean on in tough times.

Tiyano was the one who had joked with her earlier that day that she had done great, nearly an hour before she had even taken the stage for the final show of the night.

"Set the stage on fire," he'd said, clapping her on the back before sending her before the audience. Though she couldn't even remember the origins of the phrase, it had soon become their pre-show motto, replacing the common place, "break a leg."

One more delicate twirl, followed by another high-toss, and the show was brought to a close almost as quickly as it had begun.

Bowing, an indication to the fans that the show was truly over, the people below burst into a frenzy of applause. A man from the back shouted for an encore and was joined by numerous others in the crowd. The attention, the fact that her showmanship was enough to make them ask for more, brought a smile to Fura's already beaming face. There was little more she could ask for in the world.

Where her bright red hair only elicited strange stares and some mild teasing at school, here it only made her fit in. Here, in Fireswell, she truly felt like she was someone.

Just as Fura took another bow, basking in the post-thrill of her performance, her racing heartbeat drowned in the applause, a sudden flash of light, the color of a lush field of grass, lit up the night. Thunder rolled in behind it, splitting the night and echoing off every surface before being absorbed by the surrounding trees. The vibration of it made the fine hair on Fura's arms stand on end.

Each and every set of eyes, Fura's included, turned to the source of the commotion. To the east of the festival's packed grounds, just past the main square of the town, putrid colors boiled in the sky. The sickness of it danced across the overcast moon, the clouds seeming to soak up the madness of it. Never before had she seen anything like it.

The raucous crowd fell abruptly into a full-blown silence that could rival that of a graveyard. All of a sudden the darkness of the night felt overpowering, as if it would suck them all under.

Slowly, one by one, frantic whispers began to blossom throughout the festival as people leaned into one another, asking questions that no one knew the answers to. Was it some practical joke? War? A grounds for concern?

The one thing that was clear was that something huge had just occurred, and more than likely, it wasn't good.

Fura dropped the still burning torch before she even realized it was still clutched in her hand as a wave of nausea overcame her. The smoky haze of exhilaration that generally clung to her for hours after shows had melted away in an instant, leaving only one thought left: her family was that way. Her home and her life were in the direction of whatever evil had just occurred. Before the torch could roll to a halt on the stone, Fura had bolted off the stage and had begun to push her way recklessly through the tightly packed mass of people.

All she knew was that she had to get home.

"Fura!"

The familiar sound of her name brought Fura momentarily out of her daze as she turned her head reflexively. Scrambling up and over the stage to avoid the crowd, Fura could see Kieli as she fought to make her way over.

"Fura!" the girl called again.

Fura could hear Kieli's voice from behind her, clear as day despite the sudden confusion, yet she didn't stop. The obvious worry in her friend's voice didn't even register to Fura as she hustled forward, trying to break free from the group of festival-goers. She had to get out of here. She had to make sure her family was okay. Her younger brother's birthday was the following day. They were going out for breakfast. They had a whole day of fun planned for him, weeks in the making. She had even asked Apallo, nearly a month ago, if she would be able to take a day off from the festival. Fura had to make sure that would happen.

It took her what felt like hours to break free of the crowd that moved towards the festival's gates like a herd of dazed cattle, all of them with the same thoughts running through their minds. Getting out and getting home had become the number one priority, where before they had all been lost in the fun of the festival, set in simpler times. Whatever this explosion was had rocked everyone back to reality.

Racing through the streets as quickly as her long legs would allow, Fura rounded the corner into Barandor's main square. Here it was easy to see that the explosion hadn't been a mere figment of her imagination as she might have hoped. The streets that normally lay dormant at this time of night were teeming with groups of people who had left the safety of the brick and mortar of homes and businesses. Forgoing the sidewalks, many of them stood on the streets that had been paved in cobblestone to give it an old, small-town feel. Tonight though, the last thing gaining people's attention was what was beneath their feet. Instead, everyone's eyes were trained towards the sky.

Fura ignored the colors that stained the ghostly clouds, glad for once that she wasn't the focus of attention. No one paid her any heed as she rushed through the main streets of town.

As she reached the edge of the business market, sirens wailed behind her, and Fura dove to the shoulder to make room for the ambulance that sped by, lights glaring in the darkness. Not daring to slow down for breath, Fura watched the fast-moving vehicle disappear out of sight as quickly as it had approached. The further she moved out of town, leaving the hum of voices in her wake, the darker it got as the street lights became sparse.

Never had Fura been afraid of what the dark might bring until tonight. The chill of the fall breeze, and the sounds on the air brought her a devastating worry that was incomparable to anything she had ever known. In the distance, where she instinctively knew her subdivision lay, Fura could hear the screaming chorus of more emergency vehicles as they converged at the scene. Ignoring her newfound fear, she raced forward, unaware that her friends were following her towards catastrophe.

✧⌘✧

Kieli sprinted through the dark streets of Barandor, past the main square and out onto the long, deserted road out to the subdivision where she knew her friend would be heading.

Fura had bolted off the stage and out of the festival gates before Kieli had even been able to fully process what had happened. Only when she had seen the red-headed girl rush through the crowd, almost immediately followed by Apallo, had Kieli come to the conclusion that the girl's house was in the direction of the green fires.

She hadn't been too far behind Apallo, but her long legs were aching and tired from the extended festival day and she had quickly fallen behind. Pausing in the middle of the street, staring down the dashed yellow line that divided the road that led to her destination, Kieli suddenly felt the static sensation of someone watching her. The feathery hairs on the back of her neck stood on end as she scanned the darkness. With the moon proving to be an inconsistent source of light, everything surrounding her played tricks, the shadows blending with the trees and creating strange shapes.

She didn't know what it was that made her look to the bluffs, but there, just barely highlighted by the green in the air, a dark figure stood, staring down at her.

Closing her eyes and taking a quick breath, Kieli opened them again. As if it had been an apparition or a figment of her imagination, whatever had been up there amongst the trees had moved on.

The moon broke free from the clouds, casting a gray sheen over the road, but her eyes were still trained on the now highlighted trees above. The forest-covered bluffs above towered over the city, careening downward in a sheer face of rock as it met the road below, just shy of being considered a cliff.

Kieli stood stone still, her eyes scanning the lines of the trees, hoping for one more glimpse of the figure, but it was gone.

In a way, she was almost disappointed that he hadn't stuck around longer. However, it wasn't fear that caused her heart to race, pumping her body full of adrenaline.

Things were finally changing around here, heading on a crash course to better things.

As a new wave of energy flowed through her, Kieli moved on towards the fires and to a friend that needed her. The faintest trace of a smile lingered on her face, barely visible in the darkness.

✧⌘✧

Fura felt like an extra dropped onto the set of a horror movie as she fell to her knees in what had once been her front yard.

As she had rounded the corner to her street it had been apparent that her whole life had changed.

Houses – those that had boasted friends and neighbors – had been leveled. Trees stood like phantoms in the fog and ash, fires clinging to their limbs, dancing in the night and taunting her.

What felt like hundreds of people crowded the littered street, a quarter of them in uniform, as they all tried to discern amongst themselves what had happened. It was obvious that this was no ordinary house fire.

The phrase "gas leak" echoed from multiple lips, but Fura could care less the cause of all this. All she knew, looking upon the house, her house, was that there was no way anyone inside could have survived.

4
◆◆◇◆◆
IN THE BLINK OF AN EYE

Everything – the sights, the sounds – were just too much for her, yet Fura couldn't make herself look away.

The whirring of the sirens seemed far away, and the flashing red lights of the emergency vehicles moved in slow motion, as if it were all some show she were watching on TV with the volume turned to mute. Though most of the fires had been contained, a number of them still burned on, slowly consuming what had been left of the houses after the initial explosion. Their green coloring blotted themselves permanently on the skyline, leaving Fura to wonder if she would ever see another color again in her lifetime.

It all had the feeling of a dream turned nightmare, but Fura knew it was all too real. The rapid beating of her heart pounded in her ears. She could feel the remnant heat from the charred remains of the street on her face, though the sheen of sweat that ran down her neck wasn't from that alone.

Hot tears trailed down her face as Fura thought about what she had lost. Hanging in the balance was both her childhood and her future. She knew she would have to figure out the latter and quick, but she couldn't force herself to look past the present.

Hastily wiping a sleeve across her face to soak up the moisture, Fura drug in a ragged breath and looked around. Her house wasn't the only one that lay scattered across the entire block, but it appeared to have received the worst of the blow. She caught sight of a few of her neighbors who, like her, hadn't been present at the time. None of them looked her way, and the one that did turned his head immediately as if she were the one to blame.

Just as she could feel her shaking knees begin to give way beneath her, Fura was startled by a hand that fell upon her shoulder. Fighting the urge to slap it away, as if whatever had caused this mess had returned to claim one last victim, she turned to find Apallo staring back at her. Worry was stamped across his face, all the more apparent in the hollowness in the brown depth of his eyes.

Fura had heard his shouts as she had raced through the festival, but she hadn't been aware that he had opted to follow her all the way out here. She would have expected him to stay within Fireswell, helping direct the fans back home, his leadership skills kicking in as they usually did in times of need. The fact that he had followed her all this way made Fura wonder if she looked like that desperate of a mess. Not wanting him to witness her imminent breakdown, she turned away.

For as long as she had worked in the festival, Fura had taken the initiative to always appear strong, for fear that Apallo would see her unfit for the life and bid her go home. Numerous times she had mildly injured herself with the torches, receiving small scrapes, bruises, and burns, but never had she allowed herself to cry. Never had she broken down before her second family. Not when she thought she was going to fail a class in school. Not when she had been picked on ruthlessly by her classmates. Not even when her first pet, a hamster named Frank, had died.

After all that time, Fura hated to finally succumb to the misery, but it no longer mattered as she fell into Apallo's arms, her eyes closed as she buried her face in the well-worn fabric of the maroon tunic he wore on stage. His arms wrapped around her protectively as he whispered words to her that she couldn't hear over the raging emotions in her head.

A few words, along the lines of 'everything will be okay,' filtered through the space between her and Apallo, but Fura ignored them, knowing there was no truth in them. How could there be? Everything that she had ever known now lay in a pile of ash before her as strangers sifted through it, hoping to find anything left. The emergency workers couldn't know how much she wished they would find something, anything, but she could see from the grim set of their faces that that was too high of a hope.

The only thing that really registered was the burning flames. Though the fires were the wrong color, they were still just that – fires. Staring at the flickering columns of light, Fura felt herself go completely numb. Even though she knew there was something else at work here, all she could think was that the one thing she had loved all her life had turned around and betrayed her. If she never saw another glimmer of flame in her life, it would be all too soon.

A large yellow hose attached to a fire truck snaked across the yard, spraying water on the rubble as the men tried to douse the flames. The breeze caught the spray, sending a fine mist through the air, causing Fura to shiver.

"Fura?" a voice cautiously sputtered. "Are you okay?"

Pulling away from Apallo, Fura once again wiped the stream of tears from her face, red from the embarrassment of showing such sordid emotions in front of him. Bashfully turning away, she looked for the one who had called her name and found Kieli staring back at her, her eyes wide in shock as she took in the sight that claimed the street.

"I was hoping it wasn't yours..." she claimed softly as if she couldn't find the right words to make things better.

It was all Fura could do to shake her head, trying to fight the resurgence of another round of tears. Her face already burned from their saltiness.

Picking up on her friend's distress, Kieli bridged the gap between them in a few graceful steps and pulled Fura into another hug.

Though she didn't want the contact, Fura allowed it – anything to keep her eyes, and her thoughts, averted from the wreckage and the flames.

From the corner of her eye, Fura could see a figure moving towards her and the two supporters that stood by her side. With the firelight still raging in the background, the man was a mere silhouette, but as he approached she could distinguish the police uniform he wore, the badge shining in the light.

"I hear rumor that this was your house?" the officer spoke, motioning to the pile of rubble behind him as he came within hearing distance.

Shock held her voice paralyzed as if speaking of the matter would truly engrave it into reality. Fura only nodded, unable to correct him that really it was her parents and she only lived there. Her name wouldn't be found on the deed.

Glancing over his shoulder at the smoldering debris, the man shook his head. "You're lucky. It appears that no one in the vicinity at the time made it out alive." Pulling a small notepad from his pocket, he procured a pen from his shirt. "May I ask where you were at the time of the explosion?"

"A- at the festival," Fura stammered, her mouth gaping like a fish as she tested her ability to form coherent words. "I work there."

The officer nodded as he jotted the information down. "And do you know at what time you last left the house?"

"Is this necessary?" Apallo interrupted before the man could ask any further questions. "She just lost her family and you're drilling her like a murder suspect."

"I'm only doing my job. And this may be a case of murder."

"I thought I heard talk of a gas leak?"

The man shrugged. Closing the tablet, he slipped it back into his shirt pocket. "We won't know for a few days. Now," he began again, turning back to Fura, "do you have anywhere you can go? Extended family? A friend?"

Apallo could see Fura's face fall even further as she pondered the question, realizing that she didn't. It pained him to see.

"Kieli?" he said, gaining the girl's attention. "Stay here, please."

The girl nodded, her long side-swept bangs falling into her eyes with the movement.

"I'll take care of this," Apallo said to Fura before he followed the officer across the yard and out of hearing distance.

Fura only nodded in compliance, never once thinking that it wasn't his place to be discussing such things. To her it was just his natural leadership taking over, and, all in all, she was too numb to argue one way or the other.

She watched as the two men spoke, heavy words rising above the noise here and there as they talked with animated hands and gruff shakes of the head. It all came across as some bizarre ballet played out in slow motion beneath strange lights, and Fura had the sudden urge to dance to the music-less tune. Before she could do so, Kieli said something, pulling her from her daze and doing her best to engage her in awkward conversation.

"What?" Fura asked, realizing that she hadn't even heard her friend's words.

Kieli silently looked at her for a moment as if contemplating her mental health, but spoke regardless. "Tiyano," she repeated. "He wanted to come with me to make sure you were okay, but –"

"He's got family of his own," Fura said solemnly, cutting Kieli off. As much as she wanted him here, she couldn't blame him. Family came first. That had been her first thought. Though, now what?

The term ripped through her, threatening to bring forth new tears. She tried to form a list, searching through the terms – aunts, uncles, cousins – but she came up short on every try. How could she have no family? And how could it have taken her this long to realize it?

Fura knew the police officer had only been asking routine questions, but he didn't know the abyss he had just opened inside her that she was now desperately trying to fill.

Kieli was speaking again, but Fura blocked out her words. She nodded here and there, at least trying to make it appear as if she were listening. Picking up on the ruse, Kieli let the conversation fade away, resolving to simply stand by in quiet support.

The night seemed to get darker and darker as the fires were slowly put out, casting the surroundings in deep shadow. Destroyed in the blast as well, the usual glow of the streetlights was nonexistent.

"Come on, Fura."

Not knowing how much time had passed, Fura looked up as Apallo approached as if it were the first time she had ever seen him. The statement didn't register right away and she found herself looking around again.

"There's nothing left," Apallo said, gently grabbing her arm to keep her from moving any closer to the remains of the house that still radiated an intense heat.

Nodding stiffly, Fura looked up at him. "Where will I stay?" she managed to choke out. It was something that she had wondered as soon as she had come upon the ruinous street, but could only now voice.

"We'll figure that out soon, but there's nothing here. Come back to the festival. We'll discuss it there."

Nothing left.

The words resonated with a hollow echo in her mind. Though Fura made no reply, it was as if he could read her deepest secret. The thought had flickered through her mind, but only now did she come to the full realization that she had no other family.

Fura didn't even have the strength to argue as Apallo led her away from the only thing she had ever known, Kieli following in step behind them. She had nothing left. Everything and everyone had just turned to ash, and the only familiar lead Fura had was the group at the festival that treated her like family.

5

••✧••

ROGUE

"Let me see that."

Kiyani turned to see the old man staring at him, his hand outstretched as if expecting a handout. "What?"

"Your hand," the man clarified.

Glancing at the source of the throbbing pain, Kiyani could see that the blood had already seeped through the flimsy rag he had wrapped around it. Unrolling the stained gauze, he dabbed at the gash again and rewrapped it, tighter this time. "I'm fine, Kristoff."

The man he had called Kristoff crossed his arms over his chest and gave Kiyani a stern glance. "Bleeding all over my merchandise is not fine."

One glance over the table he stood next to proved the merchant's words correct. "Shit," Kiyani muttered. "Sorry." Grabbing a clean rag, he wiped the polished wood free of the drips of red.

Satisfied that he hadn't done too much damage, save but to himself, Kiyani grabbed his sweatshirt off the hook on the wall and made towards the front of the shop where people still stood clustered. Despite the sparkling wares inside, their attention was on the sky where the sickly green clouds still stood at attention.

"Where do you think you're going?" Kristoff asked gruffly before Kiyani could make it halfway across the wooden floor.

"I want to see what's going on."

Kristoff shook his head, the silver strands in his hair shining in the firelight that lit the shop at such a late hour. "There's nothing out there right now but chaos. You'd get trampled in the crowd."

"Give me some credit," Kiyani huffed. "I'm not stupid."

Looking through the heads that blocked his view, Kiyani could see the mass exodus of people as they rushed to make it to the gate of the festival. As much as he wanted to know what had happened, wanted to find out some details connected with the explosion that had nearly caused him the unfortunate loss of a finger with a jewelry awl, the thought of trying to make his way through the packed crowd didn't appeal to him.

If anything it made his stomach tighten. For one that didn't care for people, he had often found it strange that he had taken up work in one of the booths in the Fireswell festival. Wandering the crowd was one thing. Working was another. Situated behind the counter of the silver shop owned by Kristoff, he rarely thought of the number of people that crowded the dirt lanes that lay just beyond the open doorway of the shop.

"I know you want to go explore," Kristoff said, breaking Kiyani's train of thought. "I'm just as curious, but let the crowd go down a bit."

Kiyani only nodded.

"Good. Then come help me clean up the shop."

It was an hour later, after the crowds had thinned down considerably, and all that was left were the merchants and the performers, that Kristoff finally let him leave.

Exciting *K & K Jewelers*, Kiyani turned one last time and threw a wave to the old man who sat behind the elaborately carved counter and continued to polish his wares. He still couldn't say what Kristoff had seen in him when he had shown up asking for a job that had caused the man to accept, but they had fallen into a comfortable companionship over the years that Kiyani wouldn't trade for anything. The intricate jewelry-work kept his mind focused and his hands busy. Despite being leery of the trade at first, Kiyani had found that his hours at the back of the shop had become his serene getaway.

At least it usually was.

Kiyani's mind was abuzz with muddled thoughts and questions as he moved through the darkened festival grounds. Where during the day the forested area was filled with hypnotic music and eclectic buildings and characters, it became a haunted place of desolation and deep shadows at night. Yet, fear was the last thing on his mind. He had never been afraid of the dark, and the nighttime hours had always been his favorite, the moon his guiding light.

On any other night after festival hours, Kiyani would skirt the groups of remaining performers as they talked merrily of the day and wander the winding trails of the festival, with the cool dirt and grass beneath his feet. The people that paid to come loved the feel of liveliness during the day, but Kiyani lived for the solitude of the night, when groups of people and their screaming kids didn't block the paths.

However, this wasn't any normal night, and Kiyani veered away from his usual after-closing jaunt and headed towards the flickering light near the center of the grounds. Beneath the rise of the stone stage the Firedancer's Guild used for their performances, a small group of people talked frantically in the middle of a circle of torches.

Usually, Kiyani avoided this area, but already he could see the one he had thought to seek out. Moving nimbly into the circle, barely receiving a glance from the remaining performers, Kiyani paused next to a middle-aged woman, her wavy brunette hair silhouetted in the firelight.

"What happened?"

The woman jumped at his words before spinning around. As soon as she caught sight of him, her eyes widened and she stepped forward to embrace him in a bear hug which he awkwardly returned. "Kiyani, you're okay!"

"The explosion was over there, Nira," Kiyani countered when the woman finally let him go. "You know I've been here the entire time."

Monira nodded slowly as if caught in some ghostly daze. "I know," she declared. "It's just good to know you're okay."

"So," Kiyani tried again. "Is there any word on what happened?"

"The news that's coming back isn't good."

"Did you expect it to be?" Kiyani asked truthfully. He knew it would likely come across as insensitive, but rarely was he one to sugarcoat things. "Sorry," he said when no reply came.

"Sorry," Monira said, repeating his words. It was easy to see she was completely frazzled.

At least it was safe to say that she probably hadn't even heard his last remark. "So, what is the news?" he tried again.

The woman pulled her gaze away from the sky and looked at him before letting out a long sigh. "No one knows how large of an area it was, but they're saying total destruction. I heard a mention of a gas leak, but the fires..."

"There's only one other instance of green fires," Kiyani finished for her.

"Right."

"You don't really think?"

Nira slowly shook her head. "It's hard to say."

Kiyani shook his head. "But why would he risk exposure like this again?"

The Augden murders, though rarely spoken of in the small town, were something that Kiyani was well aware of, even if he hadn't been alive then. There was a small, close-knit, and tight-lipped group, mostly contained to the festival performers, that knew the truth of that event. Even if he had never acquired all the facts, Kiyani was one of the ones that knew the culprit wasn't of this realm.

He never received an answer as the chorus of whispers from the remaining people suddenly fell into complete silence. The only sound that remained was the inconsistent fluttering of the torches in the stiff breeze. It was almost as if another thunderous boom had ravaged the night.

"Oh!" Monira exclaimed from his side before bolting without a word and weaving her way through the small group.

Expecting the worst, Kiyani took a breath and followed the turn of the heads.

Coming through the festival gates, moving slowly towards the circle of torches, weary and disheveled, was the Guild's leader, Apallo. And trailing behind him, eyes glassy and feet moving slowly, as if she were merely a puppet being led by a string, was a girl with flame-red hair.

"No," Kiyani muttered as he felt his fist ball at his side.

He didn't know the full scope of the situation, but Kiyani could feel it in the air that this night could only get worse. Whatever Apallo had cooking up behind those haunted brown eyes, Kiyani had to make sure it didn't go through.

Apallo quietly led the girl over to a stump where he bid her to sit, before converging with Monira and two others in a sudden meeting. Kiyani didn't even have time to move to question anyone before Apallo broke from the group and leapt onto the stone stage in one fluid movement.

"Evening everyone," Apallo said, looking out over the remaining faces, a huge difference from the last time he had been on the same stage only hours before. "I thank you all for sticking around. As we all know, tragedy has struck us tonight. I have been to the scene of the blast we heard earlier, and I can say that a good majority of the surrounding area has been leveled."

"The Augden murderer is back?" a voice asked frantically from the crowd, causing another stir of murmurs.

Holding up a hand, Apallo called for silence before continuing. "We don't know for certain yet. I will keep you all posted on the details as they come in over the next few days. It is an unfortunate possibility that we will hold out on.

"However, I stand before you currently to announce a related topic." Sweeping his hand towards the girl who sat next to the stage, barely paying attention, Apallo continued. "All of you here know Fura. Some days it doesn't feel like she's been with us long, but she's certainly become one of the family. It is with a heavy heart that I tell you, tragedy has struck closer to home than we could have expected. Her house was among those centered in the explosion, leaving her with nothing."

Apallo let his words fall into remiss, allowing for a small moment of silence.

"After quick discussion with my council, I personally grant our good friend, Fura, full residency of Frielana, as well as Fireswell. There are tough times ahead and we all need to stick together."

"You're letting her live with us?" Kiyani suddenly blurted out, interrupting Apallo's words before they had barely had a chance to filter through the air.

The outburst was met with a harsh glare from the red-haired man, which Kiyani ignored.

Though Kiyani knew Apallo would rather ignore him completely, he replied sternly to the statement so as not to be shown up in front of his followers. "Of course."

"She's not even one of us!" Kiyani snorted gruffly just as quickly. He couldn't let this measure be passed.

He hadn't even realized Monira had come back to his side until her hand fell on his shoulder. Momentarily breaking his anger, Kiyani glanced at her to find her shaking her head, as if telling him to quit before he got into real trouble. It was no secret that Apallo had never favored him.

"And you are?" Apallo challenged immediately. "It wasn't my call to let you live with us, but I allowed it." There was a growl in his deep voice that reverberated through the air.

"It's a mistake if you let this go through."

Apallo sent a stony-eyed glare his way that would freeze most people in their tracks, however it had little effect on Kiyani. Either way, his next words were just as biting. "My mistake was letting you live with us." Kiyani made to speak again, but was cut short. "Continue to speak against me and I'll revoke that ill thought out decision."

With fists balled at his side, Kiyani took a deep breath, biting his tongue against his next words that threatened to burst forth. Shaking his head in disgust he shrugged off Monira's hand and stalked away into the shadows of the trees.

6

•••✧•••

INTO THE UNKNOWN

Fura watched the dark-haired boy as he stomped off into the shadows that lay beyond the circle of firelight. The anger that had come across in his biting words was just as evident in the deep-set scowl she had seen on his face as he had turned away, and the stiff movement of his body as he walked off into the shadows.

It wasn't until he disappeared out of sight that Fura became aware that she had been holding her breath during the conversation, as if bracing for a more physical attack. Releasing it, she steadied herself as a wave of dizziness threatened to take her down.

Out of the corner of her eye, Fura could see Apallo jump down from the stage, his speech over. The small crowd which he had addressed had all but scattered, but she still jumped when his hand came near her.

"Don't worry about him. You are indeed welcome here." Lines creased the corner of his eyes.

Fura could see that he had intended to lay his hand on her shoulder again for support, but he let it fall as he took in her reaction.

There were so many questions running through her head, but the only one she could bring forth was, "Who was that?"

More than anything, she wanted answers about why something so horrible had happened to her and her family. What had caused that fire, and why would someone do something like that. The trepidation had been apparent on Apallo's face as she had watched him talk with the police officer. Fura had heard, just as well as he had, the evident rumors of a gas leak that had triggered the awful explosion that still had her ears ringing, but even she couldn't believe the validity of it. All of it came across as too strange, too organized, for any random event such as that. There had been nothing left to sift through. No bodies. The only evidence that had been left behind had been the sickly green flames that were like nothing Fura had ever seen. It was all too clean-cut.

She wanted answers to all that and so much more. She wanted justice, and maybe even a little bit of vengeance. She wanted to walk off into the shadows, away from all these people, and be left alone to grieve.

Yet, right now, the only thing Fura could wonder about was the boy who had just spoken against her. She couldn't fathom what she had done to him to warrant such treatment, especially after what she had just been through. It was like pouring salt on an open wound, giving it no time to heal whatsoever in between attacks. From what she had been able to judge in the dim lighting, he had appeared to be around her age, and from the way he had talked, he was associated with the Guild of Firedancers as well. However, she couldn't place him to save her life.

He wasn't a performer, that was for certain. Fura would've known him if he was. As far she could recall she had never even spoken to him.

Searching the shadows, Fura tried to find him again, but found that he was long gone. Turning to Apallo, she waited for an answer.

The man sighed, peering into the trees as well as if to avoid her questioning gaze. It wasn't long before he relented and looked at her.

"His name is Kiyani, and the only thing you need to know is to stay away from him. He's nothing but trouble."

Fura didn't understand the man's request, but she was too tired to argue. Deciding to remain silent instead, she let her eyes sweep across the cleared area where a small number of people still remained. It was a far cry from the crowd that had packed the grounds earlier that day. She was just glad that each and every one of the people who had watched her performance didn't know of her current plight. Shaking off the remnant feeling of nausea that had been with her since the incident that had turned the night upside down, she put the boy's outburst out of her mind, as well as the other toying thoughts, and tried to focus on the more pressing matters at hand.

Left with a distinct feeling that that wasn't the last time she would see Kiyani, Fura told herself she would deal with it later. Right now, she had other things to figure out.

Moving back towards Apallo who had shifted to talk to Monira again, giving her space, Fura asked the first of many things that had come to her mind. "Where am I staying for the night?"

Apallo had claimed that she was now officially a part of the Fireswell group, as well as mentioning a Frielana that she had never before heard of, but that didn't take care of her living situation. The whole thing was too much to think about, but Fura knew she had to start somewhere, and where she was sleeping for the night was just as good a place as any.

Pulling away from Monira, and holding up a hand, indicating a pause in their conversation, Apallo turned back to Fura.

"You'll be staying with us."

Fura couldn't help but look around at the empty grounds of the festival and the shabby, renaissance wood-styled buildings and wonder if he meant here in Fireswell, or with him and Monira. "Right," she mumbled, confused.

Even if Apallo had meant staying here at the festival, Fura couldn't see where. The buildings surrounding them were designed for decorative purposes only. They were built well enough to keep the elements out if it happened to rain during the opening hours, giving people a place to huddle in warmth until the showers passed. A few even had nice stone fireplaces that she had visited on a number occasions, when the blustery winds off the waters of Barandor's river carried a chill with them. But that didn't mean Fura would ever choose to actually live in one of the shops. Taking in the nighttime scene, she could see that most of the buildings were already closed up for the night, awaiting the next day and a new sea of people that would pass through to investigate the wares inside. Yet, none of those specifically belonged to the Guild. Not that she was aware of, anyway. Mainly, the firedancers loitered outside during the day in small groups as they passed the time between performances. They had a small building reserved for them by the administrators of the festival to house their torches used on stage and the backpacks of 'modern' devices they kept on hand when coming in in the morning, but nothing big enough to live in.

Returning her focus to Apallo, Fura found herself taking in the man in a new light. This was the longest she had spent with him in a long while. There had been a time when the idea of being the main interest of his focus had both frightened her and been exhilarating – those times when she had first started and had been lucky enough to receive personal teaching in the art from the man that many – the audience, as well as the other performers – had genially deemed the master of fire. Revered as a near god. Now, standing behind him, waiting for him to elaborate on his answer, Fura only felt increasingly awkward. She still found it hard to believe that he had followed her all the way out to where her house once stood. She was grateful for his concern, there was no doubt about that, but she couldn't decipher why he would even bother, other than the fact that he was an exceedingly nice guy. The urge to answer calls of distress seemed to flow through his veins. One of the many reasons why she could see why he had become the group's unspoken leader.

Speaking with his hands as he conversed with Monira, Apallo glanced at his arm as if looking for a watch. Realizing that there wasn't one to be found, he rubbed his wrist and took a gander at the sky instead.

"It's well past midnight," Monira answered for him, seeming to notice his plight.

He nodded and peered over his shoulder at Fura before letting his gaze sweep across the circle of torches, counting out in his mind the people that remained. "Right," he said. "I guess we might as well head back, then. I think we've had more than enough excitement for the day."

Monira dipped her head and strolled off to join one of the other groups of people as Apallo turned his full attention back to Fura. "Ready to go?"

Trying not to think of the reason why she wasn't going home, wasn't home in bed already, Fura made an attempt to set her face in a half smile that failed to come across as care free. "I guess." Starting to follow him, she remembered something and stopped. "Oh, wait!" Diving into the shadows behind the stage, Fura found the door to the shed the troupe used for their belongings and procured her messenger bag. Feeling the familiar, worn leather beneath her fingers, she flung it over her shoulder and closed the building back up. What she had in this bag, she realized, was all she had left of the life she had lived up until now.

Attempting to come to terms with that sudden fact, Fura realized she didn't even know the full contents of what was inside. It was something she would figure out at another time, something she could do later as she stalked off into a quiet corner and tried to piece together what remained of her once vibrant life.

Approaching the circle of light again, half of the torches already blown out, Fura bowed her head slightly to Apallo who stood waiting, indicating that she was as ready as she would ever be to go. Accepting her silence, Apallo returned the gesture and moved to join the other remaining members of the troupe.

Following behind the group without a word, Fura made it to the edge of the grounds before stopping as she came to the sudden conclusion that they were headed into the Verboten Forest.

Who goes in there at night? she wondered.

The shadows lurking amongst the trees were usually of no concern to her, but all Fura could think of were the ghost stories that were said to originate from that spanse of forest. It was nothing but silliness and tall tales, but all the kids in Barandor had grown up with the chilling tales of weird beings, strange noises, and getting lost in the dark forest. Everyone knew that it was just a way to keep children from entering the forest and getting lost, scaring them into remission, but that didn't keep people from generating newer and scarier things as the years progressed.

"Are you coming?" Apallo asked, noticing her trepidation.

"Where?" she couldn't help but ask. She had been with the Firedancer troupe for a few years, but Fura was only now starting to realize that maybe she didn't know them as well as she should.

Picking up on her apprehension, Apallo held out a hand. "I know this seems strange to you, but I promise to explain in the next few days. Do you trust us?"

Fura gazed at his hand a moment, unsure of what to do. Her heart raced in her chest, knowing this was one of the deciding moments of her life. With little else to do, and nothing left to hold her back, she found herself nodding in acceptance.

"And since then we've been... Fura, are you still listening?"

"What?" Fura looked up from the ground as she walked, trying to avoid tripping over raised roots in the darkness. It was only when Apallo said her name that she realized he had been speaking for a good ten minutes, at least, yet she hadn't heard a single word. "Sorry," she murmured. Whatever this new slice of life had prepared for her, she was already failing.

Apallo shook his head. "No, don't be. I should know better. I can only assume that the last thing you want right now is a history lesson. Yet, here I am, rambling on."

"It's okay," Fura said, glad that he couldn't see the burn in her cheeks in the darkness.

Even if she hadn't been listening to the man's words, Fura found the consistent drone of his voice rather calming. It kept her mind off things as she did her best to stumble gracefully through the forest.

"It's been a long time since we've actually talked, hasn't it?"

Fura grabbed a low-hanging branch, and ducked beneath it before she had the chance to run into it, before glancing at him. The thought had crossed her own mind earlier, but she had doubted he would remember. She often caught glimpses of him running through the festival grounds during opening hours, helping others while running the group and choreographing performances during weekday meetings. He was a busy man. Fura had picked up on that quickly enough when she had first joined the group, and after she had trained with him long enough to be left on her own she had left him to his own devices, afraid to distract him.

"I guess," she admitted.

"Just know that if you ever need anything, don't hesitate to ask."

There were plenty of things she needed right now, but Fura let the conversation fall into a lull. Plowing herself into his personal life already felt like too much to ask. Apallo's gaze lingered on her momentarily, as if expecting a flow of questions, before he let it wander. He picked up his stride a bit, pulling in front of her by a few feet, though never truly leaving her behind. Fura appreciated his obvious effort to not keep her talking, yet not abandoning her either.

Watching the ground beneath her again, it wasn't long before Fura found herself trying to take in the forest. The moon still hid behind clouds most of the time, and when it did manage to break free, the dense, twisting branches above filtered the light until there wasn't much left but a hazy, gray-tinged shadow of mist. She might have been afraid, but Fura could see the small group before her, bobbing in the half light. It was the smallest comfort, knowing that she wasn't actually alone.

Hugging her arms closer to her body, burying herself deeper in her sweatshirt, Fura wished she had warmer clothing. She had long removed the lace up gladiator sandals of soft leather she wore during performances, and replaced them with a pair of worn tennis shoes she kept at the festival, but her toes were still numb from the cold. The deeper they moved into the never-ending expanse of trees, the more accustomed Fura found herself becoming to the darkness. Though she hadn't noticed it before, the quietness and the need for something to keep her occupied allowed her to realize that they weren't just randomly moving through the woods. If she squinted hard enough, she could see that the group actually followed a pathway compacted into the dirt beneath their feet. It was nearly nondescript in the dark, but it was there nonetheless.

She wondered how long they had been walking as she fantasized about some rustic city in the midst of the trees. It obviously wasn't the city they were headed towards, and when politely prompted about it earlier, Apallo had only confessed that it wasn't the most conventional style of living. His answer had left her both scared and intrigued by what was waiting for her at the end of this trail.

What they stumbled upon, seemingly by accident, not too long after, left Fura merely startled.

She actually had to stop and look twice to make sure her frazzled mind wasn't playing tricks on her in the moonlight. The path widened before her and led into a large clearing.

"Is this it?" Fura couldn't help but ask.

At first glance, it didn't appear as if much were there, nothing of living standard at least, but as Fura looked closer she could see that she was wrong. The first thing that registered was that there were no buildings whatsoever.

When she glanced at Apallo for affirmation she felt bad as she took in the look of what could have come been seen as shame on his face.

Just as she was about to apologize for her words, the man's face lightened. "I know it's not what you're used to, but wait until you see it in the daylight. It's actually quite the bustling community." He stood there, letting her quietly take in the scene before them for a few minutes before adding, "Come on, I'll show you around. I promise, it's more inviting up close."

Strolling slowly down the remainder of the path, Fura allowed the man to lead her through the clearing as he spoke of a few things while pointing out particular areas of interest.

A large fire pit of mismatched stones sat in the middle of the area, unlit. Surrounding it were roughly cut benches of plank wood and a few stumps. Off to the side stood a triage of large branches that were tented, and from which hung a cast iron cauldron. It swung ever so slightly in the gentle breeze above a fire that had broken down to gray ash, a few glowing coals scattered amongst the powder.

To the left, what Fura had originally taken for grass covered steep slopes of stone transformed into the asymmetrical and jagged arches of a series of caves – three that she could count in the darkness. Though two of them lay dark and dormant in the night, the first, and what appeared to be the largest, held a warm light that filtered through a net of vines that covered the entrance.

As she followed a few feet behind Apallo, Monira bounded up and stole him away again. Apallo promised he would return in a few moments and Fura told him it was fine. It wasn't until he had actually gone that Fura found herself paralyzed without a familiar face, leaving her alone in a nearly vacant clearing. She was half tempted to follow the inviting light into the cave, tired and wanting to crawl into a bed, or at least wrap up in a warm blanket, but also interested to see just how big the caves were. However, something else seemed to call to her, and Fura found her eyes drawn away from the caverns altogether.

Despite the lack of moonlight as it dove behind the clouds again, there was still an eerie light that permeated the place. A chill hung in the air, leaving droplets of dew that settled onto the grass, and a thin mist that hung in scattered patches just above the ground.

Lying about a hundred yards from the caves was a rather peculiar site. Despite reaching her level of dealing with the unknown for the day, Fura found herself drawn forward as if someone else were controlling her feet. She could see from a distance the height of the rocky, stone cliff from which a waterfall cascaded downwards into a shimmering body of water. As she came upon it, Fura could see that the pool was crystal clear, revealing undetermined depths as though they were a mere foot deep. Though it was bigger than what she would consider a pond, it wasn't large enough to be considered a lake.

As gorgeous as it was after such a trying day, there was something that Fura couldn't quite place as she watched a patch of weeds sway in the current from the waterfall.

"It's…"

"Green," finished a deep, male voice behind her.

Recognizing that it didn't belong to Apallo, Fura whirled around to find herself face to face with the man the leader had claimed was Kiyani. He stood in the darkness, highlighted by the strange light from the pool of water, his arms crossed over his chest as he stared at her, his eyes unreadable.

Fura couldn't help but feel vulnerable under his gaze as if he were assessing and judging her. Based on his outburst at the festival, he didn't want her here in the first place. And now he had found her alone. A perfect time to continue to tear her down if he wanted.

Unsure of how to react to his sudden appearance, or his unnerving gaze, Fura found herself glancing back at the water behind her, finding that he was right. The spring, as she had decided to call it, had an unearthly glow that seemed to emanate from the water itself, but the actual waters beneath were unmistakably a light green, intensified by the surrounding darkness.

"Come to think of it, it's always been like that," Kiyani continued without a reply from her as he appeared to think about it.

Her first urge was to turn on him and ask where the heck he'd even come from. She had assumed that he had been long gone after he had stomped off the festival grounds at least half an hour before. Yet, here he was, standing in front of her like he had never parted from the group. Fura hadn't even heard footsteps to indicate his presence.

"And no one finds that strange at all?" was all she could come up with.

"Not that I know of," Kiyani replied with a shrug. "There's actually a tale that claims it was created by a slighted witch by the name of Zena. She was angry with Mother Nature for bringing a drought that destroyed her crop of mushrooms and drove all the toads away. For payback, she cast a spell on this spring here to turn it a foul green and drive all life away from it. Supposedly her spell backfired though, and instead brought beauty to it and gave it healing powers."

Fura watched him carefully as he spoke, trying to find any hint of a smile that would indicate he was lying which, she decided, he obviously was. "You made that up."

Kiyani glanced at her with a raised brow and a slight upward turn of his lip. "Did I?"

Turning away from his gaze, Fura stared at the water again, unsure of how to counter that.

"Of course, there are also tales of a river in Trubamaere that glows purple under a full moon. I can't validate that one."

Leaving all thoughts of the spring behind, Fura stared at him. She knew his name despite him not offering it, thanks to Apallo. She wanted to strike up conversation with him, wanted to know what his problem with her was, but all she could do was stare and mull over the strange story he had just given her. Common sense automatically declared it false, but glancing at the glowing waters before her made her wonder. If anything her own sanity was at question here.

"I give you three days," Kiyani declared suddenly after a lengthening silence.

Startled, Fura looked over at him, catching his eye again. "What?" She had been so lost in contemplation of his words that she had nearly forgotten he was there. The fact that his eyes were a dazzling light blue didn't help her scattered mind.

Kiyani crossed his arms over his chest. "I give you three days before you decide you want to leave here."

And there it was again. That apparent hatred of her. Fura didn't understand. Yet, she didn't comment on it either. "I don't have anywhere else to go," she clarified.

"Doesn't matter."

Through the mist and shadows that blanketed the clearing, Fura could see a figure approaching the spring. It didn't take her long to recognize the man as Apallo.

Following her eyes, Kiyani turned to where she looking. If Fura didn't know any better and wasn't so tired, she would have said that he had tensed when he had caught sight of the Guild leader himself.

As Apallo approached, Kiyani moved away from her and began to walk back towards the main center of the camp without another word to her.

Fura could see that look of hard-edged steel in the man's eyes, watching Kiyani leave as he approached. Though Fura knew the words weren't meant for her, she could still hear the "Stay away from her," that was directed at Kiyani before they passed one another.

"Of course, my Lord," Kiyani said sarcastically as he paused in his step and gave a drastic bow.

"Don't make me dismiss you from this camp permanently," Apallo growled, visibly irritated by the display.

Kiyani wheeled around. "You've wanted to for ages. Why don't you do it already?"

"Don't tempt me."

Fura watched as Kiyani trailed off towards the caves before turning her attention back to the spring, pretending that she hadn't heard any of the conversation. She knew that that little display hadn't been meant for her.

There was a lengthy silence that followed Kiyani's departure, the tension in his words seeming to hang overhead like the fog, as Apallo approached and stood next to her. Both of them watched wordlessly as Kiyani's dark form disappeared into one of the unlit caves on the end, closest to the spring.

"I'm sorry about that," Apallo admitted a bit shamefully a moment later. "Did he hurt you?" he added before Fura could tell him that it was fine.

She shook her head, confused by his words. "Did you expect him to?" Sure, Kiyani had made it clear that he wasn't about to welcome her here, but she couldn't see him inflicting any physical violence on her. Especially if he was living under Apallo's watch. From what she had seen in the last hour, Kiyani was the one who wasn't much welcome, and quite possibly on his last line.

Apallo sighed. "I don't know with him."

"Yet you let him live here?"

"Let's just say it's one of my bigger mistakes."

"Then why don't you make him leave?" Fura asked. She wasn't about to suggest Apallo kick the boy out of his home, but it was certainly a sordid dynamic the two of them had.

"It's a long story." Apallo looked over to see a light in Fura's eyes that indicated she was interested in hearing more, but he held up a hand to quiet her words. "Let's not fan the flames of an already tainted night."

7

✦✦✧✦✦

A NEW DAY, A NEW LIFE

Fura was woken by the sounds of clinking pans and the lull of voices that drifted through the air. Rolling over, she pulled the blanket over her head as she was assaulted by the bright light of early morning that seeped in through the door she had left cracked open. She didn't know how long she had been asleep, but the warm light and the sound of life nearly made Fura wonder if those nasty green fires, and the acrid smell of charred wood and plastic, had been nothing more than a horrible dream.

If she kept her eyes squeezed shut and buried herself further beneath the blankets, she could almost make herself believe just that. However, the moment she opened her eyes and sat up, Fura was brought back to reality. The unfamiliar surroundings only set it further in stone.

After the events of the previous day, all Fura wanted to do was go back to sleep and possibly never wake up to the truth. She might have done just that, if the grumblings of her stomach didn't insist she get out of bed.

Unable to ignore it, Fura forced herself to cast off the blankets and look around. When Apallo had led her through the main cave the night before, she had been too tired to pay much attention to anything, save the bed in a quiet cavern that Monira had made up for her.

In the daylight, she could see that the dwelling wasn't nearly as primitive as she had originally thought. The curtain of vines, that had disguised themselves to look like drooping shadows of barbed wire in the darkness, had been interesting, albeit in a creepy way, but Fura had been scared to know what lay beyond them.

With the shadows melted away by sunlight that filtered into the cavern through small holes above that acted as skylights, Fura could see, that despite the bad rep of movie caverns with ceilings lined with bats, that there was nothing frightening about this one in the least. A warm fire danced in a fireplace that had been carved into the wall, the tendrils of smoke rising in small, translucent streams and filtering out the holes in the ceiling. Beneath her feet lay a colorful worn rug, the fibers of it shifting and hugging her bare toes. The frame of the bed in which she had slept was made of rough hewn timbers of wood, and the blanket on top appeared to have been hand woven. A wooden trunk sat at the foot of the bed, beckoning to her to explore and see what was inside, but Fura trumped the urge, not wanting to get in trouble. As her eyes moved away from the trunk, she could see that a multitude of patterns adorned the walls in a chalky paint that weren't instantly visible, but more blended in as if to merely add a homey accent.

Overall, it was a rather primitive living situation, but Fura found it more comforting than anything. She thought to herself that if Fireswell were to ever add a bed and breakfast for some reason, the décor within would run along the same lines as this.

Dragging herself away from the walls where she had run her fingers along the designs, wondering if there was any meaning behind them, Fura found herself digging through her bag that she had dropped next to the bed in a tired haze. The base of her fire dancer outfit was comfortable, having become something of a second skin to her, but it wasn't all that warm, and the smell of fire that clung to the fabric made her empty stomach lurch. Luckily, she often brought an extra change of clothes to the festival, and she found herself slipping on a pair of jeans and a Fireswell Renaissance Festival t-shirt she had bought years ago.

Throwing on her sweatshirt, Fura left the secluded safety of the room. Moving through the cavern, past more fires and other wood furniture, including a table and chairs and a couch, in what she assumed passed here as the living room, she shyly waved to a few unfamiliar faces. Pushing aside the curtain of vines, much more vibrant and inviting during the day, Fura had to shield her eyes as she walked into the full light of morning. Almost instantly, she felt like pulling back and returning to the quiet room and the cozy bed as she was assaulted by the sights and sounds of the group of people she assumed lived here. Apallo had been right when he had claimed the place was much livelier during the day.

Scanning the faces, Fura tried to find someone she knew. A few people waved at her invitingly, while a few others merely ducked their heads as their faces fell into sadness, as if they already knew who she was despite her never having seen them before.

Just as she began to feel her heart race from the helplessness she felt, Fura caught sight of Monira. She had seen the older woman around Frielana before but had never had much of a chance to actually talk to her, but right now she was the closest thing she could find to a familiar face.

"You're up already?" Monira said, motioning Fura over once she was within speaking distance. "I thought you would have slept longer."

Fura only shrugged, not sure what to say. As comfortable as the bed had been, hunger had gotten to her. Not to mention, the sleep she had managed to get had been riddled with nightmares, awash in raging fires. Sitting down on the log next to the woman, Fura picked up a stick from the ground and absently fiddled with it as Monira asked how she was doing – a question Fura found she never wanted to hear or answer again.

Just as Fura was trying to figure out what acceptable answer to come back with, a whistle suddenly sounded throughout the clearing, felling everyone to silence. Turning towards the sound, everyone's eyes focused on Apallo who stood on a stone stage similar to the one in Fireswell. "I just want to announce, to those of you whom this concerns, that Fireswell is closed for the remainder of the weekend. Please pass the message along."

Dipping his head as if to say 'thank you for listening', Apallo moved down from the stone and made his way to the fire.

"Morning, Fura," he said as he stopped next to her and Monira.

"Morning," Fura echoed politely.

"I can show you around this afternoon, if you want," Apallo offered warmly.

Just as the words left his lips, a call from across the camp beckoned for his help. He sighed as he closed his eyes in frustration. "Or not."

Fura gave a small smile. "It's okay. I'll be fine."

He smiled at her and gave her a nod before turning to Monira. "Take care of her."

"It gets a little hectic at times being the leader of such a large group," Monira said as she and Fura watched Apallo walk away, explaining his coming absence for him.

"How long has he been the leader?" Fura asked. She didn't even know how long he had been with the festival.

"Quite some time. Now," Monira said, eluding any follow up of the subject, "you must be hungry."

Despite the events, and trying to will the hunger away earlier, Fura found that she was ravenous and unable to remember the precise time of her last meal. She distinctly remembered stopping at one of the stands in the festival the previous day and buying a turkey leg, but that had been around noon. Normally she ate later in the evening, but the growing nerves before her big performance had masked her hunger. What had followed had driven it from her mind altogether.

As Fura ate a bowl of warm stew that Monira procured for her from the large cauldron she had spotted the night before, its contents steaming over a blazing fire, they talked of numerous things. Though it was Monira who spoke the most, Fura was happy enough to sit back and listen, appreciative of the fact that the woman didn't pry into her life, or her current feelings.

However, as the afternoon progressed, people started meandering over and sitting around her. Even though she often loved meeting new people at the festival, the strange faces and the questions and countless condolences made her nervous.

Quietly mumbling thanks to each and every one, the faces all beginning to blur together, Fura finally weaseled her way out of the group, claiming she was tired. A few faces returned to sorrow, while others looked disappointed that she was leaving the crowd so soon, but she ignored it.

Fura walked towards the cave, feeling spent though she had hardly done anything. Her first thought was to head back to the small room, but as it crossed her mind she realized she didn't want to be enclosed in a small space. Favoring the openness of the forest around her, she found herself wandering towards the spring instead.

As she cautiously approached the body of water, she was surprised to find that the eerie luminescence that it had cast during the night was all but concealed during the day. Water had never been her first love and the vastness of its size made her fidgety, but it was quiet, so Fura decided to stay.

Casting off her shoes, Fura ascended one of the flat boulders that lined the side of the spring and watched the glimmer of the falls in the sunlight. The stone wall on either side boasted patches of soft green moss, and tufts of glossy leaves grew in the wandering cracks. It was nature at its finest, and Fura found herself almost instantly calmed by the sight. It didn't make anything better, but it helped.

Closing her eyes to the sights, Fura stood and let the sun warm her face as she listened to the gentle roar of the water.

"Seriously?"

Startled by the break in the silence, Fura nearly jumped from the scare. As she quickly turned to see who had come up behind her she lost her footing on the rocks beneath her, sending her sprawling into the warm waters.

Her heart leaping into her throat at the shock of it, she flailed in the spring, sending splashes of water into the air. When she found footing beneath her, Fura willed herself to breathe. Though her heart pounded wildly in her chest, she discovered that she had been lucky enough to have only slipped into a small dip in the rocks that formed a shallow pool, and not the full depths of the spring. Clutching at the slippery stones surrounding her as she attempted to haul herself out of the water, Fura looked up to find Kiyani staring back at her, a quizzical look on his face.

"I thought Apallo told you to stay away from me," she managed to choke out when he remained silent.

Kiyani crouched on the stone above her. "Hard to do when you're following me."

"I'm not following you!" Fura insisted, though she left out the fact that her glimpse of him swimming earlier had been a small part of what had initially drawn her over.

"No?"

"No!"

Fura tried to rise out of the water again and slipped on the stones beneath. The sudden scare had brought on a feeling of sickness that made Fura wish she hadn't consumed two bowls of stew that morning.

Leaning forward, Kiyani offered a hand. "You obviously don't like water, so what are you doing out here?"

"I can't explore?" Fura asked. She was leery of the way he offered help as he called her out, but she took his hand regardless, desperately wanting free of the watery grave.

He pulled her up, holding her arm in place as she stood a few inches from his face. "Not when you're supposed to stay away from me."

Wresting her arm from his grasp, Kiyani let her go and backed away. She rubbed her arm where his hand had been, unsure of how this was all making her feel. Glancing up to find that he had moved away from her again and was now leaning against the stone wall, Fura realized that it wasn't his presence that made her cautious of him, but the warning that Apallo had issued.

"What, does this spring have your name on it or something?" Fura asked irritably as she wrung out her hair, trying to figure out what Apallo had meant by his words the night before, declaring that he wasn't sure what Kiyani would do. Despite the warning, so far all he had done was scare her because she hadn't been paying attention to her surroundings, and then rescue her from the water. Nothing that screamed dangerous.

"I'm usually the only one that comes out here," Kiyani replied, not directly answering the question.

Fura stared at him as she realized the implications of the words he had issued a mere foot from her face, his eyes piercing hers as if delivering some ultimatum.

"You think I don't know that Apallo's already told you to avoid me?" Kiyani asked, seeming to pick up on her thoughts with an unnerving awareness.

She could only stand there, speechless. After the scene she had witnessed, standing in this exact spot, between Apallo and Kiyani, she should have known that Kiyani would be well aware of the man's warning to her. Yet, it still caught her off guard. As her breathing slowly returned to a regular rate, she took the time to quietly study him. Her guess from the night before that he wasn't much older than her was only clarified in the light of day. His lean build that had been masked in the renaissance outfit and sweatshirt she had first seen him in was only accented by the jeans and black tank top he wore now. Hair as black as night fell across his face in damp strands as it dried in the breeze, a simple indicator that he had indeed been here first. Just below chin-length, Fura could see that the ends had already begun to flip up slightly as they dried. A slight goatee adorned his chin, and those blue eyes were even more dazzling now.

"I wasn't following you," Fura clarified again, breaking her focus on him when the silence filled the space between them.

"Sure."

"What's that supposed to mean?"

Kiyani only shrugged as he picked up a wet leaf from the stones at his feet and twirled it between his fingers, ignoring her stare.

"Do you really think I came out here to talk to you?"

"I think you came out here looking for something," he said, the tone in his voice implying a deeper meaning behind his words that she couldn't quite grasp.

"Some peace and quiet," Fura claimed, hoping the blush on her face wasn't too visible. The buzz of the numerous people in the clearing outside the caves had been too much for her this morning. It was true, in a way. Just as much as he was right that she had kind of hoped to run into him.

"So did I. It appears neither of us have found what we wanted."

There it was again, that biting edge in his voice that Fura couldn't understand. "What did I ever do to you?"

"Nothing."

"Then why do you hate me so much?"

"I don't."

"Then —"

"Because you shouldn't be here," Kiyani answered before she could finish her sentence.

8

♦♦◇♦♦

SEARCHING FOR SOLITUDE

Apallo only heard half of Monira's words as she stood next to him before the campfire, discussing the tragedy the night before. He had thought to spend the day with Fura, working to get her accustomed to the place, but she had already taken off when he had returned.

"She'll be fine," Monira said, noting his lack of commitment to the conversation, and the real object of his focus.

"What?"

So much precaution had been taken over the years on his own account to keep the girl away from all this, yet what good had it done? In the end, here she was, and now he hardly knew how to handle the sudden turn of events. Apallo knew the resurgence of the events in Augden, now Barandor, and what it would eventually mean here in Frielana, should have been first and foremost on his mind – the safety of his subjects – but he couldn't stop thinking of Fura. That look of hopelessness that he had seen on her face the night before just wouldn't leave him. He wanted to help her, to make her feel at home, but she barely knew him. And, despite his wishes, he knew this was probably the last place she should be at the moment. Things were stirring in the air. He could feel it. And he had the peculiar feeling that the storm would only grow rougher in the days to come.

"She's a tough girl. You don't have to worry about her."

Apallo threw a glance toward the falls again, noting just how close that boy was to Fura. "Are you sure?" He already felt bad about having left her side this morning to take care of the general business of the camp. Now that feeling was only intensified as he watched the girl speak with that miscreant.

"What do you think he's going to do to her?" Monira asked suddenly, truly interested in his answer. She didn't have to ask to know why he was so on edge.

"He's dangerous," Apallo declared without second thought, a growl in his voice. He regretted it as soon as he heard it, but it couldn't be helped. He never should have granted the kid residence. Every time he

48

thought back to that decision, he wondered what had been going through his mind that had made him accept. Everyone thought that Monira's influence had been the deciding factor, and Apallo was fine with letting people think that way, but he would never let the truth of the situation be known.

"For speaking his mind? If he was that bad that he actually threatened the livelihood of this community, you would have actually kicked him out years ago. As it is, he's done nothing to prove your accusations since he's been here, and you know it."

"That doesn't mean he won't," Apallo argued.

"When?" Monira let out a breath with a shake of her head when he refused to answer, only giving her a quick glance before looking back to the spring. The man was usually so level-headed. That was, until Kiyani became the topic of discussion. Now he was just speaking for the sake of argument. "Look around you," she said softly. "Everyone here is in their late twenties and beyond. Kiyani's the closest to Fura's age, and she could use a friend."

"Does it have to be him?"

"Just let it go and see what happens."

As if he could sense they were talking about him, Apallo watched as Kiyani broke away, leaving Fura standing next to the spring, looking solemn and lost.

Both he and Monira remained silent as the boy approached, watching as he purposely skirted the fire pit they stood before.

"I told you to stay away from her," Apallo warned as the boy walked past him, ignoring the distance between them.

Kiyani whirled around. "Then keep her away from me."

He moved to continue on, but was immediately assaulted by Apallo once more.

"And where do you think you're going?"

"Fireswell."

"Didn't you hear my announcement this morning? Fireswell is closed for the weekend."

"Well, unless the festival itself burned down overnight, Kristoff is going to want me there."

Monira laid a hand on Apallo's shoulder and he turned to find her shaking her head. "Let him go. If last night was truly a repeat of the Augden murders, then we have bigger things to deal with."

He only gave her a lingering glance of displeasure before breaking off and hurrying to regain the distance that had grown between him and Kiyani. As far as he was concerned the conversation wasn't yet done. Not until he had made his position regarding Kiyani's possibility of friendship with Fura crystal clear.

Catching up to him just as he was about to disappear into the trees,

Apallo latched onto Kiyani's arm, stopping him in his tracks.

Kiyani turned and sent him a piercing stare as he wrested his arm back, but Apallo was the first to speak.

"If you so much as think about touching her, I will kill you with my bare hands."

Kiyani's lip curled in disgust, knowing that he was speaking of the more sensual nature that lay beyond that of general friendship.

"As if I would ever be interested."

Apallo's eyes narrowed. "Keep it that way."

"Are we done?"

"One more thing." Pulling a ring off his finger, Apallo held it out to Kiyani. "Can you take this to Kristoff to have it cleaned?"

"I don't know, I might steal it," Kiyani replied mockingly.

Rolling his eyes in return when all he got was an irritated look, Kiyani held out his hand.

"I'll take it to him right away, have him put it on his priority list. You'll get it back by next weekend."

"Good," Apallo declared, seeming unsure as he handed the circle of silver over.

"Anything else?" Kiyani asked boredly.

When Apallo shook his head, he sighed and left.

✧⌘✧

Kiyani broke through the line of trees as he entered the outskirts of Barandor, heading towards the empty grounds of Fireswell. He knew he had lied to Apallo when he'd said that Kristoff would be expecting him, but he had wanted peace and quiet, and with that girl around it wasn't going to be found within the boundaries of Frielana.

Sure, Kristoff didn't expect him to come in when the gates were closed, but Kiyani knew the man would be there regardless and wouldn't deny someone to talk to. Though Kiyani had originally sought the man out for nothing more than a job to pass the time, through the age difference he had learned they had more in common than he would have originally thought.

Not only would he find some solitude in this expedition, if only for a few hours, he would be able to ask questions about the explosion the night before that he wouldn't have to worry about getting back to Apallo. Kiyani didn't mind living under the man's rule. It was better than returning to his real home. But the fact that Apallo often tore into him for nothing more than breathing was a solid case to leave now and then.

Walking through the gate, past the abandoned ticket booth, Kiyani took his time as he made his way to the familiar shop, almost by habit.

He knew he could find the place with his eyes closed if need be.

It was strange without all the people, but this wasn't the first time he had been here during such times. Plenty of days he had come midweek, simply searching for something to do.

"Lost?" Kristoff gruffed from the empty room when he heard Kiyani's steps on the wooden floorboards. He sat hunched over a large magnified lens, as he worked on fitting a turquoise into a silver setting he had been detailing the night before. Unlike Kiyani, who had succeeded in hurting himself, Kristoff was accustomed to random loud noises from the usual festival crowd, and had barely flinched when the explosion had roared through the sky.

Pulling the ring Apallo had given him from his pocket, Kiyani set it on the counter between them. "Here on request."

Kristoff raised his head and looked at the ring questioningly.

"Apallo wants it cleaned," Kiyani added with a shrug. "Don't know why he couldn't bring it himself."

"He actually let you out of his sight with it?" Kristoff asked with an amused tone.

Kiyani laughed. Apallo's treatment of him had become something of an ongoing joke between him and the shop keeper. "From the look on his face you would have thought I would walk off and pawn it."

With a smile, Kristoff shook his head. "I doubt that's the only reason you're here," he added, his smile fading a bit.

"Bored," Kiyani stated simply as he leaned over the counter to watch the man work. He had made a number of rather impressive pieces himself, but he was still awed by the old man's skill as he worked stone and metal with ease.

Kristoff looked up for a moment, a slight raise of a brow wrinkling his face further and setting the dimple in his cheek. "From what I know of you, you don't get bored."

"Looking for some peace and quiet," Kiyani said, revising his statement.

"Ah, well then. That you've got. Hardly feels like a Saturday."

Kiyani nodded. He had come here numerous times during the week when the festival was closed to visitors, but it was still strange to see the festival grounds so quiet on a weekend. Saturday was always the prime day for selling, but today not a soul was present, save for himself and Kristoff, and likely a small handful of other merchants who refused to let a day go to waste despite the circumstances.

Standing by the counter, Kiyani watched Kristoff work for awhile, exchanging pleasantries about the weather and whatnot before letting his real questions come forth.

"Have you seen the destruction yet?"

Kristoff let out a laugh. "Is that what you're here for?"

Kiyani stood and crossed his arms, doing his best to look offended at the old man's words. "No."

"It's damn near impossible to get anywhere near it with all the caution tape. I caught a glimpse of it on the news this morning, though."

"Did they say what happened yet?"

"The officials are saying a gas leak was sparked by a lit candle." Kristoff shook his head as he worked. "I feel bad for the families. I guess no one was left alive that was in the area at the time."

"And what are the unofficial reports?"

"What conspiracy theories are you cooking up in that head of yours?" Kristoff asked, setting his tools down. Turning, he folded his arms across his chest as he leaned back in the chair.

Wandering behind the desk, avoiding the man's questioning gaze, Kiyani shrugged as he grabbed the broom off a hook on the wall. Sweeping the floor for something productive to do, Kiyani answered, "I was just wondering. It's all a little too weird, don't you think?"

He purposely left out the talk he had heard about the relevance to the Augden murders. He knew Kristoff was old enough to have witnessed it firsthand, but he wasn't going to be the one to bring it up first, if at all.

"Of course. Everyone thinks that. But if it is something different, you know the police aren't going to let it go public." He caught the look on Kiyani's face as he took hold of the words. Kristoff shook his finger in the air. "Don't go snooping around and getting in trouble," the man warned. "You're one of the best workers I've had. I need you here, not in jail."

Kiyani paused and leaned on the handle of the broom. "I think I'm the only worker you've ever had," he laughed.

"Exactly," Kristoff said, rising from his chair and setting his elbows on the counter between them.

"I don't know if that's actually a compliment, then."

"Maybe it wasn't meant to be," Kristoff commented with a sly grin. Moving around the table he held a hand out. "Give me that," he said, pulling the broom from Kiyani's loose grasp. "Why don't you go on home and actually have some fun for once. You can only sweep the floor so many times, and there's nothing much that actually needs to be done."

"Whoever said this wasn't fun? I like being here."

Kristoff replaced the broom on the wall and shooed Kiyani away. "You need to get out more," he chuckled with a shake of his head. He plucked the ring from the counter and went about the business of putting it in a labeled bag with instructions to himself. Kiyani went to speak again, but Kristoff cut him off. "Go. I'll see you next week."

Kiyani could see the smile on the merchant's face as he settled back down to focus on his work again. "Fine."

Not feeling the urge to head back to Frielana so soon to be attacked yet again by Apallo, Kiyani veered off in the opposite direction, heading towards the ruined subdivision that, according to Kristoff, had been all over the late night and morning news. Despite his warnings, Kiyani still wanted to see the devastation for himself. He didn't plan on getting in trouble, and snooping wasn't necessarily in his nature, but he was still curious, wanting to see it for himself.

The long, leisurely walk through town and beyond did nothing to prepare him for the scene he came upon. As Kristoff had noted, there was caution tape strung up over the entire block, but it did little to block the catastrophe from view. The boldly worded yellow strings flapped in the breeze, providing the only real color in the area. Kiyani walked along the perimeter, leaving footprints in the thin layer of gray ash that had settled onto the ground in the wake of the fires. The blackened husks of trees and splintered timber rose from the dust like lonesome specters in strange shapes – the only real thing left, save for the stone of house foundations, and a number of charred metal husks of cars that looked like the dilapidated shells of beetles. Everything else was leveled.

Despite the chaos that had ensued the night before, only one police car adorned the scene in the distance. The man to whom the vehicle belonged looked up briefly, but ignored Kiyani afterwards, intent on going about his business and getting out of there. To the officer he probably just came across as another bored teenager that wanted to get a look at the latest excitement in town. For once, Kiyani was fine with that.

He didn't know how much time had passed as he let his eyes brush the scene when he felt the unmistakable feeling of a presence behind him. Preparing his words, he turned, expecting to see another police official, but what he found instead stopped him cold.

In fact, he would have preferred that option. Taking in the girl's form as she stood before him, her long, ebony hair blowing in the breeze as she shot him a seductive smile, Kiyani could feel the tension immediately gather in his body.

"What are you doing here?" Kiyani asked brusquely, not overly excited about her sudden presence. The fact that she had made no noise whatsoever as she had approached, practically sneaking up on him, bothered him more than it should have.

"I could ask you the same thing," Kieli purred, a gleam in her eye.

She sauntered over to him, knowing he was well aware of the low cut of the skimpy shirts she always wore. Though Kiyani tensed as she approached, Kieli knew he was stubborn and would stand his ground. Snaking behind him, she circled around and came to a stop a few inches in front of him. Leaning forward, she wrapped her arms around his neck as their lips met.

The moment only lasted a few seconds, though it was far too long for Kiyani, before he roughly pushed her away, trying to put as much distance as he could between them without actually leaving. He didn't trust her actions, and he certainly didn't trust the fact that she happened to be here the same time he was. It was like she was following him.

"You stay the hell away from me," Kiyani declared angrily, pointing a finger at her. The mere sight of her was bad enough, but her voice ground at his nerves, and her touch only infuriated him.

Kieli only smiled at his reaction. "You loved me once," she cooed innocently.

"What was that you once said to me?" he asked sarcastically. "Oh yeah, 'I *never* loved you.' The feeling's mutual."

"You say that now, but there was a time, not all too long ago, I might add, that you would have done anything for me."

Kiyani snorted. "Good thing I found some common sense. What are you doing here?" he repeated again none too kindly, not giving her the chance to reply to his comment. "And why do I have the distinct feeling you had something to do with this?"

"Like I have that kind of influence. Besides, you think I would do this to my friend?"

"You have no friends," Kiyani remarked coldly.

"Because you're such an expert on the subject? I'm here the same as you. Because I was curious."

"Curiosity killed the cat."

"Then you better watch out," Kieli said. Stealing behind him, she grabbed his arm, her fingernails digging into his skin. "The Prophecy's coming," she whispered malevolently in his ear before letting go.

Kiyani's breath caught in his throat at the words. "What do you know of the Prophecy?" he asked. But, turning around, he found that she was already gone, leaving him standing alone amongst the wreckage of so many lives.

He felt a shiver run down his spine that had nothing to do with the fall chill in the air. Not sure what to think of what had just happened, he turned away from the scene and headed back to Frielana.

His day of seeking solitude had turned into something way off the mark, leaving a sour taste in his mouth.

9

◆◆◇◆◆

A HOODED STRANGER

Fura moved through the woods, cursing herself for thinking that she would be able to find her way. She didn't have any particular destination in mind, had just wanted to go on a walk to clear her mind and get away from all the people without being perceived as rude.

The spring had been a refreshing reprieve. For a minute.

Even after Kiyani had left, she'd still had the distinct feeling that, despite no visible signs declaring such, that he felt the spring belonged to him, and that she was invading his personal territory. It was a strange thing to think, she knew. You couldn't lay claim to nature.

Either way, her encounter with him had left a bitter taste in her mouth, leading her to find solitude elsewhere.

Thinking about it as she moved deeper into the woods, she realized that despite the beauty of the falls, Kiyani was the only one she had seen near it.

Ducking beneath an over-hanging tree branch, Fura wondered why that was. She had only been in what Apallo had deemed Frielana for less than a day, but it was easy to see that there was a mysterious air around Kiyani that those living there went out of their way to avoid. It was hard to find reason why he was even living there if he supposedly harbored such ill will towards the group's leader.

She thought to ask about it, but the mere idea of approaching Apallo with the subject immediately turned her thoughts to a different path. She had seen how they regarded each other with her own two eyes, twice in less than twenty-four hours. The words that had been exchanged had been far from friendly, and if they ever thought to deal any physical blows to one another, Fura knew she wouldn't want to be there to witness the fight.

In the years that she had known Apallo through the Fireswell festival she had always regarded him as an overbearingly friendly and docile man. What she had seen between him and Kiyani had revealed something that she had only once seen a glimmer of before. And that had been when the man had caught a festival-goer trying to pickpocket an older woman. Fura could still remember him muttering to himself the rest of the day that some people took their role playing a little too seriously within the festival.

Side-stepping another branch and leaping over a small root that protruded from the ground, Fura knew that regardless of who would come out on top between the two men, it didn't much matter at this point.

What mattered right now was finding her bearings again.

It had been stupid to head out to explore on her own in the first place. That much Fura knew for certain. Of course, she hadn't meant to go out this far. It had started as a simple walk to clear the sympathetic voices from her head, the sorrow filled eyes that quietly regarded her, and the pinched lips as if none of them knew what to say around her.

The quiet of the forest was the only thing thus far that had provided any solace. So that was the figurative road that she had taken that morning. Yet, one step had led to another, the sun-drenched forest pulling her further in like a warm embrace, the calls of the birds a joyous melody that enveloped her mind and made her forget the sting of tragedy.

Truth be told, she hadn't been thinking at all when she had set off on this unexpected venture, and now she was undeniably lost.

The easiest route would have been to go back the way she had come, but, looking around, Fura didn't think that was an option. She didn't know just how long she had been out – apparently not long enough yet for Apallo to have sent a search party after her – but she was certain that she was going in circles. Unfortunately, that circle had yet to take her back past the camp.

Frustration building, Fura stopped and sat herself down at the base of a tree. Angry at herself for getting herself into this mess aside, she could see that her hands were shaking. Hating herself for knowing it was fear, her aggravation slid into a distressing sorrow that brought the tears forth from her eyes that she had been trying to hide.

Her first reaction was to hastily wipe them away, but she didn't need to look around to know that she was alone, save for the wildlife that eyed her from the highest branches of the trees. Letting herself wallow in misery, just for a moment, she closed her eyes, hugged her knees to her chest, and laid her head back against the tree.

It was what she had come out here for anyways. The solitude. A chance to get away and to cry freely without anyone around to lay judgment on her. She knew that no one would blame her if she let such emotions out within the boundaries of the camp, that no one expected her to be the epitome of strength, but she also didn't want the attention that it would likely bring. On any normal day, especially at the festival, Fura loved meeting new people. But here, she didn't want the looks of sympathy. She didn't want to be seen as the girl weeping in the corner, and she certainly didn't want to be known as the girl who had lost her family, her life.

It would be easier to start life anew somewhere than to have to deal with that stigma for who knew how long.

Sometime later, her emotion spent, Fura sniffled and opened her eyes. Letting out a sigh, wondering how long the worst of the hurt would last – weeks? months? years? - she took stock of her surroundings.

Things could be worse. It could be raining or overcast. It could certainly be much colder. As it was, bright sunlight streamed through the trees, and the light breeze that carried through the air could be considered rather balmy for the time of year.

The sun high above her head, Fura noted that at least she had the element of time on her side. It was early fall, but there were still plenty of hours of light left in the day.

Plenty of hours to attempt to back track and find her way to the camp again… or plenty of hours to get herself all the more lost.

Ignoring the glimmer of truth in that last thought, Fura pulled herself from the ground and looked around, wondering which way to go.

She still had yet to figure out just why Apallo and the others were living out here, but she could see the appeal of being so close to nature. Just feeling the warmth of the sun on her face, and listening to the twitter of the birds had a naturally calming effect that she knew nothing in Barandor would be able to rival right now.

It made her wish that she had taken the time to explore the woods before everything had changed, but like most everyone else in Barandor, the stories had driven such ideas from her mind. She had never much believed in the tales, if she really thought about it, but the ideas were still seeded in her mind, planted in the earliest years of schooling, in the drivel of fairy tales told to the youngest students to keep them entertained and in line.

Just thinking about school created a pit of hollowness in Fura's stomach. It was hard to believe that just yesterday she had been wandering the halls of the two story brick building that served as both the middle and high school for the small town of Barandor. Only yesterday had she been joking with one of her favorite teachers that she still believed in the fairy tales of old. Yet all she had received since that moment was a cold harsh slap in the face of reality. It was nearly unimaginable that so much could happen in such a short period of time, that so much could change.

The magical lull of fairy tales told her that somehow she would be okay.

Reality told her that nothing would ever be the same again.

Sometimes that wasn't such a bad thing, but right now all Fura wanted was her life back.

A part of her thought to forget about finding and returning to this Frielana, and to somehow make her way back to Barandor instead. But she had nowhere to go. It had hit her last night when the police officer had been asking her questions just before Apallo had intervened. There were no aunts or uncles living close by, no grandparents or distant relatives that she knew of.

It only made her spirits sink further. She had no home. No family. No life.

Fura thought back to the ghostly images of the smiling faces that she had seen only the day before, and had the smallest inkling of a feeling that Miss Surrei would have no qualms about helping her to get back on her feet if she suddenly showed up. Or even Tiyano from the festival. But, as tempting as it was, Fura didn't want to bring them into this, to weigh them down with her troubles.

What she had left now was Apallo and the rest of the festival troupe, who had always felt like a second family to her. As strange as it was, she trusted Apallo.

And the more she thought about it, the more Barandor felt like the wrong course of action.

It would be much too busy there. Too much familiarity to drive her back into a sorrowful depression. She briefly wondered if her face would be plastered on the news coverage of the event. If she would be listed as one of the victims or survivors. Or if she wouldn't be mentioned at all, just forgotten like a ghost in the wind.

"You seem troubled, my dear."

Fura started at the voice as she scrambled to her feet. Even deep within her mind, wallowing in her self-created miseries, she had been certain that she was alone.

Yet, there he was.

Leaning against a tree a few feet away, the sunlight reflecting off a shiny strand of dark hair that fell around a face that was shadowed in the cowl of a hood, was a man that Fura was sure she had never met before. Though it was difficult to tell with the cloak hiding most of his features.

Looking around hesitantly, Fura searched the trees, looking for any other sign of life to set herself at ease. Just because she was lost didn't mean that no one else would wander across her.

"A young lady such as yourself shouldn't be out here alone. Not in times like these."

The words did little to ease her suspicion.

Her first instinct was to run, but his words held her back, sparking her curiosity. "Times like these?" she said, repeating his words and sending them back as a question.

The man nodded solemnly. "There are things at work in these parts." He leaned on the plain stick he carried as a staff, examining it as he twirled it, speaking more as if she weren't even there. "Dangerous things. Things best not come across by wandering girls who are lost."

"I'm not lost," Fura claimed defensively.

There had been an undertone of something darker in the man's words there for a moment, making Fura briefly rethink her initial instinct to run. But she knew it wouldn't be a good idea. Sure, she could run fast, but she could tell just by looking at the man that if he caught her he could easily overpower her. It was best to wait and see how things played out.

"Forgive me, then."

Fura relaxed at his words, spoken as remorsefully as possible, making her wonder if what she had heard before had been nothing more than a trick of her mind.

"So, where is it that you're headed, my girl?"

"I – I'm just exploring."

Even to her own ears her words weren't entirely convincing, but Fura hoped the man wouldn't pick up on her faint hesitation. Only a moment ago she had been hoping to run across someone who could help her find her way back to Frielana, but now that she had been given that opportunity, Fura felt it best to keep her mouth shut. She had no idea who this man was, what he was doing out here himself, or why he had bothered to stop and talk to her. The best in her said that he was just a friendly passerby, looking for a conversational moment of companionship before setting back off on whatever trail it was that he had been on in the first place. Yet, after the day she'd just had, she couldn't help but be suspicious of his motives.

"Ah, inquisitive minds," the man said with a wry smile, obviously unaware of the turmoil within Fura's mind. "Nothing wrong with that."

"I guess."

Looking around, the sun still bright in the sky, Fura found that had she been in a different mindset, she might actually enjoy all this.

"The most promising of people are the ones who question what's before them."

Fura regarded him, the initial lull of danger falling into intrigue. Most people didn't talk as he did, his words strange, calculating and precise, but with a velvet tone that kept her rooted in place. "You really think so?"

"Trust not the ones you deem friends, for dreams are only a twisted illusion of reality."

"What?" Fura asked, confused by his words. Despite his younger appearance, he was sounding more and more like an old man who had lost his mind. Yet, it all catapulted his mysterious intrigue. A fascination that left her balancing precariously on the line of wanting to leave and wanting to stay.

The man raised a brow in reply. "Did I say something?"

"I –" Fura stammered, not sure what to say in reply. She distinctly remembered this strange man saying something mysterious, but now that she tried to recall it she could find nothing out of the ordinary, as if his last words had faded it into a ghostly memory and left her grasping for straws. "Sorry," she apologized, not wanting to come across as frail as she was suddenly feeling. "Must have been the wind."

Surprisingly, the man only smiled. "You would do well to listen to the voices in the wind… or the shadows."

"What?" Fura asked for the second time during their vague conversation, wondering if she had only imagined that last part.

"Tell me, my dear," the man continued. "What chance do you really think fire has against shadow?"

A crack in the surrounding underbrush caused Fura to turn, wondering who had stumbled upon their conversation. Nothing stirred but the leafy ferns in the breeze, causing Fura to change the *who* into *what*.

"There will be a time when you ask that question yourself."

Certain that there was no one else there, she turned to find that she was utterly alone.

Though the day was still as bright as ever, the air in the surrounding forest seemed to have darkened.

Spinning around again to take everything in, Fura had the distinct feeling that she had been in the middle of something, that someone had been there with her, but her eyes revealed that she was alone. Shaking her head in confusion as she wondered if maybe she was dreaming this whole day, Fura wheeled around as another snap sounded from behind her.

Her frantic nerves bordering on fear, she quickly scanned the ground and found a weighty branch that had long since parted from the tree it originally belonged to. Hastily picking it up, she grasped it with both hands, her knuckles white in the sunlight as she wielded it like a weapon and waited.

And waited.

Just when Fura was ready to tell herself that she was losing it, a form emerged from the dim light of the forest.

Without thinking it through, moving forward based on nothing more than instinct, she brought her makeshift weapon high above her head and attacked.

"What the hell?"

As the stick stopped mid-air, having made contact with something, Fura found herself afraid to open her eyes. Afraid to see what she might have done. The pounding of adrenaline-filled blood in her ears left Fura nearly deaf as her heart raced, but, regardless, she would recognize that voice anywhere. Opening her eyes, she nearly died from embarrassment as she took in the intense blue eyes that bored into her with question.

"Kiyani?" Fura asked breathlessly, her frantic mind still trying to register the familiar face, where before it had been certain that there had been someone out here stalking her, trying to kill her.

Repeating the thought in her mind and hearing for herself just how ridiculous it sounded, she avoided Kiyani's gaze as she tried to steady her breathing.

"Care to explain?" he prodded.

When Fura had gathered enough courage to look at him again she could see that his brow was raised in question, waiting for her answer. To say that she was embarrassed was an understatement.

What was even worse was that she could see that his hand grasped the other end of the stick that she clung to. She hadn't inflicted any damage at all except to her pride. Fura was glad that she hadn't managed to hurt him, but it made her wonder that if he could so easily dodge her attack how well she would have fared if it had been someone else she had come across. Someone that had actually intended to harm her.

Fura nearly laughed in discomfort. She was going mad, thinking that someone was after her. What was so frightening about a simple walk in a sun-lit forest anyways? It was the middle of the day, and she was seeing danger and shadows everywhere. Maybe there *was* something wrong with her.

"Waiting," Kiyani said, a hint of irritation in his voice.

"Sorry," Fura said, remembering that she had never answered him.

"So?"

"I'm essentially homeless," Fura replied irritably, letting loose the first thing that came to mind. The only thing that had really been on her mind the last few hours.

"You're acting like it," Kiyani countered.

Fura cringed at his reply, suddenly aware of how close he was to her and how she must appear to him. If she came across someone running around the woods wielding a stick, she'd probably think they were crazy too.

"Okay, so I'm an emotional wreck right now," she admitted.

Kiyani wrenched the stick out of her grasp, making her realize that she had still been clutching it like a weapon and that neither of them had moved during their whole spotty conversation. "So that gives you license to run around like a wild woman in the woods and attack innocent people with shrubbery?"

Tossing the unassuming piece of wood to the ground, Kiyani turned away, but not before Fura caught the roll of his eyes.

"And Apallo's worried about me?" he muttered irritably. "He should have checked your sanity."

Her cheeks flushed with color, Fura watched Kiyani walk away. Even if she might have entertained the idea of striking up a semblance of a friendship with him, she wasn't doing a good job of introducing herself.

"Are you coming?"

Looking up, Fura could see that Kiyani had stopped a few feet away and was looking at her.

"What?"

"I take it you're lost."

Fura grimaced, wondering if it was that noticeably written on her face.

Looking around, knowing that this was her only way back to Frielana, she let out a sigh. Apallo might not have wanted her around Kiyani, but Fura saw no sign of danger from him, only the obvious fact that he wasn't happy with her sudden presence.

And based on her recent actions, how could she blame him?

10

♦♦◇♦♦

FIRST DISTURBANCE

The walk was a silent one as Kiyani made it obvious he had nothing to say to her, and Fura was still too mortified to even try to speak to him. As she followed him she sifted through her mind, trying to find the root of why she had been so on edge in the first place. But there was nothing there, nothing but the memory of wandering, lost and alone.

It was the strangest feeling, but one that she didn't even want to dare bring to anyone's attention. Telling herself that it was nothing but her mind playing tricks on her – a combination of the recent horror she had been through, and the lack of sleep associated with it – Fura decided to leave it at that.

Now that she wasn't fearing for her life, or worried about finding her way back to civilization, she found herself actually enjoying the day – or, at least as much as she could, given the circumstances of being there in the first place. The forest was bright and alive with life, bringing the slightest of smiles to her face.

Though Barandor was a pretty small, rural town, the Fireswell festival and the short, wooded trails that wound lazily along the river that cut through it were the closest that Fura could say she had ever really been to nature. The Verboten Forest was something else entirely. Trees and leafy foliage permeated the area for as far as she could see in any direction. The ground was soft underfoot, her steps cushioned by the moist soil, kept damp by a layer of decomposing leaves. Through the air wafted that unmistakable smell of earth, yet it wasn't overpowering in the least. It actually smelled like home to her, making her think of the cedar chipped trails beneath the trees that made up the festival grounds. And then there were the colors. Never before had she seen such vivid colors of green. Fura was sure that it wasn't always so spectacular, but the area was dazzling in the sunlight.

"You should see it in the spring."

The flush returning to her face, Fura dropped her gaze just in time to catch Kiyani's eye leaving her. Apparently her streak of humiliation was nowhere close to ending. She hadn't even been aware that she had been so visibly gawking at her surroundings.

She probably looked like some ignorant child that had never seen a tree before.

But Fura was sure Kiyani was right. Certain that his attention was no longer on her, she looked closer at her surroundings. Sure enough, high in the tree tops she could see the sure tell signs of fall: the sedated reds and oranges that were beginning to creep along the leaves as if they had been dipped in a watery bath of paint.

Thinking to those early days of spring, when the sky was still mottled with the dreary grays of the season that lingered when winter couldn't yet be persuaded to leave, Fura could almost see those bright, lime green buds beginning to sprout on the end of bare branches. Just picturing it in her head made her want to see it for herself, and she wondered if there was anything in Frielana that would keep her here for that long.

Breaking away from her sudden, somber thoughts, Fura could hear the sounds of the camp begin to filter through the air, a sure sign that Kiyani had been right when he had claimed that they weren't too far away.

A moment later, the ridge that surrounded the small valley that Frielana sat within came into sight. Moving ahead of her, Kiyani ascended with ease and stood at the top of it.

Fura wasn't sure if he was actually waiting for her, or if he just wasn't keen on hurrying back into Apallo's territory, but her only thought was that he actually looked kind of pensive, standing there in the sunlight, the wind tousling his hair. A different sight than the stern-faced individual who had been arguing with her that morning.

When she came up next to him, Kiyani waved an arm across the scene as if presenting it, though in a way as if to crudely and silently declare that it had been there all along.

"Thank you," Fura said, regardless of his demeanor towards her.

Without him, she didn't want to think how long she would have been wandering aimlessly. It wasn't a terrible place, but she still didn't want to be stuck among the towering trees on her own once the dark of night set in.

Before Kiyani could make off without another word, as he seemed apt to do, Fura set a hand on his arm to hold him back.

His gaze settling on her hand, Fura immediately pulled it away.

"Please don't tell Apallo about…. that."

She stumbled with the words, not really sure how to even describe the incident, but Fura had a feeling that he knew exactly what she was talking about. It was bad enough that he had lain witness to it in the first place. What was even worse was that she couldn't recall for the life of her why she had been so on edge in the first place.

"Do I look like someone who regularly reports to Apallo?" he asked. Shucking her hand off his arm, he moved forward without waiting for an answer.

Fura rolled her eyes, wondering why he had to make play of being so damn rude.

If he was merely acting that way, he was doing a damn fine job… and if not, then he really needed to find himself a hobby.

At the least, she knew that he probably wouldn't speak of what had occurred back there in the woods.

Carefully making her way down the incline behind Kiyani, who was already a number of paces ahead of her, Fura barely had time to settle back in before Apallo came rushing over, a frantic wildness tainting his usually calm eyes.

"Fura?!" he said, his words coming across nearly as a shout as he firmly embraced her in a sudden hug. "Thank the stars, you're alive." Letting her go, he held her at arm's length, looking her over as if searching for any sign of damage. "Are you okay?"

Dumbstruck by the sudden sign of intensified and affectionate worry, Fura could only nod, her mind drawing a complete blank on what to say, or what might have caused his swift change in attitude. She didn't think she had been gone that long.

"What happened?" Kiyani asked, making it known that he was present and, at the time, the only one with a level head in the situation.

As if a switch had been struck, Apallo's face hardened as he turned to him. "And where have you been?"

Fura could see Kiyani nearly step back at the loathing present in Apallo's tone. His words weren't merely a question, but an accusation.

A shadow falling across his eyes, Kiyani replied before anything else could come from the man. "You know I was with Kristoff."

"This whole time?" Apallo asked darkly.

"He was with me," Fura claimed suddenly when she could see Kiyani grasping for a way to word his answer. She didn't know where he had been before he had come across her in the woods, yet she felt the need to vouch for him.

As if the two men had already forgotten she was there in the shadow of their hatred towards one another, all Fura received in reply to her words was the briefest hint of confusion from Kiyani, and a look of cold question from Apallo.

Brushing off both of their reactions, she only shrugged innocently. "I got lost," she confessed to Apallo in particular. She couldn't feel bad about that. It was truth, after all.

A few moments passed, the only sounds the movement and whispers of the people who occupied the site behind them, but Apallo's face eventually softened.

"You should be more careful."

Fura bit her lip, feeling like she'd disappointed him in some way.

"So, what's going on?" Kiyani tried again, devoted to getting an answer.

Running a calloused hand through his fiery hair, Apallo avoided both their gazes as he regarded the current state of the camp.

Looking past him, Fura could see that what she had initially mistaken for the general hustle and bustle of camp was actually more along the lines of controlled chaos. There was an underlying sense of fear present in the air. She could see it in the shifty eyes of those that milled about, and the creases of worry etched into the faces of individuals as they conversed with one another in hushed whispers.

"One of our own was found dead," Apallo finally confessed in a low voice, as if he were afraid that speaking it any louder would spread full on panic.

Fura pursed her lips, shocked and unsure of what to say in reply. She couldn't say that she knew many of these people, but the news still hit her hard. Wasn't it enough that devastation had last hit only yesterday?

Kiyani was the one to speak up. "Who?"

"Brieda," Apallo replied, seeming to have lost all sense of need to fight with him.

"Was it an accident?"

Watching Kiyani drill Apallo like he was an investigator in his spare time, Fura wondered who this person was and if she had potentially met them in the last twenty four hours without actually knowing it. A death, no matter who's, was always a sad thing, but it was another feeling altogether when you actually had a face to go with the name. Somehow it felt more personal, even more so if you had run across or spoken to them in real life.

Apallo looked fidgety, a state that Fura wasn't used to seeing him in. "Maybe, but it's looking more like murder."

"Who?"

"Who do you think?" Apallo replied bitterly, both his eyes and his tone taking on a shadow of darkness before he turned away.

Fura watched him leave, left with more questions than she had started with. Turning to Kiyani who stood wordlessly, she thought to ask him to try and clarify. But before she could utter a single word, Apallo stopped and turned as if he had realized he had forgotten something.

Perking up, Fura expected him to add something that would help her understand things.

"Fura, go find Monira and stay with her please," he said instead. "Now," he added a bit harshly when she faltered, thinking to still speak to Kiyani before she went to fulfill Apallo's wishes.

Feeling chastised for something she hadn't yet done, Fura winced at his tone but set her feet in motion. Though Apallo had already turned away, she found that she could only briefly glance at Kiyani before sliding past him, as if she were afraid to see what would be present on his face, afraid to make even the smallest move against Apallo.

The man was the one who had given her a home in her time of need after all. That in itself gave her reason to respect his wishes, no matter how silly they may have seemed to her. Thinking about the Apallo she had come to know over the years of working at the festival, Fura told herself that there must be a good reason as to why he consistently treated Kiyani in such a way.

She couldn't determine what it was, but it made her rethink her sudden wanting to get to know the boy.

Curiosity still playing a weakness, Fura found herself turning to look at Kiyani one last time as she approached the line of caves. He stood where they had both left him, a look of quiet, seething anger on his face as if he had been accused of the murder himself.

Wondering what Apallo had meant when he'd told Kiyani he knew who the murderer was sent the wheels in Fura's head spinning. Was it possible that he could've had something to do with it?

It only reminded her that she had no idea what he was capable of, but the way that he shook his head in disgust before stalking off told her that he was just as innocent as she was in the matter.

Letting it go for the time being and deciding to follow through on Apallo's orders, Fura glanced about the clearing. She could see Apallo amidst a small crowd that had gathered around him, as well as a few other faces that she was beginning to recognize but couldn't put a name to. But no Monira.

Though the sun still shone with the same intensity overhead, a shadow had fallen over the day with the news she'd just heard, sending a shiver down her spine and raising the hair on her arms. Her own misfortune as of late… this murder… didn't things always come in threes? She hated to think what might be next. Fura told herself that that was nothing but old superstition, but she couldn't deny the eerie feeling that something more was coming. And soon.

Shaking off the sense of impending doom, Fura moved into the opening of what she had come to know as the main cave out of the multiples that rested there naturally, intent on finding Monira. Apallo hadn't told her where the woman was at, but she was sure that if he wanted her to find her than she had to be located somewhere within

Frielana. Still not sure how things worked around the place, it was her best guess.

The mix of thoughts congealed in her mind like day old gravy, distracting her. Lost in the haze of it all, Fura barely even caught sight of the figure that moved towards her until they were in danger of crudely colliding. Startled, she managed to move to the side in the split second before they would have crashed into one another.

"Sorry," Fura hastily apologized, cursing herself for not paying better attention. If she kept this up, she would eventually find herself in some kind of trouble, whether she was actively searching for it or not. Probably of her own making. It left her to wonder if maybe she would be better off if she just voluntarily locked herself in her room and stayed there. "I should have been watching where I was going."

"Don't worry," the man stated, perking up a bit at her sudden intrusion, making Fura realize that he was just as guilty. "No one's quite thinking straight right now."

"Right."

"Nevo," he said, offering his hand.

Fura looked at it cautiously, but took it. His grasp was firm, but friendly, like the smile that adorned his face.

Under different circumstances, Fura thought that this might be someone she could be friends with, his demeanor reminding her of Tiyano back at the festival. But right now, she was too flustered and distraught to care about such things. Maybe somewhere down the line if she was still here.

"Fura," she offered in return.

"I know."

Right, Fura told herself. At the festival she had grown used to people knowing who she was. Heck, she had enjoyed it most days. But here, it was hard to get used to the fact that all these people knew her name, regardless of whether she knew them or not. When it was solitude she was seeking, it ended up being unsettling.

"My condolences," Nevo said with a small bow that sent a sheet of his pale blond hair into his face.

There it was. That sympathy that Fura had been trying to escape earlier in the day.

With a short dip of his head and a pat on her shoulder, the man moved out of the cave, leaving Fura on her own. Watching him go, she revised that thought of being friends.

"Oh, Fura!"

Left with mixed emotions after the encounter, Fura nearly shouted *what?* in frustration, until she saw that it was Monira that approached.

Not picking up on her distress, too lost in her own, Monira came forward and embraced her in a hug. It was just as awkward for Fura as

Apallo's had been, but luckily lacking the strength his had held that'd made Fura feel as if he were squeezing the breath right out of her.

Despite the strange nature of it, Fura fought the urge to pull back.

It was over as quickly as it began, and when Monira pulled away, a touch of sorrow in her eyes, Fura actually felt bad that she had initially wanted it to end.

She still only had the faintest idea what was going on, but despite the fact that she knew this sadness that had come over Frielana was because of the recent death, a part of her felt that maybe, in the deep recesses of everyone's minds that just a little of it was reserved for her and her situation as well.

Though Fura had the sudden overwhelming urge to finally cry, she kept the tears at bay. With the current news, she felt it would be inappropriate to fall apart over her own situation. Only now that she felt her time had come and gone, did she wish she had taken advantage of it.

"Apallo was so worried about you," Monira said.

The hand that rested on Fura's arm was gentle, as was the look in the woman's eyes. It was that small gesture that silently asked if she was okay, even if the question wasn't going to be voiced aloud. Sadly enough, that was one of the reasons that Fura had found herself drawn to Monira. Save for Apallo – who often appeared too busy running things and trying to keep everything in order – and Kiyani – who Fura had decided merely didn't care – she was the only one who hadn't drowned her in the sympathy that Fura was trying so hard to escape.

"How are you?" the woman asked when Fura made no move to answer.

It was that question again, yet coming from her, it wasn't steeped in that overbearing necessity to say something about her situation that seemed to come from all the others. From Monira it didn't come across as forced and insensitive.

Fura put a smile on her face that she knew couldn't fool her.

"I'm coping."

Monira nodded. "That's all you can do at this stage."

"Oh, good. You found her," a voice said, entering the conversation from the doorway.

Turning, Fura gave a curt nod in Apallo's direction.

A flicker of sadness that felt as if it was reserved only for her moved across his eyes as they settled on her for a moment. Fura couldn't quite place it, save for that he had known her for so long, but, like Monira, she knew that Apallo was one of the ones that would be the last to make mention of her circumstances.

"I've made a number of inquiries around camp and no one, save the two that found the body, saw anything," Apallo said to Monira.

Fura didn't even mind that he was talking over her, glad for the short reprieve of trying to find words to say.

"A small group of us – Nevo, Raegga, Dale, and I – are going back to the site where Brieda was found. I don't know if there's anything else to be found..."

"But it will help settle your mind," Monira finished for him with a polite nod. "Do what you need to do."

Apallo let out a short sigh. "I'll make an announcement at dusk."

The two women watched in silence as he left.

What settled in the air in his wake was something that Fura couldn't quite place, but she attributed it to what she had seen from Apallo when he had been standing there before her. That look of a leader at a loss, pulled down by troubles that wouldn't necessarily be his own in any other position. It was something that Fura was sure he would expertly disguise behind a false strength once he left the quiet confines of the cave, replacing it with that *everything will be okay* kind of air that those of authority often wore like a second skin.

It definitely took a special skill set to place your own worries and pains aside during such a time, and put on that strength before all those waiting eyes. To mask your emotions and put everyone else first. To get things done when all you wanted to do was crawl into a dark corner and hope everything would eventually right itself.

Fura had always respected the man, but it was times like this when she certainly didn't envy Apallo's job.

Looking beyond the vines that had been pulled back from the doorway during the day, she caught a glimpse of the group of men Apallo had commandeered in the short time since she had reentered the camp. Fura could feel Monira at her side, watching the same scene unfold.

"Who was she?" Fura asked.

"Brieda?"

Fura nodded.

"Brieda Morgenstein." Monira spoke the woman's name as hardly a whisper, as if trying to conjure happier memories. "She was a friend. But most of us knew her as the hunter."

"The hunter?" Fura couldn't help but question. It was an odd title to have attached to one's name.

A sad smile crossed Monira's lips. "Apallo hasn't had the time to explain much, has he?"

Fura shook her head. That was an understatement. Unlike the Fireswell festival, where he had closely mentored her and been everywhere like a shadow, Apallo had been nearly nonexistent here. Not that she blamed him. Fura didn't expect anyone, least of all him, to wait on her hand and foot. And in a way, Fura preferred it.

Her hand brushing lightly across Fura's arm, Monira directed her deeper into the cave. Into the quiet solitude and darkness. "Come. Let's go sit."

"Can we go outside?"

"Of course."

11

◆◆◇◆◆

DARK DISCUSSIONS

Sitting on the outskirts of the clearing, near the craggy opening of the caves, Fura learned that Brieda had not only been a well liked person, but an integral part of the camp. Along with so many others.

Fura had wondered from the moment that she had walked into this so-called Frielana the night before if all these people actually lived like this, out in the wilds, like some unnamed tribe on a National Geographic special. It had felt strange and almost prehistoric, barbaric even to leave yourself susceptible to the elements by choice. Instinctually, Fura had taken the early guess that maybe it was something that certain members of the Fireguild, those that were deeper into the role playing of the festival, took part in during the fall months to keep themselves in character.

In the back of her ever-reeling mind, it was still a plausible explanation.

But the more Fura sat back and watched, and the more she learned, the more she was beginning to think that maybe even that wasn't right.

Sitting on the sidelines with Monira, regrettably only half listening as she spoke, Fura watched the others move about, really taking it all in for the first time since she had arrived.

What she had first taken as a small number of people moving about and minding their own business as they took on old-world hobbies realigned itself in her mind as a much bigger picture.

On the surface it appeared as nothing more than a hub of generally organized chaos. But if you stood still and watched for more than a few fleeting moments, it was like a fuzzy picture that slowly came into focus. And what you got when you took in the milling bodies and personalities of Frielana was something akin to the inner workings of an ant hill.

Everybody seemed to have something to do. Somewhere to go. Something to contribute to the way of life that they had willingly taken on.

A few small groups of people milled about, lounging like Monira and herself in differing areas of the camp. They sat on fallen logs or stones that rose from the earth, talking amongst themselves, their conversations given life with frantic hand gestures and the occasional loud guffaw. Two women regarded one another with solemn eyes as they tended to the large fire that seemed to be ever burning in the center of the clearing. Not far from that sat two separate and smaller fires, hosting what Fura assumed would be dinner later that night. Above one, a hunk of unidentified meat spun on a spit above the flames, the juices periodically dripping down into the coals, sizzling and spitting and sending tendrils of steam into the air. Above the other stone-walled pit gently swung a giant black cauldron, steam rising from its lip as the condensed fire below licked at its bottom.

Here and there, individuals brought in branches as kindling, while a single man on the outskirts of camp stood shirtless as he cleaved thick logs with an ancient looking axe.

At the opposite end of the clearing, a group of middle-aged men sparred with stout lengths of wood.

And that was only what she could see at the moment, making Fura wonder just how many activities went on during any given day. Only that morning when she had woken up, she had walked past a woman within the caves handling the complicated workings of an old fashioned loom with ease.

Her eyes still on the men as they practiced what she could only assume were fighting skills, Fura found that watching only reminded her of attacking Kiyani earlier with no motive. Still embarrassed, she turned away.

Relieving herself of her sight, Fura found that if she closed her eyes and focused on the sounds alone, she could almost imagine herself sitting in the middle of a more authentic renaissance faire. Complete with the fully wooded natural backdrop that many sadly seemed to lack.

Essentially, it was a village without houses.

And within that primitive village was a loose system of hierarchy that Fura hadn't expected.

She had learned through Monira's words that, although titles were loosely acquired and often changed, everyone always had some sort of duty to attend to. It was what kept the place in running order.

And what made Fura feel all the more useless.

She couldn't even take a walk without getting lost.

But she had been right about Apallo being leader. His was the only irrevocable title, and one that no one dared challenge.

"So, Brieda was a hunter?" Fura asked, trying to keep everything that she was learning in order.

"Not just a hunter. She was the best among us." Monira's lip curved into a small smile, but her eyes revealed the pain of something more. "An expert with bow and arrow. She could bring down a full size deer with a single shot clear across the way."

Fura watched the woman emphasize her words with dancing hands, catching hold of something not quite said in her words, but in the lines on her face. "She was close to you, wasn't she?"

"Brieda was my brother's wife."

"Oh," was all Fura could think to say. "Sorry."

"It's alright," Monira assured her. "I lost Marcus many years ago. A wild animal attack, I suppose you could say."

Not knowing how to respond to that either, Fura could only do her best not to stare at the woman.

Before either of them could continue the conversation, a deep reverberating bellow sounded through the camp.

Nevo stood just within the tree line on the rise surrounding the clearing. It hadn't been obvious to Fura just how much time had passed while she and Monira had been speaking, until she looked upon the man's form, silhouetted in light against the growing darkness of the forest behind him.

Putting the horn to his lips again, he blew, the sound creating a stillness through the camp in its wake as it entered every last space, bringing attention to the group's return.

Just behind him, the sun glinting off his coppery hair, Apallo crested the hill, looking just as somber as when he had left. He leaned in and whispered something in Nevo's ear before giving a stout nod and moving down the hill, the horn sounding again behind him.

Like a call to arms, the eerie drone had brought together all those who had been milling about, and even more from within the caves and the surrounding area. Fura was astonished at the efficiency of such a simple thing, but she said nothing as Monira took her arm and led her to the fringes of the crowd.

Beside her, Monira unintentionally wrung her hands as they stood waiting, looking more fretful than before as the crowd grew.

"I'll be okay," Fura promised the woman.

She wasn't sure about the honesty of those words, but Fura had gathered from her talk earlier with Monira, and from simple observation, that the woman acted almost as Apallo's second in command. If that was the case, then her place was up at the front by his side, not babysitting in the back.

"Are you sure?" Monira asked restlessly. When Fura gave a nod of assurance, she paused for a moment before taking off.

Balancing on the tips of her toes, Fura tried to get a better look at things as Monira left her side. In the center of where the mass of people had gathered was the same large stone that jutted out from the ground that Apallo had stood on that morning. As she watched Apallo ascend to its edge, she could see that, much like the large rock they performed on during festival hours, it acted as a stage. It left her to wonder if there were ever any performances on this stone, or if it was reserved only for announcements such as this.

She hoped not. A stone saved only for sorrow was no way to applaud nature.

Yet, Fura already knew that that's what today's announcement would bring. Sadness and tears.

Even though she hadn't known the woman, and Apallo had yet to commence speaking, she could already feel her eyes beginning to brim with tears.

Sucking in a breath to calm herself, Fura let her eyes scan the crowd for a moment before returning her focus to where Apallo stood at the highest peak of the natural stage.

He stood, looking over the crowd with somber eyes, giving them all a moment of silence while he searched his soul for the right words to say. None of this would be easy. Yet, what made it worse, and simpler at the same time, was that most everyone had already heard the unfortunate news.

Just when Fura thought that maybe that's all this would end up being, a moment of amassed silence as the daylight faded away, Apallo cleared his throat.

Rubbing his hands together before him, his eyes far away, he let out a deep sigh and raised his head to look at those that had gathered.

"It is unfortunate that I stand before you today with such heart-wrenching news," he started gravely.

Fura felt miserable just watching him. It was a far cry from the exuberant man who she was used to watching on stage at the festival.

"I know that most of you are already aware of what has happened, but I still speak these words with a heavy heart. On this day we have lost one of our own. Our dearest Brieda Morgenstein has passed on."

"Murder," a voice spoke from the crowd.

Apallo didn't flinch at the lone word, didn't even search out the speaker. He only raised a hand to ensure silence.

"It pains me to inform you that her unexpected death was, indeed, premeditated.

"Now, before I move further into the details and what it means for our future here, I would first like to say a few words in memory of our friend."

Pausing, Apallo's eyes scanned the crowd. Satisfied that no one challenged him, he continued on.

"Brieda was not only our favored huntress, and one of the most skilled archers I've ever seen, she was a friend to many of us. Her smile could light up even the most dreary of days, and her gallant and lively spirit was infectious. As most of us know, her husband was killed during the attacks many years ago, as well as many more of our own. As the rest who have passed in these lands, she will be sorely missed, but I pray that she and Marcus are reunited on the other side."

"Fire restore us," many a voice in the crowd spoke simultaneously.

Apallo bowed his head in return. "Fire restore us," he repeated.

Holding a hand aloft again, the people before him returned to silence, patiently awaiting his next words.

"Now, returning to the matters surrounding Brieda's demise. As I already stated, it was not an accident. And upon close inspection of the body, and the surrounding area where she was found, we already know the identity of the culprit." Apallo paused, letting the words sink in before revealing the worst. "Zariah is at it again."

Just like that, the crowd erupted into a frenzy of whispers as the man before them verified what they had been speaking of all throughout the day.

"Are you sure?" one person asked. There was fright evident in the young male voice.

"It's a simple fact that he makes no move to mask his actions. All the signs were present."

"Then we're at war?"

It was a question of simplicity, but the way it was fiercely stated made it sound less of a question and more of a proclamation.

"There will be no war today!" Just like that, Apallo's voice took on a darker tone as he reinforced his position of authority. "We all know that we would be painfully outnumbered against his amassed forces.

"That being said, I don't know why he has so suddenly decided to move against us. After years of sustained peace, I fear that it's a message he's sending. It may be to all of us, or it may be to me alone.

"I have the distinct feeling that he will come forward again within a fortnight, likely to speak to me in person. If that is the case, then I shall sleep with one eye open, awaiting his presence. If nothing happens in that time, then I will go to him. Rest assured that I will not let him tear us down so easily.

"However, until matters are settled, I advise that no one leave this area unless absolutely necessary. And in such cases, I am placing a dusk curfew upon Frielana. Anyone who has viable reason to leave these grounds should do so in the company of at least one other individual. I would actually prefer larger groups. Furthermore, I ask that you please confirm with me before leaving. I hate to take away individual freedoms, but until this is settled and has blown over, I will rest easier knowing where everyone is.

"On a lighter note, however, I have heard news that, despite the events of the previous night, the Fireswell Festival is a go for this coming weekend.

"That is all for now. Stay safe, my friends."

As their leader descended from the makeshift stage, the group began to dissipate, clearing the area just as quickly as it had been filled.

Anxious to get her mind off things, but not knowing where to go or what to do, Fura found herself looking for Monira again. It wasn't until that moment, squinting to see through the dusty twilight, that she realized how dark it had gotten. The speech hadn't felt lengthy, but in the time it had taken for Apallo to convey the details of recent events – what had mostly been old news – the sun had moved well below the tree line, sinking their surroundings into deepening shadow. The remaining light came from the sliver of moon that had begun its climb to settle among the stars, and the numerous torches that surrounded the most frequented areas of Frielana in a fiery ring.

All around her, the clearing was filled with the melodic hum of voices as people discussed, in no particular order, what they had been told. It was so loud that the crickets fought to be heard over the unnatural ruckus.

But even that was short lived as the bobbing heads in the half light made their way back to the activities that had preoccupied them beforehand, taking their conversations with them. Once a majority of the bodies had cleared, it was easy for Fura to spot Monira. She stood near the base of the large stone that Apallo had occupied, her back to Fura as she spoke with the somber-faced leader.

Not wanting to interrupt what looked to be a private conversation, Fura only moved a bit closer, making sure to respectively stay out of range of hearing. After what she had been through, and what she had already heard this day, she wasn't sure she wanted to hear much more.

The conversation between the two ceased in haste time, and both Apallo and Monira disembarked from the spot.

Though he had appeared very much the leader, spinning words on a platform above those listening, Fura noticed that Apallo looked world-weary and worn as he made his way towards her with Monira at his side.

Noticing that Fura was waiting for them, Apallo gave her a light smile as the distance closed between them.

"Oh," Monira exclaimed, following Apallo's eye. "You didn't have to wait here."

Fura shrugged. "I had nothing else to do," she said bashfully. It was better than trying to explain to either of them that she still felt like there was nothing that she could do. Like she didn't quite belong here. She didn't want to make either of them feel any worse than they likely already did.

"I'm sorry you've had to witness all this," Apallo added, pausing before her. "Frielana's not usually this dark." Clapping a hand on Fura's shoulder, he quickly changed the subject before she could intervene with questions. "Come. Why don't you eat with us?"

As awkward as Fura could have felt about the invitation, she nodded and followed as Apallo and Monira made their way back to the warmth and light of the caves. Something as simple as eating was a small glimpse back into the world of the normal that Fura couldn't pass up.

Or at least she thought.

The meal itself was quiet enough, the three of them secluding themselves before one of the multiple fireplaces that dotted the stone walls of the caverns, huddled over bowls of stew. The food was good, the company pleasant enough. It was when the conversation turned toward the heaviness of politics that Fura started to feel that maybe she should have declined the offer.

"It makes no sense why he would decide to make a move now," Apallo gruffed. "Nothing has changed." Staring into the depths of the bowl in his hands as if hoping to find an answer at its bottom, he seemed to have forgotten during the course of the conversation that Fura was even there.

Monira, as friendly as she had been the past few days, was just as inclined in the current moment to remove her from the discussion. Not that Fura had made much of an effort to include herself in the first place. She wasn't in the mood for talk anyways, and now all this talk about what had happened, all these words, and people, and places that she had never heard of was just making her anxious and sick to her stomach. It was like tuning in midseason to a television show that she had never heard of before. Nothing but confusion and a growing headache.

"Maybe that's why."

Fura watched with half interest as Apallo looked up at Monira's words.

"You think he's grown tired of the complacency?"

"He never was one for idleness. We all know that."

Apallo set his bowl roughly on the floor, the ceramic chink of it echoing quietly along the walls as he ran a hand across his face. "But what does he have to gain from it?"

"The satisfaction that only comes from a twisted mind like his."

"The fires, the murders..." Apallo muttered, his mind working to piece the puzzle together. "That was twenty years ago. I just don't understand why he would do it again. It's like he's repeating past crimes. He's never struck me as one to do the same thing twice. He's much too imaginative for that."

Monira frowned, lines deepening in her face, making her look much older than she really was. "You think he's working in a pattern?"

"I hope not. Heck, if the signs of his presence weren't so remarkably obvious, I never would have pinned any of this on him."

"Not even the fires?"

Apallo shook his head, though his haunted eyes revealed that he wasn't sure. "He prides himself too much on deviating from the norm."

Fura had no idea how the death of her family back in Barandor and a single woman in the woods could possibly be connected. All she knew was that she couldn't sit and listen to conspiracy theories any longer.

Faking a drawn out yawn, she made a move to get up. "I think I'm going to go to bed," she announced, hoping it didn't come across as rude as she felt it was.

Pulled out of the delicate haze of his conversation with Monira, Apallo looked at her blankly for a moment before nodding in agreement. "Of course. You look tired. We shouldn't have kept you up so late. Especially after a day like today."

Looking down at the bowl in her hands, Fura realized that she didn't even know what to do with her now empty dish. "Thank you for dinner," she said as a way to buy time. It only made her realize just how out of her element she really was.

Monira held out her hand, seeming to pick up on her distress. "Just leave that here. I'll take care of it."

Releasing the ceramic bowl into Monira's care, Fura muttered a 'good night' and headed towards the only space that could remotely be called her own.

12

◆◆◇◆◆

UNWANTED

It didn't matter how tired she might have looked or felt, sleep was not her friend.

The blankets were warm, and the darkness was a relative comfort after what she had seen during the day. Yet, Fura still found herself tossing and turning.

And the worst part was, even through all the affirmative and light-hearted mantras she had been repeating in her head, she could still feel the tears brimming in the corners of her eyes, threatening to surface yet again. No one had made any mention of it, but she felt as if her eyes would be perpetually rimmed with red from the burning sting of the salt. If there had been a mirror present, she was sure she could quickly confirm that suspicion.

For the past hour, Fura had whiled away the time trying to clear her mind of everything but the general will to sleep, yet all she had accomplished was hopelessly twisting herself in the sheets, and mulling over things that she hadn't thought about in years. Useless memories spilling forth as if the recent tragedy had broken a damn in her mind. She hadn't even realized that she had stored that many depressing memories during her seventeen years.

With a grunt of frustration, Fura cast off the blankets and sat up. Looking around the room revealed that it wasn't nearly as dark as it had been, her eyes having adjusted to the shadows. The gray cast of half light pulled the color out of everything, leaving it as a hollow and ghostly shell of what it really was.

It was exactly how she felt.

Like a shadow of herself.

And a useless one at that.

Knowing that sleep wasn't coming anytime soon, Fura positioned herself on the edge of the bed. Her legs dangling over the side, she let her toes skim the cool stone of the floor and wondered what to do with herself. Right now. In general. She was lost on both accounts.

The logical part of her mind told her to stay put in the room, to force herself to sleep no matter the circumstances, but the other half mulled over the idea of going out to explore again. She knew that Apallo probably wouldn't approve, especially after the local murder only that afternoon. He had instilled a curfew after all. But he couldn't really argue if she stayed within the confines of the camp, could he?

Fura let the multitude of answers to that question shift and settle in her mind.

Deciding that she had nothing much to lose, save the sleep that she doubted she was going to get anyways, she got up, found her shoes, threw on a sweatshirt, and moved towards the door.

As she snuck quietly through the winding maze of the cave, Fura found it wasn't a necessity. She didn't know what time she had initially went to bed, and even less of an idea what time it was now. Her best guess was that it was after midnight.

The sheer amount of people that had gathered for Apallo's announcement that evening were nowhere to be found now. It was like walking through the remnants of a self-contained ghost town. The only sign of life present was a small line of light dancing along the wall from a door on her right.

Her curiosity lacking in the midnight hour, Fura made to stroll past the door without a second thought, not really caring what stood behind it.

Until she heard her name.

Her interest peaking at the familiar syllables, she hesitated briefly before moving closer.

The door, just as nondescript as all the others that dotted the hall, stood ajar, sending a line of color dancing on the wall from the fireplace that was still lit within. Voices drifted on the air as well, rising and falling in low, secretive tones so as not to wake anyone.

Despite the hushed whispering, there was no secret as to who the speakers were. Their voices clear as day, Fura could quickly make out that it was Apallo and Monira within. Apparently just as sleepless as she was, it sounded as if they were still in the throes of the same conversation that Fura had left them in the middle of not that long ago. The only difference was that they had merely moved from the main hall to somewhere more secluded.

In all honesty, she didn't care to hear anymore about their theories and politics on this supposed serial killer that had emerged – or reemerged, from the way they had been speaking. But she could have sworn that she had heard her name being whispered in the darkness, as if her own fate was on the block for consideration in their conversation.

Fura wasn't sure how to feel about that.

Thankful for the solid stone beneath her feet, and the silence surrounding her that made it easy to hear, Fura stood stock still so as not to be discovered, and hunched forward as she listened in.

"Do you think I did the right thing in bringing her here?" Apallo's voice rolled through the space behind the door, confirming Fura's suspicion that they were indeed talking about her. Though she couldn't see him, his tone conveyed worry.

"Only time will tell, Apallo," Monira chimed in. "You know that."

"I just can't help but think that this is the wrong thing for her. That it's been too long."

"It will take her time to adjust."

"Respectively. But now all this. It's just as dangerous as it was before."

"You don't know that for certain. You said yourself, he's just sending a message. He'll come forward in the next few days. Things will be said. Then, it'll smooth over. You'll see. As far as I can tell, he's just become bored."

"Well, that boredom has already resulted in multiple deaths," Apallo declared, his voice rising. "I can't have that. What does that say about me if I just let these recent events slide?"

"That you're not tempted into evil by evil."

"He's planning something."

"We can't go rushing into conclusions."

"And I can't just sit here and do nothing."

"Well," Monira said, her tone evening. "I've already told you what I think. We all know the man is irritable. I say he's just going through a phase."

"A phase that leaves you short another family member."

Monira sighed, making it apparent that the conversation was weighing on her. "It could have been any of us out there. I don't think he was targeting."

"Either way, he's a loose cannon. This world can't afford to have people like him around."

"That cannon's been fired. Now it'll cool off." The woman's next words were spoken lower, the tail end of them trailing off into the night. "At least until next time."

"Not this time."

"What do you mean?"

Fura could hear the frown in the woman's voice.

"I don't think this is another passing phase of his. Something big is coming. I don't know what, but it can't be good. All I know is that Fura shouldn't be here. I made a mistake."

Fura nearly stumbled back as she cringed at the comment, at the mean edge that had taken residence in Apallo's voice. It made her wonder if she was hearing someone else speaking in his place behind that door, because this wasn't the man that she knew from the festival.

"You don't mean that."

"All that I've done," Apallo continued, seeming to ignore the woman, "and nothing has changed."

"You underestimate your abilities and all that you've done for us. Give her some time. Fura being here isn't a mistake."

"Yes, it is."

"She came here willingly."

"Only because she had nowhere else to go."

"And you know why that is."

The more they argued, the more Fura wanted to leave. But that last strain of words held her in place. She had no idea what Monira meant. She actually wasn't sure she wanted to know.

"It's still a mistake," Apallo repeated.

"Like Kiyani?" There was a shallow anger rising in the woman's words as well as they silently fought deeper into the night.

Now Kiyani? Fura didn't know what he could possibly have to do with her. But this conversation was getting all the more confusing by the minute.

"Don't get me started on that miscreant," Apallo raged.

"You don't seriously think —"

"How can I not?" Apallo demanded, cutting her off, though there was a tone in the woman's halted question that seemed to immediately pick up where exactly he was going. "The signs are all there."

"How can you not see past that at this point?"

"How can you?" Apallo echoed again.

Hugging her arms to her chest, an anxious reflex, Fura turned away from the door. She didn't want to hear anymore.

She didn't know what the man's deal was with Kiyani, why he reacted so violently just to the boy's name, but that wasn't what had left her with such a hollow feeling in her stomach.

Fura shouldn't be here.

Was that everyone's basic opinion? she wondered. Did she have a sign on her forehead saying that she was destined for nothing but failure?

It was one thing for someone that she had never met to say such things, but to have someone whom she had called a friend for years say that she didn't belong out here... it hurt.

Craving the cool and quiet air of the night, Fura moved on before she could hear anymore. The rest of the way was lifeless except a few low burning fires that refused to die away.

Pushing the dangling vines to the side and standing in the archway, Fura could see the stars above the tree tops. But there was no solace in them. They looked cold and hard, their sparkling making it appear as if they too were laughing at her.

Obviously no one wanted her out here. Not even the quiet comforts of nature.

After what she'd heard, Fura's first defiant instinct was to go streaking off into the woods and never come back. Would anybody even notice she was gone? She no longer cared about the repercussions of breaking Apallo's curfew. The only thing that kept her in place was remembering that feeling of helplessness when she had gotten lost earlier in the day.

Running away wasn't an option at this point, and neither was returning to bed. The anxious feeling in her stomach threatened to envelope her just thinking about going back into the cave.

In that case, the only option left to her was to move outside.

She didn't know what to do, but the soft glow of the spring called to her, just as good a place as any. And, as far as she was concerned, it was still within Frielana's boundaries.

Like the interior of the cave, there was no life present outside either to interfere with Fura's internal confusion and spotted rage. Nothing but the soft chorus of crickets and the sound of the wind through the leaves overhead.

Taking her time, Fura moved slowly along, neither in a hurry to get there nor to leave. Just breathing in the cool night air was already making her feel better, allowing her to forget a few of her worries, if only momentarily.

To her left a noise sounded through the night and she paused, her heart instinctively racing at the unexpected disturbance. Fura waited, thinking that something might pop out of the darkness, aiming for her, but nothing happened.

Declaring herself safe, Fura turned back around. It was just the sounds of nature. All this talk of a killer and diabolical plans had her more on edge than she had realized. Now she was hearing things, twisting the ordinary into something terrifying, when in reality it had probably just been a bird in the tree.

Resuming her path to the light of the spring, Fura's shoulders fell and she paused again as she saw the dark form resting on the rocks surrounding the shimmering water.

It wasn't the potential killer that she found herself expecting to be waiting for her, but, in a way, she found that she might have preferred that alternative.

Instead, even in the darkness, she could make out Kiyani's silhouette, highlighted by the natural light of the spring. He lounged on the rocks, his eyes closed from what Fura could tell, completely oblivious to the world.

Not feeling quite as adventurous with this recent development, Fura glanced over her shoulder, back to where the mouth of the cave stood etched in moonlight. She still didn't care for the option of reentering and going back to bed, but Fura didn't really prefer the alternative of being rudely accosted by Kiyani either.

Still in the clear since he hadn't made any indication of knowing that she was there, Fura slowly turned, intent with walking away.

Stepping on a piece of brush, Fura flinched as it cracked beneath her foot, sending the sound echoing out through the darkness.

It was just enough to rouse Kiyani out of whatever he had been doing – sleeping, thinking, it was hard to tell with him. Opening his eyes and leaning back to see what had disturbed the night, she could hear him sigh irritably.

"You again?"

Cursing the unpredictability of the brush beneath her feet, Fura shrugged, doing her best to let his crudeness slide off without any permanent damage. "Don't sound so excited."

"I'm not," he quickly assured.

Letting out an irritated breath of her own, Fura moved forward, regardless of his unfriendly air. She honestly didn't know what was wrong with him. But she had been caught, and, honestly, she had nothing better to do at this time of night.

"You can't sleep either?" she ventured, testing the territory of conversation.

Kiyani only stared at her as if trying to find a way out this situation without having to reply. "Maybe I don't sleep."

"So now you're a vampire?"

"Really?"

Fura only stood, watching him. She realized how stupid it sounded, but it was the first thing that had come to mind, and she wasn't about to atone for her words. Not to him, anyway.

Kiyani rolled his eyes in reply to her silence. "You need your head examined."

"Thanks," Fura said shallowly, wondering why she had even replied in such a way.

A raised brow indicated that Kiyani wondered the same thing. "Not a compliment."

"Wouldn't expect such a thing from you."

There was little reaction from him as he sat up and rose to his feet. Fura thought that maybe he was actually being polite and talking to her face to face, but instead he jumped from the rocks and moved past her, heading towards the caves without even a glance in her direction.

"Hey, where are you going?"

She didn't even know why she was bothering. His behavior was appalling.

"Leaving."

Well, wasn't that obvious?

Fura bit back the statement, though it would have only been fitting as a reply.

"Do you have anything better to do?" she asked instead.

Fura was sure he couldn't deny her that. It was essentially the middle of the night. Apparently they were both out here for a reason. Hers was because she couldn't sleep. She couldn't possibly fathom what his excuse would be if it wasn't the same.

"Like what?" Kiyani challenged. "Wait for Apallo to come storming over? Because you know, I so love our little fights."

"Why does he hate you so much?" Fura hoped it wasn't too forward. She had meant to potentially ease into such questions, but his brutality made it difficult to get past any of the commonplace conversation pieces.

"Why do you care?" he asked a bit harshly.

Fura shrugged. "Just curious."

"If I wanted to divulge my life story, I'd write a book."

"Do you have that much material?" Fura challenged, slapping what she hoped was a sufficient amount of sarcasm to counter his own into her reply.

"You don't know the half of it."

"So," Fura started, aware that Kiyani was already making a move to leave again. "Were you telling the truth about the spring?" The story he had fed her still came across as fishy in her opinion.

"What do you think?" he asked wryly.

"I think you're full of it."

The response elicited a slight chuckle, the first genuine thing she had gotten out of him, and the first thing that had affected her so readily. Her stomach fluttered at the sound, and Fura hoped that the strange glow of the water hid the sudden blush of her cheeks.

A lonely howl sounded in the darkness and Fura stopped short, looking out into the night, half expecting to see eyes staring back at her.

"There are wolves out here?"

Kiyani nodded, an amused smile playing on his lips, as if the sight of her fear made him reconsider staying. "Big ones."

"You're lying," Fura quickly accused him, trying to hide her panic.

"Am I?"

"Why don't you want me out here?" She still wanted to know. He had made it rather apparent and now he was trying to scare her into remission.

"Because you shouldn't be here. You already saw what happened today."

Fura balked, unable to believe the possibility of what he was saying. "Are you saying that was my fault?"

"No. I'm saying that if you're not careful, that could be you."

"Are you threatening me?"

Kiyani let out a sigh, more disappointment than his usual frustration. "And Apallo's already poisoned you against me."

Looking out into the trees, Fura avoided Kiyani's gaze, making it appear as if she were searching for the wolf she had heard, when really she was trying to think of what she wanted. Maybe she should just let him leave like he appeared to be anxious to do. She had been searching for solitude after all, hadn't she? And it was definitely true that Apallo had tried to talk her down from even speaking to the man waiting on her reply.

"Are you staying, then?" Fura asked, testing the waters and seeing if he might possibly make the decision for her.

Kiyani crossed his arms, his stance just as rigid. "I don't know," he mocked. "According to Apallo I'm dangerous."

A sly smile turned up the corner of her lip. It was apparent that these two really didn't like one another, but at least Kiyani seemed to have formed a sense of wry humor to go along with it.

"I don't believe that."

Kiyani didn't reply, but Fura could have sworn that his eyes softened just the slightest.

Silence settled in as Fura watched him contemplate the alternatives. He had her so conflicted that even she wasn't sure what answer she was hoping he would come back with.

"So," he began, seeming to decide to stay, if only for a moment more. "What were you doing earlier?"

Fura felt her cheeks flush further, this time from embarrassment. She had hoped he would forget that strange encounter. All day she had mulled it over, and still had yet to come to a reasonable conclusion as to how she had ended up nearly beating Kiyani senseless with an artifact of nature.

"You ever feel like you've just lost a piece of your memory?" she blurted out, voicing the only thing that had come to her during the day concerning the event. "Like you feel like there's something you should remember, but every time you try to grab for it, there's just nothing there?"

Kiyani regarded her with a look that told her he thought she was insane, making Fura wish she hadn't said anything at all. Or better yet, made something up like he had obviously done when she had asked about the waters before them. "There are certainly some things I would rather forget, but I can't say I've ever lost full memories." His words trailed off into the stillness of the night. "There can be only one explanation."

Fura perked up, eager to know what was wrong with her. Leaning forward, she waited with anticipation for his answer.

"You're weird."

It took Fura a moment, but once she registered the sarcasm, she picked up a small stone and chucked it at him.

13

◆◆◇◆◆

THE CALM BEFORE THE STORM

The camp was relatively quiet as Kiyani meandered about in the early morning sunshine the next day. He often kept himself scarce during all hours of the day, but once in awhile he braved the moments following the early dawn. The sleep that often evaded him under the cover of night still faintly called to him, but he had found many years ago that at times there were certain rewards offered to the early risers.

Today was one of those days.

One of the things he valued the most on these rare occurrences was the peace and quiet – that absolute stillness of nature right before the birds started to sing, marking the waking of the day.

"You're up early this morning."

Kiyani smiled at the kind voice, the hint of gentle joking in its tone.

The second reward was the chance to talk to Monira without anyone else present.

Namely, Apallo.

He knew, for a fact, that she was open to conversation at all hours of the day, but there was something freeing about these particular times. There was nothing for him to hide to go to such extraneous precautions, but Kiyani simply felt better when Apallo wasn't around breathing down his neck or staring holes into him with accusing eyes.

No matter how many reassurances Monira gave him, Kiyani knew that he and Apallo would never get along. Nothing could ever change the rift that had been present before Kiyani had even officially met the man. He couldn't say it was for lack of trying. He had tried in the beginning, but it had quickly become evident that there was just no getting on the man's good side. There was no place for him there, and there never would be.

"I'm not allowed to enjoy the morning?" Kiyani asked playfully as he approached Nira.

Dew still sat heavy on the grass from the late night rain shower that had passed through, and it sparkled in a million pinpricks of light as the sun rose higher in the sky, casting its light across the clearing.

Nira, as had become normal for her, was up before the sun, tending to the large pot that contained what would be either lunch or dinner that day. It was never clear-cut.

"I'm just not used to seeing you around this much," Nira poked fun at him. "You usually stick to the shadows if at all possible."

Kiyani gave her a dark look, clearly not amused. "Not funny."

"I didn't mean it like that," she reprimanded, unfazed by his change in attitude in response to the words. "But don't think I don't notice just how much you keep to yourself."

"What else would I do?"

"Get out more?"

"We're outside," he pointed out, a sweep of his arm emphasizing just how vast the area was. "Can't get anymore *out* than this."

"You know what I mean."

"And subject myself to the torture of trying to mingle with those that don't like me? I think I'll pass."

Nira sighed, waving her spoon in the air. "You're hopeless."

"No," Kiyani corrected. "What's hopeless is a society that can't get past preexisting perceptions of people they don't even know."

Silence fell over them as Nira contemplated his words, the look on her face akin to that of a proud mother. However the gleam in her eyes couldn't quite mask the smallest hint of worry visible in the lines in the corner of her mouth. "You are way beyond your years, you know that?"

Kiyani smiled faintly. "I like to think so at times."

He had heard it from her before, but also from Kristoff back at the shop from time to time. Eighteen was only a number in his book. The way he felt most days cast him as much older. It wasn't something he was necessarily proud of, but Kiyani knew it wasn't something to be ashamed of either.

He often wondered at times though if his early growing up was the reason he generally got along better with older crowds.

"So," Kiyani ventured. "I suppose Apallo's curfew blows any plans I had."

"He didn't say you couldn't go anywhere. He just wants to know where everyone is. All you have to do is go talk to him."

"Right."

The chances of having a civilized conversation with Apallo was about the same as lightning striking on this clear morning. Not to mention he'd rather cut his own foot off. At least there might be some general excitement in that.

"You could stay and help around camp for once," Monira offered.

"I prefer to go where my help is actually appreciated."

"We appreciate your help here."

Kiyani raised a brow. "I've never heard it."

"Fura could use a friend," she tried again.

Kiyani could only look at her in shock, wondering if she had actually said those words to him. Had everyone around here lost their minds as of late?

"Do I look like the kind of person who wants to volunteer for the job?" It wasn't the first thing that came to his mind. Either way, he could only hope her answer was no.

"She's new here, doesn't know much of what's going on, and after what she's been through in the last few days… well, she's been quiet. I'm sure she could use someone to talk to. Someone her own age."

"Don't play the pity card on me," Kiyani said, violently shaking his head. "The answer's still no."

"And why not?"

"I'm not a baby-sitter."

"Do you really have anything better to do?"

Nira had always been on his side, though he had never quite understood why. Everyone else around camp had learned to simply ignore him. But not her. Yet, that comment didn't sound like she had his best interests in mind.

"Are you trying to send Apallo into a rampage?" he asked incredulously. "Because I like to be long gone in those instances."

"He's not that bad."

"He threatened me yesterday, did you know that?"

"I doubt it was an actual threat."

Kiyani crossed his arms and looked at her. Apallo had said many things to him over the years, but he still couldn't believe the man had found it necessary to stop him like that. "Killing me with his bare hands doesn't constitute a threat?"

"You know very well he just says things. He would never actually act on it."

"I don't know. He's wanted to every since I came here."

Nira shook her head as she tossed a handful of carrots into the pot and stirred its contents.

"Aren't the two of you ever going to get along?"

"Probably not."

Nira sighed, a shake of her head indicating that she wasn't quite done with the subject, though she was silently fishing for a way to continue.

"Answer's no," Kiyani declared defensively, finishing the conversation for her.

"Fine. But I still think you should consider it."

Kiyani only gave her another sordid glance as he picked up an empty bowl from a pile that sat next the pot.

Waiting until she turned to cut and gather another contribution of carrots to the mix, he moved forward and leaned into the pot, dipping out a bowl of the stew.

"Hey, get out of there," Monira said, swatting at him with the wooden spoon in her hand.

He skirted the instrument and backed away with a sly smile on his face, already forgetting their previous line of conversation. "What?" he asked with a shrug. "I'm hungry."

"Then maybe you should eat at normal times like everyone else."

"That would involve making a regular appearance."

Monira kept an eye on him as he made his way over to a log that lay lengthwise on the ground and sat on it. He knew for a fact that she wasn't actually mad at him.

She only shook her head as she watched him eat. "You little conniver. You're lucky I have a soft spot for you."

Birds started to sing just then, officially announcing the onset of morning, leaving both of them to settle into silence.

It was the call to wake up and to get a move on with the day, to get work done. Soon the camp would be alive again and crawling with life, but for that single moment Kiyani enjoyed the peace as he ate.

"You know, though," Monira started in again. "I think you and Fura would be good together."

A stream of peas and carrots went sputtering back into the bowl as Kiyani nearly choked on his meal. "That's going too far."

Nira shrugged innocently, pretending not to notice the effect her words had had on him. "Just saying."

"Does Apallo know you think like that?" Kiyani accused.

He couldn't believe she would even say something of the sort. Especially as close as she was with Apallo. She was Kiyani's friend, but she was Apallo's second-in-command. Kiyani could only imagine the fit Apallo would have thrown had he been present during this conversation.

So much for a peaceful morning.

Peace.

He nearly snorted at the thought.

It was getting harder and harder to find around here.

Going to take another sip of stew after having caught his breath, Kiyani could see Nira perk up out of the corner of his eye.

"Morning, Fura," she said perkily.

Make that impossible to find, he silently amended, bitterly dropping his spoon back in the bowl.

As the girl's form moved into his line of sight, Kiyani glared at her through the shock of hair that fell over his eyes, hoping it would give the undeniable impression that she wasn't welcome.

He smiled inwardly as she shrunk away from his gaze.

Good.

Despite his own impression on her, Kiyani knew that Monira wouldn't send her away. Just thinking about what she had said regarding the two of them made him want to gag.

"I've got to go do... something," he stated, awkwardly excusing himself before he got drug into further conversation.

"Don't you leave with my bowl," Nira reprimanded him.

Looking at the dish in his hand, Kiyani realized that he had actually forgotten he still had it.

Ignoring Fura's watchful gaze as he moved around her, he handed it back to Nira. It was just as well. He had lost his appetite anyways.

"Trying to kill me," he muttered before turning away.

"Don't be so dramatic."

✧ ⌘ ✧

Fura watched Kiyani stalk off, wondering if she had done something in particular to make him leave. It was like their conversation the night before had never happened. She had thought, in the late night hours, that maybe she was finally getting somewhere with him. Apparently not.

It probably hadn't been the best idea to sneak up on him like she had, but she had just as much right to talk to Monira as he did. Though she had to admit that that was the only time in the last few days she had actually seen him talking to anyone. She didn't quite count whatever he had going on with Apallo as talking.

"Don't worry about him," Monira assured behind her.

"Is he always like that?" Fura asked, turning to meet the woman's gaze. She didn't seem too disturbed that her partner in conversation had just abruptly got up and left.

"More or less."

Looking back to where Kiyani had stalked off, already having disappeared, Fura guessed that the more was reserved for her.

"Hungry?"

When Fura turned back around, Monira already had a bowl in her hand, offering it to her.

Smiling, Fura took it. "Thank you."

"How did you sleep?"

"Fine."

If you could call tossing and turning amongst nightmares fine. But Fura knew it was just conversation, and she didn't feel like discussing her troubles. Sitting in the quiet morning, eating, was enough for her.

"Good. It'll take awhile to adjust, I'm sure."

Nearly burning herself on the first sip, Fura settled the spoon back in the bowl to let it cool as she looked up at the woman. Those were almost the exact same words she had spouted to Apallo the night before. The repeat of the phrase left Fura to wonder if maybe Monira knew that Fura had been listening in.

But, as Fura watched her continue in her tasks, she told herself that wasn't the case.

Thankfully, Monira prodded no further as she busied herself, keeping an eye on the large pot and keeping the fire consistently stoked. After what Fura had overheard the night before, she wasn't sure what to think of the woman. Though she reminded herself that it was Apallo that had spoken much like Kiyani, declaring that she had no place in Frielana.

Fura watched Monira work as she ate, the birds providing a cheery soundtrack in the background. It wasn't until she had finished her meal – not sure if she could quite call it breakfast, or if it qualified more along the lines of lunch – and set the bowl down on the log where she was sitting, that she attempted her own venture into conversation.

"Why do Apallo and Kiyani hate each other so much?" Fura asked, drawing lines in the sand around the fire with a small stick she had found. It was something to keep herself busy as she attempted to act like she really wasn't all that interested in the answer.

Monira chuckled. "That obvious, huh?"

Fura smiled back at the woman, not expecting that sort of sentiment about the matter. "Hard to ignore."

"It's not my place to discuss. You would have to ask one of them. Though good luck getting anywhere with that conversation."

"Right." Fura chucked the stick into the fire and watched as the flames quickly consumed it. "Has it always been that way between them?"

Monira nodded, abandoning her post and sitting down next to her. "Always."

"How long has Kiyani been here?" Fura remembered Apallo saying something about letting him live in Frielana when Kiyani had interrupted his speech. Not to mention, it was quite obvious by the way that most people avoided him that, like her, he couldn't have been born into all this.

"That's something you'll have to ask him," Monira replied. "I'm all for conversation, but I'm not discussing the personal lives of others."

Tearing a piece of grass from the ground beneath her, Fura sighed. "That's impossible. He hates me."

"Oh, I doubt that."

Fura looked at the woman. She couldn't be the only one to have noticed it. Heck, Kiyani had basically made a public announcement the night Apallo had granted her living status in Frielana. "He's made it quite clear."

"I'll admit, he's a difficult one to get through to. Quiet... reserved..."

"Reserved?" Fura laughed. She hadn't seen that quality from him yet.

Smiling, Monira nodded. "So he's more than a little opinionated at times. But, trust me. He's a good person. A little hard to get to know, as I'm sure you've realized, but know that if he actually let's you in, you could never ask for a better friend."

Fura hinted at a smile. She would love that chance, with anyone really at this point, but she doubted it would be with Kiyani. It was hard to imagine his forged attitude against her changing any time soon.

"I'm sure Apallo would love that," Fura joked, attempting to mask her sadness.

Monira laid a hand on her shoulder. "Don't worry about him. Apallo's always been more threat than action. They both are."

Nodding, Fura rested her chin on her hands and looked out into the surrounding trees. It still all felt like a dream. One that she had to admit wasn't completely horrid.

"Do you think I could follow you around today? Maybe have you teach me something? Anything?"

"Are you sure you don't want to just use your free time to explore?"

"Free time isn't a friend right now."

Monira gave her a knowing smile. "I guess you're right."

14

••◇••

THE BEGINNINGS OF DISASTER

Most would have considered the day boring. To Fura, it had been a godsend.

She had done little more than follow Monira about as the woman went about her own day, helping fix meals, gathering kindling for the fires, cleaning the earthenware dishes that were scattered about, and other rather menial tasks.

Monira had laughed when she had expressed her initial excitement, calling them 'piddly little jobs' in her sing song voice. But Fura had enjoyed it nonetheless.

It may have been a far cry from a step back into the reality that she had known, but at least it had given her something to do, something to keep her mind off of things. It was a step into someone's reality. Some kind of normal routine.

Fura still wasn't sure what to think of this place. It was different. Not bad. Just different.

What helped make it okay in the end – at least enough to calm her anxiety – was that she had the smallest niche carved out that she could honestly call her own. Sitting in the room Monira had directed her to the first night, Fura looked around. The space was small, but it was still her own room. Her own secluded area that she could escape to when everything else became too much. As of yet, no one had come in to bug her. And that was just what she needed.

The only thing that bothered her was the fact that the room had no windows. The only light provided was that of a few pillar candles, an oil lamp provided on the bedside table, and the fireplace. Until her eyes adjusted, it was black as pitch at night, and if she allowed herself to think about it, it reminded her of a jail cell. Fura knew that wasn't the intent, but it was still unnerving.

The sheer primitive nature of the place left her homesick for Barandor. But, at the same time, Fura found herself increasingly scared to return. Scared of what she might find, who or what she might run into. The scene that she remembered from that hazy night showcased that her entire block had been razed to the ground, yet she still had the faintest sense of intuition that she had been the one specifically targeted.

Afraid to let herself completely succumb to the dark, she had left the door ajar, letting in some of the light from the fires that dotted the main avenue of the cavern. Even so, Fura had left the oil lamp burning for extra light.

Though she'd been told repeatedly, and had seen with her own eyes, that it wasn't a regular fire that had taken her family and her home, she still found it difficult to bring herself to look at the dancing little flame. As small as it was, it didn't appear nearly as innocent as it once had in her eyes. She used to take delight in lighting small candles in her room in the middle of the night and watching the little flames dance at the end of the wicks. So warm. So joyful.

Fura felt none of that now.

Only derision. Anxiety. Anger. And maybe just the smallest amount of fear.

Sitting on the bed, hunched over with her arms wrapped around her feet, staring at the wall in front of her, Fura wondered if Apallo had been able to sense this change in her. If he would expect her to continue to perform the remaining weekends at the festival. Right now she didn't know if she could face the stage so soon, if ever again.

It saddened her, but the thought also reminded her of something.

Crawling to the end of the bed, Fura hung over the end and reached for the bag that she had noncommittally thrown to the floor her first night in the room.

All it contained were a few things that she often took with her to the festival – a change of clothes, a couple of things to pass the time, some odds and ends that she couldn't even name off the top of her head – but it was all she had left to her name.

Resuming her position in the middle of the mattress, Fura trailed her fingers along the worn edge of the leather flap. The messenger bag, made of real leather, and hand tooled by one of the leather workers at the festival with an array of gorgeous Celtic knot work designs, had been a birthday gift from her parents a few years ago. She had never been able to get out of them just how much they'd spent on it, but Fura had seen similar pieces in the shop they claimed to have bought it at for well over a hundred dollars.

Despite their initial hesitation of letting her work within the gates of Fireswell, it had shown just how much they had cared. It wasn't working in general that had left them on edge for the longest time, as much as it was the actual line of activity she had gone into. Allowing their thirteen-year-old daughter to literally play with fire. Fura found, in retrospect, that she didn't blame them. Actually, looking back on it now, she assumed they must have gone through a momentary lapse of judgment to have allowed such a thing. Or maybe they had just grown tired of her incessant pleas.

In the end, it wasn't just a bag, but a symbol of respect. Not to mention, it was a heck of a lot better than the ratty old school backpack that she had recycled for the same purpose beforehand.

Tracing the inlaid design on the front of the bag with misty eyes, Fura finally opened it, glancing at the contents inside.

The only time she had done so since she had been here was to grab a different shirt.

Opening this bag felt like opening a doorway into another world, a different life, one that had ceased to be hers the minute those fires had lit up the sky. Fura wasn't sure if it was a door she wanted to open quite yet, but it was the only thing that she felt like she had any honest claim to.

Wiping away a single tear, she pulled out some of the contents, amazed to see just how random of an array it was.

Sitting on top was the festival outfit she wore on stage. She had stuffed it in there without a care after changing out of it, and now she tossed it aside without a second glance.

Beneath it were the things that she was really interested in. Those small objects that now made up her pathetic life. That were her remaining, fragile link back to what she had once had only a few days before.

Another shirt.

A pair of black shorts.

A small journal that was mostly empty, as she'd never thought she had anything particularly enduring to record.

An array of pencils in differing lengths of life lay scattered at the bottom. Though she could never seem to find one when she actually needed it, they collected in droves in the dark recesses of the leather satchel.

Pulling out a hardbound book, she saw it was the math book that she had crammed in there in a hurry that Friday afternoon, thinking that if she found any free time between shows, she would make an attempt to finish her homework early, instead of waiting until Sunday night as usual. School had become the last thing on her mind, and she wondered briefly if anyone expected her to go back and finish out her senior year now. Holding the heavy volume aloft in preparation to toss it aside, though she really felt like hurling it against the wall, Fura stopped when she saw the sheet of paper crammed in the middle of the pages.

She couldn't remember leaving anything within the pages. Setting it on her lap, she thumbed through the book until it fell open to where the paper was lodged. A regular piece of computer paper, folded in half, as unassuming as it was plain, Fura thought nothing of it until she unfolded it.

Her heart thudded to a halt as she took in the image before her.

A picture of her, the family dog, Barry, and her little brother, Evan, all sitting beneath the stars, the sky awash with meteors. All crudely done in blue and purple crayon, save for the scribble of red to represent her fiery hair. The stars were a hodgepodge of dots and the large five pointed stars that all kids were taught to think the stars really resembled at that age, but to Fura it was the most beautiful picture she had seen.

In the bottom corner, in large block letters, Evan had written his name.

There were no other words, but none were needed. Those four little letters were enough to reduce her to a shaking mess.

Stifling a sob as the tears came more forcefully now, Fura carefully folded the picture and placed it back in the book, setting it aside before she ruined it with the stinging, salty drops that rolled down her face.

Overcome with raw emotion, she gathered the bag's scattered contents and crudely stuffed them back into the leather bag. She couldn't do this right now. It was still too early.

Letting the bag fall back to the floor with a soft thud, Fura hugged her knees tight to her chest. She knew that staring at the wall through the haze of her waterworks would get her nowhere, but it didn't matter at the moment. All she wanted was for this pain to end, the tightness in her chest that inflicted her, like some incurable disease every time she recalled even the smallest thing from more than three days in her past, to cease.

If she could find her voice to speak, she would ask the surrounding darkness to suck her in, but what would that prove, beyond the fact that she was a coward? Afraid to face reality.

Steeling herself for the greater possibilities, Fura roughly wiped the tears from her face with the sleeve of her sweatshirt. Pushing herself to get up, she moved towards the door.

She didn't know what time it was. It didn't matter. It was late. That's all she knew. This being awake at all hours of the night was becoming a daily occurrence that she didn't look forward to.

Moving out into the shallow light that pooled just outside the door, Fura walked down the hall, glad that no one else seemed to be about, save for two men who lazily played cards at a small table near one of the fireplaces. She didn't recognize either of them, and she was thankful when all they did was throw a general nod in her direction. Returning the gesture, she moved on in silence.

What she didn't want was to run into Apallo or Monira and have them question where she was going.

She had no destination in mind. Just the need to leave her room, as it was becoming nothing but a pit of depression. It may have been hers, but it only seemed that that's where the majority of her sorrows liked to gather.

Letting the brisk, earthy smell of the fall night envelop her as she moved outside, Fura had the thought to return to the spring. The only problem was that every time she made her way there, Kiyani had already claimed it for himself. Though, she was beginning to see why he seemed to like it so much. It was close enough to be considered within the natural boundaries of Frielana, but just far enough away to be private. The ruckus of voices that generally permeated the camp were only defined as a hushed lull next to the sound of falling water, and the mosses that grew between the rocks were a lush, vivid green that looked like it would feel soft between the toes.

With Kiyani always around, Fura hadn't yet had the chance to test that theory, but it was something she wanted to find out for herself.

Setting her course for the spring, Fura decided that now was just as good a time as ever.

That was before the crash of thunder rolled through the night.

The sound sent her recoiling back into the interior of the cave from where she had just come. Clinging to the wall just inside the archway, she looked out into the night.

Deep in the sturdy cavern, she hadn't heard the approaching storm, but now that she stood outside, exposed to the elements, Fura could see the dark clouds that quietly announced its approach. Though it hadn't yet started, the smell of rain was on the breeze. And the crickets seemed to be singing with a heightened fervor as they joyously anticipated the coming refreshment.

Fura hated storms, but she found herself not wanting to go back to where she had just come from.

Cringing as another gentle roll of thunder echoed dully through the night, Fura waited. Judging by the lull in between the claps, she guessed that it was still a ways off, and she couldn't yet hear the hush of water droplets falling on the leaves of the surrounding trees. Maybe, if she was lucky, it would move on by in the distance, with just the thunder to announce its passing.

Deciding to chance it, just to get a fleeting moment of peace, Fura set her shoulders and made for the spring.

Keeping an ear tuned to the distant storm, Fura was nearly a quarter of the way there when she noticed a flickering light coming from the interior of the last cave of the procession in which she had been living.

Smaller than the other three gaping arches that led to tunnels snaking beneath the earth, it hardly looked impressive. Definitely not as inviting as the others. Which was probably why Fura hadn't noticed it beforehand, nor had she had been paying much attention.

She had just as much love for caves as she did thunderstorms. The thought of willingly placing yourself beneath the earth's surface with tons of rock overhead had never appealed to her, nor had the darkness that was said to go with it.

Granted, these past few days were the only real experience she had with such things, but it was enough to reaffirm her thought that she was a sunshine and trees kind of girl.

It wasn't the cave itself that called to her, but rather the dancing light within. It was a beacon almost, an invitation, as well as a sure sign that she wasn't the only one awake this time of night.

Looking towards the spring that sat shimmering just ahead, Fura turned away, telling herself that it would still be there tomorrow.

Though lax to talk about anything, Fura told herself that maybe it wasn't the quiet solitude of the spring that she needed, but a friend.

What she found was neither.

Slowly making her way down the crooked and misshapen tunnel, she followed the call of the light, it's soft, warm glow pulling her forward.

It only dawned on Fura as the light steadily grew brighter and brighter that she had no idea what she was even walking towards. When she finally stumbled upon the answer, she had the resounding urge to turn back and continue her original trek.

But, as always, he was quicker than her.

"What are you doing here?"

Kiyani sat before the flames that danced brightly within yet another fireplace, fire once again deceiving her. Where before he had been lounging on the floor, staring lazily into the flames, his posture was now rigid as he sat straight up, looking at her as he awaited an answer.

Feeling like a deer caught in the headlights, Fura could only shrug innocently. "Exploring?"

"In the middle of the night?" Kiyani asked, clearly not convinced.

"Couldn't sleep."

"So you decided to intrude on people's personal space?"

Fura looked at him in awe, wondering just what his problem was. "Are you always this rude, or is it just to me?"

"Do you really think I reserve special treatment just for you?" Kiyani answered, taking no time to spew forth his answer.

"So," Fura said, crossing her arms. "You really are this rude."

"If I say yes will you go away?"

Tension building inside her, Fura avoided his snarling gaze and glanced around the room instead. At least she assumed it was a room. Kiyani's from the way he was acting.

A bed sat lengthwise along the wall, a trunk resting at the foot of it. Underfoot lay a rug intended to dampen the chill in the stone beneath it.

All in all, it was similar to the room she had been given, and just as lifeless.

The lack of personal affects came across as strange to her for someone who had been living there for awhile. She wondered if, for some reason, he had as little to his name as she did or if he did it on purpose, for the room was just as inviting as he was.

"Why?" Fura asked, ignoring his last reply.

Knowing it would annoy him, she sat on his bed, her back against the wall as she watched him mess with the wood in the fireplace. As far as she could tell it was an aversion tactic. The flames were going just fine. It was just an excuse for him not to have to talk to her, or look at her.

Prodding the pile, a piece of wood fell to the side, sending a shower of sparks twisting into the air. "To keep people like you away from me."

"I'm not that bad."

"Have you met you?"

Fura sighed. "You're mean." She didn't even know why she was putting herself through this torture. She'd probably have a better time getting lost in the woods again, but something about her earlier conversation with Monira kept her from getting up and leaving. She was still waiting for the smallest sign of this potential friend the woman had spoken of.

"Yet you're still here."

That wasn't it.

"What is your problem with me?" Fura asked, walking a very narrow wall between more tears and frustration.

"I don't have a problem with you," Kiyani stated obnoxiously. "I have a problem with you being here."

Her brows furrowed as she tried to puzzle out his words with little luck. "That doesn't even make sense."

"Don't you have anyone else you can bother with your troubles?" Kiyani asked irritably.

His tone conveyed that he wasn't just talking about her sitting here with him, but about her whole situation. In a subtle way he had just asked the same thing she had been questioning herself. Why was she here?

Fura averted her eyes to the ground, keeping her thoughts private. Instinctively, she thought of Tiyano back on the festival grounds. He had always been a friend to her in rough times. Even with some financial troubles here and there, a couple of rough patches that Fura herself had helped to talk him through, she knew that Tiyano and his family would take her in. As much as the thought appealed to her, a familiar shoulder to lean on in this trying time, Fura just couldn't do that to him. It didn't feel right to impose herself on others.

Looking around, Fura felt sick to her stomach.

Like I'm doing now? she could hear herself say.

It was true. Fura didn't know half of these people. She felt absurd trying to weasel her way effortlessly into their daily lives, but it had been offered to her, hadn't it? What was worse – to launch her troubles onto a friend, or to try and make the best of what had been so quickly handed to her without question?

Fura hadn't even had time to really think on it when Apallo had given her the ultimatum. She had just agreed.

She wondered now that if she had known beforehand what kind of living conditions she would be presented with, if she would have given a second thought to the offer.

Yet, even despite the oddity of it all, there was something here that comforted her. Something that sang deep within her bones, telling her that everything would be alright in the end. That she was where she was meant to be.

"I'm only trying to get to know you," Fura stammered, changing the subject. She was confused by Kiyani's continued display of anger towards her, a remnant of that first nights conversation that had yet to abandon them.

"Why?" Kiyani asked harshly. "So you can treat me with the same disdain as all the others?"

Fura didn't know what to say. She didn't understand the meaning of his words or why he was consistently so cryptic. Her gut told her to leave, that she didn't have to listen to his anger, but her feet were rooted in place, her heart unsure of whether it wanted to answer, or stay and try to glean whatever intricate puzzle it was that Kiyani was piecing out before her, to delve into his secrets that seemed to be locked behind a stone wall with a lost key.

"Run along," Kiyani said stoically. "You don't belong here."

Accenting the end of his sentence like a bold period, a sound stormed through the night. At first, Fura thought it was just another rumble of thunder, the storm growing closer, but as the deep reverberating bellow continued, she immediately recognized it as the same horn that had called the camp to attention the other day.

It echoed through the walls of the cave like the acoustics of an orchestra hall.

Moving forward, intent on seeing what could possibly be the reason for such a call at this time of night, she gave no further thought to the sordid conversation she'd been having with Kiyani. She didn't know what she had expected to find here anyway.

The horn sounded again and Fura took a step. Not expecting it, she was immediately stopped by a hand on her arm, and she turned to see that Kiyani had grabbed her, silently shaking his head no.

Trying to weasel her way out of his grasp, his grip only tightened, leading her to the frightening conclusion that he was actually a lot stronger than he initially appeared.

"Stay here," he instructed firmly. His tone and his actions gave her no real choice.

Balling her fist, Fura tried to wrench her arm out of his grasp again with little luck. "From what I understood the other day, that indicates a meeting or something, that I'm sure *everyone* is supposed to attend."

Now that she thought about it, she couldn't recall seeing him during the last one, officially announcing Brieda's death.

"Not at this hour."

"What? Emergencies can't happen at night?" Fura asked. She might have been irritated by his sudden proximity to her, but she couldn't ignore the distance in his voice. "Maybe that guy came back to talk to Apallo. The one that killed Brieda."

"That's what I'm afraid of."

As sick as it was, she had only been joking. The adrenaline flooding her veins, Fura wondered if she had been unfortunate enough to have been pulled out of one mess only to be plunged into the heart of another. "What are you trying to say?" she asked fearfully.

"He's not here to talk."

The horn sounded again and Fura felt like she was being pulled in two directions. Her need to follow orders told her to go and see for herself what this was all about. On the other hand, Kiyani's words echoed in her mind, telling her to stay put, to listen to him despite their rocky history.

It wasn't just that, but she could feel it, like an extra sense, an air of malevolence that hung in the air.

As if to emphasize that thought, a deeper rumble of thunder sounded overhead, much closer than before.

"But, if that man's here... we're trapped in here," Fura said, looking back the way she had come. They were sitting here like rats in a cage, just waiting to be found. "How are we suppos-"

"*Hush!*"

Releasing her arm, Kiyani quickly moved into the shadows beyond the fire's glow. In a matter of moments he returned with a bucket of water and a wad of fabric.

Throwing the balled up material at her, he held out a hand. "Trust me."

Fura had all the urge to defiantly say no. To storm out of the cave and see what was going on for herself. Who cared what he had to say? He didn't like her anyways.

But his usual crude arrogance was gone, replaced by something akin to fear that was visible in his eyes.

She had no experience with his kind, but Fura could only guess that that much of a change in his attitude could only mean one thing: something wasn't right. Only a moment ago they had been arguing. Now, he was concerned with her safety.

As soon as she nodded, Kiyani cast the contents of the bucket onto the fire. The ashes spat and sputtered before throwing them into complete darkness.

Taking his hand, they fled.

15

••◇••

THE DARK ONE

Into the darkness he led her. It wasn't clear to Fura if she had made the right decision in following him or not, but it was too late to change her mind and go back now.

She wanted to ask him if he even knew where he was going. How the hell he could see.

There was nothing but black surrounding them, so dark that Fura knew she could poke herself in the eye and still not be able to see the hand in front of her face. All she knew for certain was that if she let go of Kiyani's hand she would be lost in the darkness, the night consuming her.

Thinking back to her thoughts in her own room earlier, Fura wondered if she just might get her wish of the darkness eating her up after all.

Quiet as ever, Kiyani led her through the tunnels that seemed to gradually grow smaller and smaller as they went. Though she couldn't see him, she could feel in the firm grasp that he had on her hand that he knew these passages well, navigating with ease.

Questions stormed her mind, but she was still too confused about what was even going on to try form a coherent sentence, the words scattering like minnows in a shallow pond.

Before she could think to pull back and stop this madness before it went any further, a faint light began to grow ahead. It wasn't much, but the soft darkness of natural night seemed almost blinding in comparison with the absolute darkness of the caverns Kiyani had drug her through without warning. She could see his silhouette before her now as he drug her along, following its call.

"What's going on?" Fura finally asked when they pulled themselves free from the cavernous maze.

Looking down at the cloth still clutched in her hand, she shook it out, only to realize it was a cloak, much like the ones she had often envied at the festival shops but had never had the money to actually be able to afford.

"Nothing good," Kiyani answered her as he searched the night around them.

Throwing the cloak around her shoulders, Fura watched him. "How do you know?"

"I just do."

Fura heard a scream and she looked behind her to where it had come from.

"Then we've got to go help."

Kiyani shook his head. "You don't fight a man like that."

"But…"

"If you want to go back, then be my guest. I'm going."

"Where?"

"Away from here. Before we get caught as well."

"You don't even know if there's actually something going on."

Another scream and a brief chorus of arguing caught her ear and Fura looked at Kiyani for a moment before turning and stalking forward, wanting to at least get a glimpse of what was going on.

She didn't know where the tunnel had dropped them off at, but she could tell that they were still close to the camp, the sounds of mass confusion and chaos sounding through the night. In the faint light, all Fura could see were grassy mounds and the rocky outcroppings of the caves that broke through the weather-packed dirt. None of the tall trees of the surrounding forest grew here, only small seedlings that twisted toward the sky with roots that would never find enough purchase in the rocky soil.

Ignoring Kiyani's hissed protest, Fura carefully made her way up an incline and towards the noise, desperately needing to make sure that this wasn't all a prank, that her world wasn't falling apart yet again.

Despite what he'd said, Kiyani followed her, pulling her back down into the little cover that was provided when they crested the hill. She could see now that they had somehow ended up on top of the caves. A clear view of the area below sat etched in the faintest silver moonlight.

"Do you believe me now?" he asked.

From what she could see in the horrid lighting, based only on the shadowy mass, it looked as if the entire camp had been woken by the sound of the blaring horn. Save for the time of day, it looked much like a repeat of the scene from the other day, and she wondered what it was that had Kiyani so on edge to go to all this trouble. Had he done the same thing before, watching from this vantage point?

Monira had claimed only that morning that he could be a valuable friend. Now Fura was wondering why she would want to go to such trouble. It was clear that she would never understand the man that sat crouched beside her.

However, she couldn't deny that in her gut something was off.

It was hard to see in the darkness and Fura squinted her eyes to try to see better. She caught sight of a male-shaped silhouette taking to what she had deemed the stage, but she could discern little else. The stature and gait seemed familiar, though she was certain that it wasn't Apallo, which made little sense.

The voices that she overheard calling out into the night only confirmed the fact.

"Hey, what are you doing?"

"What's this all about?"

"Where's Apallo?"

The figure held his hands in the air and the crowd before him fell into a subdued silence, if only to hear what was happening, why they had been woken from slumber. Nothing so far appeared to be out of place, nothing out of the ordinary to raise such an alarm.

"My companions!" the man shouted above a roll of thunder. "This is a night of reckoning! A night of change!"

"Where's Apallo?" a voice challenged once more, not taking the time to listen to this imposter.

Though Fura recognized the voice.

She turned to Kiyani. "Nevo?" she questioned, though she knew it to be true. He had only run into her briefly the day of Brieda's death, but Fura could recognize his canter. As if the name itself had made it clearer, she could see it now in the shape of his dark silhouette. The blond of his hair, tied up in a knot atop his head, was just visible in the low firelight of a the few torches that sputtered in the night.

"Apallo is no longer fit to lead!" Nevo's voice rang through the night, answering the question sent forth from the crowd.

"Is this a mutiny?"

"It's so much more than that."

Fura started, confused. Looking around, she tried to find the answer.

The voice that had answered wasn't Nevo's. Hadn't even come from the stage. It didn't even seem to have come from the crowd.

Not only that, it was amplified as if it had come from a loudspeaker or an intercom, echoing through the night, loud and clear as day. The cold and conceited cadence of it chilled her to the bone, even though she couldn't identify the speaker.

The noise level below rose considerably as those in the crowd turned about, searching for the same thing she was, asking questions that none of them seemed to be able to answer.

Just when it felt they would all be left in the dark, a pillar of twisting flame suddenly rose from the height of the stage where Nevo had been standing. With a brilliant flash and a loud boom that rivaled the thunder, a man stepped from the smoke and fire. He was tall and thin, clad entirely in black.

Jumping with fright, Fura latched onto Kiyani's arm, eliciting a growled "ow" from him as well as an angered glare. But both were forgotten as she looked down at what was unfolding below.

The moment the man's face became visible in the sudden light of the flames, screams broke out in the clearing, and a mad rush to leave the area ensued.

Before anyone could make light of the sudden move, the man raised his arms and a line of flames appeared on either side of the stage. Moving with frightening speed, they snaked along the ground and circled the breadth of the crowd, trapping them inside.

"Silence!" the man bellowed.

A malicious smile spread across his flame-lit face as he let his voice echo into the night, looking down upon the people corralled before him with morbid fascination painted upon his thin and sallow features.

That one word, spoken with such force, had been an obvious command, but silence was the last thing on Fura's mind. Jumping up, she was immediately pulled back down by Kiyani. Even his rough hand and stern gaze couldn't keep her seated though. Fura had known the minute those flames had lit up the night in their unearthly colors of green.

"He's the one," she cried in a hushed voice when Kiyani held a finger to his lips, indicating that she remain silent.

"*Shut up!*" he hissed, verbally emphasizing the command.

Near the point of hyperventilating, Fura barely heard him. Her vision wavered, sending the darkness and the strange glow of the flames into one unrecognizable blur. She could hardly bring herself to look back upon the man, but she had to.

"He killed my family."

Kiyani grabbed her arm again, holding her stiffly in place. But it wasn't necessary. Her legs were suddenly weak, and even if she had wanted to go down and do something, Fura doubted she could walk.

"And what are you going to do?" he asked callously. "Go down there and ask him to apologize?"

He was right. What could she possibly do? Besides lean on Kiyani and watch, helpless as ever.

The man on the stage seemed to catch wind of something, and his eyes raised to the sky, settling on something in the distance. Fura recoiled, certain that he had caught sight of them, that he had heard her talking. It felt as if his gaze bridged the physical distance between them and bored into her soul, making her feel as if he were looking right at her.

Fura felt Kiyani's muscles tense beneath the grasp she had on his arm, making her think that he had noticed the eerie closeness of the man's gaze as well. She fought the urge to look at his face to see what it said, afraid the movement would give away their position. If they hadn't already been compromised.

Slowly, a smile spread across the man's face, and he held it for a moment – that knowing look that said he had a secret – before dropping his gaze and returning his attention to the people contained within the circle of leaping flames.

Though a few people on the outer fringes of the crowd tested their luck, batting at the fiery wall, the man knew he had them exactly where he wanted.

"Distressed, sad, naïve beings," he began, his tone seeming to dance in time with the flames. "Look at yourselves! Cowering in fear before one of the fabled Sect of Seven. What kind of welcome is that?"

Fura looked to Kiyani beside her, wondering if she had just heard right. Had this man really just mentioned the Sect of Seven? Something that she had just been joking about with her teacher only a few days ago?

"You should all be ashamed. Ashamed for following such drivel." He let out a short laugh. *"Seven Lords to rule equally and peacefully to create a land of harmony."*

He was actually quoting the same story.

"Harmony? Ha! All it has done is divide us. We lay scattered like forgotten runes on a cracked table. Gathering dust."

Glancing beside her again as the man spoke, Fura looked to Kiyani, but nothing in his watchful eyes declared that he found the content of the man's words the least bit odd. Brushing it off, Fura shook her head in disbelief and returned to watching the scene below.

"Where are your gods now?" the man asked fervently. "You all obediently pray to the Stars, but when was the last time they answered?"

Heads turned within the crowd below as whispers began to break out.

"I ask that you look to me now, not as the one that the sordid rumors portray, but as something far greater!"

"Your only claim to fame is being a monster!" a man shouted out, stepping out of the crowd.

The man who held the stage whipped his head around to meet the eye of the one who had spoken out of line. As he raised a single hand, the rogue speaker suddenly fell to his knees, his eyes wide with fear, clawing at his throat as if he couldn't breathe. Gasping for air, he took one last breath before falling face first to the ground, dead. The people who had been standing around him formed a circle of dead space as they backed away from the gruesome sight.

"Then I shall play the part," the man on stage declared wickedly. "Is there any other who dare speak against me?" When no one volunteered an answer, he continued on. "Now, listen close! There is a hidden gem, left from the days of old."

Pulling what appeared to be a scroll from within the folds of his dark cloak as it billowed around him in the stormy breeze, the man held it aloft, presenting it to the sky.

"The Nyte-Fyre Prophecy! A relic from the height of our days, when wizards were our allies, when our streets were lined with gold and ambition. It was prophesized that this land would not be ruled by seven, but by one. One man. You may think me bold in my claim that that is meant to be me, but I will tell you with certainty that it is not the one that you call your leader.

"How could it be? Look at what your dear Apallo has let you become. Living in filth and disgust. Is this the man that you look up to? He's got you living like wild dogs. Sleeping in caves like bats. Blind to the fact that he spends his days driving you all into the dirt. And what do you do? You follow him... like sheep! And for what?"

Letting his words fall into remiss, the man stood tall as he scanned the contained crowd, allowing the depth of his meaning to fully sink in. The only sounds in the clearing were the intermittent bursts of thunder that accented the night with a deep sense of foreboding. The dancing fires were strangely silent, and even the songs of the crickets that Fura had heard earlier had ceased, as if they too were waiting to see what this man had to say.

"He's made you weak and vulnerable. Left you to depend on him. Well, I ask you this. Where is your leader now?"

"Apallo will hear about this!"

The man on the stage looked in the direction of where the voice had interrupted him. They all feared that he would strike another down with just as little sympathy as before, but the man only smiled.

"Oh, he knows."

Looking to the caves from where the crowd had come, he gestured with a slow roll of his fingers. From within the shadows, where all the fires had been extinguished, a small detail of four black-clad men came forth.

Fura sucked in a breath, her fear growing by the minute.

In the midst of their ranks, bruised and battered, and being crudely drug along, was a man that she had come to recognize years ago.

A frenzy of hushed voices broke out again as the crowd parted, leaving a path for the men as they made their way to the base of the stage. Reaching the end, they threw Apallo to the ground where he landed roughly on his hands and knees. Before he could even think to right himself, or to fight back, the men had surrounded him again with a brigade of sharpened spears pointed dangerously close to him. A small line of red trickled down his face from a cut on his temple, but he didn't seem to notice.

Apallo ignored the proximity of the weapons, just as he avoided the gazes of those that followed him, likely out of the shame derived by his current position.

"Zariah! Let us talk this out?" he pleaded, looking up at the man that graced the stage above him.

"*Zariah,*" Fura whispered. So this was the same man that Apallo had spoken of the other day. The one he claimed had murdered Brieda.

Jumping from the height of the stage, Zariah landed in a graceful crouch, his cloak falling around him like a shroud of misty night. In one fluid movement, he resumed his full stature, looking just as poised as ever. Nevo came scurrying from behind the stage, a long staff in his possession and paused at the man's side. Quickly bowing, he presented the length of carved wood to the outstretched hand that waited impatiently.

Tearing the staff out of Nevo's hand, Zariah made no move to thank him. Instead, he dug the staff into the dirt before him and leaned on it, looking down at Apallo who crouched, crumpled and defeated at his feet.

"The time for talk is over."

Apallo peered up at him. The look of not only shock, but fear in his eyes was something that Fura had never seen from him before.

"You don't need to do this."

"I will do as I please."

"Why?"

"You know why." Returning his gaze to the crowd, Zariah still seemed to tower above them all despite now being on the same level. "Despicable. Redundant. *Pathetic.* That is what you have all become. *Apallo* is your enemy. Not I.

"I am the one who can lead you out of this regression. Follow me and you will see glory that you've only heard of in myth.

"*Seven shall rule as one.* Well those Seven are scattered and weak! That age is *over!* It's been over. Declining year after year. And here you all sit, content to fade away into dust along with it. Pitiful humans. You all deserve your fate. But I stand before you now and give you one final chance. Join me."

"They will never join you!" Apallo announced, the fear melting out of his voice as it was replaced by hard-edged anger.

Zariah looked at him. "You don't get that choice."

"Give it up."

"Give it up?" Zariah echoed playfully. "It's only just begun."

His maniacal laughter danced in the night.

"You will follow me, or you will go the way of history, for the Sect of Seven is DEAD! Disgraced. A mere shadow of what it once was. Rotting and decayed. It is a poison upon this land."

One man stepped forth from the crowd, fires of the correct color of orange trailing from his palms and halfway up his arms.

Fura couldn't even begin to clearly describe what she was seeing play out before her.

"The only poison is you," the man shouted defiantly.

The flames growing brighter, bordering on white, the man set to act against this foe, but Zariah was too quick for him. Before the unnamed man even had a chance, Zariah brought the staff up like a skilled fighter and a bolt of green energy spewed forth from it. Hitting the rebel square in the chest, it sent him catapulting through the air before he connected with a harsh crack against the stone of the caverns in the background.

Eyes narrowed, Zariah looked upon the crowd, the smile wiped clean from his face, replaced with clear contempt. "You will one day look back upon this moment and realize the extent of the mistake you have made. Mark my words. You will live with the shadow of regret. And that moment starts now."

When no one else dared come forth to challenge him, Zariah's stance lost the smallest bit of its edge. Returning his focus to Apallo, who sat, forced into the mud by the surrounding guard, he leaned on his staff, the wood surrounding the dancing orb at its peak appearing just as twisted he was.

"And here I thought this might actually prove to be a challenge. How wrong I was."

Though the malicious grin had returned, his words were bored. Mocking.

"They will never follow you," Apallo lashed out, spitting defiantly at the man's feet.

"Oh, I shiver in fear," Zariah laughed. "They can follow me or die. I don't care which they choose."

"Then they will die fighting for what they believe in."

"So quick to decide your people's fates."

"The spirit can't be broken."

"We shall see about that."

With a wave of his spindly fingers, he beckoned Nevo over. "Gag this cur. I tire of hearing him speak."

Apallo struggled against the same guards who had drug him from the cave and thrown him at Zariah's feet with a small amount of success before he was kicked in the back of the leg and sent to his knees. Bending down, Nevo procured a rolled piece of cloth from within his shirt and stuffed it roughly in the fallen leader's mouth. None of the respect that he had shown towards the man during his years living within Frielana was present.

As Nevo moved to tie the gag, Apallo made one last ditch effort to do something. Gathering his strength, he defiantly got to his feet in one quick maneuver. In attempt to keep the man restrained, Nevo's hand moved back to the gag, intending to use it to pull him back to the ground. Instead, Apallo spit out the loose piece of fabric and bit the man's hand, sending him backward in shock. Recovering rather quickly, Nevo moved in again, but was this time elbowed in the gut. Sent sprawling to the ground, he fell in the dirt, clutching his stomach.

"THE WITNESS WILL LEAD THE WAY!!" Apallo shouted to the sky with a voice that echoed through the surrounding trees.

Zariah wheeled around at the interruption, fire burning in his eyes. Swinging his staff in anger, he caught Apallo on the side of the head, sending him to the ground.

"Enough of you!" he sneered, though he had hit with enough force to successfully knock the man out, at least briefly.

Sending a look of cold contempt to his guards, they shirked away from his rage, before moving back in to restrain the fallen leader before he regained consciousness.

"Time will tell what fate you choose," Zariah declared, returning his attention to the crowd. His voice had regained that heinous edge, his patience clearly wearing thin. "Until then, why don't you welcome your new guests."

Bringing his staff upward, he brought it down to the ground, an angered force behind the action. As soon as it made contact, the towering circle of flames lowered, creating small tornadoes of colors before vanishing out of sight without so much as a scorch mark left upon the land.

However, left in its wake, replacing the dancing barrier was a circle of men that had moved in unnoticed. They stood, shoulder to shoulder, and at least ten deep.

A rogue flash of lightning danced across the sky, revealing their grim faces and the shining metal spears they carried. All were identical in uniforms of black and silver. All cut from the same cloth and made for one purpose.

To carry out their master's orders and kill anyone who got in the way.

16

•◆✧◆•

ON THE RUN

Without the riveting light of the serpentine flames that had permeated the darkness, the camp was thrown back into the endless abyss of night.

Fura might as well have been blind with the sudden change, but even having lost clear sight of what was lying directly below her, she could still hear the sounds.

Harsh shouts and arguing were the first thing to pierce through the void, as the crowd of people who had remained diligently silent during the display began to come to their senses. Verbally fighting back, the air was filled with a chorus of shouting as they assailed the circle of armored men with harsh words. However, the words had little effect in the face of cold weapons, and it wasn't long before cries of anguish and screams of terror ripped through the fall air, assaulting Fura's senses as the circle of black-clad men began to enact their orders.

Though caught in a web of terror, Fura found herself dangerously close to the drop off, leaning forward as she tried to get a better look at what was going on. It was difficult to discern just who was fighting who as the dusty shadows began to move against one another. Subdued flashes of what appeared to be fire dotted the area now and again, interspersed with grunts and the sound of metal, followed by the soft thud of bodies hitting the ground, many to never rise again.

During one of the intermittent bursts of light, Fura's eyes trailed back to the stage where the man called Zariah had stood, this evil his own vision of what was right. She expected to see him still towering over them all, a human-shaped obelisk of horror, but from what she could see he had already vanished. Odd that a man such as that wouldn't stay to watch what he had begun. It should have been a comfort that he had left, but Fura only found it all the more chilling.

Wondering if he might still be lingering, merely choosing to watch from the same shadows where he had seemed to appear like a spectator watching a sports game, Fura nearly jumped out of her skin as a hand fell on her shoulder.

115

Too terrified to even scream, she whipped around to find that Kiyani was still with her.

"Are you coming or not?"

No longer worried about remaining quiet, his voice was stronger now, fighting to be heard over the clamor below.

Fura glanced over her shoulder, only realizing then that she was leaning forward on her hands and knees, determined to get a better view, and precariously close to the edge of the rocky overhang of the cave. "But..."

Kiyani held out a hand. "You can't do anything."

Ignoring the set determination on his face, Fura turned back to the scene below. The faintest stream of silver light broke through the storm clouds above from a crescent moon. With its half-hearted attempt, she could just make out the blond halo of Nevo's hair as the strands that had fallen loose from their bonds danced about his head in the mounting breeze. Standing upon the stage, he seemed to watch the action with a morbid fascination. With the sudden disappearance of Zariah, Fura assumed that he had been the one left behind in the man's wake to orchestrate the remainder of the siege.

Thinking back to her run in with Nevo, she couldn't believe that only the other day she had considered that one day he might be a potential friend.

At his side stood the figure of a woman. Though Fura couldn't make out any details to tell her if she was a previous follower of Apallo, as Nevo had been, she could tell that the two were rather friendly.

It was all Fura could do, trying to decipher that select piece of information, to not let her vision wander away, taking in the brutality of what was happening elsewhere throughout Frielana.

Shaking from the sheer terror that threatened to raise the bile from her stomach to her throat, Fura turned back to Kiyani. Though he had told her they had to leave, he seemed to be equally paralyzed by the events. His gaze moved well past her as he teetered back and forth in an unstable crouch.

"We have to do something," Fura pleaded.

She didn't know how she would be able to live with herself if all she did was sit back and watch.

"We're doing it now."

Fura was astonished at his easy dismissal. "We're doing nothing."

She had to admit, his words surprised her. From what little she knew of him, she half expected him to be roaring to move into battle like a majority of the men she met daily at the festival that joked about such things. But not Kiyani.

Actually, she had to hand it to him. In light of the current situation, he appeared deceptively calm and collected. His gaze was steady as he watched, unflinching, the events below. The only thing that gave her any inclination that his fear so much as matched hers was the fist at his side that she could see repeatedly clenching and unclenching in the shallow darkness between them.

Kiyani broke his focus and looked at her, just before killing the silence that had fallen between them. "We're free, which is more than they have," he claimed, pointing a finger to the clearing. "And now we do what they can't. Run."

"But," Fura argued. "You mean the only thing we can do is play the part of the coward?"

Kiyani had already moved to leave, but he twisted in response to her discriminatory dismissal, sending her a heated look that cut through the darkness.

"I am not a coward," he growled. "But there is *nothing* that we can do. Not right now. Now, you can go and join your fate with theirs, or you can come with me."

Fura barely had time to react before he turned away and began his descent into the thick cover of the tree line below.

"Wait!" she called out, her voice almost completely masked by the roll of thunder overhead.

The storm was getting closer. Already she could feel the change in temperature and sense the coming moisture that the wind carried.

Stumbling to her feet, Fura looked behind her. Her hands shook as she tried to make a quick go of deciding what to do. Kiyani's invitation to follow hadn't been the friendliest of offers. Having been given the distinct impression that, despite sounding like he had given her the final choice, Kiyani didn't really want her along, Fura knew that if she didn't hurry he wouldn't be coming back for her if he turned to find her missing

Her heart was torn in two opposing directions as she shifted her gaze between the ensuing chaos and Kiyani's shadowed form as he made his way down the backside of the caves. Just before he disappeared completely into the trees, Fura took off after him.

She despised the idea of having to stoop to such a level that allowed her to leave her friends behind, but Kiyani was right. Nothing more than two rag-tag teenagers, their chance against a plethora of armored men, trained to kill, was far from inspiring. A speck of dust pitted against the violence of a raging tornado. If they charged forth, the only thing they would accomplish would be increasing the number of captives by two.

Not to mention, they had no weapons at their disposal. Thinking back to the stick that she had unsuccessfully wielded the other day, Fura knew her thinking that she could make a difference was futile. She couldn't even defend herself against Kiyani.

Following after him, she instinctively wondered just how well he would fare.

He hadn't fought her the other day – only defended himself – and he wouldn't even fight when Apallo rallied against him, but watching his lithe stride, Fura felt that he was stronger and better adept than he led on. It was a thought that both intrigued and frightened her.

The deadly clearing, full of terror and misled trust, was already out of sight as Fura stopped to look back one last time, not knowing if she would ever see it again. It was a dark skyline that she looked upon. Only the smallest wisps of hazy gray smoke rose into the air, adding a nuance of color. The action may have been out of her vision, but the gloom couldn't mask the horrific sounds. Sounds that Fura knew would haunt her late into the night for weeks to come. It crushed her that her only option was to turn her back and flee.

"Hey," Kiyani called.

Fura finally forced herself to turn away and face him. His lips were set in a thin line, his brows furrowed in frustration, wanting to go.

"Take it or leave it," he said. "But I'm not waiting for you again."

A rumble of thunder sent her careening forward, her feet acting on reflex rather than thought.

Taking it as a sign that she had decided to come, Kiyani waved her on into the darkness awaiting them in the trees. "Stay low," he instructed.

She had only known him for a few days, but Fura didn't take him as a man who often went back on his word. So when he turned and darted forward, she followed, knowing that he wouldn't be doubling back a second time to lead her away from danger.

It was slow going, moving with extreme caution as they made their way into the heavier covering of the mature trees that made up the forest. Strangely enough, as hard as it'd been to turn away, Fura found that once she'd made that final decision, she was left only with the overwhelming itch to break out into a full run.

If leaving was their only chance, then why waste any time?

But she knew the answer, could see it in the way Kiyani moved through the shadows, repeatedly stopping, even though he had only gone a few feet. Every time he paused, he crouched low, Fura following suit. His eyes scanned their surroundings, searching.

Fura didn't have to ask what for. Each time he nimbly dove into the shrubbery, she searched the shadows herself, expecting to see the dark and human forms of scouts having been sent after them. There was no saying if anyone was even aware that they were missing, but Fura knew she didn't want to be anywhere nearby if that suddenly became the case. Her internal banter whipping her into a state of frenzy, Fura started to see her fears visualized in the murky surroundings. Not knowing if any of it was real or not, she didn't trust herself to make the official call. Instead, it was Kiyani that she looked to. As he sat crouched, stock still, she knew he was a better judge of danger than her.

Only once did one such shape appear, coming in close to them. Too close.

Where Fura knew that she would have stood, frozen in place like a deer in the headlights had she been left to her own non-existent survivalist instinct, it was Kiyani that had reflexively drug her down into cover. It felt like forever that she had stayed there, so close to the forest floor that she might as well have been lying upon the dirt.

The snapping branches the man's feet uncovered as he moved forward had seemed to have come within inches of their hiding place before he reluctantly abandoned the search and turned back around. Fura hadn't even known that she could hold her breath for so long.

After that, they seemed to glide effortlessly through the woods – or at least Kiyani did. Each and every step Fura took caused her to cringe, wondering if the sheer amount of noise she was making would alert the whole countryside. It was certainly enough to elicit a few choice glares from Kiyani. She could only assume that he was telling himself that he should have left her behind.

The further they advanced in the direction leading away from the encampment, the more Fura began to think that they were in the clear, that maybe the worst was over for the night.

And then it began to rain. As if fate laughed in her face, the excess of moisture that had been lying in wait behind every clap of thunder let loose in a sudden deluge.

Cold, wet, heavy drops crashed down on them, increasing the difficulty of sight and turning the ground beneath them to slick mud that pulled at their feet. More than once Fura lost her footing in the muck and was nearly taken to her knees, almost losing sight of Kiyani in the process through the sheets of rain.

The added complexity of travel in the dark of the night would have been bad enough, but it was the clammy cold that plagued Fura the most. Her hair was plastered to her face and rivers of water ran down into her eyes. Worst of all, even with the cloak that Kiyani had essentially thrown in her face, her clothing was already soaked through. The shivers that wracked her body made her wonder if she would ever find warmth again.

All Fura wanted to do was curl up somewhere and dry off. Maybe sleep. Looking back into the mist that rose from the ground in the torrential rains, she didn't see either of those things happening anytime soon.

How could she?

It was dank, dark, and they were completely surrounded by trees, the majesty of nature disheveled by the rain, and darkened by shadow. Fura had been wrong to think that she could enjoy living out here. Home was the only thing that called to her now. That place that had lights and electricity, a bed, a shower, a stove. All those little things that she had never thought of as something special until now.

Most of all, she wanted a hot shower and a towel.

But even beyond that, Fura wanted to know where it was they were going.

In the heat of the moment, in the midst of confusion and terror, she had followed Kiyani without question or thought. But now, freezing and alone, save for his presence, she was left to wonder if he had an actual destination in mind, or if he was just going to lead them both on some wild ride through the woods until they both keeled over from exhaustion and hypothermia.

She was thankful that he had gotten her out of danger, but what good would that prove in the end if they only found themselves worse off?

Fura was determined to get an answer. Stepping up her pace to catch up with him, she was brought to a halt as her senses caught on to something else. It was the smallest of sounds, but it was just enough to hold her attention. Not sure if it was something to worry about, an indication that something else was out there, or if it was just the trickle of rain falling through the leafy canopy above, Fura assured herself it was the latter. The second time she became aware of it was when the stirrings of panic returned.

Racing to regain the ground she had lost between herself and Kiyani, she could have sworn that a flash of gray streaked past in her peripheral vision. Just the thought that they were no longer alone sent shivers of ice surging through Fura's veins that had nothing to do with the cold torrent of rain.

Her heart pounding wildly in her chest, Fura rushed forward and grabbed Kiyani's arm. She didn't have to question to know that he wasn't an intimate person, but the physical contact gave her a comforting sense of not being quite so vulnerable.

"What?" Kiyani asked, tired and irritable as he pried her fingers from his arm.

Fura ignored his reaction and pointed to the darkness around them. "There's something out there."

"There's a lot of things out there."

"Kiyani, I'm serious," she whined. Fura couldn't believe that after what had happened he could still find ways to so easily play the sarcasm card. Had he not seen what she had?

"So am I."

She wanted to chuck something at him for taking this as some joke, but she was too cold and tired to put forth that amount of effort for the sake of injuring the only one who might actually know where they were.

"It's not like you would be able to hear much over the rain," she pointed out instead, trying to make him see reason.

He had taken a moment to search the forest silently with his eyes, but his gaze returned to her at the comment. "It's not like I can hear over your talking, either."

That's it, she was hitting him.

Raising an arm to punch him in the shoulder for being so mean, Kiyani grabbed her wrist and spun her around, just as a flash of lightning streaked overhead. Backed up against his chest, and held in place by his grasp, Fura screamed as she took in the sight of the beast that stood before them.

Any other time, Fura might have wondered if Kiyani had found a way to perfectly time the maneuver, as the sound that emanated from her lips was expertly masked by the clap of thunder that followed the light. As it was, all she could do was stare in fear at the bedraggled form in her direct line of sight.

Eyes of a light color flashed in the darkness. Wet, matted fur clung to the lithe and muscular body, the wide paws plunged into the mud by the weight they supported. However, it was the mouth of the wolf, curled into a snarl that revealed razor sharp canines, that had Fura clamoring to fight Kiyani's grasp and move behind him.

She couldn't believe it. Kiyani wasn't that mean-spirited, was he? Sure, she knew he didn't like her, but did that really justify him trying to feed her to the wolves?

"Now that you've alerted the entire forest to our location," Kiyani said in her ear just before releasing his hold, "that's what's been following us."

Fura couldn't say for certain if he had actually given her a slight shove in the beast's direction, but without his physical presence she felt more exposed than ever.

"That's a wolf," Fura said, taking a step backwards. Her finger shook excessively as she pointed to the glowing eyes and bared teeth that stared back at her.

"Congratulations on your astounding ability to state the obvious," Kiyani answered, completely unfazed.

Seemingly in response the wolf emitted a deep growl. Pulling her arm slowly back, Fura backed up into Kiyani and clung to his arm.

"That's a wolf," she repeated again.

Kiyani didn't respond as he peeled her off his arm and pushed her away again, his actions seeming to proclaim that she was acting like a child with an immature fear of the dark. When Fura went to cling to him again, the wolf let out another snarl, stopping her.

"Kiedo, back down," Kiyani declared harshly.

He was the one pointing fingers now. Fura could hardly believe it as she watched the wolf's raised fur smooth over. Its eyes moved from her to the finger Kiyani pointed, seeming to consider the words. Unexpectedly, the wolf sat.

Fura's jaw dropped, wondering if she had honestly just witnessed that. It was like Kiyani was this thing's master, controlling it with simple commands like your run of the mill dog.

Yet, wrapped in the jaws of fear, all she could manage was, "That's a wolf."

"Don't you *ever* shut up?"

How could he act like he knew this thing? This beast with teeth and claws that had been poised and ready to attack, waiting to follow through on the animalistic instinct to kill them both.

"That's a wolf!" she repeated again, her voice becoming shrill with fear. She wanted to run, but instinct told her that wasn't the best idea.

Kiyani sighed. "You've already established that."

"You have a *wolf* as a pet?"

"Can't we do this someplace else?"

Fura could see that he was eager to increase the distance between themselves and the melee within Frielana, but she couldn't get herself to move.

"You're insane." She didn't know what was worse, being left to deal with what was happening back in the clearing, or being left alone with this man. He clearly wasn't right in the head.

"Says the one who tried to decapitate me with a tree branch."

Okay, so he had a point, though Fura refused to comment.

The wolf that Kiyani had called Kiedo looked at her as if he too was trying to come up with a judgment of her. Nervous under the microscope of the animal's examination, Fura turned away, her gaze on Kiyani who ignored them both as he kept watch on the surrounding forest.

Right. So he owned a wolf. No big deal. Because that was completely normal.

"So, are you done?" Kiyani asked listlessly. "Because we've got to keep moving."

Before Fura could give an answer Kiyani let out a short whistle and the wolf rose and moved to his side.

"You knew that was what was following us, right?"

Fura still couldn't come to terms with what she was seeing, but she had to tell herself that Kiyani had to have known, that he wasn't that oblivious.

"He was keeping an eye out for us."

Great. A watch wolf.

The limbering gray form was unnerving, even more so than the entirety of the siege that she had lain witness to, but regardless of her feelings, Fura knew that Kiyani was going to move on, with or without her.

Not knowing what else to say, she followed the odd pair deeper into the trees, consciously aware of how well they seemed to fit together. Fura had first thought of Kiyani as a black cat, slinking around in the shadows, but now she thought that maybe he was more of a lone wolf, not only in spirit but in the few friends he took on. Of course, if that was the way of it, he might have been taking the comparison a bit too literally.

It wasn't long after, amidst the continuing downpour, that Kiyani finally declared that they had gone far enough.

"We're stopping here for the night."

Fura wasn't sure if he was actually speaking to her directly, or if it was for his own advantage, as a way to convince himself that it wasn't necessary to keep going for the night. She wasn't sure how far they had gone, or how much time had passed. The rain and the misery it brought made it hard to judge. However, the mixture of exhaustion and the weather conditions hadn't left her blind, leaving her certain of one thing. There was nothing around.

Not one thing had changed around them. It was still all darkness and trees. Trees, trees, and more trees, all thrown into a hazy, misty shadow, an empty void.

"Where?" Fura finally asked.

She didn't want to voice the rest of her observation, wondering if he actually expected them to sleep out in the open propped against some tree. On a languid summer night, that might have been acceptable, if you didn't count the wild animals roaming about. She looked to Kiedo as she thought it, still not sure what to think of the wolf's sudden presence. She couldn't quite decide if she felt safer, or if danger was just now lurking in plain sight. With that around, she doubted she would sleep anyways. It didn't matter how exhausted she was. Not to mention, who could sleep out in the rain, feeling like they were in a perpetual state of being washed away?

Kiyani knelt down next to one of the trees in their path. "Here."

Fura had to admit that she hadn't known what to expect when she had first entered the Verboten forest with Apallo leading the way. She definitely hadn't thought of what she had expected to come across with Kiyani leading the way. Maybe not anything resembling civilization if she was honest with herself, but some kind of shelter all the same. Another cave. A sheltered grove. At the least, a nice weft of low-hanging pine branches that would keep the ground beneath dry.

"There's nothing here," she said, giving voice to the obvious.

There was nothing special about this particular run of forest, and there was nothing unusual about the tree Kiyani had singled out either. The only thing she could make out in the darkness was the ring of bushy ferns that circled the massive trunk, bobbing in the rain.

"Exactly."

Fura let out a groan of frustration. She was too tired for his riddles, not to mention he was only making himself sound less and less stable. It was quite possible, she realized, that she had found herself alone in the woods with a lunatic and his psycho wolf-pet.

"The fact that most people think that is what's going to let us sleep without worry for the remainder of the night."

Kiyani pulled aside a bunch of the ferns just as Fura was going to ask what the heck he meant. What he revealed wasn't the wet bark at the tree's base as she would have expected, but a darker shadow than even what was surrounding them in the colorless night.

Moving forward, she crouched down where Kiyani had been just as he disappeared into the base of the tree. Without his hold, the ferns snapped back into place, leaving everything just as nondescript as it had been prior to his intrusion.

"Kiyani?" she said weakly. She didn't know how large the hole was that had sucked him in, or what might have been in it.

Pulling aside the plants, Fura searched for the opening again, not liking the idea of being left alone in the dark. The wolf patrolling the surroundings not too far away didn't make her feel any better.

Squinting as she tried to get a better view of things, Fura jumped when a face appeared in the shadows. Stepping back, she tripped over one of the ferns and fell on her rear.

Kiyani sighed. "You know, for working in a profession that requires acute agility, you have an express lack of coordination."

"You scared me," Fura shot back defensively.

Rising, she found herself glad that she hadn't fallen in one of the muddier areas.

"Are you sure this is safe?" she asked. As much as she wanted out of the rain, Fura couldn't say that she was too keen to jump head first, no questions asked, into a dark hole. Spiders. Snakes. A whole array of things that might possibly lie in wait came to her mind.

Leaning on his elbows, Kiyani watched her. "It's safer than being out there. Now hurry up before anyone finds us."

And with that, he was gone again.

Fura found her anxiety levels spiking again as she looked around, seeing shadows in the trees that she knew weren't really there. She had never realized before just how many nooks and crannies in a forest could serve the purpose of providing a hiding place, and not just for them.

Finally giving in, Fura closed her eyes, took a deep breath to calm her nerves and slid into the hollow.

To her surprise, the ground inside wasn't level with what she had been walking on and she found herself tumbling into the darkness with a yelp of shock.

"Seriously," she heard Kiyani's voice slice through the void, "how do you make it through the day?"

She knew he was elaborating further on his earlier comment about her lack of coordination. "You could have warned me."

"Do I have to tell you everything?"

Fura sighed. This was going to be a harrowing night. Apparently it didn't matter what situation she was put in with him, he would still find a way to make her feel like a trifling fool.

Swinging her legs around beneath her, Fura sat solidly on the floor and tried to will her eyes to adjust to the shadows she had plunged herself into. Even as a small child, she had never been afraid of the dark, at least, not until recently. Claustrophobia, however, was another story.

"I can't see," she commented.

"You don't need to."

Fura groaned, just wanting the night to end.

"It takes a minute to get used to," Kiyani amended, his voice taking on a bit of a softer tone as if he was finally sympathizing with her on the lowest of levels. "We should be getting some sleep, though."

"Right."

She could scarcely imagine being given the luxury of anything resembling sleep after what had occurred, but he was right. It was the middle of the night, pitch black and raining, and they were who knew where. There weren't a whole lot of options.

Using what she assumed was the wall as a guide, Fura tentatively crawled towards where Kiyani's voice had come from. Finding his form, she curled up against his side, searching for the smallest hint of warmth.

Tensing at her touch, Kiyani pushed her away.

"I'm freezing," Fura complained, justifying her actions.

"Well, I'm just as wet and cold as you are."

Feeling shunned, Fura hunkered down into a shivering ball, trying to retain some form of body heat. Pulling the damp cloak tighter she wondered if things would ever get better.

17
⋆⋆✧⋆⋆
SILVER AND BLOOD

A rumble of thunder brought Kiyani out of the shallow sleep he had managed to fall into. The rolling echo of the storm was still present, but he could tell, even without opening his eyes that the rain had finally tapered off. It was well enough. Like the night hadn't been bad enough, the incessant rain that had beaten down on them had made it nothing short of misery. Kiyani knew he shouldn't think like that, that they could have easily been captured with the rest of the residents of Frielana. But it was hard not to grumble when the damp chill still clung to him like a second skin. One he desperately wished he could peel off and cast aside like the unwanted nuisance it was.

Propped against the wall, staring off into nothing, Kiyani refused to turn to see how Fura was doing. He didn't want to look at the face that he knew would be staring back at him, full of questions that he neither wanted to answer, nor had the patience for. What had he been thinking anyways, bringing her along?

He didn't even need to pose the question.

The answer was already there.

As much as he didn't want her around, didn't think that she belonged out here in the wilderness, he knew his conscience never would have forgiven him if he'd let her succumb to the horrors of being made a prisoner along with the others.

Fine, he amended. He had gotten her out of danger.

So, now what?

He wasn't some tour guide, renting out his services by the hour. True, he often enjoyed random trips out into the forest, sometimes for a few days. But that was on his own terms, and always alone. Not with some silly girl like Fura. Kiyani could only imagine the hernia Apallo would have if he knew of the current situation. Just thinking about it sent his stomach coiling into inconsolable knots.

It was actually simple enough. There was one definitive answer, and that was to take her back to Barandor. As soon as possible. The girl had already seen far too much.

Heaving a sigh, Kiyani turned over, only to find that, save for himself, the hollow was completely empty.

Bolting upright, he emitted a curse as a wave of pain ripped through his back in response to the sudden movement. Hunched over, he allowed the throbbing to dissipate before rising. The pitch black echoes of night had become lighter in the short amount of time that had passed. Washed in the colorless tones of gray, it wasn't a huge difference, but it was just enough to help distinguish his surroundings.

His hand trailing the uneven dirt, Kiyani let the crude walls guide him through the semi-darkness to the faint light that filtered through the hollow's entrance. Issuing precaution, he listened as he looked out past the crop of ferns, searching for the smallest sign of human life, Fura's or otherwise.

There was nothing.

It was a relief that no one had tracked them this far as of yet, but it also meant that Fura wasn't in the immediate vicinity either.

Cursing his misfortune of having ended up with her in the first place, Kiyani heaved himself up and out of the hollow.

He'd been right. What the hell had he been thinking? He had been wrong to take on such responsibility.

Yet, as much as he disliked the girl, it was fear, not anger, that drove him stumbling through the mud and the slick, leafy debris of the water-logged forest.

Kiyani didn't know what scared him the most: knowing what was lurking out there in search of them, or Apallo's reaction if he ever found out that he'd lost Fura.

The rain may have stopped, but the soft patter of droplets slipping from the tips of the leaves above created a static that made it hard for Kiyani to concentrate. Regardless, he kept his senses cleared, straining to listen for the smallest crack of twigs snapping beneath a person's weight, or the wet sluice of displaced leaves as a branch was pushed aside to make way.

In the dark void of night, it was the easiest way to track, but with a single glance downward, Kiyani found that he needn't rely on such methods. There, cast in near perfection in the mud, Fura had left prints leading away from the hollow. This girl definitely didn't know a thing about staying hidden, self-preservation clearly not a trait of hers.

Following the tracks with caution, and a fair amount of concern as he kept one eye on the surroundings, Kiyani wondered just how stupid she could possibly be. Only an hour or so ago they had been on the outskirts of a hostile takeover. Now she was simply wandering the woods like nothing was wrong. He was sure that even if he hadn't been provided a distinct trail to follow that the sheer amount of noise she always seemed to make would have clued him in sooner than later.

The utter silence beyond the natural white noise left Kiyani unsettled, and though he knew it was a risk, he put his fingers to his lips, producing a high-pitched whistle that echoed out into the twilight. A lonely, singular howl answered a moment later.

What most would have considered a sign to turn and run gave Kiyani a much needed peace of mind. He was used to traveling with the wolf always in close range. When Kiedo wasn't around he was just as vulnerable and exposed as the next person. With the wolf, Kiyani had an advantage that many could only dream of. Who could argue against having a nocturnal sidekick patrol the night for you as you slept?

Just as he had guessed, Kiedo's response had come from the path he was already on. Though he knew sound carried further on cold, clear nights, it hadn't been far off. Which meant Fura was close as well.

His assumptions expertly on mark, it wasn't long after that he came across her.

Kiyani had half expected to find her cowering beside some tree, having lost her way. Maybe even cowering before Kiedo, who sat a few feet away, a mere gray haze in the shadows of the trees. Instead, she was out in the open, her face turned skyward as she watched the mist falling from the trees in the faint light of the moon.

Turning away for a moment to compose himself to keep from instinctively lashing out at her stupidity, Kiyani attempted to judge the distance he had covered.

The tree they had taken as shelter wasn't in sight, but at least she'd had the sense to stay relatively close. That didn't forgive her selfishness of leaving without a word in the first place, though.

"Oh, hi," Fura waved when she caught sight of him.

"What the hell is wrong with you?"

He had been terrified upon waking to find Fura missing, but now that he had found her, Kiyani couldn't help but be harsh in his words.

It was one thing to take a nighttime stroll to ease the mind – he did it often himself – but not when tragedy and terror lingered just hours in the past. Danger could be lurking behind any tree in this forest, and here this girl was, wandering about like nothing had happened.

Fura looked at him blankly, not understanding why he was so mad.

Kiyani wanted to turn and walk away right then and there, leave her to deal with her own problems.

"I had to go to the bathroom," she finally admitted meekly.

"So you just wandered off?"

"It's not like I wasn't coming back."

If only, Kiyani thought, not particularly regretting it as it crossed his mind.

Instead, he slapped a hand over his face, unable to believe that this girl could be so simple-minded. "Do you not realize what we just witnessed, that there could be people out looking for us right now?"

Was he really supposed to spell it out for her? Short of drawing pictures in the dirt, he couldn't possibly make it any simpler to understand. If this was what he was going to have to deal with, then maybe she deserved to be caught. Shadows take her.

It would solve the number one question for him – just what he was supposed to do with her – and give him the peace he had been endlessly searching for since she had barged into his life.

Yet, peace was hard to come by these days, and he knew that wasn't how to get it.

Thank Draimaele he had the smallest inkling of patience that kept him from throttling her.

Fura didn't reply and he didn't blame her. She looked to the ground as if she were ashamed, yet something else about her deflated stance told a slightly different story. One that indicated she didn't quite know what to say to him. Well, the feeling was mutual.

The girl standing before him was a far cry from the one he'd caught glimpses of every now and then at the festival when Kristoff sent him on some errand.

"I think your dog was keeping an eye on me."

Kiyani looked up at her to see that she was keeping a wary eye on Kiedo, who seemed to have already come to accept her presence without dispute.

"He is *not* my dog. He's a wolf. You don't own wolves. And you're damn lucky he's watching you."

"There's nothing out here but trees."

"You don't know that. I can't believe Apallo actually thought it was a good idea to bring you out here."

"Sorry," Fura muttered, crossing her arms over her chest, seeming to regain a bit of the haughtiness that went with her fiery hair. "I'm still adjusting."

Kiyani snorted. "There's adjusting and then there's common sense, which you seem to inherently lack."

"Apparently. Because common sense might have told me never to go anywhere with you."

"You want to leave, then leave."

Good riddance. Unappreciative little brat of a girl. He was beginning to think more and more that he should have taken off on his own. Heck, he would have if she hadn't been the one to intrude on his private space only moments before the siege began. Kiyani knew for certain that if that hadn't been the case he wouldn't have put himself in danger to go and search for her. Sure, he might have felt bad, if the thought ever even crossed his mind, but as it was, she had simply been in the right place at the right time. That was all.

He watched Fura gawp at her surroundings with all the familiarity of a fish out of water. It was clear to him that she would probably take him up on that offer, if only she knew where they were. The fact was, she was lost, which meant she was stuck with him. And he was stuck with her. It wasn't something Kiyani was happy about.

Even though the expression on her face was rather vacant, Kiyani could see that the wheels in her head were quietly turning, trying to figure out something.

"Shouldn't we have run into Barandor by now?"

Kiyani looked at her with wide eyes, the shock clear. "Please tell me you didn't just say that to me?" Great. She clearly lacked directional skills as well.

"What?"

He shook his head, frustration building. "That's it. You're going back tomorrow."

"To Frielana?"

It was Fura's turn to be shocked. What was he going to do, just walk in and hand her over to those wretched people that had taken her second home from her?

"To Barandor," Kiyani corrected.

Fura haughtily crossed her arms and glared at him. "Fine. Wouldn't want to spend time with you anyway."

Just as Kiyani thought to truly leave her in the woods to learn her own lesson, Kiedo rose to his feet. His fur bristled, he kept low to the ground, teeth bared as he emitted a low growl of warning. Kiyani froze and peered over his shoulder to where the wolf's eyes were leveled. He didn't see anything, but the sound of counsel left him chilled. The sensation only grew as Kiedo suddenly took off into the underbrush, leaving him and Fura alone in the clearing.

The brash tones of the previous conversation forgotten, Fura's eyes grew large as she looked to Kiyani. "He just caught a whiff of some animal, right?"

The fear was evident in her voice as if she already knew what Kiyani did.

He shook his head. "He doesn't growl like that unless there's an immediate threat." When Fura moved closer to him, he didn't complain. Instead, he loosely grabbed a hold of her arm and directed her back towards their shelter. "Go back to the tree."

For once, she didn't complain.

Watching Fura out of the corner of his eye as she did as she was told, Kiyani ignored the sudden protective instinct to closely follow her. Instead, he kept watch on her as he stood, still as stone, and waited, listening with a deeper intensity than before when he had just been on the hunt for the girl who had run off in the night. He'd spent years of his life wandering through the forests, learning on his own, through trial and error, how to track and how to discern when he was the one being followed.

Kiyani had known the moment they had broken free from the Frielana camp that the odds of someone eventually being sent after them were greater than he would have cared to admit. That time had come. He was sure of it. There was someone else out here with them, yet, what he hated the most was that he couldn't pinpoint where.

It might've been nothing at all. A lone bird taking off in the brush. An animal, like Fura had said. They were in the depth of the forest after all. In nature nothing was ever completely silent. But Kiyani couldn't ignore the way Kiedo had darted off, snarling and ready to attack. He had come to learn the meanings and take notice of the wolf's reactions, and he never overreacted. Kiyani could only hope that it was a false alarm, one of those occasions when animals seemed to sense something that wasn't really there.

His breathing steady, Kiyani scanned the shadows, waiting for something to come forth. The only thing he could hear was Fura stumbling through the darkness. His first thought was to curse her for being so noisy, but Kiyani knew it wouldn't have mattered anyway. With the lack of any other noise, indication of a silent and deadly killer, he already knew exactly what kind of evil they were up against.

Giving up on waiting the other person out – if there even was such a thing – Kiyani took off after Fura. There was already too much space between them, and he knew that any experienced assassin wouldn't go for the one who appeared to have caught on to his presence. And between the two of them, Fura was definitely weaker game.

Closing the gap, Kiyani was moments from pulling even with her when he finally heard the definitive crunch of a heavily booted foot being ground into the forest floor. Only then did he feel the unmistakable sense of a human presence behind him.

He turned just as Fura shouted his name in warning, but he wasn't quick enough. Kiyani only caught a glimpse of the stranger before the man grabbed a hold of his arm and slammed him headfirst into the nearest tree where he blacked out.

The feminine scream was what pulled Kiyani back into a state of awareness. Pinpricks of light danced before him, and he clutched a handful of dirt and decaying leaves as he fought to regain focus after the blow.

He didn't think he had been out long, but as his vision came back to him, Kiyani could see that it had been just long enough for his attacker to catch Fura and pin her to the ground. It was hard to discern any real details in the haze of night, but even so, he could see that it was a burly man, with a head of dark, stringy hair. The colors of his clothing blended almost seamlessly into the shadows, but Kiyani caught the glint of the dark chainmail that draped over his form. He knew that if it was daylight, he would be able to see that it was layered over black breeches and a silver embroidered tunic: the colors of the Shadowguard.

The sight of the man so intimately leaning over Fura as she struggled beneath his weight, his face inches away from hers as the dagger in his grasp glimmered dangerously close to her throat, made Kiyani sick.

With the proximity of the weapon to Fura's skin, Kiyani would later recognize his next move as potentially idiotic, but in the heat of the moment he acted on instinct alone. Propelling himself from where he was crouched on hands and knees on the ground, he launched himself at the man.

Catching him off guard, it was just enough force to momentarily startle the man. He released his hold on Fura, and both he and Kiyani tumbled to the ground, sliding in the slick mud that had been left behind by the heavy rainfall. They rolled a number of times, grappling with little more than arm strength. Yet, even after the impact, the Shadowguardian had managed to keep a firm hold on the dagger, refusing, even in that brief moment of confusion, to relinquish possession of the blade.

Fighting to keep the man's hand that wielded the weapon away from him, Kiyani quickly found that the man was much stronger than he had originally presumed. His own strength faltering, he was thrown to the ground again and pinned in the same fashion Fura had been only moments before. Struggling to free his arm that was immobile under his own weight, Kiyani cursed his lack of defense. He'd never had much of a reason to carry weapons of any kind, but a sword would've been handy right about then.

"You really think you're stronger than me, boy?"

His face was so close, Kiyani could smell the rancid breath that emanated from a mouth full of gnarled teeth and filled the air between them with its pungent odor. Producing the dagger from the shadows, the man laid it upon Kiyani's face, delighting in his futile struggle. He was trained in this type of thing. Two silly teenagers would be no challenge for him to take out amidst the shadows of night. His eyes shining maliciously, the man pressed the blade down, hard enough to where Kiyani could feel the cold metal wanting to embed itself in his cheek, yet not quite the right amount of pressure to draw blood. Yet, it served its purpose as a warning. Kiyani knew that if he continued to struggle, blood would be drawn.

Grinding his teeth, a grunt of pain escaped him as the man's insufferable weight continued to drive his pinned arm into the ground. Thinking he wouldn't be able to take the tingling sensation from lack of blood flow to the appendage any longer, a projectile suddenly came flying through the air. Missing Kiyani's face by a few inches, he felt the rush of air as the stone sailed past and just nicked the man's arm.

It didn't inflict any damage, but the man's head shot up, searching for the source of the attack.

A grin flickered across his face as his gaze settled on Fura.

"So, the 'lil princess wants to fight, eh?"

Kiyani shot her a look that asked what the hell she thought she was doing, but Fura wasn't paying attention. Having gained the man's attention, she took a step backward. Acting without thought, she was now left with few options, on the radar of a merciless man that had probably been sent to kill them both.

"Hey!" Kiyani shouted, diverting the man's attention away from Fura. He knew that if he did nothing the man would essentially go after Fura who was weaker fare. When the man turned, Kiyani spit into his eye.

"You little!" the man shouted angrily, falling back and clawing at his eye, fighting the sudden blindness and sting.

Ignoring the bolts of pain that shot through his arm, Kiyani rolled to his hands and knees, moving quickly to get himself back on his feet. Scrambling across the ground with his hand that wasn't asleep, he tried to find something to defend himself with. Behind him another grunt was issued and he turned to see what had happened.

This time it wasn't a rock that sailed through the air but a silver mass of fur and sinewy muscle.

"Kiedo!" he shouted. The sight of his loyal friend locked in a deadly fight sent waves of sickness roiling in his stomach.

He feared for the wolf, but Kiedo held his own as he swiftly switched from loving sidekick to defensive wild animal. Snarling, clawing, and biting, he tore at the flesh of the man, ripping fabric and leather to get to exposed skin. The Shadowguardian howled in pain, stabbing at the air and the beast with his free hand as he tried to regain his arm from the wolf's deadly grasp.

Even with Kiedo's deadly defenses removing him from harm's way, Kiyani knew it would only be a matter of time before the fight was drawn back his way. Pulling himself to a crouch, he frantically resumed the search for anything he could use as a weapon. He didn't know where Fura had managed to find the large stone from earlier, or where it had landed, but he couldn't find another to save his life.

What he was finally forced to settle with was a good sized tree branch. Looking like it had only just recently fallen from its host, possibly even in that night's storm, it still bore twigs and leafy foliage. Had he had the time, Kiyani would have stripped it, but as it was, he had chosen it for its proximity and lofty weight.

Standing, taking a moment to assess the situation before diving back in to finish things, he caught sight of Fura. Time seemed to have ground to a halt during the struggle, neither stopping completely nor moving forward. Regardless of how many minutes had actually passed, it appeared that Fura had hardly moved from the spot where the man had initially taken her down.

"Fura, run!" Kiyani shouted at her.

He could see that she was frozen in shock, her mind and body unable to process what was happening or how to react. Even left paralyzed, his words were enough to break through.

"But – "

Pointing to the trees, he refused to let her continue. "Just go!"

A sudden high-pitched canine whimper of pain sounded in the darkness, sending a bolt of fear through Kiyani. Watching Fura's form disappear into the forest, enveloped by the misty shadows, he turned, his eyes immediately falling to where Kiedo lay on the ground.

Matted fur, stained with blood, stood in spiky patches all over his lupine form, making it hard to discern just where he had been stabbed. Even injured, he tried to pull himself to his feet, snarling and showing that the setback hadn't lessened the fight in him.

The uniformed man held his own mangled arm to his chest as he stood, hunched over. His laughter at his triumph saturated the air. Sheathing the dagger, he pulled a long sword from his belt. Holding it before him, he raised it in the air, readying himself to deal the final blow to the bloodied beast before him.

Propelled into a rage, Kiyani hefted the branch in his possession as if it too were a sword and stormed forward with a cry of defiance. The man turned to face him and Kiyani struck, the end of the branch connecting with his face. Roaring in pain, the man slapped a hand over the fresh wound. He recovered quicker than Kiyani expected, and when the man turned to face him, his eyes were filled with a white-hot rage, only accented by the welts that rose on his cheek and the blood that he'd streaked with his hand.

Bracing himself for the attack he knew was coming, Kiyani had the unnerving feeling that he was facing the man that would be the death of him.

Without warning the man rushed forward, and metal met wood in a heated dance of deadly intentions and self-preservation. Both men kept their eyes locked on one another as they dodged blows and parried strikes, each intending to take the other down without mercy. The dark-clad man laughed in delight as Kiyani watched his pitiful form of defense precariously bend with each forceful blow it took from the sword. The green wood was springy, but Kiyani knew it wouldn't last, and it proved to be with a single blow that it was finally cleaved in two.

Backed up against a tree, Kiyani stared at the remaining splinter in his hand.

Sword raised and pointed to Kiyani's throat, the man advanced.

"Nevo wants you alive," he cackled, making it sound like the mere thought of such a thing was a joke.

Given the glint of murderous intent in the man's eyes, Kiyani found that hard to believe. For having orders to keep him alive, the man seemed dead-set on killing him here and now, no prisoners intended.

Despite the compromising situation, Kiyani couldn't help himself. "Are you sure, because I'm sure Zariah would prefer me dead."

That alone was enough to wipe the smile from the leathery face. "How dare you even speak his name?"

"I believe I have the right."

"You have no right," the man snarled. "Me," he said, regaining his composure as a grin spread across his ravaged face, "I don't think you're worth the trouble."

"You just said you can't kill me," Kiyani challenged.

"Accidents happen, oh mighty warrior."

It bristled Kiyani's ego to be mocked in such a manner, but the lapse of judgment from the man was just what he needed.

"Like this?" he snarled.

In one swift movement, Kiyani ducked beneath the swing of the man's blade, grabbed the hanging branch behind him, effectively tearing it from the tree, and spun to plunge it into the man's neck.

With a cry of pain and surprise, he dropped the sword and the two of them fell to the ground in a heap.

Moved to action by adrenaline and the will to survive, Kiyani drove the shaft of wood deeper into flesh, twisting it until he was sure that the body beneath him had ceased movement. Closing his eyes, he rested his forehead on the end of the branch, fighting to settle his labored breathing.

It wasn't until Kiyani's hands slipped into the bloody mess that he propelled himself backwards and stumbled to the ground, the sudden silence that had fallen over the clearing bringing him to face the reality of what he had just done.

His entire body was caked with mud, but it was the literal blood staining his hands that left him trembling.

18

••◇••

RIGHT AND WRONG

The forest felt darker and more dangerous now that Fura had truly found herself on her own. An owl cooed in the tree overhead, and she turned towards the sound, her heart leaping into her throat at the sudden disturbance. The pouring rain had ceased, leaving only a fine mist hovering above the ground, and above a sliver of the moon had finally made a faint appearance from behind the clouds. It didn't offer much light, but it was enough to make the limbs of the surrounding trees look like spindly fingers that ached to grab her as they moved in the breeze.

When Kiyani had told her to run, she'd done just that, taking off into the forest at a dead run. Sliding across patches of mud and tripping over raised roots, Fura had moved without thought, as if her feet weren't her own. There was no telling how far she might have continued had the radiating pain in her side from the run not slowed her down, finally bringing her to a grinding halt. It didn't matter how many people may have been after her, she couldn't go any further. And it was that realization that gave her the time to reflect on the fact that she had taken herself, quite literally, to the middle of nowhere.

Clutching a hand to her aching side, Fura stumbled over to a large boulder that sat among a group of ferns alongside the non-existent path she'd been following. Taking deep breaths to slow the heavy drumming of her heart and the tremors in her hands, she found herself quietly sobbing as she began to face the reality of the situation. Recalling the details of what had happened, all Fura could see in the flash of pictures that raced through her mind were the broken images of the wolf lying on the ground, injured, and Kiyani backed into a corner, trying to defend himself against an armed and armored man with nothing more than a precariously bending tree branch.

She didn't know which of the men would be the victor, the one to eventually come across her path if she stayed where she was, but the odds hadn't looked to be in Kiyani's favor the last she'd seen.

Pulling her knees to her chest, Fura tried to stave off the chill that hadn't left her since being soaked through during the rain. Peering out into the moon-stained darkness, she did her best not to see dancing images in the shadows just beyond her vision. Closing her eyes in attempt to stop her imagination from creating things she knew weren't there, Fura found herself nodding off into a hazy sleep.

When she was brought to sometime later, she didn't even have time to react or attempt to defend herself before Kiedo stalked out of the bushes, walking with a pronounced limp. Kiyani wasn't far behind. Her first thought was that she had to be dreaming, that neither of them should've had a chance against that man. The second feeling, as she shook the haze of sleep from her vision, was an overabundance of joy. Decidedly knowing that Kiyani would be against such a display, Fura fought the urge to leap up and embrace him in a hug.

For as much as they'd fought and spoken sarcastically to one another in the past few days, she had never been happier to see someone than at that moment.

"Kiyani," she said, the first words she had spoken in what felt like hours sounding like nothing more than a whisper in the night.

Kiyani looked up at her, the motion making her realize that he hadn't even noticed her sitting there.

"Fura," he acknowledged. "You shouldn't have stopped."

"I couldn't go any further."

Unexpectedly, Kiyani nodded in reply. Any other time Fura knew his reply would have been spoken in sarcasm-laced anger, but for the moment she could read the heaviness in his voice that relayed nothing but exhaustion. She couldn't blame him, not when she had scarcely believed that she would see him again. More than anything, she wanted to hear what had to be the remarkable story of his escape, but she knew that now wasn't the time.

As if to assert that fact, Kiyani waved her on, barely pausing in his own step as he passed her by. "Come on."

Fura didn't argue, or even speak, only followed without complaint. There would be time for stories later. Even what should have been on-the-edge-of-her-seat suspense over where they were going no longer seemed of import, let alone priority. She would find out sooner or later, the eventual root of their destination revealing itself to her whenever Kiyani deemed it safe to stop again.

And that was exactly what he did.

Following in quiet consent, Fura found herself so lost in the practice of watching Kiyani's gait – searching for any clear sign of injury – that she wasn't even paying attention to the gradual change in their surroundings. So when he finally declared their journey over for the night Fura was surprised to find that a small meandering river had quietly woven its way into their path.

"There's nothing here," she commented as she stood amongst the small clearing and looked around.

Save for the sudden appearance of what she actually would have considered a stream, rather than a river, it wasn't far from the truth.

Kiyani let out a sigh. "You've really got to start paying more attention to what's around you." Pointing, he added, "There's another Reln over there."

His voice sounded as tired as he looked. Yet, something else had caught her attention in his words, holding her interest and forcing her to comment on it instead.

"Reln?" she questioned. The word was utterly foreign to her, sounding just as out of place spoken on her own tongue.

Turning, Kiyani seemed to really look at her for the first time since he had reappeared amongst the trees. Maybe even all night. Fura had expected him to ignore her as usual. Instead, his face was a picture of disapproving worry. Seeming to catch himself, he pointed again. "The tree we were in earlier, before you decided to go on a little joy walk. They're of a variety that only grow out here."

Her eyes traveling in the direction he had indicated, Fura found that if she squinted she could just make out the dusty details of the tree she assumed he was speaking of. Though she could say with honesty that she hadn't been paying much attention before, it did look similar to their previous shelter. What she immediately recognized were the bushy ferns surrounding its massive base.

"Do they all have the hollows beneath them?"

It wasn't the only question on her mind regarding this particular oddity, but it was currently front and center. She'd never heard of such a thing, natural or otherwise.

Looking back to where Kiyani had been standing, Fura found that he had moved and was now crouched before the stream. Kiedo, whom she had noticed had been limping earlier, had made his way over as well. Favoring the weight of only three of his slender and muscular legs, the wolf took a long drink of the cool water.

"Not all of them," Kiyani answered. "But I know for certain that that one does."

"How?"

"Because I've been here before, and I've spent plenty of nights in that exact tree." He paused and looked out into the surrounding darkness. "Unlike you, I actually know these woods, and despite what I'm sure you've been thinking, I do know where I'm going."

If what he was saying was true, then Fura was surprised that he had actually revealed something about himself, as small as it may have been. However, she wasn't entirely convinced and she found herself voicing it, the events of the night leaving her in an unusually defensive mood.

"How do you know it's the same tree? They all look the same."

"Maybe to you," Kiyani replied flatly. "But I know this one due to the location of the stream."

"Oh," she mouthed. The argumentative feeling passing, Fura took one last glance at the tree before walking over to join Kiyani by the water. With the way the night was going she wanted to remain as close to him as possible.

Or the way the night had been going. She hadn't been aware of the passage of time, only that the darkness felt like it had been dragging on forever, but she could see now that dawn was just starting to break. The dark shadows that had followed them like an unwelcome friend were finally melting away, and in their place the dusty gray of early morning was settling in. It was one of the most welcome sights Fura had seen in days.

Too anxious to sit, she found herself hovering above Kiyani as she stared out into the growing light of the forest, silently taking in each and every detail as it slowly came into focus. It was only when she looked down to see how Kiyani was faring that she was sent careening back into reality.

He had settled onto one knee as he repeatedly dunked his hands into the water, splashing it up to his elbows and scrubbing as best he could with just his fingers. The tainted streams that trailed down his arms dripped red. Though they were still cast in muted shadows, Fura knew exactly what it was.

"Is that..." Though she didn't mean to, she found herself backing away, not wanting to finish the sentence although she already knew the truth behind it. "Blood..." she said, forcing the last word.

Seemingly startled, Kiyani looked up at her, panic reflected in his eyes. "It's nothing."

"Nothing?" Fura echoed, not sure if he even believed that.

"It's nothing," he repeated, clearly frustrated. "It's not mine."

Knowing that he'd heard the panic in her voice, she wasn't sure if his last comment was meant to put her at ease, but she was far from.

"You killed him, didn't you?" Fura didn't know why the knowledge of what she already knew was causing her such difficulty, but she suddenly found herself unable to breathe, as if the sight of the blood had finally brought everything into focus. That the true meaning of reality had hit. This wasn't some little theatrical performance like she might have initially thought. This was real life, and she was far from ready to face it head on.

Yet, there it was, so crudely staring back at her. Taunting and whispering evils in her ear like the echoes of some bad nightmare.

"What would you've had me do?" Kiyani asked heatedly, not bothering to deny it. "He was set to kill us both."

"So that makes it okay?" Fura whimpered, hating the fear in her voice. She couldn't help herself. That defensive anger that had reappeared in his voice had reminded her that she had no idea the type of man that she'd found herself alone with.

"It doesn't matter."

Fura couldn't believe him. "Right and wrong doesn't matter?" Was this the person that Apallo had been trying to protect her from?

In response, Kiyani stood in one swift movement so that his darkened eyes were level with hers. "We just witnessed a siege of Frielana by enemy forces. There are people out there who know we're not among the ranks of the prisoners, and who probably want us dead before we can cause them any trouble." He paused to take in a ragged breath. "Of course right and wrong matters, but sometimes it's the wrongs that keep you alive."

Turning, he whipped a stone that Fura hadn't even been aware was in his grasp. Missing the water of the stream from the amount of force behind the throw, it sailed off into the bushes. The sudden display frightened her, but Fura could see his generally composed façade cracking. She could see in the light of morning that he was remarkably pale, his hands trembling at his side.

"Don't think that I'm proud of what I had to do."

There was a forced strength behind his words that made Fura pity him despite her initial thoughts. She could only imagine how he was feeling in the aftermath of what he'd done, the mental repercussions that must follow such a horrible deed. As sick as it made her, she couldn't deny that it had been a purely defensive maneuver, that he had done it to save them both. She didn't want to know where she'd be now had Kiyani not been there in the first place. Fura only wondered if she would've been able to do the same.

Taking a shaky breath, she turned to apologize, only to find that Kiyani had already taken himself out of the conversation. No longer paying her any attention, he was now kneeling beside Kiedo who had remained sitting beside the stream throughout the whole ordeal of their heated words. Carefully checking the animal over, Fura could see that Kiyani had torn a strip of fabric from the sleeve of his shirt to use as a cloth to clean the wounds the wolf had sustained in the fight. It only confirmed her earliest suspicions that the man posed no threat to anybody, let alone herself. How could he when he treated an animal that most would have killed on sight with such care?

Not knowing what to do, what to say, Fura stood back in silence, waiting for Kiyani to finish his self-appointed task. When he finally rose, balling up the bloodied cloth and stuffing it into his back pocket, he moved past her on his way to the tree without a word. His only acknowledgement was a heated glance that told her to go ahead and leave if she saw fit. A challenge, really. Yet, Fura could see the pain that lingered behind it.

Even if she was lax to admit it herself, Fura knew that he was just as aware as she was that she couldn't leave, that she would never make it back to Barandor on her own. That he was irrevocably stuck with her, and her with him.

"Is that what you think I am now?" Kiyani asked, startling her out of her reverie. "That I'm just some heartless killer?"

Fura turned to find that he was leaning against the tree he had pointed out as a Reln. Bracing himself with a single arm as he faced it, he looked closer to throwing up than fighting.

"No," she answered quietly, cautiously making her way towards him. It was the truth. She didn't know what to think of him yet, but she knew that if he truly was a cold-blooded killer he never would've saved her from what could have been her fate the way he had. "I just wish I knew what was going on."

Kiyani took in a breath and turned his head to look at her. "Tomorrow," he declared, as if all of life's greatest questions would be answered in that span of time.

Fura looked up at the brightening sky overhead. "Later today?"

"Right," Kiyani agreed tiredly, not even bothering to point out that she was being a smart ass. "Right now, we sleep."

Fura gave a curt nod and followed him into the hollow, not knowing which of them needed sleep the most.

Once inside the space, Fura let out a gasp of surprise. Where the last time she had been afraid of what might lie in wait for her in the darkness, now she could see it for what it really was, as muted daylight filtered in through the fern-covered opening. Essentially, it was an underground room.

"Who would take the time to do all this?" Fura wondered aloud in amazement. She could only imagine how long it must have taken to complete such a task.

"All what?" Kiyani asked from the other side of the hollow, not paying her much attention as he rifled through some things.

Fura motioned with her arm the entirety of the space around them. "All this. Who would take the time to remove all that dirt and wood if they didn't plan on living here?"

Dropping what he was doing, Kiyani regarded her with what she could only describe as the slightest of grins on his face. "Who's to say that anyone's ever been here before me? There are actually very few that even know of these."

"These?" Fura questioned. "You mean there are more?"

"Trees like this aren't present everywhere, but they're not all that rare either." Kiyani paused a moment as he looked around. "This hollow we're in is actually a natural occurrence. Most people would pass by and classify it as an oak tree, when it's really a Reln. It's an ancient species of tree native only to these forests. One of its greatest features is that when it begins to die, it rots from the base, leaving a hollow such as this."

"When it rots?" Fura looked around, eying the wood with suspicion, wondering what the chances of it collapsing on them as they slept were.

Kiyani slapped a hand on the wall. "Still as sturdy as ever."

Feeling like she'd just stumbled upon some interactive documentary, Fura looked up to find that the space actually extended upwards a ways, though it was still too dark to determine just how far.

"How do you know all this?"

Kiyani shrugged. "You learn a thing or two when you spend the majority of your time exploring on your own."

"Something you do a lot?"

"Anything to get away from Apallo."

In the rush of things, Fura had forgotten all about the animosity between the man and Kiyani. "Why is he so against you?"

Fura should've known better than to go down that road, especially at this hour. Just as she had expected, the mere mention of it quickly deteriorated Kiyani's friendlier demeanor.

"Later," he said. "Just know that we're safe and hidden in here. So long as you don't do anything stupid."

Fura cringed at his directed comment.

"By the way," Kiyani continued heavily before she could reply. "Don't *ever* do that again."

She wanted to apologize, but knew it wouldn't make a difference to him. Yet something else registered just beyond the growl that had taken up residence in his tone. Or, at least Fura was sure she had heard it. This was the most worked up she had seen him over her situation.

"Were you actually worried about me?"

"More scared for my life if Apallo was to ever find out that I was personally responsible for your death."

A ball of fabric sailed through the air and landed in Fura's lap where it unfurled itself to reveal a blanket. She took it up in her hands, rubbing one of the soft corners in disbelief.

"Where?"

"I told you, I've been here before," Kiyani answered simply. "Now sleep."

19

✦✧✦

A MIND OF MADNESS

"So it was written and so it has come to pass…"

There was no one else on the balcony with the dark-haired man, but he smiled, regardless, as he spoke the words to himself. After all that time, things were finally falling into place, events aligning just as he'd wanted, just as he'd been promised.

The successful siege of Frielana was already hours in the past, but Zariah could still feel the excitement of having pulled it off so effortlessly pulsing through his veins. As he had expected, the cover of night had been the perfect time to strike. The sparse land, and the ignorant people he had gained in the ordeal were of little interest to him. Apallo had been the target. To make the man suffer for his past crimes. Striking fear into those that so blindly served him was only an extended reward.

In that mission alone, Zariah had succeeded with flying colors. And though he may have been content to stop there, it was only the beginning of a slew of much bigger things that had been brewing in his twisted mind for years.

From the height of one of the many balconies that protruded like great stone tongues from the sprawling Shäedenmore castle, Zariah looked out over the land that unfolded before him. He knew that if he peered to the left, he would just be able to make out the spot where Frielana – a territory that was now his – lie in the distance within the shock of shadowed trees. His gaze wandering, he only let it linger there for a moment before turning his attention to the east. On the horizon, the overcast sky that promised rain bled shades of dusty red as the morning sun made a futile attempt to break through.

Seeing that it wouldn't succeed brought a smile to his lips.

Where most would have seen the display as an ill omen, he only delighted in paying witness to the failings that even nature couldn't overcome. To Zariah, the fact that such bloody colors could permeate the dawn was just a welcome prelude of things soon to pass.

"M'Lord."

"Zendel," Zariah acknowledged dully.

He didn't need to turn to see who dared intrude upon his solitude. There were a select number beneath his reign that he allowed such privileges, and even fewer that he trusted to enact his orders. The phrase *'if you want things done right, then do it yourself'* was around for good reason.

"Apallo has been successfully restrained in the dungeons."

"Come here," Zariah said, ignoring the mention of Apallo.

A silence ensued that was broken only by the whispering bite of the wind. Without hesitation Zendel moved forward. His wavy blond hair cut across his face in the breeze, but he made no move to tame it as he stopped at Zariah's side. The fact that he knew how to follow orders without question was one of the defining characteristics that had earned him the coveted title of Zariah's second-in-command, even if he was lax to accept. The burdens were great, yet he never dared to complain. No sympathy would ever be given by the Shadowlord to a man of even his high stature, though once in a great while a glimmer of respect made itself known.

Zendel allowed himself a brief glimpse at Zariah. The man's hair, loose and blowing freely in the wind, was a change from the usual tight, braided ponytail that it was often restrained in. The curtain of black hiding the sharp lines of his face, he had the distinct appearance of being more pleasant than Zendel knew him to be. He had been a large presence in the castle long enough to not let a simple change in hairstyle fool him. There was still a look in Zariah's eye that proclaimed him a terror, a rigid set to his slender, but muscular form that dared anyone to try and double cross him. It was a thought that rarely crossed Zendel's mind, and one he would never make the mistake of putting forth. Knowing the dangers, he remained silent as he looked out across the forest, waiting for Zariah to speak first.

As if aware that he was on the man's mind, Zariah gazed upon Zendel before speaking with fervor.

"Let us take a moment to celebrate this momentous occasion before you pester me with the depravities of your position. Look at what lies before you, at what is destined to be mine. Even the sky delights in my triumph." Zariah gave a sidelong glance to his second-in-command. Zendel stared straight ahead, seriously taking in the sights. It was one of the things that allowed the man to stand apart from so many of the others. He had a mind of his own that he displayed, but only with caution. Even so, there was a continuous hint of defiance that lingered that kept Zariah on alert when Zendel was around. He hadn't seen that spark in the man in ages, but it didn't mean it had disappeared into oblivion. "There will be a time, when this is all said and done," Zariah spoke evenly, "when times have changed for the better and this land is under my rule, that despite the blood-binding you will rejoice in your position, for my continued hospitality."

Straight-lipped, Zendel turned his head, meeting Zariah's eye. He dipped his head. "Yes, M'Lord."

"Now," Zariah declared with a smile, turning to make for the doorway. "I believe it's time I paid a proper visit to the fallen Firelord. What say you?"

"Of course," Zendel agreed. "However…"

"Why must you tarry around with what needs to be said? Spit it out."

"Nevo has arrived. He requests your audience."

"Already? Very well. Let Apallo wait. He has all the time in the world at his disposal." Zariah settled a finger across his lips as he contemplated that thought. "In fact, why don't you go make sure the guard did a good job? Wouldn't want our guest leaving so soon."

Zendel gave a curt bow and moved away, stopping only to add, "Nevo waits in the foyer."

Zariah watched the man leave before looking out over the horizon once more. Entering the castle of black stone, he made his way through the halls, ignoring the furtive glances of the few he passed. The day had been going well, yet he found himself expecting Nevo and his smug attitude to ruin it with whatever news he brought.

Coming upon the foyer, he crept along the wall in the shadows, watching as the man waited impatiently.

"You have news already that calls for my attention?" Zariah said impassively as he moved into the light where Nevo stood. "Complications, I presume."

"I don't know that I would qualify it as such," Nevo declared casually.

The way the man had always remained unfettered by his influence, despite his service, had always irked Zariah, but he kept comments to himself, wanting only to discern the meaning of this meeting in as few words as possible.

"Go on."

"Frielana has been secured," Nevo started, deceptively skirting around the bulk of the issue. "The sentries are in place and are under Mrena's command in my absence."

"Letting a woman lead," Zariah balked. "A preposterous notion."

Nevo ignored the remark as he continued his report, listing the main points in short sentences as if reading from a bulleted slide. "Twenty eight deceased. Four of them ours."

"To be expected."

"I would have thought that more of them would have put up a fight," Nevo joked.

"Your arrogance will be your undoing," Zariah snorted. "Now get to the point of your wasting my time before I vacate you from my residence."

Nevo dipped his head in response, though he made no move to wipe the irritating grin from his face. "According to the roster of individuals I created during my time living in Frielana, it seems that two people managed to escape in the mayhem last night."

Zariah, who had taken to pacing, stopped. "Anybody worthy of fretting over?" He didn't know why he asked. He had taken it upon himself to visit the pitiful boundaries of Apallo's hold of land in the past. Too many times to count, and each of them a sheer waste of his time. None that he had seen had proven to be of any worth to him, let alone cause him to lose sleep at night if they were to decide to move against him.

Nevo glanced at the torch flickering on the wall, a simple maneuver of avoidance. "Kiyani and Fura."

With a sigh, Zariah's slender fingers rested on his temple. "Your incompetence never ceases to amaze me."

"Do you want me to go after them?"

Zariah turned his head, quietly assessing Nevo and the information he'd just provided. It wasn't what he would've liked to hear, but it was far from disturbing. Disappointing that the man before him couldn't complete one simple task, but far from a reason to call the whole thing off.

"Do not waste your valuable time."

Nevo's generally firm face fell. It wasn't what he expected to hear from the Lord. "But –"

"A boy that's been running from his heritage and hiding his whole life, and a girl who doesn't even know who she is are of no importance to me," Zariah declared with a raised hand.

Nevo dipped his head. "Of course."

A smile played at the corner of the Lord's lips. "However, if you happen to run across the boy, be sure to say hi for me."

"Already ahead of you," Nevo said.

Zariah's eyes darkened considerably as his mouth reaffirmed their trademark set line of disapproval. "Do not act of stupidity and ruin things. I want him kept alive."

With a pronounced bow before the man, the sure sign of submission that the Shadowlord strived for, Nevo added, "Of course, M' Lord. I only got a message to him. If he didn't know not to come back before, he does now."

"Good. Leave it at that. We have far more pressing matters to attend to."

20

◆◆◇◆◆

SWORD OF THE ENEMY

Fura stood in the mouth of the hollow and watched as Kiyani swung a sword in slow precision, the smooth, calculated movements a fluid extension of his body. He stood out against a steel gray sky that was overcast and riddled with clouds, the shadowed shapes of trees serving as a dismal background. Yet his silhouette lacked any definitive detail, save for the generic outline of his limber form.

Rain, in the form of a never-ending light drizzle, had returned during the early morning hours and had continued on throughout the afternoon and into the beginnings of evening. It had only just stopped, but the mist it left behind as drops continued to drip from the leaves overhead, and the chill that remained in the air, painted the scene before her in gloomy tones.

As it was, Fura knew that if the weather refused to give up its purchase on the remainder of the day it would be difficult to define the final onset of night. A time that she wasn't looking forward to visiting again so soon.

That single thought was enough to send a shiver through her body that had nothing to do with the rain. Yet it wasn't the only thing on her mind.

Having just woken moments before, sleeping through much of the day, Fura had yet to find a chance to speak to Kiyani, to try and pick his brain for information, anything that would help her to understand all that was happening. One thing she didn't need was to hear the confirmation in his words to know how the weapon he currently wielded had suddenly come into his possession. The dark silver of the sword's cutting edge as it sliced through the lingering rain drops only reminded her of the knife that had been at her throat, the cold steel biting into her flesh in a savage attempt to taste first blood, and the haggard man that had wielded the instrument.

She was surprised that she hadn't spent the morning fighting nightmares once sleep had claimed her without her full consent. In fact, she hadn't dreamt at all. After all that she had seen, Fura had been

147

certain as she'd raced through the muddy forest that she would never find sleep again, but exhaustion had taken her deep into the world of the unconscious the moment she had curled up in the blanket, overpowering even the cold.

Just before that wonderful distance from reality had kicked in, Kiyani had spoken shortly in the darkness, declaring that he wouldn't be there when she woke. Looking back on it, those words should have frightened her, but she'd been too numb to the living world to care. He had told her not to worry, and that was all she had needed to hear before drifting off.

In the end Kiyani had made good on his word, and when she had finally come to in the gray light of day, Fura had found herself alone. Or so she had thought. It had been the blue eyes, canine and knowing, staring back at her, that had startled her into awareness. Even though much of the night's details had settled into an indefinable blur, Fura could directly recall through the haze of semi-wakefulness earlier that afternoon Kiyani standing near the hollow's entrance, commanding Kiedo to stay and watch over her. She had watched through heavy lids as the wolf had loyally obeyed.

After that she had fallen back into the wash of sleep.

But even upon waking, before she had seen that Kiyani had returned, there had been a certain level of calm that had blanketed her and left her at ease, despite the situation. There had been no doubt in her mind that Kiyani might suddenly decide to leave her behind on a whim, but after the compassion he had shown for the animal at her feet, she knew the wolf was a different story.

As if he could sense that her mind was on him, Kiedo whimpered at her feet and Fura looked down to see that he was staring longingly at the opening. It was like he could feel that his master was back, even without actually seeing him. Fura moved aside, knowing that the only reason Kiedo was still by her side was because she was blocking the way out. Once she was out of the way the wolf exited the shelter in one powerful leap that made her forget he was even injured.

Knowing the wolf would soon break her cover to Kiyani, Fura followed suit, struggling to hike her weight – as small as it may have been – up and over the chest high wall of dirt that sat below ground level.

She finally managed without having to call for help. Though it was hardly something to celebrate as she pushed aside the ferns. A dissatisfied groan stuck in her throat as the foliage drenched her with the pockets of water they had collected during the morning showers. Kiyani's decree that she would only last three days in the wilderness was the only thing that kept her from voicing her sudden distaste of the forest.

Instead, she let the greens snap softly back into place and stretched, hoping to rid her body and mind of the lethargy she had built up over the days. Sleeping on the hard dirt hadn't helped.

Yet, as dark as the day had come to be, Fura still found it welcoming. After all that she had experienced, it was hard to believe that the world still continued turning as if nothing had happened.

Watching Kiyani move, still as oblivious to her as ever, Fura found that even though she had no idea what to say to him, she had the urge to be the first one to speak. Anything he could reply with had to be better than what she was beginning to expect from him if she allowed him the first charge. Which was to tell her to go back to where she had come from.

"You're back," Fura said conversationally, testing the waters. She didn't know what kind of mood his little side trip had left him in, but she could still sense that Kiyani wasn't all that happy about suddenly being appointed her guardian. Or maybe it was just the weapon that he brandished with expert ease.

Breaking form, Kiyani dropped the sword to his side and turned to look at her. "I said I would be."

The lack of surprise present in his gaze told Fura that maybe he had been aware she was behind him after all. The fact that he was talking to her civilly kept Fura from pointing out that he'd never actually said those words. At least not that she could recall.

"What took you so long?"

"How do you know how long I've been gone?" Kiyani asked. "You were asleep when I left." The suspicion in his tone was something Fura hadn't expected, as if he had been caught sneaking out as opposed to doing something he had warned her of in advance.

Fura shrugged innocently. "I was kind of awake. Did you even sleep?"

They had both desperately needed rest when they had finally stopped. Though Fura had no idea what time it'd been when Kiyani had quietly snuck out, she was sure it hadn't been any more than an hour or two after their arrival.

Kiyani spun the tip of the sword in tiny circles at his side without seeming to realize it. "Does it matter?" he asked callously, a sure sign he wasn't going to add any further details even if prodded.

"So," Fura tried again. "What kept you?"

Swinging the sword, Kiyani brought it to a halt directly in front of him, staring at the dark metal. The look in his eyes was something akin to wanting to throw it to the ground and wanting to keep possession of it, as if the object's mere presence was enough to wrap a shadow around him.

"I was debating whether or not my moral conscience would allow

149

me to carry a blade that had only hours before attempted to take my life."

So his eyes didn't betray his feelings. He truly was torn. Fura couldn't blame him for that sentiment.

"That's really his?"

She didn't have to specify who. They both knew.

With a slow nod, Kiyani answered, "We have to have something for protection. This forest isn't as friendly as it may seem."

Fura didn't like the sound of that, the words bringing to memory a few of the stories attached to this particular stretch of land. If there was actual truth to any of those tales, or if what she'd seen the night before was anything to go on, Fura didn't want to know what else could possibly lie in wait for her within these trees.

Telling herself that she was overreacting, Fura avoided that particular line of conversation.

"I didn't know you knew how to handle a sword."

She didn't know where else to go with the conversation, and as she spoke the words, her eyes lingered on the blade Kiyani still held before him, curious and afraid. It wasn't clear to her if he had cleaned it before bringing it back, or if it had never been used in the first place. Fura shuddered at the thought, wondering once more just who she was traveling with. She told herself that as far as she knew, it could have been the rain that had cleansed it of whatever carnage it might have seen the night before.

"A little," Kiyani answered remotely. He didn't seem eager to play up and exaggerate what Fura had just witnessed as a possible strength.

"Well, it looked impressive enough."

The smallest of satisfied grins pulled at the corner of Kiyani's mouth. He arched the blade through the air one last time before bending to retrieve a black leather sheath from the ground. "The weight of this one is actually too heavy for me," he said, returning the sword to its home. "But it'll have to do."

Kiedo came ambling over and Kiyani remained crouched near the ground as he ran a hand over the wolf's head, ruffling the fur along his back. Fura felt a general sense of unease, her instinct telling her that Kiedo could turn and bite at any time, his wild animal instinct kicking in out of the blue. However, there was a visible relaxation in his form that told her otherwise, revealing a view of the companionship between the two that Fura would never dare think to test. She'd seen enough the night before to know that she never wanted to be caught on the wrong side of the animal's rage.

Rising, Kiyani went to put something in his pocket. Seeming to think better of it, he approached Fura and made to hand her the familiar object.

"I wasn't sure if you would want this or not."

One look was all it took for Fura to back away, shaking her head. Though it didn't appear the same in the light of day, she knew it was the same dagger that could have ended her life.

"I'd probably just hurt myself with it," she said, striving to keep her words casual and joking so as not to betray the repulsion she felt towards the object. She knew it was illogical, but even just laying her eyes on the knife seemed to bring it to life. It felt as if it were laughing at her, planning to attack on its own accord. Protection or not, she didn't want anything previously belonging to that horrible man.

Kiyani regarded her with a frown, but didn't force the matter. "You play with fire on a daily basis, and you're afraid of a small knife?"

"Exactly. I play with fire, not steel."

"One as dangerous as the other, if you ask me," he said with a shrug. "If you ever change your mind, just say so."

Fura nodded. She would never be swayed to rethink her decision.

She had expected a bigger fight over it, but after witnessing a mere sliver of the inner turmoil Kiyani was facing with the sword he had decided to keep, Fura knew that, with fortune, it was one thing he wouldn't push.

Tucking the dagger into the waistband of his jeans, Kiyani crouched on the narrow bank of the stream. Laying the sword on the ground beside him, he cupped his hands and took a drink of water as he stared out into the trees.

At a loss of how to proceed, Fura followed suit. Looking down at the water, she questioned the safety of drinking it, but decided it didn't matter at this point. She was thirsty and Kiyani had no qualm about it. It was easy to see that he knew the forest better than she did. It would be a futile attempt to fight about that. Fura already knew she had nothing to bring to the table when it came to survival skills.

Unnerved by the silence, she looked over to find that Kiyani had his eyes closed, his face turned upwards towards a sun that refused to shine. For a moment he seemed to have found a sliver of peace, and Fura wished she could feel the same. Instead, the sight of his glossy strands of black hair dancing softly in the wind only brought a sensation of butterflies to her stomach.

Turning away, Fura sat and buried her head in her arms. She'd never felt like that about anybody and now wasn't the time to start. Especially not with him. He didn't even like her. Not to mention it clashed with just about everything else that was currently swirling around in her mind. How could she even think about finding happiness with anybody so soon after her family's death?

Not wanting to wallow in the self-induced paranoia that had begun to accompany her silences, Fura took in a breath and turned back to

Kiyani. Any place was as good to start as ever, and he had promised her answers today.

"Who was that man?" she asked, staring down at the sword that rested between them.

Kiyani opened an eye and regarded her a moment before dropping his own gaze to the weapon. "The man that attacked us? I didn't actually know him."

"I know that. I mean, who was he? He was dressed the same as the others that took over Frielana. Who are they?"

"Members of the Shadowguard."

"Shadow-what?" Fura couldn't believe that after he had promised her answers, he was deliberately speaking in riddles again. She should have known that he wouldn't keep to his word.

"The Shadowguard," Kiyani repeated. "The personal army of the Shadow..." His words trailed off as he silently regarded her, seeming to contemplate what he was doing.

There was no sarcasm, no joking in his gaze. But from his eyes, Fura could detect worry, a small amount of building frustration, and a look that said he would rather have teeth pulled.

"You have no idea where you are, do you?"

Fura brightened a little. She had him on that one. "The Verboten Forest," she declared jovially, determined to beat him at his own game. "Though I will say, I didn't know it was this big."

Kiyani slapped a hand over his face. "Sweet Draimaele, kill me now."

Standing, he turned away as if he couldn't even bear the sight of her, making Fura wonder what she'd done now.

"Do you have anywhere you can go?"

Fura moved to her feet as well. "Why are you trying so hard to get rid of me?"

His question might have been compassionate enough, but the hands that he clenched at his side told a different story. A visual reminder that he wanted to be far away from her.

"Because you don't belong here."

There was a growl in his voice as Kiyani turned to face her again. It made her want to step back, but she held her ground. She had to get answers, and right now he was the only one who could provide.

"That's not –"

Fura barely got a word out before Kiyani cut her off.

"You prove it with every word you say."

Crossing her arms defiantly, Fura glared at him. The words stung, as if that dagger she had refused had decided to come and play anyway, but she wouldn't let him back out of the conversation so easily. "I'm sorry that you don't like me, and I'm sorry you're stuck with me, but I don't have anywhere to go. You know why? Because my family is dead." The words stuck in her throat like the sharp barbs of a cactus, but Fura forced them out anyways. She was surprised to hear anger in her own voice. "Instead of standing here arguing, don't you think we should go do something?"

"Like what?"

"I don't know. Call the police or something?"

"And what's that going to do?"

"They can help. That's what they're for."

"Not here."

"Here?"

"Did Apallo tell you nothing, or was he too busy making me out to be a monster?"

Fura didn't know what dragging Apallo into the conversation would prove, but she had to admit that Kiyani had the upper hand. It was hard to believe that even though he had been absent most of the few days she had spent in Frielana, he still seemed to know where her short conversations with Apallo had focused, as if he had been a fly on the wall the entire time.

She was still peeved with Kiyani for so caustically turning on her – something that seemed to be a familiar habit with him – but the mention of Apallo had managed to take some of the fight out of her, making her wonder if that had been his motive in the first place.

"So what then?" All Fura could think of now was the sight of Apallo being dragged away in the mud. Her mentor and her friend.

"I'm taking you back to Barandor first thing in the morning."

That was enough to shock Fura back into the present. "You can't just drop me off like some unwanted animal," Fura shouted. But Kiyani was ignoring her, already in the process of walking away. "This conversation isn't over."

"I believe it is."

Left motionless in total disbelief over his raging attitude, Fura found herself reeling as she watched him walk away, the words taken straight from her mouth. She didn't need this non-refundable ticket to an emotional roller coaster that seemed to come from being around him. It couldn't be worth it. Maybe there was a good reason he had been left to his own devices in Frielana, why Apallo had warned her against befriending him, and why the others went out of their way to avoid him.

Fura was tempted to just let him go. If he wanted to be that way, then fine. She didn't need him.

But she knew she did.

One look around the endless forest was all she needed to remind herself of that. She wanted nothing more than to let him just storm off, to go and seethe in his own misery, but she couldn't. As much as she loathed the idea of relying on someone, especially him of all people, Kiyani was the only one who could get her out of this, show her the way back to some semblance of a home, and give her the answers she so desperately needed.

Taking a deep breath, Fura mentally prepared herself for confrontation. Not giving herself the time to think on the matter further, she took off after Kiyani before she lost sight of him. She had no idea what she would ask, or how to even start. The only thing that was clear was that she needed him to show her the way.

He hadn't had much of a head start on her and Fura saw his form coming into view sooner than she had expected.

"Kiyani!" she called. She slowed as she came upon him, breathing heavily from the sudden sprint. Pulling alongside of him, Fura panted before speaking. "You can't just run away like that!" she said, the frustration she felt around him bubbling over. "Can't you be civilized just for a minute? We can sit down and figure this out. We can go back and help."

"Frielana is not my problem!" Kiyani declared vehemently. "And neither are you! It may be in my moral center to keep you alive, but it is not my job. There is nothing keeping me from just leaving you here."

Fura was startled by the ferocity in his words, but her own reply didn't reflect it. "Then do it," she urged coldly. A part of her wondered what she was doing, what she was attempting to accomplish. If he left she was done for. No question about it. She might have been able to eventually find her way back to Barandor from Frielana, but Kiyani had effectively taken her to the middle of nowhere, and he knew it.

He stared at her for the longest time, making Fura wonder if she had gone too far, if he would take the bait and leave like he wanted. His actions answered her as he turned and walked away.

Scared to find herself alone, Fura darted forward. Standing directly in his path, she instinctively grabbed at his arm to stop him.

What happened next was far beyond what she expected, even from him.

Kiyani had left the stolen sword lying on the ground when he had left in a hurry, but the dagger was still on his person. Swiftly pulling it from his side, he unsheathed the small blade and pointed it at Fura.

Fura immediately took a step away from him. The whole maneuver had been completed with such speed that she wasn't even sure she'd seen it happen, but one look at the shining metal told her it was as real as ever. She'd been scared when the knife's original owner had tried to use it against her, but there was something about the sight of it in

Kiyani's grasp, his eyes shadowed and dangerous, that left her petrified. She could only hope it wasn't intentional. "You wouldn't."

"You don't know me."

Silence stretched between them like an eternal black hole, soundless, shadowed, and unpredictable. It was all Fura could do to not turn away, to hold her eyes to his despite the shake in her hands, as she wondered what he would do. What he was capable of.

Fura could see just out of range of her peripheral vision that his own hands were shaking. It was the smallest thing, but she hoped it was a good sign, an indicator that he couldn't go through with his threat. That it was just that – empty words.

Kiyani's eyes shifted, and just like that they softened as he lowered his arm and pointed with the knife.

"Where did you get that?"

Locked in the paralyzing jaws of dread, it took Fura a moment to follow the blade's path to her arm. She issued an utterance of surprise as she saw, not too far above her elbow, on her upper arm, the slash in the sleeve of her sweatshirt and the wound that it opened too.

"Last night?" she said weakly.

Dropping the knife to his side, the anger diffused, Kiyani went to reach for her, but Fura pulled back.

"You don't know?" he asked.

The only reply Fura could come up with was a shake of her head. The night before had been such a blur of activity that she found it hard to pinpoint anything in particular. The fight was the only logical explanation. She could remember pain shooting through her arm as she had raced through the forest, but at the time she had been certain it was just the aftermath of being smacked by tree branches. She hadn't been aware there had been any gash in the flesh, let alone blood to go with it. Not even the tear in her clothing had broken through her clouded reality. Just the stinging sensation of pain. And the need to run. To get out of the line of danger.

Kiyani let out a sigh. "You're hopeless, you know that?"

Fura ground her teeth together as she looked at the ground. She had never met a less compassionate person in her life. Yet, that wasn't the full spectrum of the case. No, she had never met someone who came across as such as mystery as Kiyani did. One minute he was trying to get rid of her, nearly going as far as to actually physically threaten her, and then the next... then the next he was voicing worry and offering help. It was mind boggling.

Kiyani had joked about Apallo checking her own mental health, but now she was wondering about his, the diagnoses of anything from bipolar to schizophrenic coming to mind. Yet nothing accurately fit him. Instead, Fura thought, it was something more akin to a battle. Of him waging combat against inner demons and fighting himself.

It wasn't the mentally impaired that she was seeing as Kiyani once again offered his hand to her, but a tortured soul.

And that actually frightened her more, for there was nothing more unstable, more unpredictable and unsettling, than being in the company of one who didn't even know himself, who was constantly waging war within. Yet, she felt for him, and in a way, it made that resurgence of strange and sudden feelings for him that she had experienced in the past few days a bit stronger.

Unsure of herself, Fura kept her arms firmly plastered to her side. But inside she wanted to reach out and take his hand, suddenly wanting nothing more than to know what it would feel like to be in his arms.

"You should have that looked at," Kiyani said, breaking Fura's train of thought.

She could only bring herself to catch his eye for a moment before turning her head away. He made no mention of it, but she could feel the heat coloring her face, the catch in her breath.

"It's fine," Fura hastily assured. "I can't even feel it."

It was a lie. Now that it had been brought to her attention, she could feel the pull of the wound as the scabbed blood that held it together threatened to flake away and leave it exposed. Prodding it with a single finger, she winced, but it was the stifled groan that gave her away.

Raising an eyebrow, Kiyani stood with his hand still held out to her, seeming to push against what her mind was telling her about him. "At least let me clean it up."

Though reluctant to take his hand and let him lead, to what she didn't know, Fura knew he was right. The wound didn't look infected now, but there was no saying it wouldn't eventually be if left alone. There was no harm in simply having him check it over.

With a hesitant nod, Fura allowed Kiyani to direct her towards the stream that continued to lazily follow their path. There he sat her down on a large boulder where he proceeded to follow much of the same procedure as he had for Kiedo the night before, stealing fabric from his sleeve and dipping it in the cool water provided to use as both a cloth and a bandage.

Fura looked through the stand of trees as he worked, at the pinks and reds that had broken through the cloud cover. The colors seemed darker and more threatening cast against the grays that had permeated the day, but she remembered one of the sayings she had learned in her childhood and a smile danced across her face. She turned to Kiyani who was taking his time tying the bandage on her arm so it would stay in place.

"Red sky at night, sailor's delight. Right?"

Securing the double knot, Kiyani's fingers lightly trailed down her arm, sending an involuntary shiver up her spine that she knew he was blissfully unaware of, as he turned his attention to the sky.

"Let's hope so."

21

♦♦◇♦♦

BEASTS OF THE NIGHT

Against all hope, danger came lurking again that night in the form of the mysterious and the unfriendly. Fate didn't seem to care to give them even the smallest of breaks, as if the mere idea of two teenagers, left to their own devices in the midst of the dark forest, was just too good an opportunity to let pass by unscathed. Maybe it was, in fact, the illusive spinner of fate herself, bored and looking for an uncanny way to pass the time, or maybe it was just the ill luck of those who had unwittingly found themselves in the wrong place at the wrong time. All that could be said was that the two would find no rest that night.

Drifting in and out of a fitful sleep, it was Fura who finally came to in response to the intrusive sound that moved through the darkness. Rolling over, she immediately brushed it off, wanting nothing more than the quiet comfort that she was beginning to realize no longer came with sleep. Over the short course of time spent in Frielana, she had begun to grow accustomed to the white noise of nature – the chirping insects, the rustle of leaves in the breeze. Yet, as she lie awake in the dark, listening half-heartedly to the sound shift and change, Fura began to realize that it was something more than just the whispering wind.

Finally pinpointing it as rustling, Fura propped herself up on an elbow and looked to the shelter's entrance, telling herself to remain calm. There were plenty of potential sources for the noise, and not all of them screamed danger. As if to further accentuate the point, the murky light that filtered in and splashed across the floor proved nothing. The rain had decided to let up for the night, allowing the light of the moon to polish the night in tones of silver and blue, but the shadows that moved in the space were only from the ferns surrounding the tree.

Ready to sign it off as nothing, the noise came again. This time closer and much more defined – the crunch of leaves beneath a weighted step. One glance around the interior of the hollow told her that the only one missing in their company was the wolf. The explanation was easy enough and Fura almost laughed at herself for overreacting. It was merely the wolf that moved about, hunting or maybe even patrolling the area.

"Kiedo?" Fura called. She didn't know why she bothered. She doubted the wolf would reply. At least not to her. Though Kiyani vehemently denied the claim, Fura still saw Kiedo as a sort of pet, his to be exact. One that she wasn't sure actually accepted her as a friend of Kiyani's, or merely tolerated her for the time being, much like Kiyani himself.

As expected, there was no answer and Fura took it as a sign that it was safe to return to sleep. Settling back onto the floor into the only spot that could be remotely deemed comfortable, she hugged the blanket close and looked over at Kiyani who had his back turned to her. She doubted he'd gotten a wink of sleep the night before, but exhaustion seemed to have finally taken its hold. It was hard to tell for certain if he was actually sleeping, but Fura assumed so as she watched the steady rise and fall of his breathing. Closing her eyes, it wasn't long before the sound returned. This time louder and accompanied by the distinct canter of voices.

All thoughts of sleep vanished as panic rose. As sweat broke out across her palms, she hoped this wouldn't be a repeat of the night before.

The image of the soulless and weather-ravaged man came to mind, bathed in silver and black fabrics. Fearing that he had returned from the shallow grave from which Kiyani had only recently placed him, or that one of his friends had come to enact revenge, Fura crawled over to Kiyani.

"Kiyani?" she whispered as she shook him awake. Despite doing her best to keep her voice low, there was an audible level of fear laced in her words and it dripped into the surrounding shadows.

He rolled over and glared at her, his face declaring more than just baseline frustration. "What?"

Fura scooted away, the picture of him with that knife pointed straight at her still fresh in her mind. Yet she refused to let him roll over and return to what little sleep he had found, sure that the only thing that had roused him in the first place was her childish tone that spoke of a sudden fear of the shadows.

She gestured towards what served as the doorway. "There's something out there."

"It's the forest," Kiyani grumbled. "There's always something out there."

"I'm serious," Fura pleaded.

"Go back to slee-" He made to return to his previous position but stopped mid-sentence, his body tense as he looked to the hollow's entrance.

Finally seeming to take faith in her words, he moved into a crouch. Grabbing Fura's arm, he whispered in her ear, commanding that she go to the back of the hollow.

Questions stormed her mind as she tried to figure out what was going on now, but the more she thought on it, the more she found she really didn't want to know, and without argument, did as she was told. Cowering in the deepest shadows the space could provide, thankful for once for the darkness that could be used to their advantage to keep hidden, Fura watched as Kiyani did the opposite.

In the time it had taken Fura to move, he had grabbed the small dagger from the floor, next to where he had been sleeping, and had slid silently towards the opposite wall. Inching his way closer to the archway, he peered outside.

As Fura watched, she tried to steady her breathing, fearing that the pounding of her heart would echo through the hollow and give them away. Maybe she'd imagined the voices and there really was nothing to worry about. It could have easily been an animal grunting, or, revisiting her initial thought, Kiedo. The wolf had no reason to answer her.

But the moment Kiyani dove to the floor, muttering a curse, she knew that her fear was far from irrational. Their eyes met in the muted darkness, the faint moonlight highlighting Kiyani's actions as he held a finger to his lips, telling her in silence to do the same. She nodded and Kiyani tipped his head upwards as the voices moved closer.

"Where did ye say ya heard it?"

"I think es' full a credge."

"I ain't. I'm a telling ya. I heard some'in o'er this way."

The strange voices trailed through the night, adding unwanted detail to the picture Fura had painted in her head. Even with the multitude of festival-goers who traveled to Barandor every year, she had never heard such thick and heavily deluded accents. The crude shapes of the familiar words they used made it hard to clearly make out what the masculine voices spoke of, yet they seemed to carry with them a masked intelligence as the unknown speakers carried on with their conversation. Fura hoped that the intruders were unaware of them, but from the snatches of conversation she could make out, it didn't sound promising.

Even painted in ghostly tones by the moon, Kiyani seemed to pale in response to their words. With no further need for spying, he made his way over to where Fura was sitting. Her eyes widened as she caught sight of what she thought to be massive legs moving across the limited vision she had of the outside of the tree.

Kiyani had barely settled in next to her before he tore into her with a hiss. "How do they know we're here?"

Fura felt ashamed. "I might've called for Kiedo," she admitted in a whisper.

160

"You didn't..."

"I thought it might have been him." She felt even stupider now. Not only that, but fully responsible for whatever might happen to them now. Maybe Kiyani had been right. She had no place out here, couldn't do this on her own. "They know we're here, don't they?" The sordid look she received was the only answer Fura needed. "What are they?"

She didn't know what had possessed her to ask what and not who, but Kiyani didn't comment, only replying, "You wouldn't believe me if I told you."

"I think ye mighta been right, Saergan."

The proximity of the voice, almost directly outside the hollow, made Fura jump. She latched onto Kiyani's arm and buried herself in his shoulder, not thinking twice about the action as she tried to block out the world. Rationality refused to make itself known behind the curtain of fear that had been draped over her. Kiyani tensed beneath her touch and made to push her away as he had done the other night, but then seemed to think better of it.

"What are they going to do?" Fura asked, her words muffled by his shirt.

Kiyani's focus remained on the doorway. "Best case scenario, they move on."

"And worst?"

Fura received her answer as a huge, hairy, and scarred arm was thrust into the hollow. The bulk of it blocked what little light they'd had, but she could hear it as it pounded softly on the dirt, trying to blindly find them. The hand retracted and was replaced by a rough face, of which Fura could only see a single eye, half a nose, and the corner of a lip curled into a fierce smile.

"Here, here, tasty little pups. Come out and play."

A scream inched its way up Fura's throat, threatening to fill the tiny space, but it stuck as if it were trying to choke her. Instead, all she found she was able to do was cling tighter to Kiyani. The fact that she might be hurting him didn't cross her mind, and otherwise occupied, he made no protest.

"They should be too big to get in here."

"Should be?" Fura didn't know what was more frightening, the lack of assurance in his words, or the fact that he had just claimed that whatever was out there was too tremendous in size to come through the gaping entrance. "So, we're safe?" She could only hope, against all odds, that the answer was yes.

The look on Kiyani's face as she looked to him betrayed the bad news. "There are other ways to flush out prey."

Just as Fura was reflecting on the unnerving fact that Kiyani had cited them as the hunted, a flare of light came to life just outside. The orange flicker of what she knew to be fire only seemed to bathe the space in a hellish glow.

"And that's what I was afraid of," Kiyani mumbled.

The light steadily grew brighter as another fire was lit, sharing life with the first. Beyond the doorway, a chorus of deep, guttural laughter sounded as the men outside reveled in their actions.

"We've got em now!"

"Can you climb?" Kiyani asked suddenly in her ear.

Fura didn't know if she'd heard him right. Yet, her moment to ask was cut short as one of the men looked in on them again before moving away and sending a fire-engulfed torch into their wake. It wasn't the greatest cause for alarm, as it sat sputtering in the dirt, but the dead pine branches that followed, catching light immediately and filling the space with smoke, was.

Kiyani was the first to react, grabbing Fura's arm and pulling her to her feet. "You do now," he answered for her. She no longer had a choice.

Blazing to life, and gaining momentum much faster than they should have, the flames rose and licked at the wood surrounding them. Fura was brought forth from her daze as the tree itself caught light. She tried to escape the intense heat but only backed into the wall, beads of sweat dripping down her face from her brow.

Plodding back and forth in the small space left like a cornered animal, Fura cried out, "What do we do?" It no longer mattered if the men outside heard them.

Kiyani grabbed her arm, pulling her as far from the growing flames as he could manage and pointed upwards. "There are footholds carved into the wood that lead to a branch outside," he hastily explained.

Fura had no time to ask for further details before Kiyani directed her to the first notch on the inside of the trunk and hoisted her up. She wasn't fond of heights, but the natural instinct to flee danger, and the sweltering heat pushed her onward. The agility that Apallo had often commended her on, saying that it made for less training for performances, allowed her to scale the wall with ease. Only once did Fura pause in her escape as she looked down to discover that Kiyani had stopped a few feet below. Following his line of sight, she could see the sword he had stolen glittering amongst the flames. For a moment, Fura feared that he would abandon his progress in attempt to retrieve it, but as their eyes met he seemed to think better of it. Though she could see the grimace on his face, speaking of something lost.

A few more feet and Fura could see the opening he had spoken of. Exhausted from the climb, it was a sudden resurgence of energy that sent her flying across the remaining distance like a spider and out into the night, where she had to quickly catch herself before she catapulted off the side of the narrow branch.

Blind from the tower of fire behind her, Fura's vision swam violently as she faced the black of night again. Uncertainty kept her rooted in place, but the cool night air was refreshing against her flushed face.

"Don't stop!" Kiyani shouted over the roar of the flames as he pulled himself free of the Reln's interior.

Fura turned to see him silhouetted against the harsh light. It was a strange picture – too vivid, and appearing to move in slow motion. Reminding herself that this wasn't a dream, she told herself she had to keep moving.

Kiyani forced the matter as he pushed her forward before she could ask where to go. She wasn't given many options, just forward or down. Looking down from the dizzying height to the dark ground yards beneath the branch she stood on, Fura didn't want to chance breaking her leg in a jump.

With Kiyani to keep her moving, Fura inched along the branch, wishing that it wasn't necessary to look down to keep her footing. The branch bent and swayed beneath their combined weight, leaving Fura to wonder if it would snap, disappearing from under them and sending them into a sudden free fall anyways. Remembering that Kiyani had told her the hollows only formed in trees that were dying didn't help. Regardless, the narrow platform underfoot was springy and pliable, never once threatening to give way. The bouncing dance of it was excruciating on the nerves, but so was knowing that they were being hunted for dinner.

"Do ye want em well done, er extra crispy?"

Fura faltered in her step as the question carried over the noise of the raging fires inside the tree. There was no reply, only the continued laughter.

They're enjoying this, Fura thought repulsively.

"Don't listen to them," Kiyani instructed, having heard it as well. "Just go."

How he could remain so calm in such a situation was beyond her. The only thing that made it easier was that they'd come out on the back side of the tree, effectively keeping them hidden from sight. The further they moved, the fainter the voices got, as they carefully jumped from limb to limb – some sturdier than others – through the network of overlapping branches.

With every new branch they moved to, Fura grew more confident. The pounding fear began to lapse, replaced with an overwhelming curiosity. Now that they were out of the line of danger, she found herself wanting to know what had been after them. She could still just hear the voices in the distance, those strange accents leaving her grasping for straws. All she knew about these predatorial people were the few glimpses of appendages she had gotten. Kiyani himself had said that she wouldn't believe him if he were to elaborate. That only left her wanting to know more.

Kiyani nearly ran into her as she stopped again.

"What are they?" Fura asked, ignoring his glare as she turned to him.

"Shush," Kiyani instructed. "And keep going."

"But – "

A deathly roar echoed through the night from where their shelter was burning in the distance. Where only a moment before, Fura had entertained the thought of doubling back to get a glimpse of these strange men, there now wasn't enough distance between them as she heard the rising voices, clear as night, as they argued fiercely.

"What do ya mean they're gone?" one voice roared.

Though it was hard to tell, Fura was sure it had come from the same one who had lit the tree on fire, the one that seemed to be the leader of the small group.

The exact words of the smaller, pleading voice that followed were impossible to make out, but they were shortly answered by the first in a thunderous bellow.

"I don't care how! Find them!"

That was all that was needed to send the fear jolting back through Fura. She turned to resume their trail through the treetops, already telling herself to move at a faster pace this time, but she was held back by Kiyani.

He pushed her down into a crouch and held a finger to his lips again. "Don't move, and stay quiet."

Fighting to balance, Fura gripped the branch beneath her with white knuckles, thinking that the only thing she wanted to do right now was move. Heck, she wanted to run, and far away from this new nightmare.

Terrified, she turned as the sound of pounding feet moved towards them. All they could do was sit and wait, hoping that the men would be so lost in the rush of adrenaline from the hunt that they would pass them right by. A scream rushed into Fura's throat as the group came into sight, yet she managed to tamp it down into a whimper.

Immediately, she wished she could take back her wanting to know more about these strange people. The only thing that Fura could see directly in the night was that they couldn't be human, though they appeared close enough at a distance. There were three of them. The first, who she assumed was the one she'd heard yelling just before, was about a head taller than the others. Though it was hard to determine from where she sat above them, she guessed them to be seven to eight feet tall. At least. Strongly built, they each had bulging muscles that rippled with each movement beneath skin that looked more like hide.

Every one of them had a cache of weapons strapped to their backs to accompany the ones they carried, ready to use.

Despite the fear making her want to cringe away from the sight, Fura didn't even know that she was leaning forward to get a better view until her foot slipped from beneath her, and she found herself grabbing at an intersecting branch to right herself. A host of dried leaves and small sticks rained down as the men stormed past. Two continued on, lost in thoughts of victory over their prey. The third stopped as the leaves fell around him and settled to the forest floor.

Turning his wide-set and gnarled face upwards, his lips formed a snarling grin. Pulling an arrow from somewhere among the weapons on his back, he nocked it on a makeshift bow and sent it racing through the sky.

This time Fura let out a full-fledged scream as it swooshed just past her ear. Moving to the side to dodge a second, she heard Kiyani issue a grunt of pain beside her. She turned to him just in time to witness him pull the projectile from his thigh, his face scrunched in misery. What Fura had assumed was a regular arrow was actually a length of white bone, whittled to a horrible point. Kiyani gripped it hard in his hand as the man below let out a high pitched, echoing whistle. Meaning to cast it aside, he seemed to decide otherwise.

Fura watched as Kiyani carefully, and painfully, readjusted his weight on the narrow foothold, the arrow's tip sending streams of his own blood down his hand. Knowing that neither of them were getting out of this to see the next day, she returned her attention to the man below as he sent out another whistling call. The sound was enough to turn her blood cold, but what froze it completely was the sight of what the man had in his hand. In the white-washed moonlight she could see that the whistle the man used looked to have been roughly carved from a human femur bone. Bile rose in her throat, threatening to make her sick.

"Ya found 'em?"

The pounding feet returned as the other two men raced each other and fell in beside the one with the bow. He smiled and pointed up to where the two teens balanced precariously in the trees.

The biggest, who had appeared dragging a massive club, made from an uprooted tree, grinned. Heaving the great chunk of wood with ease, he swung it into the trunk of the nearest tree. The impact snapped the tree like a dried bone, reverberating through the trunk as it leaned and fell through the surrounding branches, Kiyani and Fura's included.

Fura fought to hold on as the branch shook violently below her, but as intended, it was enough to shake her free and she was sent plummeting to the ground with a scream. She waited for the bone-breaking impact, but instead was caught in the cradle of thick arms as the one who had shot the first arrows broke her fall. Another scream broke loose the moment Fura realized her position and she flailed her limbs, frantically scrambling to break free from the man's grasp. Her efforts only caused him to tighten his hold, threatening to squeeze the breath from her. In a last ditch effort, her arms pinned to her sides, she bit down hard on the nearest piece of flesh she could find.

A holler not her own broke from the man and she went tumbling to the ground, stunned. She scrambled to get to her feet as one of the other men moved towards her, wanting nothing more than to recapture his dinner. A form came flying through the air, and Fura watched as Kiyani landing on the man's shoulders, stabbing the arrow he had kept into his neck. The hulking man fell, shaking the ground beneath her as Kiyani leaped before being crushed by the weight and rolled past her.

Pulling himself back up faster than Fura had managed, even with his injury, Kiyani grabbed her hand and they ran, the man with the club crashing through the forest behind them, not intending to let them escape.

They didn't make it far before Kiyani began to falter in his step, falling to his knees. Fura turned, racing to help him back up, but she was stopped short. The towering man stood before her, his club resting over a shoulder as if he knew he wouldn't actually need to use it to bring her down. She darted backwards as he stepped forward, eyes nothing but black pits in the darkness. He paused for a moment, looking down to Kiyani's lifeless form and nudging him with a diseased looking toe to make sure he wasn't going anywhere before returning his focus to her.

Preoccupied with the mass of muscle before her, Fura wasn't even aware of the second man approaching from behind until she was grabbed and lifted off the ground. She was barely given time to struggle before the pressure from the man's grasp that kept her from taking in air sent her into a blackening unconsciousness.

22

•◆•

WAKING TO FANTASY

Fura rolled over, her throat sore and her muscles aching. The deep veins of sleep refused to release her from their grasp, as snatches of conversation passed groggily through her mind from the mysterious dream she'd been lost in. Lying there, clutching the sheets, all she could remember was a heavy pressure taking the breath from her, and a darkness that had settled like a blanket, threatening to continue the suffocation. Then, all of a sudden the world had been split by a blinding light that had left her temporarily deaf in the strangest of moments, where the world had moved in slow, yet dizzying motion around her. The images that had followed had passed like still frame photos, but the voices that had carried through the air had read like a script.

"And just where do you think you're going?"

Drawing a blank as it all threatened to fade away from memory, the only image that Fura could recall with any clarity was that of the woman speaker, but even that was hazy, as if she was nothing more than a silhouette behind frosted glass. The only detail that remained was the long, dark hair that had floated about her form in a halo of waves. It had taken on a mossy green cast in the unnatural light, reminding Fura of weeds dancing beneath the waters of a crusted over pond in the winter months.

"We's gotta eat," a strange, yet hauntingly familiar male voice had spoken in reply.

There was a hard thud, the sound of someone punching flesh, and a deeper voice that overpowered the other.

"It's not ah your business," it claimed in a heavy accent.

Even with the fleeting memories that straddled that growingly faint line that separated reality from fantastical dream, Fura easily placed the men's voices. The fear that had driven her through the forest as she'd fought to escape those strange creatures bubbled in her gut as she returned to that place.

"It is when you're on my land."

167

The leader of the strange men balked at the woman's steady reply. "We ain't on ya land. And whadda ye want wit em anyways?"

"That is not of your business."

The words of the mysterious woman trailed off into silence and that was the last that Fura could recall, from dream or otherwise. Thinking on it now, with her eyes closed and warm in a cocoon of blankets, it was easy to tell herself that every last detail had been nothing but a nightmare.

Dragging a hand across her face, Fura did her best to hold back a yawn. Pulling a strand of hair free from her lashes and rubbing the sleep from the corner of her eyes, she found herself startled when she finally opened her eyes. The comforting arms of familiarity had vanished, leaving her without the faintest idea of where she was.

Infinite darkness stretched all around her.

Certain that she had disembarked from the land of dreams and had landed back on the solid grounds of reality, Fura tried to convince herself that she was back in Frielana, that someone had just closed the door to her room. But it was too dark. Even though sight escaped her, she could tell in the soft, haunting sounds that surrounded her that she was in a completely different place.

Struggling to place the faint noise, Fura finally pinned it with hesitation on water. Running water. Not the pounding cascade of the falls back in Frielana, or even the light churning of a moving river, but water all the same. Yet, as far as she could tell through touch alone, Fura was well aware of the fact that she was sitting on a bed. That fact alone left her questioning her previous observation. But even as she told herself to guess again, her other senses kicked in, reminding her that she wasn't wrong.

She could smell the moisture and feel the humidity in the air that left her skin slightly damp. The woodsy green aura of plant life and cool mosses hit her nose as well, accented by a slight metallic taste of rocks. None of it added up, leaving Fura all the more wary of her situation.

The bed was something she could handle. It was a simple creature comfort, something that she'd been dying to reacquire since the night her life had been turned upside down, yet again. But it was the addition of the remaining details that she was able to pick up on that left her far from accepting, and unable to relax in the darkness.

The biggest discomfort was that she had no idea how she had gotten here. The last thing Fura could recall was being chased by those humungous... men? Creatures, she decided. That was the only way to classify what she had seen. In truth, she still wasn't sure exactly what she had seen. But reviewing the images in her mind, trying to sort the reality from the dream, Fura's breath caught in her throat.

Kiyani...

Kiyani had been injured. The picture of him pulling that bone, fashioned into an arrow, from his leg came vividly into her mind, threatening to make her sick. They had run, trying to escape, but they had been caught.

Fighting to suppress the whimper that lodged in her windpipe, Fura looked around frantically. They had been caught.

So where were they now? Was she alone, or were those men, those creatures, just a few feet away in the dark, deciding in their foreign accents how to best prepare them for eating? Just recalling the way they had joked about how they wanted her cooked was enough to send shivers of fear racing down her spine.

Her initial reaction was to call out, to Kiyani, to Kiedo, to anyone, but Fura quickly decided against it. Following that line of action was what had landed her here in the first place. She didn't know where she was, but she knew, without a doubt, that this was her fault, and if she ever saw Kiyani again he would put on a dramatic show of reminding her. Knowing the kind of anger he would harbor made her cringe, but Fura didn't care. Given the circumstances, she would do anything to see that familiar face.

There was nothing more inviting than the thought of rolling herself back into the sheets and letting the darkness take her, hoping that it would all reveal itself to be a dream. But Fura knew better. She had been hoping that ever since those green fires had stained the sky. She had yet to wake from this continuous nightmare. Driven by the need to act, Fura poked a foot out from the sheets and over the edge of what she assumed was a twin sized bed, searching for anything that resembled a floor. A shocking cold greeted the nerves in her feet, but despite wanting to pull back, she kept it planted.

There was little comfort to be had in a night so deep that she couldn't even see her hand in front of her own face. What kept her pushing onward in slow, calculated movements was that sound of trickling water. Except for the rhythmic beating of her heart, it was the only sound she was aware of, and though the deafening silence that lingered around the edges was unnerving, it meant that there was no danger in the immediate surroundings.

Sliding the other foot out onto the floor, Fura jumped up, taking the plunge into the unknown. She landed in a defensive stance, though against what, she didn't know. She had no training in defense, and certainly nothing to defend herself with. Almost immediately she was sent screeching and reeling backwards as light suddenly flooded the room, as if whatever had been lurking in the darkness had been waiting for that moment. Tripping over her own feet, Fura fell back across the bed and tumbled off the other side, where she landed in an awkward sprawl, her legs twisted painfully beneath her.

She was barely given time to right herself before the light suddenly dimmed and started to approach, almost like the directed beam of a flashlight, but this was different, more of a radiant light. Her nerves wired, Fura crouched low, afraid to peer over the bed that blocked her view. She didn't want to know. Yet, she was given little choice. Not prepared for what appeared in her line of vision, Fura let out another scream as she hustled backwards across the floor and piled into the wall.

Ignoring her distress, the little orb of light followed her without pause. Though there was nowhere left to go, Fura tried to back further into the wall, hoping that what she could now see really was stone would swallow her and save her from this nightmare. Bobbing silently across the room, the perfectly circular ball of light came to a stop an arm's length away from Fura's face. Playing on instinct alone, she dodged to the right. Catching onto her movement, the light followed.

Not sure what to do, Fura sat still, barely breathing as she watched the light. Content to rest directly before her, it bobbed in the air as if hovering on a nonexistent current. Set and determined to wait the strange object out, Fura slowly came to the realization that whatever it was it didn't mean her harm. Hesitant, she took advantage of the sight that had been given back to her by the light's appearance. Fright fading to curiosity, she looked around.

For a fleeting moment, Fura had a sense of déjà vu, as if she fallen out of bed in the room Apallo had graciously assigned her back in Frielana. But as much as she would have liked that alternative, she knew it wasn't true. What she'd been put through since wouldn't allow it, and neither would the details that painted this as a completely different space altogether. Like the caves, stone surrounded her, but that was where comparisons ended. No lightly painted pictures graced the walls here. Instead, the sound of the small streams of water seemed to grow louder as her senses combined sight and sound. In between the meandering miniature rivers, patches of green moss clung to the crevices of the stone that was mottled in differing hues of gray, as they shifted between wet and dry. The only thing that broke the natural feel of the space was the sparse furnishings that consisted only of the bed and a small table beside it. What caught Fura's eye was the door directly across the way.

In studying her surroundings, Fura had almost forgotten about her strange floating companion until the light began to dim, casting a circle of shadow that encapsulated the furthest edges of the room. Holding her hand out, she jumped back, hitting her head on the wall as the orb sprung back to life, its brilliance returning the room to full light.

Though lackluster in nature, the room was given a magical air by the presence of the strange light. Rubbing her head where it had connected with the wall, Fura quickly forgot about the pain as she leaned forward in fascination, trying to study the orb closer.

As if driven by a mind of its own, it playfully hovered in the air, continually darting just out of reach every time Fura made to grab for it. Though she hardly ever got close, she could see that it was just big enough to rest in the palm of her hand.

Her legs still shaky beneath her, giving her all the grace of a newborn calf, Fura used the wall to pull herself to her feet. Stepping forward to chase the light, a smile formed on her face as she watched the orb react to her movement.

Dipping and bowing with the light, almost as if going through the motions of one of her performances at the festival, the orb her fire, the glowing aura it provided seemed to chase away the shadows of her mounting troubles. A happiness that she hadn't experienced in days flowed through her, making her forget for a brief moment where she was. All that had happened in the past week of no importance.

Scampering about in a near fit of giggles, Fura cried out in delight as more lights that had been hovering near the ceiling, in a state of dormancy, came to life and joined her. Spinning around and around, she stopped as she took in the sight of the door again. Breaking the spell she had fallen under, it stood out against the stone in cold contrast. Reminded of her current predicament, Fura scolded herself for letting her guard down so easily. She still didn't have the slightest clue where she was and could still be in danger.

Steeling herself against a mixture of emotions that included the possibility of disappointment, and the rising gale of fear that came with leading a one-man excursion into the unknown, Fura took one step and then another towards the ominous door. There was nothing particularly special about it, just a door set into the stone, but she had no idea what awaited her just beyond, and it seemed to mock her in response.

Catching sight of something that didn't seem to belong in the room, Fura paused at the foot of the bed as she passed. Draped across the end of the bed, she could only assume that the dress that had been so innocently laid out was meant for her. Falling deeper into the spirals of confusion, she wondered who had been here to leave such a gift. She doubted the men who had joked about eating her would do such a thing. An image of the woman from her dream came to mind, but she pushed it away, telling herself that that was ridiculous.

The idea that this was all an elegantly laid trap crossed Fura's mind. She ignored the dress, but took the felted flat shoes that sat on the floor waiting for her. There was no telling where her own shoes had gone, or why they had been taken, but Fura couldn't say that she was sorry to see the muddy tennis shoes go. They had been comfortable enough at first, but they'd been her crude shoes for after hours around the festival for the longest time. All the recent running around in them had only caused their process of falling apart, which had started some time ago, to quicken.

Fura found as she slipped on these new shoes that they were warm after having danced around on the bare stone. Wiggling her toes in delight, she couldn't complain about the fact that they felt like glorified slippers.

Finally striking up the courage, Fura raced to the door, took a deep breath, and opened it. Using caution, she stuck her head out first, only to find that what awaited her was just as empty as the room she occupied. Opening into a hallway that consisted of the same dark stone that extended in either direction, Fura couldn't help but feel a hint of disappointment. Whether her sudden flare of action sent her on the path to escape, or into the waiting grasp of danger, she had expected a bit more than echoing silence.

She didn't know what powered the floating lights, whether they were mechanical, or could be considered alive, but they were the only signs of life Fura had seen. She found herself disheartened to see that the little orb that had followed her to the doorway remained inside the room, leaving her on her own as she moved out into the hallway. As she did so a number of new lights sprung to life, illuminating the winding passageway. Keeping the door to the room in sight, though she didn't know why, Fura decided to turn left. Both directions seemed to end in darkening shadows that she had no desire to explore on her own, but there was something that called to her. Buzzing just on the edges of her awareness, she swore that she could hear water, different than that which accompanied the ribbons of moisture that adorned the walls like transparent streamers. And if she squinted hard enough, she thought she could see a faint light as well.

Light usually meant life, and Fura could feel that familiar sense of unease settle into her gut as she approached. Usually that was a good thing, but now she wasn't so sure, not knowing if she was walking towards danger or help.

Springing quietly into the middle of the arched doorway, Fura's heart sank a little bit. It was a gorgeous sight to behold – a soft flowing stream and a waterfall that cascaded down from the ceiling – but she was still utterly alone. With little else to do, she moved forward to investigate further, wondering if this was some kind of punishment. Left alone in solitude, wondering if she would ever see anyone again, familiar or otherwise.

Allowing herself to relax, Fura felt remarkably calmed by the unusual sight before her. She had been left questioning herself when she'd first seen the spring in Frielana, that strange body of water that seemed to glow warmly from within. The water before her now acted in a similar fashion, leaving her homesick for the place that she had only spent a few fleeting days in. As she approached, she could see that what she took to be a spring was actually more like a river. It flowed slowly from one end of the expansive room to the other, entering the space through a cavernous hole on one side and exiting through an identical passage on the other.

"Lovely, isn't it?"

Having grown complacent in the midst of the expanding silence, Fura jumped at the sound of the voice that echoed through the room. Even though it was obvious she had already been seen, she dove behind a large boulder. It was the only thing in the room that could provide cover, and Fura crouched with her back to the stone, her heart pounding as it frantically tried to escape her chest. She didn't know what to do. She had no weapon – not that she knew how to wield one, anyways – and she had walked herself right into a dead end. Fidgeting, she clutched the loose fabric of her shirt, knowing that she had been right. This was all a trap.

"It's okay, dear," the voice spoke again. "You're safe now, child."

Through her escalating fear, something in the words sparked a sense of recognition. Knowing there was no use hiding, Fura turned and peeked over the top of her rocky refuge. She'd heard that voice before.

Taking in the sight before her, her jaw dropped, not knowing what was the most disconcerting – the fact that the voice was the same as her dream, or that the woman who stood so gracefully before her was a perfect match as well. The only difference was that Fura could now see her more clearly, as if that frosted glass she had been hiding behind before had been shattered, allowing the remaining details to firmly settle into place.

If it wasn't for the hair, Fura might have been able to convince herself that it wasn't possible. After all, the woman in her dream had been nothing more than a hazy image, a figment of her imagination. Hardly enough to base assumptions on. But that hair was undeniable. Even with this new clarity, Fura couldn't help but compare it to watery plant life. From a distance she might have established the woman as a brunette, but beneath the multicolored orbs that bobbed along the ceiling, the dark green was unmistakable.

As strange as it was, the color didn't come across quite as unnatural as it should have. In the way that the woman carried herself, it only appeared as an extension of herself, just as unextraordinary as the eyes on her face. Half of it was pulled atop her head in a wavy tower, while the remaining mass of hair trailed down to the woman's waist. A leaf, just smaller than Fura's hand, was placed behind the woman's ear, barely succeeding in holding some of the hair back. Appearing to be made of a dark bronze, there were smaller leaves and beads that dotted the sea of green waves.

Pulling her focus away from the hair, Fura was startled to find that it was eyes the color of a copper coin that looked back at her. There was an interest there that Fura couldn't resist and she stood up, contemplating whether or not she should move any further. As friendly as she was, there was something else present. Maybe it was the set of her brow, or the painted lips that weren't fully upturned in a smile, that indicated there was more to the woman than just a friendly face.

Quietly cataloging the observation for another time, Fura was able to muster some courage in the woman's presence. Moving around to the front of the rock, her hand never leaving its surface, Fura sat on a flat section of the stone. Looking at the woman, who had barely moved, as if taking the caution to not spook a feral animal, she tried her hand at gathering answers to a few of her most pressing questions.

"Those men?" Fura asked, unsure of just how to word such a request. Just because they weren't present didn't mean they weren't around somewhere, lurking, waiting for her to be caught off guard so that they could continue what they'd started the night before.

The night before.

Had it really been less than a day ago?

The woman smiled, though Fura wasn't sure if it was as warm a gesture as she attempted to make it out to be, or if it was more along the lines of a satisfied inward smile.

"Taken care of."

The implication behind her words didn't help to calm Fura's nerves. "Who are you?" she asked, not feeling spirited enough to explore what 'taken care of' consisted of.

"The Lady Tybithera," the strange woman replied, seeming just as eager to move forward with the conversation and beyond any point that included the men. "The Fae Queen, and this is my dwelling. The expansive Fae Rue Keep."

Fura immediately told herself that she couldn't possibly be referring to faeries, but it would explain the wings. Though she knew it was rude, she hadn't been able to keep her eyes off the strange sight since she had taken notice, a fleeting moment before the recognition from her dream had kicked in. As they moved in and out of conversation, Fura couldn't figure out for herself if the iridescent appendages were actually attached. In the lighting it was hard to tell, but they seemed to appear as nothing more than an illusion. Sometimes there and sometimes not, flitting in and out of focus, like the sparkle of dust in a stream of sunlight.

"Why am I here?"

"Do not be alarmed," the woman declared softly. "I express no harm towards you or your people."

"My people," Fura mouthed silently, not understanding what Tybithera meant.

As if things couldn't possibly be any stranger. Now she was part of a people. Though she had to admit, it was obvious, dream or not, that she didn't fit in here. Wherever this Fae Rue Keep was.

Tybithera remained unaware of Fura's thoughts and playfully held a hand aloft. To Fura's surprise, one of the nearest orbs of light moved towards the woman and settled into her palm. It left Fura wondering what she'd been doing wrong earlier. When she had tried the same thing all they had done was flit away as if toying with her. Rising from the rocks, intrigue drove Fura a few steps forward.

So far, the strange woman had made no indication that she meant any harm. Yet, not unlike the lumbering men who had chased her and Kiyani out of the hollow, there was a visible indication that this woman wasn't entirely human. Driven by curiosity, and ignited by the lack of danger that Fura felt lurking here, her mind was sent reeling with questions as she attempted, with little luck, to make any headway into what this all meant.

"They do brighten the place up, don't they?" Tybithera asked, taking notice that she had caught Fura's attention. "I had almost forgotten just how gloomy it can be down this way." She released the orb, letting it settle into place where it had been prior, and held her hand out to Fura. "Why don't I show you some of the better sights?"

It was a generous offer from one who seemed to be as important as this woman appeared to be, yet Fura only glanced at the slender fingers of the upturned palm. There was still an uncertainty that left her wanting to cling to what little she knew, and right now that was the room she had woken in.

"I promise," Tybithera urged, "that it's much more exciting than here. But why don't you change into some different clothes first?"

So that was who had left the dress on the end of the bed. Fura hadn't taken the time to really study the garment, but she'd been able to tell, just with that one fleeting glance as she had passed it by, that it had been nice. Luxurious likely, compared with what she was currently wearing. Yet she couldn't find herself in agreement. There were things that she wanted to know first. Rolling the fabric of the hem of her sleeve reminded her of that.

Fura looked at the floor as she tried to figure out just how to ask the question on her mind, knowing that she was afraid of the answer that might await. Nothing had been mentioned, and that scared her just as much as knowing.

"Where's Kiyani?" she finally asked, deciding that being upfront was the best approach.

The brightness the woman seemed to carry faded for a moment, so fleeting that Fura thought she had imagined it, but Tybithera did little to try and hide the disapproval that clouded her eyes.

"He's asleep."

Fura frowned, a little disappointed by the simplicity of the answer. But it was still good news. Sleeping. Not dead. That was more than Fura could have hoped for in lieu of being in the grasp of those men as the last thing she could remember.

"So, he's here?"

"He is."

Where before Tybithera had carried a light air and had been talkative, she now spoke in short, diluted sentences.

"Can I see him?"

"In time, depending upon certain matters." Before Fura could ask what exactly that entailed, Tybithera made a quick move to change the subject. "Let him rest. As for now, go change and I shall show you around."

Fura backed away, not sure why she was suddenly so hesitant. Looking to the arch that led back into the hall, she shook her head.

"Maybe some other time," she said, hoping that Tybithera wouldn't take offense.

"Of course," Tybithera responded. "I will let you adjust first. Just know that you are not a prisoner here. If you want to explore, feel free to do so. If you find yourself lost, merely ask someone and they will direct you back to your room."

23

✦✦◇✦✦

MIND OVER MATTER

The door opened, allowing the smallest sliver of gray, shadowed light to filter into the room. It could hardly be considered bright, but after days in the dark, it was enough that Apallo had to blink back the tears that sprung to his eyes, trying to adjust to the sudden change. Struggling against the shackles that kept him within two feet of the damp wall at all times, Apallo wiped his face against his shoulder, ignoring the chains as they slapped against the floor, and the metallic ping they sent echoing through the small room. He didn't care who was coming to see him. Whether it was one of the lowly servants bringing him meager rationings of what could barely pass as food, or someone of a higher rank, all Apallo knew was that he refused to let anyone bear witness to tears in his eyes. He wouldn't let that kind of weakness be shown.

Though he had to admit, it was hard. It didn't matter what condition he was in. All he could think of were those that he'd failed back in Frielana, wondering how they were faring. Had they all survived all right? It pained him to think on it, because deep in his soul he knew that wasn't the case. The guards had dragged him away, already en route to Shäedenmore before the full melee had taken over, but even though he hadn't seen for himself, he had heard it. The cries and the screams. The explosions of energy, and the sounds of weapons being drawn and used against the ones he'd grown to care for beneath his watch. He had promised them all, time and time again, that he would protect them. But what had he been able to do? What help had he been able to offer?

Left with nothing but his own company in the aftermath, Apallo had thought of little else. Yet he always came back to one worry in particular: Fura.

Apallo knew that he should've been more careful bringing her into this world. Yet, against his nature, he had cast aside reason and had moved only on selfish impulse. There was no saying what had become of her, whether she was dead or alive. The only thing that provided any solace was that, deep in his soul, he knew that she was still in the world of the living. It was nothing more than a feeling, but it was enough. However, that's where his instinctual stroke of luck seemed to end, for Apallo knew that no matter where she was right now, it couldn't be good.

Neither the newfound light, nor the person that followed in its wake was enough to brighten the mood of the dank room.

Over a week he had spent, chained and alone. Only the rats, that he caught fleeting glimpses of as they scurried along the walls, kept him company. He may not have had any clear views of his miniature cellmates, but Apallo could hear their varied presence as their nails periodically clicked on the stone.

The moment he had been forced to his knees in submission by the Shadowguardians that had left him fettered in the dungeons, Apallo had braced himself. He'd expected immediate gloating, amidst painful sessions of torture, from the man responsible for his capture. Instead, he'd been left with only his own solitude to keep him company as he lost all sense of time and sanity, little by little, bit by bit, with each passing moment, the fight within him dispersing with it.

Now, as Apallo looked to the figure standing in the doorway, meeting Zariah's stony gaze, he came to the realization that that'd been the man's intention all along.

It burned him that even without being present, the man had pulled further ahead. Not caring to know what Zariah had to say, what he'd come to accomplish, Apallo found himself spurting forth words just to be the first to speak.

"Time has not favored you."

It wasn't true. Despite the noticeable loss of weight that had left the man's face thinner and more harsh looking, Apallo couldn't help but silently admit that time seemed to have ignored him completely.

Zariah laughed, barely giving offense to the intended insult. "Time? You speak as if the last time we met was over a decade ago, when only a few weeks have come to pass. In light of things, I would say that the days have fallen more in my favor, as I am not the one encompassed in chains and distressing in my own filth." With a slow, furtive glance at the encroaching walls of the room, riddled with moisture, and caked with mildew and decay, Zariah added. "Though I will say, I think this room suits you well."

"I think it would be better suited to one who favors the shadows," Apallo replied, his words laced with sarcasm.

He may have been in chains, but he wasn't about to bow down to the man's will, just to sate his insatiable need for those below him to live in a constant state of fear. Apallo sat up as straight as he was allowed by his bonds and looked straight into the man's eyes. This was a man of evil intentions, but the deepest part of him couldn't help but search for any sign of the person he had once known.

Zariah slammed the door shut so hard that the metal of the bars shivered in their wooden casing, ringing out around them as the sound bounced off the stone.

"Do not mock me," he spat.

The man spun back around, all of his previous jovial tone gone.

Good, Apallo thought.

"Mocking is all I have," he continued. It was a dangerous path he had decided to walk, but the man before him lived to destroy the happiness of others. Apallo felt it only right to deal the same once in awhile, even if he would pay for it, likely sooner than later.

The moment the door had been closed, the room had been cast back into the darkness that Apallo had yet to grow accustomed to. This time the darkness was short lived as Zariah spun his hands about the air, creating an undulating ball of green fire. Casting it towards the nearest torch, he waited until it lit before returning his attention back to the man on the floor.

Apallo watched, waiting for Zariah to go ahead and announce what he had come for, and get it over with.

The unnatural glow of the fires set his face in a deeply shadowed contrast that highlighted the sharp features, the sight a perfectly cast display of the dark title he so coveted.

Apallo turned away, wondering why it was that he and the others had never tried their hand at taking him from power before it had gotten to this point. The answer was right before him: because they had always seen Zariah as a man of flamboyantly ambitious talk and no action. How wrong they had all been. There was no knowing how long he had been planning this, or what his twisted mind held in store for the future.

"Keep it up," Zariah finally declared, his words cold and biting, "and that really will be all you have."

"You won't get away with this," Apallo spat, deciding to cut Zariah off before he could elaborate. He didn't care to know the details of what he was implying.

"No? I believe I already have."

"You may have taken me down, but you'll never be able to do the same with the others." At least Apallo hoped. He'd known, not long after taking on the title of Firelord, that he wasn't the strongest of the Sect. But he'd ignored that feeling, growing complacent with it over the years. Zariah's unexpected upheaval had only cemented that fact.

"We'll see."

"The Sect will always prevail."

"As it's done so far? You and I are two of the Seven, yet I'm the only one who's ever seen any sense. This world is failing because of the lot of you. Besides, who's to pass the message along? That girl?"

Apallo's eyes widened. Zariah may or may not have known her name, but Apallo knew of whom he was speaking. "Fura made it out?"

"You didn't know?" He could see a smile of relief pass across Apallo's face and it only delighted him all the more, watching the man take pride in that false sense of hope. "Not that it matters. I doubt she'll get far."

Just like that Apallo was addled with dread once more, not for himself, but for the girl he'd taken under his wing. She wasn't prepared for any of this, but he still had to believe she was capable of great things. Things that she wasn't yet aware of. "What did you do?"

"Me?" Zariah replied snidely with a snicker. "I haven't done a thing. I don't need to. You really think she can accomplish anything here? You've always been filled with foolish beliefs. She may have help, but I doubt even that will get her far. Speaking of help," the man's eyes narrowed. "What message were you trying to convey?"

Apallo wanted to look to the ground, to break eye contact with the man in the fear that his own eyes would give him away, but he knew it would only prove his guilt. Regardless, the question had startled him. He had hoped, in the spur of the moment, that his words would come across as nothing more than the frantic ramblings of a man sentenced to death. It might have successfully fooled the others, but he should've known better than to think he could deceive the Shadowlord. They knew each other too well for such deceptions to pass without notice. Despite everything he was known for, everything he had done, and the darkness that deluded his mind, Zariah was still smarter than many Apallo had ever known.

"What was that? Oh, *the witness will lead the way*," Zariah mocked. "What drivel, what…" he paused, his eyes growing wider, brighter with glee as he returned his gaze to Apallo. "No… that old wives' tale?" Zariah barked hysterically. "I must say, all that play with fire has finally addled your brain. You've gone and done my work for me, my old friend, sending them on a journey with no end."

The sound of the man's laughter was enough to set Apallo's nerves on edge, but it was what Zariah said that had caught his attention.

"Them?"

"Oh, you didn't know? So… unaware of what goes on around you…"

Apallo's breath faltered. "Kiyani…" It was the only reason the man before him would be so gleeful. Monira had been wrong. His most trusted advisor had been wrong. He should've sent Fura back to Barandor. Instead, he'd sent her on some perilous journey he could never hope to get her back from. What kind of mentor was he? Apallo already knew the answer: a selfish one.

He turned his face to peer upon the Shadowlord, his features hardening. "I suppose that was planned from the beginning." Apallo didn't bother to form it into a question.

"As if I would trust my bidding to that wretch. Amazing that he still finds ways to make my life easier, even after all these years, isn't it? I won't complain."

The turmoil in his mind as Apallo wrestled with this information seemed to transfer to the physical. He could hear the chains clack against the floor as he subconsciously fought against them.

"Where are they?" he asked, his words frantic. Apallo didn't care about Kiyani, save to spare a brief hope that death would take him, but he needed to know about Fura, to receive just the smallest piece of confirmation.

"I'm afraid I neither know, nor care."

Apallo tried to calm his labored breathing, but it was no use. Fura was alive, but she was with Kiyani. Just the thought of it was too much to bear. It was almost a sure bet that he would never see the girl again, and he felt wholly responsible for her now questionable fate.

Had that much time passed between his last meeting with Zariah that he'd honestly forgotten that words could be just as torturous as any physical pain he thought to inflict? He would've rather had the beating he'd expected.

"So, are you going to kill me?" Apallo asked coldly. It didn't matter if he was in the position to decide or not. He was done with this conversation.

"And let you miss out on all the fun? Hardly," Zariah confessed. "You will pay for what you have done to me, but it will be a slow demise. Trust me that." Seeming to be caught up in his own words, he created frightful pictures in the fires in his hands as he spoke. "There is still so much to do before that. The others will tumble before my reign, and you'll be left for last, to watch as each and every last one of your friends is destroyed beneath my hand. Though I doubt that any of them will be quite as easily taken down, or as submissive, as you've proven to be. I'll admit. I'm disappointed in you, Apallo. I had hoped for a bit of a challenge."

A timid rap at the door broke Zariah's concentration, and Apallo wondered just what could be in store for him now. As he watched the irritation of being interrupted paint the Shadowlord's face in colder tones than he normally carried, he wished that whatever was going to be done to him would just come to pass and be done with. He'd already been given all he needed to be placed in a permanent state of misery. Yet, he had a feeling that he'd only been given a glimpse of his future, that his mind would be the continued subject of torture as opposed to his body. Not that Zariah was known to favor one over the other, only working where he knew he could inflict the most pain with the least amount of effort.

"Enter," Zariah said, none too kindly after a moment's consideration.

Zendel moved into the room and stood in silence. His presence elicited a raised brow from the Shadowlord, but nothing more, as he returned his attentions to Apallo.

"Do not think that your fate holds precedence," Zariah warned.

Beckoned by the smallest twitch of a finger, a gesture that most would miss, Zendel moved forward, whispering the newest turn of events into the Lord's ear.

He had been hesitant to relay the new information that indicated the movement of the two teens into the land of the Fae Queen, not sure how the man would react, but it was only received with an amused smile that played on his thin lips. Zendel relaxed.

"Is that so?" Zariah questioned brightly. "Tybithera and I have never been allies, she'll never let him leave." He slapped a hand on his advisors shoulder before letting it fall away. "See, Zendel. Crisis averted. Not that there ever was one." Zariah's eyes returned to Apallo as he spoke the next words with a lay of malevolence. "My work has never been made easier."

24

♦♦✧♦♦

ENEMIES IN HIGH PLACES

There was someone else in the room.

With nothing but that single thought propelling him into action, Kiyani catapulted himself off the bed and into a low crouch on the floor. The pain that shot through his thigh and radiated along his right side was immediate. He issued a grunt of torturous discomfort as the room around him was suddenly thrown into a bright light, illuminating the darkness that he had woken to.

The last thing he could remember was being run down by the Streig. No. They had caught him. But this was no Streig camp. It was much too clean.

"About time you joined the waking world. I was beginning to wonder if you would ever come out of it."

The voice struck a nerve, and though Kiyani had never heard it before in his life, he didn't need the confirmation of sight to tell him who it was. The lights that danced above him in colorful circles told him enough. He had heard plenty of stories regarding the Fae but had never found the desire to discover for himself if they were true or not. Yet, he was being granted that chance regardless of his feelings towards the matter.

Resting his forehead against the side of the mattress, Kiyani heaved a sigh, wondering what the chances of this being just a dream were. The pain that issued as he repositioned his weight reminded him just how far from it was. With a grimace, he opened his eyes. Ignoring the presence standing in the shadows on the other side of the room, he studied the wound that pierced his leg. He could distinctly remember the shooting pain as he'd ripped the unconventional weapon from his skin. It was some of the worst he'd felt in some time, but definitely not among the most horrid things he'd been put through in his lifetime. Pushing the fabric of his ruined pants aside, he could see where blood had caked around the point of entry. If he were to clean it off, he knew it would've produced a perfectly circular incision.

"Looking for this?"

183

Kiyani knew for a fact that ignoring the woman wouldn't make her disappear, and he finally regarded her with slitted eyes, hoping that his distaste would come across without the need for words.

"You..."

The sight that greeted him as he finally gave in came as no comfort. Of all the people he could have woken to, of all the Fae that he was sure must live in this area, the Fae Queen herself would have been rock bottom on his list.

She held a similar arrow in her hand, twisting it so that the knuckle on the end of the bone it was formed from changed shape in the light. "A favorite weapon of the Streig, I've found. They hollow the bone and fill it with frethayne. It takes a few minutes for it to take effect as it courses through the bloodstream, but it hardly ever fails."

Frethayne, he thought. He should have known as soon as the world around him had begun to grow smaller, leaving a ring of haze dancing along the edges of his vision. But if that was the case, then he shouldn't be here. Even with the drug playing with his memory, he could remember with a specific clarity that last moment in the forest before waking up here, when the Streig had caught up with him. He should be dead, or on his way to being so. Looking up at the woman who had grown quiet, standing there in her regal dress as she regarded him with cold and contemplative features, Kiyani knew he would've rather taken the chances of waking up to the Streig.

Refusing to kneel before the woman, forcefully or in spirit, Kiyani made the painful struggle to his feet, relying on leaning on the edge of the bed only once before hobbling away from it. A defiant move to prove that he wasn't as weak as he must have initially appeared. He didn't like the situation he had woken to find himself in, unsure of what this woman expected from him. There had been a time when the Fae were known to be friendly individuals, but it wasn't in the years he'd been walking the land.

As he moved into the open space of the room, a few of the orbs that lit the surroundings floated over towards him, settling in just above his head. Most probably would have found them magical. Kiyani only found them irritating.

"Faeries..." Kiyani muttered, more of a curse, as he shooed them away with the wave of a hand.

"So, tell me, oh Prince of Shadows, how does one such as yourself end up on my doorstep, pursued by a band of Streig?"

Kiyani stiffened at the words, picking up on the accusation. "My name is Kiyani," he declared coldly, watching her with disdain.

"So it may be. That is what Fura called you, after all."

The mention of the girl's name left the smallest of cracks in Kiyani's hardened demeanor. "Where is she?"

"Answer my questions first, and only then may I consider returning the favor."

Kiyani sighed, feeling slighted. The Streig were looking more and more like the better option. At least they wouldn't have been likely to bombard him with ridiculous questions.

"She better not be hurt," he mumbled. Kiyani didn't know why he suddenly cared so much, if only to spite the woman in front of him.

"Or what?" the Fae Queen chuckled, knowing that he had nothing against her. "She only sustained a few scratches from your unfortunate scuffle. Bored, maybe. Astonished. Confused. She's plenty of things right now, but hurt isn't among them." She paused a moment, assessing him as she spoke. "However, she is not part of this conversation. It's you I'm interested in. Answer a few questions truthfully, and I may consider letting the two of you reunite."

"Consider?" Kiyani balked. He knew better than to have anything to do with the Faerie folk, let alone trust them, but that was enough to provoke him. "We haven't done anything," he tried to reason.

"I'll be the one to decide that. You can start by telling me what you were doing within my territory."

Kiyani's eyes narrowed as he watched the woman, wondering if this was a trick question. "You said yourself that the Streig are what led us here."

"That I did. You owe your life to me, you know."

He had figured as much, yet it made no sense to him. The way she was treating him certainly didn't provide an excuse for her to go out of her way to do such things. "You saved us...Why?" Kiyani questioned.

"I haven't much love for unexpected visitors anymore, but neither do I care for the Streig to devour people on my land. They have rules just like everyone else. I simply made sure that they were being enforced."

"But we weren't on your land, were we?"

Kiyani had always made it a special point to stay away from the Fae land, and though the Reln he had frequented was close, it wasn't that close. They couldn't have made it that far in their failed escape.

Tybithera smiled, though he wouldn't have considered it a warm gesture. "They didn't know that, and when they do come to the realization, I doubt they'll challenge me. Now, Faeries, you say?"

Kiyani lifted a finger, pointing at the lights that hovered annoyingly close. "Your kind are the only ones who can create lights like that."

"My kind?" She looked at him, a glimmer of a genuine smile gracing her face. Still blocking the door, she raised her hand. Though she said nothing, the light that Kiyani had alluded to drifted over his shoulder, just missing his head. Making a beeline across the room, it stopped to hover over her hand. "Not the only ones. But, the most skilled. Our lights never fade, unlike human imitations." There was a hint of contempt that failed to be hidden in her words.

"I believe that's an insult."

"Not entirely intentional, but it is exceptionally easy to insult those less superior to your own race," the woman replied airily. Raising her hand again as if giving the small light a push, it lifted and floated lazily through the air before resuming its previous location. "I take it that you can see through to what I am, then? Surprising, really. You don't strike me as one to believe."

Kiyani studied her as she daintily ignored his eye. The loose fitting material of her gown flowed about her frame, seeming to soak up the light from the glowing aura that followed her like sunshine. Her hair fell to her waist in a mass of mossy waves that were accented with hints of gold. And then there were the glimmering wings that flared out behind her in what appeared to be more of a hazy illusion than anything solid. As much as he would've loved to have declared otherwise, he knew exactly what it was he was seeing. There was no use in trying to reject what he knew to be true.

"I believe in what I know to be real, whether I agree on their actions or not. I may not like the stories I hear of the so-called Fair Folk, but I'm not going to deny your existence."

"As it should be. I must say, well spoken. Unfortunately, a quality well-preserved in your father as well." Kiyani was the only one that lingered on that comment as the woman continued on before he could speak against it. "So many go through life denying what is in plain sight because they don't want to believe the truth. I must say, however, that tall tales are aptly named for a reason. Not everything you hear resides in truth."

"You say that, but do you actually believe it?" Kiyani snidely commented. Her voice was sing-song and ethereal, but he could see past the glamour of it all.

Kiyani took a quick glance at the only thing he had managed to keep of his belongings in the wake of the Streig attack. The dagger rested innocently on a simple wood table beside the bed. It wasn't quite within reach, but it was available. He instinctively felt his back pocket, though he didn't need to to know that the knife was his.

"If you so much as think of using that against me I will be forced to take drastic measures," Tybithera spoke, a cold edge in her voice.

Fighting the urge to look at the weapon again, attempting to judge the exact distance, Kiyani kept his focus on the woman instead. It came as no surprise to him that she had allowed him to keep it.

"Besides, you would never reach it in time," she declared wistfully. "You have already announced me as Fae, so I'm sure you must also be aware of the magic I possess. I can do things you could hardly begin to fathom." She cocked her head, taking him in. "Or, maybe you do, being in your position."

"Hardly."

"No? I'm not inclined to believe that. However, I can sense that something is missing in you."

Kiyani tensed at the accusation. He could've sworn he detected pity in her words.

"Now, you already know *what* I am, but I presume that you also know *who* I am?"

Giving up on any chance of arming himself, Kiyani met the woman's eyes again. "Anyone who's heard stories of your kind would know eventually. I would say that it's a pleasure to meet you, Lady Tybithera, but given the circumstances I can't really say just how much of a pleasure this actually is."

The smile Tybithera gave in reply ran along the lines of the wicked. "You know better than to lie to me, I presume?"

"I do," Kiyani replied, wondering just how this was going to end. The queen of the Faerie race was not one to mess with, and he was already doing a mighty fine job of representing himself. He knew it would in his best interests to scale back his verbal attacks, but it was hard to do when he was on the frontlines of the opposition.

"Good. Now, I ask for the last time, for if you do not answer to my satisfaction this time I will have no choice but to suspect and try you for trespassing and treachery. Fura will be free, as I have no quarrel with her. Not to mention, she seems clueless, but you are aware. Now, please feel free to entertain me with your reason for stumbling into my territory and disturbing my peace."

Left in the middle of a disturbing impasse, Kiyani begrudgingly told her of the events that had come to pass, starting with the siege on Frielana that had started him on this fruitless trek through the woods with one of the most naïve people he'd ever had the displeasure of meeting.

Letting the last of his words trail off as he recalled his last memories involving the Streig, Kiyani hobbled back to the bed. Settling down on the mattress with some difficulty, he never let the woman out of his sight.

"Don't worry about that," Tybithera said, motioning to the wound. "Our healers can take care of that in a minute. You'll never even know it was there."

"You mean you're not going to just leave me here to rot?"

"Would you prefer that alternative?" Tybithera spoke plainly, her tone indicating that she had no qualm about visiting that route if she pleased. "What I want to know is why someone of her high status is traveling with you?" Her meaning was clear. "Eloping?"

"Hardly," Kiyani replied flatly.

What was it with people lately, he wondered, that wanted to couple the two of them? He nearly gagged at the suggestion, but figured the woman already took him in bad taste. He didn't need to help the matter along. Not if he wanted out of this stony grave anytime soon.

"She doesn't even know who she is," he continued when Tybithera didn't reply. "She knows *nothing* about this place, this world."

Tybithera took pause as her hand lifted in the air to greet one of the orbs that had floated her way. She looked at him with question. "And what is it that you're suggesting?"

"Let me see her."

"So that you can conspire on ways to escape?"

Kiyani was taken aback by the coldness of the woman's words. "You said yourself that we're not prisoners," he challenged. Though he doubted that was actually the case in terms of him.

"It's not Fura I'm worried about."

"I didn't do anything!" Kiyani said, growing more and more frustrated. The deeper he got into this conversation, the more he wished the woman never would have interfered and had just left them to the Streig.

"Not yet, you haven't."

This was beginning to feel more and more like another animated conversation with Apallo. "You can't base my potential actions on nothing more than a name."

"So, you are who you claim not to be?" Tybithera declared smartly with a raised brow, as if she knew she'd caught him in the lie.

"Half an hour," Kiyani bargained, quickly rerouting the subject. "Just give me half an hour to talk to her and try to explain what's going on." When Tybithera remained quiet, he continued. "I'm telling you, she knows *nothing*. You can't just throw her into this situation and not expect her to freak out. Half an hour," he pleaded again.

The room fell into a stunted silence as they stared at one another.

There was something in her look that told Kiyani she wasn't going to give him what he asked for, not because it wouldn't do Fura good, but because he'd been the one to ask. Yet, he didn't know what else to say. All he could think was that if Apallo had listened to him in the first place, and never allowed Fura to follow them past the gates of Fireswell, they wouldn't be in this position. Fura never would've been introduced to any of this, and though the events that had taken Apallo out of leadership would have still taken place, he would've still gotten away. Without the excess baggage that had landed him here.

"No," Tybithera finally answered.

Before Kiyani could come to terms with her response, the Fae Queen had turned and left the room, closing the door on him and their conversation in her wake.

Angrily, he rose from the bed and limped across the room, ignoring the shooting pain in his leg. Meaning to follow and try his hand at the argument again, Kiyani rested his hand on the door but stopped when he heard Tybithera's voice mixed with another's just outside.

"What is your conclusion?" a man's voice asked.

"The girl is no threat to us," Tybithera replied, "and allowed free reign. But I want the dark-haired one who calls himself Kiyani kept under close surveillance."

"Noted. I will spread the word."

Any hope that Kiyani might've had fell away as he let his hand drop without bothering to test the door. He doubted it was open. As he turned and leaned against the wall, he felt a sudden urge to throw something, but a quick survey of the room showed that there was nothing save the dagger sitting on the table. He contemplated it for a moment before deciding against it. The small knife was the only thing currently left to his name and he didn't want to risk damaging it.

Slapping the wall behind him in anger, Kiyani limped back towards the bed. Even the orbs overhead seemed to sense his mood and floated out of range of his reach. Watching, he wondered if it was even possible to capture one and throw it. If they would bounce off the wall or shatter like glass.

The voices outside floated away and he knew, after what he'd heard, that he wasn't going anywhere soon. Even during the conversation there had been something the Fae Queen had left unspoken. It was nearly impossible to pinpoint, but Kiyani vowed to make it his mission to get answers. The Fae didn't save people without reason. There was something Tybithera wasn't saying, and he intended to find out what it was.

Until he did, Kiyani had the sinking suspicion that he and Fura, if he was ever allowed to see her again, would be stuck here far longer than necessary.

25

••✧••

THE CALL OF CURIOSITY

Two days.

That was the amount of time that had passed since Fura had woken to find herself lost in the deepest abyss of the unfamiliar that she'd ever known. Left with nothing to do but get by on her own devices, she'd spent most of her waking hours letting fear run rampant in her mind. Though the woman who'd called herself Tybithera appeared friendly enough during that first meeting, and each subsequent time after, Fura couldn't push herself to leave the room. Even the misty waters of the falls held no appeal to her as she sat in the confines of the small space, her only friends the cheery orbs that floated along the ceiling.

Yet, as secluded as she was – an act of self-infliction, as Tybithera had urged her to explore – that overwhelming ache of fear had slowly but surely begun to lose purchase the longer she sat in self-imposed solitude.

As the minutes turned to hours, and she began to lose all sense of time, Fura found herself looking back and laughing at her initial reaction. There was nothing present to even be afraid of. The stone surrounding her was solid. No cracks moved along the wall to call for the possibility of a collapse. There wasn't even a single loose stone to indicate such a thing. The water that sluiced down the wall was constant, but it moved through as if just passing by, never accumulating on the floor in tiny pools as she would have suspected. The only threat that might've been had was the possibility of hypothermia from the moisture and the cool stone, but even that was only the imaginative product of her over-reaching mind. The lights that hovered above her in varying stages of dormancy posed the least threat of all.

In fact, they were the only thing, she had begun to realize, that kept her even remotely aware of the passage of time. Like the daylight that she was beginning to grow nostalgic of, the light the dancing orbs threw off seemed to gradually grow in intensity half the day, before fading slowly away during the remaining hours. As far as Fura could tell, they mimicked the rise and fall of the sun.

Overall, there wasn't the smallest flicker of danger to keep Fura from dozing off in the quiet. Boredom became such a constant companion during that short time that she almost found herself wishing for something to happen, just to have something to do. It was a short-lived thought. Returning it to the dark recesses of her mind from whence it had come, Fura couldn't help but remember what had happened the last time she'd dared think that way.

She knew that the siege hadn't been a product of her wishful thinking, but it still didn't help that the idea was there, left to linger in her mind and sprout seeds of poisonous thinking.

Only once had Fura found herself bold enough to travel outside her door. The idea to pick a direction and make a run for it had blossomed in her mind but had quickly died out. Standing in the middle of the hall, looking both ways, she knew that such an idiotic move would only result in her becoming lost.

Just ask.

That had been Tybithera's answer, to just ask someone to lead her back. Fura hadn't understood then quite what she had meant, but as the days passed by, it became murkier. Two full days, and Tybithera's short intrusions had been the only indication of life beyond her own. Sitting on the bed, listening with intense concentration, Fura couldn't pick up on any sounds that told her others lived here. There was no soft lull of conversation, not even the treading steps of someone passing by. Just lonely silence that filled the desolate halls.

Tybithera seemed nice enough, always beaming with eternal light when she made her presence known. Fura was given the impression that she could ask for nearly anything from the woman and it would be given. Yet, despite declaring that she had ultimate freedom, Tybithera was continually reluctant to allow her the only thing she actually wanted – Kiyani.

It was almost as if he didn't even exist. Tybithera refused to let her see him, and was even more dodgy when it came to so much as mentioning his name in conversation, leaving Fura to question if the woman had outright lied to her when she'd declared Kiyani alive. Maybe those strange men had gotten him after all.

Rolling the soft fabric of his shirt that she refused to part with, Fura wouldn't let herself believe that. She didn't want to relent to the belief that she'd been left in this strange place alone. Upon Tybithera's request, she had finally traded in the puffy sleeved tunic that she assumed Kiyani wore in Fireswell, for the dress that had been left on the end of the bed. Fura had worn it for awhile, happy with the fit and the flow of the delicate fabric, but in the end had layered Kiyani's shirt over top of it when she had grown cold. Treading around the room, Fura knew it must have looked silly, but she was also well aware of the lack of an audience that would give a care.

It was the sedation of being locked in such a state of mind that gave Fura reason to finally agree to Tybithera's tour of the strange place the woman called home when she returned yet again.

"Delightful!" Tybithera claimed. The ecstatic glee that permeated her features, making her look downright sunny in the dark repose of the room made Fura wonder if maybe she shouldn't have been so quick to agree.

"Come," the woman said gleefully, offering an outstretched hand. "You're sure to love it."

Fura was reluctant to succumb to the woman's wishes and rid herself of the extra shirt. Not only was it warm from having nearly lived in it for the past few days, but in Kiyani's increasing absence, it had become something like a security blanket for her. A promise to herself almost that she would see him again. Tybithera's apparent distaste over such a simple article of clothing led Fura to believe that she knew its origins.

Pulling the shirt over her head, Fura nearly strangled herself as she tried to get it back on. The gentle way that Kiyani had bandaged the gash on her arm was something that Fura hadn't begun to let go of, but the injury itself had faded from memory. At least until Tybithera hustled over, prying for information.

"It's healing," Fura claimed as she tried to pull her arm away from the woman with little success.

"Who did this to you?" Tybithera asked, worry pulling at her face, making her ageless features seem older for a moment. "Is this Kiyani's work?"

At the ill-slighted mention of his name, Fura wrenched her arm out of the woman's grasp.

"No."

She knew Tybithera was only trying to help, but Fura couldn't understand why all these people were so quick to call him out on anything that involved potentially dark motives. This strange woman was beginning to remind her of Apallo in her assumptions. It was true that she didn't know Kiyani well either, and though she had already seen that he could be caught in the thralls of rage, he didn't strike her as one to actually follow through into the realms of physical violence.

Tybithera offered a hand and Fura reluctantly let the woman take a closer look at her arm. Whether the woman had a vendetta with Kiyani or not, Fura knew she should have the injury looked at again. She hadn't bothered to unwrap it herself since Kiyani had cleaned it up for her. The fact that it barely hurt anymore was enough for Fura to guess that it was healing well on its own and didn't need any further attention, but she knew the real reason for ignoring it was deeper. She didn't want to think about what had caused it in the first place, nor did she want to lose that small thread of a moment she'd shared with Kiyani. Even if she knew it hadn't meant anything to him.

"Ah," Tybithera murmured. "Not bad at all. I can have this fixed right up in a moment. You won't even feel a thing."

"What?" Fura asked, not paying attention.

The woman spoke a slew of strange words just barely audible in the quiet room. Looking down to see what she was doing, Fura saw that the bandage had been undone. But more surprising was the fact that the wound was now entirely gone.

Staring at her unblemished arm, she was left completely awestruck. Not a single scratch or scar was left in the wake of the woman's magical workings. In a way, Fura was almost sad to see it go, as if the memories linked to it had been forced into submission, nothing more than a figment of her imagination. That single tender moment that Kiyani had allowed her to see of him as he had bandaged it. That terrifying man in the darkness wielding the knife that had been the cause of the wound in the first place.

In that simple act of treatment, it had all been taken from her. The physical remnants no longer existed, but Fura knew that the mental scars would take much longer to fade.

"Now," Tybithera started. "Why don't you come sit and tell me how that happened?"

Fura remained standing as Tybithera sat on the edge of the bed, patting the bedding beside her as if she wanted Fura to plop down next to her like friends at a sleepover as they divulged secrets. Such a small injury was something that Fura considered trivial information, but she could see that Tybithera wasn't going to let it go.

"I fell?" she lied, cringing at the fact that it came across as a question, rather than a solid answer.

Tybithera smoothed her dress and looked at her with knowing eyes that told Fura she could see through the obvious lie. The woman seemed to have an unnerving ability to discern fact from fiction.

"A man attacked us in the woods," Fura relented. She wrung her hands as she recalled the event, hating how many times she had already relived it over and over in her head. "Kiyani said he was…" Fura couldn't remember what Kiyani had said the man was. She could only recall the black and silver military dress. Looking at Tybithera's face told her it was best not to mention Kiyani anyways. "I don't remember," she continued. "But it was just after Frielana was attacked, and…"

"So, Frielana really was attacked?" Tybithera asked, standing. "It seems you and I have much to discuss."

Tybithera spent a majority of the time during her tour of the strange, palace-like Fae Rue Keep to ask questions. Most regarding the events in Frielana. Fura trailed behind the woman, feeling small and awkward in the increasingly elaborate surroundings. She didn't know how to answer half the questions asked or even if she should, wondering if Kiyani would even want her talking to this woman.

Regardless, Fura fashioned her replies as best she could. It was difficult, given that she had yet to come to reason herself. Nothing seemed to make sense anymore.

Just as Tybithera had promised, the further they moved, turning down halls and walking through grand passageways, the brighter and more fantastical things became. A sense of wonder filled Fura, but as much as she knew she should be enjoying this – would have most certainly found it thrilling at an earlier time before everything had taken place – there was something else on her mind that left a bitter taste in her mouth, ruining the whole thing.

She wasn't sure if it was the increasing number of people that they passed – all with colorful and glimmering variations of wings and dress that looked better suited for watercolor paintings in a children's book than for reality – or the so-called dress that Tybithera had urged her into that could have easily passed as a really long shirt. Fura couldn't deny that it was gorgeous, but though she had opted to keep her jeans on beneath it, eliciting a few odd stares from strangers who passed by, she couldn't help but periodically pull at the front of it in a failed attempt to make it longer.

With each step they took, Fura did her best to not look behind in an attempt to keep track of where they were in comparison to the small room. There was nothing special about it, save for, in a strange way, Fura had begun to think of the space as her own. As if the simple fact of waking up somewhere new and alone had given her singular ownership. It was a relatively comforting thought that Fura tried not to dwell on. So far, nothing that she'd begun to think of as her own had lasted more than a few days. Even Kiyani, whom she was desperate to find her way back to, had only just begun talking to her. And that was up in the air. More of a forced reaction than something borne of enjoyment. As far as she knew, if Kiyani was even still alive, he was enjoying this. Not having her as a constant, unwanted companion, leaving him free to do as he pleased.

Finding that she was chewing her lip again in thought, Fura emptied her mind of the poisonous thoughts and forced herself to look up from her feet and the smooth floor they tread upon. It was a lovely excursion compared to what she'd gone through as of late, and Fura was well aware that Tybithera had taken time out of her day to grant her the reprieve from her room. Yet Fura moved as if pulled along by a string.

Feeling flighty and out of sorts, she found that she could barely focus on anything that didn't involve Kiyani.

Not that the woman seemed to notice. Tybithera peppered the air with questions here and there, giving tidbits of information regarding the Keep, but for the most part remained silent. It was well enough. With each new thing that the woman stopped to show, Fura nodded as if she understood, when really many of the words Tybithera used meant nothing at all to her. Unable to replace the picture of the friendly and talkative woman that she'd first met with this new, quieter model, Fura told herself that the silence was just her way of giving her time to adjust to the surroundings.

Knowing that she should be enjoying herself more, Fura stopped in front of a large tapestry that hung from the wall. Covering the cold stone behind it, it added a warmth to the space that the darker tunnels where she had been living lacked. Lost within her own mind, Fura felt guilty that the only thing she'd really taken notice of was that the floor beneath her feet had grown gradually nicer. Now, as she surveyed the space, she could see that there were multiple tapestries adorning the walls. Not only did they serve the purpose of making the long halls brighter, lit almost entirely by the strange orbs and oddly burning torches in unnatural colors, but they also brought about a certain level of intrigue.

The one that Fura had first laid eyes upon depicted a gigantic, singular tree in what appeared to be a valley of stone. Walls of water fell around it, encapsulating it in a thick mist. There were no words around, on the textile or elsewhere, to declare what the picture might've been of, but Fura could see that the tree was old and decrepit, indicating its vast age.

She stood before the immaculate work of art for a few moments, contemplating and thinking to ask Tybithera about it, before moving on and leaving it behind. The meaning of some artistically rendered tree that probably didn't even exist wasn't going to help her get Kiyani back any sooner, or tell her where to go from here.

Racing forward to gain lost ground, Fura inadvertently found herself stopping before another equally artistic and confusing tapestry. The focus of this one was a large red crystal. All around it, people gathered, giving it the look of a strange ceremony. The stone seemed to glow as if activated by the presence of the people that appeared to worship it, and the fiery tones it cast off bathed the room in a strange light.

"The Blood Stone of Immortality," Tybithera said fleetingly as she appeared by Fura's side. "A story best left for another time."

"Another time?" Fura echoed as she stared at the hand Tybithera held out to her. Just how long was she expected to stay here?

"Yes. A few days from now to be exact. At the grand feast."

The casual mention of such a thing was enough to slick Fura's palms with the sweat of anxiety. "What feast?"

Just the other day she had woken alone. Now she was expected to attend some grand gathering? Fura knew it was rude, but she only stared at the outstretched hand as if it might bite. As much as she knew she needed it, she didn't want to accept any more help than she could pay back. If these were truly the faeries that she had been warned of in fictional tales, she was already beneath a mountain of debt just for the woman having saved her life.

"Why, the feast that is being prepared in your honor," Tybithera said jovially, a light shining in her eyes. "It is not often we have such esteemed guests."

Fura backed away. This was all too much.

Back in Fireswell, performing in front of all those people, she had loved the attention, but this was something entirely different. She could see it now. The eyes that had been watching her, a mixture of contempt and blooming interest, were piercing. Staring at her. Poking and prodding. Wanting to know her purpose. Her story.

This wasn't just some scripted performance. They expected something from her and she wasn't sure she wanted to know what.

Panic taking over, Fura turned and ran.

26

◆◆✦◆◆

FACT IN FICTION

When Kiyani woke again, he was well aware that he was the only one in the room and glad for it. He wanted nothing more than to get up and move, to find a way out and leave this place behind. Yet, despite being sore from lying in bed, he merely rolled over and stared at the gray haze of the ceiling and the outline of the orbs that floated overhead. The Fae lights were meant to be magical, but to him they just felt like a swarm of watching eyes, placed there to keep track of his every move. They were far from the only thing on his mind, but it was that thought alone that made it difficult to return to sleep.

Thinking about what he'd overheard from the Fae Queen, Kiyani rolled back over in disgust, letting out a groan as his head fell into his hands. Why even contemplate rising when he knew the door would be locked to him? Tybithera was the one that had brought him here, yet, for no good reason, he was the one under lock and key.

The inherent need to stretch his aching muscles was the only thing that finally forced Kiyani to his feet. Extending his arms over his head, releasing the tension in his body, two things were brought to his attention as the lights above sprung to life.

The first didn't require the presence of the orbs, just the awareness of one's body, but it was in the light that Kiyani could see that the Streig-inflicted wound that had previously crippled his movement no longer existed. Touching the skin where he knew the arrow had pierced the flesh, he could see that there was no trace of the infliction at all. No scarring. No pain. The discovery surprised him. Tybithera had mentioned that she could easily take care of it, but from the way their first and only conversation had been going, he'd been sure that she would reconsider her offer and leave him to suffer. Weighing the woman's actions, both prior and newfound, he wasn't sure if he should be thankful or angry.

With a grunt that declared a bit of both, Kiyani followed through on his second observation.

A small piece of parchment, its edges curling in the humidity, sat on the table beside him. The dagger he'd stripped from the Shadowguardian had been placed on top of it to weigh it down. It sat there, prim and innocent, acting as a decorative, yet deadly paperweight. Taking up the weapon, Kiyani ran his fingers lightly along its edge, wondering why Tybithera had left it in his possession in the first place. He already knew the answer. Despite her blatant distrust of him, she was still stronger than he was. Rolling the dagger to look at it, Kiyani knew it was just a ploy to make him think he still had some control. It was clear to him that he had none, but if she wanted to leave him with a weapon, he wouldn't argue.

Setting the dagger aside, Kiyani grabbed the parchment, positive that he didn't care to know what it said. Attempting to read the elegantly flowing script that he could only associate with the Fae Queen, he found that it wasn't quite bright enough to accurately decipher the lines. Walking stiffly across the room, bringing the remaining orbs to life, Kiyani leaned against the wall. Taking relief in the cold of the stone that permeated his shirt and cooled the burning fire in his back, he proceeded to read the note.

Kiyani (if that is what you wish to be called),

Let there be no doubt that there is still plenty I wish to discuss with you. However, I am not forcibly detaining you in the room in which you have been residing. You may not yet leave this dwelling, but you have my express permission to roam as your free will so feels inclined. I am increasingly reluctant to forfeit my decision so early, but I have reason to believe that you are correct about Fura. Not only does she request to see you every time I pay her a visit, but she also openly displays escalating levels of anxiety over the smallest things. If you wish to see her, as worried as you claim to be, I plan on coaxing her away from her room this afternoon. If you take a left and go down the hall you will find a large room with a small waterfall. We will be here if you wish to join us, which I do encourage. Just be reminded that the time allowed to you will be at my disposal.

Lady Tybithera

Kiyani couldn't help but chuckle to himself in amusement. Finally, someone had declared that they'd been wrong about him, and he had in it writing. Sort of. It wasn't exactly the kind of apology he had hoped for, but it was a start.

Rereading the note, making sure that his mind wasn't merely playing tricks on him, reading what he wanted to hear, Kiyani let his hand fall to his side, the paper in its grasp. Looking towards the door, he couldn't help but wonder if he was being played for a fool. The dull chunk of wood was uncaring to his situation, but he wouldn't put it past

Tybithera to simply pretend to give him free reign. That false sense of security was something Kiyani wouldn't allow himself to easily fall for. Even if what the Fae Queen had written was true, he was still being watched, and much more closely than he cared for.

It was because of her damned Fae nature that Tybithera knew who he was without having to explore the matter. Kiyani nearly crushed the paper in his grasp as he thought about it. Yet, it was no different here than anywhere else he had found himself over the years. The stigma of something as simple as a name seemed to follow him no matter where he went, trailing him like a steel shadow, impossible to break and even less likely to escape from.

It wasn't right that he was judged so quickly. For as little as it was actually mentioned, Kiyani could sense it in the way that others looked at him, just as much as how they treated him face to face, if they went so far as to exercise that nicety. Mostly it was watchful, wary eyes and whispers behind his back. He had learned to harden himself against the silent attacks, but even he had to admit that there were times when the clear derision got under his skin. It was unfortunate that he'd grown used to the way people went out of their way to avoid him, but Kiyani couldn't claim it was all bad. Attention had never suited him. And then Fura had come along. The girl who flaunted a clear disrespect for the personal space of others.

Kiyani closed his eyes and let his head fall back against the wall. She was a menace to his way of living. Loud, social, and a magnet for trouble – everything he did his best to steer clear of. Yet, that'd been before. Fura had retained those traits in the aftermath of the tragedy in Barandor, but in the short time he'd spent with her following the siege Kiyani could see that something had broken inside, that that carefree nature of hers had been damaged.

Glancing at the note, he wondered what he would gain in following its directions, what would be waiting for him in that room. Fura was the reason he was in this mess in the first place, locked in some room, deep underground, like a criminal. What did he really owe her? Half-heartedly rereading the words, Kiyani recalled his plea to Tybithera. He had been the one, after all, to ask to talk to Fura. But now that he'd been granted the opportunity, he wondered what he actually had to say to her.

Pushing himself off the wall, Kiyani moved back to the table and replaced the parchment, as well as the knife, as it'd been. Fidgeting as he tried to make a decision, he finally made his way towards the door. Laying a hand on the handle, he told himself not to retain high hopes. What was the possibility that Tybithera would really let him out? Kiyani didn't need to hear the exact words that would prove her skepticism towards him. It was displayed accurately enough in the measures she had gone to to keep him contained, and as frustrating as it was, he wasn't going to kill himself to change her opinion of him. There was as much of a chance of her budging as there was of him altering his own views regarding her. Next to none.

The thought that Fura must be in bad shape for Tybithera to call upon him for help was what pushed Kiyani onward. The door gave way without protest, sending him into the hall. It was more than he'd been expecting, and he found himself shocked. There weren't even guards waiting for him. Just a desolate hallway and the shadows that lingered beyond the reach of the Fae lights. The rocky tunnel extended as far as he could see in both directions, and Kiyani stood in the doorway contemplating which path to take.

If it wasn't for Fura, he would have disregarded Tybithera's note completely and ventured down the opposite hall, sticking to the shadows and hoping for an easy escape. Traveling on his own, looking out for only himself, was all Kiyani had ever known. Having someone else along, especially one as naïve as Fura, was a whole new experience for him. One Kiyani was sure he didn't care to repeat anytime soon.

As tempting as it was to forget about Fura and leave her behind, he knew his conscience would never forgive him for the selfishness of such a move. It had been his actions that had led her out of Frielana in the first place. The least he could do was get her back home. After that, Kiyani would be free, his conscience clear to continue down whatever twisted path he'd found himself traveling on his own.

Relenting as he heeded the note's command, Kiyani took a left. Taking his time as he moved down the crudely carved hall, he admired the surroundings while trying to think of what to say to Fura, or Tybithera for that matter. There was no doubt in his mind that the woman had thought of new things to hound him about since the last time they had spoken.

Ignoring the contempt that rose in his gut just thinking about it, Kiyani focused on the hall as he walked. It wasn't much to look at, but there was a functional simplicity about it that made it work. The Fae lights cast the softest glow, but it was the holes that had been drilled periodically along the ceiling that gave him the most hope. The natural light that streamed through and fell to the floor in columns was comforting, letting him know that, as far away as it seemed, the outdoors, and the freedom it spoke of, was still within reach.

Tybithera's form lingered in the entranceway of a room just ahead and Kiyani approached with caution.

The note she'd left had declared that both she and Fura would be waiting for him, but that hadn't kept Kiyani from silently hoping that the Fae Queen might have wandered off, having found something more important to do with her time. Stopping just before her, he knew he wasn't surrounded by that kind of luck.

Kiyani only met Tybithera's gaze for a moment before turning away and surveying the room she guarded. He spotted Fura immediately. She sat on a cropping of large boulders situated in front of a waterfall that looked vastly out of place within the dome of stone. Her fiery hair stood out in contrast against her surroundings, but that was the only thing that spoke of any connection to the girl Kiyani remembered. Even facing away from him, likely ignoring Tybithera, and him by association, Kiyani could see that there was a slump in her form that declared defeat. He wanted to turn to the Fae Queen and ask what she had done, but he held his tongue. Instead, he took a moment to look Fura over from afar, checking for any sign of injury, from the Strieg or otherwise.

"You decided to show up after all."

Kiyani's eyes narrowed as he returned his focus to Tybithera. Her words were far from friendly, speaking as if she'd hoped, for Fura's sake, that he wouldn't come. In fact, he had the feeling that she would have preferred that he had tried his hand at escape, so that in catching him she would've had an honest reason to lock him up for good.

"I did," Kiyani replied flatly. He wouldn't give her the satisfaction. Not when he had decided to come this far already.

Tybithera stood, unmoving, as she studied him.

It felt like he was being inspected beneath the glaring light of a microscope, but Kiyani refused to budge. He wanted to step inside the room, to talk to Fura and get it over with, but he knew that if he made the first move, Tybithera would be right there to stop him. Even if her motives weren't clear to him, Kiyani knew she was there for a reason. The thought of the woman lingering in the background, listening in on his conversation was unnerving, but it was something he would work past when the time came.

Startling him, Tybithera finally broke her gaze. Gliding forward, she leaned in close enough to speak in low tones that wouldn't reach Fura's ears.

"Your time is limited," she said coldly. "And I can end it at my own discretion."

"Fine," Kiyani replied, leaning away from her. He had nothing to add.

Tybithera stepped aside and Kiyani dipped his head in respect as he passed, though he didn't feel she deserved the goodwill the gesture provided. Her eyes burned into his back, threatening to rival the pain he was dealt on a daily basis, but that was the least of his worries. It didn't matter how many days he'd been separated from the girl he was determined to rid himself of. No amount of time could prepare him for what he was about to tell her. What he had to convince her of.

An endless ocean of silence stretched across the room as Kiyani fought to piece together the right things to say before Fura took notice of him.

Taking one last look into the hall, wondering if this had really been a good idea, he couldn't help but notice that the moss and ivy that snaked along the walls seemed to congregate around the holes in the ceiling, as if even they sought escape.

The yellow roses that bloomed along the ceiling and walls were cheery in contrast to how Fura felt. Nearly two days had passed since she had run from Tybithera and made a fool of herself, and she still felt no better about the situation. A nauseating sickness had lodged itself in her gut, answers to her questions were continuously fleeting, and Kiyani was still missing in action. Nothing added up, and every attempt to try to make things fall into place only led to more confusion.

It didn't help that Tybithera stood in the doorway behind her, lingering like a stone sentry, reminding Fura of what she'd done. She still didn't know how the woman had finally managed to coax her back out of the small room. The only place that she knew, it was where Fura had returned after the Fae Queen's sudden announcement of the feast.

Overwhelmed.

That was what she felt best described her raging emotions in the aftermath. That lonely time when she had raced back to the dark room and remained there, crying until, emotionally exhausted, she had fallen into bouts of dreamless sleep.

Fura stared at the cascading water before her, unseeing, as she wished she could fall into a deep sleep – one that took all her troubles away – and never wake from it. It was a shameful thought, but Fura couldn't ease herself out of it. Not when so much of the world had tumbled down upon her, threatening to suffocate her.

She almost wished that she had been punished for hightailing it, just to get her mind off things, but Tybithera hadn't even declared that the move had been offensive. In fact, the Fae Queen had barely spoken another word about the feast that had set Fura on edge in the first place. It was a comfort, thinking that maybe she'd been hearing things, but Fura knew it wasn't true. Regardless, she could sense that Tybithera no longer thought quite as highly of her.

As sad as it was, Fura was glad for it. She didn't know what it was that these people wanted from her, but she was sure she wasn't the one to give it. What could she possibly have to offer? Why would anyone ever think to rely on her? The daunting possibility that these fantastical creatures might expect something great from her had drawn Fura far away from herself, turning a once exuberant teen girl into an old recluse. She felt like a crab; skittish and hiding away in its shell at the first sign of anything unknown.

Yet, there was another thought that nagged at her. Maybe the Fae just found the idea of a new guest something worthy of celebration. Nothing else needed.

Pulling a leg up beneath her chin and looking to the falls, Fura watched the explosion of blue mist as it dispersed into the air. She hated herself for being such a hypocrite. What had happened to that girl that, not so long ago, had insisted she still believed in the magic of faerie tales? Now that she'd been given the opportunity to live in one, all she felt was an overwhelming fear that the seams of her reality would pull away completely, and she would be left floating in a vast field of nothing, her world having come undone.

She shook her head trying to dispel the thoughts. No. It was all nothing more than a bunch of silliness. It was time she grew up and faced reality.

But where did you start when reality had begun to mirror a land of dreams?

Just beyond the sounds of the crashing falls, Fura swore she could hear voices. Not wanting to meet any more of the Fae Queen's friends, or advisors, or whatever they were called in this place, she childishly pretended not to hear a thing. For all she knew Tybithera was talking to herself, and she was perfectly fine letting herself believe that. It wasn't until Fura heard a stone skittering across the floor that she finally turned in frustration, wondering just how rude it would be if she asked Tybithera to leave. Surely there was something more important for the woman to do than keep an eye on her.

But Tybithera wasn't the only other person in the room.

Fura's breath caught as she took in the familiar sight, wondering if she had begun to hallucinate now. Telling herself that her vision wasn't failing her, she could feel the smile growing on her face as she suppressed a squeal of delight. Oblivious, Kiyani scanned the floor, searching out the stone that had given him away.

It wasn't until he gave up and their eyes met that Fura finally bounded off the rocks and raced towards him. Without thinking, she threw her arms around him, glad to be reunited with someone she knew. Feeling Kiyani tense beneath her grasp, Fura released him and backed away, heat rising in her cheeks. Tangling her arms behind her back, she stared at the floor. Her face burned in embarrassment, but the blood that flowed through her veins had turned to ice, hoping that she hadn't destroyed any possibility of conversation with him in that one bold move.

"Sorry," Fura mumbled. Digging her toe into the ground, afraid to meet his eye, she added, "You're okay…"

Kiyani nodded simply. "You?"

Relieved not to hear the anger she'd expected, she looked up, giving a faint smile and a nod of her own in reply.

"Good."

Fura had spent the better part of a week waiting for this exact moment, but now that it had arrived she only felt awkward as she shifted uneasily in the silence that had fallen between them. A silence that Kiyani made no move to remedy. Facing the reality of the situation, Fura didn't know what she'd honestly expected. Surely not that he would jump for joy at their reunion. Chancing a second look at him, Fura could see that he wasn't even fully present. There was a shift in his eyes that told he was deep in thoughts hidden to her. Reminding herself not to set her hopes too high, Fura came to the conclusion that he was probably plotting how to get rid of her again.

"What are you thinking?" she finally asked when the silence became too much to bear.

"That it would be better for both of us to drop you off in Barandor, and hope that you forgot any of this ever happened."

The admission left Fura wanting to cry. So, she'd been right. In the first few words spoken to her, she could see with crystal clarity that Kiyani was devising a way to relieve himself of her presence. Crossing her arms, Fura hugged them to her chest, the gesture offering no real comfort.

"You really think I could just forget all this?"

In a way it was a lovely notion, but highly unlikely. This was one of the strangest dreams she'd ever found herself in, and Fura knew that even if she were to wake up one morning to find that it had been just that, that the events it had spoken of would never leave her memory.

"Wishful thinking," Kiyani declared.

Glancing at her, he held her gaze for a fleeting moment before walking to the water's edge.

Fura followed, not knowing what to say. "You know that's unlikely."

"Barandor is where you belong."

There was a callous edge to his voice that Fura couldn't ignore. It reminded her of that fleeting moment before he'd unexpectedly drawn that dagger on her. He had never used it, and Fura couldn't see it on his person, but she still took a cautionary step away from him.

"You can't just drop me off like some unwanted animal," Fura said. The words came across as more confrontational than she had meant them to be, but she didn't take it back. All she wanted was answers. To anything. To everything. Nothing had made the slightest bit of sense in her life since the explosion and that first blazing fire.

Kiyani turned on her. "And just where do you expect to go here?" he asked angrily, his eyes taking on a darker shade, as if a storm brewed in their blue depths.

"Just tell me what's going on," Fura pleaded. It was a small hope that the softness in her tone might diffuse the anger she could see was lying in wait.

"Like you would even believe me," Kiyani huffed.

"You don't know that."

Kiyani crossed his arms. Standing tall and tense, the look on his face bordered disgust, making Fura wonder what she had done to earn this sudden change in him.

"I'm sure of it," he declared scornfully before turning away.

Fura watched him as he took to pacing before the running stream, giving off the appearance of a trapped animal seeking escape.

"Try me," she begged.

She didn't understand what the big deal was. After everything that she'd seen as of late she was beginning to question her own sanity anyway. What more did he think he could add that she wouldn't believe?

"Fine," Kiyani declared roughly, approaching her for a moment before turning on his heel and walking away again, continuing his prowl. There was silence as he searched for the best way to begin, but as promised he continued speaking. "Have you heard of the Sect of Seven?" he asked. "I believe they talk about it a bit in school."

As if he needed to refresh her memory. When the teachers weren't busy cramming the necessities of life into their malleable minds, the Sect of Seven, and the related stories, often took over. Like some strange cult mythology, it had almost become Barandor's equivalent of Big Foot. Fura was fascinated by the fact that Kiyani would bring up such a subject, but it was what his words implied that caused her to stray from the topic.

"I don't remember you," she said, looking at him closer as if that might jog her memory. "Did you go to school in Barandor?"

"Once upon a time, yes. Now, yes or no?"

"Yeah, sure," Fura said brightly. "The one with the seven lords of the elements or whatever." For once it was something she actually knew about.

Kiyani stopped mid-step and looked at her with shock just before his gaze hardened in response. For a moment it had appeared that he might quell his usual sidelined anger and stop his pacing to actually talk to her, but now he just turned away, roughly shaking his head in disgust with the situation.

"No," he declared suddenly, clearly fed up. "I'm not doing this." Kiyani pointed a finger at her. "I don't know how, but you're going back. You don't belong in this place."

Fura's heart sank. She had expected a bit of anger following the events of what had happened on her account. Yet, after not seeing him for days, she'd thought he might have at least tried to be a bit nicer in light of the situation. Instead, it was only the same clear contempt that he seemed to hold in reserve for her.

"And where do I belong?" she asked, trying to still the tremble in her lip.

"Not here," Kiyani said irritably. Spinning on his heel, he stormed towards the entrance where he was well aware Tybithera stood, listening to their conversation unfold. It didn't matter to him. "Damn Apallo for not telling you anything," he spat. "This was his job, not mine!"

Despite the unfriendly air of the words she'd just been able to make out as he had disagreeably muttered them, Fura followed. They had only just been reunited. She couldn't lose him again.

For much different reasons, Tybithera moved into the center of the doorway, blocking Kiyani's path. Though Fura silently thanked the woman for successfully accomplishing what she knew she couldn't, she wasn't sure she wanted to know just how far the Fae Queen would go to implicate the measure. It was hard to tell without words to confirm, but Tybithera's face seemed to declare that she was searching for a way to restrain him.

It was disrespectful, she knew, but Fura ignored Tybithera and focused instead on the black-haired man that she had come to regard as a friend, despite his open difference in opinion.

"Kiyani," she shouted, afraid to approach him any further. "You're all I have!"

Fura hated the tears that could be heard in her voice, but there was no taking them back. There was no telling without the presence of a mirror just how frantic and disheveled she must have looked, or what he was thinking, but it was enough for Kiyani to take pause. He turned his head just far enough so that she could see the profile of his face over his shoulder. Though he didn't actually look at her, he seemed to be waiting to see if what she had to say was worth his time.

"I've been alone and confused," Fura started shakily, speaking words that she doubted he cared about. "I have no idea where I am, or what's going on. All I know is that something isn't right. If you want to make up some story to satisfy me, that's fine. I just need to hear something."

"There is nothing I have to say that you would believe," Kiyani said, his words forcibly calm.

"I believe that your time here is done," Tybithera interrupted. The darkness of her voice was a warning as she moved forward, intent on breaking them up and taking Kiyani away.

Fura knew that she should have felt a deeper level of fear... from Kiyani... from interfering with the Fae Queen's wishes... but the sinking feeling in her gut urged her to take action before it was too late.

If she let Tybithera separate the two of them again, Fura was certain she would never have answers.

Making a rash decision, Fura rushed forward and grabbed Kiyani's arm, forcefully turning him to face her. If looks were strong enough to kill, she would have dropped dead from the intensity in his eyes. Ignoring both Kiyani, and the intrigue on Tybithera's face, Fura let the brunt of her emotions spill forth, before either of them could speak.

"You keep telling me that I don't know where I am," she said with haste, speaking only to Kiyani. "That I don't know anything. You get mad at me for no reason, and you keep trying to drop me off in Barandor for reasons I can't understand, when you know very well that I have nowhere to go. Apallo let me stay in Frielana for a reason." Fura took a breath. Ignoring Tybithera who hovered just behind him, the only thing she could focus on was Kiyani's eyes, trying to judge his reaction to her forwardness. There was nothing in his face to say that his anger had lessened, but he was listening as far as she knew. "You say I don't know where I am... so tell me."

The pounding water from the falls was the only thing that cut through the silence in the wake of her outburst. Biting her lip as she held back tears, Fura was sure that despite her pleas, Kiyani would turn and leave. If Tybithera didn't escort him out first.

Time was still as Kiyani stood poised with narrowed eyes as if cementing his final judgment of her, but to Fura's surprise, he was the first to make a move. He peered over his shoulder at the silent Fae Queen before strolling past Fura without a word.

"One more outburst like that and you're never leaving that room again," Tybithera warned him.

Though it wasn't directed at her, Fura cringed at the comment. She looked at Tybithera but didn't wait for confirmation before turning and following Kiyani.

Shadowing his movements, Fura waited until he'd settled himself on the rocks not far from where she had been sitting earlier, before following suit. Keeping a wary eye on him, unsure of what was going to happen, she kept herself just out of his reach as she moved in front of him. She was reluctant to sit beside him, but there was something about his defeated posture and the contemplation in his eyes, as he stared past her and into the falls, that told Fura she wasn't in any immediate danger.

Minutes elapsed at a mind-numbing crawl, yet Kiyani was as silent as the night sky that he so often reminded Fura of. It was as if he had shut himself down in order to recover from the blast of rage that had poured from him like a stream of molten rock. Though every passing moment only increased her fear of the answers she might receive, Fura finally took it upon herself to urge him into conversation.

"Say something. Anything."

Kiyani looked at her, but still remained quiet.

"You mentioned the Sect of Seven. Start there. What can that possibly have to do with any of this?" Fura asked. It was strange that he had mentioned such a thing. This wasn't exactly the time for bedtime stories. "It's just a fairy tale."

That seemed to be enough to stir Kiyani back into words. "And where exactly do you think fairytales come from?" There was still a gruffness in his voice.

Fura shrugged. "Someone's head when they're bored? They're just stories someone makes up. They tell them to people and eventually they get passed on, details get added... I don't know." She wanted answers, not intellectual conversation on strange topics to pass the time.

Kiyani clasped his hands together and rested them beneath his chin, avoiding eye contact. "A few tales start that way, I suppose," he began quietly. "But most stories start with at least a seed of truth. Someone gets bored with reality, and they add a few fantastical elements to the mundane and start a story. And like you said, over time, more and more things get added until the whole thing is so ridiculous that it's passed off as some tall tale with little left to believe in."

"What are you trying to say?" Fura asked, wondering what all this talk of stories had to do with her current situation.

"However, not all of these stories are as far-fetched as they may seem," Kiyani continued as if he hadn't heard her. "There are a few tales out there that are completely true, but they're passed off as fiction because no one is truly willing to believe in such things."

Connections began to form in Fura's mind, but she could hardly believe what he was trying to say. "You don't seriously think that the Sect of Seven is real?"

Kiyani buried his head in his hands with a heavy sigh.

Fura stood. There was no way he was speaking truth. "I know I told you to go ahead and make something up, but you don't have to blatantly lie to me," she said shakily, fighting off tears. The last thing she wanted to do was anger him again to the point of leaving, but he was making it hard.

"I'm not," Kiyani replied sternly. "Look around you," he gestured. "What part of this comes across to you as a lie?"

"You're not kidding..." Fura muttered. "Come on, you can't seriously believe that?"

"See. I told you."

"Don't you think if that story were true we'd know it? Seven Lords controlling the elements around us? Don't you think we'd see one of them every now and then? That they'd make an appearance?" Fura was actively working to convince herself of the logic as much as she was him. Maybe he really was crazy. "What does this have to do with me and not knowing where I am?"

"You're in it, Fura. That story that the teachers of Barandor try so desperately to weave into fantasy. You may think that you're wandering somewhere within the depths of the Verboten Forest, but you're far from. You've already met one of the Seven."

Fura nearly choked. "Lords?" she questioned. She didn't know if she could handle this level of crazy. Besides, wouldn't she know if she had met some high Lord? "What, you?"

"You think I'm that high up?" Kiyani nearly laughed. "Not quite. Apallo, however…"

"Apallo is one of the Seven?" Fura asked. She took a deep breath, trying to stay on track with him for just a moment, weighing the plausibility of any of this actually being true. "And what element does he control?"

"Do you really have to ask? What does he do for a living?"

"Fire…" Fura mumbled. "You're saying that Apallo is the Firelord?"

"He doesn't always act the part, but that would be his official title."

Fura nodded as she started pacing, feeling like she was picking up where Kiyani had left off. "Okay. That I can possibly believe. But as for the rest of it… you say I'm not in the Verboten Forest. So, where am I? 'Cause that's what any map would claim."

"Izandüre."

"I've never heard of it."

"No, I'm sure you haven't. But it's where the Sect of Seven resides. It's a world within yours, yet separated from it."

"Wouldn't I know if I was in a different world?" Fura asked, skeptical.

Without skipping a beat, Kiyani answered calmly. "The portals that connect the two worlds are nearly seamless."

Confused and bewildered, Fura was unable to do anything but stare at him. It all sounded so ridiculous, but Kiyani rattled off answers like they were nothing, not the slightest hint of toying with her in his voice, like when he'd been speaking to her by the spring that one night. She wondered if it was possible to make up that elaborate of a tale in the short time they'd been separated.

"I told you you wouldn't believe any of this," Kiyani said as he watched her. He had taken on a distinctively calmer demeanor than before when he had been controlled by his anger.

Fura shot him a look of contempt. If this was his way of trying to get rid of her, then she would play along. "It's about as far-fetched as your purple river," she claimed, remembering the first night she had met him.

"Then it resides in truth."

Fura groaned. That was hardly the reply she was expecting. "You're saying that Frielana is a part of this Sect of Seven story?" she asked, trying a different approach.

"It's not a story, and yes, it is."

"Oh come on," Fura balked. "No one really lives like that."

"So this last week was nothing?" Kiyani asked, rising to meet her at eye level. "You're saying that all of that was a lie? Apallo would be disappointed to hear that from you."

"Why would he care what I think?"

Kiyani's face fell. "Did he tell you nothing?"

27

••✧••

SURPRISES

Faeries. Worlds of fantasy. Lords that possessed magic.

Fura's head was still reeling the next morning as she strolled down the hall on her way to the falls. The conflicting thoughts had kept her up all night as she'd tried to squeeze any sense out of what Kiyani had finally told her. She wanted to pound her fists against his chest and make him apologize for lying to her. The thought that maybe Barandor was her best bet after all had crossed her mind more than once. At least there the rules of reality weren't bent like a zig-zagging wire.

But there had been something about the way Kiyani had spoken to her, none of that playful joking that she remembered, that told her to at least give this crazy idea a chance. What did she really have to lose at this point?

Rounding the corner, Fura stopped, surprised to see Kiyani. Sitting on the rocks that she'd occupied the day before, his back to her, it was difficult to discern what kind of mood he was in, or what might have brought him back. But it was the lack of Tybithera's presence that left her wondering what was going on. The Fae Queen had never discussed with her where Kiyani had been during her emotional week of feeling helpless and lost. The feeling that he'd been purposely kept from her, akin to a prisoner, had been her own. Yet, from what Fura had witnessed the day before, she couldn't say it was far from the truth.

Standing in the doorway, she looked down the hall, but the woman was nowhere in sight. Shrugging it off, Fura moved forward, glad for her sudden disappearance. Tybithera wasn't bad. In fact, Fura had started to grow somewhat fond of the strange, winged woman, but her absence allowed for the one thing Fura had sought to seek out all night, and that was more time to question Kiyani. Without her listening in. It was bad enough that she was struggling to come to terms with what Kiyani had so calmly told her. Fura didn't want anyone else privy to their line of conversation. Or, if this was indeed all real, aware of just how much she didn't know.

Not knowing how to address him after their conversation the day before, Fura simply put one foot in front of the other and moved forward.

"No Tybithera?" she asked conversationally.

Kiyani turned, seeming to have been pulled from thought. "Scary, isn't it?"

Letting out a breath, Fura smiled. At least he was in a decent mood.

"Still don't believe me?" he asked, barely giving her a moment to think.

Fura crossed in front of Kiyani and sat next to him on the rock.

Believe.

She honestly didn't know what to believe anymore. "I have no idea. It's a lot to take in."

She pulled her legs up before her and closed her eyes, listening to the hum of the water. Fura didn't expect him to reply. It had been a quick discovery from the moment she had met Kiyani that he wasn't big on conversation. At least not with her. Not that she'd ever really seen him conversing with anyone else, either. The fact that he was even sitting here with her was a big deal. Though, Fura had to admit that she was the one that had intruded on his time alone. Had their roles been reversed, she was sure that he would've walked away from the room without a single thought of entering.

As it was, when Fura looked up to see how he was handling her presence, she was left to wonder if he was even awake. His eyes were open, but he stared off into the waters as if he could see something far beyond. Yet the way that he spoke, when he did take his turn, was lucid enough to declare that he was well aware of her and his surroundings. It was like he was two places at once, balancing the line between memory, coherent thought, and physical awareness. The past, present, and future.

Fura quietly watched him, afraid to impose as he absentmindedly fiddled with the necklace at his throat. As much as she craved answers, she wasn't sure she wanted to brave the choppy waters of his ever-changing mood. She had to admit that she'd never met someone who could turn so quickly. It was frightening at times, but not enough to entirely scare her away.

Taking a breath, she braced herself. If she wanted to talk it would have to be soon, before Tybithera returned.

"Those men… those things that attacked us. They weren't human, were they?" Fura asked. Even with all the time she'd been given with Tybithera she hadn't felt right asking such questions. Not knowing when she would return, this seemed the only time to try her hand at getting some straight-forward answers.

She was still surprised at just how forth-coming Kiyani had been the day before. Her only hope was that some of that might continue on into today. Fura no longer had any idea what to expect from day to day, but centering herself would be a big start in this new life where nothing made sense.

"No," Kiyani confessed simply. "But neither is Tybithera."

It wasn't the biggest shock to Fura. She had known that the minute she'd met the woman, unable to deny the obvious, but to hear Kiyani confirm it did little for her shriveling sense of reality.

"I didn't think so," Fura said with a sigh. "So, faeries... they're real?"

"As real as you and I."

"Is the food safe?" She hadn't dared to ask Tybithera for fear of offending the woman, but it was something that had been on Fura's mind since she had introduced herself as the Fae Queen. A remnant of the stories of her childhood that claimed to eat any food of the faeries was to trap oneself in their realm for eternity.

"Tell me you haven't spent the last three days not eating?"

"No," Fura huffed. She couldn't imagine how hungry she would be now if she had refused to eat all those days, though she certainly hadn't gorged herself either when food had been presented. But, the lingering thought had been with her with every bite, making everything taste like ash in her mouth.

Given Kiyani's reaction, she was sure she could thankfully cross that off as a lie.

"You can still go back, you know."

"I don't think so."

Fura didn't have to ask to know that he spoke of Barandor. A part of her wanted to go back to what her head told her was still home. Another told her to stay just to spite Kiyani, and to follow the new feeling that had begun to form in her gut. One that told her there was something more to this place. After her conversation with Kiyani the day before, Fura now knew that to be truth. But that still didn't explain the feeling that she was suddenly a part of something so much larger than she ever could have fathomed.

"Why do you hate me so much?" Fura said, breaking the preliminary silence that had crusted over between them again, building upon what felt like a permanent frost that waited continually in the wings of their conversations. Despite everything else, it was one question that continued to front itself before so many others.

Kiyani flinched, finally broken from the depth of his reverie as he turned and looked at her with furrowed brows. "I don't."

Fura looked at him, finally allowing herself to meet his gaze, those startling blue eyes reminding her of a frozen pond. They currently held a hint of confusion, as if he really wasn't aware that his words affected her so strongly, that they made her question herself continuously.

"You make it seem that way," she mumbled, suddenly feeling self-conscious for even bringing it up. "Despite what you seem to think, I really have nothing left in Barandor. The only people I considered friends, and that I could count on, were the members of the Fireswell Firedancers, and I don't even have that now. I honestly have nowhere to go."

"And you think I do?"

His answer shocked her. In the dancing chaos of her growing confusion, she had never stopped to realize that he was just as much of a fugitive as she was, with no life and no home. Fura had just assumed, given that he wasn't actually from Frielana, that he had somewhere to go. That he was being slowly drawn to where he'd come from in the first place.

She wanted to say something, to apologize, but Fura couldn't form the words. She knew so little about the man beside her, but from what she'd gathered, she didn't see him responding well to sentiment or sympathy. It reminded her that one of the reasons she had been drawn to his company in the first place had been his lack of sympathy for her situation.

"I just think it would be better than you wandering around here," Kiyani continued. "There's danger lurking around nearly every corner here. Things that I can't even begin to explain, others that would take too long, and even more that I wouldn't even think to try because it's just something I grew up knowing."

"You could try," Fura offered expectantly.

With a sigh, Kiyani leaned back against the rocks. Searching her face, he seemed to contemplate what he was doing. "You're not giving up, are you?"

Shaking her head with a sad smile, Fura hoped that whatever this conversation might hold it wouldn't end in near disaster like the last time they had spoken. "Do you really blame me?"

"No," Kiyani responded, running a hand through his hair. "So what do you want to know?"

"Everything?" Fura answered warily, aware of the hesitation in Kiyani's voice.

"You might want to start a bit smaller than that. I'm telling you, you have no idea what you're getting yourself into."

There was a sinking feeling in Fura's gut as she looked at Kiyani. Even if he wasn't going to continuously hound her about her decision regarding his determination to send her on a one way trip back to Barandor, it was apparent in his words that he was still trying to convince her, albeit a different fashion.

"I'll manage," Fura tried to assure him. She couldn't deny the itch she felt to return to the one place she knew, but she wasn't going to take the bait.

Kiyani raised a brow. "We'll see."

"You said those men weren't human," Fura started, determined to not allow him the chance to reconsider his offer. "What were they?" She found herself suddenly afraid of the answer she might receive. Faeries were one thing. Deadly races of strange creatures that could almost pass for human were another. "Trolls?" she tried. It was the only thing she could come up with that might accurately describe what she had seen.

"I suppose that's what the fairytales would deem them, but they're not quite the same. They wouldn't think too highly of you if you were to call them that, for one."

Fura snorted. Those things had joked about eating the two of them as if it were normal conversation. "I don't think they thought too highly of us, anyways. They looked almost human, but they weren't. So, what *would* you call them?"

"They're a race called the Streigvaiine, but most commonly just referred to as the Streig," Kiyani began without hesitation. "They're probably where your modern mythology of trolls originates, but they're far from the textbook stories. I guess you could say they have some of the same menacing features that you would associate with trolls – the wide-set faces, the minimal clothing made of animal hide, strong build. They're a lot skinnier than people claim trolls to be. Also, a lot closer to the look of humans, and a hell of a lot smarter than the bumbling oafs of your tales. They live in fancier accommodations than under bridges, too."

He showed no sign of fear connected to that night. Something that surprised Fura. She had chills just thinking about it. What else had he seen in his lifetime, she wondered, that could so harden him to something like that?

"And I take it they eat us, that that's not a fairytale rumor like the Fae food?" Fura shuddered as she recalled some of the conversation she had overheard from these Streig.

"Humans, among other things I'm sure. Though, I'm no expert on their race. I've only heard of them, might have seen them from afar once, but I've never had a real encounter with them before."

Fura looked away. "That's my fault, isn't it?"

"No," Kiyani said, surprising her yet again. "They have a heightened sense of smell, so they likely would have detected us, regardless."

"Why didn't Kiedo warn us?" Fura asked, suddenly remembering the wolf. She had never thought, upon first meeting the beast, that she would actually find one day that she missed his presence. Especially, so soon.

"As much as I enjoy having him around, he can't always be there for me. He is a wild animal, after all. He was probably out hunting."

An image of the Streig passed through her mind and she had the brief thought that the wolf might've accrued the fate that was meant for them. "Where is he now? He's okay, right?"

Kiyani nodded, not appearing overly worried. "Should be. Kiedo knows better than to follow into danger when he's not going to be able to help. He's probably patrolling close by though."

"How nice to see the two of you getting along so well this morning."

Both Kiyani and Fura turned to find that Tybithera stood in the archway, beaming brightly.

"I'm sure you have plenty to talk about, but there is a big day planned for both of you. The day of the feast is upon us, and you simply can't attend as you are."

Kiyani perked up. "What feast?" There was a sudden hardness in his voice that demanded to know what was going on.

Fura hugged her knees tighter to her chest. "Is that today?" She had been trying to forget about it ever since Tybithera had first mentioned the occasion.

"What is she talking about?" Kiyani asked, turning to her. His eyes narrowed as if accusing her of withholding knowledge from him.

"Come, come," Tybithera beckoned, ignoring all questions. "There's a long day ahead and simply no time to waste." She spoke the words as she moved out into the hall, hardly bothering to look back to make sure that she was being followed.

Fura met Kiyani's eye, and though she was almost certain that he would refuse to follow the woman, whether out of caution or pure spite – something that she'd been able to pick up on between the two the previous day – he only looked back at her, seeming shell-shocked.

"Do we follow?" Fura asked.

Kiyani didn't appear too happy about the sudden announcement. "I don't think we have a choice."

28

•• ◇ ••

PREPARATIONS

Fura trailed just behind Kiyani, watching his stiff gait as he followed Tybithera wordlessly. From what little she could see of his face as he actively looked around, he appeared bored. None of that hard-edged irritation that had been present when Tybithera had made the announcement of the feast seemed to remain. But Fura could see that he was still on edge, and she guessed that as they walked he was committing each twist and turn in the stone hall to memory, keeping a continuous ledger on how to return to point A. She wished she'd had the sense to do the same. It was a miracle that she had been able to find her way back to the small room where she'd woken the first time she had been led beyond the falls. Fura doubted she would be that lucky if she decided to bolt a second time.

Ignoring that thought as she wondered just how Tybithera must see her in lieu of her prior reaction to this same trip, Fura decided that this time she would make a point to enjoy herself and pay closer attention to what she was being shown. Here she was in some fantasy land that every girl dreamed of, surrounded by Faeries and magic, and she was locking herself away, letting herself drown in fear. She told herself that there was absolutely nothing to be afraid of. Besides, she had Kiyani with her now. Fura kept an eye on him, using his reaction to all of this to judge the situation. He was callous and cross most of the time – something that she was beginning to see wasn't just with her – but he seemed to know a lot more than she did.

Even if he held an active distaste of her, Fura found that she trusted him, regardless.

Her melancholy feelings were quickly washed away as they continued on, each turn they took revealing brighter, more elaborate settings. The stone underfoot gradually grew nicer before full white marble floors emerged beneath their feet, slick and polished to a high shine that reflected her figure. A mass of glowing orbs floated overhead, a few breaking free and following in short spurts. Unlike the lights that lined the halls where they had been sleeping, these weren't the same pale yellow orbs that merely gave off enough light to see by. These were a multitude of colors. Brighter than their counterparts. Greens, reds, and blues danced merrily in the air and Fura watched them with bright eyes, allowing herself to move deeper into the dream with each step she took. Different smells, none reminiscent of the mossy waters in the darker hallways, wafted through the air, making Fura realize just how long it'd been since she'd eaten a decent meal.

Without warning, Tybithera stopped in the middle of the hall and Fura ran into the back of Kiyani, eliciting a stern glare from him.

"Don't you ever watch where you're going?"

"Sorry," Fura mumbled.

When Kiyani turned back around, Fura looked up from the floor, her cheeks flushed with embarrassment as she waited for the Fae Queen to speak. She wondered why they had stopped here of all places. Nothing in the vicinity looked worthy to even slow down for. There were no windows to the outside world, no doors that could lead to other halls or grand new rooms. Only the quiet stone of the surrounding hall.

Tybithera stood quietly, her flowing gown having fallen still around her. Before Fura could ask questions, she began to speak.

"Before we go any further," Tybithera said, addressing the two teens. "I want you to realize that I don't do much in the way of favors for anyone who passes into my territory without fair reason, or invitation. I understand, however, that neither of you planned to pass those borders. Especially you," she said, nodding at Kiyani, "as I discern that you, at least, know where those particular borders reside.

"Most who enter my lands without valid reason are dealt with most brutally. I do not appreciate unwanted visitors interrupting my time with their quarrels and problems. The two of you, however, were victims of circumstance, unfortunately residing in the wrong place at the wrong time.

"I watched from a distance what was most likely not the beginnings of your problems, coming in at the right time to disrupt what would have become an easy meal for the Streig. I will confess that I kept the two of you separated for a reason. I wanted an account from both of you on how you came to be here. I fully expected to hear two completely different stories as you scrambled to make something up that would sound legitimate. However, from what I was able to gather from both of you, both accounts have been too similar to have been hastily fashioned on the spot, and according to my sources, have checked out."

Tybithera paused in her words as a slender faerie with green-streaked blonde hair passed by. With a smile, the young girl nodded her head in greeting. Tybithera returned the gesture before the girl's quick stride allowed for a rapid disappearance down the hall.

Fura glanced at Kiyani as she waited for the Fae Queen to continue, trying to judge from him how he was taking all this. She was glad to get answers, but Fura had been completely unaware that the woman had felt this way. It didn't fit with what she had been shown. Questions piled up, all fighting for a voice, but Fura dispelled each and every one of them, not wanting to rudely interrupt the only Fae Queen she'd ever met. She nearly laughed. Only a week ago, she would have argued that such material was only found in books of fiction.

"Now," Tybithera started again, her voice solemn. "If what you tell me is true, and the fate of Frielana and its inhabitants, as well as the Firelord that watches over them, hangs in the balance, then the journey ahead of you is sure to be filled with danger and difficulty."

Fura swallowed. She had hardly begun to think about where her life would lead after this, but the word 'danger' hadn't been a contributing factor.

"I will help you while you are here, but I will warn you now that beyond my own borders I have little remaining influence. If I can help you get on your way, however, it would be my honor.

"There will be a feast later this night in honor of the success that we hope awaits you. But first, there are some things that must be sorted out. One is your lack of equipment, and the second is your dress. As I'm sure you know, Kiyani, what the two of you are presently wearing would lead you to be the subject of questioning that I'm sure you would much rather avoid. Many towns nowadays are unfriendly towards outsiders, especially ones that noticeably don't belong."

"I had clothing before the Streig decided to destroy everything," Kiyani huffed, though he nodded in acknowledgement of her words, unable to deny their meaning.

Tybithera turned and began to walk again. "It will be taken care of. In the meantime, I have a few things to show you before the celebration, and a few more to give if you are willing to accept."

Fura smiled. She didn't know what the woman had in store for them, but she actually found herself looking forward to what awaited them at the end of the day, thinking that she really had overreacted before. This wouldn't be that bad after all.

As they moved, another Fae strolled down the hall. This one, a male with curly blond hair pulled back into an unruly ponytail, stopped at Tybithera's side. Save for a wayward glance, he gave little notice of the two that trailed behind his queen.

"My Lady," the man said with a flourished bow, holding what looked like a clipboard tightly to his side. Without waiting for a reply, he stood straight and continued on. "Preparations are moving ahead on schedule."

Tybithera nodded. "Very good."

"Gifts," Fura whispered in Kiyani's ear while the Fae Queen was distracted. "Do you think she means to give us gifts?" A small part of her was still in denial about this whole thing, her mind laced with fear and confusion, but it didn't keep her from wondering just what kinds of fantastical things Faeries could give if they so felt inclined.

Kiyani glanced at her briefly before returning his narrow eyed gaze to the man who was speaking to Tybithera. "I really don't know, Fura," he said. "I don't see why she would. Don't expect anything. If you think about it, we're lucky not to be locked up."

Fura's shoulders fell at his proclamation, wondering just what had been done to him that he held such a dark view of the woman who had saved them from death. Sure, she had to admit that the Fae Queen wasn't necessarily on the most subtle of sides, but Fura didn't think anything from her actions during the last few days declared she would do such a thing. Ever since Fura had woken, Tybithera had done nothing but try and make her stay more comfortable and exciting. It was through her own stubbornness that she had spent the passing days on her own inside the little room she'd been provided, refusing escape from the intolerable silence.

Fura paid no attention to the continued conversation between Tybithera and the man. It was wrapped up in due time and the man bowed again before moving off down the hall from where he had come. In his place another Faerie appeared, this time one that Fura was sure she recognized from the other day.

The two of them exchanged a few quick words and then Tybithera turned back to Kiyani and Fura.

"This is Saiva," she said, introducing the other woman. "I hope you don't mind, but I'm going to separate the two of you for just awhile longer. Fura, Saiva is going to get you into some more acceptable clothing and give you a tour of my dear Fae Rue Keep. Kiyani, you shall remain with me. We will convene once more at the feast."

Separated? Again? Fura felt the nerves creeping in again, like a cold stone had been dropped into the pit of her stomach. She had only just been reunited with Kiyani. Fura looked at him for conformation, hoping that maybe he would speak up and tell Tybithera it wasn't necessary. Instead, he only met her eye and gave her a short nod, telling her to go ahead. That it would be fine.

Fura looked back once as she followed Saiva away from Tybithera and Kiyani who remained in the same spot, talking. Kiyani watched her as she left, his face unreadable as he stood next to the Fae Queen, looking tense and uncertain.

She wondered, as she followed Saiva silently, why Tybithera was so set on keeping her separated from Kiyani, and why he was so on edge, blatantly not giving trust to the situation they had found themselves in. This was all strange, sure, but Fura didn't sense anything threatening in their current state of affairs.

Reminding herself that she'd vowed to enjoy this day – no matter what twists were presented to her – Fura turned and allowed Kiyani to disappear from her sights. Thoughts of the impending feast filled her mind as she wondered what it would consist of, what food they would have, and just how many Fae lived here. Interspersed was the question of how she and Kiyani had received such a high honor. She doubted that such a grand affair was prepared for just anybody. Reviewing all that she knew of Faerie lore, Fura wondered just how much of it was true.

"You don't have to walk behind me, you know," Saiva suddenly declared. She paused in her step until Fura moved in beside her. "I'm not superior to you. Some may claim to be, but not me."

Looking at the woman's shining blue eyes, only a little lighter than her short, blue-tipped black hair, Fura could feel her enthusiasm. Saiva's beaming smile was contagiou,s and she found it mirrored on her own face in short time.

"What's it like being a Faerie?" Fura asked out of the blue, hoping such a question wouldn't be taken in offense.

She didn't even know what had prompted the question. It was certainly something she wouldn't have thought to ask Tybithera, but there was something different about Saiva – younger, not so aware of her place in life. She struck Fura as someone who had the ability to laugh at herself and not take things so seriously, whereas Tybithera elegantly displayed the title bestowed upon her, in both speaking manner and the way she carried herself. Yet, there was just something about watching the Fae and their graceful movements and sunny dispositions that left Fura burning to know.

Saiva slowed her pace as she contemplated, the excited gleam in her eye never fading.

"Fura, is it?" When Fura nodded, Saiva continued playfully. "It's hard to say, since I've never known anything else. I could ask you what it's like to be human."

Fura laughed. "Fair enough. Faerie dust?" she asked following a short silence, wanting to continue the conversation.

"Stuff of myth," Saiva confirmed, making Fura wonder if anything that was written in books was truth. "I guess it's real enough, but it's actually just flakes of color that shed from our wings." As if to prove her point, Saiva reached back, touching the tip of one of her wings and then Fura's hand. Fura looked down to see that a shimmering line had been left on her skin. "No magical properties whatsoever," Saiva continued, her voice musical. "But people, humans especially, seem to think it's pretty."

"It is," Fura said, unable to look away from the back of her hand.

Who had she been kidding? This was going to be one of the best days ever.

She followed Saiva, blissfully unaware of the passing time as she joked with the woman, asking questions as they came to mind. Before Fura knew it, between answers and special things pointed out as they wove their way through Fae Rue, they stood before a large mahogany door.

"Now," Saiva said, lifting the iron ring that adorned the simplistic structure and letting it fall a few times, rapping it on the wood and listening to it echo. "Let's get you into some fancier clothes."

Stopping short at the proclamation, Fura looked down at her own clothes, thinking that they weren't that bad. She was still wearing her jeans beneath the stubbornly short dress, but as strange as she was sure it looked, it was beginning to grow on her. Taking in Saiva's colorful attire that consisted of a short, sleeveless ruffled dress, trepidation began to gather in her stomach. Fura didn't think she could pull off something like that. Not only were both the dresses she and Saiva wore short, but one look at the way the woman accessorized, told Fura that she would look even more out of place if she were to dress in similar fashion. Striped tights and spiked hair weren't her thing.

Saiva seemed to catch on and laughed. "Don't worry. We won't go so bizarre," she declared, motioning to her own outfit.

Fura smiled as Saiva knocked on the wood again, leaving her to wonder if anyone was actually in the room.

"Myrian doesn't like to be bothered," Saiva explained. "But Tybithera sent word ahead that we would be in need of her services."

"Her services?"

"She's the seamstress here. One of the best if you ask me. Though you should see the looks she gives me every time I commission something new. You have no idea the number of times she's tried to stuff me into something more 'appropriate'."

Fura grinned as she tried to imagine the woman next to her, with her outrageous hair and dress, in what would be deemed appropriate. It was a failed attempt that only left her laughing quietly to herself. Even though she'd only just met the woman, Fura couldn't see Saiva's bubbly personality contained in one of the long, flowing dresses that Tybithera seemed fond of.

Her smile subsided and the two went quiet as the door in front of them slowly moved from its resting place, creaking on its hinges. The wood slab didn't move far before it stopped, opening just enough to allow the woman inside enough room to peer out at the intruders.

"What do you want?" her gravelly voice demanded.

Whereas Fura would have taken such a greeting as a sign that visitors weren't welcome and left, Saiva only shook her head as if this was a common joke between the two. "You know what we're here for, Myrian. This is Fura. She needs some proper clothing."

The door opened further and out poked a head. Fura was startled by the sight. Far from what she would have expected, the woman's age-wrinkled face was framed by a mass of frizzy silver hair. Myrian's gray eyes flitted between the two young women as if, despite Tybithera's suggestion, she still contemplated letting them pass into her domain. The silent moments that followed felt like ages to Fura as she did her best not to stare, afraid to see what would be reflected in the old woman's eyes. Regardless, she could feel the woman's gaze taking her in – tearing her apart and forming judgment – and she twisted nervously under the pressure.

Without a word, the door was pushed open to reveal the darkened room beyond, covered with skeins of fabric in a vast array of colors.

"Come in," Myrian said, turning into the room.

Still frozen in place from the encounter, Saiva was the first to make a move.

"Don't mind her attitude," Saiva whispered to Fura. "She always seems uninviting at first."

Convinced that Saiva knew the woman better than she did, Fura took in a breath to steady herself and followed the two into the room. Lit not by the orbs that she had grown accustomed to, but by a few burning torches on the walls, the room was darker than Fura would have expected. Her first instinct was to balk at the fires that burned a blue-white instead of orange, but instead Fura found herself in awe at what the room contained.

Though Myrian herself was dressed rather plainly, in a simple, straight-cut, floor-length beige dress with fitted sleeves, Fura was surprised to find that many of the fabrics that lay piled on tables and chairs and every free surface, were of rich velvets, silks, and chiffons in an array of gem-like colors. A few dresses, looking near to completion were lain carefully atop mounds of fabric. One dress in particular caught Fura's eye and she moved to stand in front of it. Crafted of a dazzling emerald green velvet and trimmed with gold embroidery, it pooled on the floor in a shining mound as it stood displayed on a mannequin. Long, gauzy fabric made for arms that belled out, the fabric resting only inches from the floor. It was one of the most beautiful creations Fura had ever seen, and she smiled as she gazed upon it, almost forgetting all the hardships that had led her here.

"Do you think you live in a damn barn?" Myrian declared from the corner, startling Fura back into the present. "Close the door!"

Fura turned away from the dress and quickly did as she was told, muttering a 'sorry' as she did so.

"Good," Myrian said. "Now, come here and we'll see what we can do to get you out of that."

29

♦♦◇♦♦

SILENT INTERROGATIONS

Kiyani wordlessly went through the motions of following Tybithera, keeping his thoughts and comments to himself. He didn't dare voice his opinion, one that consisted of the general grievance that, as nice as all this was, he and Fura really needed to get going. It didn't matter that he hadn't the faintest idea of a direction in mind. All Kiyani knew was that this wasn't it.

Tybithera proceeded with a quick tour of Fae Rue Keep. In that time, he had tried to keep proper judgment of the passage of time but with little success, sure that despite her friendly air, she was keeping him well away from the major sights of the place, and away from the majority of others as well. It was hardly lost on him that they had only passed by a small number of Fae on their circular journey through the passages of stone.

He'd only just been forced back to her side after a small reprieve on his own in a small room where he'd been given the chance to find some more suitable clothing. The short time he'd been allowed, taking the time to reflect quietly, as he searched for just the right clothes that would not only be suitable for the journey but actually fit correctly, had been the only time he'd been given away from Tybithera's prying eyes.

He had kept silent in the halls as she'd recited story after story about Fae life, lore, and history. Kiyani kept a wary eye on the woman as she talked, knowing that the thin ice that remained between them was as fragile as ever. It was obvious that she didn't trust him, and in turn, he didn't trust her. The Fae were known to be devious creatures at times, after all.

As he had donned his old clothes once more, saving the finer ones for the feast and beyond, Kiyani wondered if Fura was having a better time than he was. He was certain that on that level he had drawn the short end of the stick. Fura had no secrets she felt better left unrevealed. She still had barely begun to grasp that this wasn't the world she had grown up in. He could tell by the shine in her eyes that all of this, despite the horrors she'd been exposed to, was a dream world to her. The faerie that Tybithera had sent her off with had looked like some punk girl out of a magazine, a giant smile on her face, and a gleam of joy in her eyes.

Kiyani sighed, knowing for a fact that Fura was having a better time. How could she not? He could see directly through the front that Tybithera put on. It was an artificial smile that she kept on her face as she tried, again and again, with chatty stories and other talk, to initiate conversation, when he knew in the back of his mind that this was all just so that she could keep a close eye on him. Luckily for him, the talk had subsided a bit as Tybithera began to realize that she was failing to get much information from him in her digging. At least nothing that she was deliberately searching for.

They had fallen into an increasingly uncomfortable silence as he had left the room to continue on with the elaborate tour of the unknown. Down one hallway and then another, everything seemed to drift together in Kiyani's mind as he became less aware of the surroundings, and instead dug deeper into his thoughts, wondering at just what point things had begun to change that had led him to this current unwanted position. Every last route of thought seemed to return to Fura. The raging fires in Barandor had been one thing, but it hadn't been until Apallo had brought her into Frielana that his life seemed to have taken an undesirable turn. Her name a ghost on the lips of nearly everyone in camp, as they had spoken in whispers of her fate, had been enough to irritate him, unable to completely tune out the gossip. Especially when Monira, the one person he was apt to talk to, was just as much a culprit. But it was the fact that she always seemed to be lost, always intruding on his space and moments of peace that were difficult to come by in the first place. It had taken him years to develop a sense of solitude in the hectic droll of life in Frielana, to find a place where the other inhabitants had finally begun to ignore his presence. And then Fura had come along to stir it all up. It was enough to grind his nerves. Her wandering into his room in the middle of the night had been the last straw. Yet, Kiyani couldn't keep himself from wondering just what would've become of her had she not been in the shadows of the cave he had called his own at the time of the siege.

The fact that the orbs that bounced lazily overhead steadily decreased as they moved along was almost completely lost on Kiyani. It wasn't until the light grew brighter, and he found himself blinking back tears as his eyes attempted to acclimate themselves to the change that he took notice of the difference in his surroundings.

The Fae lights had disappeared completely, replaced by a natural light that filtered into the space. Looking ahead, Kiyani began to understand. At the end of what was actually a tunnel, was the first glimpse of the outside world that he'd seen since the Frethayne had taken him under, the last picture in his head the toothy grin of the Streig.

Standing in the archway, Kiyani squinted, trying to adjust to the radiance of the sun after spending a week in the recesses of the mountain with only artificial lighting to guide him through the day, as Tybithera moved out into the open.

Beneath his feet, grass sprouted in the cracks of the stone floor as it faded away. He wanted nothing more than to move forward and enjoy the crisp breeze, but something held him back. As good as it was to feel the warmth of the sun on his face again, Kiyani couldn't bring himself to enjoy it. Instead, he questioned Tybithera's hidden agenda as he watched the Fae Queen stroll forth into the light, the silver-gold of her wings fanning out behind her like a shimmering mist. It made little sense why she would quell his imprisonment deep in the mountain and lead him into the daylight if she didn't have faith in his actions.

"You would do well to follow me," Tybithera said sternly. Even though she'd made no move to turn and check on him, she seemed aware of his apprehension.

Kiyani steadied himself with an inhale of breath and took a last fleeting glance down the hall from where they had come.

It all suddenly fell into place. Kiyani didn't have to ask to know why she had brought him out here. A single glance told him that there was no one else around. He had no idea where she was planning to lead him, or to what purpose, but he also knew that he'd been left with no option but to follow. Tybithera had him trapped. As long as they remained on her land, his death would go unpunished, if that was the path she saw fit. And even if he tried to escape, there was no one to help, no one to carry his secrets but the animals of the land.

As if it had suddenly become the story of his life, Kiyani knew that there was no other option but to move forward. Taking his first steps into the depth of his unknown future, he wondered if he would ever step foot back in the mountain.

The gaping tunnel that led back into the mountain soon disappeared, yet the two kept moving on in silence that was only broken by the calls of birds. Golden leaves drifted down around them as they fell from the highest branches of the trees, shedding their weight in preparation of the coming winter. The scenery seemed to go on forever, as did the time spent walking. Following Tybithera's beck and call without voiced argument Kiyani had found himself hopelessly lost in the web of what-ifs in his mind. It was the only voice present to keep him company. Since leaving the mountain, the Fae Queen had been as silent as stone, as if she were a drifting statue, leading him to his grave. No longer did she hold the pretense of keeping up conversation that they had both known was meaningless.

227

With each added footstep, their consistent plodding on the compacted dirt below seeming to keep time, Kiyani steeled himself for what he was sure was coming. He had always known that his death would come sooner than most, but he hadn't expected it to take this form.

Another few steps, patiently awaiting the end, Kiyani stopped, unsure of what had happened. He glanced at Tybithera who kept walking as if nothing had occurred, thinking that having been set on this trail so early, that maybe his mind had been the first to go. Though there were no physical boundaries marking the land of the Fae Queen, he was sure, somehow, that they'd just crossed that line back into unclaimed land. He wasn't sure what made him so certain of that fact, but there was something different in the air, as if a consistent sense of static had suddenly just disappeared, lifting from his mind like a morning fog burned off in the light of afternoon.

"No, we're no longer on my land," Tybithera confirmed.

Kiyani looked up to find that she had taken pause as well, stopping to look back on him with what he swore was a grin on her face. The longer this went on, the more Kiyani realized that he really didn't care for the situation he'd found himself in. That Fura had put him in.

Tybithera turned and commenced walking. "If you'll bear with me, it's not much further."

Not much further, Kiyani repeated in his mind. *What? My grave?* he thought morbidly.

Yet, he followed regardless, nothing in her stance giving away what she really meant to accomplish out here.

On high alert, Kiyani followed, not sure if he felt better or not, now that they'd left her land behind. All of that was forgotten as things around him began to grow in familiarity, lending him the answer to what this was all about. He had been in this particular stretch of forest enough times to easily recognize certain landmarks: trees, the river that ran through the underbrush. And then, suddenly right before him, was something that he'd never thought to see again.

The sight of the burned out Reln stopped him cold in his tracks, shock taking over. He had never expected to see such devastation lay to waste such a mighty tree. Even in the process of dying, the Relns easily held their own against the tortures of the elements, of strong winter winds, and impetuous summer storms. Now, the Reln that had been an excellent hiding place, that he'd frequented on numerous occasions, had been degraded to nothing more than a desiccated pile of sunken and smoldering ash.

Tybithera stood quietly off to the side as Kiyani walked around the gaping hole that had once been hidden from the outside world and the prying eyes that wandered by. It was hard to come to terms with, but there was nothing left. Nothing but a charred shock of wood that still stood crookedly, and a few blackened branches that had fallen during their escape.

"This is all that's left?" Kiyani asked faintly, completing a lap around the hole. He knew the disbelief must have been present on his face, but he didn't bother to try and mask it. If this is what the Fae Queen had brought him out here for, then she had accomplished whatever wicked task it was that she'd had in mind.

"It is," Tybithera said. She moved to his side like a specter. "You've been here before, I take it."

Kiyani nodded. "More often than not, it seems like."

"I can tell."

There was a small nuance of what might have passed as sympathy in those words that allowed Kiyani to return his thoughts back to what was left of the Reln. Though the fire that had destroyed it had to have been almost a week in the past, there were still a few small areas, down along the wall in the hollow, protected from the wind, where the ash still smoldered, emitting heat, while wisps of smoke reached into the air with spidery tendrils.

Pulling a stick from the ground beside him, Kiyani knelt along the edge of the depression, poking around in the ashes. Given the extent of the damage, he didn't know what he expected to find, but he still hoped for the smallest remnants of anything worthwhile of the provisions he'd stored there between trips. Something from the life he'd once had.

"It's already been sifted through," Tybithera said.

Kiyani looked up to find that her attention wasn't on him, but on the swirling dust that circled in the exposed hollow in tiny tornados.

"Nothing?" he asked, knowing there was no reason to remain hopeful.

The Fae Queen shook her head. "Everything was beyond saving. I don't know what you're looking for, what you might have had, but there was little left. It was the tree itself that we had hoped to save, but even that was beyond our help when we arrived."

Throwing the stick into the ashes, Kiyani ran a hand through his hair. "I had provisions," he declared angrily. Standing, he refused to face her. None of this was making sense. "I had money, if the Streig didn't get to it. I had a small home here. I should have known better," he said, kicking another branch into the depression, not sure if he was angrier at himself, or at Tybithera for bringing him here. "I should have had it all packed up and ready to go the minute we got here. If it wasn't the Streig that found us, someone else would have."

"There's nothing you can do about it now."

Her words were sincere enough, but the rage was already flowing within, and Kiyani turned to face her, determined to get straight answers no matter what it took.

"Why are you helping me?"

He wasn't afraid of the potential repercussions of being so straight-forward in his questioning, having already found solace in the face of death.

Tybithera stood tall. "Who said it was you I was helping?"

Kiyani was taken aback by her admission, but was hardly given the time to reply before she cut back in again.

"It's Fura we're interested in. Not you." Kiyani tried to speak but was intercepted yet again. "Now, go."

"What?"

Kiyani had followed the Fae Queen out into the depths of the forest expecting death, not freedom. Somehow it was worse.

"You heard me," Tybithera declared coldly. "You wanted freedom. You have it. Now go, before I change my mind. I'm sure it's more than you came out here expecting."

It was. There was no doubt about that. But all Kiyani could do was stand there, thinking that none of this was adding up. He turned and looked around. At the glittering rays of the sun that caught particles of dust floating through the air. At the vivid colors of green, and the sky, stained in the colors of the setting sun. Tybithera was giving him a free pass, was letting him move through like a shadow that had never been there in the first place. It was an invitation Kiyani knew he should take. But he couldn't.

Steeling himself for the repercussions of his actions, he stood up straighter, his arms folded across his chest. "No," he declared simply. "I'm not leaving Fura behind."

Tybithera's eyes narrowed, her head dipping to the side, clearly surprised by his answer.

"She means nothing to you."

"It doesn't mean that I'm leaving her behind," Kiyani said, surprised to hear the words coming from his mouth. Tybithera was right. He owed the girl nothing. But even as a distinct non-believer in fate, karma still had its ways, and Kiyani was positive that if he left now, that even locked up, Apallo would find a way to destroy him if Fura came to harm. Taking in a breath, he stood with his shoulders high. "She has no idea who she is. Whatever you think it is she can do for you, you're wrong. She belongs back in Barandor."

"And who's going to take her back? You?"

"If I have to."

"You really think she's going to agree to that?"

"She doesn't have a choice." Why couldn't anyone else see that? Fura was too far removed from this world. She had to go back before she found that she no longer fit in in either realm.

"Are you saying, then, that you're taking her place in all this?"

"Her place?" Kiyani gazed upon the woman more intensely, trying to figure out what it was that she was deliberately keeping from him. Even without the concrete knowledge of what was going on, he didn't like the path her words were taking. "I thought all we had to do was attend this feast, and then we could leave?"

"You said yourself that big things are taking place. You don't think that our survivability doesn't depend on this world not falling apart?"

What difference does it make? Kiyani wondered. The world had begun to unravel before he'd even been born. Everyone knew it, just nobody spoke of it aloud.

"Why are you helping me?" he questioned once more, redirecting the conversation. He'd had enough of this toying around.

"I'm helping both of you."

"I told you. Fura's not coming. And even if she was... why? Anyone else, and you would have strung them up without questioning for being this close to your land, for bringing trouble into your region. I know the stories. I know what you're capable of. This friendly façade doesn't fool me."

"It's often customary to be thankful for help, rather than rude and questioning," Tybithera spoke calmly.

"Is it wrong to question that which I don't trust?" Kiyani asked. "I never asked for your help, for your supposed generosity."

"Would you have rather died?"

"If you have to ask that of me, then you don't know me as well as you seem to think."

"Even if death is what you were seeking, which I don't believe it was, I doubt the Streigvaiine are the way you would've chosen to go."

Kiyani followed Tybithera with his eyes as she began to walk away, his heart sinking with each word she added to the conversation. She knew, just as well as he did, that he was currently caught between truth and lies.

"I know more about you than you know," Tybithera said, turning to meet his eye. "A lot of people do. You should know by now to expect it, for you're going to run into it more often than you like."

Kiyani turned away from her, looking back into the desecrated hollow, full of black ash, his thoughts just as dark and angered. Hundreds of things ran through his mind, but none of them were feasible in this situation, not to mention he wouldn't get far with many of them, either. Instead, he proceeded to walk.

"You would actually lay your trust in me?" he questioned, falling back into line with Tybithera's stride.

"That is yet to be determined."

Kiyani stopped again, growing tired of this game. There was nothing more confusing than a person who kept changing their view.

"Either you trust me or you don't, and I'm sure I already know the answer. You may pretend to give me all these supposed freedoms, but I've learned how to read people over the years. You don't have the smallest inkling of faith in me. Don't have a clue what I'll do the minute I leave your land…" Kiyani looked around, remembering where he was. "Again."

"I have no intentions of locking you up, of keeping you from whatever you plan on doing. I have come to the unfortunate realization that, whether we like it or not, the future of the Fae race just may lie in your hands."

Kiyani huffed. "Unfortunate. You say unfortunate, yet you're still willing to put blind faith in me? Willing to let me make choices that you say are going to affect you? I could be a traitor for all you know."

As soon as the words left his mouth, Kiyani stopped pacing, realizing what he'd just said. It was hardly truth, but now he was condemning himself.

"I'm well aware," Tybithera said after a stunted silence. "You're certainly in the position to go down that road." Her words were calm and measured. "But I don't think you will. I can read people rather well myself. I find your distrust in me, not an indicator of you trying to hide your intended actions, but rather a precaution of not knowing what my own intentions are."

Kiyani raised his head to meet her eye again. He had expected the conversation to go further downhill after what he'd said.

"Even if I find you hard to read, Fura doesn't prove to be as much of a challenge. I don't feel as if she would have come this far with you if she didn't trust you for some reason."

Had she really even had a choice? Kiyani wondered. It had been one thing after another ever since the siege, hardly giving either of them a moment to stop and think where any of this was taking them.

"I doubt she does."

"You don't think so?"

"Even if she did, do you really think she could tell you why?"

"Intuition is often better followed than common sense," Tybithera proposed. "Now, speaking of Fura, we should head back. The feast is quickly approaching, and if Saiva hasn't talked her ear off, I'm sure she'll be asking about you."

Just like that? Just like that this whole sordid conversation was over? Kiyani found that difficult to believe.

"So, you're not going to kill me?" Kiyani ventured boldly, finding that he wasn't necessarily afraid of the answer.

Tybithera glanced over at him, seeming to weigh the options. "The repercussions wouldn't be worth it in the end."

"It's not like anyone would miss me."

"You seem to bargain for the wrong side," Tybithera said, regarding him with a sudden interest.

The trip back was quiet as Kiyani followed the Fae Queen of his own volition, wondering just what had happened.

Tentatively crossing back into the Fae's territory, Kiyani was uncomfortable, yet glad for the silence that ensued as he followed Tybithera back to the Keep. He still wasn't sure what she had meant to accomplish with such an extravagant jaunt out of the way, or what had happened during that time. If she had meant to confuse him, and scramble his brain with conflicting thoughts, before tossing him headfirst into an event meant for royalty, then he had to admit that she'd effectively won that round.

As the entry back into the maze of stone came into view, Kiyani found himself trying to come up with excuses not to enter. Knowing that he had no choice, all of them fell short. Focusing on the surrounding forest, washed in the rich hues of the setting sun, Kiyani committed the sight to memory, telling himself that this wouldn't be the last time he would feel the sun's warmth.

He didn't know for certain if Tybithera had been speaking the truth about giving them freedom, or if he would have to steal Fura away in the middle of the night and find it himself. What he did know was that he couldn't spend much more time in this place.

Before entering the tunnel, Tybithera paused and turned to him.

"Given your origins, I didn't think you would hold up so well when tested."

Kiyani stopped suddenly, more confused than ever. "What?"

The Fae Queen only flashed a wicked smile before turning and moving on.

Watching her saunter away as if she'd accomplished something great, Kiyani stood, flabbergasted.

Test?

With all the things he'd said that shouldn't have seen the light of day, he wondered if he'd passed.

30

♦♦◇♦♦

A BLADE OF A DIFFERENT NAME

Standing in front of the full-length mirror, Kiyani could feel his lip rise into a snarl at the reflection that stared back at him. It had been a long time since he'd been forced to really look at himself, and he could declare with perfect honesty that he still didn't care for what he saw. There was too much of a resemblance to a man that he held so much hatred for that it threatened to consume him. Those same blue eyes that spoke of an abyss of secrets stared back at him. And the hair, as black as the shadows that he had cast himself from – though much shorter than it had once been – still couldn't make him unsee what he knew to be true; that he was his father's son, no matter how much he wanted to vehemently deny it.

But it wasn't just that. The clothing he sported did little to change his distasteful opinion of the stranger that gazed upon him.

He knew it was more fitting for his place in the world, that it was closer to the average dress for men around Fae Rue – though the only other man he'd seen was the one he assumed was Tybithera's advisor. Earlier that day was the first time Kiyani had seen the unnamed man, but he'd recognized the voice from the conversation he'd overheard that first day he had woken here.

Either way, it didn't matter. Clearing his mind, Kiyani forced himself to look himself over, ignoring the unease he felt at his own reflection.

There was a time that his current attire would have been normal, would have suited his day to day needs, but that was long gone in the past. Living in Frielana for so long, he had grown far too comfortable in the jeans, tank tops, and t-shirts that had passed for normal in Barandor that lie so close by. The only time he'd been dressed in something similar to what he currently sported was at the Fireswell festival, where the merchants were required to dress the part of the period.

But even that had been toned down compared to what he wore now. Standing straight, he sucked in a breath of air and turned to the side, still not sure if he was gazing upon himself. Gone were the jeans that had become torn and blood-stained, courtesy of the Streig, replaced by black fitted trousers, and boots that went to the knee, their polish so high that they gleefully reflected the surroundings. The navy blue shirt that he had chosen over two similar ones in different colors boasted sleeves that Kiyani felt were entirely too puffy. Instead of the general simple belt tying it altogether, he had opted to go for a dark vest that looked closer to black than the blue it was meant to be, embroidered with silver thread. As sad as it was, it felt like the only true decision he had been allowed to make since arriving here.

It was definitely different, giving him a certain regality that he wished he could adequately strip himself of. But alas, it was something Kiyani knew he would have to get used to.

He sighed, turning away from the mirror. If it made Tybithera happy and got him out of Fae Rue Keep faster, then he would deal with it. Luckily this outrageous finery was for the remainder of the day only. He had chosen substantially plainer clothing for the actual journey. Wherever that ended up taking him.

Readjusting the vest so that it lay flat as he moved towards the door, Kiyani wondered just how long he could possibly spend in the room before Tybithera came in to ask what was keeping him. His precious moments of free time were ticking by, bringing him closer to this grand feast that the Fae Queen continued to speak of as if it were the event of the century.

Kiyani couldn't claim he felt the same, wishing instead that he could skip it altogether. He'd rather be attacked by the Streig again than sit all prim and proper before a thousand wishful Fae eyes. The trip back from the Reln had been quiet and uneventful, and even when he had tried to ask what this whole ordeal was really about, Tybithera had remained exceedingly vague on the details. He no longer had any idea what to expect from one minute to the next, let alone throughout the following days, but Kiyani had a feeling that whatever was coming tonight wouldn't be something he would be happy about.

"It took you long enough," Tybithera said when he finally emerged from the room.

Kiyani just shrugged. "I'm not used to this," he said, his arms in the air to indicate the fine clothing.

Tybithera took a step back, a finger to her lips as she looked at him, seeming to judge his ability to dress himself. "I thought you might have gone with the red or the green, but the blue was a good choice. It brings out your eyes."

Uncomfortable with the comment, Kiyani looked to the floor, waiting for wherever the next step in their journey would take them. It had to have been late enough by now for the feast to have already started, and Kiyani found himself rearing to go and get it over with.

"Is it time yet?" he asked, changing the subject, and trying to move things on a little faster.

"Almost," Tybithera promised. "But first, I have one more thing to show you."

Kiyani's shoulders fell as he fought the urge to yell 'now what?' What other tortures could she have possibly concocted for him to fit in a day's period?

"Or, I should say give?" she amended.

Without clarifying her meaning, the Fae Queen strolled down the hall. Far from intrigued, Kiyani followed without question, knowing that even if he did ask she wouldn't say much.

It wasn't long before they stopped before a nondescript door in a quiet hallway, far from the main halls of the Keep. The only thing that seemed to differentiate this door from all the others they'd passed were the ornate iron hinges and crossbars that decorated its heavy wooden surface.

Her hand on the wood, Tybithera turned to Kiyani. "I will admit that I wasn't entirely truthful when I said there was nothing found in the ashes of the Reln."

Kiyani straightened a bit at the revelation, her words peaking his interest.

"What could have possibly survived?"

He couldn't think of a single thing that he'd had stored in the tree that wouldn't have succumbed to the flames and the heat of the raging inferno he'd escaped.

"Come with me. I'll show you."

Not bothering with the iron knocker, Tybithera pushed the door open and entered the dark interior of the room.

Not knowing what to expect, Kiyani followed, Tybithera's admission grabbing his attention for at least a moment. He was still far from comfortable with this woman, and this feast and what it meant for him, but if she'd found something of his worth saving, then he wanted it back.

The first thing that struck him was how out of place this room felt compared to the rest of the Keep. Unlike the halls, and many of the single rooms that were lit by masses of Fae lights, Kiyani could see that not a single orb resided within. It almost made him smile. Instead, the only light provided came from a number of torches on the walls, and a large fireplace at the far end of the room.

But it was what the room contained that caught Kiyani's eye.

"Yes," Tybithera proclaimed merrily from behind him. "Despite all our magic, we still have an armory. I can see you're impressed. Now, Sauvalle should be around here somewhere."

Kiyani was sure from the look on his face that what she spoke was a definitive understatement, but he couldn't help himself.

A vast array of weaponry, in all shapes and forms, filled the room for as far as Kiyani could see, all glimmering in the muted light from the fireplace. The orange flames danced along the blades of short swords and long swords, bounced off the metallic tips of spears and arrowheads, and shimmied across the walls and ceiling. Walking over to the nearest sword, displayed on a rack, Kiyani could see his reflection in the molded metal. Drawn forward by an unknown call, his hand hovered over it.

"Don't touch anything," Tybithera said, quickly ending the spell Kiyani had fallen under.

He gave her a cross look, but said nothing. Instead, letting his hand fall, he searched for the man the Fae Queen had deemed Sauvalle.

Kiyani found the man easily as he watched him rise from a leather chair positioned near the fireplace. Middle-aged, with short brown hair and a bushy beard, the man boasted a spry step as he moved towards them. As he approached, Kiyani could see that streaks of silver accented his hair, and his face was lined with wrinkles, but the shine in his dark eyes spoke of a man that loved what he did.

Sauvalle gave a toothy grin. "By all means, touch it all. It's made of metal, wood, bone…"

Kiyani paled. "Bone?"

"One of the most durable substances I work with. With a touch of magic, it doesn't break, it doesn't burn…"

Upon the man's request, Kiyani had picked up one of the blades closest to him. Now he slowly replaced it on the rack.

Sauvalle didn't seem to notice as he continued to ramble on.

"Wolf bones. The occasional Ves. I think I even have a handle made out of a bone from one of your Strieg friends around here somewhere," the smith explained enthusiastically. "It's meant to be played with. Carefully and with caution, of course. But that's a given." He looked to Tybithera, shaking a finger. "You Fae seem to think this is all nothing more than wall adornment, but it sings to be carried, to be used. It's what it's made for after all. The challenge is finding the right person to carry the responsibilities tied with such a convenience."

"I've never seen so many in one place," Kiyani said, mostly to himself, still shell-shocked at the glimmering beauty of it. "It's amazing."

"Surely at your father's estate?" Tybithera said, watching him.

Kiyani shook his head. "I was never allowed. Besides, his focus has always been more on magic, and what you can do with your mind. Not what you can accomplish with strength and a good weapon."

"I can see you feel differently."

Sauvalle slapped a hand on his shoulder. "My kind of man!" he declared. "Any bumbling idiot can wield a sword, but it takes a good mind to be able to truly master it." Producing a hand, he held it out to Kiyani. "So, you must be the one that everyone's been talking about."

"Everyone?" Kiyani asked as he took the man's hand, though his eyes narrowed as they met Tybithera's.

The Fae Queen shrugged. "You and Fura had been somewhat of a hot topic as of late. It's nothing much," she declared with a wave of a hand. "It's just that, with visitors being so rare, the folks around here aren't used to having new people in the Keep."

"I wonder why," Kiyani huffed before he could stop himself or think about what he was doing. "You aren't that inviting."

His words seemed to catch Sauvalle off guard, the smile falling from the smith's face, but Tybithera remained as complacent as ever. Kiyani couldn't decide if she had merely grown used to his exceedingly callous nature, or if she was still keeping something big from him that kept the tables turned in her favor. Either way, Kiyani had the feeling that with that one small sliver of new information that he'd drawn the short stick yet again. All he knew was that this thin bond that had just begun to form between him and the Fae Queen was bound to be short-lived.

"Speaking of everyone," Tybithera said, seeming to accentuate further that she was ignoring Kiyani's childish outburst. "You'll be meeting a lot of new people during the feast shortly, which brings me to the reason I brought you here." With a small nod, Sauvalle moved back into the shadows. "There was one thing left in the ashes of the Reln that was salvageable. Though it was quite charred, it takes a massive amount of heat to destroy a work of metal."

"The sword," Kiyani said, finally understanding.

He couldn't believe he hadn't thought of it sooner. Going over and over the Streig attack as he had lain alone in the room, the image of the sword lying on the ground had come back to him again and again, and Kiyani had cursed himself for leaving such a valuable object behind.

"I wasn't sure if it was you that had been carrying it, not until I found that you were in possession of a dagger of the same make." Tybithera paused, her eyes boring into him, all sign of prior friendliness gone. "One might wonder why it is that you're carrying weapons forged by the enemy."

"I *knew* you still didn't trust me!"

"Hold," Tybithera declared, her voice a warning to him to go ahead and try anything. Even in a room full of weapons, Kiyani knew she outmatched him. "I'm not accusing you of anything just yet. You cannot honestly blame me for pursuing caution. You come in here, followed by a band of Streig, carrying weapons that only members of the Shadowguard, a common enemy among many, have access to. So, please, enlighten me, *Kiyani*."

Kiyani cringed, the strict emphasis on his name hardly lost on him. Taking in a breath to calm himself, he gathered his thoughts, trying not to take too long, making her think he was stringing together a lie. Something Tybithera seemed certain he liked to do.

"We were attacked the night of the siege," he started, realizing that this was the first time he'd been given the opportunity to really speak openly about any of it. "It must have gotten out quickly that we weren't among the prisoners, and they sent out a scout... an assassin, really. Fura wandered off by herself, and I had to go save her ass. We're lucky it was only one guard."

"You truly resent having her by your side, don't you?" Tybithera asked, noting the edge of anger in his voice.

"Babysitting wasn't my first choice of action."

"So I can see. So, this guard... what became of him?"

"A one way trip through the void," Kiyani said, avoiding her gaze as well as the use of the word death. He still felt like he couldn't get the blood off his hands.

"I see," Tybithera spoke flatly, seeming to weigh her options of what to do with him in lieu of his confession. "Well then, let us hope that no one else happens to get in your way."

As if on cue, Sauvalle returned, interrupting the awkward conversation. In his hands he held a bundle wrapped in velvet, and secured by a gold cord. Kiyani didn't have to ask to know that it contained a sword.

Forgetting Tybithera's presence, he watched the man unwrap the blade, the folds of fabric falling away to reveal the polished metal gleaming in stark contrast.

"It was quite the sight when it was brought here," Sauvalle said. "Looking like it had been pulled straight out of the pits of hell, but it was nothing a little work and polish couldn't take care of. Given its origins I hate to say it, but it really was a beautiful sword in its own way. I'm sure that even you know that carrying a blade, easily recognized as one of the Shadowguard, is not only dangerous but can invite some rather unpleasant conversation."

Kiyani nodded, wondering what the man could have possibly done to it, and why he couldn't have just been presented a new sword altogether. Let the weapons of the Shadowguard rot where they had been made. Looking around, Kiyani felt a pang of jealousy at the racks of blades that seemed to wink at him in the dancing light of the fires, wishing that the accursed sword he'd picked up had melted in the blaze.

"Now, it would have been easier to give you one of my own creations," Sauvalle said, seeming to read Kiyani's mind. "But I must say, I love the thought of a challenge, and this was certainly one. And now, especially after hearing how it came into your hands, I feel that you deserve to keep it."

Sauvalle waved Kiyani closer.

"I don't know how well you looked it over in the short time you had it, but you may have noticed, or already been aware, of the etchings in the blade that mark it as one of the Shadowguard's. Those engravings go rather deep, so it was impossible to fully rid the metal of them without weakening the blade. And then the hilt was another story. The black iron cross, surrounded by the entwined silver snakes was rather conspicuous, so I had to change it out completely."

The smith paused for a moment, taking the time to finally reveal the whole of the blade. Kiyani gasped, wondering if the man was simply joking with him by claiming that it was the same sword. Flipping it gracefully, Sauvalle presented it hilt first to Kiyani, who took it, weighing it carefully in his hands before turning it and running his hand along the newly fashioned hilt.

It was stunning. The course black metal, that had been rough under his hands, had been replaced by a dark antiqued silver, the metal looking almost like liquid despite being solid. A large, pale blue stone sat embedded in the pommel. As promised the menacing snakes were gone. But what Kiyani found the most dazzling were the veins of blue that ran along the length of the blade. Wondering if the light was merely playing tricks on him, he ran a hand along the cool metal.

Sauvalle grinned. "Couldn't let it leave without the smallest touch of magic. That sword will never break on you."

"This is really the same sword?" Kiyani asked, astounded by the level of craftsmanship.

"Hard to believe, isn't it?" It was clear the man was proud of himself.

Leaning in, Sauvalle studied the blade along with Kiyani.

"I don't do reconstructions often. Messy work. But I must say this is one of my best. Probably because the Shadowguard swords are so thick to begin with, favoring weight over form. The best can get some wonderful hits in with even the thinnest of blades, but even the worst swordsman can do some considerable damage with something that's heavy. Give it a bit of a razor edge and you've really got something, if they don't injure themselves first, that is.

"The thickness gave me a lot of metal to work with, though. As you will notice, it's considerably lighter than before. However, as I mentioned, I wasn't able to completely rid the blade of the symbols. They're not as noticeable as before. You have to look closer now, and know what it is that you're looking for, but they are still there."

"This is the first I've seen it since it was brought in," Tybithera said, moving in closer as well to get a look at the sword. "It really is some amazing work, Sauvalle."

"Any idea if it had a name before?" Kiyani asked suddenly, not knowing what'd sparked the thought, or why he'd brought it up.

Sauvalle handed the sword back to him. "A lot of weaponry fashioned for a large army such as the Shadowguard is mass produced, not made individually to fit each man's fighting style. So, my guess is probably not." He paused to stroke his beard thoughtfully. "However, even if it did, it's yours now, so a new name would be in store."

"I wouldn't know what to call it," Kiyani said shaking his head, trying to get the conversation back on level ground.

However, Sauvalle wouldn't let it go so easily. "I was thinking Betrayal."

In his strange accent it came across as 'bet-ray-awl' but Kiyani heard the word for what it really was. He looked up, his eyes meeting Sauvalle's.

"Why would you say that?" he asked warily.

"What would be more fitting to kill the Shadowguard, and their leader, than a weapon forged by their own hands?" the smith replied without pause, as if he'd actually spent time prior to their arrival thinking of the same thing.

"Oh," Kiyani said, relaxing a little. "It fits, doesn't it?" He let his voice trail off, wondering however, if it wasn't meant to have a deeper meaning, one more directed towards him, though he didn't dare mention it.

31
♦♦◇♦♦
A FEAST OF FANTASY AND LIES

"Well, isn't that pretty?" Myrian said from across the room, commenting on Fura's hair as she and Saiva reentered the space.

Fura beamed at the compliment, knowing just from her time spent with the seamstress earlier, that coming from her it meant something special.

The fitting with Myrian had taken longer than Fura had expected, yet had ended up being a joyous affair. Saiva's tour of the Keep had been spectacular, as had been their ranging conversations, but the hours spent with the two women in this very room, trying on dress after dress, had easily topped it. Fabrics of taffeta, velvet, silk, and velour had been sent flying about the room as Saiva and the seamstress had put together Fura's new wardrobe. And though Fura had felt akin to a doll being played with by a rambunctious little girl, she couldn't deny that it was the most fun she'd allowed herself to have in what felt like ages. Forgetting about the spectacular scenery, and the fact that Saiva and Myrian weren't human, Fura thought it felt like a genuine girl's night out, a time when she could let herself go and simply enjoy the moment.

After a few hours of trying on different dresses, and musing over fabrics and colors, feeling like she had taken the place of a princess, Saiva had led Fura down to an underground spring not far from the room where she'd been staying. A thorough soaking, and another hour of pampering later, where the two girls had fallen into a fit of giggles, Fura felt rejuvenated and refreshed.

Settled down in another room following the trip to the spring, Saiva had demonstrated some of her magic, transforming her hair into a multitude of colors and styles, even going as far as copying Fura's orange locks. Finally, she'd sat Fura down, and had somehow managed to transform her usual limp, straight hair into a gorgeous up-do. Her bangs swept across her face, Fura had gazed into the mirror. Half her hair had been wound into a loose bun, secured with sparkling pins and emeralds, the rest left to cascade around her shoulders in loose curls.

"And thank you," Saiva said with a coy smugness as she raised her chin and grinned at Myrian, making sure that the woman knew just who had done Fura's hair.

"Yes, yes," the old woman replied with a shake of her head. "I know it's your work. Not that anyone would ever guess by looking at you."

"I happen to like my style," Saiva defended. "It's unique."

"That's one word for it," Myrian laughed. She turned to Fura. "Now, I know we had a dress picked out for you, but I think I just might have something better for you to wear."

Walking over to one of the piles, Myrian carefully took up a bundle of fine fabric and brought it over. Fura's breath caught the moment she noticed the deep emerald shimmer of the velvet. Her eyes shifted to the mannequin in the corner that now stood bare.

"I couldn't help but notice you admiring it earlier."

As much as Fura longed to see herself in the elegant masterpiece, she found herself shaking her head. "I couldn't." She didn't deserve it.

"Of course you can." There was a warmth in the woman's eyes that Fura hadn't expected to find. "I didn't make it for anyone in particular, and if my measurements are correct, it should fit you like a second skin."

It wasn't long after, following a short spout of argument that ended in a two against one vote, that Fura stood speechless in front of the mirror, wondering if the girl that looked back at her was really one in the same. She had never felt more elegant in her life.

The hour of the feast finally dawning upon them, Fura and Saiva bid Myrian goodbye before strolling out the door and down the hall, lost in another round of laughter as they walked, joking, arm in arm. Chatting merrily, Fura fought the urge to twirl around and watch her dress dance around her, the sleeves floating in the air, despite the fact that Saiva danced about.

The woman had momentarily allowed Myrian to change her into a floor length gown of bright red in response to the seamstress's prodding that she don something more appropriate. But to Myrian's dismay it hadn't been long before Saiva had wiggled into something closer to what she'd been wearing in the first place.

"Isn't Myrian coming?" Fura asked as she followed Saiva, feeling excited and nervous at the same time. She had never attended something so extravagant, leaving her with no idea what to expect.

"She might make an appearance. Though I doubt it," she replied. "Myrian isn't much for social gatherings. She already knows what it's about anyways."

"What is it about?"

It was a splendid thought that all this trouble was being taken just for her, but she doubted that was the full reason for such a gathering.

Saiva stopped mid-twirl and began walking backwards. "Tybithera hasn't told you?"

Fura shook her head innocently. "Just that it was in honor of Kiyani and I."

"Oh," Saiva said flatly, falling back into line beside Fura. The energy she had been exuding all day suddenly drained. "I guess you'll know soon enough. Besides," she declared with a wave of a hand. "We're here."

Lost in the pleasant dance of cheerful conversation, Fura had hardly noticed the grand entrance that they'd stumbled upon, and that now opened before the two of them like a giant gaping mouth. But rather than threatening, the towering arch was wholly inviting. Noise streamed from inside, and bright light, more intense than Fura had witnessed her entire time spent within Fae Rue, poured out onto the marble floors, making them dance as it caught the shimmering flakes of gold in the stone. Elegantly carved moulding framed the arch, and sprouting from it were what looked like vines that trailed along the walls. Fura couldn't tell if it was merely painted, or if magic had given it real life. Either way, it set off the gold veining in the floors.

Two young men stood on either side of the entrance. They held golden staffs that dwarfed even their tall height, making Fura realize that they were guards, something she hadn't come to expect in such a fantastical place. Tall and limber, with straight hair in the respective colors of light blond and brown that fell loosely about their shoulders, Fura could tell they were Fae. The time spent with Saiva and Myrian had made her forget that there must have been male counterparts within the Keep, even if she had hardly seen them.

They smiled and each gave curt nods as she and Saiva passed through the doorway. Color stained her cheeks and Fura quickly moved to catch up with Saiva, embarrassed by how easily such attention affected her.

However it was quickly forgotten the moment Fura stepped inside the massive room. It was far more than she'd found herself imagining throughout the day, the real life version immensely surpassing anything she could have possibly dreamed up. Balling the fabric of her dress in her hands and pulling up the hem so she didn't trip over it, not wanting to make a spectacle of herself, Fura looked around, trying to take in every detail so she never forgot this moment.

Ignoring the sheer amount of Fae gathered in a single place, Fura found that the biggest surprise didn't come from the number of people, but from the lighting, or lack of. There were no sign of the orbs that she had grown accustomed to, yet the room held a dramatic luminosity as if Tybithera had found a way to trap the sun's radiance. Peering closer, determined to find the light's source, Fura let out a delighted laugh. Large, white flowers, the size of her head, hung from the concave ceiling, the leaves and vines trailing along the stone in an intricate weave. Reminiscent of lilies, Fura could see that both the leaves and the vines were pinpricked with light, but it was the flowers themselves that appeared to glow internally. Despite everything she had been exposed to since waking in the mountain, Fura had to admit that it was the most fantastical thing she had seen all week.

Only when Fura pulled her gaze away from the ceiling did she realize the true immensity of just how many people could fit in a single room. Long tables were arranged in lines covering the majority of the allotted floor space. Numerous individuals gathered around all of them. Many were already seated, but, here and there, small groups of Fae stood as they convened with friends to talk. Hundreds, maybe even thousands of them, all dressed in an assortment of colors, their shimmering wings only adding to the otherworldly radiance of the room.

Fura knew it was merely a figment of her imagination, that not every set of eager eyes were focused upon her. But as Saiva led her up the middle aisle in what felt like a grand procession, the thought still left her with a flutter in her stomach.

Wondering just what Kiyani would think of all this, Fura realized that she'd hardly thought about him all day. As if a switch had been thrown in her head, making her feel guilty having forgotten about him, she found herself searching the faces, wondering if he was already present.

She was met with her answer as she looked forward to the rise of stone at the end of the room that appeared to have been constructed as a throne-bearing stage. A single, long table sat crossways along its length with five chairs situated behind it. Two chairs sat empty. Fura guessed for herself and Saiva. Tybithera sat in the middle, looking at home behind the elegant table. Her face was soft as she gazed down upon her people. Scanning the room, the Fae Queen caught Fura's eye and gave a warm nod. Fura smiled, returning the gesture, but it was the end of the table that caught her attention.

The name of the man sitting at the furthest end was unknown to her, but Fura's heart skipped a beat as she caught sight of Kiyani, sandwiched between him and Tybithera, the clothing he wore giving the illusion that he was born into this wonderful race. The rush of heat gave Fura pause as she looked at her feet, thinking that, even in the gorgeous dress she wore, she could never hope to fit in so seamlessly.

Ascending the stairs, Saiva allowed Fura to pass before directing her to sit beside Tybithera. Wondering just how she had found herself in such a place of honor, Fura was hardly given time to think on just what it meant before Tybithera turned to her.

"I take it you had a lovely day?"

Fura could only nod, left speechless by the overwhelming immensity of the room and the patient crowd that filled it. She fought the urge to lean behind the Fae Queen and talk to Kiyani, wanting to share with him all the amazing things she had seen, and to gossip like two school kids in a lunch room after hours of boring lectures. It was only a passing fantasy, she knew, coming to the realization that the way his moods went she would be lucky if he spoke to her at all. Before she could even think to give it a try, Tybithera stood.

Her mind went blank as she watched all the eyes in the room turn to acknowledge their queen. The din of countless conversations coming to an abrupt end, a stillness swept over the room.

Waiting for the woman to speak, Fura watched Kiyani at the opposite end of the table. He sat absentmindedly chewing the fingernail of his thumb. A nervous tic, she guessed. Yet, somehow he managed to look bored and uncomfortable at the same time, an uncanny ability of his to be able to wear two opposing emotions within one single moment. Though she was hardly within whispering distance from him, Fura could sense, just in his posture and continually searching eyes, that he desperately wanted this to be over so he could leave.

"It has been a long wait," Tybithera began, her voice echoing around them as it bounced off the stone. "And an even longer day preparing. We all know what we are gathered here for, and I assure you that you will receive the full details of this exciting news in short time. However," she laughed airily, "I'm sure that our guests, seated on either side of me tonight, are not the only ones here who are famished. So I say, let the feast begin!"

Tybithera had no sooner returned to her seat before Faeries descended in ubiquitous numbers, their arms laden with platters, heaped with food. It was as if they had been hidden in the crevices of the stone, silently awaiting the word to come forth and begin serving.

As the meats and leafy greens were set upon the tables, and plates filled, the mouthwatering aromas saturated the air with sweet spices and decadent glazes. Looking around in wonder as food appeared before her – some things that Fura recognized, many others she didn't – she found that all intentions of talk dissipated in the wake of the tantalizing dishes that teased her senses.

It wasn't long before the chorus of chatter and laughter, interspersed with the clatter of silverware and chinking glasses, rose from the Fae guests below. From somewhere within the room, music began to play, filling the air with hypnotic sounds. Fura dug into the food presented to her, not realizing, until that moment, just how hungry she had been. Food had been one of the last things on her mind since arriving, but now she found that she was consumed by it. The tastes, the smells, the sounds. If she closed her eyes, Fura could almost imagine herself back in Fireswell.

Back home... and just like that Fura paused, choking back the sudden lump in her throat as what she assumed was a bit of a leg of turkey turned to ash in her mouth. Setting it back on the edge of her plate, she took up a glass and looked down at the mass of people enjoying themselves. Fancy clothing and fine food. All the extravagances she had been enjoying suddenly rained down on her, making her feel guilty as she thought back to what had happened to her home, to the people she had loved, and just how far she'd gone to abandon their memory, if only for a moment.

As the knot twisted harder in her stomach, Fura found herself catapulted back in time, wondering just what she would have been doing were she still in Barandor. Her answer fell short. She didn't even know what day it was anymore, had lost track of that monotony of life a long time ago. Even the time of day was lost to her, having been inside for so many days. Fura guessed that it was evening, but for all she knew it could have been three in the morning.

"Fura?"

"Huh?" The voice had stirred her out of her string of depressing thoughts, bringing her back to the dancing chorus of sounds that made up her current reality. Fura could see that Tybithera had paused in her own consumption of food and drink, and was now looking upon her with lines of worry etched in her face.

"Are you okay?"

Fura forced a smile. "I'm fine. Just so much to take in."

The woman's gaze rested on her for a moment longer, but seemingly satisfied with the lie, turned away again and resumed talking to the man at the end of the table. Watching, Fura caught Kiyani looking at her and she turned away, though not before catching the concern in his eyes.

She spent the remainder of the feast silently picking at her food and half-heartedly listening to Saiva, the thoughts of home lingering on the edges of her mind and tainting what had been a good day. It was as if a match had been taken to her thoughts, burning away the good. As excited as Fura had been about all this just that afternoon, now she just wanted it to be over, to sit alone by the falls near her room, left in the throes of her own misery.

The thoughts eating away at her, Fura cast a few furtive glances at Kiyani, but his attention had been snagged away from her by the man at the end of the table. She desperately wanted to ask him what to do, though she already knew the answer. From the few times she had really gotten to talk to him, he had made it clear that he would do anything to get her to return back to Barandor.

✧⌘✧

Kiyani poked at his food, finding that the culmination of the day's events had left him far from hungry. Given the circumstances, he should have been ravenous. Instead, he dined only on caution.

Listening as Tybithera and Sauvalle spoke over him, Kiyani took in everything he could, as useless as it may have seemed. There had to be something in their words that gave him some kind of insight as to why exactly he was here. Most people would have been ecstatic to find that such a grand celebration was to be held in their name. He was just worried.

Because a celebration was exactly what this was. But there had to be a reason to celebrate, and everything Kiyani could come up with stunk of ill-intentions. Tybithera had declared, time and time again, in the moments that she'd spoken to him alone that she didn't trust him, leading Kiyani to actively reason that his mere presence wasn't avid motive. Stealing a sidelong glance at the Fae Queen, he knew that even the supposed test she had placed him before earlier, and the way she had seemed to warm up to him just the slightest in the smithy, wasn't enough to warrant this kind of attention.

There was a specific reason. One that she wasn't openly announcing without a fight. Kiyani tapped a finger nervously on the table. He felt like an animal being fattened for slaughter and all the people below were the waiting wolves, ravenous and expecting more than he could possibly give.

His hand coming to a stop as he looked over the crowd, it came to him that he was right. Tybithera had him trapped in a corner yet again. As everything fell into place as he worked the puzzle in his mind, Kiyani knew that she did have something unsatisfactory to his tastes hidden up her sleeve, and she was due to reveal it before all these people.

He had the sudden urge to get up and just leave, to take Fura and get the hell out of this stone-filled maze before it all came crashing down on them. Judging the distance to the entrance, and the fact that he would have to move past Tybithera to even get there, Kiyani knew it was too much of a fruitless attempt to even dwell on. Casting destructive notions aside, he peered over at Fura again, wondering what was going through her mind. The last time he'd looked, he had noticed that her own demeanor had changed suddenly, the gleeful smile wiped from her face as if she'd started to feel sick. He had wanted to turn to Tybithera then and tell her that he'd been right, that all of this was too much for her.

Unable to take it much longer, he turned to Tybithera, vying to steal her attention from Sauvalle.

"You said that people have been talking of me and Fura." He let his words trail off into remiss, leaving it as more of a comment than a question. No matter what it came across as, it was enough to catch the queen's ear.

"Yes," she said simply. "It waivers between good and bad, but a lot of people are counting on you."

Counting on you. Kiyani didn't like the sound of that. No one had ever counted on him for anything except to effectively fuck up his own life.

"For what, exactly?"

Hidden within the copper-colored eyes was an edge of darkness that Kiyani couldn't ignore. "It's nothing much. You will see shortly."

He didn't want shortly. He wanted to know now. "I don't know what you expect me to do, but I doubt I'm the person to do it, and probably the last that anyone would ever count on."

"Are you saying that your loyalties are to be questioned?"

Silence ensued as she stared at him. Kiyani finally allowed himself to be the first to turn away. It was clear that she didn't care to prolong the conversation, and he knew he should quit while he was ahead. Taking a breath, his gut filled with trepidation, he looked ahead, his eyes unseeing. He wanted to leave, to be free of all this deception. The fantastic food set before him might as well have been rotted filth, for this wasn't a feast of fantasy, but one of lies, and he was about to become the liar.

Tybithera's eyes continued to bore into him, but Kiyani ignored it, refusing to give in to her, even if that was the only defiance he could currently offer. Knowing that his appetite had shriveled into nonexistence, he picked up the goblet beside his plate, filled with some kind of berry wine concoction, as a last resort to occupy his mind and give his hands something to do.

It seemed that it was only a handful of moments later when Tybithera rose, leaving Kiyani to wonder if he had managed to find a way, yet again, to foul up the situation, as if his mention of it had acted as a catalyst.

The hall fell silent once more as all eyes turned to their queen. Standing tall, looking completely composed, Tybithera began to speak.

"Again, I welcome all of you," she began with a lightness in her tone, a glimmer in her metallic eyes. "The food, the drink, the merriment... we are grateful for all of this. For a moment it almost feels like old times." Those last words took a darker turn. "And maybe, just maybe, we will have a future, for once, to look forward to where those times return to us as if they never left. However, we are at the crossroads between the here and now. I know that the exciting news of our grand jury is what has caused you to gather here today, waiting on the edge of your seats, so I shall delay this no further.

"It has been a long time since we have had reason for such grand celebration. Too long indeed. Merely a decade, and fifteen years, ago this was not to be the case. Then we acted as if we had the world in our hands, for did we not? Lavish meals, decadent balls, and exquisite fineries were a part of our everyday lives. And though we still retain some of that grandeur − through strict tradition and self-imposed exile from the world we once loved − it is nothing like it once was. To fully recognize the degree of this downfall, and to bring our guests up to speed, I recall one of the many legends of our race, and the story that relates."

Tybithera smoothed the folds of her dress, catching Kiyani's eye for a fraction of a second before turning away, as if instructing him to listen closely, that her next words were sure to make him see eye to eye with her. Or else.

"In the dawn of time, a stone was born of this earth − of rain, of dirt, and of fire. Though some merely saw it as a lovely jewel, it was a gem like no other, for bestowed upon it was great power and magic. Most outside of our influence," Tybithera said, waving a hand to Kiyani and Fura, "believe that those of the Fae race are born with magic, granted upon birth the gifts of beauty, grace, and immortality. As we look upon ourselves now, though, we know that truth does not hold in this. We are beginning to age, some of us distinctly more than others. Our magic is beginning to fail us, made clear by the dimming Fae lights in the halls... that of which is some of the simplest magic known to us.

"That glorious gem of crimson red, marked by the black star within, was given to us as a gift so long ago that the name of that person, that god, has long been forgotten. Though our gratitude has never faded. Some have declared that it was the Draimaele themselves that granted us such a precious gift. One fact that has never been questioned is the name. The Bloodstone of Immortality. It is what created the Faerie race, for those born beneath it, within the stone of this mountain, our beloved Fae Rue Keep, were given lasting life and vast magical talents.

"But all of that is no more, faded away through time to remain as only a ghostly tale for sleepless nights, a mere whisper on our lips for fear of the memories consuming us in deepening grief. For it was about this time of year, with fall coming to a close, twenty five years ago, that a mysterious man came to us in need. Compassionate and giving, the mark of Fae nature, we took him in and helped him to get back on his feet. He spent two months here, shielded from the icy tendrils of winter, wandering our halls and taking advantage of our hospitality.

"Whatever he asked of us, we gave. Material objects. Information. It didn't matter to us. No request too petty in our eyes. We gave it all of free will, our judgment clouded by our trust in that which resided outside our walls. We told him our tales, our stories and legends, the Blood Stone included. Always have we believed that possessions, whether small or grand, are to be shared in one way or another. The stone was no exception, displayed with pride in the Room of Return, a relic of our race.

"I frequently noticed the man spending time in that room, staring intently at the stone, nothing short of admiration in his eyes. At that time I was unable to read that look in his gaze for what it really was, for the trouble that would come to us. Had he come to us now, I would have questioned his intentions. But then, I was naïve. We all were. What I mistook for adoration, was nothing more than lust and greed. We woke one morning to find that the man was gone, as were all his possessions, and with him the Blood Stone. Not wanting to intrude on privacy, we never asked him his name, and in return he never offered it. When we went to inspect his room however, there were two words carved into the stone of the wall: Nox Rean.

"Since that day, we have secluded ourselves from the outside world. Under law, no one of the Fae race crosses outside of the borders of our territory, and no one comes in without a merited invitation, unless they warrant for themselves an untimely death.

"So what, you may ask, is so special about these two humans sitting beside me? I will tell you, it was never my intention to let them out of this domain alive. However, they did not deliberately cross these borders, but were forced by Fate's hand. I do not blame Fura, for her naivety is apparent. Of Kiyani, I had much different thoughts.

"Yet, even separated, when thoroughly questioned, their stories matched, and an interesting account it was. Things in this world are changing, and we can no longer stand back and watch it fade away. The Shadowlord has finally made a move." There was a collective gasp from the crowd below as the name echoed throughout the hall. "On the run, these two are now rogues, cast from their home and sent searching for answers of their own. I see a future where we may join to fight this evil that shadows our land, but we cannot do so with the fading powers left to our name.

"With the onset of this news, however, I see not sorrow, but opportunity. Kiyani and Fura find themselves on the beginnings of a long and harrowing journey, a quest into the unknown. Though our humanitarian natures beg for us to assist, it is with much grievance that I declare we cannot. We do not cross our borders, not just because of our laws, but because Fae Rue Keep is the only source of power left to us. Stepping foot outside these boundaries leaves us stripped of our magic, of everything that is known to us. We are decaying, slowly over time, but dying nonetheless.

"There is only one way to stop this deterioration and the eventual extinction of the Faerie race. Yet, it is beyond our reach. Until now. The restoration of the Blood Stone is the only way to regain our former glory. The only lead we have been left with is that name. Nox Rean. Though we still do not know the man's origins, I have reason to believe that there is only one land in all of Izandüre for a man of that nature." Tybithera paused for effect, letting her words sink in, before allowing the last word to fall like a stone. "Skeltonshire."

Another gasp sounded just before a frenzy of whispers rocketed through the hall. Though he'd spent the majority of the time staring at the table, Kiyani's head shot up. He knew the place, the dangers of it. Just the sound of it receding into the air left his fist balled around the goblet he held with a viselike grip. But it was the fear of what was yet to come that left his breathing labored. Trying to conceal his shaking hand he raised the glass to his lips.

"Even if one of us was to go," Tybithera continued, paying him no attention, "even stripped of our magic, we would stand out. What we need is one who can slip into the shadows unknown and retrieve what is rightfully ours. One who is accustomed to the deceitful nature and lies of others. One who has been given an allotment in this life with nothing left to lose. The man that sits beside me, by the name of Kiyani."

And there it was. Kiyani nearly choked on his drink, spitting half of the red liquid back into his cup as the words left her mouth.

"Are you insane?!" he shouted, slamming the cup on the table and standing to face her, his chair rocking back to the point of nearly falling over, the wine splashing out and trailing down his hand like blood. He didn't care about the thousands of eyes trained on him, about the cold malice in Tybithera's gaze. "That's a death sentence!"

The Fae Queen stood calmly, unperturbed by his raging outburst. "There are still details that need to be smoothed out, preparations to take place in the days to follow," she spoke evenly as if they were talking privately about the simple rise and fall of the sun.

"Absolutely not!"

"There is no need to be hasty. A lot of people are counting on you."

"Lies and deceit is right," Kiyani spat, blind to the happenings beyond Tybithera and himself. "Was it too much to make mention of this beforehand? Or did you know that I would never agree to such a half-assed plan that you figured you'd just force me into it?"

"Kiyani…" Tybithera said, her voice taking on a tone of warning.

"Do I have no say whatsoever? You don't even care that you would be sending me to my death on a mission that is hardly even possible. All you care about is saving your own ass, about reinstating the legacy of your land. You don't care about Izandüre as a whole, or the people outside of your jurisdiction."

"You have no right to speak to me as such."

"Don't act like you own me. I have big enough problems of my own. There is no way, in the name of the Starlord, to the darkest depths of the Hell that Skeltonshire supposedly lies upon, that I will ever agree to this madness!"

32

•• ◇ ••

NEGOTIATIONS

Without another word Kiyani stormed off, moving past a stern-faced Tybithera and down the stairs. All eyes were upon him but his only focus was the archway and the freedom that lay beyond. Freedom he knew he would never be allowed. But he didn't care. He had to get out, to at least find a moment's reprieve to gather his thoughts, to think.

The night of the siege that had torn down Frielana. The attack of the Streig. The story of the Blood Stone. And now, the Fae Queen's proposition that directly involved him... he couldn't handle it all. Then there was the ever present image of Fura's expectant face to top it all off. Kiyani's life had never been easy, but he'd sure seen quieter times in his eighteen years.

Reaching the end of the walkway, Kiyani's path was blocked as a group of male Fae stood before him, their expressions unreadable as they crossed pikes to keep him from passing. It wasn't the faces of the men that he focused on, so much as the sharpened points at the ends of the poles, knowing that they were likely crafted by the maker of the sword at his hip.

The way was impassable, but Kiyani refused to turn and make amends. Which left him standing, still as stone, as he tried to think of a way out.

"Let him through," Tybithera suddenly claimed from behind him.

It wasn't what Kiyani had expected, but it was the leverage he needed. The guards were hesitant, but they did as they were told, lowering their weapons and stepping aside. As soon as the poles touched the floor once more, Kiyani moved past, making a break for the hall.

He didn't know where he was going, simply letting his anger drive his feet forward as he searched for escape – from Tybithera, from Fura, from Fae Rue, from everything. Down one hall and then another he walked, his pace quick but never breaking into a dead run.

The one thing that he found he couldn't elude was the Fae Queen who had followed him from the grand hall and quietly remained on his tail. Kiyani didn't know what more she could possibly find to say to him, but he didn't care to know. Though he refused to turn and face her, the one thing he was curious about was why she hadn't immediately stopped him. Instead, she let him take them both on a wild journey throughout the tunnels.

"You can run all you want," Tybithera finally declared, shattering the silence that had only been broken by the sounds of their feet crashing on the tile below. "From this, from your family, from the trouble you left behind in Frielana…" she continued the list as Kiyani turned down another hall, refusing to acknowledge her. "But you can never run from who you are." It was that declaration that finally brought Kiyani to a halt, though he still didn't turn to meet her burrowing gaze. "You think that you can just run from life, that it will never catch up to you? That none of what I spoke of will affect you? Or is it that you're hiding something? Maybe you don't actually plan on going on this grand journey to help those that you left behind," Tybithera ventured coldly. "You managed to escape, and now you're running from it all? Is that it? You don't plan on going back, do you? You're just like your father, but at least he has drive."

Kiyani wheeled around at the comment, unwilling to let that deep stab of the knife go unheeded. "The only thing that I ever claimed to be doing was taking Fura back to Barandor. Besides, if that's what you believe I think of those that I've lived amongst for years, then what makes you think I would do anything for you and your people?"

Avoiding her eyes, Kiyani looked down another hall, knowing he was lost. With no other options available to him, he crossed his arms and leaned against the wall, waiting for Tybithera to continue to tear into him. Wondering what she would do. There was little she could say to make him rethink what he'd already voiced as his decision.

"You're avoiding the subject."

"Am I?" As far as Kiyani was concerned, she didn't deserve answers from him anyways. Not after backing him into a corner with no option out. "Why should I bother when you're so sure that you already know what I'm going to say?"

Tybithera looked down on him. Every last ounce of her gentle nature had been wiped from her face, leaving nothing behind but cold lines, and even harsher eyes. "Answer me," she threatened. "Do you plan on helping them, or not?"

"I don't know," Kiyani said. "I honestly don't see why I should. None of them have ever done a damn thing for me, and I can tell you for a fact that if they were in my position not one of them would make a move to help me."

"You don't know that. People may surprise you."

"I've found that most are full of disappointments rather than surprises." Kiyani turned to continue walking, needing the movement to keep him centered. "You're avoiding the larger subject here." And that was this ridiculous journey she'd so thoughtfully signed him up for without his approval.

"How foolish of me. However, I'm not the one running from my tasks."

"I'm not running from anything 'cause I never agreed to this! You made no mention of this stone to either me or Fura, and now I can see why. I will not be some pawn in this ridiculous scheme of yours." Kiyani found that he could barely look at the woman, his rage at her one way proposal reaching full force again.

Tybithera followed him in a fury of her own that was reflected in the rippling colors of the Fae aura that seethed around her, her dress flying about her form. "I don't need your consent," she stormed. "I can make you do whatever I want, though I would much rather have you willing."

"That makes me want to agree," Kiyani laughed. "I'm accustomed to pain, to torture. You can't do anything that I haven't already experienced."

"Maybe not to you."

Kiyani stopped, his thoughts immediately eclipsing the image of a certain girl with flame-red hair. He turned, wondering if the woman was serious. "You wouldn't."

It was obvious that the Fae Queen seemed to have a vendetta against him, but Kiyani hadn't seen anything throughout the past few days that would indicate she would take her anger towards him out on Fura.

Tybithera seemed to brighten. "So you aren't completely void of weakness."

Shock filled him as he looked to her, wondering if she was really inferring to what he assumed she was. "That's ridiculous," he said callously. As if he could ever have feelings like that towards that girl.

There was a glimmer of intrigue in Tybithera's eye, having caught him off guard. "Is it?"

"Saving someone's life and keeping them alive is a declaration of love now?" Kiyani nearly gagged on the words.

"It's a start."

There was a slyness in her tone that Kiyani couldn't ignore. "Not only is it forbidden, but Apallo would have my head."

"If what you speak of the sudden incurrence of fate over Frielana is true, then he no longer holds that kind of power over you."

Kiyani couldn't believe that the conversation had taken such a turn. "Doesn't mean I'm going to take advantage of the situation, as you would be so apt to have me do."

Tybithera held a finger to her lips as if judging, staring at him through thick lashes. "Just how far has it gone already?"

"Just what are you accusing me of?"

"Merely trying to show you, that as much as you seem to think, that you're not invincible to the downfall of feelings. You care about this world and your part in it, even if you don't think you do. As for my request, I saved you and Fura from certain death. Is it not fair to ask for something in return?"

Kiyani hated the truth that resonated in Tybithera's words, but it wasn't the only thing that irked him. "What you're asking of me is not a fair trade."

"Your lives for a little bit of help?"

The charmed innocence in her voice only touched Kiyani's last nerve, as he wished once more that the Streig had found them earlier and saved them from this tortured madness. "What you promised them of me, of us, is more than just a little bit of help." He wondered if having lived in a bubble for so long, if she really knew the depth of what she was asking. "Fura's probably never heard of Skeltonshire, but I have. I've been there. What you may consider a little bit of help could very well cost us our lives. I'm telling you, it's certain death."

"If you refuse this, it will be death for us all, and not just the Fae race. You may be too young to see it, but Izandüre as a whole is fading away. There is a darkness taking over that, if left unheeded, will tear this world apart until there's nothing left here to save."

"Then who's to say I won't just jump ship?" Kiyani questioned. Though he knew it was hardly an option for him, there was always the world that Barandor was a part of.

"We both know that there is a bond that links those born of this realm to the land here. It's not easily ignored by those who decide to abandon." She paused a moment, seeming to regather her thoughts. "We will help you in this venture, in the end fight, but until that stone is restored we are next to nothing."

"You're nothing more than I am right now," Kiyani retorted, hardly convinced.

"That's not what I mean."

"If you have such a strong disregard for humans, then what makes you think I can do anything?"

"You're different than most. You fight for what you believe in, and rage war against what you don't."

"Everyone does that."

"No," Tybithera said with a shake of her head. "I'm Fae, remember, I can see past outward appearances, see bits of truth in what I've heard. You're not like most others. You go beyond the point where most people, humans especially, would have given up. The Fae are keepers of their word. We *will* help."

The fact that she claimed to know him so well hardly began to make amends for how she'd treated him thus far, not to mention it sent an involuntary shiver down Kiyani's spine. He preferred to keep his world private.

"Say I do help... all you have is a name inscribed on a wall from ages ago. This Nox Rean could be dead for all you know. If that's even his name. Besides, what makes you so sure that he's in Skeltonshire?"

"I know the place. Been there myself, once. If there's a single place in this world that a creature of his disposal would inhabit, it would be that hellish rock."

The returning walk back to the grand hall was far from comfortable.
I can make it so that you and Fura never leave this dwelling...

Moving forward, Kiyani found that he hated Fura all the more. He didn't care about his fate. If Tybithera wanted to be the one to end his life, then so be it, but he wouldn't be the one to carry Fura's blood on his hands.

The guards at the doorway moved aside without being ordered as he and the Fae Queen entered. The room beyond fell into complete and utter silence, but Kiyani walked in front of Tybithera with his head held high. He may have been defeated, but he wouldn't show it. He refused to look around to meet any eyes, and did the same with Fura as he ascended the stairs and reclaimed his seat.

Tybithera stood before her chair, not bothering to sit as she gazed down upon her subjects. The silence seemed to last forever before she finally began to speak once more. "I must apologize for our guest's rude behavior," she said, her gaze lingering on Kiyani for a moment, throwing the blame on him without speaking the words to do so. "A small misunderstanding is all, but we have now come to a decision. Kiyani," Tybithera called on him, motioning with her hand for him to stand. "If you would."

He rose, wary. "Would what?"

"They need to hear it from you," she whispered, just loud enough for him to discern her words.

She wanted his honest declaration, for him to sign his life away. The mere thought of it made Kiyani sick.

"This wasn't part of the agreement."

"Do it," Tybithera said warningly, though Kiyani could see the playful satisfaction of making him surrender in her eyes.

Irritated, Kiyani couldn't bring himself to look to where he knew Fura was sitting, expectantly watching him. Instead, he stared out at the prying eyes that peered back at him.

"I agree to help..." he declared, not knowing, or caring, if it was loud enough to carry throughout the room. He wasn't accustomed to pretentious speeches to large crowds, and didn't care to be.

"With?" Tybithera prodded.

"Finding the Blood Stone."

He made to sit back down the moment the binding words left his lips, but the Fae Queen's slender hand on his shoulder stopped him.

"You can do better than that," Tybithera said. Grasping the goblet of wine before her on the table, she held it up, motioning for everyone to do the same. Kiyani watched as those below followed suit before he hesitantly did the same. He didn't like where this was going. "Now, loud and clear so everyone can hear... even the spiders lingering in the darkest corners... repeat, word for word, my each and every word, starting with your full name."

"Are you serious?"

"Say it."

Shooting her a look of hatred, he turned back towards the eager eyes below. "I, Kiyani Nyte Ridanthu…"

"Swear upon my life, and all that I find sacred, that I will find and restore the Blood Stone of Immortality."

"Swear upon my life, and all that I find sacred, that I will find and restore the Blood Stone of Immortality," Kiyani repeated obediently, the woman's gaze upon Fura as she spoke not lost on him.

"Unless, and only unless, death may find me first."

"Unless, and only unless, death may find me first."

Tybithera raised her glass high. *"Täemaen stryktfäere.* And so it is done!" Sealing the deal with a swig from her goblet, a chorus of laughter and cheers rose from the crowd. "Now that wasn't so hard, was it?" she asked Kiyani.

"The key word was to *help*," Kiyani hissed. "Beyond that I make no promises."

"Oh, but you just did," Tybithera laughed wickedly.

Kiyani glanced at the drink in his own hands before tipping it back and downing what was left as he dropped back into his seat. He allowed himself a quick glance at Fura, only to find that it was a mistake. Turning away, he dodged the look of worry painted in her eyes. Sauvalle next to him laid a hand on his shoulder in reassurance, but Kiyani shrugged it off. His vision fogged with anger as he stared out across the room, he couldn't rid himself of the image of the smile on Tybithera's face. That smug satisfaction with the finality of the matter.

33

◆◆◇◆◆

WORDS AS SHARP AS STEEL

His anger seething just below the surface, threatening to make a rise, Kiyani found that though the festivities continued on as if he'd never made a move against the Fae Queen, he couldn't sit and enjoy himself. Not like he had found enjoyment in the matter in the first place.

The hall was too brightly lit, the airy echoes of the Fae below, as they rejoiced in the aftermath of the announcement, too joyous. Kiyani tried to shut it all out, to dig deep within himself, but he just couldn't ignore Tybithera's grating laugh as she spoke to the nameless advisor who had returned to her side. Her airy tone seemed to convey the irritating fact that she'd just gotten what she had wanted all along.

Kiyani wondered if it had been her plan from the moment she'd seen him in the woods to shorten his lifespan by implicating some stupid task on him. It was fishy. For one that declared that the Fae never left the boundaries of their land, what had she even been doing there in the first place?

He didn't care to know the answer. All he wanted was out.

"Are you done abusing me for the night?" he asked callously, interrupting Tybithera's conversation with the man he found himself hating just through association with the woman.

Tybithera turned to him, regarding him as if she'd forgotten he was even there, though Kiyani knew better. "You may go. Just know that there are still things to discuss."

Kiyani stood, giving a half-hearted sarcastic bow. "I can hardly wait."

Walking behind the table and descending the stairs, Kiyani couldn't bring himself to look at Fura as he passed, his thoughts too scattered and teeming in turmoil, racing to find a loophole to whatever it was exactly that he'd just agreed to. He didn't know when Tybithera would finally let him out of this horrific rat race, but he vowed that as soon as he was granted the sight of the outdoors once more he'd be gone for good. He'd take Fura back to Barandor, and then find something to do with himself. Something that involved staying as far away from Fae Rue as possible. Tybithera claimed that she never left her land. Good. Let her find him once he disappeared. He had spent most of his life living in the shadows. She'd never see him again if he had any say in the matter.

Making it past the guards this time without so much as a single movement from them, Kiyani turned in the opposite direction then he'd chosen beforehand, determined not to get lost this time. Not that he particularly cared. As long as Tybithera wasn't going to follow him, he would wander the whole night. Sleep was sure to elude him, anyways. And if he happened to come across one of the tunnels that led him out of the mountain, then all the better.

As the planned hope for escape crossed his mind, Kiyani stopped. Some of the fight left him as he leaned against the wall, wondering what would happen to Fura if he just left her behind. Would Tybithera keep her around, continuing to treat her like a princess, or would she go as far as to hurt her as recompense for his actions?

She had given him the option to leave once. He wasn't sure she would do it again.

Pushing forward, Kiyani let his feet lead the way. He couldn't wait to get rid of the girl. All this having to plan his course of action around the protection of another was getting old fast. If he happened to come across an exit, he knew it would be hard to pass up, but regardless, he also knew that he wouldn't be leaving until he had the opportunity to take Fura with him as well.

Mumbling irritably to himself, Kiyani looked back the way he'd come. As it stood, he refused to go back to the hall. To sit in that empty chair beside the Fae Queen, listening to and taking part in her twisted ways of getting what she wanted. Fura would be escorted back to her room at some point. That much he knew.

Besides, he amended, that spiky haired faerie was with her. In the mean time, Fura was better off without him, which left him with time to spare.

As if the sword at his hip was drawn back to its previous home, Kiyani found himself standing before the door of the smithy. He looked around, contemplating entering. It hadn't been that long since he'd left the grand hall and he assumed that Sauvalle was still sitting at the table, jovially talking with the queen as if nothing awkward had transpired in his presence.

Kiyani felt a surge of guilt for intruding on the man's space without being offered the luxury, but found himself pushing the door open anyways, the thought of the wonders that waited inside drawing him forward against his better judgment.

261

Just as it had been before, hundreds of weapons glittered in the darkness. Kiyani let the door fall shut behind him. The fire in the hearth burned lower in the hours it had been left unattended, but it still shed enough light in the room to see by.

Settling into the comforting embrace he often found in silence, he strolled through the room and made his way towards the fireplace. Standing before the fading embers, he watched the shimmer of colors before finding a set of pokers beside the hearth and prodding the flames back to life. Satisfied, he fell into the large leather chair where he had first seen Sauvalle. It was a comfortable seat, but Kiyani found himself perched on its edge, hunched over with his head in his hands as he tried to sort through the mess inside his head.

He didn't know how long he sat like that, each failed train of thought threatening to push him closer to the edge. Giving up on reflecting on the day's events, Kiyani rose from the plush leather embrace of the chair and poked at the fire one last time before moving away to find something else to occupy his thoughts.

Not yet wanting to leave the room, Kiyani moved quietly between the racks of weaponry, trying to lose himself in their silence. None of these instruments would ask ridiculous things of him. They would only sit in quiet reprieve, waiting for eternity to find a home, silent as the shadows of death, after being brought into the world in such a noisy fashion, pounded flat from bars of steel.

He ignored his reflection as it bounced from blade to blade with his movement. Nothing that greeted him in a mirror had ever met his satisfaction. The medium made no difference. He would always hate what he saw, what looked back at him, reminding him too much of home and things best left forgotten.

The door to the forge opened and closed in close fashion, and there was an intake of surprise that left Kiyani feeling more defensive than he should have been.

"Oh," Sauvalle said. "Pardon me. I wasn't aware that I had company."

"Going to go report me to Tybithera now?" It was rude, he knew, but Kiyani couldn't help it.

Sauvalle only moved forward with a warm and welcoming glimmer in his eye, not once looking back at the door that would lead him to his queen. "Not at all. Stay if you wish. I have no quarrel with you. Whatever has happened is between you and her."

Kiyani didn't know why he'd come here in the tumultuous wake of the feast, but the man gave good reason to stay. Maybe it was why his feet had led him here in the first place. Yet, as friendly as the smith was, had always been, Kiyani couldn't help but feel a certain sense of unease as the questions gnawed at him.

He kept Sauvalle within sight from the corner of his eye, watching as the man strolled past and tended to the fire that heated the room. "Did you know?" he asked as he ran a hand along a hilt of one of the many swords.

After the childhood he had been forced to live, Kiyani didn't come to trust easily, and he found himself fearing the man's answer, even if he already knew what it was going to be. He looked up to see that the warm smile had been replaced by a tight-lipped frown. It was as he'd expected.

"I did," Sauvalle confessed. "But I thought when Tybithera brought you here earlier today that you already knew. You must excuse her, she's not always this way. She is a good person, but I will admit that she can come across as rather callous at times. Especially when she feels she is close to getting something she wants. You must understand that this is a very important matter for us. To say that that stone is our everything doesn't begin to cover it. It's our life force, and without it we're fading. Tybithera's reached a point where she's willing to do just about anything to get it back."

"Including backstabbing and betrayal?"

Sauvalle lowered his head as he picked up a sword, looking it over as if searching for dust. "Aye," he admitted wanly. Replacing it on the rack, he turned to Kiyani. "She may threaten you, but she would never harm Fura, and given your position in this world, you need not worry either."

The addition of she won't kill you was implied, but Kiyani doubted the unspoken just as much as what Sauvalle had actually said. He liked the man, but he was biased. A half-hearted smile took to Kiyani's face. "No one would ever miss me."

The smile returned to Sauvalle's fatherly visage. "Fura would."

✧ ⌘ ✧

Back in the grand hall, the festivities continued as if nothing out of the ordinary had transpired. Fura sat stiffly in her seat beside the Fae Queen as she watched those below shuffle about in excitement, their eyes full of delight following the unexpected news. She could only imagine what was being spoken of them within the mingling groups. Beside her, Saiva continued talking, yet Fura barely heard a word. All she could focus on was the empty chairs at the end of the table.

It had been over an hour since Kiyani had left abruptly for the second time that evening, this time failing to return. Fura was certain that she wouldn't see him again that night, at least not in the grand hall, surrounding by swooning Fae. The image of Kiyani surrounded by women, even ones of a whole different species, left a stabbing jealousy deep in her gut. Not that it was anything to worry about. Kiyani seemed indifferent to such attention, hers included. He hadn't so much as glanced her way as he'd passed, removing himself from the festivities as Fura wished she could do. She desperately wanted to leave as well, but Kiyani's actions had left her paralyzed, afraid to chase after him. Even after the mix of feelings in her stomach had settled to a reasonable calm, Fura had been too afraid to move to announce her need for escape to Tybithera. So she remained.

Catering to nervous hands, she smoothed the fold of her dress, fingers trailing over the lush velvet. Anything to distract herself as she wondered when the feast would be declared over. No one had given her tips on Fae etiquette, therefore Fura didn't know if she awaited the moment when the Fae Queen would formally dismiss her, or if she was allowed free leave. Kiyani had left without repercussion, though he seemed to live in a world all his own, governed by an entirely different set of rules. Even so, Fura hadn't been able to ignore the thickness in the air between him and Tybithera, or the cruel gaze the woman had fixed on him as she'd watched him make his way down the aisle and out into the hall.

In the wake of the decree he had offered the Fae people, and his following absence, Fura had continued her descent into depression-driven panic. After his previous outburst, she had been sure that Tybithera would have kept Kiyani at her side, under close watch. Or at least followed him out again, maybe even to direct him back to the room he'd been occupying and telling him to stay there. Luckily, the woman had remained seated. Fura hadn't been able to make out the last words of their conversation, though she had strained to hear – going so far as to realize that she was leaning in her seat – but she had been able to make out the callous tone that both had used to arm themselves against one another.

The moment Kiyani had risen from his seat to leave, Fura had wanted to follow, but he hadn't even bothered to look at her, passing by as if she didn't even exist. It had left her weighing the options between what appeared to be two equally deadly options: staying with the Fae Queen, or trailing after an angry Kiyani. She had opted to remain in the hall, thinking that the continued conversation with Saiva, and the lovely atmospheric music would help her return to a time earlier in the evening when she'd actually been enjoying herself. Instead, Fura had discovered one of her own nervous tics as she wondered if maybe her second option of trailing Kiyani wouldn't have been such a bad idea.

It was Saiva that finally spoke up, allowing her release.

"It's getting late," she said, loud enough to gather Tybithera's attention. "I think Fura's getting tired."

"Huh?" Fura perked up at the sound of her name, unaware that she had drifted off so deeply in her thoughts that the only thing that remained of reality was the music that continued to play.

Tybithera held a hand aloft to indicate a pause in her conversation with the same curly-haired Fae that Fura had seen earlier, before turning to face them. "My apologies," she said with a dip of her head. "You must be exhausted."

"I am," Fura said, forcing a smile. Though she envied the thought of a comfortable bed in a quiet room, she doubted that sleep would come with ease tonight. Not wanting to come across as rude, or ungrateful for what could have been a magical night, and wanting to smooth some of the tension Kiyani had left behind, Fura curtsied and added, "Thank you for the wonderful night."

"You're welcome."

It wasn't until Fura had risen and begun to follow Saiva towards the stairs that the woman spoke again. "If you see Kiyani, make sure to tell him that we still have matters to discuss."

Fura didn't turn to face the Queen, but she could feel the woman's eyes boring into her back as she scurried after Saiva, suddenly wanting to place as much distance as she could between them. A certain sense of unease crept into the hollows of her stomach as she walked, realizing that Tybithera's sunny welcome was starting to wear thin. No thanks to Kiyani. What had started out as a delightful celebration had quickly escalated into one of those days that Fura found she would rather forget.

A number of the remaining Fae smiled and bowed as Fura moved past, the length of her dress keeping her from escaping as quickly as she wanted. There was excitement in their eyes that Fura might have mirrored when she'd first walked in, but not now. She didn't know just what had happened earlier between Kiyani and Tybithera during their absence, or what he had essentially agreed to in the end, but she could see that it meant a lot to these people. She only wished she could share their excitement.

Once in the hall, the tremor in her hands began to fade and Fura found she wasn't as stricken by paralyzing fear. The cool stone seemed to calm her nerves, and compared with the clamor in the bright room, walking alone through the halls with only Saiva as company was a welcome reprieve.

Fura breathed a sigh of relief, though it still wasn't enough to make up for the night that had turned out far from what she'd expected.

Just ahead of her, Saiva looked close to tears, a far cry from the bubbly personality she had showcased earlier.

"A little tense, huh?" she commented weakly, seeming to search for something to fill the silence.

Fura nodded, unable to force herself to look upon the girl she had thought was her friend. It was childish, but all she could think was how satisfying it would be to send her a look that said 'you could have warned me.'

"I really am sorry," Saiva continued before Fura could find the words to speak. "I swear that I had no idea that neither of you knew."

"It's okay," Fura said, her words far from meaningful. Even she could hear it, and she cringed, hating how cold she had become in that short time.

Saiva shook her head. "Everyone I talked to knew what it was about. I just assumed that Tybithera had told you..." Her words trailed off as if she didn't know what to say, simply trying to keep the conversation from dying out, and their early friendship along with it.

"It's okay," Fura repeated, her words weaker, as if exhaustion had suddenly taken place of the sudden surge of betrayal she had felt.

Saiva was right. It wasn't her fault. Why would the woman have thought that her Queen would leave her guests in the dark? As it was, the more Fura thought about it, the more her tiny room, and the solitude it provided, seemed like the perfect remedy for the night.

She followed Saiva without question, trusting her to get her back to her room without any further confrontation. The conversation fell flat, neither of them making the effort to revive it. It was clear that every word following would be nothing more than forced syllables presented only in a faded attempt to combat the silence.

It wasn't until a few minutes had passed that Fura began to question their destination. Though the labyrinth of twisting tunnels still had her confused, she knew something wasn't quite right.

"This isn't the way back to my room," she declared, certain that she knew that much.

Saiva peered over her shoulder. "I know," she quietly admitted. "But I wanted to show you something first."

Fura had had enough surprises for one day, but she followed regardless, sure that if Saiva wanted to show her something of her own accord that it would be okay. She felt no ill will towards the woman, just mildly disappointed that she hadn't shared what she knew. It was Tybithera that had kept her in the dark, yet Fura couldn't even find herself mad at her. Maybe if she knew this world better, things would be different.

This world.

She still couldn't grasp the concept that she wasn't walking the same land where her hometown of Barandor resided. How was one meant to come to terms with such information?

Too tired to argue, Fura continued on, each step taking her further from her intended target. When they turned into another tunnel, she stopped, uncertain of what was happening. This hall was dark and depressing, a gaping black hole waiting for them at its end, looking as if it silently waited to swallow them whole. Trepidation deepening her step, Fura moved forward as Saiva waved her on.

It wasn't until the shadows surrounded them and they reached the end that Fura came to realize that it wasn't as dark as she'd thought. Popping out of the stone and onto a grassy plain, Fura felt a smile drag at her lip as she sucked in a deep breath of the cold night air.

"Are you allowed to bring me out here?" she asked, wondering if Saiva was risking getting herself in trouble in an attempt to atone for the villain Fura had callously accused her of being.

Saiva shrugged, the gleeful grin reappearing on her face. "I figured you could use a change of scenery."

"Thank you."

"I really am sorry," Saiva said again, standing beside her as they both looked to the sky. The bright moon above cast its light upon the ground, making the blades of grass that danced in the wind look like silver hair sprouting from the earth.

Fura nodded, feeling sorry that she had ever accused Saiva of malcontent. "I know."

It was hard to pull herself away from the energizing light of the moon when the time came, but Fura knew she couldn't hide outside forever. Sooner or later she would have to talk to Tybithera again, to make sense of everything that had happened. She had decided that even if this did all prove to be a dream in the end that she had to make the best of it while it lasted, for it felt like she was never going to wake up.

Upon reentering the mountain dwelling, Saiva faithfully returned Fura to her room. Bidding her friend a good night, she opened the door, knowing that all the fun she'd had earlier that day had been overshadowed by the meaning behind the feast.

Once inside, the orbs lit up, chasing the shadows away. Looking up at their cheerful circular forms, Fura wished for once that they would remain dark. As she moved to settle herself on the edge of the bed, wondering what to do next, something caught Fura's eye. At the end of the bed, the new clothes she'd picked out earlier with Myrian had been brought to the room and neatly folded in piles. In a smaller stack next to them were the clothes of her past that she had cast off in favor of the gown, as well as Kiyani's shirt that she'd left strewn on the bed that morning.

She let her fingers slide over the array of fabrics. None were as elegant as the dress she wore, the thicker pieces made for the wear of travel.

Travel.

Fura nearly snorted in contempt at the thought of her on some crazy adventure. As much as the idea intrigued her, she knew it would never happen. Kiyani was just as apt to dump her off in Barandor, hoping to never see her again. She'd been lost in the throes of daydreams earlier as she had pranced around in the clothing in the company of the Fae, not bothering to think what reality had in store for her instead.

Falling back onto the bed, Fura stared up at the ceiling, her mind too full of conflicting thoughts to even try to go to sleep.

Unable to calm her mind, and favoring a change of scenery, she left the room. Wandering slowly down the hall, Fura passed a few doors similar to hers, and she wondered for the first time if anyone else resided in this hall. The lack of activity and the dim lighting told her the answer was probably not. However, it made her realize that even after all this time, she didn't know where Tybithera had placed Kiyani.

Her thoughts focused on him once more caused her to unwittingly relive the events of the feast again, and Fura wondered what had become of him in the hours that had passed.

Turning into the room that housed the waterfall, she found her answer.

34

••◇••

IN THE ARMS OF A STRANGER

Standing before the plummeting stream of water, his back turned to her as he shifted from foot to foot, Kiyani had all the appearance of a trapped animal. Feral and ready to attack. The nervous tap of his foot. His tense stance. None of it deemed him approachable.

As if searching for escape, he periodically paced the length of the slow moving stream.

Though Fura reckoned with herself that even if she hadn't been straightforward in searching him out, her subconscious had drawn her to him, wanting to talk. Even if that was the case, she stood frozen in the doorway wondering if it was safe to enter. He had thrown off sweltering waves of anger during the feast and even now, over an hour later, that heat didn't appear to have faded.

Fura didn't have to look across the room to reveal the unassuring fact that there was no one else present. Silence consumed her as she stood motionless in the stone-faced arch, debating on whether or not to proceed. Her common sense told her to turn around, but her gut begged her to stay. Though, for whose sake she wasn't sure. She was torn, standing in the middle of a two way street. In one direction lay peace and solitude, and in the other, uncertainty.

She took a single, hesitant step forward. Unable to get a good read on his current mood, Fura wasn't sure she wanted to brave approaching. But, time after time, he had proven one thing to her. Even if brutally at times, Kiyani was honest.

It wasn't just the time spent with the Fae that Fura realized things were being kept from her. She had begun to notice it right away in Frielana, that feeling that no one around her could trust her with the truth. Despite his crude behavior, Kiyani was the only one that had never tried to sugar-coat his words to make her feel better.

Certain that the only way to get answers to any of her questions resided in taking the path that led her forward, Fura moved further into the room. Unsure of how to announce her presence, she lifted the hem of her dress to keep it from rustling against the floor. She could see that

Kiyani had opted, as well, to not change out of the fineries he had donned at the feast. Almost as if it were a declaration of some strange kind of connection between them, Fura silently thanked him for it, no longer feeling so out of place herself. The sword he'd been carrying now rested on the rocks behind him, and Fura glanced at it, suppressing a shiver as she wondered if, as much as the woman hated him, it had been one of Tybithera's gifts.

Lacking the nerve to initiate conversation, Fura sat on the rocks behind Kiyani. She realized as she watched him pace, that sneaking up on him was far from the best move, but she couldn't think of anything to say. The meaning of the night's events continued to elude her, as did a way to fix it.

She was examining the sword with her eyes when Kiyani spoke.

"I suppose you had a nice chat with Tybithera after I left."

His voice was dark and accusing. Fura flinched away from its tone as she looked up to find that Kiyani had stopped in the middle of the room, looking back at her. It hadn't been a question.

"Actually, we didn't talk," Fura said. "Tybithera told me as I was leaving though to tell you that the conversation wasn't done," she added, relaying the message from the Fae Queen. "She said there was more to discuss."

Kiyani snorted. "I can only imagine."

Looking preoccupied, Fura could see that Kiyani had something in his hands. It gave her a certain sense of comfort to know that he focused his anger more onto the dance of the object than on her.

"Things didn't really go as planned, did they?" Fura asked warily.

"There wasn't a plan to begin with," Kiyani declared, tossing the object into the water with a splash. "I knew when Tybithera announced the feast was in our honor that it couldn't have been anything good, but I had no idea it would end up being something like that."

Hugging her knees to her chest, Fura looked away from him as she wrapped the folds of fabric around her legs. In the midst of her building confusion she hadn't realized that he'd been caught just as off guard as she was. Even going out of her way to not meet his eye, Fura could still feel Kiyani's gaze on her.

Unable to bear it, she looked up, afraid of what would be reflected in those icy blue orbs that she'd found herself dreaming of at night. Having cast aside whatever had been in his hand, she could see that he now fiddled with the necklace he wore, but it was the eyes that left her wondering what she'd done. She had noticed the strain in Kiyani's voice prior as he'd done his best to keep the anger leveled. Fura doubted that it had faded so quickly, yet there was now a certain softness in his gaze as he regarded her.

"What?" she asked, finding herself uncomfortable with the sudden attention.

As if her words had broken the spell, Kiyani shook his head, before answering, "Nothing. I've just never seen you in a dress before."

"Never?" Fura couldn't help but laugh. "I've only known you for two weeks."

"I've known you longer," Kiyani admitted. "Well, known of you."

Fura's smile subsided as she found herself looking at him more closely. "What do you mean?" His admission shocked her, and she wondered if it was possible that she might have met him before. That the reason she found herself so drawn to him was merely a side effect of her subconscious recognizing a familiar face.

Kiyani shrugged as if to declare that it was no big news. "We both work in Fireswell. I've seen you around."

"Why have I never seen you?"

"I work at the opposite end of the grounds, but I've seen you perform before."

"Oh." Maybe she had seen him before, though Fura still couldn't find any sign of remembrance to tell her so. "How come you've never performed?"

"Me?" This time it was Kiyani who laughed, causing Fura's heart to dance. "I have no talent when it comes to fire. If you haven't noticed, just because I live in Frielana, doesn't mean the others associate with me. Besides, I don't have that kind of elemental magic."

Fura perked up, not sure if she'd heard right. "Magic?"

"Yeah…" Kiyani paused, a darkness shadowing his eyes again as he looked at her. "Some of the people that work in Fireswell have actual talent to be able to play with fire like that and not pay the price. There are a number of people in Frielana however that carry an inborn connection with the element, and if taught correctly can learn to bend it to their will. Some might call it magic, others don't necessarily think of it that way."

"That's sil –"

"Silly? Bullshit?" Kiyani declared, his voice rising as he cut her off.

"It just doesn't make sense," Fura said, hoping to steer the conversation away from the edge of the cliff. She didn't want it to go awry so soon. This was the first time she felt like she was getting anywhere with her questions.

"Maybe not in Barandor, but this isn't the world you grew up in."

My world.

There it was again. Fura watched Kiyani run a hand through his hair as he stared off into the waters, seeming to search for a sense of calm before continuing. She couldn't believe how dedicated to this lie he was, but with each passing moment, she knew it was far from.

"Are you really going to question that after what you've seen lately?"

he spoke again, trying to keep his tone calm.

"I guess not," Fura said weakly as Kiyani turned to face her again. "It's just all so new."

"When you've grown up elsewhere, I suppose it would be. For me, it's nothing special."

Even as Kiyani tried to ease her into the information, Fura found that what she clung to were the smallest things he revealed about himself. So he didn't belong in Frielana, but he grew up in this strange world. Telling herself to stay on track, Fura stored the information for a later time, knowing that if she brought it up now he'd probably leave, and then she'd be left dead in the water again until the next time she could corner him alone.

But where to even start?

"So, does everyone in Frielana have this... magic?" Fura asked, struggling to apply the word to reality.

"No. But a majority of them possess at least some level of latent talent."

Fura felt relief, hearing that not everyone in this world was superior to her.

"What makes Apallo the Firelord, then?" Fura still couldn't grasp the concept that in all that time she'd spent with the man as he'd taught her the trade in Fireswell, she had actually been in the presence of one of the Sect of Seven. If this was all true.

"I thought you were familiar with the stories?"

"Exactly," Fura said. "Stories. None of them go into great detail." What was a fairytale without the mystery?

"Right. Well, there used to be a grand ceremony that went into the choosing of each Lord, but nowadays it rides more on skill set and family ties. When one Lord dies, the next presiding family member takes over." Kiyani's eyes skirted her, seeming to calculate her worth. "Though I'm not sure how that would work in this case, seeing as this is the first you've heard of any of this."

"What does any of this have to do with me?"

Kiyani's fist balled at his side. "You really don't know, do you? Didn't Apallo tell you anything?"

Fura shook her head, wondering why Kiyani was so insistent that Apallo should have told her more. He was a busy man, why should he have taken time out of his day to cater to her? "He only spoke to me a few times... mostly to warn me about you." She felt embarrassed admitting that last part, but was sure that Kiyani was already aware of that fact.

Kiyani rolled his eyes and resumed pacing. "Too worried about me as always," he muttered.

It was easy to see that that shallow anger Kiyani harbored was surfacing again, but Fura found herself crawling off the rock, meaning to follow him. She wasn't sure she liked where this conversation was going, but she felt she was on the verge of discovering something big.

"What does Apallo have to do with any of this?" Fura pushed.

"Everything!" Kiyani declared roughly. "You have no clue at all about your family, do you?"

Fura had put up with a lot from him, but she couldn't let that pass. "Don't insult my family," she found herself shouting. "If you haven't noticed, they're dead." Fura cringed. It was only the second time she had spoken the truth out loud, and though it didn't hurt any less, she refused to let him tear at a wound that was still so fresh.

Letting out a sigh, Kiyani turned. Walking back towards Fura, he paused in front of her for a moment before moving around her as he spoke. "Who have you been living with?"

"My parents," Fura answered, wondering what kind of ridiculous question that was.

"I mean names," Kiyani clarified. "Last names."

"Mary and John Keeple."

"And what do you go by?"

"Fura Feuer."

Moving back into Fura's line of vision, Kiyani shook his head in disbelief. "And you've never wondered why your name wasn't the same? Why you had no other relatives? Why you were forced to seek out Apallo and the other firedancers when your 'family' died? Why you had no other place to go?"

With each word he spoke, Fura felt the heavy weight of dread pulling her further down, that feeling of learning something that she had always known in the back of her mind, but had never accepted, pinning her in place. "What are you saying?"

"Sit," Kiyani commanded, directing her back towards the stones where she had been sitting. It wasn't until he was sure that she was firmly in place that he continued, too antsy to do the same. "You wouldn't know this, but Apallo rarely lets anyone into Frielana without some sort of test. It's a process he overrode specifically for you. I can't believe that you never noticed though that you share that same shade of red hair, the same name…"

"Name?"

"Apallo Feuer. Didn't you know that either?"

Fura ignored his remark as she fought to put two and two together in a way that made even the slightest bit of sense. "We're related?"

"You can't get much closer."

Fura's hands shook in her lap and she watched them, telling herself that this couldn't be happening to her. Apallo had warned her. Kiyani was trouble, a liar. But why had he taken the time to tell her that again and again?

"Apallo's your father, Fura."

A single hot tear rolled down her cheek. Fura bit her lip as she met Kiyani's eye, shaking her head. A long period of deafening silence stretched before them, neither knowing what to say. All that Fura had learned in the past few days had been a lot to process, but this was a whole new level of insanity. She wanted to reach over to where Kiyani stood, watching, waiting, and hit him. Ask him why he was toying with her like this. She wanted him to tell her it was all a lie, that he was just playing some cruel joke on her to deal with his anger towards Tybithera, but the more she thought it over, the more she allowed herself to realize that it all made sense. At least most of it.

"Why was I living with the Keeple's, then?" Fura asked, choking on the words. She didn't know what was the most disturbing; that she was from this world, or that she'd had family this whole time right under her nose that refused to claim her. All those days under Apallo's tutelage at the festival, and he'd never spoken a word to even indicate such a relationship. It all felt like a betrayal now. What had she done to cause him to cast her aside?

"That I don't know," Kiyani said with a shake of his head.

Fura could tell that he was just as lost on the subject as she was, but it wasn't enough. She wanted answers. She wanted the truth.

"Why didn't Apallo care enough to raise me himself? And what about my mom? Where is she?"

"I'm sure he wanted to," Kiyani said, surprisingly attempting to justify the actions of a man who had helped condemn him to a life of solitude. "Apallo's the one you need to talk to about this, not me. But from what I've heard through talk in the camp over the years, your mother died not long after you were born."

The tears flowed freely now as Fura tried to collect the words Kiyani issued and place them in a neat row. So, that was another family member down.

"He placed you in Barandor so he could keep an eye on you," Kiyani continued, filling the silence. "I doubt he expected you to find him."

Fura had always thought it had been the fire itself that had drawn her to beg the man for a job, but now she realized that maybe it had been that connection to Apallo, even if she hadn't known it at the time. She stared into the falls, watching the water cascade down the wall into a shimmering mist where it met the rocks. She couldn't believe the words she'd just heard. None of it made sense, yet, in a way, everything seemed to fall into place. Needing something to keep her hands busy to keep from tearing at her nails, Fura picked at the pins holding her hair in place.

"Why didn't he tell me, then?" she asked, deciding to play along with it for a moment, entertaining the possibility of the statement. The first pin came out smoothly, the second one stuck. Fura let out a whimper as she fought restlessly with the knot it was forming as she tried to yank it out. The pain just increased the tears.

Kiyani sat down next to her. Forcing her hands back to her side, he freed the pin from her tangle of orange waves.

"I think he was waiting for the right time, and he was probably afraid of the look on your face."

"What look?"

"Like the one you're giving me now."

Fura could only stare at him, unsure of what he meant.

"Like there's a spider on my face," Kiyani said, attempting to clarify, short of making her move forward to look at her own reflection in the water.

She turned away from him, embarrassed, but allowed him to remove the rest of the pins, slowly releasing her hair to fall free around her shoulders.

"I'm sorry," Kiyani said, placing the last pin atop a small pile between them. "I shouldn't be the one to tell you any of this, but you needed to know."

"So what now?" Fura sniffed. "I'm going to lose my real father after losing the only family I've ever known?"

"Not if we save him."

Kiyani watched as Fura nodded half heartedly. It sounded like a good idea, but he knew the chances of pulling off such a coup were thin. There was nothing more he could think to add to the conversation that would be appropriate following that revelation. He could only imagine the conflicting feelings that could follow such a discovery. To find out, so late in life, that you had family living under your nose. Though he knew he would give a lot to find that the family he'd been placed alongside was actually false.

"You should get some rest."

Fura silently agreed with a nod of her head. She didn't know how much else she could handle. Following him out of the room, leaving the splendor of the waterfall behind, Fura allowed him to lead her down the hall.

They hadn't gone far when they stopped before a door that looked strikingly similar to the one that led to Fura's room. She looked down the hall, knowing that they hadn't walked far enough. It was when he whispered good night and slipped into the room, leaving her alone in the hall, that she realized it was his room.

"Night…" Fura said weakly to the closed door before moving on to her own room.

Once inside, she stripped herself free of the formal gown. A quick survey of her new clothes left her missing the comforts of home and the joys of a simple pair of cozy pajama bottoms. Searching for the closest thing, she ended up in a pair of soft leggings and Kiyani's shirt.

It wasn't until she had thrown everything else to the floor and lay on her back, staring at the ceiling, trying to come to terms with her family heritage, that Fura realized there wouldn't be any peace in being alone. The room surrounding her suddenly felt cold and uninviting, the stone closer and more confining, as if it threatening to cave in around her.

Barely giving any thought to the matter, she moved barefoot out into the hall.

The short walk from her own room to the one where Tybithera had placed Kiyani wasn't nearly enough time to think of what to say, and Fura found herself standing before the door, at a loss.

The element of surprise was the only real thing she had at hand, at least until she opened the door. As soon as it swung in on its hinges and she entered the room, the Fae lights that hovered in the air came to life.

"No, bad lights," Fura hissed, trying to keep from waking Kiyani. "I'm sorry, go back to sleep," she said, continuing to speak to the orbs.

Cringing, she turned to see just what damage she had done. Whether Kiyani had been asleep or not, she had his attention now. He sat, propped on an elbow, looking at her with a raised brow that asked what the heck she was doing. Fura expected him to yell at her, to tell her to leave, but he remained silent as if waiting for her to explain.

"I…" Fura's eyes flickered towards the door. It had been stupid of her to leave her room, to expect anything further from him, but she was here now. "Can I stay with you tonight?" she asked shyly, embarrassed to have even uttered the words.

The answer would be no, she just knew it. It didn't matter what was racing through her mind. She would be alone tonight with nothing but the turmoil of her own thoughts to keep her company. Kiyani had pushed her away that first night wet and shivering in the Reln. This wouldn't be any different.

Fura didn't know what it was, but to her surprise, Kiyani let out a tired sigh and nodded. Standing in shock, wondering if he'd honestly just agreed to her request, she watched as he sat up and ran a hand through his hair, messing it up even more than it had been. It wasn't until he leaned over the opposite edge of the bed and retrieved a ball of fabric that she realized he had been shirtless.

Heat flushed her cheeks as she cautiously moved forward, hoping that despite triggering the lights, that it was still too dark for him to take notice. It wasn't until that moment that Fura realized the awkward situation she was walking herself into, about to crawl into bed with someone she barely knew. Someone who didn't even like her. Sleeping with the enemy jumped to mind, but Kiyani wasn't even that, stuck someplace in between that and friend. He just didn't care to have her around.

Fura stopped a few feet from the bed, watching him wrestle into a dark tank top. In the flash of skin she saw before he pulled it down, she thought she saw something amiss, but told herself it was just a trick of the lighting.

"Maybe —"

"Don't wake me up if you're going to change your mind," Kiyani interrupted her, making no mention of the fact that he hadn't been asleep in the first place. That he'd been wide awake in the dark, twisting the dagger Tybithera had left him in his hands, as he tried to quell his own thoughts. "Get over here and go to sleep."

"Right. Sorry."

Scurrying forward, Fura sat on the edge of the bed for a moment before burying herself beneath the covers and claiming the space that Kiyani had given up for her. It was the simplest of gestures, but coming from him it meant the world. Even his last words hadn't been harsh, just exhausted. Though maybe that was the basis of his change in mood.

Fura curled herself into a ball and faced the wall. She remained so until the lights began to fade from inactivity. She knew she had promised to go to sleep, but even here her mind wouldn't stay silent.

Rolling over, she could see that Kiyani was turned away from her. Silence seemed be the best policy around him but Fura couldn't keep herself quiet.

"Do you think Apallo is still alive?" Fura could barely keep her voice from cracking, tears threatening to break lose again. How was she supposed to deal with losing two families in such a short period of time?

Kiyani heaved a sigh before rolling over to face her. Fura couldn't blame him. He had never wanted to be stuck with her in the first place, and now here she was intruding on his evening, practically kicking him out of bed. She waited for him to tell her to leave, but the words never came.

"I really don't know," was all he said.

"So he really is my father?"

"I think you've always known."

Fura nodded, finally letting herself admit it.

There was the longest silence that followed, making Fura think that Kiyani had closed his eyes and returned to sleep, or was at least trying to. Her mind was busy sifting through questions, her body buzzing from exhaustion. So when he finally spoke again, Fura jumped, surprised to hear his voice.

"You want to go home?"

Fura couldn't see Kiyani's features well in the dimming light of the orbs, but she could hear the concern in his voice clear as day. He was still trying to get her to go back to Barandor, that much she could tell, and though it hurt to be so crudely pushed away, especially after what she'd learned, Fura was starting to see glimpses of a whole different side of Kiyani. One that she'd been sure existed, but had never thought to see firsthand.

"I don't even know where home is anymore."

"Barandor…"

"Kiyani," Fura scolded weakly. There was a time when she would have reacted more vehemently to his continued attempts to push her in that direction, but right now she was too weak from the vast scope of information that she'd had to take in over the past few days.

"You could go back to the life you had," he said, continuing to argue his point. "You could forget that any of this ever happened."

Another tear rolled down Fura's cheek and she ignored it, not caring anymore to try to wipe it away before he could see it. Kiyani had seen enough of her tears already that evening, and though she wasn't sure if he could clearly see them now, Fura was aware that he could likely hear her sniffling in the dark. She was surprised that he hadn't yet physically pushed her away, disgusted by her presence and her weakness, like he'd done that first night directly following the attack on Frielana.

"Go back to what life?" she questioned. "You seem to know, just as well as I do, that I have no family to go back to. I have nowhere to go."

"You think I do?"

His melancholy tone faded away into the shadows, leaving the room empty. Distraught, Fura couldn't keep the sounds of her tears from echoing against the surrounding stone. She winced as each sound came back to her, magnified. Though she was sure that Kiyani had had enough of her and was contemplating telling her to leave, she moved forward against her own better judgment and buried her face into his chest.

Kiyani went rigid in response, yet distraught and ravaged by raw emotions that tore at her from the inside, Fura didn't even take notice. Nor was she aware when he relented with a tired sigh, his body softening as he attempted to make himself as comfortable as he possibly could. She was lulled into sleep not too long after, the warmth of his body and the protective drape of his arm chasing away all coherent thoughts.

35

◆◆◇◆◆

RECONSIDER

When Fura opened her eyes the next morning, the scene was much the same as it had been the past few days. Dark stone walls, the slow-moving trails of water slicing down the uneven rock, and the eerie colors of the faerie lights that illuminated the moisture. Yet, Fura instinctively knew that it wasn't the same room.

As if to prove she wasn't fully mad, she rolled over to find Kiyani sitting at the end of the bed.

Just the sight of him brought back the memory of falling asleep in his arms the night before. Fura's face flushed at the thought. In the darkness it had been a tremendous comfort. But now, in the semi-light of what she assumed had to be day, all she could think of was how she must have come across to him. If he hadn't thought she was some sad, needy little girl before, then he surely must now.

Not that it much mattered.

Kiyani had made it clear early on that his initial opinion of her was set in stone.

Fura doubted that there was much she could do to change that.

All it felt like was that she was continually digging herself deeper into the same hole.

Glad that he hadn't yet noticed her, Fura could see that his attention was on the glittering blade that he carefully caressed. The one that he'd said the Fae's blacksmith, Sauvalle, had created for him.

If there was one thing that Fura knew absolutely squat about, it was swords, but if what Kiyani had said was true – that the one he currently held was the same as the one he'd stripped from the Shadowguard man who had attacked them – then she was impressed.

That knowledge aside, there was something else that nagged at her, making it impossible to go back to sleep. As much as it sounded like a good idea, Fura knew that sleeping her life away wouldn't change what had happened recently. Wouldn't change what she had learned.

"You stayed," she finally said weakly. Even after everything, it was the only thing that immediately came to mind.

279

Fura almost expected Kiyani to jump, startled by her voice, but he only turned his head slowly as if he'd already known that she was awake.

He shrugged, indicating it was no big deal. "I'd rather sit here than go brave running into Tybithera by the falls."

His words stung, but Fura had come to expect nothing less from him, becoming ever more aware that she wasn't the only one he spoke so caustically to without a second thought. Not sure what else to say, she only nodded in return.

She still wasn't sure what kind of opinion she had of the Fae Queen, but Kiyani had made his quite clear. Not that she blamed him. Helping them escape from those strange creatures that Kiyani and Tybithera both had called the Streig, and then offering to help in their journey had been very kind of her. But what had happened last night at the feast had thrown things into a whole new perspective. Fura could still see the sadness on Saiva's face as she'd told Fura that she was sorry. As mad as she'd been then, Fura realized that she didn't blame the bright-eyed, blue-haired girl in the least. All in all, she still wasn't even sure what had occurred, but Fura had a good idea that Kiyani knew more of what it all meant than he was letting on.

"You don't like her much, do you?" Fura finally asked.

Kiyani's eyes darkened as he looked back at her again. "I don't take kindly to those that force people into submission."

"Is that what that was?" The look of shock on his face before he'd made the announcement to the Fae had stuck with her throughout the night.

Lowering the sword in his grasp, Kiyani placed it so that it lay across his lap, as if the shine had just worn off and he no longer knew what to do with it.

"You don't think so?"

Fura shrugged. She still didn't know what to think. About the feast. About this new world or her family switch. About any of it.

Not knowing what to say to him, she let her thoughts drift, wondering if she would ever be able to come to terms with what he had told her the night before. Her introduction to the Fae had been a strange and cumbersome experience. But Fura had gotten through it, even finding herself able to deal with it quite readily if she just let herself go and enjoy the moment. But how was she ever supposed to be able to just wake up one morning and be okay with the fact that she had never been related to the people she had always called her family?

It was true that she'd never known of any relatives, that every now and then she had felt out of place in her own household. Yet, only now was it finally all clicking into place, like someone had dumped a shower of puzzle pieces on her that contained the missing pieces of her life when put together. The bonds of family were one thing she had never questioned, but now it was the only thing Fura could think about. How could she have been so closed-minded to not notice something so glaringly obvious? Did everyone else know? Was she the only one who'd been blind to this information all along?

"So, how are you?" Kiyani asked, breaking the silence and changing the subject.

Fura was still unsure herself. "I feel like my life has been put through a cheese grater."

She didn't know how else to describe what she was feeling.

"I bet. I don't assume you would even think about going back to Barandor now?"

The mere suggestion hurt, but Fura let it roll off her shoulders. Just before falling asleep she had made a final decision, and she wasn't going to let him talk her out of it. "If there's any chance of me being able to see Apallo again, to rescue him, then I want to be a part of it," she declared boldly.

Kiyani looked back at her, startled by her sudden change in demeanor. He raised a brow in question. "Do you really think you're up for it? This world's bigger than you realize."

Fura could hear in his tone that he was trying to sway her decision. "All I can do is try," she admitted. "It's not like I have anything to lose at this point."

"Just your life," Kiyani replied flatly.

Fura cringed. His voice held the experience of a thousand jaded lifetimes all wrapped into a few syllables. It left her cold, and she found herself deep in contemplation about just how much she was willing to risk to look into the eyes of a man that had given her up. And for what?

"Do you know why he left me?" she asked. It was hard to issue the words, to hear such a devastating revelation in her own thin voice. It wasn't so much a question of wanting to know, but the need to have an answer to fuel her accusation. Only the day before she had still looked upon the man as a fatherly figure, the same as she had for years. Only now that there was truth behind the feeling, Fura couldn't bring herself to look upon him with the same affection. Instead it was like a poison that dripped inside her, eating away at those fond memories and replacing them with something irreparably tarnished.

"I don't know that he did."

That simple statement left Fura confused. Had she really just heard that sentiment from the one she had seen fight with Apallo tooth and nail over nothing? Apallo had supposedly looked down upon Kiyani the whole time he had been living in Frielana, yet now he was defending the man. This side of Kiyani was foreign to her and Fura wondered if maybe she was still asleep. "What do you mean?" she asked, seeking clarification.

"You have to realize that he's the Firelord. He's got a lot of responsibility."

"What about my mother? What exactly happened to her?"

"Look Fura, that was all before I even knew of Frielana. I don't know your family history."

"But you do know more than you're telling me."

There was a sense of faded sorrow in the glance that Kiyani pinned her with, but he refused to say much more. "You ask questions that I don't have the answers to."

Questions that he didn't have the answers to.

Kiyani had already turned away from her, his attention drawn away by the detailed, swirled carving in the leather that made up the sheath for the sword. Fura stared at the line of his back, the soft flip of the dark hair that skimmed his neck. She knew he didn't have the answers, but it couldn't keep her from wanting them regardless. She didn't even care who gave them to her. She realized then that maybe it wasn't the bond of family that drove her to take on this wild journey on little more than a whim, but the overbearing need to hear the excuses from Apallo himself.

Excuses. Fura couldn't believe that her view of him had changed so dramatically in such a short period of time. She knew the man and he didn't strike her as a mean spirit. Knew for a fact that he didn't have an evil streak in him at all. Yet, here she was condemning him based on nothing more than a few facts from Kiyani, mixed with her own raging feelings. The only thing Fura wanted to hear was that she hadn't been a mistake to him. There had to have been a reason behind his decision. Everyone had reasons for their doings.

Looking at Kiyani again, Fura could see a patch of skin, marred and bearing a scarred line, just visible as it peeked from under his tank top at his right shoulder. But it was the black ink, so vivid against the pale skin at his neck that truly caught her attention. The tattoo, depicting a curled snake with wings protruding from its body, was different than anything Fura had ever seen, even on some of the crazy characters in the festival. Sitting forward on her knees, she looked closer at the striking detail of the crescent moon and the flames that surrounded the creature.

She wanted to comment on it, to ask him of its origins, but Fura didn't want to turn him against her so early in the morning. The only time she had ever gotten anything out of him regarding himself was what he offered freely without the poking and prodding of curiosity.

It only reminded Fura how little she knew him.

Most of the time, he struck Fura as a bomb waiting to explode, but then there were times when he completely surprised her, like the night before. The one thing Fura couldn't deny was that he was certainly an interesting individual. Hot headed at times, and temperamental, but all she could think of was that haunted look in his eye back in the forest when he'd had that knife pointed at her. As dangerous as he may have been, she wanted to know more.

Her eyes sliding away from the tattoo and back to the scar – glyphs of a past that she wondered if she would ever become privy to – Fura vowed that she would withhold judgment of both him and Apallo until she knew more.

"So what do we do now?" she asked.

Kiyani stood and walked around the end of the bed to the table. He placed the sword alongside the dagger that rested on its surface. "I guess we go to the falls and see what Tybithera has to say about the fiasco last night."

"Do you think that's where she'll be?" Fura wasn't sure she wanted to understand any further.

"If not, I'm sure she'll make her way there sooner than later."

"She hasn't found you yet?" Fura had assumed that the Fae Queen would have been the first to search him out. Especially when she took into account the cold distance in Kiyani's voice when he so much as spoke the woman's name.

They both made their way down to the falls, only to find that the room was as quiet and empty as ever. Fura thought to leave, maybe go back to her own room and change before suggesting that they go seek the Fae Queen out themselves. Kiyani on the other hand continued into the space. Fura watched as he walked along the waterline, gathering loose stones.

"Do you think we should go find her?" she asked, voicing her thoughts.

Kiyani tossed a rock into the water as if making a wish before turning. "Tybithera? And say what? Nice stay and all but we've got to go?" Tossing another stone and watching the ripples in the water, he gave a distant laugh.

"We're leaving?" Fura asked, moving to his side. She hadn't even been given time to think about when their journey would actually start.

"Do you think we're going to find Apallo if we stay here?"

"No... I..." Couldn't she at least be allowed some time to think? "When?"

"I don't know yet."

"What is Tybithera going to think if we just up and leave?"

"What does it matter?" Kiyani asked irritably, his voice rising. "I'm regaining my freedom, and then I'm leaving."

"Do you really think that's such a good idea to go back on your word like that?" Fura didn't know how Fae politics worked, but she was sure Tybithera would have an overtly different opinion on Kiyani's sudden jest.

"I never had a say in the matter."

"So you're just going to up and leave after you offered your help? Why?"

"Why? Because I'm tired of being poked and prodded about my decisions, about my life, of being used like some game piece with no feelings. Maybe I didn't have a goal in mind when we fled Frielana, but I can say that this little stop was unintended. I don't know what else Tybithera has waiting in the wings for us, but I'm not going to be a part of it!"

"I'm sorry to hear that," Tybithera's clear voice announced from the doorway. There was no saying just how long she had been standing there, listening to Kiyani's tirade.

"Maybe you should have thought about that before you blindsided me," Kiyani fired back, turning his head to shoot her a look of blind hatred. It was obvious that he was uncaring of the rank of the one he was so rudely talking to.

Tybithera floated into the room, unfazed by his anger. Her hands clasped gracefully behind her back, her chest puffed out in pride, she looked every inch the queen she was.

Fura returned a silent nod from the woman as she passed by, before making her way over to the rocks to sit, not sure of how this would end. Badly, she guessed. As soon as the Fae Queen had entered the room, all Fura had wanted to do was quietly leave, making her way, unnoticed, back to the safety of her room. This was a fight between Kiyani and Tybithera, and both were incredibly volatile. Fura had no desire to get muddled up in the middle of it.

"Blindsiding, as you would call it, is not what I do," Tybithera said, her gaze unwavering as she stopped before Kiyani. "You made an oath to restore power to this dying race and I expect you to uphold it."

"*Help*," Kiyani corrected. "I promised to *help*. If I remember correctly, that oath was whispered in your own words which you forced me to repeat."

"I will see to it that you follow through on that promise." Her words were cold and calculated, no hint of give to be had.

"A promise I have no recollection of ever making. Words repeated from someone else's lips hardly hold the same strength as those spoken from the heart of the one talking. That was not my promise, therefore I don't need to do anything in the way of helping you or your people."

"Trying to find a loophole in your agreement will get you nowhere," Tybithera said with a sly smile.

Fura sat with her knees drawn to her chest and her eyes to the floor as she listened to the two argue. She didn't dare look up, afraid of what she might see. It felt like she had disappeared from the room, or had become a fly on the wall, somehow dodging the lines of fire.

"I believe that part of the criteria for this little suicide mission of yours was someone who had nothing to lose," Kiyani said smugly. "That's just another way of saying that I either have nothing going for me in this life, or I'm unafraid of death. Either way, it's going to be hard to convince me."

Tybithera laughed. "It wasn't that difficult last night."

Kiyani shook his head. "That was a cold move and you know it." Sauvalle's words rang through his head, though he doubted they were true. "This is between you and I. You have no right to involve her."

Though desperately wanting to retreat, Fura perked up, sure that even though her name hadn't been specifically mentioned, she had just been brought into the conversation.

"That is past us, is it not?" Tybithera asked, her voice smooth.

"So you retract your claim now that she was invalid to your cause, that her life meant nothing?"

"Who's?" Fura couldn't help interceding as she moved cautiously from the rocks, her curiosity dampening the fear.

"Yours," Kiyani confirmed, his eyes never breaking from Tybithera's.

Fura's eyes widened in shock as she looked to the Fae Queen as well. "What?"

"That's low for one of the Fae to use lives as bargaining chips, don't you think?" Kiyani continued, a sly grin on his face as if he'd been the one to break through the woman's glamour, revealing her for what she really was.

"Don't listen to him, honey," Tybithera said soothingly, painting Kiyani as the dark horse as she returned to her charming air.

"How dare you try to sweet talk her after the words that came out of your mouth last night. Who do you think she's going to trust?"

"You? Why would she trust someone who's name she does —"

"Don't," Kiyani warned.

"We can play this game all day. You won't win."

Eyes moving back and forth, weighing the opponents, Fura watched as they let the heated argument fall silent. The boiling rage had left Kiyani shaking, but she knew he wasn't about to retreat.

"There's no reason that you can't do this yourself," Kiyani lashed out suddenly, breaking the short reprieve. "It's not like you're going to turn to dust the moment you step free of your land. You proved that yesterday. You would be just as defenseless as we would be, which is unknown to you. So what makes you think that I could get the job done? Or is it that you're just too self-centered to ever think of putting yourself in danger?"

"The things I could do to you, not only physically, but mentally, are beyond your level of comprehension."

"So the tales are true," Kiyani said. He stood tall, facing the Fae Queen without flinching in response to her threats. "The Fae are deceitful and devious."

Fura bridged the gap between them and pulled at his arm. "Kiyani," she begged, wanting him to stop before he got them thrown into whatever could qualify as a dungeon in the Keep.

Tybithera grinned. "At least someone knows their place. Smart girl."

Kiyani was unperturbed by the comment. "My place is knowing the truth in a situation," he replied with dead calm.

The Fae Queen regarded the two of them, taking in the sight of the frail girl attached to Kiyani's arm, trying in vain to protect him.

"And just what would you have me do? Gather everyone and announce that all of this was a lie, crush the only hope they've had in years? Do you want to be the one to make that call? I cannot allow you the precedence of deciding that." Tybithera broke her gaze with him and walked along the length of the stream, watching herself in the reflection cast back from the water.

"They don't need to know," Kiyani said simply.

Tybithera paused in her step. "You would have me lie to them?"

"I'm adamant about keeping my promises, but this is one that I never intended to make."

"What exactly are you proposing? For me to free you?"

Kiyani could hear her speak the words around a laugh that sounded to have gotten stuck in her throat. "Yes," he replied simply. "I will help, if I can, but not under order."

"What difference does it make?"

"I will not have my name tied to any variance of a promise that I'm not sure I can keep. I will not sell my soul or risk my life to save another race when I can't even help my own."

Fura was astounded by the amount of diplomacy that he seemed capable of conveying when only a moment before he'd been yelling.

Approaching him yet again, Tybithera's lip turned up into a small smile. "You doubt yourself," she guessed accurately. "How noble of you."

"My oath?" Kiyani commanded, not wanting to wait to hear if anything had actually been accomplished in the heated exchange of words.

"You are released," she relented after a long moment of silence, her voice conveying that she was far from happy about the decision. "However, I do not plan on letting any portion of this conversation leave this room, and I suggest you do the same. Help is all I really ask for. If you can promise me that, then you are free to go."

"Good," Kiyani said with a rough nod. He knew it wouldn't be the last he heard from her, but for a brief moment, the game was once again on a level playing field.

Though he was satisfied, there was a fire still blazing in his eyes as he turned and stalked out of the room.

36

♦♦◇♦♦

CAGED AND DROWNING

Fura watched as Kiyani turned the corner, the scene playing out as a sense of déjà vu from the night before. The way he had spoken to the Fae Queen left her speechless. She didn't know if he had a death wish or if he was just crazy.

Feeling like she had just been dropped to the curb like unwanted trash, Fura braved a look at Tybithera. The woman's gaze had followed Kiyani as he'd taken his leave, but in his absence the metallic eyes shifted to meet hers. The look on her face seemed to declare she was pleased with the outcome of the conversation, despite ultimately relenting to Kiyani's request. Uncomfortable, Fura turned away, no longer feeling quite as safe with the woman as she had before. Though Tybithera had been almost motherly in the time Fura had spent with her alone, she was beginning to pick up on a different side of her through the conversations overheard between Kiyani and the Fae woman.

Shying away from Tybithera's stare that seemed to challenge her to pick between Kiyani and the Fae, Fura turned and bolted out into the hallway, intent on catching up with Kiyani.

Despite being driven by his anger, Fura discovered that Kiyani hadn't gone far. As she approached, she frantically wondered what to say to him. Though she still wanted questions answered, she had the feeling that now wasn't a good time to continue their on-going conversation.

"Are you insane?!" Fura challenged anyway when she caught up with him, not knowing how else to breech the subject.

Kiyani simply turned and looked at her with a raised brow, questioning her as if the prior conversation had never happened. "Not that I'm aware."

She couldn't believe him. This new side of Tyibithera had only begun to emerge within the last few days, and it scared her. Yet, one thing she'd noticed was that she only glimpsed it when Kiyani was present. As if he were a magnet for dredging up the darker side of people. With her high stature, and who knew what abilities she had as a Faerie Queen, Fura never would have thought about challenging Tybithera like that. Kiyani didn't seem to think twice about it.

"It's like you try to make trouble," Fura vented. "Like it's some big game to you. Are you really that unafraid of retaliation?" She had never met anyone quite like him, and Fura wasn't sure if that might have been a good thing.

"I'm generally the one retaliating."

"You do know that you've nearly crossed the line twice now, right?" At least twice that she was aware of. There was no telling what he might have said to the woman while she had spent the day with Saiva. Fura cringed just thinking about the possibilities. "Is it because you know she can't do anything to you, or something? Do you have some form of immunity that I don't know about?"

"Relax," Kiyani said nonchalantly, cutting her short. "We're both still alive, aren't we? I see that as a good sign."

Fura let out a growl, wanting to hit him for being so cocky, when he knew damn well he could have just gotten both of them killed.

"The Faerie race is weakening," he continued, repeating Tybithera's words from the night before.

"So that gives you free range to try your hand at offending them?"

Kiyani gave a noncommittal shrug. "On her own land she can do some significant damage if she so pleases, but I don't think she would go that far."

Staring at him, Fura fought for the words to reply. It was apparent that he knew the dangers, yet he seemed to enjoy walking that perilous line, to feed off the raw thrill of it. She shook her head, trying to figure him out. It was as if the longer she knew him, the more of a stranger he became.

"Is there a reason then that you try so hard to make her mad? She's a Faerie Queen! Does that mean nothing to you, because here you are playing cat and mouse, seeing who can mess with the other's head the most."

With a groan, Fura leaned against the wall. Just one day that held any semblance of normal, that's all she asked. She hadn't known that in the present company it would be such a difficult order to fill.

"You're insane," she whimpered, trying to calm her nerves. Fura didn't know how much more she could handle, here or anywhere else. "Maybe Apallo was right."

"About what?" Kiyani asked harshly, all sense of joking aside.

Fura's head shot up, wishing she could take the words back. She hadn't even been aware she'd spoken them aloud, but Kiyani's rigid stance told her there was no way he hadn't heard that.

"If you're so worried about it, then stay the hell away from me!" he shouted, disappearing into his room and slamming the door before Fura could even think of a way to apologize and tell him she hadn't meant it.

She should have known better than to so much as mention Apallo around him. A raging inferno in the center of an active volcano... that's what Kiyani was. Fura just wondered how long it would be before she got too close to the edge and fell in.

The sensation of eyes boring into her pricked at the skin on the back of Fura's neck, and she turned to find that Tybithera had moved into the hall. Though she hoped against it, the grin on the woman's face declared that she had witnessed the whole argument. Her strange copper eyes glimmered in the light of the Fae orbs, silently saying, 'I told you so.' Fura didn't know what was going on between Tybithera and Kiyani, having only begun to bear witness to the rage that seemed to be harbored between them. All she knew was that she didn't want to be involved any further than she already was. Before the woman could say a word, Fura darted into her own room, hoping she wouldn't follow.

When Fura emerged over an hour later, the Fae Queen was nowhere in sight. The falls called to her, telling her to come out of the small room and stretch her legs. Tempting as it was, Fura turned left instead, not wanting to brave the possibility of running into Kiyani so soon. There was no saying for certain that he would have returned to the falls, but it wasn't unlikely. If she knew anything at all about him, it was that he seemed to be drawn to water. Meandering down the hall, she thought about returning to the underground spring Saiva had brought to her attention the day before. Water didn't have the same calming effect on her, but it was solitude she sought.

Though the thought of seeing Kiyani again left a raw, yet almost thrilling, terror in her gut, Fura couldn't put him out of her mind. She wondered where their conversation might have ended up had she not spoken her last words. There was no saying that it would have gone much further, but it might have at least ended with them still on speaking terms. The fact was, Fura didn't even know if that'd been considered a fight. He was so quick to anger that every word spoken to him felt like a fight if she thought about it. All she knew was that he hadn't been happy with her, the slamming door speaking louder than anything he could have said.

The look that Tybithera had fixed her with afterwards had almost spoken just as loudly, reminding her of Apallo and his own warnings. Just the thought of the man left a hole in Fura's heart. Though she didn't know how long it would take for her to come to terms that he was her father, she still thought of him as a mentor and friend. Not only was she determined to see him again, no matter what it took, Fura amended that she would prove both him and Tybithera wrong in regards to Kiyani.

He had his moments, that was for sure, but Fura was certain that he was defined by more than just his anger. She just had to decipher the maze he'd built around himself. He carried a latent anger on the surface, hidden at times, but ready to strike at any given moment. Yet, as off-putting as that should have been, Fura had seen the side of him that he went to extensive lengths to hide. It was in the most fleeting of moments, but she had witnessed it all the same. The easy route would have been to simply walk away, but the mystery just left Fura determined to crack the code. Especially if she was going to be traveling with him from here on out.

As she strolled through the halls, poking her head around corners and glancing behind her, trying to judge how far she'd gone, Fura felt her senses begin to return to her. Something that she'd been lacking ever since she had arrived in Fae Rue. As she took in deep breaths of the mossy air, she stopped periodically to stare at the streams of water running down the stone. Out of the corner of her eye she could swear that she kept glimpsing patterns and pictures left in the wet trails. Watching it trickle down the stone, Fura wished that getting the answers to her questions were as simple as decoding the watery glyphs before her.

When no help appeared in their silence, she moved along.

It wasn't long before a shimmering light danced along the walls ahead, announcing that she was close. Knowing that the spring lay just around the corner, Fura quickened the pace. The distraction it would provide was exactly what she needed at the moment.

Walking around the corner and ducking under an overhang of stone, that had the unnerving possibility of decapitating someone if they didn't know where they were going, Fura squinted as she looked into the unnatural light. She'd only been to the underground spring once, but she was sure that this was right. The only confirmation she needed was the dancing mist that bellowed out into the hall, clinging to the walls in shimmering beads. The sound of water that followed was just further proof that she'd made it on her own.

As her eyes adjusted to the change in light, Fura took an involuntary step back, surprised to find that she'd stumbled upon the one person she had meant to avoid.

Kiyani stood waist deep in the steaming water, stark naked. Yet it wasn't the lack of clothing that caught Fura's attention. With his back turned to her, her focus was immediately drawn to the meshwork of scars that decorated his back. Trailing along his skin in deep veins of angry red, they looked like they might bleed at any moment. Though crude at times, Fura had begun to grow accustomed to the way Kiyani acted on a daily basis. Yet, the way he carried himself left her with no indication that he could've possibly been injured so badly. Drawing in a silent gasp, Fura couldn't take her eyes off the grotesque lines. They couldn't have been more than a few days old. Knowing they had to hurt, Fura found herself thinking back to any signs that he could have shown.

Water splashed at her feet and Fura cringed as she looked down, knowing that Kiyani's sensitive hearing would surely take notice, the sound indicating that he was no longer alone. Sure enough, Kiyani tensed. It was the shallowest of movements at first, but it was enough for the sickness in Fura's gut to bottom out. After her last meeting with him, this was the last thing she could have hoped for.

Wheeling around, Kiyani ducked deeper into the water, a look of shock spreading across his face for a brief moment before the lines hardened into the scowl she was growing far too comfortable with. The irritated set of his lips was something she could contend with, but it was the darkness in his eyes that left Fura unnerved.

Holding her hands aloft as she backed up, Fura found herself apologizing in a slur of murmured words. "I'm sorry," she said quickly. "I didn't know you were down here."

She'd assumed that he would have stayed holed up in his room for the remainder of the day, stewing in his own self-imposed exile. Or, that in the Fae Queen's absence, he might have taken up residence at the falls again, seeking the solitary companionship of the falling water. Never did she think that he would end up down here. In fact it hadn't even occurred to her that he knew of this place.

Though, now that she saw him in this setting, she could see why he had wandered down to the spring. In a way, it had him written all over it. Like her, peace and quiet had been what he'd sought. Once again, Fura had found herself the intruder. Just like at the spring back in Frielana. Yet, it wasn't clear if he was angry at being disturbed, or if it was because she had been the one to break into his solitude.

"Get out…" Kiyani finally growled, his voice lower and more collected than Fura expected, leaving her deeper in the throes of fear than if he'd straight out yelled at her.

Left speechless, she was torn between wanting to move forward and help him, knowing he had to be in excruciating pain, and wanting to bolt to escape his impenetrable rage. Yet, all Fura could do was remain frozen in place, paralyzed by the darkness in his eyes and the way he looked shirtless, the dark hair falling around his face in wet strands. Plastered to the back of his neck, it was almost long enough to cover his tattoo. But all Fura could think about were the scars. It was the one thing that kept her from running, her compassionate nature kicking in, as scenes of moving forward to help him as he'd done for her ran through her mind in unruly pictures. Ones that, even so early in their sordid relationship, she knew would never happen.

He shied away from her presence just as often as her touch, which was practically every waking moment. It was a response he seemed to share with everyone. Everyone except Monira and the wolf that he refused to call a loyal friend. Even so, Fura doubted she could ever get that close to him where he would share such a dark secret.

Granted that it was a secret at all.

Regardless, it was her heart that drew her forward, ignoring the caution in her head as she gingerly took a step into the water. It was like approaching a rabid animal.

And he reminded her of just that. Kiyani drew back further into the water and the steam, a wild look in his eyes.

"I said leave."

"But, your back..."

The mention of it seemed to startle him, as if he hadn't even been aware of the flayed skin. As if the pain that much have been wrought from such a travesty wasn't his own.

"It's nothing," he declared forcefully, retreating back into the anger he wore like a mask, almost always dashing behind it when a situation wasn't to his liking. "Now go!"

Fura cringed at his tone, knowing that it would be stupid to press any further. She may have caught him in a compromising moment, but she knew, even in his current position, she was defenseless against him if he decided to take that anger out on her. Fura couldn't see him going so far, but she didn't want to test the limits of his boundaries either.

Teetering, she took a timid step backwards.

"Get out!" Kiyani bellowed.

This time Fura took heed and bolted.

A startled doe. That's what she reminded him of.

Kiyani watched tensely as his words finally registered and Fura bolted out of the water and around the corner, quickly disappearing from sight. His heart pounded in his chest and he took a deep, yet ragged breath, trying to calm himself. A useless endeavor.

He didn't know what was worse, that she'd caught him in such a compromising situation, or that she had genuinely startled him. Something that he wasn't used to. Remaining acutely aware of his surroundings, no matter what was going through his head, was one of the few things he prided himself on. The fact that she had so easily snuck up on him was just a reminder of how complacent he had grown while hiding away in Frielana.

Muttering irritably, Kiyani lay back and let himself sink under the water, wishing that it would just drown him. It would remove him from all the problems that had come to light in the past few weeks. The siege. His troubles with Apallo. Tybithera would disappear, as would Fura. He wouldn't have to worry about it anymore. All the things that shouldn't have been his problem in the first place. He could just pass away into nothing, all his stress and worries following him into the void.

It was a tempting escape...

Opening his eyes, he stared at the wavering clouds of mist, refracted in the water covering him. It came across as a strange, yet comforting dream.

... but one he couldn't easily allow himself.

Coming up from his submersion, Kiyani cradled his head in his hands for a moment before wiping the water from his face and squeezing out his hair.

As tempting as it was, such an act wouldn't change anything. The world around him would still be the same crap shoot as it always was, and Fura would be just as lost as ever.

Even if he didn't care, such a release wasn't that easy. Besides, he was too good of a swimmer to allow himself to succumb to the fatality of drowning. If he were to choose to go, he would have to find another way.

Looking to the empty doorway where he almost expected to find Fura peeking around the corner, Kiyani felt a sudden sense of loss. Even if she wasn't still lingering, it didn't matter. The secrets he would have rather kept hidden were slowly coming to light in her presence. His fingers trailing the path of the scars on his back, Kiyani grimaced. The pain was something he had grown accustomed to, but the look on Fura's face haunted him.

Sitting alone on the rocks, staring at the water before her, Fura wished she'd come to the falls first. What had she been thinking, seeking out the spring, anyways? She didn't even like water.

There was no solace in it.

No joy.

Only the terrifying fear of drowning.

Yet, it wasn't the waves she was sinking beneath, but her mixed emotions.

Staring into the crashing water of the falls, she reminded herself that what had happened wasn't her fault. How could it have been? There was no reason she ever should have expected to run into Kiyani there.

Her intent hadn't been to pry further into his personal life. She'd only wanted a quiet place to think, to mull over all that she'd learned in the last few days. To glean any sense out of the recent events. Instead, she'd only been dealt more confusion.

With each day spent in this Izandüre, Fura felt like she knew herself less and less. Not only did she no longer know herself, she didn't know *what* to do with herself, either.

Apallo was not only the Firelord, but her father.

Those two facts alone left her world spiraling out of control.

Barandor was no more a home to her now than this strange land of fantasy creatures.

Myth and magic aside, the one person she felt she could talk to about any of it currently harbored a tornado of emotions, and had never wanted her around in the first place. Even Tybithera no longer felt like a safe option. After that last fleeting glance she'd received from the woman, Fura felt uncomfortable discussing the matters with the Fae Queen. Following the events of the feast, she no longer knew if the woman actually cared about her situation, or if she was simply looking for a couple of low-lifes for a dangerous quest, as Kiyani had declared.

Hearing noise beyond the falls, the low drone of a voice, and the shuffle of feet, Fura turned her head to see Kiyani disappearing back out into the hall.

Though she knew he'd left because of her, she stumbled off the rocks and raced after him.

"Wait!" she called, catching him before he could make it back to his room.

"What?"

"I'm sorry," she quickly apologized, fumbling with the words. "I swear I didn't know you were going to be there."

Kiyani looked down on her as she nervously wrung her hands, hating that she was purposely avoiding eye contact with him. She knew she should have just let him go. It was obvious that he didn't want to talk to her, and she didn't know what to say anyways. Yet, Fura knew she couldn't just leave it like that. Even if all she could manage was a brief apology, she knew it would make her feel better, at least.

"It's fine," he declared through gritted teeth, making to leave for a second time. Her increasing fear of his presence wasn't lost on him, making him want to leave on that fact alone. Though Kiyani knew he should accept her apology and move on, offer one in return, he remained silent. He knew he shouldn't have been mad in the first place. Yet, none of this should have been on him. He was meant to travel alone, not have someone prying into his personal life.

"I don't believe that," Fura answered meekly, stopping him again.

The best answer was to simply walk away without any further words, Kiyani knew that. He was quickly finding that Fura was one of those people that would try to continue a conversation at any cost, when he was, in fact, quite the opposite.

Let her have the last word, Kiyani thought. He didn't care. His place in life had left him used to people refusing to talk to him at all. It made no difference to him if he had the last say. Only in certain matters, and this wasn't one of them.

"Kiyani," Fura pleaded as he took another step closer to his room. She knew that if he got past that door she wouldn't see him for the rest of the day. Despite her bold move the night before, she didn't dare follow him in again. Not in his current mood. "Please don't go."

She cringed at the childish tone in her voice but she didn't dare speak again to correct it. It was easy to see that Kiyani already wasn't in much of a mood to deal with her, leaving her to wonder why she was even trying. What did she really have to gain from any of this save for more misery?

"There's nothing to say," Kiyani answered.

"What about your back..." Fura tried again but Kiyani immediately cut her off.

"I said it was nothing," he growled. "Leave it alone."

Fura took note of the sudden intensity in his tone. She had already discovered that there were a number of things that could set him off, but she hadn't thought that that would have been one of them. Then again, she should have known that sympathy didn't gain her any points either.

"Okay," she relented meekly. "But you should have it looked at."

He may not have wanted her, or anyone to know about his injuries, but he had to know how bad it looked. Fura didn't take him for one that would risk his life on pride. At least she hoped not.

"Its fine," he argued, intent on settling the matter. "That's my decision, not yours."

Fura watched him turn on his heel again, knowing he'd been done with the conversation before it had even started. Yet, she couldn't allow herself to let him have the last word in the matter. Even if she was willing to let the issue of his back slide for now, there were still plenty of things left to discuss.

"Why do you have to be so mean to me?" Fura asked, surprised by the power behind her usually timid voice. She didn't know where the words had even come from, but as embarrassed as she felt for uttering them she didn't feel the need to take them back. She could understand his dislike of her, but not how far he took it, almost to the point of cruelty at times.

"I'm not making you follow me," Kiyani declared harshly, finally turning around to face her. "If you want to leave, then go right ahead."

"And go where?" Fura couldn't believe that he was going down that path again. She thought she'd finally gotten him to give up that fight.

"Do you think I care?"

"I know you're not as mean as you try to be."

Kiyani seemed taken aback for a moment at the sudden declaration. "You don't even know me, Fura."

Fura felt a flush in her skin again that she knew she had no chance of hiding. It was a mystery even to her how she could feel this way about someone who was so decidedly against her. "Maybe not," she admitted. "But I feel like I can trust you."

"Then your judgment of character is faulty," he said simply.

"How can you say that about yourself?" she asked, wanting to know why he was so at war, not with just the world around him, but himself as well.

"You don't know me," Kiyani repeated as if trying to make it clear that he was against the idea of the two of them being anything that resembled friends. "Not. At. All. I'm a mystery to you, and most of those that surround you. I could be the shadow that haunts your dreams, or the silent killer that ends your life in the middle of the night."

Fura shook her head. "I don't believe that," she said, unwilling to admit that he already haunted her dreams at night. But it was the fact that that was the most she had heard him speak at one time that kept her going. "You could also be a newfound friend. A shoulder to cry on. A guiding light in the darkness. There's two ways to look at it."

In fact, he had already proven to be one of them, though she had to remind herself that that very well could have been a flash of something entirely foreign to his nature.

"On a probable one way street. Trust me, Fura, you set your standards way too high. The last thing you need to do in this world, whether you believe it exists or not, is lay your trust in the wrong people. There are more here than you could count who would take advantage of someone like you, and nothing good could come of that."

Was that worry for her? Fura wondered, startled by Kiyani's words. Or was it simply him trying a different approach of getting rid of her?

"Not everyone is like that," Fura said, trying to get him to see the view that she had of him. One that didn't paint him as the monster that Apallo had been so adamant he was.

"You're in a different place now. Trust is not to be taken lightly. It could cost you your life."

"Not always."

"Fura…"

"You're not one of those people. I refuse to believe that."

It wasn't until her back hit the solid stone of the wall that Fura realized that as they had been talking she had been slowly moving away from Kiyani. Once it was clear that she was trapped, he moved forward in a flash and caged her against the rock, his face inches from her own, those intense blue eyes staring straight into her. She couldn't help the shiver of fear, mixed with an electric surge of desire, that coursed through her spine.

"You're afraid of me," Kiyani declared, his tone low and intimate. "Whether you care to admit it or not. Apallo made sure of that."

"It doesn't mean you have to play the part." Fura's words came across stronger than she could have hoped, but she still couldn't keep her eyes from straying away from his.

"You can't even look me straight in the eye, and you know it," Kiyani said, commenting on the one thing she'd hoped he wouldn't notice.

Just the words made Fura want to shy away and she hated herself for it, for the fact that she was making it so blatantly obvious. And what was worse was that Kiyani was right. Had it not been for Apallo's warning, she couldn't have said that she would feel so conflicted about the man she had found herself keeping company with.

Sure, Kiyani had his moments that left Fura to wonder just what kind of man he was, but it was her father's warnings, repeating on an endless loop in her mind, that forced her to keep her distance for fear that those words would someday ring true.

"Placing your hopes too high just sets you up for failure," Kiyani said remotely, before breaking the cage of his arms and walking away.

As he walked away, Fura was left frozen in place, clinging to the wall to keep herself standing despite the shake in her legs. Trying to catch her breath in the aftermath of that unexpected move, she tried to convince herself that Kiyani's words weren't true. That she wasn't afraid of him.

Yet, her reaction only proved his point.

Looking down the abandoned hall, Fura peeled herself off the stone and moved towards the inviting doorway of her own room on unsteady feet.

She only made it a few steps before stopping and turning.

The best thing to do would be to forget about any reconciliation with Kiyani for the night. Simply return to her room and either go to bed early, or curl up in a blanket and use the silence to try and settle her mind. It was the safest bed.

However, Fura couldn't go of the fact that Kiyani hadn't returned to his room either, as he'd been so apt to do. Instead of disappearing into the room, slamming the door in her face again, he'd gone the opposite direction. Leaving her out in the hall, he'd taken the chance to steal the solitude of the falls for himself.

Solitude may have been the better option, but Fura still had questions that needed to be answered, and she was certain that Kiyani was the only one to do so.

Bracing herself for the possibility of more argument, Fura took the path less traveled.

37

◆◆◇◆◆

FALSE LEADS

Despite the determination in her mind, there was still something in Fura's gut that held her back as she lingered in the doorway.

Everything in her told her this wasn't the time to approach him, let alone with a load of questions in tow. It'd been easy to see that he'd never meant for her to become privy to his injuries, which had left her in shallow waters with him. That alone would have been enough to put him in a bad mood. Coupled with his leftover sour arrogance from his last argument with Tybithera, the road best traveled would be to just leave him alone for a bit. Maybe even wait until the next day.

It sounded like a solid idea, except that Fura had become increasingly aware that she didn't know what the next few hours would bring in this strange world. The way things had been going, she wasn't even guaranteed to see the next day.

Whether she was ready for more blunt conversation with him or not, she knew she couldn't put it off. He had once told her that in this place he called Izandüre, information was safety. Fura still didn't understand everything, but after what she'd been through, she knew the truth of that statement. So many things might have played out differently if she'd only known a few key things.

This had to be done now.

She just wished there was someone else around to act as a buffer.

The problem with that was that she was running out of options. She hardly knew anyone within Fae Rue Keep. Saiva wouldn't understand, and Tybithera was starting to morph into someone she wasn't sure she trusted.

Then again, she could have said the same of Kiyani.

The only difference with him was that from the first night he'd made an appearance in her life he'd never given her the impression that he was on her side. Which meant his current behavior was nothing new.

Her hand on the wall, as if it offered some cold, quiet support, Fura took a breath and moved forward into uncertainty.

The fact that she now had to mentally prepare herself to talk to

Kiyani left her wondering if maybe he hadn't been wrong in claiming he wasn't trustworthy. Yet, her only response to that was that if he really wasn't to be trusted, would he have made it known? Didn't the questionable ones lure others in with false pretenses before showing their true colors? That was something that Kiyani had never done.

Yet, each day spent with him felt like a battle. He was no more a stranger to her than he was a friend.

Each step muted by caution, Fura slowly moved into the room, trying to decipher his mood. Something easier said than done. Attempting to judge when his outbursts of anger would flare up was like trying to judge precisely when lightning would hit during a storm. You could feel the electric charge of it, but couldn't determine just when it would strike.

To her relief, however, Kiyani had already taken a seat on the rocks. She didn't know what was going through his mind, but it gave her a better peace of mind than when he'd been anxiously pacing the room the night before. From what she'd seen, anger drove him to movement. Though she knew he couldn't have calmed down that quickly, Fura felt better approaching him when he wasn't actively fidgeting.

As a matter of fact, as she rounded the rocks and sat beside him, she saw that he wasn't even paying her any attention, though she was certain he knew she was there. There was no way he couldn't. His eyes were open, but Fura guessed that his thoughts were as far away as the look in his eyes.

Struggling to think of a way to edge her way into conversation with him, Fura found herself staring at her feet. When the silence ensued, she dredged up the courage to peer at him out of the corner of her eye.

Though he had been closer to her in the hallway, fear and shock had kept her from picking up the details that were clear to her now. She didn't know how much longer he had remained at the spring after she had bolted, but it was easy to see that he hadn't made much of an effort to dry off. His hair still hung around his face in wet strands, and the loose tunic he wore clung to the damp skin beneath. Even with the tension between them, Fura couldn't help the rise of heat in her face as she thought about what she'd seen.

Despite the scars, and the instability of his temperament, she couldn't deny that she was still attracted to him. Against her better judgment. Against Kiyani's own judgment, even.

Then your judgment of character is faulty.

Those strange, self-condemning words of his rang throughout her head, leaving her as confused as ever. What kind of person warned people away from himself?

She was slowly falling in love with a man who didn't want anyone in his life, let alone her.

Angry at herself for holding onto such silly notions, Fura turned away. It didn't change anything. The fact was that he still saw her as nothing more than a little girl, and a lost one at that. He was insistent that she didn't belong in the world that he called home, and though he hadn't mentioned it since the night before, Fura still knew that, one way or another, he couldn't wait to be rid of her. She was kidding herself if she thought that there was anything there. Or ever could be.

Father or not, maybe Apallo had tried his hand at warning her away for a reason.

The thoughts burrowing into her mind like a poison, she fought the need to wipe away tears that hadn't even begun to fall. Though she would've preferred not to cry in front of him, it no longer mattered. She'd never met a more compassionless person in her life.

And yet, she knew that thought wasn't rooted in truth.

"So," Kiyani spoke, his voice sounding like thunder as it suddenly rumbled through the silence. "Are you going to say it, or what?"

Startled, Fura looked up at him. "What?" she echoed.

His hands clasped beneath his chin, he looked at her with knitted brows, seeming to contemplate the ever-raging war of his own thoughts. Though, if Fura had any guess in the matter, she would say that he was currently doing a better job than she was at fighting inner demons.

"You're sticking around for a reason."

Though she knew it was a childish maneuver, Fura crossed her arms over her chest and glared at him. She hated how easily he seemed to read her mind. "I can't just sit here?"

The tiniest shadow of a grin played at his lip as he shrugged and got up, so discreet that Fura wondered if she were seeing things.

"Fine," he said simply, rounding the boulders, indicating that if she wasn't going to offer any entertainment, then he was leaving.

Twisting, Fura followed him with her eyes. "Wait!" she called, knowing she was playing into exactly what he'd been expecting from her. As if playing a game, Kiyani stopped, his eyes centered on her as he waited. "Can't you stay?"

"I see no reason to."

Fura flinched, hurt by his comment and the quickness of it. He'd either had those cutting words waiting in reserve or had just tossed them out carelessly, not caring about their repercussions.

"Can you please just talk to me?"

Kiyani eyed her suspiciously. "I feel like we've done this before."

It was true, Fura realized. Nearly word for word, it was almost like a replay from the day he'd given this mysterious world a name. A moment in time before that ridiculous feast had taken place and changed everything. It was that implication that finally gave her reason to give up. What was she doing, anyways?

"Right," Fura muttered as she turned away. "Why bother. It's not like it would turn out any different," she said, trying to feign indifference, as if nothing had happened before that would lead to unsettling awkwardness. Though she yearned to know more about the marred skin she had seen, it wasn't just that.

A deafening silence settled over the room, broken only by the hush of the falling waters, leaving Fura to realize that she had done it now. He had taken his leave, and if she didn't know any better, she was certain it was for good this time. She had always known that it would only be a matter of time before he tired of her.

Pulling her knees up to her chest, she hugged them tight, waiting for the tears to fall. With no one around to see them, there was no use in fighting to hold them back.

It wasn't until she saw the flicker of shadow out of the corner of her eye that she realized Kiyani was still keeping company with her. Forcing herself to look up at him, she caught sight of the questioning concern in his eyes, though the words he spoke hardly reflected the same emotion.

"It depends," he said remotely, his tone more level than Fura had expected.

If he was confused by her actions, she was just as equally so with his.

"What?"

"I'll stay, but it depends on what you want to talk about."

"I," she faltered, still not knowing what he meant. "I'm not going back to Barandor, if that's what you mean."

"I didn't say anything about that," Kiyani replied, seeming to be stunned by the comment, leaving Fura to realize that he was fishing for any sign of her lingering concern regarding his personal life, past or present.

Fura studied his face, searching for any indication that he was lying about Barandor. "Not yet."

Maybe he hadn't been forthright in mentioning it, but she knew it was still on his mind.

"Fine," he relented. Sitting back down, he looked at the falling water before them. "I won't say anything more about it. Though I still think it would be for the best."

And there it was. Biting her lip, Fura let the conversation ride the lull as she looked back at her feet, at a loss.

"Why do you hate me so much?" she finally asked after a few moments, breaking the silence and spouting the one question that continually fronted itself before so many others.

For once, it was Kiyani that flinched, taken aback as he looked at her with furrowed brows, the smallest reaction that left Fura surprised.

"You keep asking me that, but I don't."

Fura looked at him, finally allowing herself to meet those startling blue eyes that currently held a hint of confusion. She didn't know that such a simple statement would affect him so much, but it was truth.

"You sure make it seem that way," Fura said meekly. "Despite what you seem to think, I really don't have anything for me in Barandor. As you were so apt to remind me last night, I have no family. At least, not there. And the only friends I really had, that I could count on, were the other members of *Pyropheric.*"

Pyropheric.

Fura thought back to first time she'd seen them perform, that she'd seen Apallo take to the stage with absolute confidence and a large grin on his face that told the story of a man that loved what he did. She didn't know if it had been the fires themselves that had called to her, or that image of Apallo, that had drawn her in, but from that moment on she had wanted nothing else in life but to live in that small slice of fantasy.

So caught up in the draw and the thrill of festival life, she hadn't bothered to put any other prospects into play. Thinking on it now nearly made her laugh in nervousness. How stupid she had been. She had been so close to the end of her senior year of school and yet had nothing planned beyond that moment of taking her diploma in hand. She had never had any other job, no real knowledge of the world outside the gates of Fireswell, no concrete idea of relationships.

The room around her was silent, filled only with that deathly emptiness that allowed one to explore the deepest recesses of their mind. Even the calming sounds of the trickling water and the deep, earthy smell of the moss couldn't remedy the turmoil that boiled within her.

The day before had started out so promising, now Fura had no idea what she had been left with. Just shreds of ravaged memories, and throes of raging emotions that she didn't know how to deal with.

Thinking about Apallo, Fura wiped a rogue tear away as it moved down her face. All the time she had spent with him at the festival, how could she not have known he was her father?

Every time her mind brought it forth, Fura pushed it away, telling herself that it wasn't true, that Kiyani had been lying. But there was no reason for him to lie to her like that, and deep down, she knew it was the truth.

"Lies…" Fura murmured. "My whole life has been lies." Caught off guard by her line of thinking, Kiyani stared at her as if he wanted to say something, yet he let her continue. "I don't even know who I am," she said, shaking her head. "Or what I am… I can't possibly have magic. Is that why Apallo didn't want me?"

"He never said he didn't want you," Kiyani pointed out, finally speaking.

Fura shook her head with a crazed laugh that turned to a choking sob. "No, he did. You weren't there, but I overheard him talking to Monira. He said it was a mistake bringing me into Frielana."

Avoiding eye contact with her, Kiyani looked up to the falls. "Because it was. He knew from the moment those fires touched the sky that night that something was happening that would spill over into Izandüre. He never should have brought you into it."

"But I was already a part of it. Not that it mattered. He didn't want me anyways. He proved that when he gave me up in the first place."

"Fura..."

Lost amidst her hysterical rant, Fura barely heard Kiyani. "And then the Keeples... how much of this did they know? Is that why they kept me on such a short leash? Did they know I was some freak from another world? Did they really not have any other family, or were they just embarrassed by me?"

"Fura," Kiyani said, breaking her train of thought with a rough shake of his head. "Stop. You're searching for excuses to hate them that aren't there. I'm sure Apallo had his reasons. As for the Keeples, they obviously treated you well enough that you never questioned them."

Fura knew it was true. The Keeple's had always played the part of loving parents true. But just the thought that her whole life thus far had been a lie was enough to keep her on the defensive. "What would you know about it?"

Kiyani turned his head to meet her eye. It was only a moment before he turned away, but she could see that he chewed his bottom lip in contemplation.

"More than you know."

Fura looked at him questioningly.

"I ran away from home at five," he revealed morosely, seeming to know from experience that she wouldn't let the conversation end there.

"And you never went back?" Fura didn't know what this had to do with their conversation, but his admission was shocking to her. Such a thought had never once crossed her own mind, let alone at such a young age. She couldn't even think of what she had been doing at five. Possibly eating crayons.

Kiyani shook his head. "There was nothing there to draw me back. Nothing that was worth subjecting myself to the torture."

"All this time you've been in Frielana? But, Apallo hates you."

Kiyani shrugged as if it wasn't that big of a revelation, but she could see that it pained him to even bring it up. If it was anything like what she was feeling, she couldn't blame him.

"It was better than going back."

"I'm sorry."

"Don't," he warned. "Just be happy with what you were given, because I would have done anything to have had the same."

Fura nodded, not knowing what else to say. Kiyani kept himself so bottled up that she had to remind herself that she wasn't the only one with problems. He was just better at making it appear as if he were fine.

"So, where does that leave us?" she asked.

"What do you mean?"

Shrugging, Fura looked at the sparkling waters before them, reflecting the orbs above in a moving shimmer. "What do we do now?"

"You know my stance on the matter," Kiyani reminded her. "I still think it would be best for you to just forget about this place and return to what you know."

Fura wanted to argue with him, but she had lost some of her steam during her rant. Now she just wanted to curl up and cry over the things she had lost. Yet, for as much that had changed, there were still a few familiar threads left that she didn't want to sever.

"You really think that I can do that, knowing that Apallo's still out there somewhere? That he's my father?"

Kiyani cracked a small smile that told her he doubted it, though he kept his eyes trained on the floor. "You can't really blame me for trying. As fantastical as you think this world is, no one should have to live like this, surrounded by constant danger."

"Then why do you?" Fura asked. "Why not live in Barandor?"

"It's not that simple."

Deciding not to pry further into that statement, Fura stuck with the rest of the conversation. "You really think Barandor would be any safer? There's danger everywhere. Just different kinds. Look at what's already happened there."

Running a hand through his hair, Kiyani sighed as he turned to her. "I'm fighting a losing battle here, aren't I?"

"I'm not trying to be a burden, Kiyani," Fura began. "If I had something going for me back there, if I had somewhere to go, then I would think about it, but I honestly have nothing." She shrugged half-heartedly. "I suppose I could still go back, but I don't have anything to lose by staying here, either."

"Just your life."

Fura looked up at him, wondering why he had to draw the most extreme negatives out of everything.

"I can't protect you from everything," Kiyani added solemnly.

"I know," Fura said with a nod.

"Right."

"Does that mean I can come?" Fura asked, excitement creeping into her voice despite everything.

Kiyani glared at her.

"You have to know I'm not changing my mind," Fura said with a forced smile. The meager possibility that he might shift his line of thinking kept her from reminding him that he'd promised not to bring Barandor up.

Heaving a deep sigh, Kiyani shook his head as he got up and strolled over to the edge of the water. "You really don't know what you're getting yourself into. You've already seen more than you should have."

Standing, Fura wandered over to his side, crossing her arms and rubbing them against the chill from the mist. "I know the risks."

"I don't think you do."

"I'm not changing my mind," Fura reminded him, adamant in getting that across to him.

"Fine," Kiyani relented, though his tone revealed that he was hardly enthused about her decision.

Fighting against the grin she felt growing over winning, Fura gave a single nod, not taking him as one to seal the deal with a formal handshake. "So, where do we start?"

"Well, first we get out of here."

"Already?"

She didn't know why, but his answer surprised her. She didn't expect to stay in Fae Rue forever, knew that they would have to set out on the road at some point if they were to make any headway in attempting to free her father. Yet, Fura hadn't expected it to be so soon. They didn't even know where to go to start.

"Already?" Kiyani questioned. "We've already been here far longer than necessary."

"When would you have us leave?" Fura asked, suddenly dreading the answer. As uncertain as she was becoming about Tybithera, she didn't look forward to returning to cold nights spent out in the forest.

"I was ready to leave the moment I woke up," Kiyani huffed.

Though that came as no surprise to her, Fura still cringed at his tone. At this point she wasn't sure if he hated Apallo or Tybithera more. "I'm sure Tybithera would let us stay longer," she offered weakly.

"Did you not just hear me?"

Fura shrugged. "At least until we know where we're going."

"Tomorrow," Kiyani said matter of factly. "We're leaving tomorrow, and we're going east."

So soon? Fura felt cold at his proclamation. She didn't know what else they could accomplish within Fae Rue, but their departure felt rushed. Though she had no doubt that Kiyani really had been thinking about leaving the moment he had woken here, Fura couldn't help but think that he had just made that decision in the heat of the moment.

"Why east?"

"Because," Kiyani replied, his voice darker and calculated. "It takes us further away from Frielana and makes Tybithera think that we know where we're going."

That was one of the least convincing answers Fura had ever heard.

"*Do* we know where we're going?"

"We'll figure it out along the way."

For someone who seemed to mull over every possible answer to things, Fura wasn't sure she liked how reckless Kiyani was acting all of a sudden. "Don't you think we should stay here until we get things sorted out?"

"Let me rephrase that," Kiyani said, tossing a stone into the water before them. "*I'm* leaving tomorrow. Whether you decide to follow is up to you."

"You really don't like it here, do you?"

Fura didn't really expect him to answer, already guessing what he'd say. A difference in him had been visibly present ever since Tybithera had first allowed them to see each other. He was quieter, even more subdued than usual. But beneath it all, something else pulled through, a general sense of anxiety that Fura could see in the way he continually played with his hands, ran a hand through his hair. His eyes may have been far off, but he was actively thinking. Most likely of a way out.

"I don't like feeling trapped like this."

"Trapped?" Fura couldn't say she felt the same. This place had an ethereal charm about it that she'd spent the last few days trying to comprehend with little luck. She had no urge to leave though. "You act like we're prisoners."

Kiyani glanced at her, his eyes fully present for once. "You don't think so? When was the last time you saw the sun?"

Deflated, Fura looked around at the endless stone. Even if she was lax to admit it, he might have had a point.

Saiva had whisked her away the night before to stand beneath the moonlight for a few moments, but save for that, Fura honestly couldn't remember the last time she'd been outside. But that hadn't really been Tybithera's intent, had it? It wasn't like she had ever asked to leave. That very well could have been miscommunication on both their parts.

Or, maybe Kiyani was right.

Fura didn't want to think of the Fae Queen in such negative terms, but the more she witnessed the serrated conversations between the woman and Kiyani, the more she learned things about both of them. Most of it condemning.

"It may be a large cage," Kiyani continued. "But it's a cage all the same."

38

♦♦◇♦♦

MASKS OF DECEPTION

In the early morning hours Kiyani stood in the doorway of Fura's room, the cold shadows of the fading Fae lights in the hall at his back. Leaning against the stone of the archway, he remained still, knowing that if he moved into the room the Fae lights waiting inside would spring to life, waking her long before he was ready to start that part of the day.

Just because he'd had a fitful night of sleep didn't mean he intended to interrupt what would likely be her last good episode of slumber.

Taking in the calm reprieve of Fura's face as she slept peacefully, rolled up in the blankets, he wondered if he had made a mistake in relenting his opinion that she should return to Barandor.

It wasn't just that he didn't want to deal with her naïve nature and her outstanding lack of knowledge in this world. All his life he'd made it a point to push people away, preferring the solitary nature of being alone. He feared people getting to know the real him and the history that he fought relentlessly to hide. Only once in the past year had he allowed himself to get close to anyone, and it had ended in utter disaster. He wouldn't do that again.

No, his only friends were the wolf who stayed close to his side and Monira, though that was questionable at times.

Thinking back to what Monira had said the second day Fura had been in Frielana, Kiyani had to stifle an angered laugh. What did people see between him and Fura? Even Tybithera had made mention of it. It was all madness. He was certain that his views about the girl should have been blatantly obvious. So why didn't people see that?

Despite the fact that there were days when he could hardly stand her, it wasn't the only reason he wanted her to leave Izandüre as soon as possible.

Witnessing the sight of her, still wearing his shirt like some form of security blanket, he already knew she would continue to cling to him in the days to come.

Something that he didn't have the first clue of how to deal with.

But what was worse were the things she would encounter. A quest such as theirs – reclaiming her father from an evil lord – would be no walk in the park. Already, she had fallen privy to too much darkness. Yet, the way that she seemed to view life – that there was to be good found in everything – told him that she likely assumed that the worst was over. He had warned her only the night before, and yet, she had seemed to have taken his words with only a solemn reprieve and nothing more. As much as she had tried to fight it, he had still seen the light of excitement in her eyes. She had witnessed a handful of horrid events in the last few weeks and still she was filled with the curiosity of adventure.

For all he knew she was expecting a journey filled with sunshine and fun, when the truth was that she would be introduced to far worse horrors. And what was worse was that he would be the one that would end up being the reluctant teacher.

He knew the darkness this world held. What he didn't know was if he could handle watching that spark of life being slowly stripped from her, cracking and peeling away like old paint.

It was a painful process, but he had gone through it at a young age, leaving him a little rough around the edges, yet keenly aware of his surroundings and the happenings around him. It was why he was alive now in such a vindictive world. Yet, being forced to undergo that transformation from naïve child to world-weary adult on your own, learning to make due, was far different than suddenly playing the mentor.

That responsibility should have been left with Apallo, not him. His fist clenching at his side, Kiyani couldn't completely clear his hatred for the man. It was one thing to be so against his living under his roof, but it had been made clear in the few days Fura had been present in Frielana that the man had no more idea of how to be a father than his own had ever had.

"So innocent, isn't she?"

Aware of the increasing presence behind him, Kiyani barely flinched, though the voice sounded like thunder as it broke through the quiet he had been enjoying. But the voice of the Fae Queen had become far too familiar to him over the course of the past week. Looking over his shoulder to find Tybithera standing just behind him, her gaze resting on Fura as well, he resolved to simply ignore her.

At least, until she spoke again.

"Too bad she won't stay that way for much longer."

"What do you mean?" he asked darkly. He'd been about to turn away, but now he wanted an explanation for her words. It might not have been intentional, but he decided that it was too much of a coincidence that that sentiment had sounded so harshly directed

310

towards him. A fact he didn't appreciate. It was as if, after all this time, Tybithera still felt as if he posed a direct threat to the girl before them, left unaware in the throes of sleep.

"There are things in this world that she will be exposed to," she began, ignoring his callous tone. "And whether you like it or not, you are likely going to be the one tasked with explaining it. Just be careful that you don't end up breaking her spirit in the process. Izandüre, as beautiful as it may be, is not for the faint of heart."

"I'm well aware," Kiyani scoffed, wondering if one of the more unnerving attributes of Fae magic involved mind-reading.

"Then do not let your feelings for her interfere with common sense."

"I do not have feelings for her," Kiyani stressed. "You know who she is, and you know who I am. We both know it would never work."

Not to mention, the ridiculous idea of it had never once crossed his mind.

"You remember that," Tybithera warned.

Kiyani crossed his arms in agitation, ready to be done with the conversation. "Any other useless advice you can offer me?"

Tybithera silently regarded him for a moment before speaking. "The secrets you most want to stay hidden are the very ones that find themselves revealed in the worst of ways."

Gritting his teeth, Kiyani avoided her eyes. He wanted to say that he had no secrets, but that was far from the truth.

"Whether you do care for her or not," the Fae Queen continued as if she'd never spoken the previous words, "remember that you can't protect her from everything."

Kiyani cringed, hearing the same words he'd spoken to Fura the night before handed back to him.

"And that includes the truths that you hide."

Kiyani looked at the woman, knowing the shock was apparent on his face. In Frielana he'd been used to this kind of treatment, but not so much in travels abroad, depending on how much he decided to reveal. She was sounding annoyingly like Apallo. And just as it had been with the Firelord, it boiled down to one thing. "What do you think I'm going to do to her?"

Tybithera regarded him with slitted eyes that did nothing to soften her features, as if she could decipher the answer in his actions.

"You tell me."

"I thought the Fae didn't judge," Kiyani challenged.

"And I thought Shadows only destroyed."

The words sending a chill through his body, he turned to find that Tybithera had already gone, the only sight left the trails of her dress disappearing around the corner. Though he hated to admit it, he returned his gaze to Fura, knowing that the woman was right.

✧⌘✧

From Kiyani's first knock on the door, and onwards into the afternoon, the day moved by in a frenzied blur.

Sitting in the spring one last time as per Kiyani's request, Fura tried to take the moment to relax before the real journey began. Hugging her knees to her chest, feeling exposed in the shallows, she found it a hard task to accomplish. Taking in the sight of the beads of water gathered on the walls and the warm mist hovering above the water, all she could think about was her encounter here with Kiyani the night before.

It left her far more uncomfortable in the water than she would have normally been with just her phobia of the depths. No, dealing with water had never been her strong point, but what really bothered her was the image that she hadn't been able to get out of her head all night. And that was what she'd seen here, in this very spot. Though it had quickly become apparent that Kiyani wouldn't openly talk about his marred back, it didn't leave Fura caring any less. If anything, the sheer mystery of it left her wanting to know more.

Kiyani had been an enigma from the moment she had first met him – one moment vehemently rallying to get rid of her, while the next, playing the part of a caring friend, though Fura knew that they were far from. He had painstakingly made his stance on that front clear as well.

And yet, every little thing that she learned about him, despite throwing him deeper into the shadows, left her all the more curious. Who was he, really? And what was this past that he fought so hard to keep hidden? Because, as far as Fura was concerned, a dark past was one of the only reasons for him to act the way he did – so callous and closed off from the people around him.

It was an incredibly vague excuse, she knew, but it was all she had to go on. It should have been enough to make her want to walk away, to run in the other direction, to forget about the whole thing. Yet, although she'd never been the most confident of people, what she was, was persistent, and to turn away from him now would leave so much unanswered. Highest on that order was how someone that Apallo so openly despised had ended up living under his rule with what appeared a free pass.

Her sudden knowledge of those scars didn't help matters along. Without his consent to hand over the facts on the matter, Fura found herself devising her own truths to explain the situation. Though what she came up with only darkened her view of the people around her.

Namely, Tybithera.

Though Fura was still grateful to the woman for saving their lives and intervening when she could have easily left them to the Streig, an unnerving feeling had begun to grow in her gut simply upon the mere mention of the woman. Part of that was due to Kiyani's extreme, and often times overly verbal, distrust, but she had also begun to see things on her own ever since the conclusion of the feast. The horrific scars decorating Kiyani's back had only solidified that. Fura had no substantial evidence that Tybithera had been the culprit, yet she couldn't see who else could have done it. She may not have gotten a good look at Kiyani's back, but it had been long enough to tell that the injuries weren't that old.

Had she been given the option, Fura would have guessed that they had been Apallo's doing. However, the flayed skin had been far too fresh for that. It was hard to believe that the siege was already two weeks in the past, but that cleared Apallo's name. A simple fact that Fura was grateful for. Even if they'd been acquired during the Streig attack, they would have at least begun to heal over, still looking grotesque, but not nearly as close to bleeding at any given moment. No, the skin she had seen had still been raw.

In the scheme of things, that left Tybithera.

Or, so Fura assumed. From what she had gathered in her few minced conversations with Kiyani, he hadn't been given the freedom to leave these halls as she had. And from what Fura had seen, Tybithera was the only other individual that visited these otherwise quiet and secluded caverns.

Letting her head fall into her hands, Fura tried to clear the thoughts from her mind. She didn't want to take sides without the proper evidence for a fair conviction, nor did she want to falsely accuse the Fae Queen after all that she had done for them.

Knowing that the heat and steam from the spring was only clouding her mind further, Fura decided that she had lingered long enough. Though her main goal had been to try and clear her mind, she didn't know how far she had gotten with that. Ever since leaving Barandor it felt as if she were consistently being attacked by a barrage of knowledge, most of which she was still struggling to comprehend.

Traversing the cool, empty halls, her hair dripping about her shoulders, Fura made her way back to her room. Opening the door to the familiar, warm glow of the Fae lights, Fura smiled, knowing that despite everything, there were definitely a few things she was going to miss.

It didn't take long to pack the few meager belongings she had accumulated, no thanks to Tybithera, leaving her with one last dilemma of what to wear.

Out of habit, she nearly donned her firedancer's outfit. Catching her mistake, Fura reminded herself that they would be viewed as out of place in this land, or so she'd heard. In fact, Fura realized that it would probably be a long time before she donned that attire again. If Kiyani were in the room with her, Fura knew he probably would have argued that she leave them behind for the sake of saving room in her pack. Fortunately for her, he wasn't present. Unable to give up all ties to that life just yet, Fura unpacked her bag and shoved her *Pyropheric* attire deep into the bottom.

Looking at the sad bundle of clothing was a glimpse of reality.

Yet, as much as it scared her, Fura had already decided that the only way to go now was forward. What other choice did she really have? Going back to Barandor was no longer an option. Not after all she had learned.

Even if Kiyani despised the idea of her tagging along, she would see her real father again if it was the last thing she did. She had to speak to him, face to face. To hear the truth from him. Until that time, she wouldn't be able to rest. At least not peacefully.

Even with that motivation spurring her on, it still wasn't easy picking something to wear. Just like her performance outfit for the Fireswell Festival, she knew Kiyani's shirt that she'd taken to wearing like a second skin, and the gorgeous green velvet formal dress she had worn to feast were out of the question. Carefully arranging them at the bottom of the bag as well, she looked at what was left. It wasn't much, but what made it worse was that save for her little side trip with Saiva to view the nightscape a few nights ago, Fura had no idea what the weather was like. All she knew was that winter was just around the corner, the chill that came along with it slowly creeping in. Finally settling on a plain, dark brown, long-sleeved dress, Fura added a pair of leggings beneath as an afterthought.

Quickly repacking her remaining possessions and moving to leave, Fura paused in the doorway, wondering if she would ever see this place again. Even though she hadn't been in Fae Rue long, in a way it had begun to feel like home. She had her own room with a cozy bed that had become something of a sanctuary. Trying not to remind herself that she'd had that back in Frielana as well, Fura closed the door and made her way down the hall, hoping that she wasn't destined to accrue the same fate with every good thing she ran across.

Thinking back on that morning when Kiyani had popped into the room, urging her to visit the spring one last time before meeting him at the falls, Fura made her way slowly down the hall, not knowing what to expect. Before she even turned the corner to the room, Fura heard familiar voices, telling her that Kiyani had been right when he'd mentioned that Tybithera would likely be there as well.

When she had joked with him earlier, declaring that she better hurry before the two of them killed each other, he had simply rolled his eyes in response. Now that the time had come, a vision of the intense argument Fura had witnessed the day before between Kiyani and the Fae Queen came to mind, and she shuddered at the thought of witnessing a repeat performance. That was certainly something she didn't want to see again, from either party. She was still amazed that the Fae Queen hadn't punished Kiyani for such insolence. Though, thinking back on it now, it had seemed like the woman was amused by his outburst. Something that left Fura all the more confused.

A sudden burst of laughter brought Fura out of her dark thoughts as she realized that the vibe that emanated from the room was considerably brighter than the last time she had been there. Thankful for that, Fura smiled as she entered the room.

Just as Kiyani had warned, Tybithera lingered by the falls, the flowing trails of her white chiffon dress puddling around her feet, making her look far more approachable and magical than the stern fixture of her copper eyes had the day before. Realizing that the laughter she'd heard had come from the woman, Fura found herself afraid to move into the room, not wanting to disrupt the moment. Yet, when she realized that it was Kiyani that the Fae Queen was talking to she had a sudden desire to be a part of the conversation. If there was something that the two of them could actually discuss in a civilized manner, then Fura wanted to know what it was.

Fura never got the chance before she was distracted by a colorful streak of blue that flashed across the room. Tackling her in a giant hug, Saiva nearly lifted her of the ground, squeezing the breath out of her.

"Fura!" Saiva exclaimed, releasing her hold. "I was afraid I would miss the chance to say goodbye. Are you really leaving so soon?"

Rubbing her arms, Fura hadn't been aware that the small woman had that much strength in her. Yet it was the bright sparkle in Saiva's eyes that left her wanting another hug. Though she and Kiyani hadn't been living in Fae Rue long, she had grown close to the little firecracker of a Fae.

"We are," Fura admitted sheepishly, almost embarrassed by the fact. Though she knew they had to move on if they were to get anywhere close to saving her father, Fura suddenly found herself lax to leave one of the only friends she'd made since the fires. Thinking back to her days in the Barandor schools, she had a hard time remembering anyone, save for a few of the teachers, that she had truly thought of as a friend. The closest she'd had was Kieli and Tiyano in the *Pyropheric* troupe.

Though the smile on Saiva's face faltered, the joy never left her silver eyes. "I'm going to miss you."

Fura smiled in return, glad that they shared that sentiment. She almost wished she could ask the girl to come along with them, but Fura knew that Kiyani would never agree to that. It was apparent that he didn't want to deal with her most days, she couldn't imagine the bouts of frustration he would fall into with two hyper women at his side. Even with that knowledge aside, Fura recalled both Kiyani and Tybithera mentioning that outside the borders of Fae Rue Keep the Fae had no powers. Fura didn't know what that would do to Saiva, but she didn't want to find out.

Instead, Fura nodded. "I'm going to miss you, too," she replied, surprised to find just how much it hurt to utter those words.

Save for Kiyani's unwilling presence, nothing had been stable in her life since the explosion in Barandor. Though she tried not to think that far into the future, not knowing what trials this journey would bring, Fura knew that nothing would be for some time.

"Will I see you again?" Saiva asked, her eyes alight with the possibility.

Drawing her from her thoughts, Fura found herself startled by the simple question. "I..." she faltered, not knowing how to answer. She still had no idea where they were even going, let alone if they would make their way back along this route.

"It's a possibility," Kiyani answered as he showed up at her side, saving her from the awkward conversation.

From the grin on his face, Fura could tell that he was amused by her dilemma. Wanting to comment on that fact, Saiva interrupted again before she could even think of a snarky reply.

Giddy with excitement, Saiva surprised her with another hug, this one a lingering goodbye. "I already can't wait." Pulling away, the girl seemed to remember something. "Oh, shoot!" she exclaimed. "I promised Myrian I would meet with her this morning." Tackling her in one last quick hug, Saiva waved as she sprinted towards the door with all the giddy energy of someone who was quickly approaching a deadline. "I'll see you soon!"

Watching the girl disappear around the corner, Fura almost felt as if that excitable energy had been taken with her. Feeling a sudden sadness threaten to overwhelm her, she turned to Kiyani. "Do you really think we'll come back?"

The smile fell from Kiyani's face, giving her all the answer she needed. "I'm not sure," he replied, though she wasn't sure if he was being honest or simply offering her a small lie to make her feel better. "If we do, it won't be anytime soon."

Afraid of that answer, Fura clung to the fact that he hadn't said never. If they wouldn't return here in the near future, then it was a far off possibility that she would cling to.

"Such a sparkling personality, isn't she?" Tybithera said, popping into the conversation and laying a hand on Fura's shoulder as she looked to archway where Saiva had last been seen. "A bit contagious, really."

Though Tybithera seemed ready to continue on with the day, Fura could feel Kiyani's eyes lingering on her, asking if she was okay.

"Are you sure you're ready to go?" he asked instead, taking note of her sudden change in demeanor. "You can still go back to Barandor if you want."

Looking him straight in the eye, Fura shook her head. "I told you, there's nothing there for me."

"You don't know if there's anything here, either," he retorted coldly.

Trying to ignore the cold cut of anger in his voice as he made one last attempt to get her to return to Barandor, Fura glared at him, hating him for turning the day sour so soon. "I'll take my chances."

Kiyani's fists balled at his side, his body rigid, though he kept his voice steady as he spoke. "You have no idea what you're getting yourself into," he explained, trying once more to deter her from the path she was determined to take. "The dangers, the –"

"You promised you wouldn't do this," Fura said, cutting him off. "You said I could come as long as I thought it over. Well, I've thought about it, and I'm coming."

Before Kiyani could reply with anything more than a heavy sigh, Tybithera interrupted their conversation with an abrupt clap of her hands. "The two of you have a long journey ahead, and fighting isn't going to get you anywhere. So, I suggest you quit now."

Though they both still carried the urge to speak, Kiyani and Fura remained silent as the Fae Queen stood before them, her posture demure, her face serene, though there remained a nearly hidden light in her eyes that dared them to run with defiance. Nodding in approval, she smoothed the flowing fabric of her dress.

Her eyes falling on Fura, it was Kiyani that she spoke to. "Fura is not your enemy. The rage that you've shown me these past few days, and the anger that seems to be sparked by this never-ending disturbance between the two of you, needs to be reserved for a different time." Turning her attention to Kiyani, she continued. "To focus that bottled up rage upon one that actually deserves the title of enemy would be deadly in itself. Remember that. Now, I take it that the two of you are ready to start your journey?" she asked, her voice taking on an airier tone.

Though there was still a fire in Kiyani's eyes, he nodded in compliance, Fura following suit.

"Good," Tybithera said. "Grab your things and I will lead you out. It can be difficult to find the way on your own." As they moved into the hall in a line, she glanced over her shoulder. "I'm sure that seeing the sunlight again will brighten your moods."

Taking in the stiff lines in Kiyani's form as he walked in front of her, it was obvious to Fura that although they were about to start a long journey together, he was nowhere close to accepting her as a companion for any length of time. He may have fallen silent for a moment, but this wasn't the last time they would argue.

✧ ⌘ ✧

Though he'd vowed to keep his opinions to himself in attempt to find a less obvious and obtrusive way of getting Fura to return to Barandor, Kiyani knew he'd spoken too soon about the matter. Yet, he hadn't been able to help himself. Not after witnessing the sorrow etched on her face as she had spoken to the cheery, blue-haired Fae. After their talk the night before, he had thought that maybe she could deal with this, but now Kiyani wasn't so sure. All he knew was that the further they both ventured, the less likely it would be for them to turn around and go all the way back to the beginning. It was a simple fact that Fura didn't seem to fully understand.

Even he wasn't sure if he was ready for this massive undertaking, but at least Kiyani was aware that he contained the mental capacity to handle whatever was thrown at him. He'd already had to deal with so much in his life that he couldn't imagine much fazing him. Fura may have made it this far, dealing with evil leaders and the Strieg, but he was still convinced that she'd be done with the whole ordeal at the drop of a hat. It was just a matter of time.

The only thing he was truly waiting for was to see what it would be that finally tipped the scale, leaving her crying to return home.

Home.

It was such a viable term. For both of them.

What did either of them really have left?

Pushing the thought aside, Kiyani focused instead on the woman before them. Only once peering over her shoulder, Tybithera seemed well aware that both he and Fura were following close behind, though he was the one that was more eager for escape, where Fura had appeared more inclined to stay another few weeks if she'd been given the chance. The way the Fae Queen had been speaking just the other day, Kiyani was still surprised that she was even letting them leave. Compared to that first meeting with her when he had still been under the influence of the frethayne, it seemed completely out of her nature. As much as he questioned it, he wouldn't ask, not wanting to tempt fate or give her reason to change her mind.

It wasn't long after that the hall began to brighten ahead as sunlight streamed into the tunnel, granting them the first sight of the outdoors since the day of the feast.

Drawn forward by the sight, Fura streaked past him, her former excitement returning with full force.

"Fura!" Tybithera called to the girl, stopping her before she made it too far out into the open. Ashamed, Fura stalked back, only to be drawn into a motherly embrace by the Fae Queen. "I wish you luck in whatever comes your way," Kiyani heard the woman whisper to her. "Be safe. Now, go on," she said, letting Fura go with a smile.

Still put off by her quick changes in demeanor, treating Fura one way and him the complete opposite, Kiyani watched Fura dash down the hall and out into a grassy clearing as soon as she was dismissed. Suppressing a smile, he watched as she danced and twirled in the sunlight, her copper hair radiant in the full sunlight. Walking ahead of Tybithera, he paused at the end of the hall where the grass began to grow into the stone, suddenly not sure if he was ready to begin what would surely prove to be a trying journey.

"This is where your journey truly begins," Tybithera said as she appeared by his side, echoing his thoughts.

"I know," Kiyani said solemnly. "I just wish I knew for certain how it will end."

"No one ever knows the answer to that," the Fae Queen mused. "So," she asked, regarding him with her unnerving copper-eyed stare. "Have you decided whether she's going with you yet? You seemed rather adamant that she return to Barandor."

"I still am," Kiyani confirmed, feeling the smallest sliver of guilt as he looked out into the clearing again where Fura danced around like a giddy child seeing sunshine for the first time. He may have promised her the night before that he wouldn't speak of it anymore, but he'd made no further agreement that he wouldn't find other ways to get her to return to the town where she had grown up. Simple persuasion hadn't worked. His newest relay involved nothing more than showing her just what a living hell this place could be until she came up with the idea to double back on her own.

At least that had been his plan. Now he wondered if he was right to adhere to such a diversion.

They were both children of worlds denied to them. Who was he to direct her away from the one thing she had left in either realm?

"A conflicted mind is never a good thing."

Kiyani glared at the woman, cursing her Fae nature and her ability to read him with ease. Something so few could accurately do.

Yet, as much as he wanted, he couldn't argue against her.

"I don't think she even sees Barandor as an option."

Tybithera let out a musical laugh, seemingly intrigued by his dilemma. Was that why she was letting him go so easily? Because she knew that having Fura along would keep him in check?

"I can't imagine she would. You've got to realize that from her standpoint, it must feel like she's walked into some fairytale dream. So many fantastical things that are new to her."

"Like the Streig?" Kiyani scoffed. What person in their right mind would view this land as fantastical? "Fairytale, no," he continued. "Most people would find this all a nightmare. She's been shaken up by current events, I can tell. She questions me and every bit of information I give her, but she quite literally plays with fire on a daily basis. This is an adventure for her. No matter what I say, I don't think she's walking away without a fight."

Not when Apallo's life is on the line, he added to himself.

A part of him wished that he had never revealed her relation to the man, hadn't given her that incentive to hold on to this crazy idea she had implanted in her mind.

"You just might want to keep her around, then. You never know when that fighting spark might be of use."

Kiyani nearly snorted. Tybithera didn't know the first thing about it. "So far, all its done is get us in trouble."

"You don't think that you're equally to blame for all that's befallen the two of you?"

Kiyani glared at her for a moment before returning his gaze to Fura who seemed to have forgotten them both. He wouldn't deny her this moment, for he knew that it would end all too soon. Knowing that he would get no motherly send off like Fura had, Kiyani took a deep breath, his hand gripping the sword at his side.

Just as he was about to step into the sunlight to join Fura on the true beginning of their journey, a slender hand held him back. He could feel Tybithera behind him, her face hovering next to his, her wild hair tickling the skin of his neck.

"Just remember what you promised," she whispered malevolently in his ear, the tone of her voice taking a drastic turn from the airiness she usually portrayed. "Don't even *think* of returning for help unless you have the Bloodstone. Now, go!" she hissed, pushing him out into the light.

Whipping around, Kiyani made to face her, but she was already making her way down the hall, her back turned to him. Only once did she pause to glance over her shoulder. Shocked, Kiyani took in that same sly smile of ill-sought victory that he'd witnessed from her the night of the feast. And it was in that moment that Kiyani knew; the wispy folds of her white, gossamer gown, and that serene smile were merely a mask, fabricated to hide the ugly soul she harvested beneath the Fae glamour.

39

❖❖◇❖❖

JOURNEY ONWARD

Taking in the lush grass beneath her feet with a new fervor, Fura watched the billowing flare of her skirts as she spun in circles in the clearing. The sun beamed overhead, promising a lovely fall day, perfect for traveling. Yet, all she could focus on was the warmth on her face. Closing her eyes against the bright light, Fura smiled. The birds twittering in the surrounding trees. The whisper of the wind through the tall grasses. Despite the circumstances, she felt lighter than ever.

Though she couldn't deny that the elaborate, twisting caverns of Fae Rue Keep were magical, Fura hadn't realized until now just how much she'd missed the fresh air and wide open spaces of the outdoors. Only once in the week and a half long stay in Tybithera's dwelling had she been allowed outside, and that had been Saiva's doing. Yet, as much as she had needed the cool, fresh air that night, the light of the moon, painting everything in cold, silver shadows hadn't been nearly as reviving as the sun felt now.

Kiyani had claimed that Fae Rue was a cage. Though Fura still didn't agree with him, she realized now that he might've had a point. Wondering what was taking him so long, she looked to the tunnel opening where he still stood with Tybithera. The sight surprised her. After so many arguments with the woman, she had expected him to be the first one out of the labyrinthine mountain, not daring to look back until he knew it was out of sight. She could only guess that they were discussing last minute preparations. Or that Tybithera was reminding him of whatever it was that Kiyani had agreed to without his consent. Unable to see Kiyani's face, it was hard to tell. However, his lax, yet mildly stiff posture deemed that the conversation was going as well as could be expected, given the history between the two.

Not wanting to interfere, Fura returned her gaze to the dense network of trees at the clearing's edge, wondering where the road would take them next.

East.

That's all Kiyani had said. Yet, she didn't even know where east was.

Nor what lie in that direction that would prove to be a draw in the first place. Trying to recall the conversation, Fura found herself coming up short. Her mind had been a flustered mix of emotions at the time – anger at Apallo and her so-called parents, as well as worry, and a lingering fear after coming across Kiyani unexpectedly at the spring. Though, sifting through the debris of that tumultuous day, Fura could distinctly recall Kiyani claiming that east was simply a cover to keep Tybithera from asking questions.

The fact was that Kiyani might not have been planning to go in that direction at all, leaving her to come to the unsettling conclusion that she was just as much in the dark as when she'd first started this journey, following him into the dead of night. Hating herself for continually proving to be so naïve, Fura barely heard Kiyani's approach.

"Would you stop prancing around like a child?" he said irritably as he moved past her, hardly giving her a second glance as he made his way towards the tree line. "Nobody is that excited about clothes."

Watching Kiyani move forward in a huff, Fura continued to play with her skirts. "Maybe not you," she murmured, wondering what had gotten into him.

All throughout their stay, he'd done nothing but gripe about wanting to leave. Now that Tybithera had finally bid them farewell and pushed them along towards new adventures, she had expected him to lighten up a bit. Instead, Kiyani appeared to be on edge, and just as feral as ever. Taking in the weight of the provisions she carried on her back, and the bright, sunny day, Fura was left to wonder why. Everything appeared to be in order. So, what did he know that she didn't? Though she wanted to deny it, there was an unmistakable shift in his attitude compared to that morning.

Knowing that it had likely been brought on by whatever words had been exchanged between him and Tybithera, Fura turned to give the woman one last wave only to find that she was already gone. Confused, she turned and scurried after Kiyani before he could disappear as well.

Though she was curious, Fura couldn't muster the courage to ask Kiyani what Tybithera had said, nor was he any more forthcoming in offering up an answer on his own.

In fact, he barely uttered a single word as he silently and hastily made his way towards the trees and the unexplored wilds beyond.

The further they got from Fae Rue, the more Fura realized that, despite their brief moments of companionship, it would be more of the same old thing between her and Kiyani: misunderstanding, silence, and tempered arguments.

The day might have been sunny and bright, but her mood

dampened quickly the longer she followed in Kiyani's intangible wake. Having expected the day to go much differently, Fura found herself at a loss, not only for words, but for action as well. It didn't take long for the silence between them to begin to gnaw at her, and yet, she couldn't push herself to face him and his sporadic moods to ask just where it was that they were going.

The only thing she could do was follow blindly, hoping that, in time, he would reveal his true motives.

It was easier said than done.

Not only did Kiyani continue the cold shoulder treatment throughout the day, but the land proved to be uneven and difficult terrain, leaving Fura consistently tripping over roots and sticks buried beneath deadfalls of leaves. More than once she had to stop as she contemplated how to get over fallen trees or down steep, mossy slopes. Kiyani, on the other hand continued to move along with the same ethereal grace he'd always seemed to carry. It was almost as if he were a mere spirit, or maybe even one of the Fae they'd just left behind. A comparison she knew he wouldn't care to hear.

Though they moved on at a good clip, the land seeming to fall away behind them, Fura couldn't help but notice how strange Kiyani was acting. She had reason to believe that his words exchanged with Tybithera were still taking center stage in his mind, but she'd thought he would have forgotten about it the further away from Fae Rue Keep they got. Glancing behind her, she could see that the rise of mountainous stone that made up the Fae Queen's dwelling had already disappeared from view.

That brief chapter of their journey was now in the past, yet Kiyani's stiff gait told her that he was still worked up about something.

He barely checked to see if she was okay, or even still following, seeming to be either ignoring her presence altogether, or simply wishing that she wasn't there. However, even without his speaking to confirm her suspicions, Fura couldn't help but notice Kiyani continually looking around, as if expecting to run into trouble at any moment.

If she didn't know any better, she would have said he was spooked.

That thought left her on edge, and before she knew it Fura found herself paranoid, startling at the smallest sounds, and walking closer to Kiyani than before. An hour later, though, when nothing had presented itself, she finally backed off. She didn't know what had gotten into him, but she was certain that, even with her lack of survival skills, there was no one else around.

Trailing further behind, Fura found her mind wandering again.

She still didn't know if it had been the best idea to follow him, but she shuddered, thinking about where she might be now had she not. Things could have gone so much differently. She could be in Frielana right now, enduring whatever torture was befalling its citizens.

Or, maybe not.

Had she ever really had a choice in the matter? The whole siege had happened so fast, leaving her with no time to think. She'd simply taken Kiyani's hand when offered and gone off into the night. Reliving the event, she realized now how stupid of a move that could have been. What had she known about Kiyani at that point besides his name? He could have easily been one of the infiltrators as Nevo had proven to be.

Fura shook her head. None of it really mattered now.

A stranger or not, if it hadn't been for Kiyani, it was possible that she wouldn't even be alive right now.

Yet, the one thing that haunted her still was Apallo's warnings that Kiyani was a darker individual than she'd ever know, that trouble followed him. She didn't know what the man had meant by that, but it left her questioning how Kiyani had known to flee when they had. It was almost as if he'd known that that particular night was a good time to not follow direction. She wanted to ask more about it, but she kept her questioning at bay.

It was easy to see that Kiyani wasn't in the mood for regular conversation. She didn't want to assault him with accusations.

Despite the raging call for answers, Fura had no desire to put herself on the frontlines of that battlefield, knowing that any attempt to talk to him right now would ultimately end in yet another fight. It seemed to be the way with him, and though she still knew little about him, Fura had quickly begun to pick up on Kiyani's little nuances that screamed to leave him alone if she didn't want to endure the consequences. Silence may have been far from what she was craving at the moment, but the last thing she wanted was to delve into another round of his excuses on why she should return to Barandor. Though Kiyani had actually spouted off a few that had made clear sense, Fura knew that her answer wouldn't change. Not now.

Not after learning that Apallo was her father. Three days after that shocking revelation, heard from Kiyani of all people, and Fura still had reasonable doubts. And yet, no matter how much she tried to deny it, it all made sense. All those jagged puzzle pieces that had been missing in random parts of her life had suddenly appeared out of nowhere and fallen into place, filling in those places that had been vacant for as long as she could remember.

Why she couldn't recall any extended family.

Why she looked nothing at all like her brothers, or the one's she'd called her parents for so long.

Why, when all the other girls in her class had been drawn to boys and makeup, she had gravitated instead towards the dirt and grime of the Fireswell Festival and the raging fires of the *Pyropheric* show.

Thinking of her fellow firedancers, Fura paused in her step, wondering what had become of them and the festival that they had all loved so much. None of the other members had been any more related to her than she and Evan had been, and yet, she had thought of them as a kind of second family. Looking back at it now, Fura found it darkly ironic that the leader of that secondary family had in fact been her biological father.

Thinking about where Apallo probably was at this moment left Fura feeling sick, and she momentarily pushed thoughts of him aside. Though the ones that replaced them weren't much better. She may have had an idea of where Apallo was, of what he was being put through, but what she didn't know was what had happened to the other members of *Pyropheric* she had known. Only a handful had made their way through the trails of the Verboten Forest, claiming that they lived in Frielana. The others, like Tiyano, Fura knew to live in Barandor. The double-edged nature of the whole situation was enough to leave Fura's head spinning.

She remembered Apallo's announcement that the festival would continue the following weekend – a date that had already come and gone – but Fura didn't know if that had really been the case. Maybe the festival itself would continue on as normal, but what about *Pyropheric*? Would they cancel, not knowing where their troupe leader was, or would they continue on as if nothing had happened? Would any of them even know?

Fura knew the truth of the matter now. It was likely that the whole troupe would simply think that her and Apallo were no shows. There was no reason at all that they would know what had transpired in the depths of the dark forests surrounding Fireswell that were said to be haunted. It just reminded Fura how far removed from that world she had become.

That world.

It still felt like such an odd thing to say. After all that she'd heard and witnessed, it was the one thing that Fura still found hard to wrap her mind around. The fact that the world she had grown up in was not the only one, let alone the one she apparently belonged in.

How was it even possible that there could be this whole separate place, full of different species and animalistic races, living parallel to her own world?

Next she would discover that she was a damn princess. Fura let a few moments pass before letting out a derisive snort that elicited a raised eyebrow from Kiyani as he looked at her over his shoulder. Waiting until his focus had drifted away again, Fura continued to shuffle along, reminding herself that in a way, she already was.

Fireheir.

That had to be as close to a princess as she could get in this world.

Looking up at Kiyani as he resumed ignoring her, she wondered, briefly, what world it was that he was from. He was human. Fura had no doubt about that. However, the way he carried himself in such a quiet, wanted solitude, and the way he would stare at nothing, lost in some other place within his mind, was far different from anyone she'd ever met.

Unable to get much information out of him, it left him all that more difficult to pin down.

Especially when he was being so ornery. Something that was uncalled for in their current situation.

Though she'd expected things to be a bit different after some of their last conversations, it was as if things hadn't changed at all. As if that night spent sleeping in his arms had never happened, proving only to be a far-fetched dream.

Watching the tense line of his form as he strolled onwards, unaware of the troubled thoughts on her mind, Fura wondered if he wished that night hadn't happened, thinking that he should've turned her away instead.

If he was to talk about it, she was sure that he'd only declare that it'd been a moment of weakness on his part. Something that wouldn't happen again. He might have been angry with himself for that moment, for all she knew. But, to Fura that had been a glimpse of the man that Monira had mentioned. The faithful friend in troubled times. If anything, it had been the faintest of hints at the man he tried so hard to keep hidden from the world. The softer side that Fura knew was hidden beneath the rough, give-no-shits exterior he wore like armor.

In a way, Fura knew that it might have actually been better if she had never witnessed that from him. All it had done was give her a false sense of hope to continue to follow as they journeyed into the unknown.

However, no matter what she might have felt for him at times, currently Fura was annoyed with Kiyani's behavior. It very well might have been Tybithera that he was angry with, but the Fae Queen was miles behind them, leaving Fura to take the brunt of it. She knew she should have been happy enough that he wasn't actually raging at her, his callous tone and barbed words making her feel worse than she already was, but as it was, Fura didn't care for his secondary method of dealing with things any more, which was to ignore it completely.

And right now, he was definitely ignoring her. It hadn't bothered Fura too much at first, but as the hours had passed and the sun had hit its peak in the sky, she'd come to the unnerving realization that it wasn't just ignorance. She had the unsettling notion that if she fell over from exhaustion, or was snatched by some creature that he wouldn't even notice. In fact, he would probably keep right on going at the same quick pace that he'd set early in the morning. And whenever he did notice she was missing, she had the feeling that he would continue sauntering onward through the trees with a smile on his face, happy that she was finally gone.

Maybe.

Though she currently wanted to think of him as a heartless individual just to sate her souring mood, Fura couldn't forget about him searching the shadowed forest of night just hours after the siege. He had been pissed that she'd left the hollow without telling him – as a matter of fact, she was certain it was something that Kiyani still thought about, probably one of the deciding factors of sending her back to Barandor. Yet, he had still come after her. He could have continued on without her that night, but he hadn't.

Even if he wouldn't be forthright in admitting it, Kiyani cared about her well-being to some degree.

Letting out a frustrated sigh, Fura kicked at a rock in her path, sending it skittering ahead of her and past Kiyani. Her mind was a muddle of conflicting thoughts. Though she hadn't meant to, her little burst of annoyance elicited the mildest of reactions from Kiyani as he glanced at her over his shoulder, a raised brow questioning what she was doing.

Catching his eye for only the briefest of moments, she found she couldn't hold his gaze and Fura let her attentions drift away, feigning sudden interest in the ground beneath her feet.

✧⌘✧

It wasn't until that night, when they finally stopped to search for shelter, that words were finally exchanged.

"I don't see any Relns," Fura commented as she looked around, wondering if she could somehow spot one before him. A way to potentially prove her worth on this journey. It was her first real attempt at striking up conversation with him since they'd left Fae Rue.

As if they'd been speaking all throughout the day, Kiyani simply pointed. "There's one not far that way."

Fura sighed. Though he'd answered, giving her reason to believe that he was far more aware of her presence than she'd initially thought, he still couldn't be bothered to so much as give her a passing glance as he spoke.

Watching as he stalked off in the direction he'd indicated, she wondered if this was how the whole journey would play out. With him doing his best to pretend she wasn't there, as she trudged along in silence like a dog on a leash, only speaking in as few words as humanly possible when the need arose.

Not wanting to be left alone in the dark for too long, Fura followed his lead. Kiyani may have waited for her the night of the siege when she'd hesitated, but she had a feeling that he was no longer offering that incentive. Not with the way they'd been fighting as of late. And without Kiedo tagging along, Kiyani was unfortunately the only one she could rely on at the moment.

A short distance later, Fura stood in shock as she looked up at the only Reln she'd seen in hours.

"How..." Fura muttered, wondering if he had some extra-sensory radar that picked up on the Relns and the hollows they contained.

"I told you, I've been out here before," Kiyani said with a shrug as he made to set up camp before the full onset of night.

"This far from Frielana?"

For the first time that day, he looked over at her. "I'm not tied down to Frielana," he said, his tone indicating that he was actually offended at the idea. "I've taken a few trips before."

Trips or not, it still didn't explain how he knew so much. "So," Fura tried again as she started to gather sticks for a fire. "Where exactly are we going?"

Kiyani glanced at her, seeming to take notice of her not so subtle change in direction of conversation. "I'll let you know when I figure it out."

His words hit her so hard that he may as well have actually slapped her. "You don't know where we're going?" Fura asked, trying to keep the shriek out of her voice. Her father, her own flesh and blood, was in grave danger, and Kiyani's grand plan was to lead them aimlessly through the woods until he came across a path that suited his fancy? Until he came up with a better idea or a sense of where they should go next?

"I never said I did."

"You said east," Fura reminded him, though she had long since deciphered that that'd been nothing more than a cover for Tybithera as he'd claimed.

"We are going east."

Fura shook her head in disbelief. "But to nowhere in particular?" At least he hadn't been lying about their direction.

"You don't have to follow me," Kiyani snapped impatiently, before stalking away.

So much for the bright new start to our journey, Fura thought.

Watching him go, she couldn't help but think of all the things that had changed in her life recently. Everything that she'd known to be truth had been revealed to be nothing more than cleverly crafted lies, while all that should have been contained to the pages of a storybook had fallen on the wayside of reality.

Faeries. Wizards. Magic.

Fura had suddenly found herself in a world of fairytale enchantment. She should have been happy. Ecstatic even. So, why did she suddenly feel so sick?

40

•◆•

LONG DAYS, LONGER NIGHTS

The days that followed were no better.

Three days and Kiyani had continued to acknowledge her only in short, quipped conversations. None of which were all too friendly in nature. A few words here and there when they stopped for the night. A grunt of recognition, maybe followed by a nod if she was lucky, when she attempted to ask a question.

Fura had thought that leaving Fae Rue Keep would have brightened his spirits, that his lack of dire conversations with Tybithera would direct him towards a better mood. Yet, if anything, Kiyani seemed to have reverted further towards the same annoyed boy that had wanted her gone the night of the fires in Barandor.

Yet, even returning to that standpoint would have been an improvement.

As it was, Fura may as well have been traveling with a ghost.

Kiyani may have been leading the way through the dense maze of trees, but save for acting as a guide, he played the part of a phantom well.

Marked with treacherous terrain, the hilly landscape hurt Fura's feet, but she found that it was the awkward friction between her and Kiyani that kept her on edge throughout the days. Every time she made to say something to break the ice, she faltered, realizing seconds before she voiced the words just how stupid they would sound. She knew nothing about this world and nothing about him. There should have been plenty to fill the silence. Yet, Fura already knew from experience that Kiyani wasn't prone to answering questions without giving her that condescending look that appeared to be permanently plastered on his face, as if he was simply counting down the minutes until he could get rid of her for good.

He hadn't asked to take her on as a hindrance, but in her own defense, Fura hadn't asked for her life to be turned upside down either. Neither of them had drawn the winning cards. The only difference was that Fura was more apt to try and make the most of it, even while her heart remained shattered, the tears far from dried up. She didn't know how much more she could handle, but what she did know was that she couldn't do it alone.

She definitely couldn't traverse this winding forest by herself. She knew that much as she stopped to scrape a hunk of mud and leaves off her boot.

Not a moment later, she ran into difficulty again.

Kiyani looked back this time as Fura tripped over another raised root, sending a resounding crack throughout the immediate surroundings. As she lost her balance and tumbled into a pile of brush, he shook his head. He couldn't understand how this was the same girl that took to the stage every weekend in Fireswell in the summer and fall months to play with fire. He never wanted to be saddled with such responsibility, but he'd expected the girl to be a little more graceful. So far, she'd proven to be quite the opposite.

Moving along, it wasn't long before Fura stumbled again.

Finally stopping, Kiyani turned, taking in the sorry sight of her trying to untangle a rogue number of leaves and a good sized branch from the hem of her cloak.

"For the sake of my sanity, would you carry a walking stick or something?"

Placing a hand on a nearby tree trunk to keep her balance, Fura looked up at him in surprise. It was the first thing he'd said to her all day.

Unable to determine what kind of mood he was in, she decided to play it by chance.

"The last time I had a stick, I nearly hurt you," she said wryly, a grin playing on the corner of her lips. She still didn't know what had been going through her head that day, but looking back at it now, it was kind of funny.

The look on Kiyani's face did little to reflect her playful nature. "I was hardly in danger," he mocked. "If anyone was going to get hurt, it was you."

The smile fell from Fura's face as she crossed her arms. Did he really have to be so cross with every little thing she said? If that was the case, then this was bound to be a long trip. Things had to change, or else she was going to crazy before this whole thing was over.

"You know," Fura started, feeling her frustrations rise. "You gave me three days out here before I went running home and I made it way beyond that."

Kiyani shook his head. "Hardly. You haven't had three days to yourself to truly experience what this world is. If I were to walk away right now, you'd be done within the hour."

"You don't know that," Fura argued.

331

"I do."

"No, you don't. You said yourself that I haven't been given the time to really see. Maybe I would surprise you."

Crossing his arms, Kiyani's eyes narrowed. "Why don't I just leave right now, then?"

Fura felt the color drain from her face. "You wouldn't." Even if she wanted to prove a point to him, she didn't want him to leave. She didn't want to be left in this place alone.

"You don't know that, do you?" he asked.

Cringing, Fura looked at him, searching the planes of his face for any indication that he was messing with her. She didn't like the darkness in his tone, or what his words were insinuating. "Please don't," she said weakly.

"And why not?"

Her eyes skirted the forest surrounding them, desolate and quickly growing shadows as the sun continued its evening descent. "Just because I might be okay doesn't mean that I want to be alone out here," she said, hoping he wouldn't be able to pick up on the fear laced in her words. He had threatened to leave her once before, and yet he had stayed. Fura could only hope that this would be the same. "Would you want to be out here alone?" she added, hoping to further sway him towards her side of the matter.

Kiyani simply shrugged. "I've done it before. It wouldn't bother me."

"It would me," Fura muttered as he turned and starting walking again, his silent way of saying he was done with the conversation for the moment.

Taking in how dark the forest had become in just the few minutes they had stopped to talk, Fura scrambled after him before he made good on his word.

✧⌘✧

Waking that night from another nightmare – this one focused on Kiyani's threat – Fura stared out into the darkness surrounding her.

Though a single glance proved that Kiyani still remained by her side – lost in the throes of his own fitful sleep – Fura had never felt any less alone.

As if sensing her sorrow, the smallest flicker of orange beckoned to her from the pile of ash leftover from the fire they'd started earlier that night in the middle of the Reln hollow. Though Fura felt as if she'd been asleep for a few hours at least, she realized it couldn't have been that long. Not when embers were still alive.

Scooting forward, she pulled herself into a crouch before the ashes, feeling the remnant heat that emanated still. Though it wasn't nearly what it had been when the flames had fully encased the sticks they'd gathered to burn, Fura knew that she could have it started again with just a little bit of prodding.

Shivering against the night air, she leaned forward and blew ever so lightly on the embers. To her excitement, she was rewarded almost instantly with a twisting spindle of smoke and a flare of flame as the oxygen shocked it back to life.

Careful to avoid Kiyani, she gathered a few of the remaining sticks scattered around the hollow and went to work building the fire back up. It didn't take long for it to start blazing again. Proud of her accomplishment, Fura sat cross-legged before the fire, extending her hands over it to warm her fingers. She was glad for the warmth and the light it provided. Smiling, she let her thoughts drift, thinking, for once, that maybe she could survive on her own.

Kiyani's harsh words and her nightmares be damned.

"What the hell do you think you're doing?" Kiyani suddenly hissed behind her.

Shaken from her warm bubble of light, Fura looked over her shoulder, wondering when he'd woken. She'd done her best to keep quiet, though it didn't look as if it had been enough. Yet, what startled her the most was the look of seething anger on his face.

Rising, he rushed over, flinging dirt on the fire with his feet, rapidly putting it out.

"Hey," Fura said, shocked by his actions. "I was using that!"

"Not anymore, you're not."

She couldn't understand his sudden anger. Only a moment ago he had been sleeping. Now he was wide awake and filled with rage for something that she couldn't even begin to understand. "I was cold," she argued.

"Then wrap up in your cloak!"

"What was wrong with the fire?" Fura complained, doing her best to ignore the fury in his eyes and the harsh bite in his tone. These moments with him still left her heart beating rapidly in her chest, fear filling her and making her tremble, not knowing what he would do. Yet, she'd found that if she backed down at times like this, nothing got answered.

"There are still people looking for us," he replied, glaring at her. "Nothing's more inconspicuous than a glowing tree, wouldn't you say?"

"This far away?" Fura argued. She saw her mistake, but she still didn't think it was that big of a deal. At least nothing to get so upset about. "We're days away from Frielana."

Kiyani shook his head in what appeared to be disbelief, though Fura found it difficult to decipher. With the warm glow of the fire replaced by the cold light of the moon that filtered through the hollow opening, it was hard to tell the exact details of his mannerisms. She didn't need to see him clearly though to feel the heated anger he carried.

It left her once again wishing that Kiedo was present, though Fura wondered who's side the wolf would take. Kiedo may have appeared to have taken a liking to her, but when all was said and done, Kiyani was still his master.

"That doesn't mean anything. Don't think that they'll stop looking for us just because we're not within a mile radius of Frielana."

"Why would they even care?" Fura continued, trying to understand Kiyani's distinct worry. "If they wanted us that bad, wouldn't they have found us already?"

"Did you already forget your last experience with the Shadowguard? We're the only escaped witnesses to a siege on the lands of one of the Sect of Seven, by another Lord no less. Do you really think they want us wandering the countryside?"

Sitting with her knees folded to her chest, staring at the floor so as to avoid Kiyani's dark gaze, Fura pondered his words. "Another Lord..." she muttered. Fura had found it strange as she'd listened to the man's dark speech that night, mentioning the Sect of Seven that she had known as nothing more than a fable. It was something she had tried to forget as the days had gone on, but now that she thought back to it, she realized the man hadn't been crazy.

"What are you even doing up?" Kiyani asked.

Fura looked at the floor again, embarrassed by the reasoning. "I couldn't sleep," she admitted, sheepishly. "The ground hurts." It might not have been the initial reason, but it was still truth. It didn't matter how tired she may have been, it was difficult to find any comfort on the cold, hard ground of the hollow.

"You would hurt more if the Shadowlord or the Streig had caught us," Kiyani snapped.

He offered no condolence for her discomfort. Not that Fura had honestly expected any, though she found his rude words unnecessary. And though she had come to expect it from him, she couldn't help the tears that brimmed in her eyes in response.

"You could stand to be a bit friendlier," Fura muttered.

"You could stand to talk less," Kiyani replied, his tone picking up a new air of annoyance.

"I've been quiet all day," Fura complained. Though it had left her stuck in the doldrums of a never-ending boredom, she'd left him alone, hoping that he'd eventually come around on his own. He couldn't ignore her forever. "It wouldn't kill you to pick up some conversation once in awhile."

"I've told you before," Kiyani snarled. "You don't have to travel with me. If you don't like it, then leave."

"You would like that, wouldn't you?" Fura shot back, angry that he was doing this to her again.

"Yes, actually, I would."

Fura cringed at his comment, knowing he meant every word. Backing down before she dug herself further into trouble, Fura wondered how she had gotten herself into this mess in the first place. Of all the people she could have been stuck with, why did it have to be Kiyani? She didn't think she deserved this kind of treatment, but what other option did she really have?

"I hate you…" Fura muttered beneath her breath, pulling her feet to her chest and staring at the ground.

Ignoring her, Kiyani ran his foot over the cold coals again, making sure they were out, before making his way towards the entrance of the Reln.

"Before you decide to do anything else stupid, wake me up first," Kiyani declared, giving her one last ultimatum before exiting the hollow.

Sitting before the pile of expended ash, feeling shattered and abandoned, like a forgotten doll, Fura watched him go, his words from that evening lingering in her mind.

Why don't I just leave, then?

She was afraid that he wouldn't return, yet too terrified to follow him into the night.

41

◆◆◇◆◆

A HARSH REMINDER

A chilled breeze danced through the trees, but it wasn't enough to cool Kiyani's raging emotions. Half-heartedly glancing over his shoulder at the Reln hollow he'd just left, he knew he was overreacting. Yet, he couldn't force himself to return.

Anger drove him into the darkness, fueled by the inability to truly register what had just happened. Though he knew he should stop and evaluate the situation, all he could comprehend was that he'd woken to more of Fura's latent stupidity and incompetence.

He didn't know if it had been the light or the smell of smoke that had woken him, but all he could remember for certain was opening his eyes to the sight of an incredibly unnecessary fire. Ever since he'd begun unwillingly traveling with the girl, Kiyani had taken note of the multitude of traits that she inherently seemed to lack. Surprisingly, for hearing, and seeing on occasion, that she was one of the best performers at the festival, coordination seemed to be front and center. Lately, however, good old common sense was an equal contender on that list.

Even now that he'd separated himself from the situation, he couldn't help but wonder who in their right mind thought it prudent to light a blazing fire in the dead of night when there were people out there somewhere that wanted them dead. They'd been knocking on the door of death with the Streig, and yet she couldn't seem to face the reality that they were in danger. All the time.

They may have gone a few days with no incident, but Kiyani knew better. All his life he had kept himself keenly aware of his surroundings, knowing that danger could be anywhere. Now was no different. In fact, since the siege of Frielana, he'd had to employ those skills more often than he'd ever wanted.

Thinking on it, he wanted nothing more than to keep walking, to leave all this nonsense behind. He may have felt like the majority of his life was an on-going trial for worse things, but he had never expected to be saddled with the responsibility of a naïve girl. Of all that he had been through, that was something he definitely wasn't made for.

Just walk away and leave it all behind.

Just leave.

That was the incantation running through his head.

Yet, something kept him at bay.

Grumbling as he halted in his frenzied step, Kiyani took to the trunk of a nearby tree. Its gnarled bark was far from comfortable, but it brought him careening back to reality, reminding him just how uncomfortable life was. Nestling himself in one of the long, unwieldy crevices, he looked up to the sky and the moonlight that filtered through the sparse cloud cover. Much like Kiedo, the moon had always proven to be a quiet companion. Its silver light had always been calming to him, though he didn't know what help it would prove to be now. Too many emotions welled just beneath the surface, coiling and threatening to break loose.

Unlike the simple silver friendship of both the wolf and the moon, Fura had burst into his life in a mess of flaming red hair and spirit, upsetting a balance that had taken him years to achieve. Where Kiedo and the light of the night never asked him questions of his past, Fura was quite the opposite, wanting to know everything about him. It wasn't something he was used to, nor found himself wanting to indulge in.

But he found himself thinking that he could possibly give in to the endless barrage of questioning, if only she would stop doing ridiculous things that placed them in constant danger.

Fire… in the dead of night.

What an idea… he scoffed internally.

Closing his eyes, he inhaled deeply, taking in the cool, musky scent of the forest around him. He knew it wasn't likely to be as calming as it generally proved to be, but he could still try.

Attempting to clear his mind, Kiyani listened to the gentle rustle of the wind through the trees, trying to enjoy the natural calm of the forest that he'd always been able to count on. It was one of the few things that had never let him down.

However, that peace was short-lived as the distinct crackle of steps over the brush littering the forest floor brought him out of his reverie. Letting out a frustrated sigh, he hoped that Kiedo had decided to return, though he knew it was probably Fura, coming after him.

Opening his eyes, he discovered neither.

"And just what do we have here?"

As angry as Kiyani may have been over Fura's recent and questionable antics, seeing her would have been preferable to the man that stood just out of reach of the moon's light. What made it worse was that it was his being out in the open that had given them away, not the small fire of Fura's that he had chastised her for before extinguishing.

"Look at you," Nevo said slyly as he stepped out from the shadows of the subsequent stand of trees. "Just traipsing around the forest like nothing happened."

He was the last person Kiyani had thought he would see out here, and though he wasn't at the top of the list, Nevo was definitely among the last he would have wanted to. Even arguing with Apallo would have been preferable to this.

Refusing to sever eye contact with the man as he approached, Kiyani surreptitiously scanned the surrounding area, searching for any sign that he had brought reinforcements to kill him.

"You're remarkably quiet tonight," Nevo noted with a practiced smile. "Usually so full of witty and sarcastic comments. I have to say, I'm a bit disappointed. But, come, what is this look? If I didn't know any better I would almost say you were scared."

Kiyani glared at him, but remained quiet.

"A pity, really," Nevo said, waving a hand at the moon overhead. "Such a lovely night to run across old friends."

Narrowing his eyes, Kiyani wondered what it was the man wanted. He had lived with him for far too long. Apallo may have never seen the darkness Nevo harbored, but he had.

He was too terrified of what this man might have planned to do to him that he could hardly find it in himself to scoff at the idea that Nevo had just called them friends.

"What are you doing here?" Kiyani asked, finally finding his voice to speak.

"What am *I* doing here?" Nevo asked, almost sounding offended by the question, though there was a distinct chuckle in his voice that claimed he simply found the conversation amusing. "I could ask you the same thing."

"How did you find me?" Kiyani amended.

The man's hair was such a pale shade of blond that it looked white in the light of the moon, giving him the appearance of a specter. As much as Kiyani wished that this was simply a ghostly dream, he knew it was a futile hope.

This time the man emitted a genuine laugh, though Kiyani hardly saw what was funny. In fact, hearing such laughter from him left him more chilled that his initial presence.

"Do you honestly think that your father doesn't have ways of finding you?"

Though Kiyani had been planning his own sarcastic reply, that remark took his own words away, leaving him far colder than the night chill that nipped at his exposed skin.

"So," Nevo continued, his tone darkening. "How is it that you were lucky enough to escape?" Drawing closer, he grinned again as Kiyani made to back away from him. "Oh wait, that's right, because you knew."

"What good it did me," Kiyani shot back, trying to regain his composure. Though none of these situations were ideal, he was generally able to act casual in such instances. He didn't know why Nevo's sudden presence had him so spooked.

The Streig should have easily topped the unwarranted arrival of a man that he'd lived beside for so many years. It had been an unwilling relationship, more of a general acquaintance than anything, but it had given Kiyani the time to inadvertently be able to pick up on and decipher the man's mannerisms.

"I take it you're here to kill me, then."

The grin widened on Nevo's face. "You don't know the pleasure that would give me."

"I have a mild idea."

"As much as I would enjoy having your death on my hands, I don't have the liberty to make that decision."

"Still following orders," Kiyani mocked.

A sudden snarl replaced the smile on Nevo's face. "Maybe it's something you should have learned to do. As a matter of fact, you may still have one last chance to join the movement."

Searching the man's face for any sign that he was lying, Kiyani wondered just how much effort that statement had taken. He had been given the chance once before and had denied it – just as he intended to do yet again – and he had been ignored and berated ever since. Once again, Kiyani decided that it was strict orders that were talking, rather than what Nevo truly had on his mind.

"I'll pass," Kiyani declared. He'd heard the plans Nevo and Mrena had spoken of, and he wanted nothing to do with it. The fact that it would leave him tied to the Shadowlord made such a thing even less desirable.

"Then let me tell you something," Nevo said darkly. "If you ever return to Frielana I'll deal with you as I see fit."

This time it was Kiyani that showcased a mocking grin. "I don't think Zariah would like that." If there was anything that he knew of this group of people, it was that the Shadowlord himself had first dibs on his death. It wasn't a pleasant thought, but it gave Kiyani an idea of the limits of what those working for the man were capable of.

"You don't deserve to even speak his name," Nevo snarled insidiously.

"Yet you're here trying to recruit me."

"Not my idea. If I had the clearance, I'd drop you off a cliff, myself."

"But you don't," Kiyani reminded him, glad to have the upper hand in the conversation, if only momentarily.

"Not yet," Nevo said, the grin returning to his face. "Do you really think I came all this way to tempt you back to our side?"

"You came searching for me for something," Kiyani said, sure that he didn't particularly care to know what that reason was. Just seeing the man again was more than he wanted. Words weren't really necessary.

"Of course," Nevo admitted. "I came to give you a personal warning."

"I thought you'd already taken care of that," Kiyani ventured, thinking to the roll of parchment in his back pocket.

"I did, didn't I?" Nevo mused. "But it's so much more fun to give it in person."

"Fine, point taken. You can go now."

Warily searching the forest behind Nevo again, Kiyani finally realized why it was that this man's presence had him so on edge. It wasn't Nevo himself, it was the fact that he had come alone.

For nearly eight years Nevo had ingratiated himself into Frielana, playing the part of a needy victim of circumstance, searching for a place to live. Apallo, being the generous man he was, had taken him in without question. For just under a year, it had been that way, until nine months later when Mrena had shown up in much the same way. After that, the two had been nearly inseparable. The other citizens of Frielana had viewed it as a friendship, but Kiyani had heard them on numerous occasions as they schemed. Had anyone else had given the man warning, Apallo might have done something about it, but because the accusation had come from his lips, it had been shrugged off as nothing important.

Kiyani wondered if Apallo saw his mistake now.

Nevo laughed. "As if I came to merely exchange words."

Too busy trying to decipher the riddle behind the man's twisted words, Kiyani didn't see the fist that had formed at Nevo's side until it was too late. Unable to dodge the blow, the man's fist connected with Kiyani's face, sending him flying to the ground.

As Kiyani scrambled to a crouching position, aware of the trickle of blood running from his nose, Nevo stepped closer. Crouching by his side, he took Kiyani's moment of weakness to snatch the dagger from his back pocket.

Grimacing, Kiyani wished that he'd thought of the weapon when the man had first appeared, not after it had been taken from him. Better yet, he wished he hadn't left the sword lying on the floor of the hollow. He wondered what his chances were of getting the dagger back, but didn't dare attempt the maneuver.

"You know," Nevo said with a smile as he ran a finger along the blade's edge. "It's interesting, really. You're so much closer to becoming what you've been hiding from all these years than you realize. Killing a member of the Shadowguard. Carrying his weapons. That's just a few steps away from leading the whole damn mob, isn't it?"

"Hardly a job I want."

"You best remember that," Nevo said, his eyes dark as he rose to tower above Kiyani. "By the way, where's Fura?"

Hoping that Fura had the common sense to stay in the hollow if she was witnessing this, Kiyani played the innocence card. "How should I know?"

In fact, if he was lucky, Kiyani hoped that she'd returned to sleep and would never know about any of this.

"Are you saying that she didn't escape with you?" It was evident in Nevo's tone that he didn't believe Kiyani, yet he played along for the entertainment value, seeming to bide the time before delivering his next blow, whatever it was he had planned. It was becoming evident that he had simply come to mock.

"Please," Kiyani scoffed. "Do I look like someone who would take on a traveling companion?"

It was truth. The last thing he wanted was Fura tagging along like a lost child searching for a parent. Yet, that was exactly how it had ended up. Nevo didn't need to know that, though. As far as any of them knew, Fura had simply vanished.

"You should keep it that way," Nevo sneered. "I'd hate to have to kill her like I did Kiedo."

Kiyani didn't know just how much the man could say that would make his blood run cold, but the mention of Kiedo's name from his lips had turned it directly to ice. Forcing himself to look at the man, he searched for any sign that he was lying, but all that was present was a practiced stoicism and that haughty ass grin he wanted to carve off his face.

It was only because Nevo had lived alongside him in Frielana that he even knew of Kiedo. Monira was the one that knew Kiedo was probably his only trusted friend. Kiyani hadn't been aware that anyone else had been paying attention to the strange man and beast relationship that had formed between him and the wolf over the years.

"I don't believe you," Kiyani forced himself to say, feeling sick at the thought of what Nevo was telling him. It was nothing more than something to throw him off guard. That's what he had to tell himself.

Remembering the night that Kiedo had alerted him to the Shadowguardian that had been after him and Fura, he told himself no one could even get close enough to the wolf to injure him, much less kill him.

Pulling something from his pocket, Nevo carelessly tossed it to the ground. "Let that be a reminder of what I'll do to anyone who befriends you. And if you haven't taken the hint by now, let me tell you plain and clear that you're permanently exiled from Frielana. If I ever catch you lurking around, I'll be far less lenient."

Looking down at the hunk of bloodied gray fur on the ground before him, Kiyani found himself at a complete loss for words. He had expected that this far from Frielana, they would have given up on them, that they wouldn't care. Now he wondered otherwise.

"By the way," Nevo said, pausing as he walked away. Tossing the dagger, the blade embedded itself into the soft dirt before Kiyani. "He will *always* find you."

Still on the ground, his face throbbing with pain, his mind a catastrophe of thoughts, Kiyani glanced up at the man. He may have wanted the last word in this sordid conversation, but just like the ghost he resembled so fairly in the moonlight, Nevo had already disappeared into the trees as if he'd never been present in the first place.

If only.

Kiyani wished that it'd been nothing more than a figment of his imagination, but the blood running from his nose told otherwise.

Too stunned to wipe it away, Kiyani remained motionless, the fight drained out of him as he stared at the fur on the ground, blowing in the breeze. With that image burned into his mind, Nevo's parting words echoed menacingly in his head.

✧⌘✧

Staring into the night in utter awe at where Nevo had disappeared without a trace, Fura found herself leaning against the inner edge of the hollow, desperately trying to catch her breath.

She hadn't played any part in the confrontation, yet it'd effected her far more than she would have thought. One moment she'd been anxiously pacing the empty hollow, trying to work up the courage to go after Kiyani and apologize, the next she had been caught completely off guard as Nevo had appeared out of nowhere.

The man had come out of the trees with more stealth than even Kiyani seemed capable of, and it had shown in the terror Kiyani had done his best to keep out of his eyes. Even then, Fura had wanted to dash out and help, but she had remained, frozen in place, unsure of what action to take. In the end, all she'd been able to do was stand there, hidden in the hollow, pretending to be invisible. Never before had she felt more useless.

Even knowing that Nevo had gone, she still couldn't force herself to move out into the night to confront Kiyani. It didn't matter that she felt sick just looking at his crumpled form that was nothing more than a shadow in the darkness.

And yet, as he finally rose, appearing weak and disoriented, all Fura felt was anxious, not knowing how to approach the subject with him. She knew that the easy route would be to quickly feign knowledge of the whole incident. As far as Kiyani knew she had returned to sleep after he'd stormed out, though she doubted he would believe that. Even she couldn't believe that lie. There was no way that she could have so easily gone to sleep after Kiyani's latest rampage, his words still ringing in her ears.

Not to mention, he had mentioned only that afternoon that he might just up and leave. As much as she didn't want to reflect on that possibility, she was starting to not doubt his words so much. How could she possibly sleep with that potential outcome in her mind?

Reentering the hollow, Kiyani surprised her. So lost in the frantic disarray of her thoughts, she hadn't even seen him start to approach. Now not only was she at a loss for actions, but a complete loss for words.

Casting her a cursory glance, Kiyani's eyes appeared questioning, but his tense form and deafeningly quiet arrival dared her to say anything about what had happened. Either way, it was apparent that he knew she had witnessed the whole thing. A fact they both would have preferred not to be true.

Keeping quiet and to herself was her best option, yet Fura found herself speaking regardless.

"Are you okay?" she asked. It was probably the dumbest thing she could have asked, yet it was too late to take it back. All she could do was wait for his general biting reply, sure to cut even deeper after what he'd just been through.

Though he appeared shaken, for good reason, he ignored the trickle of blood from his nose, as well as her concerned gaze, and walked past her without a word.

Watching him now, as he fumbled about, pretending he was fine, Fura cursed herself for her earlier decision. She had wanted to follow him, to apologize, to talk to him until he had at least calmed down. As much as she hated to admit it, she had been too afraid, the thought reminding her of one of their last lengthy conversations after she had discovered the scarred back he went to lengths to keep secret.

Admit it, you're afraid of me.

Of all the things he could have said to her, that was one that she didn't want to prove as truth.

And yet, as she had watched him storm off, leaving her in the dark, all she had been able to picture in her mind had been that dagger he had pointed directly at her and the dark look in his eyes. He hadn't hurt her then, and she didn't know for certain that he would now, but it was still enough to leave her wary of Kiyani when his mind was clouded with anger.

Peering at him through the fringe of her bangs, she hated herself. She should have followed him. She should have been there.

Yet, she wondered just what good that would have done. She wouldn't have been anymore of a match against Nevo than Kiyani had been. The fact of the matter was that she probably would have only been in the way. Something that Kiyani could have raged about later.

Even if that was the case, it didn't make her feel any better.

"Kiyani..." she tried again, not knowing what to say to him, but feeling incredibly uncomfortable in the deadening silence.

"I'm fine," he finally declared, though his voice was a gravelly growl that warned her against inquiring any further into the situation.

42

•◆•

RIDDLES AND SORROW

In the deep shadows of a dark, stone room, a man sat shivering. Though his red hair was matted with blood and stuck to his face, he didn't seem to notice. His attention wasn't focused on his plight, but rather the menacing dark form that stood across the room, looking down upon him with a malicious smile.

The tall man leaned against the opposite wall next to the only window in the close quarters. His pale face, framed by long black hair was lit by the cold moonlight that streamed in, his dark eyes fixed on the man on the floor. The two appeared to be locked in a stare off, though the figure by the window seemed rather unamused, his fingers clicking together as if in thought, contemplating his next violent move.

Seconds later, though the man hadn't made a step to move, he was standing directly in front of the man on the floor, peering down at him. With one flick of his spindly hands his victim was screaming in pain, writhing in agony on the cold stone beneath him. The man committing the violent act smiled, his lips peeled back in a satisfied grin, revealing pointed teeth.

Moments later, the scene changed. It was still dark, but Fura found herself standing alone in the middle of the woods. Partially covered in viney foliage, a green neon sign reflected the moonlight.

WELCOME TO AUGDEN, it boasted.

At first glance, it looked like any normal road sign, but something about it wasn't right.

Moving closer, Fura noticed a strange residue covering portions of the green, darkening it as if it had recently rained. Extending a hand to wipe it away, she instantly pulled back, realizing that handprints were visible, sliding down the slippery surface as if it had been a last, faltering lifeline.

Backing away, she turned, suddenly feeling as if she weren't the only person present. However, as her eyes scanned her immediate surroundings, she found that there was nothing but her and the darkness.

Returning her focus to the strange sign, she let out a high-pitched scream, nearly tripping over her own feet as she continued to back away from the sign, taking in the new scene that was presented to her.

Where before there had been nothing but the lonely darkness, the sign a reflective contrast against its shadows, now a pile of broken and bloodied bodies had appeared beside the cheery greeting. Many of the faces Fura didn't recognize, but there was one body lying near the top with its face turned towards her. Letting out a gasp, Fura told herself to stay where she was, to not move any closer, that she wasn't seeing what she thought she was. Fighting the rise of bile in her throat, she also battled the conflicting urge to step forward and lay her hand on the mans, wanting to know that he wasn't dead. The vacant gaze told her otherwise as she stared into the cold and vacant eyes of her older brother, Josh.

Feeling the tingle of being watched, Fura found herself startled yet again as she looked up. Beside the sign, a man had appeared. Silent as the night surrounding them, he stood, watching her. Though the cold moonlight had disappeared behind thick clouds, and a dense mist had begun to gather, he was recognizable. His dark hair floated around his face, dancing on a nameless wind. Eyes that were pools of black, leading into the abyss, looked back at her, and decorating his face was that same sinister, satisfied smile that revealed teeth filed to a frightening point.

Waking in a cold sweat, Fura shot up, fighting the heavy folds of the cloak she had wrapped up in to fight off the chill. Her hands shaking, she felt along the floor as she tried to calm the frantic beating of her heart. As her fingers sifted through the loose dirt of the hollow's floor, she felt herself returning to the safety of reality.

Though she could tell herself in the morning light that it was only a dream, Fura knew that the images would haunt her throughout the day. It hadn't been just a run of the mill nightmare. It had been filled with far too many images of reality: her father, broken down and bloody, that terrifying man from the siege of Frielana that had called himself the Shadowlord, and one of her brothers, dead. Even the sign boasting the city of Augden had appeared familiar, though she couldn't determine why.

The terror of it left her torn between wanting answers, and wanting to forget all of it. She briefly thought to ask Kiyani about Augden at least, but looking around the hollow, Fura found herself faced with another problem… Kiyani was gone.

Feeling scared and lonely, she slowly picked herself up off the ground, cringing as she moved her sore body. She had never known before just how nice it was to sleep in a bed as opposed to on the hard ground. Telling herself she had far more pressing problems, she found the smallest hint of relief as she discovered that Kiyani's belongings were still piled against the far wall of the hollow.

She hadn't heard him get up, but that was nothing out of the ordinary. If Fura ever had to compare him to an animal, it would have been a cat, a black cat, despite his lupine friend. Just like a feline, he was unnervingly quiet and evasive.

Looking to the hollow entrance and the light of afternoon that seeped through the ferns outside, she wondered just how long he'd been up. She had come to notice that Kiyani didn't ever seem to sleep well at night, and yet, despite that, he was always up before her. She wasn't sure if that was his general routine, or if he was that desperate to find some time to himself that he purposely woke up at the crack ass of dawn.

Another thing she wanted to bring up in conversation, but thought better of. Letting out a tired sigh, she looked back to the sun-filled entrance, finding herself scared to approach. The last time she had looked out, the scene painted before her hadn't been a good one. Daylight may have taken over, but she still feared that Nevo might come back.

What if he already had, and he and Kiyani were playing the same cat and mouse game as the night before, only painted in the tones of the light of day?

Telling herself that that wouldn't be the case, Fura took in a deep breath and made her way outside.

Taking a moment to adjust to the light of the sunny day, Fura found it amazing just how much the lay of the land changed in relation to the differences in light. Where before the landscape had been dark, cold, and ghostly, now it appeared a whole different place. One that she barely recognized as the background of Kiyani and Nevo's encounter.

Scanning the area, she quickly found Kiyani perched on the trunk of a fallen tree. Before him a small fire burned. She didn't know why, but the sight of it slightly angered her. Who would've ever known that a small fire could be such a cause for contention? Only the night before he'd chastised her for the fire she had coaxed back to life, searching for relief from the cold chill of the night air, and now here he was with a fire of his own. Gritting her teeth, Fura reminded herself that there was no use in being angry. As much trouble as her actions had caused her, she couldn't argue against what he'd said. In hindsight, it had been a terrible idea to pinpoint their location with firelight. Especially in their current predicament.

Briefly, she wondered what would have happened if Nevo had shown up earlier. Would he have passed them by, or would he have cornered both of them in the hollow? Just how different would things have gone if she had been present? She'd heard her name during the conversation, and had wondered why Nevo cared.

Once again, she was brought back to her brief meeting with the man in Frielana, back when she had assumed that he was a nice person. How wrong she had been.

Shaking the thought from her head, she returned her focus to Kiyani.

It was strange to be looking at the man that her father had so vehemently hated, and yet he was the one she was traveling with. The one essentially taking care of her. It wasn't ideal, but after the night before her current situation didn't seem so bad. It was better than living under Nevo's rule with the rest of the prisoners in Frielana.

Approaching Kiyani, she could see that he held a stick in one hand, twirling it absentmindedly. Though she could see that he had written a message in the dirt before him, she couldn't tell what it was. Even he appeared to give it no thought.

Instead, he seemed to not focus on anything in particular, his eyes shadowed, staring out into the trees across the way. Though his mind appeared to be blank, Fura knew it was far from. He was a quiet person, but she had watched him fight with himself, had witnessed his tossing and turning at night. Anyone with a settled mind wouldn't have exhibited such behavior. At least not on a constant basis. His mind was always churning, even if he never said anything.

Most of the time, whatever was on his mind was a complete mystery to her, but today she had a good guess. In his opposite hand, he clutched what looked to be a hunk of gray fur. Though she hadn't asked him after Nevo had left just what he had tossed at his feet, Fura had heard the man's admission that he had killed the wolf.

Seeing Kiyani now, she hoped for his sake that the man had been lying. Though the hair in Kiyani's hand looked dreadfully familiar in color.

"Do you think it's his?" Fura asked, breaking the silence and cringing at just how awkwardly she had chosen to do so.

Chastising herself, she wondered why she couldn't have at least commented on the weather first like a normal person, instead of just bombarding him with dark questions that neither of them really wanted an answer to.

Slowly turning his head, Kiyani regarded her silently.

"I think Nevo was lying," he replied, not sounding confident as he ran his fingers through the fur.

Fura nodded as she moved a few steps closer, judging that he wasn't in a particularly volatile mood. She hoped he was right. Even though she had only just gotten used to the wolf's presence, she still found that she missed him. Kiedo may not have been able to warn them of the Streig, but Fura had still felt safer with him around.

Looking at him closer, Fura could see the exhaustion present in the black circles under his eyes. The mild bruising from his fight with Nevo only accentuated that fact. Wishing that she could do something to help him, she knew it was best to not even mention it, and yet, Fura couldn't help herself.

"Are you sure you're okay?"

"I'm fine," Kiyani sighed, the irritation present in his voice telling

Fura that he was far from.

Though she wanted to inquire further, Fura told herself to leave it alone. If he wanted to talk, he would. She had never gotten anywhere in the past trying to force information from him. Now would be no different. If anything, she assumed the late night incident would leave him even more closed off.

Ignoring her instinct to care for him, she moved to stand beside him. Glancing at the ground, she read what he had scribbled there. Surprised, Fura found herself blinking, wondering if she was seeing things. She had expected that it might have been a note to himself, or possibly just some mindless nonsense to keep his mind off things. Fura hadn't expected what stared back at her.

"What does it mean?" Fura asked, reading it again. "The witness will lead the way…" she said, repeating the words that had visited her dreams time and time again, ever since Apallo had shouted it on that fateful night. Her father. She realized that those were possibly the last words she would ever hear from him. Holding back tears, she tried to focus on the meaning of the message instead.

"I've been wondering the same thing," Kiyani muttered, twirling the stick in his hand absent-mindedly. "I thought I might have heard it wrong, but that's what you heard as well?"

Fura nodded as he looked to her for confirmation. "Wasn't everyone there a witness, though?"

"I could see him searching the crowd with his eyes," Kiyani said. "I think he was looking for you."

"So he could have known that we weren't there?" Fura asked.

"He doesn't give a rat's ass about me," Kiyani reminded her sullenly. "He was looking for you."

Searching for words, Fura shook her head, shocked at his accusation. "You don't think he meant that I'm supposed to lead the way, do you? You've said yourself that I don't know anything about this place. You were a witness too."

Kiyani shook his head. "I may know more about this place than you do, but I don't know what he meant either. Besides, Apallo would never rely on me unless he absolutely had to. And even then, he'd think twice about it. In fact, he'd probably rather face his death than leave his life in my hands."

Fura looked at him incredulously, wondering if he actually meant that.

"You've seen the way he treats me," Kiyani claimed before Fura could comment.

Not knowing what to say to that, Fura remained silent. Falling into the regular silence that seemed to permanently lurk between them, she watched as Kiyani moved the stick in the air, invisibly retracing the words in the dirt.

Keeping quiet as she mulled over the words herself, she perked up as he stopped writing once he reached the word 'witness.'

"Witness…" he whispered to himself.

"That's what he said, 'the witness will lead the way,'" Fura said, repeating the cryptic sentence from memory, rather than reading it from the ground.

Only mildly glancing at her, Kiyani didn't say anything before returning to the word.

"Witness…" he said again, jabbing at its written companion on the ground. He stared at it for a moment before speaking again. "What if the witness isn't a person?"

Fura looked at him questioningly. "What else would it be?"

Ignoring her question, Kiyani began to write another word below witness, muttering to himself as it took form. "Not N-E-S-S, but N-E-I-S. The Witneis Reln."

"Isn't the reln a kind of tree?" Fura asked, spouting off what little knowledge she'd managed to retain in this wild journey. "How could that be a witness?"

Kiyani shook his head. "It's not, it's the name."

"You're saying that a tree will lead the way, will tell us what to do next?" Fura didn't know whether to laugh at what he'd just said, or take it seriously. She could never quite tell when he was joking, and was usually too afraid to ask. "Now I know you're insane."

Kiyani looked up at her, stick still in hand. "Apallo is the one who said it."

"There must be something else," Fura said. "Do you really think the Firelord would send us to a tree for help? It's got to be a person."

Tossing the stick off into the tall grass beyond the fire, he shook his head again. "No, I'm sure this is right. Of course it doesn't make sense. It's not supposed to. It was a message of help to anyone who hadn't been captured. It had to be vague to prevent anyone else from comprehending it."

"Have you looked around?" Fura asked, still unconvinced. "We're surrounded by trees. Even if it's a reln, there are hundreds, probably thousands of them. We're in a forest. How are we supposed to find the one he was talking about?"

"There *is* only one."

Letting the words settle in her mind, Fura tried to think of how any of this could have made sense. Even if Apallo had spoken of a single tree, how could he have possibly been seeking her for his message. He had to have known when he'd spoken that she knew nothing of this world.

"Only one…" Fura said weakly. Looking out at the forest

surrounding them, she had no idea how they were supposed to find a single, special tree, if such a thing existed. "I don't suppose it glows in the dark or something?"

Kiyani eyed her, obviously not entertained by her attempted humor. "I doubt it."

Dropping her eyes to the ground, she felt embarrassed for even trying. Though it would have been nice to know if it had some distinguishing feature that would make it easier to find. "So, how do we find it?"

He shrugged. "Your guess is as good as mine."

In other words, they were never finding it, Fura thought. He was the one that knew this land, not her. If he had no clue where to look, then what use could she possibly be?

"Maybe we should go back," Fura suggested.

"Absolutely not," Kiyani shot back.

Fura cringed at the intensity in his tone. She knew it sounded like a stupid idea, but was it really any worse than wandering the land with no goal in mind?

"Why not?"

Angrily wiping out the message in the dirt, Kiyani spun around on the log to face her. "And do what?"

"I don't know," Fura admitted. "Find Apallo?"

Kiyani shook his head. "He's not even there."

Fura wondered how he could possibly know that, though it did make sense that the man that had organized the takeover wouldn't have kept the previous leader there. However, there was something about Kiyani's sudden evasion that bothered her.

"Maybe not," she agreed. "But what about the others?"

"What about them?"

That was it, Fura discovered suddenly. "You never planned on going back, did you?"

As Kiyani looked away, she knew she was right.

"There's nothing we can do," he argued.

"Why are you so against going back?"

Fura was already aware that he didn't care much for Frielana. It was apparent in his interactions with Apallo. But the leader wasn't the only other person living there. From what she'd been able to take in during her few days living there, he had taken it upon himself to stay away from the general population, but he spoke frequently with Monira. He had Kiedo, and a space to himself. She couldn't find it in herself to believe him when he said he had no ties to the place. It might not have been ideal to him, but it was still a home.

His isolation was self-induced, she thought, leaving her to wonder if he'd ever even tried to talk to anyone else there. Yet, even as she questioned his actions, she was reminded of her own. Even she had spent most of the time hiding away from the general population. The only reason she had gotten close with Monira was because the woman was one of the first to approach her, acting as a motherly figure. Thinking on it that way, she wondered if she would have ended up much like Kiyani had nothing happened to make them leave so suddenly.

Fura hated to think so, remembering how open and friendly she had always been at the festival, but there was no way to know.

"Kiyani..." she said warily, trying to approach the conversation from a new angle. One that at least got him to utter a single word, as opposed to simply turning away from her. His silence was a solid answer in itself, but she preferred words, preferred to hear his voice, even if it was laced with anger most of the time.

"We can't go back," Kiyani declared vehemently, finally meeting her eye with a dark gaze that said the decision was final.

Angrily crossing her arms over her chest, Fura glared back at him. "Just because you don't like the people there –"

"I never said that," Kiyani replied defensively as he stood.

"Then why?"

As he moved towards her, Fura instinctively stepped back, his form looming larger now that he had risen. Ignoring the gesture, Kiyani quickly pulled something from his pocket, grabbed her hand, and placed it in her palm. "Because, it's too damn dangerous."

Confused, Fura looked at her hand where a small, weathered roll of paper now sat. Not knowing where it had come from or when he'd acquired it, she held off on questioning for a moment. Unsure of what to expect, she unrolled it slowly, revealing a single, hastily written word in thick black ink, followed by a single letter.

Exile
    - N

The edges of the paper were worn, the ink smudged and dotted as if it had been left in the rain. Trying to decipher what the word pertained to, Fura found herself unable to look away from the single letter scrawled at the bottom like a taunting signature. She could only recall one person she knew from this journey with that initial, but he hadn't handed Kiyani anything other than the hunk of fur, had he? Racking her brain, she couldn't come up with a clear answer.

"Who is this from?" she asked, sure she already knew the answer.

"Who do you think?"

Nodding, knowing that he had just confirmed her suspicions without mentioning the actual name, Fura glanced at the ominous word again.

"He couldn't have just told you this last night?" Actually, now that she thought about it, she was pretty sure she had heard Nevo say something about Kiyani being exiled. So, what purpose was the written note supposed to serve?

Seeming distracted, Kiyani crossed his arms over his chest and looked out at the woods surrounding them. "It's not from last night."

Narrowing her eyes, Fura watched him for any sign that he might be lying, but there was nothing. Looking at the note again, she wondered just how long he'd been carrying it. However long it was, it would explain why it appeared so worn.

"Then when?"

Kiyani sighed as he held his hand out. Not knowing why she suddenly felt so protective of the scrap of paper, Fura reluctantly handed it back to him.

"It was pinned to the tunic of the man I killed," he finally admitted, his words so low they were close to a mumble. "I found it when I returned for his weapons."

"You've had it all this time?" Fura asked, wondering why he had deemed it necessary to keep it from her.

That night felt like ages ago, leaving Fura to wonder just how long it had actually been. She had hardly been able to kept track of time in Frielana. All sense of time beyond that had gone out the window. She didn't even know what month it was anymore.

"I half thought to leave it there," Kiyani said, rolling the edge of the note between his fingers, wrinkling the paper even further. "It's like he knew I would come back."

"How could he have?" Fura asked. Trying to recall more details from that night, all she could honestly remember was just how sick Kiyani had looked afterwards in relation to what necessity had forced him to do.

Kiyani shook his head. "I didn't even know," he said, confirming her suspicion. "It was an afterthought. It just felt prudent to have weapons at that point, and where better to obtain them? I never expected that I'd find a note waiting for me as well."

Grimacing, Fura realized that Nevo had left one of his own men, dead and rotting, in the middle of the woods, simply to give Kiyani a message. The more she learned about this man, the more she feared ever meeting him again.

What Fura also realized was what had suddenly changed in Kiyani, between the time he had snuffed her fire and the time he had returned. He had left in anger and returned, burdened with fear. Even now he exuded the symptoms; the lack of conversation, the nervousness.

However, it was only the nerves that tipped her off, the way he continued to fidget with the object in his hands as if he didn't even realize he had regained possession of the note.

Finally glancing down at it, Kiyani ran his finger over the word one last time and tossed it into the fire. Watching it quickly take light, he internally bid it good riddance, though he knew the message would continue to haunt him, even after the physical evidence of it had disappeared.

"I thought that would be the end of it," he said, continuing as if speaking only to himself. "I never expected he would continue to follow me, just to make sure he had gotten the message across."

"What do you think he'll do if you go back?" Fura wondered aloud.

Shaking his head slowly, he replied, "I don't want to know."

Fura watched him cautiously, suddenly understanding something she didn't want to take as truth. "We're not going back, are we?"

"No," Kiyani replied simply, his eyes on the fire.

"Kiyani…" Though she knew why they couldn't go back now, Fura couldn't face the fact that they might never return. How could he just turn his back on all those people?

Ignoring her gaze, he continued to watch the edges of Nevo's note curl and burn. "I'm only saying that had I not made a promise to you to find Apallo I would have no reason to go back. Not one of those people would do the same for me."

Fura watched him speak, searching for any sign that speaking such words aloud pained him, yet his face was as stoic as ever, his eyes reflecting only the flames between them. She doubted that that was true, but whether it was or not, he seemed to think so.

"Monira would," she tried, knowing that at least was an honest observation.

At the mention of the name Kiyani's eyes moved to meet hers for a moment, but his lips still remained silent.

"She spoke highly of you, you know," Fura continued. She had seen them talking, joking the morning of the seige. Why Kiyani was so apt to deny what was probably his one and only friendship was beyond her. Yet, she couldn't help but speak of it. "She told me that you could be a great friend."

"You shouldn't always believe the things people say."

43

•◆•◆•◆•

ACCUSATIONS

Zendel stood in the shadows of the room, watching Zariah as he quietly mulled over the images reflected in the basin before him, depicting the two teens that had once again fallen just out of his reach. Yet, where Zendel had expected rage from the man, there was, instead, a strange and eerie calm about him.

It had always been his way to wait until the Shadowlord spoke, but for once, Zendel couldn't hold his tongue.

"Would you like me to go after them?" he offered, not knowing why he'd even spoken. Or maybe he did. Taking a hesitant step forward, he could just see the silvered image of the two teens, one of which he had grown relatively fond of.

His slender hands folded along the edges of the bowl, Zariah turned his head ever so slightly to take in the man who had interrupted his blissful reverie.

"No," he declared simply. "I have already deployed a small group to attend to that task. Besides, I would rather have you here, where I can keep an eye on you."

"Excuse me, sir?" Zendel questioned, though there was no need. He may have felt slightly offended, but he knew exactly what the man spoke of, why there still remained a fission in the level of trust between them.

"Do not feign ignorance," Zariah spoke coldly, waving his hand over the basin to erase the images before turning. "I am not unaware of what you do behind my back, Zendel."

Grimacing, Zendel bowed his head. "Of course." It shouldn't have been a surprise to him just how much Zariah knew of his life. In fact, as the man's advisor, he was probably watched far more closely than the other's that worked for him.

Reminding himself that the accusation wasn't out of place, Zendel moved onward before anything else could be said.

"M'Lord..." Zendel spoke carefully. He had been uncertain of the man's demeanor when he'd first walked in. That statement hadn't helped. "Nevo is here with a report."

The blond-haired tyrant in training had arrived not long before Zendel himself had been summoned. He knew he should have mentioned it the moment he entered the room. A good advisor would have done just that, and yet, he hadn't been able to deny the opportunity to make the smug man wait around for just a bit, just to inconvenience him.

Turning to look at him from where he had moved to stare out the window, his hands behind his back, Zariah fixed him with a cold gaze.

"How thrilling," he declared unenthusiastically.

Zendel had always found it amazing just how bored a person could sound at any given moment. If there was an award for such a thing, Zariah had certainly earned it. Then again, from the years he had worked for the man, he preferred that state much more than the quiet controlled anger that appeared to be the only other option. Only so often did he incite full blown rage, and Zendel knew from experience that that was a time to stay far away.

Gazing about the room, Zariah appeared to take his time, as if mulling over the exact shade of gray in the stone surrounding him held more appeal than speaking to one of his subordinates.

"Sir?" Zendel approached cautiously, reminding the man of his newest call for attention.

The eyes that met his were just as wicked as ever, though the words that followed were relatively harmless, considering what generally came out of the man's mouth.

"Yes," Zariah agreed mildly. "Let us see what pathetic report Nevo has brought to us this time. Bring him in."

A moment later Nevo sauntered into the room, acting as if he owned the place, or was at least destined for the spotlight.

Zendel could see the Shadowlord didn't share the man's opinion.

"Nevo," Zariah said, his voice a dark and mocking sneer that made even the usual haughty man turn his gaze to the floor like a scolded dog.

"M'Lord."

"You're bleeding," Zariah declared pointedly.

Glancing down at the arm he hadn't been aware he'd been cradling with the opposite hand, Nevo fought the grimace that wanted to surface as he moved to drop the appendage. Plastering a smile on his face instead, he answered wittily. "I didn't know you cared."

It wasn't often that the Shadowlord brought attention to such grievances.

"Of course," Zariah mocked. "It would be a shame to stain the carpet."

Grimacing, Nevo averted his eyes. Checking the rug beneath his feet, he was glad to see that he hadn't managed to drip blood on it. Based on Zendel's cowering in the corner, Nevo already knew that he was in trouble. He'd hardly said a word, and yet, Zariah already knew about his indiscretions.

He was meant to rule this place, he knew it, but Nevo knew he wouldn't get anywhere if Zariah killed him first. It was all a matter of playing the right cards at the right time. Taking a deep breath, he fell back on his usual cocky manner, pretending that nothing was awry.

"Get it together, you twit," Zariah continued before Nevo could even think of a word to get in. He cringed at the comment, expecting the brash manner, and yet still mildly offended by the man's tone. "You mistake me for someone else entirely."

"It's okay to admit your sympathy," Nevo pressed, smiling over gritted teeth.

Zariah looked just as unflustered as ever, the only sign of his growing annoyance the mild snarl that raised the corner of his lip. "Feelings are the downfall of man. You would do well to remember that."

"I knew you cared."

"You are dispensable, just like everyone else around me. Quite possibly even more so. Especially if you can't deal with a single wolf without consequence."

This time Nevo cringed noticeably. So the man did know where he'd been and what he had been doing.

"But it's the annoyingly detestable fact that you cannot seem to follow direction. I would suggest returning to your post. However, if you can't handle it, I can easily find someone more competent to take over your task as overseer of Frielana."

"I beg your pardon?" Nevo said, though there was a fear in his eyes that betrayed him.

Zariah looked over at him, letting the silence linger longer than necessary, watching the man sweat. "You know exactly what I speak of," he finally said, drawing out the words.

Zendel remained motionless in the corner, waiting for the man to formally release him from the room. Nevo wouldn't have been able to pick up on the nuances, but Zendel was painfully aware of the daunting similarities between the current conversation and the words Zariah had spoken to him only moments before. It was said that the Shadowlord had eyes and ears everywhere. Whether that was true or not was up in the air, but what remained an indiscriminate fact was that you didn't betray the Shadowlord without expecting repercussions.

If you were to ask Zendel, he would have acquitted it to Zariah's unnatural ability to read people. But, even if that was the full truth, Zendel knew that that was his numaejic mind working. He didn't have magical abilities, leaving him with little knowledge on just what the Shadowlord was capable of, despite working for him for years.

Nevo may have been numaejic as well, yet that never seemed to have bothered the man much. Or, maybe it was simply his nature to think that he could get away with damn near anything. Something that Zendel knew Zariah had never been fond of. He himself had learned very quickly not to push the Shadowlord.

"I clearly recall requesting that you not go after the two of them," Zariah said darkly.

Though Nevo looked paler than usual, the conversation clearly not going as he had expected, he continued on. "I thought I would take initiative –"

"I would advise against such actions in the future."

"Only Kiyani was present," Nevo claimed, as if in correcting his superior he made the situation better. "Fura was nowhere to be found."

"What makes you think that she wasn't nearby?"

"Kiyani was alone," Nevo tried again, this time sounding unsure of himself.

"Did you bother to look?" the Shadowlord sneered. Moving back towards the scrying bowl in the center of the room, he brought up the image of the two teens walking side by side amidst the forest.

Nevo's eyes dropped to the ground, answering the question in silence. "I…" It was easy to see that he'd been wrong.

Zariah snorted. "I didn't think so. Your naïve insolence never ceases to amaze me."

Waving his hand over the bowl to clear the images again, Zariah wheeled around to face Nevo, his eyes dark. "Not only did you disobey my orders, you also left Mrena in charge of Frielana while you were gone, knowing very well that I do not trust that lying witch of a woman. You are not doing well in reminding me why I keep you around."

Though he would have been better off to remain silent, those words seemed to spur Nevo into a refreshed sense of fight. "You have me watching peasants," he said, his words declaring that he felt the job inferior to his qualifications. "There are so many other things I could be doing. Things that would serve you better."

"I will be the judge of that," Zariah said coldly.

Crossing his arms in defiance, Nevo cringed as he brushed against his injury. "What do you want me to do?"

"What I *want* you to do," Zariah declared, "is return to Frielana and stay there as I initially commanded. No more of these little excursions without my permission. I left you in charge of Frielana, however, if that is proving to be difficult for you, I'll gladly find someone to replace you."

"I assure you," Nevo said with a short bow. "I'm more than capable."

"Then prove it and do your job. I shouldn't have to remind you."

Appearing more frantic than he had ever seen him, Zendel had to suppress a smile. Though he often didn't approve of Zariah's methods of dealing with people, it was nice to see that haughty air of Nevo's deflated for once. Though he was still dwelling on Zariah's words to him, that alone brightened his day.

"Now, get out of my sight," Zariah spat, watching as the man inched his way towards the door, seeming to now want to leave as quickly as possible.

"Yes, M'Lord." Though it appeared that he had more to say, Nevo bowed his head and quickly left the room.

"And Zendel," Zariah said as his second in command made to leave as well. "Refrain from betraying me. I've had my fill of such nonsense."

44

•◆•

SIGNS OF CIVILIZATION

Despite finally having a name for their seemingly unattainable goal, the days that followed passed by in an agonizingly slow blur. Fura watched the sun set each night, and woke to daylight each morning. Yet she couldn't have made a single observation about any of those days if someone had asked.

Though she'd never been so dreadfully bored in her life, she kept that thought to herself, knowing what Kiyani would have to say if she mentioned it. She only had to listen to him say that if she didn't like it, then leave, so many times before she took the hint. If anything, she guessed that he was doing it on purpose, trying to drive her away by making her time spent with him just shy of miserable.

Even if she did have the choice of finding another path, Fura felt like she would have stuck with the charade, just to annoy him. He may have created it, but two could certainly play at that game.

However, the longer that time drove on, the more Fura found that she simply missed conversation in general. It didn't even have to be with Kiyani, but unless she wanted to start talking to herself, she found herself short on options. She couldn't even have a one-sided conversation with Kiedo.

Thinking about the wolf, Fura cringed, hoping once again that he was okay. Kiyani may have claimed Kiedo was fine, but she could see it on his face when he let his guard down that even he wasn't sure. Nevo's appearance and words had left Kiyani downtrodden. Even the way he walked ahead of her, looking as if he were carrying the weight of the world on his shoulders, told her that he had little else on his mind.

For once, she couldn't blame him.

Trying to keep herself from bothering him, Fura let her mind wander, its tendrils encompassing a multitude of subjects. Yet, even with the new revelation about the Witneis Reln, Fura still found her thoughts returning to Kiyani.

She knew so little about him. Only that he was one of the most confusing people she'd ever met. Thinking about the strange individuals

360

she'd met at the festival, that was saying a lot. The way he acted often left her reminding herself that they were around the same age.

It was almost as if he had lived a multitude of lives, where she was still trying to figure out the one. As odd and closed off as he was, Fura still felt a remarkable trust in him, though she couldn't figure out why.

The only moderate verification of such a feeling was that he had, in a way, saved her life. Had it not been for him, she would have been trapped in Frielana, not out on the road – bored and confused, but free.

She could only imagine what it would have been like had they been caught amongst all that chaos. Shuddering, Fura knew she didn't want to experience that. Still, she couldn't help but wonder why she had been spared, and how Kiyani had known to run the other way, rather than to follow the beckoning of the horn like all the others. Had he truly known something bad would happen that night out of all the others, or had he been expecting it for years? Or, was he really that distrustful of people?

Fura banished such thoughts from her mind before she could come up with answers she didn't want. Though Kiyani's actions were questionable at times, she didn't want to think negatively of him. He'd made it known time and time again that he didn't want her around, and yet he was still there. That had to count for something, right?

So why was it that when she'd revealed that trust, he'd turned her away? Not only pushed her away, but had told her point blank not to trust him, going so far as to claim that he could be the one to end her life. Apallo might have agreed, but even after hearing it from Kiyani himself, Fura couldn't find any potential truth behind that statement. There were times when he seemed to reveal a darkness that he kept hidden, but all Fura could come back to was the image of just how shaken up he'd been after their run-in with the member of the Shadowguard. Fura just couldn't see it in him to kill someone in cold-blood without a reason.

Allowing her mind the freedom to ramble and ruminate, she wondered why he would say such a thing about himself in the first place. In all their conversations she had never been able to get him to reveal much about his personal life, but maybe that was because, like herself, he didn't think there was anything worth mentioning.

Fura had always been drawn to fire, but had learned to keep that budding interest to herself outside the festival over the years, knowing that very few found it nearly as fascinating as she did. It was all in who you spoke to, she supposed. Trying to talk to someone who didn't have the same level of appreciation and vigor for the subject just didn't make for good conversation, no matter how hard you tried.

It made her wonder if that was it; that he had never found anyone interested in talking to him, so he'd simply taken up the habit of remaining silent when others were around. It was a possibility, Fura thought. Even distraught and anti-social at the time, it hadn't taken Fura long to realize that Frielana was populated by an older demographic. Kiyani had appeared to be the only exception.

That alone was one of the main reasons she'd gravitated towards Kiyani, herself. Though, as she glanced at him, Fura knew it wasn't the only one. Her numerous hours spent with the *Pyropheric* troupe in Fireswell, made up mostly of people in their late twenties and early thirties, hadn't prepared Fura for the group that had surrounded her with their condolences and sympathy in Frielana.

Fura had expected that the group she had gone to for support after losing her family would be the same one she performed with during the festival months. A group she'd been part of since age thirteen. Instead, she'd discovered a whole different world, surrounded by people she had never seen in her life. There had only been a few faces she had recognized, Apallo's being one of them.

Though Kiyani had recently admitted to knowing of her before, working in Fireswell himself, Fura was sure she had never seen him before that fatalistic night. That night when he had so rudely called her out for not belonging with them. Even after that, Fura couldn't help but feel a certain connection with him, couldn't control the way her stomach flipped when every now and then she caught that crooked smile of his, as rare as that was.

Growing angry with herself, Fura cleared her mind of all thoughts, previous and forthcoming. She knew better than to let her imagination create freely, at will, what it wanted. Allowing it to paint a picture of what she wanted wouldn't bring it to life.

Kiyani didn't like her. There was no denying that fact, yet her mind wouldn't settle with that. It should have been enough that he even tolerated her. He'd made it known that the only reason she was even allowed on this journey with him was because her father was involved. Fura sighed. There would be nothing more between them. The way things were going, she would be lucky if she could muster a mild friendship.

Something she wasn't doing a good job of so far.

"Would you stop?" Kiyani gruffed, startling Fura.

It'd been so long since he'd spoken that she wondered if she'd even heard him correctly.

"What?" Fura asked, confused. As far as she knew she hadn't done a thing all day, save for follow him without a word, despite the array of things in her head.

Kiyani eyed her as if to dare her to question it again. "I can hear you moping back there."

So she hadn't been nearly as quiet as she'd suspected, Fura

concluded, looking away.

"I can't help it," she finally said. "I'm bored."

"Then find something to do."

"Like what?" Fura asked, gesturing to the forest surrounding them. She'd always found the woods fascinating, but when they were simply trailing through at a steady clip, it left much to be desired. The only excitement was the small animals that skittered away into the brush once in awhile as they passed by. With Kiyani so quiet, the only thing Fura had found to keep her company were her aching feet and the constant grumble in her stomach, both of which continued to go ignored by her traveling companion.

"Figure something out."

Glaring at him, Fura sighed. It was another typical answer from him.

"What do you want me to do about it?" Kiyani asked, still watching her.

"I don't know," Fura admitted. "You could be a little more sociable."

"I'm not a conversationalist."

Fura had to chuckle to herself. As if she didn't know that already. He was the least sociable person she had ever met. Though she hadn't been able to ask where he worked in Fireswell, she concluded that he had to be lying. No one that went to such lengths to avoid people could possibly work in such a crowed and noisy place.

"Fine," Kiyani relented, startling her. "What do you want to talk about?"

Wondering why he was suddenly giving in, Fura looked at him. Now that he'd given her free reign, she couldn't think of anything to talk about.

"I... I don't know."

Raising a brow, Kiyani studied her, slowing his walk so that she could finally catch up to him. "I'm sure there's something in that head of yours."

Not knowing whether to be offended by his tone or not, Fura shook it off. He was right. She should have been able to think of something to talk about. Yet, the only thing she could think to pursue was the dark subject of her dream the other morning.

"What do you know about Augden?" Fura asked cautiously, deciding to just go for it.

Kiyani faltered in his step at the mention of the name, telling Fura that even if he hadn't wanted to talk, she had at least caught his attention.

"Where did you hear that?" Kiyani asked, peering over his shoulder, taking her in as he walked.

Fura shrugged as if it wasn't a big deal, though it had been haunting her since that morning, the images of that sign all too fresh in her mind. Actually, now that she'd dredged forth the memory, she seemed to recall the name being thrown around between the remaining crowd of the Fireswell festival following the explosion.

"Apallo told me a bit about it."

"Then why are you asking me if he already told you?"

Appearing just as antsy as ever, Kiyani seemed ready for her to drop the conversation. It might not have been the cheeriest of subjects to start with after days of so little exchange, but now Fura couldn't help but wonder just how much he knew if he was already attempting to evade the subject.

"I wasn't paying attention," Fura admitted sheepishly.

Eliciting a disapproving groan, Kiyani shook his head. "That's typical."

"Excuse me?" Fura asked, confused by his answer and his darkening tone.

"You've hardly paid attention to a thing since you've been here."

Though she wanted to argue against his comment, or at least swat at him for it, Fura held herself back. It wouldn't have done anything to move the conversation further. Taking a deep breath and ignoring him, she continued on as if she hadn't heard him.

"So, you *have* heard of it, then?" she said, wondering if this was even a safe conversation to delve into with him.

Kiyani nodded. "Not many people know of it. Or, maybe they do and just don't talk about it. Then again, it's not as big of a deal here as it is in Barandor."

"Barandor?" Wondering how her hometown factored into this conversation, Fura hoped that he wasn't trying to weasel back into the game of trying to get her to return. However, if he brought it up, she assumed there was a reason. He seemed to have a reason behind everything. "Where is Augden?" she asked, thinking that maybe it was the name of some obscure town close to where she had grown up.

"You've been living there."

"What?"

"Augden was the name of your town, twenty-some years ago, before it was changed to what you know it as now."

Fura fell quiet, wondering how she'd never heard this before. Though she had lived in Barandor all her life, she was pretty sure that Apallo's mention of Augden was the first time she'd ever heard the name. Kiyani peered over at her, but she avoided eye contact as she mulled over this information. A part of her wanted to call him a liar, much like the night he had revealed her relation to Apallo, but the ease of his answer, in that level voice of his when he knew something for a fact, told her it was truth.

Walking along beside him, the wind blowing her hair in her face, Fura knew what her next question would be. Even so, she wasn't sure she wanted to know the answer.

Taking a breath, she asked anyways, knowing that Kiyani was probably waiting for it. "Why was the name changed?"

Kiyani ran a hand through his hair, his fidgety behavior an indication that he was trying to figure out how to put it into words. It was a few moments before he spoke. "To rid the town of its bloody reputation." Either allowing the words to sink in, or trying to determine how to continue, another short silence followed, though he was speaking again before Fura could interject. "There was a series of murders, ranging from bloody and gruesome, to some that could be blamed on mundane things, like a gas leak, perhaps."

"A gas leak is what the fire at my house was blamed on," Fura muttered.

"From what I've heard, it only spanned a two month period, but a lot of people were killed," Kiyani continued, ignoring her comment. "There's still speculation now and then if they caught the actual killer. It was enough to tarnish the name of the town though, and keep tourists at bay, so they changed the name in an attempt to bury the past."

Walking with her arms crossed, Fura contemplated the information, trying to figure out how her dreams could have pieced this together when she'd known so little. Though Apallo had made the first mention of it, she couldn't recall him revealing much about it. "I guess that's why I've never heard of it."

"Once again," Kiyani said, not seeming to be overly thrilled with the conversation. "You didn't ask Apallo about this why?"

Fura shrugged. "Because, I wasn't dreaming about it then."

"Dreaming?"

"Just the sign saying *Welcome to Augden*," she said, nodding. "I thought the place looked familiar though." Even as she admitted it, she wondered if that was why the dream had affected her so much. It wasn't just Augden she'd been seeing, it was her own hometown of Barandor.

"Is that why I woke up to a fire the other night?"

"It wasn't just the sign," Fura tried to explain, detecting a hint of disbelief in his voice. She didn't dare tell him that that night had been the product of a different nightmare. "The man that took over Frielana was there as well."

"The Shadowlord?"

Looking at Kiyani, she wondered why his question surprised her so much. If anything he'd just verified what she already knew, but didn't want to believe. "So, he really is the Shadowlord? I thought he might have been delusional at the time..."

Kiyani snorted. "Delusional is one word."

Startled by his sudden quip, Fura looked over at him, studying the dark and disgusted look on his face.

"You speak as if you know him."

Momentarily glancing at her, he was quick to look away. Though for once he actually replied in due time. "He's one of the Seven, as is Apallo," Kiyani decreed. "Meaning he's visited Frielana from time to time."

"Oh," Fura mouthed, wondering why it'd never occurred to her before. Even when she'd overheard the conversation between her father and Monira regarding the man, she hadn't assumed that they had known each other so well.

Shuddering, she came to the conclusion that she no longer wanted to be a part of this conversation. Thankfully, Kiyani appeared to be just as uncomfortable as she was with the topic.

As if offering reprieve, Fura noticed something come into view just ahead. Dropping away from the mention of Lords and towns with dark histories, Fura scurried ahead of Kiyani, wanting to know what it was.

Taking it in as she approached, she almost had to look twice, wondering if what she was seeing was real.

"Kiyani," Fura said, "a town."

Following days of what felt like endless forest, Fura had begun to wonder if there was any civilization in this strange world beyond that of Frielana and Fae Rue Keep.

"I see it," Kiyani confirmed dully.

Peering over her shoulder, Fura wondered how Kiyani couldn't feel the same elation she did. This was the first sign of human life they had seen in days, reminding Fura that they weren't alone in this place.

But it wasn't just that. Though they'd just been speaking in tongues of darkness, at the first sight of the town Fura's head had filled with cheerier thoughts.

People.

A hot meal, and a long shower. Both of which were overdue.

Or a hot bath, Fura thought, squinting as she tried to imagine what amenities the town might hold.

Pausing in her step, Fura wondered for the first time just how technologically advanced this world of Izandüre was. Since leaving Barandor, her mind had been in a constant haze of confusion and question. Only now did it occur to her how much she'd gone without since that time.

Cars. Computers. Televisions. Cell phones.

All were non-existent in this place

As she thought about it, Fura realized that Izandüre as a whole seemed to be lacking electricity, and, save for the natural falls, running water as well. From what she'd seen, those living in this parallel world were still one with nature, either unaware of modern advancement, or simply preferring to ignore it.

As Kiyani came up behind her and paused at her side, Fura thought more on the subject. Running a tongue over her teeth, she tried to think back to the last time she had been able to brush them.

Even her clothing was something she hadn't had the luxury of cleaning regularly. Not once since leaving Barandor had she been able to wash what she'd been wearing. Thanks to Tybithera she had the makings of a new wardrobe, but it was still only a few menial pieces that she had to routinely change out, attempting to rinse them here and there in small streams.

Fura wrinkled her nose, suddenly wondering how bad she smelled to others. Not like she had been around many people, she thought, glancing at Kiyani beside her. Though the people in Frielana had the spring, it still hadn't appeared to have been a big deal.

Fura was beginning to see that in this world you simply had to learn to deal with what was given to you. A way of thinking that she was quickly falling into line with herself.

Yet, despite the lack of daily hygiene, Fura found that the longer she traversed these lands, the less she cared, even with her attraction to her traveling partner. Though tragedy had brought her to this place, Izandüre was proving to be a place of freedom.

Catching movement out of the corner of her eye, Fura turned to watch Kiyani veer away, back to the path they'd been traversing. One that moved away from the town below.

Confused, she skittered after him. "Wait," she said, grabbing his arm as she caught up to him. "Aren't we stopping?"

Kiyani looked past her to the town. "No."

A single word, yet laced with such finality. Fura cringed at his darkened tone, wondering what was going through his mind.

"Why not?"

"Because I said so."

Fura looked back at the quaint little town sprawled out between the valley of trees before turning to watch Kiyani's stiff gait as he stalked away. She didn't understand how the simple mention of what looked like a nice place to stay could set him off so easily.

"And why can't we stop?" Fura asked, trailing after him. It was true that they would probably be best served by continuing on. Fae Rue was barely a week behind them, leaving them with a lot of time that needed to be made up. But what was wrong with stopping for one night? For preferring the comforts of a soft bed to the hard ground the Relns provided?

His eyebrows furrowed as he looked at her questioningly. "Why would we?" The biting tone of his voice made it sound like a ridiculous acquisition.

It seemed like a relatively normal move to Fura.

"I don't know," she began. "We could get a hot meal, sleep in a real bed for a day or two, stock up on food..."

"We're not stopping," Kiyani said harshly. "And we're most certainly not staying." Turning away from her, he resumed walking.

"Someone there might know something about the Witneis Reln," Fura prodded.

Kiyani paused and turned to face her. "We're going *around*."

Fura folded her arms stubbornly. "I don't see why we can't stop."

"You wanna know why? Because that's extra time that we don't have, wasted on a probable false hope that they have a tiny bit of the information we need. Not to mention they could be on the lookout for us. There's no knowing where that town's loyalties lie."

"Are you serious?" Fura asked, not understanding why he was being so unreasonable.

His voice was flat as he turned around, mumbling, "Completely."

Fura kept the town in her peripheral vision as she walked behind Kiyani, his gait noticeably quicker than before.

There was nothing menacing about the neat rows of houses below, some with thatched roofing, others with tiles the color of muted rust. A long stretch of wooden buildings with windows was situated in the middle of the town, what Fura assumed were storefronts.

She could see people milling about, wandering here and there, and talking in small groups. They were too far away to distinguish any features, but Fura could see, even from a distance, what Tybithera had meant by changing their clothing to keep from attracting unwanted attention.

It was almost like looking down at a scene from Fireswell. If you added a few people dressed in the more flamboyant dresses of richer fabrics, generally reserved for those of the upper classes in the medieval age the festival represented, she would've sworn that it was Fireswell that she was looking upon. However, her own dress and the lack of a cheering crowd told her otherwise.

Looking back at Kiyani, Fura asked hesitantly, "Are you sure we can't stop?"

"Yes," he snapped back, the biting edge of his voice no softer.

"Why are you so against people?"

Kiyani whipped around, "Why do *you* feel like you can trust everyone you run into?"

"Because that's what people do."

"Not people that stay alive."

Fura looked at the town longingly. It wasn't just the comforts that it potentially boasted, but what the mere sight of it represented, and that was a sense of excitement to disrupt the doldrums they had fallen into.

In comparison with the past few weeks, life had almost become boring. Ever since the explosion, Fura had felt like her life was stuck on fast-forward, never allowing a spare moment for thought. Now it felt like it was stuck on pause, moving so much slower and leaving Fura with far too much time to brood. With the lengthy lulls in conversation, and nothing else to keep her mind occupied, Fura had found herself mulling over things that she preferred to not think about.

The fire.

The siege.

Her father.

Her recent onset of nightmares.

It wasn't just the comforts she sought, it was the distraction that the town could provide. Looking down on the inviting streets, Fura knew she couldn't let the opportunity pass by. She needed this more than Kiyani could ever know. What she didn't know was how to get that across to him. He wasn't always the easiest person to talk to as Fura had discovered, leaving her to keep more and more to herself. Her fears and worries were killing her slowly from the inside. The way she was going, she felt she could die in her sleep from the poison with a smile on her face, no one on the outside ever knowing.

"Kiyani," Fura whined as she raced to catch up with him. "I don't get why we can't stop. It's already mid October. Winter is coming. We can't sleep in cold Relns forever."

Kiyani stopped so suddenly that she nearly ran into him, not expecting such a jaded reaction from the mere mention of the month.

"It's the middle of October?"

Fura nodded, not knowing what else to say as she took in the tense tone of his voice.

"Are you sure?"

"I think so," Fura answered, though his reluctance to accept her answer left her faltering. The last date she knew for certain was the date of the fires back in Barandor. Every day since then had passed by in an indistinguishable blur of memories that she would have rather left to decay and fade away. The only thing worth remembering in that time was meeting Kiyani, and even that was sketchy at times.

The further they traveled together, the more Fura wondered if maybe she would have been better off had they never met.

"October..." Kiyani muttered as he returned his attention to the town he had been so adamantly ready to bypass. Taking a number of steps closer, he leaned against a tree, his back to her.

Confused by his sudden change in demeanor, Fura followed suit, taking note of the defeat in his posture. Though he'd grown irritable the moment she had suggested stopping in the nameless town, he now seemed to be thoroughly considering it.

She wanted to know what had essentially changed his mind, but left it alone, knowing better than to pursue the answer. If she was lucky, she would eventually find out.

Later that night, Fura still hadn't received her answer. Only more confusion.

She had expected that once Kiyani had changed his mind they'd immediately go down to check the town out. Instead, they were sitting beside a tree in the growing darkness, looking down on the people below.

Leaning forward to try to get a better look in the fading daylight, Kiyani held an arm out to keep her from moving any closer. Even if by an inch.

"Wait."

"Why?" Fura questioned. "Shouldn't we try to get a closer look?"

"Not if you want to be seen," Kiyani said. "If we can see them, then they can see us. Though, right now we have the advantage of being camouflaged in the tree line."

Though Fura had been entranced by the sight of human life besides her own and Kiyani's, her attention had been fully reverted. Intently watching Kiyani as he spoke, she found herself wondering about him again.

"Where did you learn all this?"

Kiyani gave her a cursory glance before shrugging. "It's just common sense," he declared, making it sound as if it were no big deal.

"Maybe," Fura agreed warily. "But most people don't think like that."

"Maybe they should."

Shaking her head, Fura looked to the town. The lights in the windows looked warm and inviting, and here she was, shivering against the cold. She still didn't understand why they couldn't simply walk down, find whatever qualified as an inn, and get a room for the night. They could've left in the morning. Instead, Kiyani had decided to make a production out of the whole thing.

Pulling her cloak tighter around her shoulders, Fura looked over at him. His eyes were focused on the people milling about in the streets, leaving him unaware of her discomfort.

"How long are we going to sit here?" she said with a sigh.

"Go back to the Reln," Kiyani offered. "I'll be there shortly."

Unable to stand the chilly breeze any longer, and fighting exhaustion, Fura nodded. Rising, she made her way back to the shelter

Kiyani had chosen over anything the town below could offer.

Kiyani watched Fura walk away, waiting until she was out of sight before returning his focus to the town below. Though he kept a watchful eye, his thoughts remained scattered.

The town and the potential dangers it held should have been first and foremost on his mind. Yet, three days later, he was still trying to comprehend his unexpected run in with Nevo. No matter how he looked at it, it made no sense why the man had wanted Fura. He might not have said it in those exact words, but there was no other reason as to why he would have asked.

It might not have been Nevo that cared. It could have been the Shadowlord that wanted her. But, why?

Leverage...

It was the only thing that came to mind.

Apallo wasn't the kind of man to easily give in to a situation, nor betray his friends. But, despite the title of Firelord, he was human. He could still be persuaded. And that was where Fura could become useful.

Gritting his teeth against his thoughts and against the cold, Kiyani told himself he was over-thinking the situation. It was Nevo. For all he knew, the man had simply wanted to blow off some steam and he'd chosen him as his victim.

The fact of the matter was that the whole thing could have turned out much worse. As it was, Nevo had gotten his message across and had left. If Kiyani was lucky, that would be the last time he'd see him.

Running a hand over his face, Kiyani tried to set his focus back on the present.

He had a feeling that it wouldn't be the last time someone would come after them, but what mattered now was trying to figure out if stopping in this nameless little town was a good idea. His gut told him no, but if Fura was right about the date, then what choice did they really have?

The breeze that whispered through the pines rustled his hair, but he remained stock still as he scoped the town. He didn't like the looks of it, the armed guards milling about the perimeters, gazing out into the darkness beyond the light the lanterns hung on buildings provided. Though it felt as if they could see him, more than one having paused to stare directly at where he sat, Kiyani told himself he was completely invisible. If he had learned anything over the years, it was how to hide in the shadows.

Every fiber of his being told him to move on, put this town behind them, forget it had ever come into view. However, that didn't change the date of the Hunt. Even if they stepped up the pace the following day – something he knew Fura would struggle with – Kiyani knew that the next town was a least a week or more away. Not enough time.

Whether the number of armed individuals below was due to the impending Hunt, or if it was a regular habit, Kiyani wasn't sure. What he did know was that it didn't make for the friendliest of impressions. Then again, the hours of night weren't for impression making anyways. At least not good ones, he thought, recalling the Shadowlord's midnight siege of Frielana.

That wasn't the kind of impression he wanted to make here. Anyone coming in the night was usually bad news, which was why he'd told Fura that they would wait until mid-afternoon the following day before making themselves known.

If they had to.

Slowly piecing together the passage of time in his head, Kiyani knew they had no other choice.

The changing weather was the least of their worries.

45

◆◆◇◆◆

NOT SO WELCOMING

The following morning was dank and gray, the air damp from impending rain. A bitter wind streaked through the sky, adding to the misery.

However, Kiyani sat, still as stone, outside of the shelter where Fura still lie sleeping. The cold, howling winds of changing seasons would have been enough to keep anyone from sleeping, yet it wasn't what had kept him awake.

There was no telling how long he had knelt alone in the darkness on the outskirts of the town, watching its inhabitants fall into their habitual night time hibernation. As he'd watched the armed guards patrol the dirt streets, Kiyani had kept another wary eye on the skies above.

When he'd finally returned, Fura had been fast asleep. He hadn't bothered waking her, knowing that if he did he would only be bombarded with questions. He already knew that she was confused about his sudden turnaround.

He'd made his opinion on the town clear the moment they'd first stumbled upon it. He hated that he'd been forced to change his mind, especially knowing that Fura was probably gloating on the inside. She was the one that had wanted to stop in the first place, no thinking involved.

Though Kiyani had planned on getting at least a small amount of shut-eye, his plans hadn't quite followed through. Instead, his mind had kept him up throughout the night. Tossing and turning, he had tried extensively to find a way, any way, around this stupid, last minute plan. His mind, still laden with questions regarding Nevo's visit, worry about Kiedo, and stress over upcoming events and unavoidable stops, had offered no new insight.

As soon as dusk broke, Kiyani had made his way back to the vantage point he'd staked out the night before. He'd hoped that the brisk walk in the cool, morning air would help clear his mind. Yet, one last look at the town only solidified the fact that he had no other options. To his dismay, and Fura's delight, they would be making an unintended stop.

One thing he knew for certain, as he listened to Fura begin to stir, was that whatever welcome that town would show them it would be nothing compared to what they would encounter in a fortnight or so if they remained out in the open.

✧⌘✧

"So, tell me again why we're sitting around doing nothing?" Fura murmured as she lay on her back in the small, grassy clearing beside the latest Reln shelter watching the clouds roll by.

She had woken up full of energy, ready to head out and see what the town had to offer. Even if they couldn't find any information regarding the Witneis Reln, at least it would be a welcome change of scenery. As calming as the forest was at times, Fura missed the clamor of people that was prevalent in Fireswell. She didn't need a crowd, but she found herself craving light conversations at dinner as opposed to the deafeningly quiet meals she shared with Kiyani. At least when one of their conversations didn't leave him stalking off beforehand.

Maybe the change of pace would do Kiyani good as well.

A bed with an actual mattress would be a bonus, she thought to herself, seeking not only companionship, but the comforts of home that she had taken for granted.

Yet, Kiyani had taken no time in quelling her excitement, telling her instead to relax a little while longer before they went. He hadn't given any reasoning for the strange decision. In fact, he had been quieter than usual throughout the morning.

"I told you," Kiyani began in a tone that was a mixture of weariness and irritation. "It's better to show up asking for shelter later in the day than early in the morning."

Fura rolled over onto her side, propping herself up on her elbow, and looked at him. She was pretty sure that he hadn't said much of anything earlier, aside from announcing that it would be a few hours before they left.

"It makes it more believable that we've been traveling for the past few days," Kiyani added before Fura could say anything.

How does he do that? Fura wondered.

Where she'd been enjoying what sun she could get in the overcast morning, taking everything in, he sat in the shade, his back against the tree that had been part of the night's shelter. Though his eyes remained closed, it was as if he knew when she was watching him, when questions were about to be thrown out into the open. Without pause, he seemed to deflect them before they were even asked.

Moving again so that she was lying on her stomach, her elbows propped on the ground, Fura watched him. The sight of his hair blowing across his face in feathery strands made her want to pull the strands of her own unruly hair out of her mouth. Kiyani, on the other hand, remained blissfully unaware, no more annoyed by the wind than he was with her at the moment. Anyone who happened to wander by would probably think he was sleeping.

If he hadn't answered her question so quickly, she might have thought the same.

Yet, even if he hadn't, Fura wouldn't have been completely convinced. She had no idea when he'd come back the night before, or if he'd even slept at all. All she knew was that he had been sitting outside when she had woken up. Lack of sleep was probably a factor, but she had a feeling that his lack of motion was, in part, a ploy to avoid questioning.

"You know, we have been traveling," Fura said. "For a week now." She didn't know why he was so convinced that they had to pretend. "Why would they need to believe us?"

"Because, from what I saw last night, the people there aren't all too friendly."

"What do you mea –"

"We get in and we get out," he replied firmly, cutting her off before she could finish her question. "We're going to get a room at the inn, get a hot meal, a night or two of sleep and then go on our way."

"Fine," Fura relented, having lost her initial enthusiasm. "But, is that really necessary?" She saw no reason why they couldn't have walked into the town the night before, yet she had trusted Kiyani and waited until morning. Now here they were, still camping out on the fringes of society, waiting for what, Fura didn't know.

Finally opening his eyes, Kiyani sighed. "This isn't Barandor. Things are different here."

Breathing her own frustrated sigh, Fura flopped dramatically on her back. "So you keep reminding me."

"For good reason," Kiyani said, his words picking up growing annoyance.

Sitting back up, and picking loose pieces of grass from her clothing, Fura glanced past him to where the town lay, just out of sight from their camp. "I know, I know," she decreed before he could say it. "If I don't like it, leave, right?"

Though he appeared mildly shocked by her admission, Kiyani simply shrugged. "You said it, not me," he declared, as if the change in perspective made all the difference. "All I'm saying... all I've been saying... is that this is a far different world than you're used to. You belong in Barandor more than here."

Fura shook her head. "If what you say about Apallo being my father is true, then I belong here just as much as you."

"You still don't believe me?"

Hearing him say it that way, Fura suddenly felt ashamed. "It's just a lot to take in," she said, knowing that in part it was truth. However, it wasn't just that she had grown up thinking two strangers were her parents, it was more that she couldn't find it in herself to believe that she was the daughter of a man she'd looked up to for so many years. In Fireswell, Apallo's name had become legendary. Though she had recently begun to hear her own name being chanted by the crowd, the onlookers seeking more, Fura felt that she could never live up to such greatness. On top of that, she now knew he wasn't just a spectacular performer, but a member of the fabled Sect of Seven. How could she ever grow into such expectations?

"You don't believe it," Kiyani prodded, seeming to pick up on her twisting thoughts.

Fura sighed. "How can I?" she asked, feeling deflated.

"How can you not? There's no detesting the red hair, and you're just as stubborn as him, if not more."

Casting an emotionless smile, Fura looked up at him, trying to determine if he was messing with her or not. Even if he was, she couldn't shake the sadness the conversation was drowning her in. If Apallo really was her father, there was so much she wished she'd said to him. Yet, it wasn't the only thing on her mind. "Do I belong here, or not?" she asked woefully, suddenly verging on tears.

So many times he'd said she didn't. Had bid her to go home. Yet, just when she thought she had Kiyani pegged, he seemed to change course.

Meeting her eyes for only a fraction of a second, Kiyani's gaze wandered off into the woods to his right. "You know my stance on the matter," he reminded her brusquely. "But, honestly, that's for you to decide."

Where she'd expected his usual argumentative confrontation, Kiyani's level reply left Fura speechless. Watching him as he finally rose, she waited for the rest of it.

Instead, Kiyani's focus veered to where the town sat. "However, that's a conversation for another day. Right now, I guess we might as well pack up camp and get this over with."

Half an hour later, as they made their way down the steep embankment leading into the town, Kiyani turned to Fura one last time.

"Remember," he said sternly, with a warning glance. "We're not here to make friends. We're not here for information. If any questions are to be asked, they will be from my lips, not yours." The edge in his voice made Fura wonder if, in his mind, he had added an 'or else'.

Not sure how she felt about his sudden placement of rules on this side trip, Fura decided to stay quiet. Trailing a few feet behind him, she didn't see how something as simple as one little town could put someone so on edge. It looked like a nice little rustic town, something that you might find in one of those cozy historic communities where you could vacation and get away from the real world for a few hours, or a few days, if you pleased.

It wasn't until their feet hit level ground once more that Fura began to understand his initial hesitation.

They had barely begun to approach the line of outlying buildings when, one by one, men emerged from the hazy afternoon shadows. Crudely trained in the defense of their small town, they formed a crooked, but tight line across the main road that trailed through the town.

A barricade, Fura realized.

Where she would have thought Kiyani would take pause to reassess the situation, he kept up the same pace as if he'd been expecting this. Fura, on the other hand, could feel herself shirk away from the stern gazes of the guards. They bore no armor or plated military gear, but the pikes they brandished, the hand-sharpened metal tips glinting in the muted sunlight, were too reminiscent of the men who had overtaken Frielana. A small number of the men brandished swords at their hip as well, their earth-worn hands lingering all too close to the hilts.

It wasn't until a single man stepped out of line, ushering a firm "Halt!" that Kiyani slowed, coming to a stop a few feet before him.

The man had close-cropped blond hair and thick, heavy-set eyebrows that shadowed his light eyes. He scanned Kiyani for a moment, deducing his threat level, before focusing on Fura.

"Come forward, m'am," he commanded.

Fura did as she was told, though she moved slowly, her feet feeling like lead. She couldn't remember stopping, though she must have froze as soon as the men had begun to assemble. It was a slow and tenuous walk as she encompassed a good twenty feet before hesitantly coming to a stop at Kiyani's side.

She threw a quick sidelong glance his way, but his pale eyes were unduly focused on the men before him.

The blond-haired man's eyes returned to Kiyani. "What brings you to Skirvynmire?" he demanded, his voice uninviting.

Fura had thought that Kiyani had been severely overreacting the night before, but he was right. Strangers weren't welcome here.

"We've been traveling for days," Kiyani said calmly. None of the exalted fear that clung to Fura like moss on a damp rock showed through on his demeanor, and for once she was glad of his general lack of emotion. "We merely ask for a hot meal, and a place to rest."

With heavy-lidded eyes, the man who'd emerged as the leader studied the two, contemplating Kiyani's answer. His eyes flickered towards the sky as he flexed his hand that held the pike perfectly perpendicular to the damp ground. "The Hunt is nigh, is it not?"

Fura was sure that she caught a quick flash of concern distort the man's face, but it was gone as quickly as it had appeared. She had no idea what he was talking about, but one look at Kiyani and the even set on his face told her that he did.

A few of the men shifted anxiously in the line, as if their leader's question had set them further on edge than their sudden visitors. A forewarning rumble of thunder in the distance seemed to confirm the answer, despite no one actually lending their voice.

"Very well," the man finally spoke after a long silence. He looked over his shoulder for a brief moment, as if seeking clarification from the now nervous guards before continuing. "Come with us. The Magisard will determine your fate."

If Fura could see the blond man's face as he silently led them through the small town, she would guess that his eyes were still wary, shifting uneasily as they passed building after building, the alleys between them dark and shadowed. The way the other men followed through on their orders, hasty and tense, as if they wanted nothing more than to run back to their homes and lock the doors behind them, seemed to confirm her suspicion. Though, he still carried about him the rough air of leadership, the pike remaining in his pale hands as he walked rigidly, the threatening demeanor he'd initially brandished had fallen lax.

Yet, he wasn't the town's leader. He hadn't declared it outright, but he had mentioned someone called the Magisard. Fura had no idea what that meant, but it sounded important.

Trying to calm herself, Fura attempted to follow Kiyani's unruffled lead. A task she found exceedingly difficult. Their fate was going to be decided by a man who held a title she'd never even heard of.

Fura shivered at the thought. This wasn't going at all as she had imagined. In all the fairytale books she'd read, in all her daydreams, strangers would come upon a small town such as this and be welcomed with open arms. A small, yet cozy room would be offered for a few coins. And a hot meal would be available in the tavern as the locals told merry tales and shared drinks. The atmosphere always light and airy.

But there was none of that here. Though it was a chilled breeze that drifted through the buildings, the air felt stifling, as if the men surrounding them had claimed all the oxygen for themselves, leaving her light-headed and anxious.

It was the eyes, Fura knew. The eyes that watched them with caution as they were led past, surrounded by armed men like prisoners. What little talk there was between people out on the streets was instantly hushed as they looked up, watching the brigade usher the two strangers by. There was a morbid fascination, mixed with fear and anxiety, in their glassy eyes, wondering who these people were and why they were here.

Fura shifted her eyes away from a pair of women, focusing on the dirt under her feet instead. She didn't feel as if she looked threatening, but there was no knowing what thoughts lay in their heads beneath the silent stares. Somehow she couldn't help but wonder the kind of inquisitive stares she would be receiving now had she still been wearing her worn firedancer's clothing stuffed into the bottom of her bag.

Stealing a glance at Kiyani as he walked beside her, she watched in amazement as he strolled along with a confidence that surpassed that of their guards. Rather than the wandering eyes of the men that caged them in, he kept his eyes forward. Whether he was keeping watch on the blond-haired man who was leading them or looking past him to see where they were being taken, Fura wasn't sure.

As if he could sense her questioning eyes, he turned his head slightly, hissing, "Are you happy now?" The words were low enough that only she could hear, but the dissatisfaction was well received.

Fura shrank back for a moment, caught off guard by his pent up anger, though she knew she should have expected it. Just like the Streig, this was her doing. But, he had agreed to it in the end though, hadn't he? He couldn't lay the full blame on her.

When Fura dared to look at him again, she could see that his lips were set in a straight line. Though it gave him the air of annoyance, she knew he was on edge. At least this time he was rightfully so. Yet she was left again with the unsettling feeling that he knew something she didn't. What was this Hunt that the man had spoken of, and why hadn't Kiyani even flinched at the mention of it like the others had?

The group came to a sudden stop. "Luke and Heinlan," the blond man said, "follow me. The rest of you can return to patrolling the perimeters."

There was a nearly synchronized nod from the men before they rapidly dispersed, leaving two behind. One man was taller than the one giving orders, both of his hands resting on the pike on his right side. A full beard covered his face, while a tangled mop of brown curls hid the rest in shadow. The other man, who stood taller, despite actually being shorter than the man at his side, resembled the blond. His eyes were the same color, his hair the same shade. The only thing that decidedly set them apart was that his hair was longer and pulled back away from his angular face into a ponytail.

With the uninviting nature of this town, seeming to prepare for an oncoming attack that could strike at any moment, Fura was expecting to be led to a grand building, maybe of dark, chiseled stone, with a name, possibly of the town, engraved into it. Cold, shadowy halls would then lead them to a room where a heartless man would interrogate them.

Instead, they stood before a sturdy, two level building made of dark, weathered boards. Oak-hinted wood smoke poured out of the chimney, staining the already gray sky a deeper charcoal before dissipating into the air. There was a thrum of chatter that came from inside, people deep in conversation unaware of what was happening just outside the doors.

A sign above creaked as it blew in the wind. The *MEAD MILL* it read. And a mill it was. As if merely reading the sign had brought it into focus, Fura watched the half circle of the giant wheel that was visible from this side of the building slowly churn water from a small stream that she hadn't noticed before.

"Follow me," the blond man repeated, this time directed towards her and Kiyani.

They were led inside, flanked by the two remaining guards, weapons still at the ready. Fura wondered if they really believed they would need them. Kiyani could put up a good fight, but she knew she stood no chance if the time came when things turned from discouraging to a downright fight for life.

Entering the building, the crowded room fell into complete silence. As the door thudded shut behind them, Fura found herself squinting to adjust to the darkness.

Despite outward appearances, what lie before them was a decent sized room. Lanterns hung at regular intervals along the walls, shedding dim light. Above, a large wrought-iron chandelier hung in the center of the room, between four thick posts nestled into the dirt floor, its candles casting shadowy light.

Smoke hung thick in the air making it hazy, and the smell of food made Fura's stomach ache with longing hunger. Plates of heaped meats and potatoes, nestled amongst glasses of amber liquid beckoned to her from mismatched tables. Groups of men and women alike sat at square tables, their tops glossy from sloshed drinks.

A few people here and there continued on with conversation, but most had ceased as they turned their focus towards the newcomers. Fura could feel a knot of anxiety beginning to form in the pit of her stomach. She was used to being the center of attention only when she was in Fireswell, and then the focus was generally on the whirling flames in her control.

The blond-haired man paid no heed to the change in atmosphere as he walked along the wall and led them into a fire-lit hallway. As soon as they were out of sight, Fura heard the clamor rise, louder than before.

Not too far down the hall, they paused before a heavy looking door. A sharp knock was answered by a gravelly *'come in'*. Ushered through the door they were brought to a halt in the center of a much smaller room. Sparsely furnished, its only distinguishing features were the impressively large desk, and the few plush chairs before it. A small window in the far wall cast barely enough light to care for a scraggly plant in the corner.

Behind the desk, a man sat in a large cushioned chair. Though they had been ushered in, he paid them no attention as his hand scribbled something on a worn piece of parchment before him. A dark shock of lanky brown hair hid his eyes from view. His mouth was set in concentration as he wrote, his nose twitching above his wiry beard and moustache.

The door slammed shut behind them, pulling the man from his work. Fura looked over her shoulder to find that Luke and Heinlan had dispersed, leaving them with the man that had led them here. Looking around, she could see that there was no other way out.

"What have you got here, Maven?" the man asked, placing his pen neatly next to the paper.

The one called Maven held his head high, shooting a quick look of disapproval towards her and Kiyani. "Spies, Aldam."

"What!?" Fura heard herself squeal in disbelief.

"We are *not* spies," Kiyani said calmly, a thick growl lurking in his tone.

The man's hands were wrapped so tightly around the shaft of the pike that his knuckles shone white. "Why else would you be here?" he said sharply. Any caution he had harbored before was now gone.

"Maven!" The man behind the desk commanded. "You can wait outside."

There was a flash of shock on Maven's face. Quickly shaking it off, he nodded once. "Yes, sir."

Another muted slam of the door left only the three of them in the room. "Sorry about that," Aldam apologized. "What *is* your business here, if I may ask?"

Though it was Fura the man seemed to be staring at, it was Kiyani who answered, much to her relief. "Shelter from the elements," he said curtly.

When neither he nor the man behind the desk spoke, Fura blurted out, "We're looking for the Witneis Reln." As soon as the words left her mouth, she wished she could take them back.

Kiyani's eyes bored into her, but he let his expression fall flat almost immediately.

Aldam leaned forward in his chair, his hands clasped together beneath his chin. "I have not heard of it." The momentary glare was not lost on him, though he said nothing.

"I'm so sorry," Kiyani muttered suddenly, wrapping his arm around Fura and pulling her into a half embrace. She froze, not knowing what he was doing. He hardly ever looked at her, let alone gave frequent hugs. "My wife is not all there," Kiyani continued, his finger momentarily pointed at his head, worry in his voice. "She was in an accident awhile back. Poor thing doesn't know what she's talking about half the time."

Letting her go, Fura shot him a stark look, but his focus had already shifted. Aldam's eyes narrowed.

"Please," Kiyani said before Aldam could resume speaking. "We've been traveling for a week straight. All we ask is for a room and a few meals. We'll be out of here in a day or two."

"That is most unfortunate," Aldam said, leaning back into his chair. There was little concern in his voice, though his tone held warning.

"What?"

"Anyone who asks for residence within this town is required to stay for a week. During that time you will work for your board doing whatever tasks are assigned to you. There will be no free time to wander about on your own accords. I'm sorry, but this is not a town of leisure for unexpected guests."

"We don't have a week to spare!" Kiyani argued, his voice rising.

Fura looked at the floor, not sure if she was allowed to speak. She never should have suggested this. Listening, she hoped Kiyani would regain his composure before he got them into deeper turmoil. She wasn't sure what it was about him, but Kiyani seemed to have an issue with people of authority. Something she wished he would remedy before he got them into trouble because of it.

"Then you should have bypassed Skirvynmire," Aldam declared sullenly, as if he almost regretted the harsh nature of the rules he himself had set into place. "You are free to leave if you so please," he offered, waving a hand towards the door. "However, if you intend to stay, then you will be subject to the rules, just as anyone else would be."

"Are there any other towns nearby?" Kiyani questioned. "One that's perhaps a bit more accommodating?"

Though Fura wanted to shove him out the door for being so rude, Aldam hardly seemed offended. "I wouldn't call any nearby, though I suppose that would depend on the time frame of which you speak. Fae Rue Keep lies about a week west. Medoria, two weeks south. There's not much out this way."

As much as Kiyani wanted to turn around and leave, he nodded methodically, realizing defeat. "Fine," he declared through gritted teeth.

"Very well," Aldam said. "In that case, Maven will show you to a room." His eyes flitting towards the door, he silently indicated that the conversation was over.

Kiyani mumbled something that sounded like a curse under his breath as he turned and shooed Fura towards the door.

"The winds warn of a coming Hunt," Aldam said as Kiyani reached the door. He turned to look at the man. "If you cause any trouble, you won't be here the full week."

46

••✧••

ASSIGNMENTS

Outside in the shadowy hallway, Maven waited for them, a haughty smirk set on his face. Luke and Heinlan were no longer present, leaving the passageway exceedingly desolate. Though he wanted to, Kiyani said nothing, instead shooting Maven a disapproving glance that spoke in itself.

He had the feeling that the man had known beforehand what would become of them if they entered the town. Instead of warning them to turn around and go about their way, he had led them through the unwelcoming streets to hand over to his Magisard to throw into slave labor.

Aldam's number one pet.

That's what he was.

Even after reminding himself that Aldam had given them the chance to leave, Kiyani wasn't settled. Both men had known that the two of them had no choice but to stay. If the Hunt hadn't been so close on the horizon, Kiyani would have quickly accepted the alternative route and left the town without a second thought.

Following Kiyani closely, Fura's eyes scanned the ground, no longer finding interest in looking around. She'd seen what the town had to offer, and it was nowhere near what she had expected. What was worse was that she knew she'd forced Kiyani into this. He hadn't wanted to stop, but she had persisted. Trying to catch a quick glimpse of his face, she knew that as soon as they were alone he would waste no time in reminding her. Either that, or he wouldn't give her the time of day for the rest of the week. Fura didn't know which option was worse.

His spells of anger frightened her, but she also didn't want to imagine the week of awkward silence if he did decide to ignore her.

A week...

A lot could happen in a week.

Or a whole lot of nothing, Fura thought, hating herself all the more for placing them in this situation. Who knew how many miles they could have traversed in that time period. It didn't matter that they didn't yet have a specific destination. They could have managed to accomplish something in that span of seven days. Now they would be caught, stagnant. A week of wasted time. Lost time in which they could have come closer to finding her father.

Dozens of eyes followed their progress as they were led back into the tavern the mill contained. Instead of returning to the daylight, Maven took them past the entryway. At the opposite end of the building, a stairway sat nestled in the shadows.

Up a single flight of stairs and three rooms down a candlelit hall, Maven opened a door and pointed them into a room. "You'll be here for the next week," he said with a sly smile. Keeping a watchful eye on the two of them as they entered, he tossed Kiyani a key, before adding, "Aldam will be up in a few minutes to give you your assignments."

His duty done, the man took his leave.

The door falling shut behind him, they listened to Maven's receding footsteps as he disappeared down the hall.

Fura took the moment of silence that followed to quickly scan the room, taking in the sparse furnishings, consisting simply of a bed and a dresser.

Ignoring the feeling in her gut as she told herself that this was where they would be spending the next week, Fura turned her focus to Kiyani.

"At least they gave us a key," she said brightly, eyeing the ornate piece of metal Maven had given Kiyani before taking off. It was all that was needed for Kiyani to turn on her.

"Do not talk to anybody!" Kiyani hissed harshly, a fire burning in his eyes. "Don't mention Frielana. Don't tell them what we're doing, where we're going, anything!"

"I —" Fura began, attempting to justify herself, though hardly knowing where to start.

In his usual way, Kiyani cut her off before she could even begin to spit out some excuse.

"I introduced you as slow for a reason," he said. "Keep it that way. It would be better if you didn't talk at all, but I know you can't manage that."

"That's not fair," Fura retorted, cringing at the slip in her voice. "You know I'm smarter than that!"

Kiyani pointed a shaking finger at the door, gesturing to all those that lie outside their private bubble in this confusing world. "But they don't! Trust me, it'll work out better in the end. With some of the shit that spews out of your mouth without thinking, it'll be better if they just think you don't know what you're talking about. And don't you *dare* mention the Witneis again!" he said angrily.

"But, it's what we're here for, isn't it?"

"No, it's not."

Fura had thought that the potential for information regarding their journey was what'd prompted Kiyani to stop after all. If that wasn't the draw, then she had an even harder time understanding why he'd petitioned them to remain chainless prisoners for a week when that time could have been put to better use.

She wanted to ask, but decided better of it. If they were stuck in this place for seven days, then there would be plenty of time to corner Kiyani for information. Yet, she couldn't justify remaining stagnant that whole time.

"It couldn't hurt to ask since we're here."

"I said no. That tree is more of a mythical legend than anything. Asking about it so openly would only lead to accusations and questions about us that we wouldn't want to answer."

"Why are you so closed to everyone?" Fura asked, shaking her head. His circular answers were making her dizzy.

"I may be closed, but you're far too trusting of people," Kiyani said through gritted teeth.

The conversation was brought to an abrupt halt by a sharp series of knocks on the door. A hollow echo sounded briefly in the small room as Kiyani stood frozen, staring at the source of the disruption. He hadn't even heard anyone approach.

Fura watched him closely, wondering what he was thinking. It was apparent that Kiyani wasn't done reprimanding her, yet she knew he wouldn't continue with an audience present. Thankfully, she had the feeling that he was cut short on his tirade for a little while.

"Not a word," Kiyani warned as the knob turned.

Neither of them had spoken, no mumbled *come in* had fallen from either of their lips, but the door opened inward with a drawn out, droning creak. Aldam let himself in before blocking out the view of the hallway once more as he shut the door behind him.

"I hope I didn't interrupt anything," the man proclaimed, furtively glancing between the two of them.

Kiyani shook his head. "Of course not."

Fura watched him closely, searching for any sign of the prior darkness of their conversation, but there was nothing. It continually amazed her just how quickly he could drop it, falling into the ruse of the calm individual in the presence of others.

"Good," Aldam said with a nod. "I hope that the accommodations are suitable."

"They're fine."

"Then if you don't mind, you will be sent to your duties now," he proclaimed, not bothering with the formalities of a simple hello. Though the words were friendly enough, it was clear that his demands weren't optional.

Silence ensued, though Aldam remained rather indifferent to the matter. He scratched at his beard nonchalantly before taking a few steps to pause before Fura.

Holding his hand out in a welcoming gesture, Fura found herself lax to take it, her eyes remaining on the floor. After her outburst earlier, which Kiyani had quickly covered, she no longer knew how to act or what to say. She didn't know if she was allowed to be herself here, or if she was meant to follow an act decided by Kiyani. She hadn't had the time to ask, about that, or why Kiyani had been so quick to proclaim they were married.

"What might your name be, my dear?"

Though it was a simple question, Fura was caught off guard. She hadn't expected him to approach her first, nor did she care for the pet name he'd attached to the question. Her eyes met the man's for a moment before darting over to Kiyani, as if asking permission to answer. Yet his own gaze was focused on the Magisard, tense and waiting out the situation. "Fura," she managed to squeak when Aldam's hand fell back to his side.

"I'm sorry," Kiyani declared, moving closer and laying a hand on Fura's shoulder, shocking her further. "Strangers frighten her."

Holding a hand to his heart, Aldam gave a half bow. "My apologies. And your name?" he asked, turning to Kiyani. "I realize I didn't ask."

"Kiyani," he answered simply.

Taking in the name, Aldam looked Kiyani over, as if trying to discern if he believed his answer. "Have we met before?"

Kiyani's eyes narrowed. "I don't believe so."

"Maybe not," Aldam agreed. Veering away from that line of conversation, he continued, surprising both Kiyani and Fura with his next notice. "If I may be so bold as to ask," Aldam began. "Why is it that you and your wife don't wear rings."

Glancing down at her bare hand, Fura wondered if they had been caught in the act so early in their stay. Then again, though the thought might have briefly crossed her mind before, even she had to admit that she and Kiyani hardly looked or acted like a married couple.

Yet, Kiyani was just as quick to answer as ever, unruffled by the question. "We were robbed not too long ago on our journey," he said, his voice picking up a hint of sorrow as if remembering that false day. "Haven't had the money to replace them yet."

"I'm sorry to hear that," Aldam said, a hint of sympathy permeating his voice. "Better luck in the days to come." Giving a passing glance to the strength of sunlight that streamed through the window, the man folded his hands behind his back, standing straighter, appearing all the more a leader, even if it was of such a small town. "Look at me, talking the day away when I came to give you your assignments for the week."

Turning to Fura first, he continued on as if suddenly aware of the mission he'd come to complete. "You'll be working downstairs in the tavern," he explained. There was an underlying condescension in his tone as he spoke to her, reminiscent of an adult speaking to a child that didn't yet fully understand the world. Cringing, Fura desperately wanted to send a look of hatred towards Kiyani, but forced herself to keep her eyes trained on the floor. "I'm sure you can handle washing dishes and cleaning tables. Go down to the bar and ask for Wanda. She'll let you know how things work."

Fura nodded before heading towards the door, doing her best to avoid his condescending words and Kiyani's watchful gaze. She knew he didn't want her to leave his sight, afraid of what she might say or do in his absence.

As soon as the door shut, leaving just the two of them, Kiyani turned to the town's leader, waiting to hear his job assignment. He knew he wasn't going to be let off as easily as Fura. Though he seemed friendly enough, there was a mildly threatening look in the man's eyes that left Kiyani feeling uneasy. It was as if the man recognized him, though he had no idea how that was even feasible.

"Are you sure we haven't met?" Aldam asked, the first to speak.

"Certain."

Staring deeper as if he could discern his answer from simply looking long enough, the man seemed unwilling to let it go. "You look generally familiar."

"I seem to get that a lot," Kiyani replied flatly, skirting the subject the best he could. It wasn't far from the truth.

Aldam's eyes bored into him. "I imagine you would," he said, momentarily dropping the subject. "If it were spring, I would have you working primarily in the fields, however winter now approaches. Therefore, I'll start you in the fields, finishing the harvest and beginning the plowing under of the compost. From there you'll have assorted duties depending on what needs to be done."

Standing with his arms crossed, Kiyani mumbled, "Fine."

It wasn't the worst thing he could be put through.

"Maven is downstairs waiting for you."

At least until that factor was added.

Keeping his thoughts to himself Kiyani turned and made his way to the door, rolling his eyes. Just what he wanted... to spend more time with Maven. He just hoped that they wouldn't be working side by side. It was bad enough that he was being supervised like some criminal. He knew it wasn't fair, but he had developed an instant distaste for the man, and he knew from experience that feelings like that were best not ignored.

"I will be watching," Aldam added.

"We're not here to make trouble," Kiyani attempted to argue.

"Time will tell if that's your motive. Just remember that I will not hesitate to put you out on the night of the Hunt if your actions prove me to be correct."

Then you'll find yourself rather disappointed... The words floated dangerously close to his lips. It was what Kiyani desperately wanted to say. "Yes, sir," was what he said instead.

Kiyani had wanted to turn tail the moment they had first approached this town. Now, less than an hour in, that feeling had only grown stronger. The Magisard was already suspicious, and he was sure that any relations with Maven were a lost cause. Fighting an annoyed sigh, Kiyani knew it was going to be a restless week.

"Then welcome to Skirvynmire," Aldam said with an awkward attempt at a smile. It was easy to tell that he still wasn't happy with having Kiyani and Fura under his roof, invading his town like some pests better left to extermination.

The conversation reaching the end of its life, Aldam followed Kiyani out the door, blatantly directing him to where he was supposed to go. As soon as they made their way down the dark stairs, Maven stepped forward, announcing his presence once again, as if he were hard to miss in the first place.

There was a darkly satisfied look on the man's face that Kiyani did his best to ignore. It wasn't until he'd scanned the dark room, searching out and finding Fura talking to a dark-haired woman he assumed was Wanda, that he finally turned to Maven. It was easy to see that Fura felt out of place here, but there was little he could do. She may have hated him for what he'd said of her, but at least it would give him a grain of solace to know that it would help keep her out of trouble. If anything was certain, it was that she would have a far easier week than him.

"Come on," Maven said, taking control. "The day is young and there's plenty of work to do." His tone of voice was entirely too cheerful, Kiyani decided. There was no way that he was going to like this man.

As he moved to follow, a hand fell on his shoulder. Turning, he found that Aldam was still lingering, thoughts seeming to be eating at him. "What did you say your last name was?"

"I didn't," Kiyani declared with a grin before following Maven out the door.

47

♦♦◇♦♦

WHERE IS HOME?

The day was long and tiring, far from what Fura had expected when the town had first come into view. She didn't know how long she'd been working, only that she was exhausted, and had the inexplicable feeling that whatever shift she had been commandeered for was far from over.

Wiping the sweat from her forehead, she looked around the bustling tavern, wondering where all these people had come from. The criminal parade through the main street just that afternoon had shown what a small town it was, yet the room was flooded with individuals. Crowded around short, dark tables they shared conversation, food, and copious amounts of drink, lending a boisterous appeal to the establishment.

Fura had thought that such a place would experience a lull once in awhile, but from the moment she had somehow found Wanda and begun working around the noon hour she had been kept busy. Though she'd never worked a similar job in her life, Fura had found herself immediately tossed into the fray.

Skirting between serving food, wiping down tables, once manning the bar for a few moments, and trying to keep up with the endless piles of dirty dishes, Fura was constantly on the move. Even at the festival she had never been so tired. She was sweating profusely. Her feet were aching, and more than once Fura found herself going cross-eyed from exhaustion.

Letting out a sigh, she scanned the room, making sure that nothing needed to be tended to, before ducking into the relative calm of the kitchen. Though it was just as busy in a way, cooks dancing around one another, Fura found it quieter.

Taking in the growing pile of dishes, Fura rolled up her sleeves and went to work tackling the stuck on food of the dinner plates and the mugs sticky with beer. It wasn't how she cared to spend the day, but she preferred the simple task of washing cutlery to mingling with the mildly intoxicated guests. It was a fact that surprised her. After multiple years of working in Fireswell, walking amongst a similar crowd, Fura felt that she should have taken to this situation just as easily. Yet, instead of the constant clamor that she'd come to enjoy before and after her stage show, here she discovered that the thought simply gave her anxiety.

Wondering if it was simply because she was out of her element, it wasn't long before Wanda appeared at her side. Feeling nervous under the woman's gaze, Fura continued what she was doing, hoping that Wanda was merely checking up on her to make sure that she was working. The woman had been friendly enough when she'd first introduced herself, and had quickly answered any questions Fura had throughout the day, but no thanks to Kiyani, Wanda kept a wary eye on her as if she might hurt herself doing the simplest of tasks.

Without a word, the woman moved to stand beside her, pulling a towel from a nearby table to help dry glasses. Though Fura didn't appreciate the constant watch, she had to admit that the woman was pretty much the only one who'd spoken to her so far besides the customers.

Thinking that Wanda had just come to help for a moment, Fura didn't expect her to strike up conversation. Yet, with only a handful of plates washed and dried, the woman began speaking.

"So, where are you and your husband from?" she asked nonchalantly, setting a glass aside and reaching for another.

Dropping the plate in her hand back into the water with a splash, Fura quickly grabbed for it, trying to cover her reaction. The woman's assumption that she and Kiyani were that close made her cringe, yet recalling his claim that they were married, that wasn't what bothered her the most. Gripping the plate, she was left stammering for words. Kiyani had never mentioned such a thing. Though they hadn't had much time to create a story for themselves, Fura had a feeling that he wouldn't want her mentioning that they'd come from Frielana. In fact, now that she thought about it, he had said those exact words before being whisked away for his own job assignment. But where else could she claim? These people living in this strange parallel world that she'd only come to realize existed... Fura doubted the woman had ever heard of Barandor.

"I –" she tried again, fishing for something, anything. "I don't know."

Even as she said it, Fura knew she would hate herself afterwards, though not as much as she currently despised Kiyani for the label he had given her. Thanks to him, it was certain to be a long week.

Her hands falling lax, Wanda turned to look at her, confusion and passion mixing in her eyes. "You don't... Oh, you poor thing," she mumbled with a shake of her head.

Dreading where the conversation could go, Fura was grateful when the sound of shattering glass filtered in from the tavern. Offering an apology, the woman scurried off to take care of the mess, leaving Fura alone with her thoughts.

Frozen in place, feeling like she had dodged a bullet, Fura could feel tears brimming. Quickly wiping her face on her shoulder, she tried to forget about the conversation, instead busying her hands and her mind with the work that remained.

A few hours later, Wanda approached again, still appearing wary.

"You may go now, dear," she declared sympathetically.

"What?" Fura asked, startled.

Though the woman's face carried a sense of worry, she repeated her words carefully, as if she were a mother speaking to a distracted child. "You can call it quits for tonight. We're closing down in a little while, but most everyone's gone already."

After her last botched conversation with the woman, Fura had dove into the work presented to her with far more conviction than when she'd started. Focusing completely on each task, she hadn't taken in the passage of time. Only now, as she looked around the room, did she understand Wanda's words.

At the front of the room, the door shut behind a customer, momentarily revealing the darkness of night beyond the warmth of the building's interior. Inside, a few diehards remained, huddled around a table in the corner amidst a collection of empty glasses. Deep in discussion, they appeared unaware of the lessening noise and thinning crowd. Around them, chairs had been stacked on tables that'd been wiped down for the night, a silent nudge that closing time was drawing near.

"Oh," Fura mumbled, not knowing what else to say.

Returning the rag she had been using to Wanda's outstretched hand, Fura untied the apron she'd been given.

"Come back tomorrow around ten, please."

Fura nodded before heading to the side of the room where the staircase lay, thinking that she couldn't have done too badly if the woman wanted her back again.

With sore and aching feet, she took one tread at a time, her ankles wobbling with each step, threatening to send her careening backwards down the stairway with the smallest misstep. Not realizing until that moment just how much the endless work day had taken its toll on her, it was all Fura could do to make it to the top.

Even then, the looming corridor of the second floor hallway appeared just as daunting, though she knew it only looked longer than it really was in the darkness. If she hadn't been so tired, the desolate, candle-lit hall probably would have been spooky. As it was, the only thing she could focus on was the door near the end that led to the room they'd been assigned.

Though the thought of a bed called to her, Fura suddenly found herself uncertain if she wanted to enter as she approached. Her last words with Kiyani hadn't been the friendliest, leaving her scared to continue the conversation. Even if he hadn't said so, she knew that conversation wasn't over.

Yet, maybe she would be lucky and he would leave it alone. At least for the time being. The last time she'd caught a glimpse of him, an hour beforehand, he had looked tired. Returning from whatever work he'd been given, she had briefly seen him walk through the tavern door, closely followed by Maven. The hours spent with the man hadn't seemed to change Kiyani's opinion of him. And though she had thought that maybe she would see Kiyani again when he returned for dinner, that had never happened.

For all she knew, he had returned to the room and simply passed out from exhaustion, just as she felt like doing.

Between his wavering moods as of late, Fura could only guess that him being asleep was the best that she could hope for.

Yet, as soon as she entered the room to find him perched on the end of the bed, wide awake, she attacked, no longer content to let him rest.

"I hope you're happy!" she said sharply, not knowing what had suddenly come over her. Where just a moment ago she'd been afraid to talk to him, now she was in full confrontation.

Turning away from the window, Kiyani simply regarded her for a moment before returning his attention to the darkness beyond the pane. "I should have pretended to be asleep," he muttered, unfazed by her attack.

"I have never been so embarrassed in my life!" Fura continued, ignoring his remark as she closed the door and moved into the center of the room. "I had to tell the woman I was working with today that I didn't know where I was from. The look she gave me…" she shook her head, still trying to forget the encounter. "She hardly spoke to me after that."

"Good."

Fura groaned, hating that he was so complacent in the matter, as if none of what she was saying was a big deal. "Did you really have to introduce me as slow?" she asked, trying a different approach.

He was silent for a few moments, his reply veering away from the subject when he did speak. "If you want to go back, I'll take you."

"The only reason you're willing to take me all the way back to Barandor is because you don't want me around," Fura argued, annoyed that he would bring this up again. "You said you were done with this." Though she threw it out there as a reminder, she realized that he'd probably never meant those words, only casting them at the time as a diversion until he could find the time to utter them again in a different way.

"You should have gone back a long time ago," Kiyani replied, raking a hand through his hair. He wasn't even paying attention to her plight, yet his words were remarkably pointed. "I just don't like having to worry about you throughout the day. Trying to keep you alive. Wondering if you're alive… it's nerve-wracking."

Momentarily silenced, Fura looked at him. He was a loner in his own right. She knew that much just from the few days she'd gotten to observe him from afar in Frielana. Yet, she hadn't known until now that thoughts of her safety preoccupied his mind. It didn't make sense.

"You could have easily just dumped me off somewhere," she said weakly, not knowing why she was reminding him just how simple it would be.

"I could have," he agreed, his voice far more level than she was expecting.

Unable to read him, his face turned away from her, Fura didn't know if he was blatantly ignoring her or just tired. From the lack of conviction in his tone, she guessed a bit of both. Taking a few steps forward, she glanced past him. Peering at the encapsulating darkness outside the window, she couldn't figure out what it was that had him so entranced. Moving ever so slightly, she found that he wasn't staring out the window at all. His eyes closed, she knew it was his own mind that he was lost in.

"So, what do we do now?" she asked, the anger she'd been cultivating when she had walked in dissipating. Though she was still mad at him, Fura knew it was useless to continue arguing.

Kiyani sighed, finally pulling away from his own thoughts. "We're here for a week, whether we like it or not. We ride it out, and then we get the hell out of here."

Sounding more like himself, Fura cautiously continued to prod him for more information. "Until then we're married?" she mused, still not understanding his earlier motives. It was something she'd been wondering about all day, but hadn't gotten to ask him about before he had been whisked away. He couldn't stand her most of the time, yet he'd told strangers that they were happily hitched.

"A traveling couple is looked upon more kindly than a pair of wandering rogues."

"Why not just say we're brother and sister?" Fura asked, thinking that might have been the easier route, or at least more believable. Though, even having a younger and an older brother, she had never fought with them like she did Kiyani.

"Like we look related..."

Fura shrugged.

Kiyani glared at her surreptitiously. "I panicked, okay?"

"But, I've never seen you panic," Fura said, wondering if it was possible that the thought of them being together had crossed his mind as it had hers.

"We all have our moments. Don't read into it. As for right now, get some rest. Enjoy the comforts while we have them."

Fura nearly laughed as she watched him rise from the corner of the bed. "Comforts?"

Striding across the room, he paused before the dresser. Pouring water into a basin from a pitcher she hadn't noticed prior, Kiyani dipped his hands in the cool water, running them over his face and through his hair. "I think even you would agree that this is better than sleeping in a tree."

Though she was certain that Kiyani had no preference one way or the other, she couldn't deny that. The Relns offered adequate shelter, but they certainly didn't provide the most comfort. It was something that she had done her best not to mention thus far, though the thought crossed her mind nightly as she lay on the rocky ground, trying to fall asleep.

Not sure what to do with herself in such a small space, Fura watched Kiyani as he turned towards the bed. Fighting a yawn, he went to remove his shirt. Almost immediately he stopped, glancing at her over his shoulder as if remembering something.

"I already know about the scars," Fura offered, realizing why he was so hesitant on the matter. Even if he refused to elaborate on their origins or just how much they pained him, it didn't take away the fact that she had seen them. The image was burned into her mind, as were the scripted questions she'd stored away for a later time if she could ever get him to talk about it. Something she doubted. "You don't have to hide them. If it's better for you to sleep shirtless, then do it."

He almost seemed to contemplate it for a moment, at least until Fura caught sight of the exposed skin of his back. With a sharp intake of breath that she tried to hide, Fura could see that the lines marring his skin hadn't aged a day.

Throwing her a heated look, Kiyani let the fabric of the shirt fall, thinking better of his prior decision. Ignoring her, he quickly pulled down the covers of the bed and sat on the mattress.

It was only then that Fura became starkly aware of the situation.

Looking around the room as if seeing it for the first time, panic rose in her chest as she took in the lack of furnishing.

"Wait," Fura said, her eyes widening, though she realized she was only now seeing what should have been obvious. "Are we sleeping in the same bed?"

"If you want to sleep on the floor, then be my guest," Kiyani offered, unperturbed by the fact.

All Fura could do was stare at his form as he stretched out on the bed, a sure sign that he was more than ready to find some semblance of sleep. Though she was still rattled, she didn't know why his rude nature was suddenly a surprise to her. Yet, she couldn't seem to let his words go without a menial fight. "Why would I be the one sleeping on the floor?" she asked, feigning irritation, though the squeak in her voice gave away her fear.

If Kiyani had heard that mild infliction, then he chose to ignore it, much to Fura's relief, though the words he did issue weren't much better. "Because you're the one making a big deal of it."

"Maybe because it is a big deal," Fura said, fidgeting anxiously, unsure of what to do.

"You didn't have a problem with it before," Kiyani said evenly.

Heat colored Fura's cheeks as visions of that night in Fae Rue rose to memory. That horrid night when the truth had been laid out for her, when she had lost all sight of who she was, and when she had sought out his company in distress. It hadn't been so much sleeping beside him as cradled in his arms.

Dredging up the memory, Fura felt as if she were looking upon someone else in that moment. Someone a lot bolder, and less afraid than she could ever hope to be.

"You know," Kiyani declared. "If I had wanted to take advantage of you, I could have easily done it already."

Cringing, Fura knew he had a point. Of all the time she'd spent with him, traveling alone with only Kiedo as extra company alongside his master, this was the first time the thought had ever crossed her mind, and she knew why: because it wasn't something she'd ever expect of him. He had largely ignored her from the moment they'd met. She didn't expect that to change any time soon.

Steeling herself against her own thoughts, Fura moved woodenly towards the bed, keeping an eye on Kiyani's still form. Unfettered by the possibilities of such a situation he had rolled over to face the wall, already having moved on from the conversation.

Settling daintily on the edge of the mattress, Fura tried to tell herself that she was over thinking all of this. Kiyani had proclaimed them a couple and the leader of the town had given them a single room with one bed. What other option did they really have?

Sighing, Fura slipped off her shoes and sat cross-legged on the bed, all thoughts of sleep having fled from her mind. Seeking something to do, she quickly got up, extinguishing the light of the oil lantern, only to discover just how dark the room was without it. Fumbling to return to the bed, she heard Kiyani grumble in the darkness.

"Would you go to sleep?"

Cringing at his tone, Fura got herself settled again. "You were nicer the last time we slept together," she said, pulling her knees to her chest, then flushing in embarrassment as she realized how that had come across.

"Don't make me regret that."

Though she knew she should heed his words and just go to sleep, Fura yawned, fighting to stay awake after the long day. Telling herself not to lie down just yet, that that'd be the end of it if she did, she stared out the window, trying to determine how to approach the conversation.

Kiyani was certainly ready for the day to be over, but there was still something on Fura's mind that gnawed at her. She could have asked at any point during the last few weeks, yet she hadn't been able to bring it to light. Though she knew the effort would be futile, she was intent on trying anyways. From what she'd gathered, sometimes Kiyani actually gave a decent answer to her questions. Most of the time, however, he refused to answer at all.

"Can I ask you something?" Fura tried anyway.

"Can it wait?" Kiyani grumbled.

"I don't know when I'll be able to talk to you again," Fura said. "It's like they don't want us to have the time to talk."

"They don't," Kiyani confirmed. "They run you to the bone so that you're too tired. People have less time to plot devious crimes if they spend most of their free time asleep."

"Devious crimes?" Fura echoed, confusion in her voice. "Is that really what they think of us?"

"I told you, small towns aren't always welcoming of strangers."

Though she hadn't believed him when he'd first said it, he had warned her. She hated to admit that he was right, but she wished now that she had let him talk her into moving past the town. Either way, it was too late now.

Knowing that she was quickly losing her opportunity, Fura posed her final question, despite Kiyani never giving her the go ahead.

"I don't know why I was thinking about it, but I was trying to remember some of what the Shadowlord said," she began, momentarily reliving the siege of Frielana, and still trying to believe the man was who he said. "What is the Nyte-Fyre Prophecy?"

He didn't say anything. The words hung in the air, as Fura waited, wondering if he would even answer. "Basically, what we're here for," Kiyani said, finally. "What we're out to stop, to destroy."

Fura looked at him with furrowed eyebrows, confused. "So, it's real..."

She had tried listening to the Shadowlord's words, trying to figure out what exactly it was he was saying and to gain a better perspective on the situation, if anything. But it had all sounded like the ramblings of a mad man to her.

"Depends on who you're talking to, really. Many have heard of it, but only a select few actually believe in it."

"Who?"

"Those who want it to come to life," Kiyani said darkly. "The Nyte-Fyre Prophecy is the downfall of the Sect of Seven."

Fura stared blankly at the wall, not knowing if she'd heard Kiyani correctly, or if maybe it had been the Shadowlord's words she'd twisted in her fear.

"Wait... is he for or against it?" Now that she'd brought it up, she couldn't honestly remember.

"He's one of its main advocates."

"But he's one of the Lords... why would he want his own downfall?"

"I don't make knowing his motives a priority in my life, but I believe even you can puzzle that out."

"Absolute power..." Fura mumbled, understanding.

Kiyani nodded.

Good and evil. Darkness and insidious plots.

"I really have fallen into a fantasy land, haven't I?"

"There are evil people everywhere. It doesn't matter what world you're in."

48

♦♦◇♦♦

PRELUDE TO A STORM

The sun had only just begun to filter through the window when Fura rolled over, woken by sounds of movement on the creaking wooden floorboards. Sitting up, she willed her blurry eyes to come into focus.

Darkness still shrouded the room, leaving her to wonder if she had merely been hearing things. As the surroundings came into focus, she could see that a candle had been lit. Sitting upon the dresser, it cast a small halo of light just bright enough to discern that Kiyani was already awake. Standing before the piece of furniture that also served as a table, he splashed his face with water from the basin she'd noticed the night before.

"You're awake already?" Fura asked with a yawn. Despite the early hour, he was dressed, appearing ready to go numbly through the motions assigned to him by the Magisard.

Glancing over at her, Kiyani's eyes trailed towards the window. "Of course," he replied, though his tone was mocking. "When you work outside, the day begins with the sun."

The words sounded textbook, as if he was simply repeating what he'd been told the day before. Though she didn't dare ask, she had a feeling that that was a direct quote from Maven. If anything, it would account for the distaste in his tone.

Kiyani may have been awake, but Fura could tell that what he really wanted was to crawl back into bed for a few hours. His words were slow and measured, his actions forced, and she was certain that she had managed to catch the eye roll that had accompanied the last statement. Yet another indication that Maven was involved in such ideals. She'd barely met the man, but Fura was sure that another day with Maven probably wasn't what Kiyani could have hoped for. Judging from their brief meeting the day before, she was certain that the man wasn't of the kind that Kiyani easily got along with.

Then again, she had to ask herself if any such person existed.

"What time did Wanda tell you to come back?" Kiyani asked

wearily, his words piercing the faint light of the room. He seemed to be talking just to keep himself awake.

Fura pulled the sheets around her exposed feet, fighting off another yawn. "Ten."

"You have a few hours, then. It's only about five-thirty now."

Fura sat up taller, a little more awake now. "You can tell that without a watch?"

He cracked a slight smile, the first she had seen in days. "I don't think I've ever used one of those. You live outside in a world like this for long enough and you learn to judge based on the sun."

Looking out the window, Fura wondered how long that took. All she could decipher was that the sun was beginning to cast out the shadows. Her heart fluttered for a brief second as she looked back to where he was standing, paying her no attention. Whether Kiyani liked her or not, he never ceased to amaze her. That was for sure.

"Of course," Kiyani spoke mildly, "if you want to verify, there's a sundial in the main square that's visible from the window."

"What?" Wide awake now, Fura crawled to the edge of the bed to look out the window to see if he was messing with her again. She could hear him chuckling behind her, but he was right.

It wasn't very large, but right in the center of the circle of buildings that created the main center of town, the tavern one of its cornerstones, sat a sundial carved of ivory stone. In the early twilight of morning, it wasn't yet useful in telling time, but sunlight had just begun to stream into the square, lighting up its corners. Fura didn't know how she'd missed the fixture the day before, but thinking back, they had been a bit preoccupied with other dire thoughts.

Watching the color begin to seep back into the town, casting away the hazy gray of dawn and replacing it with livelier hues, Fura almost found it hard to remember the horrifying moments of first arriving in Skirvynmire. Though she still shuddered at the thought, she told herself that today would be different. It was merely protocol. Surely the longer they remained, the more welcoming the town would become. Kiyani may have been hard to read, but they certainly posed no threat.

Wrapped up in the blossoming beauty of the town below and tangled in her thoughts, Fura nearly missed the squeak of the door opening behind her. Turning, she saw that Kiyani was leaving. Locking eyes for a brief moment, he paused as if he'd been caught.

Stepping back into the room, he let the door quietly fall shut behind him.

"Naquaelin," he said faintly, as if he still contemplated even mentioning it. "We're from Naquaelin."

Staring at him, Fura wondered where this had suddenly come from. "Are you just making a name up? Because I could have done that." She couldn't help but ask herself why he was doing this now. He'd made no mention of a solution to her plight the night before, acting like he didn't even care.

Kiyani shook his head. "No. Naquaelin is a large town far east of here. We might actually end up there at some point. For now, we can say that's where we're going. If prodded further, just claim we were visiting family in Andor."

Fura nodded, dazed by his sudden declaration. The answer had come out of nowhere, a cryptic and delayed solution to an exchange of words that she'd wanted to forget. Lying wide awake beside Kiyani, trying to fall asleep, she had resolved that she wouldn't think of that particular exchange with Wanda. At least now she wouldn't sound so lost if the subject came up again. She could simply claim that she'd had a momentary lapse in memory.

"Thank you," Fura said, grateful to him for answering at least one of her questions.

Looking towards the door, she discovered that Kiyani had already left.

✧⌘✧

Kiyani didn't know how much time had passed. More than a few hours, he guessed, from what little of the sundial was visible to him. Leaning on the weathered garden hoe that he'd chosen as his weapon of choice against the sun-baked soil, he paused in his duties to take a quick glance towards the mill and the tavern it housed.

Though he was grateful that Aldam hadn't allowed Fura to work alongside him, saving him from the monotonous questions, he still wished she was within his sight. Creating the lie of her mental instability had guaranteed her light and incredibly supervised work, but he still worried about her loose lips and the never-ending questions that he swore she spent the day, and sometimes the night, conceiving. She may have done a relatively good job of brushing off the difficulty she had faced during that first day of work, but he had seen beyond the anger she'd shown him. Wanda's words were of the kind that he'd grown used to ignoring, but they had probably been eating at Fura since they had been spoken. Even so, it wasn't until then that Kiyani realized just how elaborate of a back story they might need to efficiently cover their asses. Just another reason why he had always skirted towns in the past. Especially small ones such as this. Larger villages only cared if you had coin, not where you came from. Places like Skirvynmire on the other hand, wanted to know why you were passing through.

As he had lain awake, something that was hardly out of the ordinary for him, he had mulled it over, attempting to come up with an answer to give her in case the question arose again. He knew the names of a good number of towns he had passed in previous travels, yet not always the specifics of where they were located. Only the largest of cities came to mind, having learned from experience to stay out of most centers of civilization. Generally he kept to the woods, only approaching towns to stockpile food and other supplies when the need arose.

It had taken him longer than he would have liked to sort it out, but the city of Naquaelin had finally come to mind. He'd never actually stepped foot on its streets, but he had passed close by once. Not only was it in the general direction they were heading for the time, but it was a good cover. With its high stone walls and sprawling cobble-stoned streets, it was more than large enough that no one would ever know if they lived there or not. Unlike the smaller towns, cities like Naquaelin didn't concern themselves with knowing each and every man, woman, and child that lived within its boundaries. If someone from Skirvynmire were to ask about the likes of him and Fura, it wouldn't be unusual that no one could recall them.

Catching a hint of blond hair out of the corner of his eye, Kiyani rerouted his thoughts and resumed work before Maven could call him out for being lazy. He wasn't the only one working the tough dirt, but he was the only one that Maven was watching like a hawk. There was nothing that he was doing wrong as he followed the examples of the others, attesting to the back-breaking work of tilling under dead vegetation from a recent harvest, but he could tell that the man was simply searching for something to say to pick a fight.

He didn't have to do anything wrong. The day before had proven that. Though it hadn't been oppressively hot, it had been warm enough to break a sweat. Even so, Kiyani had held off on taking a break for as long as possible, feeling that as soon as he took a moment to cool down, he would be ostracized. Low and behold, despite watching one after the other of his fellow workers take brief leaves of absence from field work, the minute he had ceased plowing Maven had brusquely stalked over. Calling him out louder than necessary, the scene had not only gained a small audience, but had elicited a wave of gossiping whispers. Kiyani couldn't recall the exact words used, but *useless* had been among them.

As much as that incident had left Kiyani wanting to punch the man in the face, he had kept himself in check. Not only that, he'd done the man one better by simply not speaking at all in return. Maven was the kind of man that found thrill in getting a reaction from his deeds, therefore Kiyani had resigned that he wouldn't give him the satisfaction. Instead, he had quietly gone back to work in his designated area, pretending that he hadn't heard. It may have been hard to let such words simply roll off his back, but the tense jaw and gritted teeth that

Maven had sported the rest of the day had been well worth it.

Maven may have taken an instant dislike to him, but Kiyani could say the same in return.

After that, the man, as well as the others, had left him alone for the most part. Much to Kiyani's relief. Even though Maven continued to shoot him dirty looks once in awhile, it made working much easier.

That had been the day before.

Thankfully, today was proving to be far less eventful. Not only that, but the winds were considerably cooler. Though the morning had started out crisp and sunny, gray clouds had begun to gather around the noon hour. Steadily building, they brought with them a promise of rain. Doing his best to keep his mind on the work before him, Kiyani couldn't help but look to the sky now and then. The clouds seemed to grow darker by the minute, the humidity thickening to a dense soup. It wouldn't be long before rains would drive them inside, likely shortening the work day.

Though the coming storm had nothing to do with the upcoming Hunt, it still felt like a foreshadowing of the darkness in the days to come. He wasn't the only one to feel it. A quick glance at the others easily betrayed the mix of fear and anticipation etched on their faces. Many were on edge, while all of them simply wanted it to be over so they could continue on with their lives. Even Maven was noticeably subdued today, appearing anxious and distracted.

The man still kept a wary eye on Kiyani, as Aldam had likely instructed, but he had yet to throw a snide comment his way. There were other things on his mind as he patrolled the edges of the field... first and foremost, just how many would be left for him to supervise in the following days.

It was midday when flashes of lightening began to tear through the sky. The clouds, nearly black, began to emit a drizzle of rain, before opening up to a torrential downpour. Thunder roared in soon after, the final sign that the rest of the day would be a wash.

Though plenty of work remained, even Maven knew that it would be futile to continue. Calling it early, he stood to the side as the small work detail quickly stored their tools in a small shed on the edge of the field. The ground turned to mud as the group scattered. Most took off to their houses and their waiting families. Only a few, including Kiyani and Maven, made their way towards the tavern.

It was a short distance to what Kiyani had discovered was the town's hotspot, but he took his time walking back. He didn't mind the rain. Never had. And though he mostly found himself not wanting to deal with Fura so early in the day, he also knew that it would mean Maven would be stuck in the rain longer, refusing to let him out of his sight. By the time he entered the building he was soaked. Half holding the door open for Maven as he came in behind him, Kiyani met his angered glare with a satisfied grin. The man was just as drenched as he was.

As soon as the door shut behind them, effectively blocking the wind and the rain, Maven stalked off, his duties done for the day. Taking in the bustling activity of the room, packed with people seeking shelter from the rain, as well as company and food, Kiyani turned to the stairs. The smell of roasting meats made his stomach ache with hunger, but he waved off the temptation in lieu of the peace he would find in the empty room upstairs.

Dinner was in the near future, but he wasn't sure if wanted to see Fura just yet. The field work may have already been taking a toll on his body, but he was thankful for the quiet it gave him. Many of the days he'd spent traveling he wished he could listen to the wind through the trees rather than Fura's incessant chatter.

Even though Skirvynmire had been an unexpected, not to mention unwarranted, stop he had enjoyed more solitude in the last day than he'd been allowed since their journey had begun.

He would return to the dining room to eat and watch Fura work later. At the moment, drying off and changing clothes seemed more important.

Upstairs, standing in the doorway, Kiyani looked at the spartan room before him. The bed called to him, but he knew he wouldn't get any rest, even if he tried. Sleep had never been much of a friend to him at night, let alone during the middle of the day. Though it was a tempting offer, he left the room after quickly throwing on dry clothes, meagerly working his way back down to the lively room below.

In just the short time since he'd come in from the rain, the tavern had filled considerably, everyone else seeming to have contrived the same thought: a hot meal and drink to ward off the chill of the storm, as they mingled with friends.

Kiyani took one of the smaller tables that inhabited the shadows in the corner of the room. He could hear the pounding storm outside if he concentrated enough to tune out the noise of the people around him. The rain had gained strength, the winds momentum, and the lightning and thunder sounded like it had become more frequent.

It was going to be a rough night for a lot of people.

Kiyani cracked a wry smile, though there was no one to see it. At least no one paying attention to him. It was during nights like this, when storms were running rampant, that he accrued the best of sleep. The lashing rains did wonders to drown out all thoughts of the cruel world around him, giving him a wonderful static silence and a relief from the tangled thoughts that haunted him day in and day out.

Only a few wondering eyes passed over him. Already, Kiyani had become one with the shadows, becoming a piece of the puzzle that was the background of this town. A strange piece, but no one questioned it. It was what he did best.

Kiyani sat at the table, glad for people's continued ignorance. Only a few wandering eyes settled upon him, but mostly people had already resolved that he wasn't a threat, and therefore unworthy of their attention.

It was fine by him.

If any of these people caught sight of his tattoo, eyes would shift away out of fear, but hidden, he was just another face in the crowd.

Despite Maven, and possibly Aldam, thinking that he and Fura were plotting espionage, it looked as if the majority of the townsfolk didn't harbor the same feelings. If anything, it looked like they could care less. As long as no one messed with their routine drinking habits, all was well in the world.

Every now and then a pair of curious eyes would scope him out, lingering for a moment. It was to be expected. A new face in the crowd always gained unwarranted attention for a short period of time. As long as you gave no one reason to suspect you of anything, you were generally left to your own devices.

"If you want, I'll let your wife have a break so you can eat together."

Kiyani looked up. He hadn't heard anyone approach the table, but a woman stood before him, waiting for an answer. She held a tray laden with ale-filled glasses, meant for a table that wasn't his.

"It's fine," he said. He could hear her foot tapping impatiently on the wooden floor. "I'm not going to take her from her work if she's needed."

Wanda looked at him, a small glimmer in her eye. "I think I can afford her a few minutes. I'll send her with food."

As she walked away, her pony-tailed hair bobbing behind her, Kiyani mumbled a 'sure'. He wasn't sure what had just happened. The mention of *wife* had caught him unaware. The lie had been his own doing, but he knew he couldn't take it back now. He only wished that he'd been quick enough to come up with something else. Something that wouldn't give Fura the wrong idea, though he knew it was far too late for that.

It was another necessity. However, it wasn't one he cared for. If anything, he knew Fura was probably enjoying it. Though he did his best not to encourage her, he could see the way she looked at him. She did a rather poor job of hiding the fact that she wanted more in what little relationship there was between the two of them. Most days, Kiyani just wanted her to go away. He had spent the majority of his life in silence and he didn't plan on changing that anytime soon.

A moment later, Fura plopped down in the chair across from him, sliding a heaped plate of steaming meats and potatoes his way. He slowly pulled it closer, trying to avoid her stare, briefly conflicted by her presence.

"I guess you got out of work early," Fura said, an awkward attempt at conversation.

Kiyani did no better as he took a hesitant bite before replying, "Yeah. It started raining."

"I can hear it."

They both sat in silence, picking mildly at the food before them. Even though no one paid them any attention it felt as if there was a flashing sign above them, pointing out to everyone that they weren't a couple, let alone a happily married one. The lie felt like it would instantaneously fall apart, that with one sidelong glance anyone in the room would be able to tell it was an act, and that would be the end of their escapade.

Oddly enough, it wasn't the thought of being caught and jailed that bothered Kiyani, but the simple act of sitting across from Fura, eating together. It felt nothing short of awkward. The single thing that went through his mind, over and over, and what was beginning to be a daily mantra, was *I should have taken her back to Barandor.*

Luckily, as the storm grew stronger so did the number of waiting customers. It wasn't long before Wanda scuttled over, beckoning Fura back to work.

Though it was easy to see that she didn't want to leave, she nodded methodically and took up her plate. "See you later," she said with a half-hearted wave before disappearing into the crowd, leaving Kiyani alone again. Though there had been a smile on her face as she'd said the words, it had been forced as if even she could feel the sudden rift between them.

Cringing, Kiyani finished the plate that he'd practically left untouched in Fura's presence before taking to the shadows, making his way back to the room where he would find short-lived solace from everything but the storm outside. The rising number of people in the so-called 'cozy' room was making him increasingly nervous.

49

◆◆✧◆◆

STORMS AND SCARS

Taking her time as she made her way down the hall, Fura found the darkness encapsulating. Though the stretch was just as lonely as it had been the night before – all the more so now, due to the lightning visible from the window at the other end of the corridor – it was calming in a way. After another long day spent elbow deep in dishwater and liquor, scurrying between the tables full of obnoxious people, the quiet was just what she needed.

If only her mind would allow her such freedoms.

Cringing as a roll of thunder echoed in the empty space, Fura sorted through the conflicting thoughts in her mind. Making her way towards the room where she knew Kiyani would be waiting, she still wasn't certain if she wanted to face him.

That morning Fura had thought everything was fine with him. Now she wasn't so sure. Before he'd left, he had surprised her, offering a solution to her dilemma with Wanda from the day before. He'd even been joking with her, something that Fura hardly ever saw with him. From the moment she had first spoken to him by the falls, Kiyani had been a dour personality, appearing to be worn around the edges from a life filled with darkness. A fact that she couldn't verify, due to his aversion to speaking about himself.

So what had happened between then and when she had seen him earlier?

Fura had tried to tell herself nothing, but there had been no denying the awkward tension between them as they had dined together. She hadn't even seen him long enough during the day to do something wrong in his book, and yet he had been far more remote than usual, avoiding her gaze as if she had committed an atrocious crime.

After he had left, Fura wondered if maybe he'd only just begun to understand the awkward situation of sleeping side by side, regretting his claim to marriage. As much as that made sense, Fura had a feeling that that still wasn't it. Or, at the least, that it wasn't the half of it.

Kiyani's mind was a torrential whirlwind that she had no idea how to approach on the best of days. It was an even harder task when she knew he was in a dark mood.

Fura glanced out the window one last time as she stood before the door to their room. She didn't know what time it was, only knew that it was late. Darkness had fallen long ago, the heavy storm clouds bringing its onset much earlier than usual.

On the fence about whether she hoped Kiyani would be awake to talk, or sleeping so she wouldn't have to deal with whatever was going on with him, Fura entered the room.

Slipping into the space, and closing the door quietly behind her, she found herself encapsulated in a deeper darkness than even the hallway had provided. A quick glance across the room told her that Kiyani had taken to sleep early. Despite feeling relief, Fura found it strange. She'd only known him for a month, but it hadn't taken long to come to the conclusion that he was a genuine night owl. To see his still form in the bed, dozing long before she could even attempt to close her eyes for the night was a sight she didn't see too often.

As she cautiously stepped closer, she could see that the oil lamp on the table had been doused, replaced by a stub of a candle that appeared to be on its last leg, the small flickering flame threatening to go out on its own at any moment.

Distracted by its dancing light, Fura stubbed her toe on the corner of the dresser, scraping the piece of furniture across the floor as it shifted. Cursing her clumsiness and the possibility of a broken toe, she saw Kiyani move out of the corner of her eye.

"Are you ever quiet?" he gruffed.

Rubbing her foot, Fura took note of the aggravation in his voice, realizing that he probably hadn't been sleeping in the first place.

"Sometimes," Fura mumbled, feeling that familiar air of annoyance that emerged whenever he had something to say about her apparent lack of grace.

It wasn't just that he had to comment on every one of her missteps. Fura couldn't figure out where the girl from the festival had disappeared to. It had taken her years of practice to get each and every one of those routines down. So she had a bout with clumsiness every now and then. She hadn't always been that bad. Glancing over to where Kiyani now sat up, pulled from whatever sleep he may have been attempting to get, Fura wondered if maybe it was only in his presence.

She didn't seem to have as much trouble around other people. It was as if he brought out the worst in her.

Issuing a frustrated sigh, Fura watched as Kiyani reached for a wadded up shirt at the end of the bed.

"You don't have to bother, Kiyani," she reminded him. It wasn't as if she didn't know about the scars. "If you had been sleeping already, it wouldn't have made a difference. You don't have to hide what I already know about."

Though she expected him to have a snide remark about the matter, Kiyani remained silent. Seeming to take the option of remaining shirtless, he tossed aside the covers. Rousted from any chance at rest, he scooted to the end of the bed and leaned against the wall, staring aimlessly into the stormy night beyond the window.

Uncertain of what she was walking into, Fura carefully moved across the room, avoiding any further incident with furniture. Keeping a wary eye on Kiyani, she could see that he'd already taken his regular stance of ignoring her. Doing what she could to ready herself for bed, she did her best to return the favor.

It was only as she settled herself onto the edge of the bed that she noticed how quiet the room was. Being so close to Kiyani hadn't been the only thing that'd kept her awake the night before. A muted clatter had risen from the tavern below, making it hard to find peace in the darkness. Tonight the only sound in the room was the heavy rain on the tiled roof above.

Exhausted, Fura stuffed her hands beneath her thighs and swung her legs, trying to decide how to approach any kind of conversation with Kiyani. The easiest route would have been to simply retire for the night. Go to sleep and contemplate conversation the next day. However, the awkward moments they'd shared over dinner only hours before had been lingering on her mind ever since. She knew if she didn't at least ask, it would keep her up throughout the night.

It was as if the man she'd met then, the one she now sat beside, was a completely different person than the one she had spoken to only that morning.

Wondering if there were a slew of things on his mind – a new set of worries – or if it was something else entirely, Fura rearranged herself. Turning, she pulled her legs up beneath her, staring at his dark form and the way the flickering light cast a muted orange glow on his hair.

With his attention drawn to the drowning world outside the window, it was the only feature she could make out besides the shadowed planes of his face hazily reflected in the glass.

"Are you okay?" Fura finally said after a few moments of contemplation. It was a rudimentary question, but she had no idea how else to approach the matter.

It was possible that, much like her, he was simply exhausted.

Yet, it felt like more than that.

Seeming to be practiced in the art of being a statue, Kiyani shifted ever so slightly, as if momentarily startled by the break in the silence. Despite that small form of recognition, he didn't reply, her words not strong enough to warrant a response.

"Kiyani?" Fura prodded, feeling increasingly uncomfortable as the time passed.

"I'm fine..." he mumbled, his words forced. An obvious effort to keep her from moving forward with the conversation.

Still unwilling to go to sleep as her body demanded, Fura simply allowed herself to silently watch him instead.

Though she still knew so little about him and his changing moods that he could accurately be considered a stranger, even she could see that he was far from festive spirits. Despite wanting to cheer him up, Fura couldn't blame him. Kiyani might have been the one who'd made the final decision, but she still held herself accountable for their being stuck in Skirvynmire.

He had immediately declared they bypass it, while she had been adamant they stop. Never before had she been so disappointed to have gotten her way.

When she wasn't distracted by thoughts of Kiyani, her mind bombarded her with thoughts of where they could possibly be had they remained on the road.

Fidgeting, Fura brought her knees up to her chest and stared at the wall. Though she tried her best to ignore him, she kept Kiyani in her line of sight, thinking that if she remained quiet long enough he might actually initiate conversation.

Yet, nothing was ever that simple with him. Thinking back to the days of traveling following Fae Rue Keep, Fura knew she should've known that already. It was no secret that Kiyani would probably be content to complete the entire journey before them without exchanging a single word.

Fura, on the other hand, couldn't stand the mere thought of such a thing.

"So, what about you?" Fura finally asked, shattering the stillness in the air as she desperately sought the companionable lull of conversation that she had come to crave. It had been such a constant thing on the busy weekends at the festival. Out here, in this strange world, alone with this even stranger man, those moments had become few and far between. A simple treat when it had once felt like the shower of candy thrown out at parades.

The weight of the thin mattress shifted as Kiyani pulled his gaze from the window.

"What about me?"

There was a wariness in his voice that questioned why she would want to know anything in regards to him. As if it were unusual to want to know more about the odd person she had found herself traveling with.

Fura shrugged, almost embarrassed for bringing words to the

darkness.

"I don't know," she admitted meekly. "I don't really know anything about you."

Kiyani looked upon her with a nearly blank expression, his brows cinched just the slightest, asking what the problem was.

"There's nothing much to know."

"Come on. You can give me more than that," she urged. His reluctance to offer up anything only made her all the more eager to know what he was keeping from her.

"No," he declared simply.

"That's not fair," Fura whined. "You know all about me."

That night back in Fae Rue, when he'd revealed Apallo's relation to her, was one that Fura had revisited almost every day since. How was it that a man she had never met before the siege knew more about her life than she knew herself?

"It's not my fault that Apallo kept your heritage a secret."

There was a distinct and jagged truth to that. Fura still wondered why Apallo had kept her in the dark, but it wasn't the secrets of her own life that she was currently interested in.

"Can't you tell me something?" she pleaded. She couldn't understand why it was such a big deal. Though she wanted to know about his life, his past, at this point she would've settled for simply knowing his favorite color.

"There's no point."

When Fura looked at him, she found that Kiyani had already returned his gaze to the night-covered town outside the window.

His words left her confused, but they also left an underlying feeling of unease, detecting a specific meaning behind his cryptic reply.

"You're not seriously still thinking of leaving me back in Barandor, are you?" Why else would he think it would be pointless for her to get to know him? "You promised you wouldn't say anything else about that."

"And I haven't."

"Oh…"

She still didn't know what his words meant, but Fura found herself releasing a breath of sudden pent up anger. He'd scared her for a moment. She couldn't go back. Not now.

Though that didn't quite erase his threat of leaving her in the dark of night.

Silence filled the room again as if it had never been washed away in the first place.

Even more awake after her sudden outburst, Fura fished for something more specific with which to question him.

"Apallo obviously doesn't like you," she ventured. "So how did you end up in Frielana in the first place?"

Fura couldn't help herself. Kiyani was the one who'd brought up Apallo's name, only causing her to reflect further on the fact that she had come to the early conclusion, given the nature of both men, that he couldn't have originally been from the secluded little village.

The darkness shadowing Kiyani's eyes as he turned back towards her spoke of a man who didn't want to answer questions, let alone discuss anything that bordered personal.

"Don't you have anything better to do?"

Breaking eye contact with him, Fura looked around the sparsely furnished room. Nothing of particular interest had shown up in the last two days.

"No," she answered simply.

Kiyani sighed as he raked a hand through his hair and rose from his spot. Rounding the edge of the bed, he began to head towards the door.

"Where are you going?"

"If you're going to continue to pester me, I'm going to find somewhere else to relax."

"You're not going to find relaxation in the tavern." She wasn't positive, but Fura had the sneaking suspicion that under Aldam's orders it was the only place they were allowed beyond their room.

"I won't here, either."

Scared to follow him, Fura perched dangerously close on the edge of the bed, waiting for his final move.

"I'm asking a simple question, not pulling teeth," she said, trying to redirect the conversation to smoother waters.

Kiyani's hand rested on the doorknob, leaving Fura to believe that he really was going to walk away that easily. He might've been on his way to dreamland when she'd entered the room, but now he was wide awake, willing to forgo sleep in exchange for a moment of peace. He stood, rooted to the spot for a few moments before turning around and leaning on the door. The candlelight highlighted his hair, but left his eyes shadowed as he looked back on her, leaving Fura to question what was going through his mind.

"I left home at five, my mother was murdered when I was eight, and my father's an ass. Satisfied?" he said in one agitated breath.

Fura could only stare back at him, taking in the tense silhouette of Kiyani's form, as she fought the shock that had silenced her. When she'd asked him to give her a spare detail of the life that he so vehemently kept shadowed from her, she hadn't expected him to comply, let alone reveal something so dark.

Words backed up in her throat, threatening to choke her, to drown her in the silent syllables. How could she possibly reply to that?

"I'm sorry," Fura finally managed. Yet, her words were so faint they barely had the power to make it past her lips, let alone echo in the darkness of the room.

Kiyani gave a shunted grunt that was the only indication he'd heard her.

"Don't delve into things you know nothing about."

His words, softly spoken and carefully measured like the first quiet snow of winter, yet carrying that same biting cold, sent shivers down her spine.

She could sense that she had angered him, but if that was the case, then why hadn't he lied about it? Fura never would have known the difference.

But it was in that one little spiel that Kiyani had managed, in a way that only he could, to give her a briefing on his sordid background yet distance himself even further from her at the same time.

Taking in the sight of his hand on the doorknob, on the verge of leaving, Fura contemplated rising from the bed to block his way. Yet, she hardly knew how to approach him on a good day. This was far worse.

Seeming to be caught on the edge of his previous conviction to leave the room, Kiyani moved away from the door. Stopping before the dresser, he absent-mindedly fiddled with papers on its surface, seething in silence.

Fura could almost feel the heat from him as she sat frozen, watching him and feeling like a terrible person for pushing him. For making him reveal what he probably never wanted to think about, let alone discuss with others. Now that the words were out in the open she couldn't give them back to him. Couldn't pretend that she hadn't heard.

Though Fura had no words to offer to make the situation better, she still wished there was something she could do. Though, she knew from experience that even if she could formulate the right words, he wouldn't accept the apology. He didn't know how to deal with pity, with concern. From the shake visible in his hands and the way he avoided eye contact with her, Fura knew that any attempt to rectify the situation wouldn't go as she hoped.

Yet, she couldn't keep herself quiet. Couldn't simply allow him to walk out the door.

"Kiyani, I didn't know," Fura murmured, unable to look at him.

"There's no way you could have known," Kiyani responded.

Though his words were calmer than she had expected, she could hear the strain in his voice.

"You could have lied," Fura said, still wondering why he hadn't. It would have been so much easier. He could have played it off jokingly, like he had with so many other things. Instead, he had given her what could have been the darkest part of his history.

His hands still flat on the dresser, Kiyani turned his head to look at her. "To what point?"

Her eyes falling to the floor, Fura knew he was right. She might have wanted him to talk more, to give her something more personal once in awhile than how he knew where specific Relns were, but was that what she really wanted? For him to lie to her?

Not knowing how else to respond, she simply shrugged.

That should have been the end of the conversation. Fura had exhausted her lines of communication, had had the words taken from her mouth and crushed. Just like any other night when she'd made the mistake of pushing him too far, Kiyani would leave for awhile, and in the meantime she'd go to sleep, hoping for a better day when she woke. That was how it should have gone. That's how it always went.

So, when Kiyani's feet came into Fura's line of sight, she looked up, surprised to see that he'd moved closer to the bed. She was shocked even further when he sat beside her without a word.

Of all the unexpected moves he could make, that definitely topped the list. Fura had been certain he'd leave. Even if he wasn't the angriest she'd ever seen him. His emotions were still raging unchecked beneath the surface.

Not knowing what to think, Fura remained quiet, waiting for him to say something. Wondering if he would say anything. Or if they were just going to sit in silence, neither of them knowing where to go... with the conversation... with the journey... with any of it.

Suddenly self-conscious about sitting so close to him, their legs nearly touching, Fura chanced a look at him.

Though he sat hunched over, his elbows on his knees and his chin resting on interlaced fingers, her movement was enough to catch his attention. Where he'd been staring across the room, lost in thought, he now looked over at her, his eyes meeting hers, his gaze unfaltering.

"Would you stop?" Kiyani said after a moment, his voice a mild growl in the darkness.

"What?" Fura asked naïvely, certain she hadn't said anything.

"You know what." When Fura remained silent, only searching his face for confirmation, he shook his head. "Do you really think I don't notice the way you look at me."

Her eyes falling away, Fura was glad for the darkness, feeling the flush of embarrassment spread across her cheeks in response to his words. "I don't know what you're talking about," she claimed, her reply too quick, too forced, to sound like the truth.

"You're a terrible liar, Fura," Kiyani said with another shake of his head. "I hope you realize that."

Fura cringed, though she wondered if that was really such a bad thing. There were worse things she could be. "I don't have feelings for you," Fura said, nearly fumbling on the words as she tried to tell him what he obviously wanted to hear. She could feel her hands shaking in her lap, knowing that she'd almost declared the opposite, wondering what he would've said.

"Are you trying to convince me, or yourself?" Kiyani asked, telling her in those few words that she'd been unsuccessful in her attempt. "Not that it matters," he continued. "It wouldn't work, anyway."

"You don't know that," Fura said weakly, knowing he wasn't seeking a reply.

"We're too different," Kiyani claimed.

Though Fura was certain she was hearing things, she could've sworn that his voice had picked up the briefest hints of sorrow. Yet, she couldn't focus on that. "Then why did you bring me along?"

Kiyani snorted. "The only reason I brought you along is because your father is involved. Anything beyond that is a figment of your imagination."

"I don't believe that."

"Believe what you will. It doesn't matter to me."

"Yes, it does," Fura said, surprising herself.

"You don't know anything about me," Kiyani shot back.

Continuing with her unexpected bold streak, Fura kept the conversation going, even when she knew she should let it fall silent. "I'd know more about you if you'd talk once in awhile. We're traveling together," she reminded him. "It's not uncalled for to want to know more about the person I'm stuck with. To notice things that you don't want seen." Though she was still shaking, Fura brought her hand up and let her fingers trail along the bare skin of his shoulder, brushing across his tattoo at the nape of his neck.

Kiyani grabbed her wrist before her touch could find the scars on his back.

"I just know so little about you," Fura said, afraid to look at him. His grasp was firm, leaving her without the option to escape, but it was the intensity of his gaze that she couldn't contend with.

"I'm not the kind of person you want to know," he said darkly.

Fura shook her head, frustrated with him. "You don't know that."

Spurred on by the catch she'd heard in his words, telling her that he didn't quite mean what he said, Fura met his eyes. Though she couldn't read him, there was something different in his expression. As if this was the first time he'd ever really seen her as something beyond the title of Apallo's daughter.

They remained, frozen in time, looking at one another, before Kiyani finally spoke lightly. "Neither do you."

The move was so sudden that Fura could hardly recall how it'd even happened. One moment they'd been arguing as usual, and the next their lips had met. She could feel the pressure of his body pressed against hers, his lips upon her own, a hand trailing through her hair. It was something that she had wanted in a way since the first time she'd laid eyes upon him, but for how she had come to view him, it was completely unexpected.

In that fleeting passage of time all coherence was gone. The passion he exhumed was something Fura had never fathomed existed in his world of meditated solitude, though she guessed that it was from that solitude from which it was derived.

It was Kiyani who abruptly stopped the madness as quickly as it began.

Opening his eyes, he froze in place, his face inches from hers. There was a look of terror in his pale eyes as if the lapse in judgment had faded, leaving in its wake the crystal clear realization of what was happening.

In a desperate attempt to retain the moment, Fura tried to pull him closer. But, like the flip of a switch, he was back to his angry, distanced self. He tore himself from her grasp, his feet hitting the floor in a quick acrobatic dance that made Fura forget all about the pain he seemed to have been in moments before.

It was only as another flash illuminated the shadows, that she was sent careening back into reality. The thunderstorm outside was still raging, pelting the window with heavy drops. In the brief flash of light, she could see Kiyani shaking from pent up rage as he stood far away from her, bent over the dresser, his palms flat on the wooden surface. Her heart raced, feeling like it was going to escape from her chest, the dizziness it created amassed from more than one source. From fear. From longing.

She watched Kiyani, afraid of what he would do. His hair hung in a feathery sheet, hiding his face and the burning eyes she knew would be present. It looked like he wanted to grab something and fling it... at her, at the wall, at nothing in particular... Fura wasn't sure. Instead, he left the room so quickly that his form was a mere blur of monotone color in the darkness. He slammed the door so hard on the way out that Fura was afraid it would fall off the hinges.

Though Fura knew she should've been relieved that he had vacated the room before he turned his anger on her, it did nothing to relieve the pain and the sudden pit of emptiness in her stomach. Despite his outburst and the tangible display of his resentment towards her, she could still feel the ghost of his lips on hers. The remnants of that sudden spark of untamed passion wouldn't leave her mind.

However, the moment was long gone. No matter the lengths she went to recover it, she was still left alone and heartbroken.

✧ ⌘ ✧

Hastily throwing on the shirt he had somehow managed to grab in the confusion of rage before leaving the room, Kiyani stormed down the hallway. He paused at the top of the stairs, leaning against the wall and staring at the ceiling, trying to regulate his breathing and get the shaking to subside. He knew it would take awhile for it to fully recede, but he didn't want to draw any more attention than necessary. Already, he had done a fine job of that. Though there was no one else present in the hall, he could still feel the reverberation from the slammed door that was sure to have echoed throughout the entire building. His best hope was to pray that others had mistaken it as thunder.

As he slowly made his way down the stairs, pausing on the landing, he was surprised to see the lack of impression he'd made on the few left in the dark, fire-lit room. No one gave him a second glance as he made his way back to the small table in the corner he had inhabited earlier.

When the waitress came by he ordered a drink so as to not be rude. Rather than actually drink it, he found himself fiddling with the glass when it was dropped off. It was a menial tic, spinning it around in the ring of moisture it left on the table, something to clear his mind.

"Spying, are we?"

Kiyani turned to look at the man standing behind him, his arms crossed, a stern look on his face with a hint of concern, not for Kiyani but rather for the other customers.

"Thinking," Kiyani replied. He had recognized Aldam's voice but knew better than to ignore the man, no matter how much he may have wanted to. At least it wasn't Maven. Kiyani couldn't handle much more of that man. Especially at this hour of the night. Nor after what had just happened.

Though he'd turned his attention back to the glass on the table, Kiyani could still feel the Magisard's eyes upon him. Rather than leaving him be, as Kiyani would've preferred, Aldam walked around the table, pulled out the chair opposite him and took a seat. Kiyani looked up at him with a raised brow but said nothing, waiting instead to see what Aldam had to say.

Seeming to have the same idea, they both remained silent for the longest time as Aldam leaned forward, his elbows resting on the table as he looked Kiyani over. When the waitress came back around he calmly declined her offer to bring another drink.

Waiting until the woman was out of distance, busy with another table, Kiyani finally spoke, feeling increasingly nervous under the man's scrutinizing gaze, though he was sure that was Aldam's intention. "I'm minding my own business," he commented, as if he had to speak it outright to prove it.

"I didn't say you weren't." Leaning back in the chair and crossing his arms, Aldam almost looked like he was simply having a normal conversation with an old friend. "You always come down here, amongst all these people to think?"

"I can't imagine I'm allowed to go anywhere else."

All Aldam said was a mumbled, "Mmhmm..." as if to confirm Kiyani's answer. Another silence set in. Aldam's eyes never left him as Kiyani fiddled with his glass again, wishing the man would go away. There was just no getting any relief lately.

Finally, the governor stood up and pushed the chair back towards the table. "Don't stay down here too long," he advised. "You wouldn't want to be dead tired while working tomorrow. The rain should be done by then."

"And if it's not?" Kiyani wondered aloud.

Aldam shrugged before leaving. "You've heard of working rain or shine, haven't you?"

Kiyani sighed, shaking his head as he watched the man leave. Heaven forbid if he were allowed a day off again for a little water and mud. He finally picked the tankard up and took a swig of the liquid inside as he listened to the mumbles of conversation about the Hunt.

✧⌘✧

Fura lay awake in the dark, sleep refusing to grant her a reprieve. She stared at Kiyani next to her, his back turned, revealing the angry red lines that trailed across his skin. She wasn't sure if he was awake or not, unable to discern any movement beyond that of his breathing in the monotone shadows.

He had come back not too long before. Still shaken from his outburst she'd feigned sleep as he had quietly slipped under the covers. He hadn't say anything, hadn't made any attempt to wake her, and when she finally found the courage to open her eyes, Fura discovered that he was facing away from her, as if he favored the sight of the wall over her.

Rolling onto her side, Fura let her hand float over the scars on his back. She didn't dare touch them for fear of sparking another burst of rage from him, though it didn't keep her from wondering what they felt like.

Faltering for a fraction of a second, momentarily distracted by a flash from the continuing storm, Fura's hand brushed lightly across his skin. Whether he was awake or not, it was just enough to accrue a reaction as Kiyani whipped around, grabbing her wrist.

"Just stop," he growled.

Fura flinched, trying to pull away from him, but he kept his grasp tight, anger burning in his eyes. "I'm sorry," she whimpered.

"This fascination with me has got to stop. Now, leave me alone," Kiyani said, glaring at her before releasing his hold.

She rubbed her wrist, working to rid it of the flash of pain Kiyani had caused. It was something he probably didn't realize, Fura thought as she looked at the wall behind Kiyani, afraid to meet his eyes. She had heard his words, yet Fura still found them hard to absorb. All this time she had been so sure that her real feelings for him were kept secret.

"Would you just talk to me?" Fura asked meekly, fighting off tears as she watched him turn around again.

He stopped midway and turned his head. "About what?"

"I don't know. Could we just, for once, have a normal conversation that doesn't end with you storming off?" She didn't know what it was about him, but no matter how angry he got with her, Fura just couldn't make herself stay away.

He regarded her for a moment, watching her flinch as a bolt of lightning split the night sky, illuminating the room for a brief second before plunging them back into darkness. "You don't like storms, do you?" His voice was level, but she could hear him fighting against that hard edge that remained in it.

Fura shook her head no as she cringed again with the onset of the thunderous boom.

"It'll pass," he said. Rolling back over to face the wall, Kiyani listened to the sudden downpour outside.

Sitting up, her knees drawn to her chest, Fura watched him breathing. She knew for a fact that he wasn't asleep now. Though her mind warned against it, she let her fingers brush across the scarred skin again, surprised at how warm it was.

"Fura…" Kiyani growled in warning.

"When did this happen, anyway?" Fura asked, ignoring him. Her heart was beating frantically in her chest, a mix of excitement and the fear of his reaction, and she hoped he couldn't hear it. "It had to have been in Fae Rue. It's hardly even begun healing."

"Must you pry into people's personal lives?"

"I'm just wondering," Fura countered, glad to hear the anger fading, even if it was irritation that was replacing it.

Despite the lack of bite in his previous words, Fura wondered, after a steadily growing silence, if he was done with her for the night. It felt like the passing of eternity. Fura's eyes kept returning to Kiyani as she listened to the winds and the lashing rain outside, the steady ebb of white noise.

Kiyani took in a deep breath and let out a heavy sigh, as if it was a difficult decision to continue. "Since I was eight."

Her eyebrows furrowed. "Eight?" she asked, confused.

"How long I've had those scars."

Her breath caught as she looked at them again. The marred skin was still red with inflammation, the irritated cells working to repair themselves. "That's not possible, Kiyani. They barely look a week old, two at the most. That would mean you've had them…" Fura faltered, realizing she still didn't know his age.

"Nearly ten years, now," he answered for her.

"How…?"

Whether Fura had more to add or not, Kiyani spoke before she could say much else. "Injuries through magic don't heal like normal wounds do. The one who caused the damage can control the rate at which it heals, allowing it to heal quicker than normal, or not at all. Most people either don't know that or, if they do, don't know how to control it anyways. Unfortunately, my father is not in that category."

Kiyani was silent a moment, either reliving the moment or letting the information sink in.

"Your father?" Fura said, shocked. *My father's an ass.* That had been mentioned in his tirade, but she hadn't expected that. "He's the one that did this to you?"

"There are reasons I left home at such a young age. He's not a kind person. I can't see them, but I know that those scars have only healed enough to keep them from bleeding. As long as he's alive, though, they'll never heal past that point."

Silence filled the spaces between them, Kiyani feeling he'd revealed enough, and Fura not knowing what to say. Only that evening, she'd been pushing him to give her something about his past. Now, she found herself sorry for asking. Realizing why he hadn't wanted to talk about it.

Despite the depth of the conversation, Kiyani had barely moved during its length. Even now, he had his back turned to her, his eyes closed, as if still trying to escape into sleep. Fura knew she should leave him be for the night. Yet, staring at the marred skin, she found it hard to believe what he'd just told her. Even in a world of magic, how was it possibly to retain such an injury for ten years.

"They do hurt then, don't they?" she asked.

Kiyani opened his eyes slowly and peered over his shoulder at her. "Some days are worse than others. It's a constant pain that I've learned to live with."

Fura shook her head in disbelief. "You shouldn't have to live like that."

"No one should," Kiyani argued. "But that's the way of life."

Wishing she could rid him of the pain, she settled for simply laying a hand on his shoulder. "I'm sorry," she whispered.

"Get some rest," Kiyani said.

Though she could tell that he was done with conversation for the night, wanting to go to sleep, Fura couldn't help but get in one last word before she tried to do the same. "Thank you," she said, staring out the rain-streaked window. "For bringing me along... I know you didn't want to."

"I didn't have much of a choice," Kiyani declared roughly.

"And that kiss?" Fura wondered, knowing that it probably wasn't even a good idea to bring it up.

"A product of clouded judgment, sleep deprivation, and lust. Don't read into it. Now, go to sleep."

50

••◇••

LONELY MORNINGS

It was expected. The cold bed. The dark room. The feeling of loneliness.

After the strange, unexpected night she'd had with Kiyani, she couldn't imagine it starting any other way. Trying to ignore the emptiness in the room, Fura stared out the window. She knew the sundial wouldn't be able to give her a time. Shadows still enveloped the world beyond the glass, the sun far from chasing them away.

Sighing, she laid her head on her knees and closed her eyes.

In all the books she'd read, in all the movies she'd watched, this wasn't how things were supposed to develop. After such an emotional night, the heroine of the story would wake up with the man still by her side, ready to comfort her, if not confess his love. But not him. Not Kiyani. She shouldn't have expected anything less.

She'd spent so much energy trying not to think of Kiyani like that, keeping her thoughts hidden, and telling herself that there was no hope in such an idea. Then just like that, he'd destroyed it all.

Fura still didn't know just who had initiated that kiss, but she'd felt that shift in him. Even though he vehemently denied it, something had changed.

Hugging the sheets close, she tried not to cry. Already, she had shed tears too many times around him, though she did her best each time to mask the reasons. He already saw her as weak. She didn't need to confirm that image. This was the first time, however, that those tears were specifically for him.

Though she knew it was destructive to think on it any further, Fura recalled those few scary hours following the incident. She'd been afraid that he wouldn't come back after storming from the room, that he would decide to leave, despite Aldam's claim that they had to remain in the town. Kiyani had threatened to leave her to fend for herself before. Fura had been certain that that time had finally come.

She didn't know what had been more terrifying: the thought of being on her own in this strange place, or the idea that she would never

422

see him again.

Even if they were only ever friends, Fura couldn't deny that she needed him around. It didn't matter how many times she tried to claim that she could handle herself. The truth was that he was right. She knew nothing of this world. How could she?

As soon as they'd started their journey, trudging continuously through the woods, the scenery had blended together in a muddled mess. Tearing through the darkness and the rain the night of the siege had been a recipe for disaster. And the following morning hadn't shed any familiar light on her surroundings. The truth of the matter was that she could have confessed to him an hour after they'd begun that she was lost in this place. But she'd kept that fact to herself, not wanting to fuel Kiyani's stubborn pride. It was bad enough that, even now, he was still trying to find ways to get her to go back to Barandor. A home that she would never be able to claim as her own again.

Though she hadn't known what to say to him upon his return, Fura had been relieved when Kiyani had come back. Yet, even after their unexpected talk, involving things she could have barely imagined, she had a feeling that they were no longer on good terms. If they ever had been in the first place.

Every day was different with him.

Still feeling the ghost of that kiss on her lips, Fura chastised herself for getting so involved.

The storm outside had ended long ago, but the storm in her heart was still in full force.

Knowing that sleep was out of the question, Fura rose from the bed and lazily got dressed. Though she was trying to keep him off her mind, she wondered where Kiyani had gone. She hadn't heard him leave, but she didn't need her eyes to tell her that the room was vacant, leaving her as its only occupant. It was too dark to have started work in the fields. Yet, Fura had no clue where else he could have gone. She had a feeling that they weren't allowed to wander the town freely, especially at odd hours of the morning. Which left one place... the tavern below.

Fura had contemplated heading downstairs early to see if breakfast was available yet, until that thought had crossed her mind. Even with the possibility of immersing herself in work a few hours ahead of schedule, Fura knew she wasn't ready to face Kiyani. Not so soon. She didn't even know what to say after last night.

Sitting on the edge of the bed, dressed and ready to face nothing, she looked out the window. Dawn approached, turning the sky a hazy gray that matched her mood.

It wasn't long before Fura forced herself to rise again before she fell victim to her anxiety. She could either face the fact that she would run into him eventually of her own accord, or hide in bed all day, awaiting his return. The outcome was the same.

Catching sight of a scrap of white that looked out of place on the top of the dresser, Fura walked over to investigate. Pulling the piece of parchment from beneath the basin of water, she looked down at what she could only assume was Kiyani's writing. His name scratched beneath the bulk of the writing confirmed it, but it was the message itself that made her heart drop.

If you want to get your own room, it's ok with me...

Her hands shaking, she dropped the note back on the dresser, not wanting to read it over again. So that was it. One misstep and he wanted her gone. Wiping a tear from her face, she turned away, from the piece of paper, from the room that now held painful memories, and made her way out the door.

Not knowing how to even begin to deal with the day, Fura cautiously made her way through the hall and down the stairs. Approaching the tavern, she kept to the shadows as she looked around, knowing that the first sign of Kiyani would send her skittering back up the stairs. Stepping down from the last tread, she found it wasn't necessary. Scanning the room once, and then again to make sure, she came to the conclusion that Kiyani wasn't there.

As much as she had dreaded the possible encounter, her heart still sank with the realization that he'd completely disregarded her existence today. It was like spending her time with a ghost. One minute he was there, and the next he was gone, nowhere to be found, slipping soundlessly in and out of life. Fura almost wondered, if asked, if anyone would even remember him.

The only sign that he'd even been present was that heart-wrenching note.

'Maybe he's right,' she told herself, thinking back on the conversation from the night before.

'This fascination with me has got to stop.' It was one of the first things he'd said to her after his return.

Even before she had set foot in Frielana, her judgment had been clouded around them. She hadn't even met him before he'd stormed into her life, telling her she didn't belong, and yet she'd wanted to know more then. She had known, but hadn't wanted to admit, that she had felt something more than she should have. Then Apallo's warning, and Kiyani's continued rude words had followed.

It should have been enough to make her turn the other way.

He'd made it clear from the get go that he didn't want much of anything to do with her, and yet she had kept running into him at the most inconvenient times.

Maybe she would have eventually gotten the hint, but then the siege had taken place and she'd been sent on a journey with him, rather than setting her on the path to forgetting him. Though she should've been more concerned about what was going to happen, the one thing that had been on her mind was that she would get to spend more time with him. It had been her hope that the more time they spent together maybe he would return her feelings.

Thus far there had been nothing of the sort. Nothing but consistent yelling and fights, words that nearly brought her to tears, and mannerisms of his that made her fear for her physical safety. Yet, he'd done nothing to harm her. Even when he had pulled that knife on her, Fura knew he hadn't actually meant to hurt her, only scare her into submission.

Mulling over the past, Fura half-heartedly wished that she'd taken her father's words into consideration. Had she known just how close Apallo was to her, she might have. But none of it mattered now.

She had been pushed off the ledge into the unknown with Kiyani and there was no turning back. Fura only hoped that she had a chance to talk to him again before his statement of leaving her to fend for herself proved to be truth.

"Fura," a friendly voice called from nearby. "You're up early this morning."

Looking up, pulled from the haze of her thoughts, Fura found Wanda heading her way. The woman had a bright smile on her face for such early hours. Her wavy mass of dark hair was tied into a loose bun, keeping it out of her face as she worked.

Fura had discovered in the two days of apprenticing with the woman that nothing got in her way as she flitted about the tavern.

Masking her feelings with a smile, Fura nodded. She hoped she would be able to make it through the day, though she knew there was no pulling it through as effortlessly as Wanda managed day after day.

"You have a few more hours, you know," Wanda declared, wiping down a nearby table as she spoke.

"I know," Fura said with a shrug. "Just not tired, I guess." She watched the woman work as she stifled a yawn that threatened to contradict her words. The time seemed to drag as Fura waited to see if Wanda would ask her to start work early.

The hours that Fura had worked already had led her to believe that the busiest time of the day was early evening and beyond. It seemed that the majority of those who came in for a hearty dinner stuck around for hours after the plates had been cleared to enjoy drinks with friends as they traded the latest gossip. A quick surveillance of the scene seemed to confirm the fact. There were only a few tables filled with people at this ungodly hour of the morning.

Though Fura waited for Wanda to say something, anything, one question lingered in her mind that she couldn't help but ask. "Have you seen Kiyani?" She scrunched her forehead as she closed her eyes, not believing she'd actually asked that after last night. The woman would probably think she was mad.

Opening her eyes, however, Fura found that the question had had little impact.

"Of course," Wanda answered. There was no inquiring look in her eye, no change in the tone of her voice. "He came down to eat and left about an hour ago."

Fura wondered about the lack of change in her composure before she realized that the only ones who knew about the fight, if it could even be classified as such, were Kiyani and herself. There was no reason that anyone else would be aware of such a thing. It was strange, she thought, that something that'd had such an impact on her, completely ravaging her emotions, had encompassed only a few fleeting minutes that everyone else would remain oblivious to.

"Must have decided to start work early so he could finish before they got called back indoors due to the Hunt."

"The Hunt?"

Wanda looked up at Fura, noticing the confusion. "Oh yes," she said. "The beasts come out tonight."

That barely began to answer her questions, but Fura didn't pursue it. "Right," she said, talking as if she'd just remembered what the word entailed. "The Hunt."

As if she was still picking up on the discomfort, Wanda asked, "Didn't he tell you he was leaving?"

"He probably just didn't want to wake me so early," Fura said, avoiding the woman's gaze as she threw on another faked smile.

As much as it bothered her that Kiyani had left without a word this morning, the thought no longer took precedence. This wasn't the first occurrence of someone talking about the hunt, yet she still had no idea what they were speaking of.

The first few times she had brushed it off as a normal hunt, a few men out with weapons taking down some animals. However, as she continued to hear of it, Fura wondered if there wasn't something more. The way these people spoke of it, it wasn't some good time out in the woods between comrades. It was more... ominous.

"Would you like some breakfast before you start your day?" Wanda asked, not seeming to notice that Fura was off in thought again.

Fura nodded. As she watched the woman walk away to put in an order, Fura sat at a table and contemplated what she knew, and all that she didn't.

✧ ⌘ ✧

The nasal blow of a horn called the town to a meeting at midday. With the echoing call, the entire workforce was brought to a halt, as one by one people ceased what they were doing to look up towards the source of the noise.

Following suit, Kiyani leaned on the hoe that he'd just stabbed into the damp soil of the water-logged field. Looking to where the noise had originated, he watched as people began to gather, heading towards the center of town where the sun dial sat.

Much like the last time the horn was blown in Frielana, Kiyani had a feeling that he already knew what this gathering would entail.

Though Kiyani was set to ignore it, Maven made it clear that it was mandatory. As the echo of the horn's second call faded through the streets, Maven barked out orders, his eyes focused on Kiyani as if daring him to do anything other than follow his word.

Not feeling his usual argumentative self, Kiyani simply nodded as he took the weather-beaten tool he'd been using and leaned it against the shed alongside the field. Falling in line with the others, he moved along with the group, keeping his eye on Maven as they made their way to the town's center.

Kiyani knew there was nothing the man could call him out on, leaving him to relish the silent rift between them. It was better than the incessant orders and oversight he'd received from the man the first day he'd been on field detail. The work, though tiring, was simple, allowing Kiyani to pick it up easily, and improving with each day. This morning he had been the first one on the site, and though he could tell that Maven had wanted to throw some well conceived comment his way, the man had kept his mouth shut, knowing that there was nothing to argue.

Though Maven remained quiet, he still kept a close watch on him, waiting for that one moment, that one slip up, that he could report back to Aldam. Careful to do little beyond what he was told, Kiyani knew there was nothing so far that would condemn him to the Magisard's punishment. As far as he was concerned, it could stay that way.

The sight of Maven flustered at his compliance with the rules and ways of Skirvynmire was one of the few things that got Kiyani through the long days, and kept his mind off of other things. He was sore from the sudden workload, but he had come out early, working twice as hard as the days before. Despite his muscles complaining, the pain kept him from thinking about the night before. Kiyani knew he would have to deal with it later, but for now the labor was the least of his stress.

He had kept his pain in check throughout the morning, keeping himself as the only one aware of its presence. Though Kiyani hadn't really planned on taking any breaks, he was relieved to have a few

427

moments to do nothing but listen.

As the small group came into the center of the square, they joined the waiting crowd. People whispered to each other in a hum of mixed voices that seemed to drown out everything else. However, as soon as Aldam appeared from the tavern and made his way through the crowd, silence fell over the town. Approaching the center of the mass, Aldam stepped up onto the stones that surrounded the sun dial and created a raised border. Given a miniscule height advantage, the man began to speak.

"I'm sure that you are all well aware of the date," Skirvynmire's leader began in a somber tone, skipping the droll of the usual formalities. "November seventeenth. As you know, the annual Hunt ensues tonight. I just want to remind you that, no matter what your duties are, no matter what task you have in mind, no matter the things that you may feel you need to achieve before the day's end... as soon as dusk begins to settle, the moment the shadows begin to creep in, I want everyone and every living thing inside." Everyone in the square gave the man their full attention as his voice darkened, knowing the seriousness of the matter. It was the one day of the year that it was not only dangerous to be out at night, but deadly. "I don't care what you feel your emergency is after that. Once you are inside, you are under lockdown, and under orders to stay where you are until the sun has risen again tomorrow morning. Make sure that the place you go for refuge is a place that you can remain comfortably, because once you are there, you are forbidden to leave, less you want to risk your life.

"We have all been through this before, and will do so many times in the future. I just want all of you to remain safe. Once tomorrow comes, our daily lives will resume as usual. Until then, remember... dusk."

As the last word hung ominously in the air, Aldam stepped down from his post and weaseled his way out of the crowd, hurrying as if he had other important duties himself to complete before the day's last light. There were some that remained rooted to their spots, talking feverishly to their neighbors. The rest slowly made their way back to what they'd been doing beforehand.

Turning to follow his own group back to the field that seemed to harbor never-ending work, Kiyani was stopped as Maven stepped into his path.

"And just where do you think you're going?" the man asked.

"Back to work," Kiyani replied starkly. He hardly felt like dealing with the man.

Maven shook his head. "Not so fast." Tossing a scrap of paper in his direction, Kiyani had to fight to catch it before it fell to the ground. "Don't take all day," Maven said snidely before walking away, leaving Kiyani confused.

Watching him as he rejoined the work detail he oversaw, Kiyani made sure the man wasn't returning before glancing at the paper in his hand. Only then did he see that it was a note from the Magisard.

KIYANI,

PLEASE SEE ME IN MY OFFICE FOLLOWING THE MEETING ABOUT THE HUNT. I WOULD LIKE TO SPEAK WITH YOU.

- ALDAM

Groaning inwardly, Kiyani began to make his way towards the tavern, wondering what he possibly could have done. Nothing came to mind, yet he was left wondering if he and Fura would be tossed out of the town on the night of the Hunt.

Entering *The Mead Mill,* he didn't bother looking for Fura. Instead, he traced the path that they'd walked the first day, down the side hall to the room at the end. Standing before the door, Kiyani took a moment to compose himself before knocking.

Almost immediately a *'come in'* was uttered from beyond.

"Please, come in, come in," Aldam said as Kiyani opened the door and walked inside. "Good to see that Maven remembered to give you the note."

Ignoring the offered chair sitting in front of the desk, Kiyani stood. "Can I ask why I'm here?"

"Nothing bad, I assure you," Aldam declared, seeming to sense his hesitation at being in the room. "I just wanted to pull you aside to let you know that the day after the Hunt is declared a work holiday in Skirvynmire. Only those working in the tavern are exempt. As much as I would prefer keeping you busy with work, I seem to have little choice."

Kiyani nodded, knowing where this conversation was headed.

"I simply wanted to remind you —"

"To not make any trouble," Kiyani said, finishing the Magisard's sentence.

"Yes," Aldam replied simply, paying no mind that he had been cut off. "I still ask that you keep to the tavern, however."

"Anything else?" Kiyani asked, wondering just how much of a holiday it would prove to be. He was certain he would rather be stuck with the back-breaking work in the fields than be sequestered to a single building.

Aldam shook his head. "Not at this time. You may go."

Quickly taking his leave, Kiyani left the room and began to make his way back to Maven's watch. Exiting the tavern, he looked to the sky as he walked, calculating the hours of sunlight remaining before the setting sun brought the beasts.

It was the countdown that was on everyone's minds.

But for him, it was a countdown to something entirely different. Not only was danger on the horizon, but in roughly six hours he would have to face another danger: coming face to face with Fura. And that, to him, was worse than what the darkness would bring.

"If you want your own room..."
How could Kiyani say that? Fura asked herself.

The words had been with her all day, their image and cadence distracting her from her work. Spilling yet another tankard of beer as she wiped down a table, she knew she appeared a worse waitress than she had their first day here. Yet, it didn't keep her from mulling over Kiyani's note.

Was that really what he wanted? Or was it simply a maneuver for him, his own way of dealing with the situation?

She had expected him to leave early in a way, yet the note still surprised her.

Clearing another table, Fura dragged an arm across her forehead and sighed. As if dealing with her personal issues wasn't enough, the day had been busier than usual. Ever since the announcement in the square, the tavern had been filled with a consistent wave of people, coming in for their meal or nightly drink before the mandatory lockdown was established for the day.

Her fingers were pruny, her body was sore, and she was tired beyond reason, the night before having provided little rest.

'So much for staying here for a night to rest and gain some strength,' she thought, recalling her initial plan when the town had come into view.

Yet, as much as the idea of rest called to her, Fura knew she would work all night if it meant keeping herself out of the small room upstairs.

She'd caught a glimpse of Kiyani earlier during the town meeting, opposite of where she had been standing. As far as she knew, he hadn't seen her... hadn't bothered to look, even.

All Fura knew, was that, for now, despite having a billion more questions she wanted answered, about the Hunt especially, she wanted to keep her distance from him.

Moving to another cleared table that demanded cleaning, a boisterous bellow rang through the tavern, nearly causing her to topple another glass as she picked it up. Glancing across the room, she could see the man that had issued the laugh. A large tankard was grasped in thick hands, his wild, wavy hair amassing his head in a frizzy halo, and what appeared to be the neck of some strange instrument was visible propped next to his chair. Immune to the noise he created, he was surrounded by a small crowd of people, all appearing to egg him on further.

"Who's that?" Fura asked, leaning over towards Wanda who had appeared by her side.

The woman gave the man a cursory glance before returning her focus to her work. "A traveling bard that came in last week. Still haven't gotten a name off him. I'm surprised this is the first you've seen him, though."

A bard.

Pausing in her work, Fura looked the man over again, suddenly seeing him in a new light.

Though she had just resolved to stay away from Kiyani for the night, she now had the overwhelming urge to talk to him, wondering if the mention of this man might raise his spirits. Bards were known for stories, weren't they? Was it possible he might know something of the Witneis?

Trying to return to her work, Fura wondered what the next few days would bring.

51
♦♦◇♦♦
A NEW KIND OF ANIMAL

It was pitch-black, a heavy rain pounding noisily on the roof above, when Fura's eyes flew open. There was noise beyond that of the rain. Not the regular white noise of night, but something that reeked of danger and disturbance. If she focused hard enough to cancel out the rain, she could just barely make it out.

All day Fura had heard terrified whispers of the Hunt. A hunt that she still knew nothing about, only that it scared everyone enough that the governor – the Magisard, Fura reminded herself – would put the whole town under lockdown.

She didn't know what this hunt entailed, but what she was hearing now was *inside*. Fura clutched the sheets closer as she listened, her heart racing in her chest, not knowing what was out there. She could hear something out in the hall, banging around, stumbling, and knocking on doors.

Then she heard it. The voice. The slurred words.

It was a man out there.

She almost chastised herself for being so frightened of another human. Fura hadn't questioned anyone the past few days, not even the past few hours, about this dreaded Hunt, but that hadn't kept her from creating notions of wild and mangled beasts in her mind.

At first she had passed it off as some recreational hunt that the townspeople waited all year for. It wasn't until the recent morning that Fura had taken from the sparse and varied information that it wasn't the people hunting the beast. As far as she could tell, it was quite the opposite. Why else would so many people be scared, despite possessing weapons of steel, iron, and powder? So scared that they would lock themselves in the darkened recesses of their homes, hoping that they would be overlooked on this particular night.

It was a terrifying thought.

Right now, though, the Hunt wasn't on Fura's mind. It was what was just outside the door, mere feet away. It didn't matter what the people here were afraid of, what was coming. This man, whoever he

432

might be, was nothing short of danger himself.

His tone was angry and laden with liquor. Fura couldn't make out the exact words, but he seemed to be making his way down the hall, pounding on the walls and the doors, calling out to someone, for someone, all the while throwing out every expletive in the book.

Seconds later, it was her door the man was beating on, creating a terrible racket.

"I know you're in there!" the voice shouted. It was loud enough that if she didn't know any better, Fura would have guessed that he was in the room with her. "Come out here, now!" the man slurred again, his voice rising.

Fura cowered under the sheets, her heart pounding, fear increasing ten-fold. There was no telling what he wanted or if he was armed, if physical harm was his goal.

She was so absorbed with what was happening outside the room that Fura nearly let out a terror-filled scream when an arm wrapped around her. Visions of tombs and death materialized in her mind until the voice instantly wiped them away.

"Don't make a sound," Kiyani whispered harshly in her ear, barely inches from her face. It wasn't a suggestion, but a command. One that Fura was more than willing to obey.

She'd forgotten he was even there. As much as she had been dreading their next encounter, terrified of the mood he'd be in, their meeting that night had been rather uneventful. Now, Fura was glad to know that she wasn't alone, thankful that she hadn't taken the suggestion written in his note that morning.

Kiyani stayed huddled over her, unmoving, his eyes focused on the door and the danger that lurked just on the other side. "If he doesn't hear anything, he'll just move on," he whispered, barely loud enough to hear through the sheets of water pounding at the window and the man's drunken tirade.

"Get out here, you bitch!" the man stormed. Fura flinched at the anger behind the curse as she cowered closer to Kiyani. "I know you're in there." He pounded at the door again with so much force that the door wobbled on its hinges. "I know what you did!"

Fura prayed the man would move on. Though she knew he would continue on his path of drunken madness, knew he should be stopped before he hurt someone, Fura just wanted him gone. There was nothing she could do besides hope that someone else would take care of it. All she wanted was the man to leave their door.

Seconds later, just as the boisterous drunk was starting in on another series of incessant knocks, her wish was answered. The sound of hurried feet, barreling up the stairs at the end of the hall was followed by angry voices and shouts.

The commotion intensified briefly, as numerous men added their voices to scene in the hallway. Shouts and harshly stated commands to calm down, or to back off were issued. But the words seemed to do nothing but go through one ear and out the other, rolling off of intoxicated and dying brain cells. If their proceeds were met with anything, it was a heightened audio level as the man's screaming continued. Fura could only imagine, just from listening to him, how glazed his eyes must be, how red in the face he was, how many veins were bulging beneath his flesh. As the disturbance continued, his words became increasingly longer as the syllables began to blend together.

Then suddenly, almost in the same manner as when Fura had been startled awake, everything went eerily quiet. She could hear her heart beating frantically in her chest, could feel Kiyani's breath on her neck.

Though she hadn't heard much of anything intelligible, something must have been said. Given the quick silence, Fura could only assume it was a threat.

And then it started up again.

"You can't do that to me!" the drunk began, his slurry of misspoken vowels and consonants changing from outrage to fear.

It was all that Fura was able to make out in this new tirade. He repeated the phrase several times, each time his volume rising another few decibels until it was a high-pitched yell.

There was a sudden change in the racket. Fura heard what she thought was a gasp before the onset of shouting set in, filled with nervousness and ill-intentions.

And then the shot.

The metallic ring of the bullet leaving the burning barrel split the tense air.

Fura's heart sank, as an overwhelming notion that she was going to die set in. Though she wasn't in the hallway herself, she could feel the ringing echo in her bones. It wasn't until the delayed wail of pain, easily distinguished as that of the drunken man, that Fura realized she had stopped breathing.

Sucking in a deep lungful of what unexpectedly seemed like stale air, she lay there, tense in Kiyani's protective grasp, as she listened to the procession make their way out of the hallway, taking their business downstairs.

The slow whine of the creaking door and the crack of light that appeared as it swung inward made Fura sit up defensively, ready to flee if need be. Kiyani did the same behind her, though the vibe that emanated from him was more suited to fighting.

As Aldam's form came into the room, Fura let out a sigh of relief, knowing that neither action was needed.

"Is everything okay in here?" he asked, playing the role of Magisard and protecting his people, even if the two of them weren't considered as such.

Fura wanted to answer but she found she still had no voice. She nodded instead, unsure if he could even see them clearly enough to make it out.

It was Kiyani who lent his voice. "We're fine." Fura was mildly jealous. His voice was as clear and level as any other day, lacking hesitation or fear.

Aldam stayed only momentarily, as if assessing the answer and seeking the truth behind it. Apparently satisfied, he closed the door and moved on, checking on the others that were taking residence in the hall.

As quiet as it had become on the upper level of the mill, there was still unsettled noise below. Moments before, Fura had heard the unmistakable slamming of the heavy door to the entrance of the building.

Now, outside there was a new wave of commotion. She could hear the drunk screaming, but this wasn't the same as before. The pain from the gunshot wound seemed to have disappeared, replaced instead by a belting wail of terror.

Only then did a new sound become apparent to her. Out of nowhere, inhuman growls filled the night, followed by low howls that sent chills down her spine. Though Fura had no idea of their origin, she knew they weren't like the warning signal she'd heard from Kiedo when he'd been set on protecting them. These were that of animals on the hunt, catching the first scent of frightened prey.

Instinctively, Fura turned her head towards the window to get a better look, to add visual to the sound. Her body must have moved along with her focus, because before she knew it, Kiyani grabbed hold of her, pulling her back. As quick as it was, it didn't keep her from catching the smallest glimpse of the scene outside.

"Don't look," Kiyani warned.

But it was too late. Despite the moonless night, she had seen what she hadn't wanted to. The gnarled animals of her creation weren't even a fraction of what was actually out there, prowling the night.

Dark forms, taller than the average human, and masses of what she assumed was dark, wet, and tangled fur advancing on the man that had been so cruelly tossed out. The hunter becoming the victim.

The darkness allowed for no details but Fura was sure she didn't want any. She could feel herself beginning to hyperventilate with a sudden onset of unmanageable panic.

Kiyani pulled her closer into his arms. "I *told* you not to look," he said with a hiss of disappointment.

Too upset to even take notice that Kiyani wasn't only being nice to her, but protective, Fura pushed away from him, trying to form frantic words into some sort of sentence but falling short, her voice in hysterics. "What in the *HELL* is that!?" was all she managed.

Meeting his eyes, Fura discovered something she didn't want to see. As she watched him avert his eyes from her waiting gaze, she knew that his earlier lack of fear hadn't been imagined. "You *knew*..."

The screams outside changed again. Not pain this time. Not terror. Death. The high-pitched gurgling wails of the last moments of life being painfully torn away sounded as the animalistic growls of joy in the prize hunt intensified. Whatever was out there was tearing this man apart. Alive.

Fura stiffened, her voice and her anger lost.

Kiyani grabbed her again. This time she nuzzled deeper into his embrace hoping to block out the terrible sounds. His arms were around her protectively, but Fura could tell that his focus was outside. She didn't dare look up, afraid of his level of interest in what was happening beyond the window.

"I thought it would be better if you didn't know," Kiyani said. "I was hoping that you would sleep through it, that they would just pass by without incident."

Fura didn't reply as she listened to him try to explain his motives.

The sounds came to a crescendo and then waned back into muffled growls and groans, noises that Fura tried not to justify with mental images. She remained huddled against Kiyani as she attempted to regain control of herself. Both of them were silent.

Though she knew that Kiyani's disgust with her was still there, still burned fresh in their rocky lack of relationship, the events of the night temporarily masked it. There was no way that he was going to let her forget about his angry outburst from the night before, and Fura knew, that unfortunately, there was no way that she would ever be able to.

Despite that high level of inbred hate towards her and the instability of his manner, Fura felt oddly safe in his arms. Somehow she knew that, as long as it remained in his power, he wasn't going to let anything happen to her, no matter the terminal status of their coexistence.

"What are they?" Fura asked, shattering the silence as she found some power to finally spit out the words.

Kiyani released his hold on her and let his arms fall away. The sudden lack of extra body heat made Fura shiver, but she didn't dare move back towards him. The moment was gone.

"They're called Werebeasts, for lack of a better name," he said. His eyes scanned her in the darkness, as if trying to judge her mental stability. "In their own language it's something completely different, but it's hard to pronounce," he added as an afterthought, as if it wasn't really important, but it was something to say.

There was something that prodded at the back of her mind. "So that's why you changed your mind," Fura commented, just now realizing that this must have been why he'd so quickly changed his mind about the town days ago.

"Trust me, I really didn't want to stop. The only reason we're here is because I knew we wouldn't make another town in time."

Of all the questions she'd built up and stored the last few days, Fura found that she was falling short. "So, buildings are safe?" she threw out just to keep the conversation going, all the while trying to make sense of the situation.

Kiyani shook his head. "If you were in some abandoned shack in the middle of nowhere, you would have the same chance of survival as if you were out wandering the woods alone. Next to nothing. They generally stay out of the towns, but anything out in the open is free range."

"Then why are they here?" Fura asked, flinching as another scream pierced the night. A new victim.

"Because there are still meals to be had. Anyone unruly like that is thrown out and sacrificed. Some towns actually use it as a chance to free up the prisons."

Fura looked at him, disgust in her eyes. "That's sick!" She was just beginning to gain ground on what exactly this Hunt meant for this world and the people in it.

Kiyani just shrugged, unfazed by the matter. "Here, it's a way of life."

"So, are they where werewolves came from?" It was the closest thing that she could categorize them as from what little she'd unfortunately seen.

"Probably not," Kiyani answered, shaking his head again. "These are a bit different."

"How so?" As much as Fura really didn't want to add detail to what she'd already seen outside, the ongoing conversation helped keep her fear at bay.

"These have wings."

"They can fly?!" It was pitch black outside. Wings hadn't been present in the one image she had managed to get of them.

"Afraid so. There are three different types too... one is a large, hairy, human-like wolf, like your werewolves. The second is more squat and cat-like, and the third is a large snake." He listed off the types methodically, as if reading from a text book.

"Like your tattoo..."

Kiyani subconsciously reached to the back of his neck. "Yeah..."

Though Fura cringed, realizing that this was the first she had ever actually mentioned his tattoo, Kiyani said nothing more. Then again, she knew Kiyani had to have been aware that she'd seen it.

"How do you know?" Fura asked, trying to keep the conversation going. "Have they been through Frielana before?"

"No, only heard and read of them. They don't pass through Frielana because it's one of the Lord's. A part of the pact we have with them, I believe."

There was another scream outside, followed by a beast-like snarl.

"I guess you'll be cleaning that up tomorrow," Fura said faintly, referring to the ruckus outside. The sarcasm was an attempt to hide her fear, though it was poorly executed, the complacent mask cracked by her shaking voice.

"They're won't be much to clean."

52

⁜

THE BARD IN THE BAR

The screeching and shrieking of ravens ascending upon a meal startled Fura into awareness.

Sitting up in response to the noise, she rubbed her eyes and looked to the gray dawn that filtered through the window. She didn't know how much time had passed, nor when she'd managed to fall into a fitful sleep filled with nightmares, but night was over. Stretching her aching muscles, Fura recalled that she had fallen asleep curled into a ball and wrapped in the protective cage of Kiyani's arms. The memory of it almost felt like a dream, especially as she took in Kiyani's prostrate form beside her.

Stretched out on his side, one arm stuffed under the pillow with his back to her, it was hard to tell if the birds had woken him as well, or if he somehow remained asleep through the terrible ruckus.

Cringing at the sound of the feathered scavengers, she glanced out the window again, just catching a glimpse of dark wings charcoaled against the shadowed clouds.

Carrion crows.

As they continued to squawk in delight, Fura knew she didn't want to know what they were feasting on.

"Cursed birds," Kiyani grumbled, rolling over as he was finally woken by the noise.

Watching him dig himself deeper into the blankets to block out the growing light and the commotion of the crows, Fura knew there was still plenty of time for sleep. Despite the need, she knew she wouldn't be able to get anymore rest, even if she tried.

After what she'd glimpsed out the window, she didn't know how she had managed to get any sleep at all. Just thinking about the bone-chilling animalistic howls and ghastly growls that had dotted the darkness for hours sent shivers down her spine. She hadn't even gotten a good look at the beasts, but that hadn't kept her imagination at bay as it had attempted to fill in the blanks with frightening faces and features. Especially after Kiyani had mentioned the wings. That had only brought more terrifying images of them flying through the second floor windows.

Glancing over her shoulder at the unlit candle that sat on the dresser, Fura recalled thinking that lighting it would cause the beasts to do just that. As much as she'd feared the darkness, she had feared the possibility of attracting their attention just as much.

"Are they going to come back?" Fura asked, hoping Kiyani hadn't fallen back asleep. "The Werebeasts..." she added, the fear that was associated with the term causing her to fumble over the words.

Kiyani had claimed during her short briefing of the creature's history that what'd occurred the night before was a once a year event. True or not, Fura needed to hear it again. If not to verify the information, then to reaffirm that it hadn't simply been a horrific dream.

Looking at him, Fura waited for an answer. Though his eyes were closed, she had a feeling that he was still awake. He couldn't have slept much better than she had, yet she was beginning to wonder if he slept at all.

It seemed that whenever she found herself awake at night, lying there and counting shadows, Kiyani was awake as well. No matter what odd hour of the night it might have been. Most of the time he simply lay there, his eyes closed to the world, listening. Resting, maybe, but not sleeping. Yet, for all Fura knew it was simply a tactic of his to keep her from asking questions.

"Kiyani?" Fura prodded lightly, needing to hear something from him.

Opening an eye, he looked at her. "No," he answered simply. Seeming to know that his chance for rest was over, Kiyani pulled himself up to a sitting position and looked around the room as if judging what time it was. Knowing that she wouldn't be satisfied with such a short reply, he continued sleepily before she could ask anything else. "If they did, they would be violating law."

"Law?" Fura had never heard of these creatures before, let alone knew the rules they were meant to abide by.

"Yes," Kiyani said, running a hand through his hair. "The race might be a couple hundred years old, but they're bound by a pact created by the Sect of Seven. Once a year, they're allowed to hunt freely, to feast on human flesh. The rest of the year, they're forced to spend scavenging like rats."

"You sound like you sympathize with them," Fura said warily as she watched him. She wondered where the sentiment was coming from, recalling that he'd claimed to have never seen them before.

"I don't. I pray I never see them again in my lifetime. However, it's the reality of the situation. What you saw last night might not be right, but it keeps the carnage to a minimum. There was a time, not that long ago, that they used to run rampant."

"Oh…" was all Fura could manage to utter, unable to think of anything else. Just how many more creatures were out there, with rules and histories all their own? How many of these things would they run across as time wasted on?

It was bad enough that Fura knew so little of this world, but she was trying to learn. What she hadn't expected was that this strange realm of Izandüre would be so dangerous. Though she had apparently been born to the realm, Fura wondered if maybe her father hadn't been in the wrong to squirrel her away in Barandor.

Though she still wanted to ask him face to face why he'd done it, it was the first time she had seen reason in his decision.

Telling herself that, real family or not, she'd still had a nice childhood, Fura couldn't help but recall her conversation with Kiyani from the night of the kiss. He may have kept it from her with relative ease, but now that it had been brought into the open, she could see the smallest wince in his face as the scars etched into his back pulled with movement. The practiced maneuver of someone who had grown used to pain. She knew she couldn't do anything about the scars, nor the pain that plagued him because of them, but she still felt bad that he'd been put through so much torture.

In a way, it helped to explain why he was so apt to push her away. He'd already been hurt by life. In more ways than one, she assumed.

Casting the thoughts away, Fura closed her eyes, listening to Kiyani rise from the bed and move towards the dresser.

Thinking back to the man in the tavern the night before, she realized, despite her initial frustration with him, why he'd gained her attention. Unlike Kiyani, his bright-eyed demeanor and loud voice reminded her of the festivities in Fireswell. The warm spirit the place held. He may have been distracting, but that was exactly what she could have used right now.

"Did you happen to notice the bard in the tavern yesterday?" Fura asked, posing the question simply to change the topic.

"Not that I'm aware."

Turning away from the window, Fura moved to sit on the edge of the bed, swinging her legs. It was easy to see that it was much more exciting for her than it was him. Even so, she continued the conversation.

"You should talk to him."

Kiyani leaned on the dresser, silently regarding her. "And just why would I do that?"

Fura shrugged. "Why not?" She'd heard from Wanda the night before that those in the tavern would be among the few working, the others taking the day after the Hunt as a holiday. It wasn't fair in her mind, nor had she asked Kiyani to confirm, but she could guess by the fact that he was still present that he was free from work duty for the day. "Maybe he might know something about the Witneis."

"Or, he might not," Kiyani replied, his voice colder than Fura would have expected given the topic of conversation.

"It's not like you have anything else to do today."

"I'm sure I can find something."

Fura looked at him with question. He'd said he hadn't seen the man, right? "Why are you so against a man you've never met?"

"Don't ever trust a bard," Kiyani gruffed.

"Why?" she asked, not understanding Kiyani's problem. "I thought he was kind of entertaining."

Kiyani shook his head as if the answer should have been obvious. "Exactly. He's a bard... they make shit up for a living. You think they would be half as entertaining if they told the truth?"

Fura sighed. It was a typical Kiyani answer. She shouldn't have expected anything less. Glancing out the window to where the light was growing on the horizon, she knew work was approaching fast. "Just think about it."

✧⌘✧

Sitting outside, clutching a cup of tea he'd managed to pilfer from the kitchen, Kiyani listened to the cheerful melodies of the songbirds. The small sliver of peace was all he could ask of the morning, yet it felt hard-won. Sunlight flooded the streets, but it wasn't enough to wash away the fear that still clung to Skirvynmire in the wake of the recent Werebeast visit.

"It seems surreal, doesn't it?"

Kiyani barely moved, only peering over his shoulder to verify that it was Aldam.

He'd hoped that his brief conversation with the man that morning would have sated the Magisard's curiosity, but he hadn't counted on it. A simple vie for wanting to be outside had ended in Aldam offering him the use of the second floor balcony of the tavern. It wasn't quite what Kiyani had hoped for, but with a day of canceled work, it beat the alternative of being cooped up in the tavern.

Kiyani shrugged, knowing the man expected some kind of response. "The world goes on." It was true, and as harsh of a fact as it was, it was one that Kiyani had grown used to.

"That it does," Aldam solemnly agreed. Moving to pull up a chair, he seemed to rethink that option, instead opting to lean on the balcony rail. "You know," he mused, "most never even see them," he said, speaking of the Werebeasts. "Only hear the screams in the middle of the night."

"That's enough," Kiyani said. He had already known what they looked like, what the species was known for, but he still wished that he hadn't seen them the night before. Or, at the least, that Fura had remained naïve. Even if she'd only glimpsed them through the second-story window, it had been more than enough. Surely, she would have nightmares for days to come – a side effect that he would be left to deal with, because whether he liked it or not, he would be the only one present to comfort her. It wasn't a job he looked forward to, especially when no one had ever been there to offer the same to him. How could he reciprocate an emotion he'd never been granted?

"You know," Aldam said, breaking his meandering thoughts, "I wouldn't have taken you for a tea drinker."

"Most people don't take me as a lot of things."

"People are funny like that."

Glancing out over the waking town, Kiyani didn't find that 'funny' was the word for it. Granted, he wasn't overly fond of the man intruding on his silence, either. What appeared a simple conversation was a façade for other things.

"I assume you came out here to make sure I wasn't burning down the town." He didn't bother to phrase it as a question, or sugar-coat the obvious.

Turning, the man's face fell, as if he'd been given the word that he no longer had to keep up pretenses.

"Simply doing my job. You can't really blame me when strangers roll into town."

Aldam's words reminded Kiyani of the confusion present on Fura's face the other night when she'd asked him if people really thought that lowly of newcomers. What they'd experienced thus far was only a fraction of what they could have been dealt. Then again, there was still time.

Knowing that there must be blood staining the grass somewhere in the town, Kiyani was well aware that those shallow remains from the night before could have easily been them in the right circumstances.

"If I may ask," Kiyani said, testing the waters. "Why such harsh measurements?"

"These are harsh times," Aldam replied curtly.

"Surely not enough to treat travelers with such disdain."

"You may be aware of the unrest in the west?"

"Maybe we're running from it," Kiyani declared, wondering if he was speaking of the Firelord's downfall, or if something else had happened that he wasn't aware of.

Aldam fixed him with an unreadable stare. "Maybe, in running from it, you also bring it with you."

Kiyani watched as the man turned away, leaving him at a loss for words. Without hardly ever speaking to one another, Aldam had echoed one of his own fears. The night Nevo had found him was still fresh in his mind. *"He'll always find you,"* he'd said. Just how true was that? Just how long would they be hunted?

Pausing in the threshold, Aldam gave him one last lingering glance. "I ask that you refrain from causing any trouble today."

As the man disappeared back into the building, Kiyani wondered if that was even possible.

With both Aldam's and Fura's words lingering in his mind, Kiyani discovered that the peace he'd initially sought wasn't much of an option. Usually he relished the quiet, preferring to stay far away from others. Yet, the solitude of the open air only left him to reflect on conversations that he'd rather of not had in the first place.

Given the few options open to him, Kiyani didn't know how he could make the day worthwhile, only that sitting by himself wasn't it. The mug he'd abandoned to the porch railing after Aldam had taken his leave now sat half filled with cold tea, gathering dust in the sunlight. Overhearing the din of voices from below, he knew the tavern was likely packed. It was the last place he could have wanted to be in this town, yet listening to the canter reminded him of Fura's last words.

He didn't know what she expected him to glean from such a man as a traveling storyteller. From his few prior experiences, he already knew that they were liars and con artists, only out for coin. Fura could listen to the mysterious man all she wanted, but Kiyani had no use for him.

What he did need, he discovered with the raging growl of his stomach, was food. Whether he wanted to talk to the man or not, he was still going to be forced to reside in the same room. Resigning himself to that fact, Kiyani rose from his chair and looked out over the town one last time before grabbing his cold drink and heading back inside.

Moments later, he gingerly made his way down to the tavern. Dropping off the mug he had taken earlier, he took to the table in the corner again, surprised to see that there was even a seat left. As expected, despite the early hour, the place was nearly packed to the brim. With hardly a soul working, it was easy to see that the *Mead Mill*, with food and drink aplenty, was the favored hang out of the town.

Taking in the rowdy bunch, talking and laughing loudly, he thought once again that no one would ever know about the events from the night before given the atmosphere in the room. But that was exactly what this holiday was meant for – to forget.

Settling in and hoping that no one asked to share his table, Kiyani ordered a meal when the waitress came by.

Expecting the high volume of traffic, it wasn't long before she returned with food and drink in hand. Nor did she stay long to chat before she was off to attend to another customer. It was fine with Kiyani. Even Fura, whom he saw briefly out of the corner of his eye, her red hair a beacon in the crowd, only offered a quick wave before she was whisked away to another task, much to Kiyani's relief.

After such a sordid week, he hardly knew what to say to her anymore. It was bad enough that he'd initially panicked and claimed they were married. Every time Aldam or Wanda mentioned the term *wife* it threw him off momentarily. Too late to revise that blunder, he begrudgingly went along with it.

As if that wasn't bad enough, then he'd had to incite that kiss the other night. Though he tried to put it out of his mind, he still didn't even know how exactly it had happened, nor did he want to. Only that it didn't need to happen again.

He knew Fura was still filled with questions from that incident. Questions that he had no idea how to answer.

If anything, the Werebeasts and the Hunt left him in the clear for a little while, certain Fura would question him on that first given the chance.

Everything aside, he paid no particular interest to his surroundings. Even his food went untouched after a few bites. Instead, he aimlessly fiddled with the glass of water he'd requested, trying not to think too hard about how people might see him.

As a matter of fact, Kiyani knew that no one would look at him twice, let alone assess him as a threat based on his appearance and actions. Already, he was nothing new, just another fixture on a bar stool. He'd left his weapons back in the room, having no need for them in such a place, not to mention he was sure Aldam would prefer he didn't carry them on his person. He hadn't even taken any real pride in getting dressed, forgoing any fancy attire given to him by the Fae Queen and sticking with the loose shirt he'd been wearing out in the field. If anything, any passersby would mistake him as the town drunk.

Fine with me, he thought, nearly laughing at the image.

Staring at the wall across the way, Kiyani listened to bits and pieces of conversation, seeking anything of use. Talk was varied, as were the speakers – menial tellings… worries about family… about the crops. There was nothing about the Shadowlord's sudden move, nor anything about the fate of Frielana. He wondered just how long it would be before the news reached the outlying areas.

Even the Hunt was only mentioned now and then in hushed whispers.

The Hunt.

If there was anything in this world he would have rather kept from Fura's knowledge that would have been it. It was bad enough that she knew of it now, but she'd also caught a glimpse of the beasts.

The land taken by Apallo as his home as Firelord was endowed as sacred and off-limits to the Werebeasts. Though Kiyani had never taken it as an ideal living situation, living in Frielana for most of his young life had meant that he'd never witnessed firsthand the terror, sick anticipation, and worry that the Hunt brought. He'd never had to lock himself indoors on that one night, hoping that their keen noses wouldn't sniff him out. Even with a dedicated night to run free, the Werebeasts still had limits, only able to hunt what was out in the open. However, that didn't keep them from sniffing through doors and cracks in poorly structured buildings. Though the beasts may have gone, the danger over, deep gouges from deadly claws and teeth could still be found the day after in whatever had stood in their way.

Even with being sheltered from the murderous Werebeast rampage for so many years, Kiyani couldn't believe that he'd nearly forgotten about it altogether. The date was the same, year after year. Though he had never been taught to put much stock in it, it was a date that people outside of the sacred lands learned to dread from the time they could talk.

He'd nearly put both Fura and himself in danger. No Reln hollow would have protected them from that… though he did have something that would deter the beasts if presented. Yet, rubbing the back of his neck where his tattoo resided, he knew it wasn't a card he wanted to play.

Leaning forward in his chair, Kiyani sighed. As stupid as it had been, there was no use beating himself up over it. They had escaped that danger… this year, at least. This time next year, he had no desire to still be hauling Fura around.

Dawdling with the silverware before him, Kiyani began to fiddle with his food again. Even if he wasn't nearly as hungry as he'd thought up on the balcony, he knew he had to eat something.

Fork in hand, he was just about to vie for a second attempt at his dinner when a figure caught his eye. Across the room a man sat, staring. Kiyani told himself that it was someone else the man was interested in, but a nonchalant survey of the room verified the feeling in his gut. He was the sole focus of the man's intent gaze.

It was easy to tell that, like Kiyani, this man also wasn't from Skirvynmire. Dressed in dark tones, bordering on black, the man stood out among the earthen tones the people of the town seemed to favor. He looked even more out of place than Kiyani currently felt.

Like Kiyani, he occupied a table by himself, seemingly drawn to the shadows, even amidst a vibrant room. His hands, sheathed in a pair of thick, black leather gloves, cupped a glass of half-downed amber liquid. Repeatedly clenching his fists, he appeared to have something far more sinister on his mind than having an aimless drink in the middle of the day at a strange tavern. No food rested before him, declaring that hunger hadn't brought him in either. Only a hunger for what looked like vengeance.

Kiyani held his gaze for only a fleeting moment before casually returning his focus to the rest of the room. Scanning the layout of the room, noting the number of people that currently resided within the building's lower half, he scratched his neck, hoping that his actions would come across as not having really noticed the man. However, his mind was racing, wondering what to do.

The noise in the room was overwhelming, but Kiyani suddenly found himself thankful for the amount of people. The sheer number of witnesses had to be enough to keep the man from doing anything rash. Or so he hoped. It should've been a soothing fact, yet he was just as anxious as ever. As much as Kiyani wanted to casually walk out, leaving the room and the busy suffocation of it, to go back upstairs, he knew it wasn't a good idea. He had a good feeling that the man would only follow suit, leaving him in a far worse predicament.

No, Kiyani knew it was best to stay put and pretend the man's presence didn't bother him. At least for now. A crowded room was better than a dark and empty hallway.

Appearing to decide on a course of action, the dark clad stranger suddenly rose from the table, his glass now sitting empty. Kiyani tensed as the man began to deliberately make his way towards him, his eyes shadowed, darkness seeming to cling to him like an invisible shroud.

Halfway across the room, the man suddenly paused as Fura plopped herself down in the chair across from Kiyani.

"Did you talk to the bard yet?" she asked, sounding out of breath.

"No," Kiyani replied. Keeping his head down, he watched the man warily through the curtain of his hair, waiting for his next move.

Seeming to sense that his moment had passed, the stranger appeared to change his mind. Throwing one last dark glance Kiyani's way, one that Kiyani met full on this time, and that forebodingly announced that they'd be seeing one another again soon, he strode out the door, heavy black boots clodding noisily on the floor.

"Why not?" Fura asked, unaware of what was going on behind her.

It wasn't until the door closed on the man that Kiyani let out a long breath that he hadn't been aware he'd been holding. "I told you, I don't plan on bothering."

Fura gave him a stern look that wasn't like her. "You'd rather kill someone with a fork?" she said, nodding to the utensil he gripped tightly in his hand.

Looking down, Kiyani set it next to his plate, cursing himself for panicking yet again. What was happening to him all of a sudden?

"Fura! We need you!" Wanda announced as she flashed by, sloshing overfilled drinks onto the floor.

As she sighed, Kiyani could briefly see just how much waitressing was wearing her down. Quickly rising from the chair, Fura only glanced at him before walking away without a word. Watching her blend into the crowd, he knew that any appetite he might have had beforehand was now completely gone.

Arguing with himself, Kiyani tried to pinpoint all the reasons that Fura was wrong in her assumption. He may not have seen the man in question the day before, but it hadn't taken him long to hone in on the bard today. Fura had never mentioned what he looked like, but details aside, the man's booming voice echoing off the tavern walls was more than enough to draw Kiyani's attention. The lute by his side was another sure fire sign, though he had yet to see the man pick up the instrument. For all Kiyani knew the man didn't even play, simply using it for show. From what he'd seen from afar, the man preferred to simply recite stories to his adoring and growing crowd, dotting his spoken landscape with jovial laughs and flamboyant hand gestures.

Keeping a keen eye on the tavern door, Kiyani waited, wondering if the devious stranger would make a return. The man couldn't have known that Fura would only stay at his table for a few minutes. So, even if he did make a return, it probably wouldn't be anytime soon. Though Kiyani hoped he wouldn't see the man again, he had a feeling that wouldn't be the case. The lingering glance he had sent his way had almost guaranteed a second meeting. One that would likely be far more deadly.

Looking to the amount of people gathered around the bard, Kiyani sighed. He didn't care for such people, but the throng of listeners could easily act as a safety net. Even if the stranger came back, he wouldn't be as keen to approach Kiyani with so many potential witnesses.

Abandoning his half finished plate, he laid down a few coins. Gathering up his drink, he made his way to the other side of the tavern, doing his best to keep from bumping rudely into people.

Trying to avoid the bulk of the crowd, he found an empty stool and took a seat, leaning against the wall behind him. Not all that interested in the man's tales, he stared off into the distance, only half listening to his words. Sitting across the way, he'd sought out any conversations that might have been of importance. Here, the only thing he could hear was this man's booming voice and the crowd's excited reaction to his word-weaver's tongue.

Though he remained for safety reasons, Kiyani kept a careful watch on the door, feeling with each passing moment that he was simply wasting the day away. The longer he sat there, the more he almost wished that he'd been out in the field working. At least that gave him something to do. His only saving grace was that Maven wasn't breathing down his neck. Even better was that he hadn't seen the man at all since his departure the night before.

Knowing there was no way he could fall asleep amidst such clamor, Kiyani closed his eyes, blocking out the world.

He didn't know how much time had passed when he was brought back to the present. Opening his eyes, he could see that the number of individuals surrounding the bard might have thinned a bit, but the tavern was still relatively packed. Yet, it wasn't the crowd he was interested in. He was certain that the man had made mention of a tree.

Leaning forward on the stool, he listened, catching what sounded like the last verses of a hastily written sonnet.

There stands a tree,
So tall you hardly see,
The branches that touch the sky.

Yet, attempt to find, you'll surely die.

Intrigue and danger, wrapped in one.
It's time, however, is certainly done.
So, pay no mind.

Search, and death you'll find.

But those that reach the prize,
Gleaned only with pure eyes,
Will come to discover,

That what they sought was nothing other,
Than what was already known...

To them,
To all,

The future, written in the past.
Tales of tomorrow that can never last.

As the man finished his shoddy ballad, his words trailing off, the tavern burst into another round of applause and praise. Rolling his eyes, Kiyani watched as the man took a bow.

Just as he'd expected, there was nothing to be found. Only made up tales and riddles that left questions unanswered.

Regardless, he slid off the stool and moved in closer. If anything, he could appease Fura by saying that he had spoken to the man.

Lingering as the crowd thinned considerably, Kiyani waited until the man sat down to take a break from his adoring fan base before moseying up behind him. "You spoke of a tree," he declared simply, forgoing any formalities.

Looking up at him, the man smiled over the rim of his beer. "Aye. The Tree of Knowledge."

"Would that be the same as the Witneis Reln?" Kiyani asked, getting straight to the point. He didn't trust this man any further than he could throw him, or any others like him.

"Mayhaps," the bard said with a shrug. "Mayhaps, not."

Kiyani groaned. Fura may have found the man charming with his stories, but this was why he preferred to keep his distance. These men spoke in riddles, telling tales that often weren't true. His mind was filled with doubt that he would be able to get anything of worth here. Yet, as much as he would have liked to turn right around and return to his room where peace and quiet could be found, Kiyani could still feel the eyes of the dark clothed man watching him, even though he had failed to return. To go back to the second floor where no one else could be found would be stupid at this point. Irritating or not, he knew his best bet was to remain among the crowd of people surrounding this storyteller.

Ignoring Kiyani's reaction, the man leaned back in his chair and propped his feet on the seat next to him. Gesturing to another chair beside him, the bard invited Kiyani to sit.

Begrudgingly, he took the offer.

"Rowan McVaar," the man declared, offering a hand.

Though Kiyani shook the man's hand, he didn't offer his own name in return.

"The Witneis Reln, you say?" Rowan continued. "I haven't heard that name in a long time. So few know of it."

"Right," Kiyani agreed. "So, what do *you* know about it?"

Taking a swig of his beer, Rowan shrugged, almost appearing embarrassed by the topic of conversation. "Honestly, not much. I've never seen it in person, nor do I know anyone who even knows its location. It remains just as much of a tall tale today as whenever it first came into mention."

"How useful."

"If it does exist, I can only imagine that the gods don't want it known."

Rising from his seat, Kiyani made to leave. He knew this wasn't going to get him anywhere. "Thanks for nothing," he mumbled.

"All that anyone who's even heard the name knows is, *the knowledge lies within the words of knowledge.*"

Kiyani turned, silently regarding the man. "A riddle…"

Dropping his feet back to the ground, Rowan leaned forward, peering into the froth of his beer as if trying to glean further information. "I know it's not much," he admitted. "I wish I could offer you more, but that's all I know. Why so interested?"

"Not really your business."

"No, I suppose it's not. But, you strike me as someone who might actually be looking for the thing. All I've got to say is that you should be wary. The few tales that I know describe the tree and the land it sits upon to glow with ethereal beauty, but the lands around it are said to be dark and dangerous. Many have gone in search of it, but few have returned. And those that have, never did find what they were looking for. The small handful that did claim to find it were scarred from the experience, both mentally and physically. I don't know what you seek it for, but I'd think twice about it if I were you."

Rowan's concern sounded genuine enough, yet Kiyani couldn't help but be offended by his words. The sentiment of some stranger wasn't going to deter him.

"I'm not you."

Turning on his heel, he walked away, all the while wondering just what Apallo had been thinking to send Fura on such a journey.

53
•• ✧ ••
CAST INTO THE NIGHT

Slipping into the room on aching feet, Fura did her best to stay as quiet as possible. She didn't know exactly when Kiyani had returned to the room, nor how long he'd been resting, but from the darkness shrouding the space and his still form sprawled on the bed, she guessed it had been awhile.

Closing the door, she realized that the interior of the room wasn't nearly as dark as she'd first thought. In fact, it was no more shadowed than the hallway that had led her there. A single candle, burned down to a small nub, still shed just enough of a flickering light to see by. Even so, Fura managed to stub her toe on the corner of the dresser. Again. Though she kept the curses to herself, the scrape of the disturbed furniture across the wood floor was enough to rouse Kiyani.

"That's the second time you've done that this week," Kiyani declared, though he'd barely moved.

Fura only glared at him as she moved across the room. She didn't want to admit that he was right. Especially when it shouldn't have happened the first time, let alone again. There was hardly a speck of furniture in the place.

Plopping herself down onto the corner of the bed, she slipped her shoes off and rubbed her tired feet. "It's not fair that you didn't have to work today," she huffed.

"I don't make the rules," Kiyani offered groggily.

Looking back at him, Fura wondered just how long he had been sleeping, or had allowed himself to sleep. She had assumed when she had first entered the room that he'd been pretending, as he had so many times before. However, the tired drawl of his voice gave her reason to believe that she'd just woken him, leaving him clinging to semi-consciousness.

"It's still not fair."

"Field work was canceled today. Not much I can do about that."

"I was aware. But I had to slave away all day, working harder than usual because of the extra people, and you got to spend the day

452

napping."

"You know very well I didn't lie in bed all day. I spent half the day listening to your over-dramatic bard."

"Aldam could've had you work the tavern as well," Fura argued, though she was actually impressed that he'd done as she'd suggested.

"As I've said before, I'm certain that he doesn't want us working together. He separated us in the first place for a reason."

"Then he could have made you work and given me the day off."

"The fact that you're bitching to me about it now means that you made it through the day."

"You're mean."

"Truthful," Kiyani reminded her, echoing one of their previous conversations. "Besides, the way Aldam talks to me, you'd think he expected me to poison the town. So I doubt he would have let me anywhere near food that was being served."

Fura sighed as she dropped the conversation and looked out the window. She didn't know why she always put herself through this. No matter what she found to argue about, Kiyani could always reason his way out of it. And though she was sure that at least some of it was eloquently fabricated bullshit, it sounded plausible.

The truth of the matter was that as much as she had resented catching glimpses of him sitting in the tavern – when he hadn't been elsewhere – as she'd been scurrying about, she knew that he'd been working as well. She had heard the bard speaking of an array of things the day before, but today she was certain that she'd heard him mention a tree of great importance. Whether Kiyani believed in what the man did or not, she knew that he had hoped the same thing: that this grand tree the man spoke of was one in the same as the Witneis Reln that they were now hunting down.

Fura wanted to ask all about it, as she had seen Kiyani speaking with the man – something that she knew he had to have done with much reluctance. Yet, despite her argument, she also knew that whatever sleep Kiyani had managed to get in her absence had been much needed. She only wished she could have done the same.

After a night like the one before, the cries of the Werebeasts still echoing in her head, she could've used it.

"So," she mused aloud, hoping that it would come off as casual conversation. "How did you sleep?"

Kiyani opened an eye, as if questioning where that inquiry had come from. "Fine, I guess. Same as every other time I sleep."

"Right."

"What is that supposed to mean?" Kiyani asked, propping himself up on his elbows.

"You don't talk about yourself much, but there are things that I can't help but notice just from being around you, and one of those is that you don't sleep worth shit."

"I'd advise you to stay out of other people's business," Kiyani said darkly.

Fura looked back at him, taking in the shadow of his form in the half light. She could tell by his tense posture that he wasn't overly fond of this particular conversation. Then again, he tended to avoid anything involving himself.

"The mental health of my only traveling companion kind of is my business."

"Mental health…" Kiyani scoffed. "Is that all Apallo ever spoke to you of when he pulled you aside? Listing all my misgivings?"

"No," Fura answered truthfully. "All he ever told me was to stay away from you."

"Maybe you should have listened."

"You're not as bad as you make yourself out to be."

"How do you know?"

Shirking away from his tone, Fura returned her focus to the darkened town outside the window. The truth was that she didn't know for certain that her father hadn't been right about Kiyani. It didn't matter. What did was keeping Kiyani on her side, and delving into such conversations wouldn't help his set view of her. Telling herself not to dig a deeper hole, she remained quiet, even as she felt the bed shift as Kiyani sat up and leaned against the wall.

It wasn't until the candle burned out some time later that she finally spoke again.

"I'm hungry," she sighed, her eyes fighting to refocus with the sudden shift of light.

Though it hadn't been that long since she'd left the tavern behind, Fura had made it a point to get out of there as quickly as possible when Wanda had finally released her from work. She hadn't wanted to give the woman time to think of anything else that needed to be done. Unfortunately, between that and being busy all throughout the day, Fura only now realized that she hadn't taken the time to eat dinner. Her light snacking between the heaviest loads of work on small hunks of bread and the occasional shred of pork seemed to have accounted to very little, her stomach reminding her of the fact with a protesting grumble.

"Well, you're going to have to get used to it," Kiyani said, his voice gruff in the darkness. Though his tone was still weary, Fura could still detect that level of underlying anger left over from a few nights back.

"Why, 'cause they don't serve food all day?" Fura asked, trying to ignore it. Working in the only building in the town that could be considered a restaurant, she knew that to be true. Though she had a feeling that if she wanted to go down in the middle of the night and try to rustle something up, she wouldn't necessarily be turned away.

"That, and there's going to a lot of times out there," Kiyani began, nodding to the darkness beyond the window, "that there's not going to be much food. Scavenging can only get you so far. Sometimes, it can be days before you eat."

"You really don't want me to come with you, do you?" Fura asked. She couldn't believe he was pulling that card again so soon. After his last attempt, Fura had been sure that he'd finally given it up. She had blatantly resisted his numerous offers to direct her back to Barandor, and after learning of Apallo's relation to her, there was no way that she could leave this world now. Not even if she wanted to, and there had been more than a few times she had yearned for home.

Glancing his way, she found that he'd turned his attention toward her, his eyes seeming to wonder what had prompted that of all questions. "Why do you say that?"

"Because, you're constantly pointing out all the negatives of being out here. Here in the world *you* live in. Can't you think of one positive?"

"What if there are none?" Kiyani asked, giving her something to contemplate.

His blue eyes on her, he waited for an answer.

"There must be," Fura said. She just couldn't figure out what it was with him. No simple answer was ever enough. "People go hiking and camping in the great outdoors for a reason."

"Because they know they can go back to the place they call home."

Resting her head on her arm, Fura stared hazily at the wall. She wanted to throttle him some days, but for such a pessimistic person, he was rather level-minded. If she had a question, he had an answer... even if he didn't always feel like replying, even if she didn't like the answer, and though she hated to admit it, he was right.

Where was home now?

Unable to look him in the eye, Fura turned back to the window. Though the room had gone dark, she discovered that her eyes had adjusted enough to make out the hazy shapes of the town below. She hadn't understood beforehand why Kiyani often staked out the spot at the end of the bed, but now she saw its appeal. Sitting there in the darkness was reminiscent of being a shadow. People hardly ever looked up, therefore no one ever saw you as you watched like a hawk the happenings below.

Not expecting to see anything of interest at such a late hour, Fura was surprised to see movement on the street leading into the main square. A single individual, out for a late night stroll, or late in returning home, might not have raised suspicion, but a line of four men spanned the roadway, all walking in unison.

Squinting, Fura leaned closer to the window to get a better look. She didn't know who these people were or why they were out at this hour, but she had a bad feeling.

Not one of the men stuck out with any distinguishing features. All of them were dressed in dark colors, swords hanging at their belts. It wasn't until the stray light of the moon caught the small amount of inlaid silver on their uniforms that Fura let out a squeak.

It can't be...

"Kiyani..." Fura said, her voice barely more than a whisper.

He only grunted in response, an indication that he still didn't feel like talking to her.

"Kiyani," she pleaded. "You need to see this." Glancing over her shoulder, Fura could see that even from what was visible in the weak light, his face was unreadable. "Please tell me this isn't what I think it is."

Though he seemed apt to ignore her, the growing fear in her voice gave him reason to scoot over to the window to at least give her the benefit of the doubt.

Peering outside, Kiyani instantly tensed. There was hardly enough time to ask what was wrong before he turned to her, a look of intensity replacing the indifference in his eyes.

"Hurry up and pack your things," he declared, his voice a harsh whisper.

Startled, Fura found herself unable to move, let alone follow his orders. "Who are they?"

"Shadowguard," Kiyani said, confirming her suspicion as he swiftly jumped from the bed. His feet quietly hitting the floor, he shot around the room like a ghostly shadow, taking up any of their belongings that had strayed from their bags.

Forcing her shaking limbs to comply, Fura followed suit, though where he was racing, she felt as if she were moving in slow motion, unable to keep up. All she could hear was the sound of her heart beating frantically in her chest. It wasn't meant to end like this.

Filling one bag, Kiyani dropped it into her arms, leaving her to stand awkwardly in the center of the room.

"What are we going to do?" Fura stammered, watching him pull on his boots.

Grabbing for his sword that had leaned against the side of the dresser since they'd arrived, Kiyani pointed to her shoes, trying to get her to move faster. "Get out of here."

Swallowing her anxiety, she moved over to the bed on wooden limbs. "But, Aldam said we have to stay here a week."

Kiyani shook his head. "It doesn't matter anymore. If the Shadowguard are here, it means they know where we're at. Stay in this room and we'll be captured for sure."

Putting her first shoe on the wrong foot, Fura struggled to fix her mistake. "You don't think Aldam will cover for us?"

The town of Skirvynmire might not have given them the warmest of welcomes, but now that they were faced with no other choice, Fura didn't want to leave. She hadn't formed any attachment to the small village, but she didn't fancy returning to living in the woods so soon, either.

"No," Kiyani replied. "There's no reason he should. We're essentially trespassers here. Why would he protect us? Besides, you don't argue with the Shadowguard."

"He might…"

Scanning the room one last time, Kiyani turned to her. "If you want to stay here, then stay. But, I'm leaving."

Watching him stride towards the door, Fura felt a strong sense of déjà vu, his words nearly identical to the ones he had spoken the night of the siege. Taking a breath, she knew her path was already laid out for her.

She had trusted him then, and it had gotten them this far. She felt she had no other choice but to trust him yet again.

Moving out into the hallway, deserted the same as any other night, Fura followed closely behind Kiyani. Though her feet itched to take off at a dead run, to race down the stairs and away from this town that no longer offered safety, she remained by Kiyani's side. Slowly, he inched away from the room and eased the door shut. Fura didn't know what his plan of action was, or how he could remain so calm in these situations, but she knew better than to question his motives. Though he had his moments, more often than not, he was right.

Only when he began to move away from the stairs that would return them to the first floor did she begin to wonder if he had a plan at all. Grabbing his shoulder, she looked at him with a raised brow, pointing to the stairway behind them.

Shaking his head, Kiyani pointed to the opposite end of the hall, where faint moonlight streamed through a small window, offering the only natural light in the space. "If we went that way, we'd run right into them," he whispered.

"Then how do we get out?" Fura asked, staring at the window. He did know they were on the second floor, right?

"This place used to be a mill," Kiyani explained as he continued to inch forward, giving Fura no choice but to follow if she wanted to be able to hear him. "The water wheel may no longer be in use, but it's still there."

The water wheel.

Fura had only caught a glimpse of it when they had first come into Skirvynmire. Hearing him mention it now made her wonder if he'd been planning escape from the beginning. All this time, she had thought he was simply obeying Aldam's orders, dealing with Maven's uncalled for crudeness. Yet, behind that aloof façade, he'd been calculating all along.

Even so, as they approached, Fura had to ask herself just what he had in mind.

It may have been an alternate escape route, but the window was still small, and two stories above ground. If it was their only option, it wasn't any less dangerous.

As she watched Kiyani fiddle with a latch that looked like it hadn't been opened in ages, Fura heard voices rise from the tavern below. Though the dining area had been busier than usual, due to the holiday, Wanda had let her leave early. When she'd handed off her apron and returned to the room she shared with Kiyani, at least a quarter of the tables in the *Mead Mill* had still been surrounded by people not appearing any closer to leaving. The atmosphere had still been jovial, the bard still spinning tales, his voice growing louder with each drink.

Fura didn't know how many of those people were still down below, but though she hadn't listened for the Shadowguard to enter, she swore she heard a distinct shift in the manner of words. Most of the noise was simply that, just noise. But as she listened harder, she could hear Aldam's words take precedence over the others.

"How dare you enter my town! There's no reason for you to be here."

They were here.

Hearing the decree, Kiyani paused and turned his head, listening as well.

Laughter ensued.

"You don't have the right to speak to us as such," one voice snarled.

"Stand aside!" another declared, overpowering the first and taking charge as he spoke to Aldam. "You are not the one we seek, and therefore of little importance to us. However, lead us to those that we were tasked to find, and you just might be compensated."

As the conversation fell into a mixed lull again, Fura struggled to listen while Kiyani returned his attention to the window.

Finally jiggling it open, he swung it outwards and stuck his head outside. Sidling closer to him, Fura wondered just how far he had planned this escape. Looking at the hole, she didn't even know if she could fit through the window, let alone climb down the wheel without falling to her death. She had a feeling that the Shadowlord didn't particularly care if they were brought back dead or alive. If this went wrong, they just might make the Shadowguard's job easier.

"I do not know those that you seek," Aldam said, his voice rising again. "Maybe you should try the next town."

Breathing a sigh of relief, Fura caught Kiyani's eye, giving him a look that said she had known the Magisard wouldn't hand them over. At least not without a fight. She still wasn't sure what exactly the man thought of them, but he didn't strike her as one to throw away a human life, be it one he'd known for years, or had only just met.

"Why do you protect those that don't even belong here?" another voice asked.

This one caught Kiyani's attention. Witnessing the clench in his jaw, Fura knew it was Maven speaking.

"The man lies," Maven continued. "They're here. I'll lead you to them."

It was then that Fura's heart dropped. This was really going to be the end for them, and all because one man had taken such an instant dislike as to betray them.

"Come on," Kiyani hissed, bringing her back to reality. They weren't done for yet.

Shoving her towards the window, Kiyani looked back to the opposite end of the hall. It wouldn't be long before Maven would appear, leading the group of shadowed men, his heart just as dark as theirs.

Hoisting herself up, Fura looked down at the ground, so far down that she could barely see it through the shadows and the mist that swirled above its surface. She shivered as the cool, damp air hit her skin. But it wasn't just the weather that had her on edge. Peering at the rickety wheel before her, she wondered again just how safe this could possibly be.

"Are you sure about this?" she asked.

Growing more frantic with every wasted second, Kiyani nodded. "Trust me. Now, go!"

Terrified, Fura kept a firm hold on Kiyani's hand as he helped her out the window. Her legs shaking just as badly as her hands, she nearly slipped on the rotting wood of the wheel. Clinging to the structure, knowing her life depended on it, she reminded herself not to look down. Frozen in place, she watched as Kiyani moved out beside her, taking his time to maneuver himself, his belongings, and the sword he carried at his side through the tiny opening. Once through, he quickly closed the window behind him, doing his best to make it appear as if it had never been disturbed, leaving no trace of their escape.

Sidling closer to her, Kiyani leaned in. "One step at a time," he reminded her, making the first move.

Wanting nothing more than to return to solid ground, Fura moved slowly. As her foot hit another blade of the wheel, she heard the sound of heavy boots stamping through the hall just above them. Though they were free of the building, they were still too close to their potential captors.

"Liar!" a voice rang out moments later. "This room is empty!"

"You would dare interfere with our mission?" another shouted.

"I... I swear to you," Maven pleaded, his voice sounding far weaker than usual. "They were here. They must've escaped."

"Find them!" the first voice shouted.

As the hall was filled with commotion again as the men raced back down the stairs, Kiyani and Fura continued downwards.

Though tricky and slow going, both knew they had limited time. The first thing the Shadowguardians were apt to do was search the perimeter of the building. Knowing this, Fura hurried. Catching her foot in a rotted out hole, she teetered off balance, finally falling the last few feet and tumbling to the ground in a heap. Deliberately jumping from just above where she had been, Kiyani landed with the skilled practice of a thief.

Expecting him to call her out on her clumsiness, Fura was surprised when he simply offered a hand. Taking hold, she allowed him to help her up, only catching his eye for a moment before looking away in embarrassment. Though she wanted the moment to last, she knew there was no time to linger.

Adrenaline pumping through her veins, playing the part of the hunted yet again, Fura only looked around for a second before taking off towards the woods, the only thing in her mind the fact that they needed to escape.

Instinctively, Kiyani reached out, grabbing her shoulder and pulling her back into the shadows. He could see the confusion on her face as she turned around, but he simply put a finger to his lips and shook his head.

Instead of heading towards the tree line as Fura had intended, he led them in the opposite direction. Pointing towards the alleyways that snaked between the buildings, he stuck to the darkness that clung to the back of the structures. Taking them along the back of the tavern, he continued behind a number of other buildings before finally turning into an alley. Moving between homes and other businesses, they ducked behind woodpiles and weaseled their way through paths cluttered with crates and other cast off items.

Only once did Kiyani stop them, pulling Fura down behind another woodpile. Shushing her before she could ask questions, they watched as the group of four men hurried past. The hands on their swords told Fura that she was right that it didn't matter if they were caught dead or alive. Though it didn't surprise her, the realization left her mouth dry and her blood racing. With each day that passed, with each trial they faced, this was becoming all the more real.

As the fantasy of it began to fade, the more Fura realized she really did want to go home, to the place where the most dangerous thing she had to worry about was slipping on ice in the winter.

Slowly peering around the corner, checking to see if the Shadowguard were gone from sight, Kiyani hurried Fura across the main road through town. To her right, she could see the tavern where she'd grown used to working, and the sundial that sat useless in the night. As much as she wanted to stop and take it all in, only appreciating it now that they were being forced out, Fura scurried after Kiyani, not wanting to be left behind.

Stopping again amidst another alley, Kiyani scanned the outlying buildings and the open land that lay between them and the safety of the dense forest. Seeing that the path was clear, he made to move, until the smallest crunch of gravel sounded behind them.

"There you are," a voice sneered.

Turning around, Kiyani recognized the man from the tavern. He had known when he'd first seen him it had meant trouble, but he hadn't expected Shadowguard. But now that it was staring him in the face, he knew he shouldn't have expected anything less. He already knew they were being hunted. Nevo had said so himself that the Shadowlord wasn't done with them. Yet, maybe that was what had thrown him off. Why hadn't Nevo tried to move against them himself? Why simply threaten them and then leave?

Then it hit him.

Complacency.

He'd wanted to give them that moment of false security. In a way, the man had done both that, almost giving them a reassurance that they were safe, yet putting them further on edge.

He will always find you.

It didn't matter how far they ran, that statement would always be true.

The man standing before them proved that.

As did the sword he drew from his belt.

Pulling the blade from the sheath at his side, the man approached, a wicked sneer painted on his face. Peering over his shoulder at Fura who looked petrified, and beyond to the woods that were just out of their reach, Kiyani wondered if they could make it if they simply turned and ran. It was the two of them against one man. Or so he assumed. He didn't know where the others had gone. Either they had split up, each searching on their own, or they were still working collectively as a group, the others waiting in the shadows to ensnare them.

It could have gone either way.

Though he knew it would have been better, simpler actually, to turn tail and run, Kiyani drew his own sword. If anything, he could act as a diversion, giving Fura a head start. Cockiness wasn't in his nature, but he was sure he could hold his own against this man. If only in the simple act of self defense.

An invitation to a fight, the man stormed forward, intent to kill burning in his eyes.

"Run!" Kiyani hissed at Fura. Dodging the first attack, he wondered yet again if the Shadowlord's orders were to actually kill the two of them, or if it was only the caliber of men working for him that just wanted to wet their blades in blood.

Taking a few tentative steps backward, Fura found herself locked in place, watching the fight. She didn't want to witness this again. Especially when she still wasn't certain if Kiyani's win the previous time had been a fluke. She had no doubts about his sword-fighting abilities, but he was also going against men who had probably trained far harder than he had. Willpower and inherent skill didn't always put one above dedicated learning.

Even as the thoughts raced through her mind, the fight took a deadly turn. She hadn't witnessed what had happened, but the dark stranger had somehow caught Kiyani off guard, or had taken a lucky blow. With a curse, Kiyani's sword went flying into the shadows. Backing off, he held his right wrist as if in pain, leaving Fura to guess that the man had either nicked him or caused him to twist the muscle.

Steeling himself against the injury, Kiyani quickly pulled the dagger from his belt, his eyes just as focused as ever. As he and the man circled each other in a strange and deadly dance, the Shadowguardian dove forward again. This time standing his ground, Kiyani ducked the oncoming blow and slashed at the man as he came within reach.

The man uttered a feral cry of pain. Though the sword remained in his grasp, he looked up at Kiyani with a hand held over his left eye, blood seeping through his fingers.

"I'll remember this, Enderline," he spat.

Panting with raw energy, the drive to kill now even stronger, the man made to move again. Gripping his dagger, preparing himself for a new attack, Kiyani was confused when the man suddenly tumbled to the ground. Standing behind him, Fura looked terrified, a length of wooden board in her hands.

"What did I do?" Fura asked, her voice barely a whisper in the night, its syllables nearly drowned out by the breeze. Looking down, she dropped the chunk of wood to the ground as if it could burn her at any moment. She didn't know where the idea had come from, nor where she had gotten the courage to go through with the act. All she had done was move as her body had told her.

"You helped," Kiyani replied, sounding just as shocked as her. Quickly retrieving his sword, he grabbed her hand and pulled her away from the man's limp body. "Now, come on."

Racing through the remaining stretch of alleyway, they streaked up the hill that led to the woods beyond Skirvynmire, neither of them looking back. Only when they reached the tree line, did they pause for breath.

Had it not been for the gunshot, they would have kept going.

As the metallic shot echoed through the cold air, they both turned and looked down on the town. Neither knew where it had originated, nor who had received the blow, only that it sounded like it had come from the direction of the tavern. The sound of their racing feet was replaced by an eerie silence. One that only followed violence, and that stillness of shock and awe. Of witnessing the unbelievable.

Her eyes scanning the town, searching for any sign of shadowed men moving through the streets, or ensuing chaos following the shot, Fura heard Kiyani mutter what sounded like *shit* beneath his breath. Glancing over at him, she found him staring up into the night sky. Her gaze following his, she wondered what else could possibly be coming for them, what else could go wrong on this night.

Silently, crisp, white snow had begun to fall around them.

54

•• ◇ ••

THROUGH THE STORM

Down below, the town began to wake in response to the violence. Lights in nearly every household came to life as the sound of gunfire reverberated through the night, shattering what should have been the peaceful silence of night. One by one they came alive, pulling the valley from the darkness of sleep to a frenzied state of awakening. Though Fura's first instinct was to stand on the hillside and watch the scene unravel below, Kiyani pushed her forward.

She wanted to argue, to race back down to help. But what could she do?

With a sickening feeling, she knew that her and Kiyani were responsible. If they hadn't come here, the Shadowguard wouldn't have either.

Swallowing her guilt, she turned and followed Kiyani, knowing once again that she had no other choice.

As they moved quickly and silently through the towering trees Fura began to realize why Kiyani had been worried about the snow. It was the first storm of the season, and though it had just begun the white powder was already accumulating at a dreadfully fast pace. Not only were they leaving easy to follow tracks in their wake, but the wind had picked up as well. Though it helped to cover some of their prints, it made for dreadful visibility. Not to mention, it was terribly cold. It whipped around them, finding purchase to chill even the smallest amount of skin left uncovered to the bone.

There would be no way of knowing if the Shadowguard was near in this horrid weather. The group of men could easily come upon them with no notice, leaving their chance of escape at next to nothing. Their customary black and silver dress would blend in with the surroundings as if the men were merely another part of the background.

Shadowguard, Fura thought.

They would be just that, too.

Shadows.

Ideally, the men probably would have preferred to capture them in the town with little fuss. But, Fura guessed that even in the expanse of the forest they wouldn't have a hard time tracking them, and she wondered if that had been a part of their plan all along. If they had purposely waited to flush them out when a storm was on the rise. She didn't dare mention it, but she knew that if the snow kept coming down like it was, they wouldn't be able to make it far. Even Kiyani, in all his stubbornness, had to know that.

Yet, what also bothered her was that following the siege, only one man had come after them. Now, they had several on their tail. Had whoever sent the previous guard really thought they were so weak and defenseless as to be overpowered by a single man?

Though she was initially offended by the thought, Fura wished that they'd maintained that mentality. The truth of the matter was that she didn't feel any stronger now than she had when they'd been forced out of Frielana. Now there were four men on their tail, while her and Kiyani were still only two. She didn't know why a single man had broken from the pack earlier, but she didn't want to think about the results of that fight had they run into the group of three instead. They had gotten lucky.

Time and time again they seemed to just miss out on the worst of what fate could deal them. One of these days they wouldn't be so lucky, and Fura didn't look forward to that moment.

Struggling to keep up with Kiyani, Fura couldn't help her rising sense of paranoia. She had a hard time keeping up with his pace on a normal day as she meandered behind him. Now his gait had increased ten-fold as he streaked through the trees, trying to put as much distance between them and the Shadowguard as possible. As much as she wanted to stop and rest, Fura painstakingly followed Kiyani as closely as she could. Wheezing for breath in the frozen air, she ignored the pain that had developed in her chest and side from the sudden sprint.

She didn't know what was worse at the moment; the sense that they were being watched by those they were running from, or her fear that she would lose Kiyani in the blizzard. If she lost sight of him, she'd be done for.

The little sense of direction that Fura normally had was all but gone in the darkness and blinding snow. Though she didn't even know if they were actually being followed, her heart beat rapidly as if they were already in the chase. It had been hard to tell if the gunfire within the tavern had been from the Shadowguard, but Fura already knew for certain that one of the men had seen them flee into the woods. Or would have. Shuddering, she still couldn't believe what she'd done. Yet, she was certain that Kiyani had actually praised her in his own way.

If anything, though the man had been unconscious when they'd made a break for the trees, he still knew where they'd be headed. She didn't take the Shadowguard as ones to give up easily. It would only be a matter of time before they were out in the woods with them, intent on finishing their mission.

Despite sweating from the physical exertion, Fura was freezing. The moisture on her skin froze instantly as they plowed ahead. Wind whipped around them creating an incessant whine that rung in her ears, making it difficult to listen for signs of the Shadowguard, while flakes of snow and icy drizzle bit at Fura's skin.

Though the work that she and Kiyani had been assigned to for the past few days had been tiresome and seemingly pointless, Fura would have given anything at this moment to be back within the tavern walls. A night full of rowdy men, rambunctious in their drunken state, would have been infinitely better than this.

It'd been just over a month since they had fled Frielana, but the few days of sleeping in an actual bed with pillows and sheets had been a welcome reprieve. Now they were on the run again.

Fura couldn't help but wonder, as they raced through the sheet of white, when she would come across such comforts next.

The initial excitement of actually sleeping beneath the stars and becoming one with nature, even if it was beneath the various Reln trees rather than in a manufactured nylon tent, had worn off long ago. Her family, or the ones she'd thought were her family, had never gone camping. Had never even talked about it. Now, Fura knew she wouldn't be all that disappointed if she never went camping again in her life.

Fear driving her forward, she tried to ignore the condescending voice in her mind.

Three days... I give you three days.

It didn't matter how many days past that initial deadline Fura made it, Kiyani's condescending voice just wouldn't leave her alone. She had proven him wrong, hadn't she? Yet, the taunt remained.

Kiyani had finally let the matter fall out of favor, only repeating the words once in awhile in times of severe argument. Even the talk of her returning to Barandor had decreased for the time being.

No, he had reverted instead to labeling her as slow and making her feel useless. She still had difficulty determining if he'd done it for her own good, as he had claimed, or if that was how he really saw her. Either way, it hurt her deeper than she let on.

Three days...

Fura forced the words back into submission as she fought to find a second wind to keep herself going. However, the thought lodged itself in the back of her mind, blossoming to include further accusations that if it wasn't for Kiyani she wouldn't have made it past that three day mark at all... not out here. He'd said so himself.

Though the arguments in her head helped to keep the fear at bay,

Fura swore that every now and then she could hear the cracking of twigs and the rustle of dead leaves. Looking ahead, watching Kiyani intently lead the way through the darkness that he so well blended into, Fura could see that he was no more alert than before she had caught on to the noises.

It's just us, Fura told herself.

It made sense. She couldn't expect to run full speed through a wilderness snow storm and not make any noise at all. As much as Fura wished during times like this that she were as silent as stone, she knew better. It would take a hell of a lot of practice, and probably more time than she ever wanted to spend out here, to be as experienced as Kiyani as he expertly weaved his way through the woods with little sound.

Ignoring her gut feeling, she steamed ahead, working her legs harder through the growing burn, trying to bring herself into closer range of Kiyani. If anything were to happen, Fura didn't want to be too far away from him.

Would he even protect you?

Her mind just wouldn't stop relentlessly posing questions she didn't even want to think about, let alone know the answer to.

How can I even think that? Fura scolded herself.

But it'd already taken root.

If they were attacked from behind, would Kiyani turn around and help, or would he continue on, happy to be rid of her?

The realization that she didn't have a clear answer left Fura colder than she already was.

A few more yards ahead, just as Fura thought her legs would finally give out, Kiyani began to slow down, before coming to a stop. Leaning against the trunk of a nearby tree, he wearily slid down onto his haunches, ending up in a squat at the root base.

Slowing down as well, Fura tiredly trotted the remaining distance, closing in the gap that had formed between them. Coming up alongside Kiyani, she fell to her knees in the thick powder, gasping for breath. The bitter air burned at her lungs. Her muscles spasmed from over-exertion. Her hair, wet with snow and sweat, was plastered against her face, and her heart pounded from the adrenaline of being pursued, but she took the time to try and regain her strength before turning to Kiyani.

"Did we lose them?" she asked, knowing it was almost too much to wish for.

Her head still hung low, Fura looked over at him. Following him as close as she possibly could, she hadn't thought the breakneck speed he'd instilled had affected him. Now, sitting just an arm's length away from him, listening to his ragged breathing, Fura could see otherwise.

Kiyani shook his head. "I don't know," he said breathlessly. "They won't give up easily though. Especially if one of them saw us." His words only confirmed Fura's earliest suspicions. "You might have knocked the man out, but he won't be out long. They might have already left Skirvynmire."

"Should we even be stopping, then?" Fura asked, looking around restlessly as if she expected one of the men to jump out of the brush at any moment... a silent, snow-filled ambush. The game of cat and mouse was a lot more fun when it was imagined on a school playground.

"Even if they moved into the woods not long after us, I doubt they've been running the entire time," Kiyani answered, knowing that his early decision had bought them some time, though just how much was yet to be determined. "They tend to move with stealth, not speed."

Fura wished that she could take that as a welcome statement. "But they could still be close," she countered.

The blatant truth of it was met with a nod. "We're not going to make it much further tonight."

Looking back, Fura wished that she had taken the time she'd spent watching the sun rise that morning to sleep more. Or that she'd at least eaten.

If I had known... she stopped herself mid-thought. If either of them had known ahead of time, they could've skipped the whole running for their lives part of the chase entirely. They could have slipped out of town, unseen, before the Shadowguard had even come strolling in, acting like they owned the world.

Would they after this was all said and done?

With a heavy sigh, Kiyani picked himself up. Fura watched him painfully stand, losing the clarity of his face in the flying snow.

Sitting stagnant for just the short time they had deemed acceptable to rest an inch of snow had accumulated around them.

"We have to get out of the open," Kiyani's voice declared through the wind.

Brushing the snow off of her thighs, Fura struggled to get her tingling limbs working again.

Standing, Fura wavered as she felt a sudden onset of wooziness. She hoped that Kiyani wouldn't notice the weakness, but it was his hand that rested on her shoulder to keep her steady. Fura grabbed his arm to keep herself from falling back to the ground as she let the feeling pass.

Kiyani surveyed the surrounding area as he waited, trying to determine how to continue. They both knew they had to find shelter and soon. Even if they weren't exhausted, the snow would eventually lead them astray, following their own masked footprints in circles.

Fura let up on the pressure on Kiyani's arm before letting her own arms fall limp to her side, embarrassed by the display.

He looked back at her, his eyes seeming to ask if she was okay rather than voicing the words, but she kept her gaze to the ground. She knew that the red hue of her cheeks wasn't just from the biting wind.

Thankfully, Kiyani paid no heed. Instead, he turned and began to lead the way again, decidedly slower this time.

Picking up a foot to follow, Fura stopped immediately.

There it was.

"That!" Fura grabbed at his shoulder again. "Did you hear that?"

She'd heard it again.

Kiyani paused. Turning back, he looked at her questioningly.

Fura could tell that Kiyani, although still on edge, didn't quite believe her. However, they both stood in silence, focusing on any foreign sound that overpowered the howling of the wind.

A moment passed. And then another.

Maybe I am going mad, Fura thought.

Just as she was about to apologize for crying wolf, it came again. There was no way, with both of them standing still, that the crunching of leaves and popping of small sticks that carried on the wind was them.

It was behind them.

Kiyani held his arm out in front of Fura protectively as his free hand rested on the sword at his hip.

Weaponless, Fura cowered behind him, holding her breath for fear that releasing it would welcome attack. This was it. The Shadowguard had found them.

It was next to them.

They shuffled their feet, facing it head on.

The brush before them trembled.

Almost forebodingly, the intense wind momentarily died down to a calm breeze.

And then a flash of gray streaked out of the darkness.

Kiyani instantly drew his sword as Fura shrieked.

Reflexively, Kiyani held the mass of steel above his head, ready to strike. However, recognition let him lower it as he let out a sigh that was a mixture of relief and irritation.

When sounds of a fight didn't ensue above the racket of the wind, Fura opened her eyes.

Before them a gray wolf looked up at them with clear blue eyes, his body hunched down as if readying for further attack.

"Kiedo," Kiyani scolded, his body relaxing, "How many times have I told you not to do that!"

Fura released her deadly grip on Kiyani's arm, embarrassed again by her overreaching fear. Certain that the Shadowguard couldn't be close if Kiedo was so lax, she knelt down and held out her hand.

Kiedo cocked his head, studying her before rising from his crouch and moving forward to nuzzle her palm. She had missed his quiet company and the extra sense of security he brought. It allowed both Kiyani and herself to let their guard down at the same time without worry. At the least, he was an extra set of eyes.

Leaning in further, Kiedo allowed Fura to pet him and scratch his back a moment before breaking away and going to Kiyani for further attention.

Fura would have thought that Kiyani would simply give the wolf's fur a quick ruffle and move on. Instead, he looked at Kiedo with a mixture of frustration and sorrow. Dropping to his knees, he hugged the beast, his face buried in the thick ruff of fur at his neck. Only then did Fura recall Nevo's words, claiming that he'd killed Kiyani's companion.

Not wanting to interfere with the moment, she kept an eye on the shadows surrounding them.

"We still need to find a place to rest," Kiyani said, releasing his hold on the wolf and rising.

The further they went, the colder it got. Though Kiyani had set a walking pace this time, slow enough for her to keep up despite the exhaustion, Fura had to fight the urge to grab his arm every now and then to keep from losing his form in the blizzard.

She didn't know how long they'd been out in the darkness. With the snow there was no way for her to gauge time, nor distance. She'd thought that everything had begun to look the same during their daily travels. Now, their surroundings were nothing but a white wall of blinding snow and ice, only made worse by the onset of night. The world surrounding them was nothing more than a formless deep gray haze with nameless shadows that danced in the wind.

Whether Kiyani knew where he was going or not, he seemed confident with the path he was blazing. The only difference now was the gray beast that followed alongside them. Hunched against the wind and ice, Kiedo trudged on in the snow that was already more than half way up his legs.

He moved with them, silent but alert. At least with the wolf as added company Fura felt a bit safer, knowing that his ears would pick up on any danger before either her or Kiyani would hear it.

Stifling a yawn, Fura tried to find something to keep her attention so she wouldn't fall asleep while walking. Yet, all she could see through the thick snow was the black silhouettes of the trees, writhing like spindly apparitions in the darkness. The sights, and the images her mind created out of it, did little to ease her fear.

Just ahead, Kiyani came to a halt again. It was only the second time he'd stopped since they had raced out of Skirvynmire. Fura's hopes rose as she prayed that they could finally call it a night. She had long lost most of the feeling in her fingers and toes and now the lack of feeling was beginning to creep further into her body.

Lost in her own mind to pass the time, Fura hadn't realized that Kiedo had moved silently ahead of them, becoming just another shadow against the muted white of the snow. Now he stood, rooted to the ground, his feet lost in the powder, as he sniffed the base of a large tree trunk.

Kiyani glanced around as if making sure that no one was waiting in the darkness to claim what they'd found. Seemingly satisfied, Kiyani joined the wolf at the tree base. He patted Kiedo's head affectionately before crouching down and digging away the snow drift that had formed. The ice covered ferns at the base crackled in resistance as Kiyani moved them aside, revealing a dark cavern that was nearly invisible in the night.

Fura didn't have to be told that they'd been lucky enough to have stumbled upon another of the rare Reln hollows. At least that was one piece of knowledge she had been able to retain since being thrown unexpectedly into Izandüre – the rarity of their occurrence.

Though she knew the hole was their safe-haven for the night, stowing them away from searching eyes, Fura was still wary.

Kiyani, not so much.

He didn't say a word before diving into the hollow, clearly done for the night.

Fura walked over and stood before the grand tree. Looking past the ferns, she tried to make out something, anything, in the darkness. The pale outline of a figure showed itself and Fura jumped back, startled, as Kiyani poked his head out.

"Are you coming?" he asked, ignoring her reaction.

"It's dark in there," she mumbled, knowing she sounded childish.

"Well, you can't stay out there."

As if to prove a point, Kiedo pushed past the foliage, rubbing against her leg as he passed by, and disappeared into the hollow.

She knew he was right. Taking a deep breath, Fura tried to calm her nerves before following. At least it wouldn't be windy in there, she tried to assure herself as she shivered against the howling cold.

Sitting on the ground, in the midst of the hedge of ferns, Fura let her legs dangle over the ledge that dropped inside and then pushed herself forward. Though it was a short fall, Fura felt as if she'd jumped into the abyss. If what had encapsulated them before had been darkness, then this was the absence of all light. This was death.

She leaned against the dirt wall in a sudden wave of paranoia, hoping that her eyes would focus to the change sooner than later. As a hand fell upon her arm, Fura choked on a scream. Though she assumed it was

Kiyani, she had no visual reference to reassure her.

"Come on," Kiyani said, pulling her away from the wall.

Fura dragged a hand along the solid vertical surface, trying to find some sense of stability as she allowed him to draw her forward.

"Kiyani, I can't see a thing."

"Your eyes will adjust. Come on, I think we stumbled upon a real rarity."

There was no mention of his lack of vision, and Fura wondered briefly if he could somehow see. He couldn't have had that much time to have explored the dark hollow already.

"You might want to duck," Kiyani warned before pulling her down into a crouch behind him.

Fura followed wordlessly letting her hand slip from the wall to trace along the floor.

"What is it?" she asked. The darkness hadn't let up at all.

"There's another cavern," Kiyani explained, "just outside the hollow. I don't know if it's natural or if it was dug out, but it'll offer us extra protection from the storm."

Stopping in what Fura assumed was the center of this extra underground room, Kiyani dropped her hand, leaving her feeling alone in the dark. She could still feel his presence not far away, but it was unnerving not being able to see him. It allowed her mind too much freedom to create illusions.

Not knowing what else to do, Fura settled herself cautiously onto the floor. Bringing her knees to her chest, she wrapped her arms around them tight and curled into the cloak she wore.

"Now what?" Fura asked. She knew it sounded stupid, but it was something she had to ask. The one good thing about the surrounding darkness was that she couldn't see Kiyani's reaction to her questions.

"We rest," Kiyani answered.

By the sound of his voice, he was only a few feet away. Though his answer was short, it lacked the irritation he usually instilled in his replies.

If there was one word to sum up the night, Fura knew it would be exhaustion. The lack of sleep. Little to eat. A long day of work. She was supposed to be in the bed in the room above Skirvynmire's tavern. Instead, she'd spent the night running for her life while dodging snowflakes and being battered by bitterly cold wind.

She shivered, trying to ignore the fact that she felt like she was frozen solid.

"Can we start a fire?" Fura asked.

She already knew Kiyani's answer, but she had to ask anyway. It was either be spotted by the Shadowguard or freeze to death beneath a dead tree. Fura couldn't fathom which he would choose for them.

A heavy sigh drifted through the air. "You know we can't"

"So, we're just supposed to freeze?"

"The glow would attract attention, and then we'd be dead anyways."

Fura huddled deeper into her cloak, trying to cover every square inch of her body with it with little luck. Though it was warm, it wasn't nearly warm enough, caked with ice and snow.

Is this how it's going to end? she wondered.

On the opposite side of the hollow, Fura thought she could hear Kiyani mumbling to himself. Uncertain, she attributed it to the wind outside, its howling giving voice to the night.

Beside her, a rustle made her jump. As Kiedo sidled up next to her, Fura held out her hand, allowing him to nudge his head into her palm. Running a hand along his back, wet and caked with melting flakes of snow, Fura knew that even his thick fur wouldn't offer her much warmth. Regardless, he lay on the floor, settling himself onto her feet.

A small flash of purple-tinged light illuminated the room for a brief moment before immediately sending it back into the abyss. Fura jumped again, startled by the display. Though she still couldn't see, the sudden flash of light killing what little of her night vision had developed, Fura frantically looked around for the source.

Moments later a similar flash lit the darkness before quickly fizzling out. This one was accompanied by a gravely growl of "*shit*".

"Kiyani?" Fura probed.

"I'm fine."

Fura hugged Kiedo closer, wondering what was going on. She wasn't sure whether to be amused or afraid.

For a third time the purple light came to life. This time, however, it stayed alight.

Though it wasn't extremely bright, Fura had to blink a few times before her eyes were able to adjust to the strange light.

Finally given the advantage of sight, Fura's nerves calmed a degree. She could see that where they sat, in the cool dirt below ground, was similar to the hollows they'd frequented since their journey had begun. Not far to her right, Fura could see the dark shape that acted as the doorway into the actual hollow beneath the Reln. She wondered briefly if they were still under the actual tree or directly beside it.

However, those questions quickly lost relevance as more, of a completely different matter, filled her mind.

Looking up, she found that Kiyani was just shy of where she had imagined him to be while under the cover of the darkness. His back was turned to her as he focused on something before him. The light and the strange pulsing glow of it seemed to be coming from Kiyani himself, casting his frame in an eerie silhouette.

Almost forgetting the cold and the raging storm outside entirely,

Fura leaned forward, wondering what she was seeing. As Kiyani turned back to her, she could see that the light that brightened the hollow came from an orb that floated within his hands.

Scooting towards the center of the space, Kiyani let the writhing globe fall from his trembling grasp. It slowly cascaded a few inches before settling in the air a foot above the ground. The glow that emanated from the strange mass wasn't bright, but it cast a muted purple ambiance that was just enough to see by, reminding Fura of the novelty black lights that people used at their Halloween parties.

There were so many things that Fura wanted answered, but she couldn't find the courage to voice any of it. She was almost afraid to speak, as if breaking the silence would cause the light to go berserk.

It looked almost similar to the dancing Fae lights that had lined the ceilings in Fae Rue Keep, yet this looked different... darker.

Huddled against the cold, it appeared as if the light had drained Kiyani of all the energy he'd had left.

It was only then that Fura realized what she had witnessed.

Magic...

Though it sounded ridiculous, even in her mind, Fura could think of no other explanation. She was certain that Kiyani had all of a sudden discovered a device to give them heat. If Tybithera had given him such a thing, he would have used it during those cold nights before they'd stumbled across Skirvynmire. And they'd had no free time to wander the small town they'd just fled to do any kind of shopping.

No, it had to be magic.

Fura's mind told her to be realistic, but in a world that was filled with Werebeasts and Streig, Faeries and elemental Lords, magic was only a given.

"Kiyani... your hands," Fura said. Though she wanted questions answered, wanted to know all about magic in this world, she couldn't help but comment on the injuries Kiyani had sustained that had only come to her notice with the light.

His hands looked raw, the purple cast of the strange orb making it appear more grotesque than it probably was. Though he ignored her, Fura could see his hands shaking as he rubbed them together, wincing as if in pain.

The sound of her voice, rampant with concern, caused him to snap his head up. He looked at his hands for a moment before letting them fall to his lap, playing it off as if the marks were nothing. "I'm not pyropheric, so it bites back," he said by way of explanation.

"Pyro-what?" Fura asked. If she wasn't mistaken he had just mentioned the name of the fire-dancer group back in Fireswell. Not only was she extremely tired, now she was extremely confused. She eyed the ball of light that hovered just above the floor, not sure what to think of it. She could feel the heat coming off of it, was thankful for its light. But if that really was magic, she now questioned it after seeing what it'd done to Kiyani.

"Pyropheric," Kiyani said again. "It's the technical name of the power that's associated with the fire element. Power that you should possess, actually."

"I can make that?" Fura asked, realizing that if all of this was true that Apallo had likely named the group after his own powers.

"I don't know," Kiyani claimed. "*Noxfae* or dark fire isn't really in the realm of normal pyropheric powers. It delves into a darker sanction of that magic. I don't even know if Apallo would dabble with it."

"Dark fire..." Fura repeated, dazed.

"It gives off heat but doesn't cast any real light."

Fura eyed him. "I don't think I want it if it does *that*," she claimed, indicating his hands.

Folding his hands out of sight, he shook his head. "I don't have that inbred power. That's why it fights back. You wouldn't be affected the same."

A storm of questions rose in her mind like a cloud of angry bees, all of them fighting to be let loose.

Though she wanted to know more, a yawn reminded her just how tired she was. Knowing that Kiyani probably felt the same, she looked around the hollow that would be their shelter for the night. She had Kiyani and Kiedo, and for once, some heat. It wasn't ideal, but it was better than some of the alternatives.

"So..."

"We get some rest," Kiyani said, seeming to expect her questions. "We'll leave in the morning when the storm breaks."

55

⬩⬩◇⬩⬩

BREAKING POINT

Three days later the storm continued to rage on.

Nothing was going as planned on this trip, starting with the fact that this journey hadn't been planned in the first place. It'd all gone downhill from there.

Being saddled with Fura.

Numerous run-ins with the Shadowguard.

Beasts that wanted to kill them, and devious Faerie queens.

What they'd been put through would've been more than enough adventure to last a lifetime, all conveniently packed into the span of a month.

It was a wonder he hadn't yet died from the stress.

And what was worse was that they'd only just begun this fruitless trek into the nothing. They didn't even know where they were going, driven forward only by the simple need to outrun danger, and spurred onward by the ramblings of a man on death row, and the useless words of a bard.

The knowledge lies within the words of knowledge…

What the hell was that supposed to mean, anyways?

Lying on his side on the hard ground, Kiyani stared at the wall, contemplating. Three days lost in his own thoughts. It was enough to drive him stir crazy, but then again, so was spending three days stuck in a small space with Fura as they waited out the storm. There was only so much he could handle.

Most of the first day had been spent sleeping, both of them exhausted from the lack of sleep from the night of the Hunt, and the hasty escape from Skirvynmire.

Though there was plenty they could have discussed after that, Kiyani had quickly discovered that it was far easier to feign sleep than to continuously deal with Fura. Hounding him with questions, sighing from boredom, looking at him with eager eyes as if he was the one that was supposed to know what to do.

No, it was better to simply lie there with his eyes closed, letting his

476

thoughts wander.

Not that they gave him any more peace.

Through the long days three things continued to hound him over and over.

First and foremost was that they were still too close to Skirvynmire. He didn't know just how far they'd traveled that night, the Shadowguard on their tail, but he knew it wasn't far enough. They should have been days away by now. Instead, they were practically camped on the outskirts of a town that probably never wanted to see them again. Aldam had offered them modest hospitality, and in return they'd brought death to the quaint little village.

As much as that thought killed him, it was the knowledge that the Shadowguard could still be out there, searching the woods just beyond the Reln they sheltered in that took precedence. He didn't know what the men's orders were. They could have given up pursuit that night, or they could have continued the patrol, intent on finding them, no matter how long it took. Though he hoped for the first, Kiyani would've put his money on the second option.

The moment he'd woken from the deep, exhaustion-induced slumber the day after, he'd been ready to leave. Yet the weather hadn't cooperated. Snow had continued to fall, blanketing the land in heavy sheets of white and deep drifts. Hardly suitable for traveling. Even if they could have somehow made it through the few feet of snow without exhausting their energy, the biting wind would have left them susceptible to hypothermia. As much as he'd hated it, the hollow had remained the better option.

The threat of the Shadowguard and the unforgiving weather were their main problems. The question of the bard's riddle was mere annoyance.

Kiyani didn't know who he was angrier with at the moment – the bard for handing over useless information that offered little help, or for Apallo for mentioning the Witneis in the first place. What good had his message proven thus far? And just what would it accomplish in the end if the trail was a dead end to begin with?

He almost wondered if that hadn't been Apallo's message at all. If, somehow, it had been something Zariah had forced the man to say. Sending them on an endless journey would definitely keep them from interfering with his plans, whatever they were.

Dispelling that thought from his mind, Kiyani returned to Rowan's cryptic message.

The knowledge lies within the words of knowledge...

Just what was he supposed to do with that?

The only thing that he could think of was that he needed to look in the pages of books, but just where was he supposed to find books in this cursed realm? It wasn't as if there were libraries dotting the hillside. Even living in Izandüre, there were only a few he could think of, and he certainly wasn't going to go knock on the door of the Shadowlord's castle asking to borrow a book. Which left…

"Du Reizlan," Kiyani muttered, as he sat up, the idea only now coming to him.

Yet, it made sense. In fact, it was already in the direction they were heading. He may have started heading due east just because it was far away from the commotion in Frielana, but maybe he'd been moving towards the school all along.

"Du Reizlan," he said again. It was perfect. Not only would it provide a sanctuary, but he was certain that they had one of the largest libraries in Izandüre. If they couldn't find something there, then there likely wasn't anything to be found. Not only that, it would keep Fura occupied and away from him.

Realizing that he'd probably woken her up with his sudden proclamation, Kiyani turned, expecting to see her sitting there, looking at him with questioning eyes.

Instead, he was met with the sight of an empty hollow.

A flashback of that first night they'd been on the run ran through his mind. Waking to find Fura gone. The man that had been waiting for them in the night. The man he'd killed.

He couldn't do this again.

Flinging off the cloak he'd been using as a blanket, Kiyani stood, anxiously raking a hand through his hair to get it out of his face. Telling himself to breath, that he wasn't reading the situation correctly, he looked around and listened.

Momentarily setting aside the fact that Fura appeared to be missing yet again, he hoped to hear silence; that wondrous sound that would mean the snow, and the storm that'd brought it in, had finally ceased.

Instead, all he could hear was the wind that still howled outside with such intensity that it threatened to bring the whole tree crashing down. The night was filled with the creaks and groans of icy branches being forced from their frozen state. Though they were rounding out the end of October, it sounded more like the middle of January.

Regardless of the weather outside, inside the hollow it was quiet. Though the hollow was a bit breezy at times, a chill set into the damp soil that wouldn't budge, the adjacent room was calm. The dark fire he'd managed to create flickered soundlessly, and Kiedo was out for the night. On the hunt and fending for himself, as his animal instincts called for.

Any other night, Kiyani would have appreciated the calm nature of it all, but right now, it was too quiet.

Ignoring his shaking hands, he quickly donned an extra shirt and the heavy cloak Tybithera had supplied him with before moving out into the actual hollow beneath the tree, hoping that Fura had simply moved into the other room to stretch her legs. As his eyes adjusted to the unlit room, he found that wasn't the case.

Cursing the fact that he was dealing with Fura's stupidity yet again, Kiyani moved to the hollow's entrance and peered outside. As he crawled out into the open to begin his search, he could see that the snow was still falling steadily. Gusts of cold wind created swirls of powder at Kiyani's feet, but he barely noticed, his mind already beginning to writhe with a growing anger.

How could she be doing this again?

Had she not learned the last time? Had she not seen his confrontation with Nevo?

No matter how many times he told her to stay put, to at least let him know before she left, she never did. The girl just wouldn't listen.

She was definitely Apallo's daughter, Kiyani thought, as he stood amongst the frosted ferns, letting his eyes scan the darkness that surrounded him, searching for any clue as to which way Fura had gone. She was just as stubborn, if not more so, than Frielana's leader. And holding that same fiery attitude that made her feel as if she was right in any given situation, when in reality she didn't know a damn thing. Only a month ago she'd never even heard of Izandüre, now she just thought she could go traipsing about its dense tangle of maze-like forests by herself. In snow, no less.

Clenching his fist at his side, Kiyani let out a heavy sigh that turned to fog before drifting away on the winds. He was livid, yet worried about her, alone in this storm, probably freezing.

And probably attracting unwanted attention.

Looking at the ground before him offered little help. There was nothing to gauge the amount of time she had been gone. No trails. No footprints. The wind was still too strong, the flakes that fell too powdery to do much besides cover tracks and pile the inches of white in foot-high drifts at the bases of surrounding trees.

He didn't even know what Fura might have come out here for, besides boredom. They had food. They had heat. They had shelter.

Glimpsing what he thought may have been the remainder of a footprint, Kiyani began to move forward.

Looking around for any sign of movement, Kiyani couldn't fathom what, in this monotone, frozen wilderness, could possibly be of intrigue to Fura's mind. She had complained periodically about being cold while in the hollow. Out here it was ten times worse. The wind, alone, had already driven a chill into his bones in the few moments he'd stood contemplating his course of action. Kiyani placed the discomfort in the back of his mind, as he did daily with his pain.

Creeping stealthily through the frozen tundra, he did his best to leave as few tracks as possible. The whine of the wind would cover the crunching of the snow beneath his feet, but the tracks would still be there. Kiyani didn't know at what rate they would blow over, hidden from wandering eyes, but he still hated being out in the open, taking chances. Even if they hadn't seen nor heard the Shadowguard in the last few days, he and Fura were still being hunted.

The men employed by the Shadowlord were a ruthless lot. The inclement weather would bother them, but they would trudge through it anyways. It was expected of them. To not follow orders would lead to worse things than being out in the unrelenting snow.

Just like their leader... merciless to the end.

Did Fura not know the danger that she was putting them both in? Or, did she simply not care?

The smallest of movements up ahead drew Kiyani's attention. Hunching down closer to the ground, he paused, watching and waiting. There was no moonlight to help his sight, only the wavering shades of gray and black, dotted with the flickering white specks of snow.

Regardless, he recognized Fura's small frame in the darkness.

Bringing himself back into a full stance, Kiyani stormed forward. All sense of caution, of worry about her condition, was now clouded by his anger.

"Fura," Kiyani said, trying with little luck to keep the growl out of his voice.

Fura turned around, a small smile on her face. "Hi," she said, before turning around again. Her face was turned up towards the sky, watching the snow fall in amazement as if she was taking it in for the first time. She was leaning against the trunk of a shadowed tree, looking as if she had no care in the world.

Though Kiyani knew the sight of Fura actually looking happy for once should have made him want to forgive her, it only enraged him further.

"*What* do you think you're doing?" he asked, his voice low and dark as he approached her.

It was enough for the smile to fall from her face. "I..." she stammered, looking around as if she'd only just realized what she'd done. "I checked to make sure there was no one around..." she offered, as if that made the situation any less volatile.

"Did you?" Kiyani growled, hardly believing her.

"I... I think," she answered sheepishly, her eyes falling to the ground, unable to meet his gaze.

His blood boiling, he stalked forward and grabbed her arm, whipping her around to face him. "Is it so hard for you to listen?" he stormed. Trying to free herself from his grip, Kiyani only held on tighter. Though he knew it wasn't the time for this, that he should just forget it and return back to the hollow, it was as if the flood gates had let loose, all the feelings he'd been bottling up since this fated journey had begun spilling forth.

"I told you to stay put, to stay in the hollow, out of the open, because there are people out here after us!" he hissed, his voice low as his cold hands curled around her wrists. "Yet, here you are, out in the open, playing in the snow like some child. Do you hear my words at all when I'm talking to you?! Why is it so hard for you to get it through your damn head what's going on? You prance around in this world like all the danger's just going to pass you by because you know nothing about it. Well, let me tell you, you naïve little brat, that's not how things are. The less you know, the worse off you are, and one of these days I'm not going to be able to save your ass because you're already going to be too far gone. And to tell you the truth, I don't even know that I would be too upset to be free of you!"

Though Fura could only begin to fathom what she'd done this time, it was easy to see that Kiyani's anger had returned in full force, rivaling even the darkest moments she'd seen of him thus far. Trying to escape the rage in his eyes, she didn't even realize that she'd been backing away from him until she felt the bark of another tree dig into her back. Scared senseless, she couldn't even form any sensible words to counter his. Thinking to get away from him, Fura never had the chance before he shoved her against the tree, pinning her in place as his fingers dug into her wrists.

"Why is this so damn hard for you?" Kiyani continued, ignoring her whimpering. "Don't you remember what happened the last time you did this? You would never make it here by yourself. If I would have left you like I said I was going to you'd be dead already. Murdered by that Shadowguardian. Food for the wild beasts that wander these woods. Ripped apart by the Werebeasts as one of their yearly sacrifices."

Fura could feel the tears welling up behind her eyes. His nails were digging into her skin but she could barely feel it, too taken aback by this sudden outburst of pent up anger. "Kiyani," she pleaded. "You're hurting me..." the words came out in a half sob.

Yet, he didn't seem to hear her words as he continued on. "Did you so graciously forget already why we're out here, what we're running from?" The more he said, the darker his voice became, rising above the wind, no longer caring about the imminent danger. "I admit, I don't have a clear idea yet of where we're going, but the dank dungeons where the Shadowguard would take us if we were to get caught are not on my agenda. You're setting yourself on a clear path to go down the same damn forsaken road that we would already be on had we not left Frielana when we did! Is that what you want!?"

Fura's body went limp as she slid down the tree, ending up in a crouch at its trunk, her knees up to her chest. Tears ran down her cheeks in hot streams. She couldn't bring herself to look at Kiyani, at the seething fury in the blue pools of his eyes.

His fingers seemed to dig deeper as he shook her. "Why can't you just listen to me, for once?"

She prayed for it to stop, her body shaking in shock and in fear. She could hear the pounding of her heart in her ears. Could feel the angered heat off his body, far too close for comfort in his current state.

As much as Fura fought against it, their eyes met.

"You don't belong here," Kiyani said, his voice dropping in volume. As if he'd seen something in her eyes that had changed his mind, his train of thought, he quickly looked away, letting up on his grasp and allowing his hands to fall. Only then seeming to realize how they were tangled at the base of the tree, how much his own hands were shaking.

As soon as the physical contact was broken, Fura lurched forward. Looking at him, his eyes suddenly distant and vacant, his body lax, she paused for a moment before bolting like a frightened deer released from the grip of the headlights.

Though she wanted nothing more than to run off, full throttle, into the night, never looking back, pushing herself as far away from him as she could, Fura knew better. Instead, she ran back towards the Reln, stumbling in the snow, to the hollow it hid and the warmth of the strange fire inside.

Kiyani didn't turn to watch her flight. His eyes were to the ground, his vision blurred as he sat on his knees in the snow, the powder drifting about him. His body was shaking from the anger that was still coursing through his veins. He couldn't even remember all of what he'd said to her. But he knew the words were rage-driven, even more hurtful due to the red-tinged intensity of it.

Leaning forward, his elbows on his thighs, he sunk his face in the cups of his hands, taking the time to steady his breathing and to regain his composure. The look in Fura's eyes when they had finally met his had been nothing short of fear.

Fear...

Her lips had been moving at some point, but Kiyani couldn't recall for the life of him what she'd said as the tears had streamed down her face. What would he have done if he had let himself continue, if the look in her eyes hadn't brought him crashing back to reality?

He didn't want to know.

This journey was slowly killing him, eating away at his sanity and turning him into the person he'd fought so hard against becoming. He didn't want to be anything like his father, yet it seemed like the path he was destined to take. Trying to steady his breathing, he wondered if he and Fura would even be able to make it through this journey alive.

Running a shaking hand over his face and balling it into his hair, Kiyani heard a crunch of snow beside him. Not knowing what, or who, to expect, he looked up cautiously.

Kiedo stood alert right next to him. The wolf was close enough in range for Kiyani to see the slight cock of his head, the knowledge of what had transpired reflected back in his blue eyes.

"What?" Kiyani asked, almost defensively, though even he knew he didn't have a good reason for what he'd just done.

The wolf only briefly glanced at him before turning and heading back towards the Reln.

Kiyani sighed as he picked himself off the ground and dusted the snow off his legs. As if he didn't feel bad enough, now he was being slighted by man's best friend.

Back in the hollow, Fura sat on the floor of the adjacent room with her knees drawn up to her chest, the dagger of Kiyani's shaking in her white-knuckled grasp. Though she'd wrapped up in her cloak, it didn't quell the nerves that wracked her body in the aftermath of Kiyani's recent outburst.

Her heart still pounded in her chest as tears streamed down her face.

She didn't know what to do, or where to go. What options did she even have at this point? It wasn't like she could up and leave in the middle of the night. She had no idea where they were.

Yet, it couldn't keep her from wondering if maybe she'd be better off on her own. She no longer knew where safety lie. Tangling with the Shadowguard wouldn't be pleasant, but neither was being the focus of Kiyani's rampages.

Sniffling, Fura realized that this was the man that Apallo had tried to protect her from.

Useless... a bother... incompetent...

It wasn't just the physical terror he'd inflicted on her, it was his biting words as well. Was that really what Kiyani thought of her? Everything that she had feared, he'd just voiced aloud. Fura had known that Kiyani hadn't cared to have her around, but she hadn't known, until now, just how deep that thread ran.

Movement in the shadows outside the room caught her attention, but she barely looked up, knowing that she had nowhere to go anyways.

Kiedo sauntered into the light first. Sitting beside her, licking the beaded snow from his paws, he appeared to be content to settle in for the night.

Kiyani followed not long after.

Standing in the doorway, his eyes fell on the dagger in her grasp.

"Put that down," he urged.

Though she had every reason to keep hold of it, his demeanor had changed completely. Looking drained, his voice weak, Fura only met his eye for a fleeting moment before tossing the dagger onto the floor in the middle of the room.

Deeming it safe enough, he walked over to the mess of pine boughs and clothing that'd made up his make-shift bed for the past few days and slowly sat down. Staring at the floor as he warmed his hands near the strange, purple light, he only briefly looked at her before turning away, ashamed.

"I... get some rest," Kiyani said, changing his direction mid-sentence, his voice lacking any sentiment. "We're leaving tomorrow," he continued. "No matter what the weather is like."

56

♦♦◇♦♦

WORKING IN OUR FAVOR

The shadowed, gray cast of the surrounding stone complemented the winter-esque weather outside. The men were finally out of the unbearable winds that had accompanied the first storm of the season; Izandüre's warning storm before the actual winter blew in on its heels. Not one of the members of the small group would ever admit it, but it was a welcome reprieve to be back indoors, warming their frost-bitten limbs, if only for a minute.

In reality, however, as the troupe waited inside the thick surrounding walls that muffled the storm's force to a low droning hum, it didn't feel much different. A fire burned within the stone inset in the wall, though it hardly succeeded in warding off the cold. In fact, it didn't seem to radiate any heat at all throughout the room. Even the light that it cast was dark and murky. The water that managed to melt from their boots left dark pools on the smooth stone floor, reflecting the men's travel weary and fearful faces.

Not that the dank atmosphere was the fault of anyone in particular, lest the weather.

It was the castle.

The building itself, carved out of the darkest black stone, as if it were forged in the pits of hell, seemed to drench any bystander with cold and fear, sucking the warmth out of the soul. If the mere sight of the dark palisades hadn't already done so upon entering the towering structure set into the mountain, the interior would finish the job.

It was precisely why those who'd had the unfortunate luck of finding themselves a prisoner within the slick onyx walls of the Enderline castle, known as Shäedenmore, were quick to become a trembling heap. If they didn't die within a few days, they were generally void of emotion within a week. Any unwarranted stay of more than a couple of days was enough to leave most men welcoming the onslaught of death, rather than fearing it.

No, the fear of death should have been the last thing on their minds. Darkness lingered in these shadowed halls that made death appear to be a friend. A friend far more comforting than the lord that lived there.

The sun will never shine here
The rain will always fall
Full of dark and desolate souls
Hopes and dreams are lost to all

The short mantra flitted through Tyvan's head as he stood at attention amongst the three others, waiting. He couldn't remember where exactly he'd read or heard that particular poem about the castle he stood in, but it was fitting all the same. It took a rare breed to walk the lengths of its winding corridors and retain their sanity.

Seeming to think the same thing, Tyvan thought he saw the man beside him shiver. Whether it was from the actual chill wrought by the surrounding stone or fear, he was unsure. The man was relatively new, and his inexperience as a loyal member of the elite Shadowguard showed.

He, himself, had served for years. The castle, with its damp chill and dark stone passageways was nothing to him, save for just another part of the day. He'd become accustomed to its discomforts early on in his service to the Shadowlord. As far as he was concerned, the living and work situation was how the man weeded out the weak ones. Besides, there were other things to keep first and foremost in his mind than the unsuccessful attempts from one of his fellow servicemen to hide the growing apprehension of coming to terms with why they were standing here in the first place.

The man's eyes seemed to flit back and forth. Wary. Searching. Scared. Other than the blatant unease that littered his features, the man was rather unmemorable with his mousy brown curls that stuck to his face, wet with snow, and his mud colored eyes. Tyvan still didn't know his name after all this time. Now that he thought about it, he couldn't remember ever hearing it mentioned. Not even during their recent mission to Skirvynmire and back.

As the ornately carved doors before the group of four opened, sending an echoing squeal throughout the chamber, Tyvan put the inconclusive thoughts aside. Made of thick, age-darkened wood, past the point of being petrified, the moving set of doors seemed to set in motion the snakes engraved into its surface. The ruby eyes of the two largest snakes, accentuated with silver filigree, danced in the firelight, making them seem all the more alive.

The cold-blooded creatures, close cousins of the feared dragon of myths, acted as the castle's, as well as the family that had laid claim to its walls and the happenings inside, unofficial mascot. Images of the snakes were ever present in the building's intricate design work.

The man beside Tyvan jumped, the fear and the dread even more apparent now that things were under way.

Tyvan turned his attention away from the man again. That little display only made him all the more adamant that he didn't care to know him.

Instead he looked ahead, his head held high, standing straight in anticipation, waiting for the appearance of his Lord.

The Shadowlord's second in command, Zendel, was the first to stride through the double doors of dark wood and black iron. His blond hair slightly askew, he looked anxious, as if he could already anticipate the outcome of this late night meeting. A gathering to relay words that would no doubt displease the man he served.

Close behind, dressed in his trailing fineries, Zariah stepped through the entranceway, doing well to take his time. His ebony hair was slicked back in a half ponytail, revealing the full force of his sharp features. The Lord's silver eyes were a shade darker than usual, taking on the cold hue of the walls and making him appear as if he'd stepped straight out of the stone rather than through the doorway.

Though it was bad news that Tyvan had to relay to the man, he still felt a thrill of being within such close proximity to the Lord in which he served. He'd glimpsed the man plenty of times in passing through the halls, but had only been in his full presence, allowed the privilege to speak, a handful of times.

The Shadowlord had a close council of those that he trusted most to attend to the matters of highest importance and share his voice with. Tyvan knew he was too busy otherwise to even take the time to spit on the ground in which he currently stood.

But now, now it was finally his time to speak.

Tyvan could feel his heart hammering in his chest from the sheer excitement of it all.

Zariah stood before the four men that waited in the room. They were dripping wet as the snow and ice melted off their garments in what little heat the room provided. Wind-whipped and most likely famished after the chase they'd been sent on, they cowered like sniveling puppies with the smallest hope that they would be thrown a scrap, but knowing it was really another beating they were waiting for.

A half smile crept onto the Shadowlord's face as he strolled slowly in front of them, studying their faces, making it a point to drag out the moment longer than needed. His spider-like hands appeared, the long fingers clicking together as he moved, the pale, nearly white, skin a stark contrast to the black velvet cloak that feathered out behind him.

He could already tell by the demeanor the four men carried that the news they harbored wouldn't be what he was hoping for, but Zariah savored the minutes of drawn out silence beforehand. They were all well aware of their training. No matter the circumstance, he was to be the first one to speak.

Until then, they had to wait, haunted by whatever thoughts infiltrated their weak minds. Though he knew he could be in and out of this drafty room in a mere matter of minutes, Zariah relished this time, taking a certain amount of pleasure from the situation. It was amazing how just his presence in the room could reduce those that served him to quivering masses.

Zariah studied the four of them carefully as he wandered by, his back straight, only his eyes boring into each and every one of them. Most of them succumbed to the urge to let their eyes fall to the ground as they met his own, the fear they so desperately tried to keep to themselves easily surmised.

One man in the midst of the group stood out, however. Feathery hair, stringy from the weather outside, fell to his shoulders in a dark mass. As Zariah paused before him, the man's hazel eyes bored into his own. There was no hesitation, but rather a slight glimmer in his eye.

At least one of them bore potential for greater things, the Shadowlord thought. He had seen the man before, going about his duties. The name escaped him, but he thought it might start with a T. Though he rarely paid attention anyone one person beneath him, Zariah couldn't help but notice the difference in this man. A difference that was accented by the fresh red gash that adorned his face, running from the middle of his left brow down to his cheek. Even with a recent injury, he appeared willing, excited even, to continue in his duties.

As much as he could tell this particular man wanted to talk, Zariah addressed the man next to him instead.

"Report."

The man jumped as he looked up to meet the Lord's eyes only momentarily, realizing, to his horror, that he was the one who'd been called upon. He looked to the men on either side of him nervously, as if hoping he'd merely heard things.

"They... they escaped us again," the man finally stuttered. He kept his eyes to the ground, afraid to look the Lord straight in the eyes. He had failed in his mission. A rather simple one, too. How hard was it really to bring in two teenagers? "We will send out another team right away," he said, quickly trying to counter his first words.

Zariah held up a spindly hand. "Leave them."

The man looked up. "Excuse me?" He wrung his hands uneasily, knowing he had just spoken out of line. The Shadowlord never left business unfinished though, especially not such easily accomplished feats.

"We have more important things to attest to than to try and track two scrambling teenagers to a destination that even they don't currently know. You did your job. They know they're being followed. Watched. They know the fate that eventually awaits them. At least one of them does. That paranoia will manifest into fear soon enough, making my job that much easier. Mark my words, he will show his face eventually," Zariah concluded, making the target of his intentions clear in his wording.

"And the girl?" Tyvan asked, unable to keep his voice out of the conversation.

Zariah looked at him with a raised brow, heeding the interruption. It wasn't too often that anyone took the liberty of speaking over him. They all knew what would befall them if they did. But he let it slip. This one definitely had spunk.

Tyvan let his head fall, indicating that he was done. He knew better than to speak to the Shadowlord before being called on, but the tremulous waste of life next to him wasn't doing his job.

Just as he'd wanted, the Lord's eyes had now descended upon him. However, the silence that ensued was nearly unbearable as it rained down heavily upon him. Tyvan had the overwhelming feeling that he would be dragged down to the dungeons by one of the higher guards for being disorderly, just as they'd done when he was still in training. It had been a long time since he'd been a guest in one of those dank cells. Though he knew he'd survive if he paid a visit to the cellars again, Tyvan was ready to proclaim that his time would be better spent above ground.

"She follows him without question," Zariah declared as if it were common knowledge, finally adding his voice to the room again. "Wherever he goes, she'll be there."

Tyvan tried to make sense of what the Shadowlord was saying, mildly shocked that there had been no repercussion from his outburst. They'd been given the task of hunting down the two teenagers that had escaped from Frielana during the Lord's siege. The two were traveling together, that much was apparent. But it didn't mean they'd continue to do so.

"What if they eventually take separate paths?" He couldn't quite understand the Lord's certainty on this matter. How could he be so sure of the path these two would take when he'd already so boldly claimed that they didn't even know where they were headed.

The question was more than viable. They were from two completely different walks of life. From what he'd heard, and what little he had seen from afar, the two had little in common; definitely nothing that would keep them moving together on the same road.

"They won't," Zariah claimed confidently.

"How can you be sure?" He was in the wrong, he knew it. If anything, he should have remained quiet, losing himself in the shadows like the others, but Tyvan wanted the answers to these questions that had all of a sudden flooded his mind. The Lord questioned them, not vice versa, it was the way things worked, but Tyvan couldn't help himself. He wanted to know more about the brat that'd cut up his face.

"Kay tells me that there is the possibility of something more."

"A romance?" Tyvan questioned, picking up on the Lord's inference. It couldn't be. "But, that's forbidden."

Zariah smirked. "As if I care. It plays well in our favor. Let them grow close. It distracts them, makes things easier, and all the more pleasurable when I tear them apart later. No, this will certainly work in our favor. More so than I had ever hoped. "

57

♦♦◇♦♦

LEFT BEHIND

When Fura woke the next morning to a new day, she was far from rejuvenated. The hours preceding had been filled with horrific dreams, forcing her to relive, over and over again, her most recent fight with Kiyani. A groan of discomfort escaped her lips as she rolled over and stretched her legs. The despair and anguish in the aftermath had left her sleeping curled up in the fetal position, tangled in the rough fabric of her cloak, with only the unwelcome memories from the night before to keep her company. Now she was paying for it. Her muscles were stiff and cramped, her mind still foggy, and her right arm was asleep from using it as a cushion from the hard ground for so long.

However, even through the haze, Fura just couldn't shake the remnants of Kiyani's outburst that lingered within her mind. All night the images had floated through her consciousness like a grainy black and white horror film. Even upon waking she was left with the bitter taste of a nightmare that refused to leave. She doubted that even the intense light of a new day would be enough to burn away those memories. Or to realign her feelings. Even though she might have been attracted to him, there was no denying that he wasn't right for her. Her own father had seen that, long before she'd even realized she'd wanted a relationship with Kiyani. Yet, the night before had finalized its death. She didn't even know if she could look him in the eye anymore, let alone continue to nurture any romantic feelings towards him.

Not that it mattered. This was what Kiyani had wanted all along.

Sitting up and rubbing her eyes, Fura wondered how she'd even been able to sleep. What little rest she'd found had been fitful, interspersed with nightmares. And all the while, the anger that had raged in Kiyani's blue eyes had haunted her. His hurtful words stabbing her deeper and deeper with every reoccurrence, chipping away at her already fragile self-esteem until it left her crumpled in a useless ball of self pity.

Useless...

There it was again. That jab of hate... of truth.

491

Shaking her head, she tried to get rid of the poisonous thoughts and the headache that came with it.

That fear and self-doubt had been the concurrent theme of her dreams since this journey had begun, mirroring the emotions of her waking life.

Yet, she'd had to face it head on, day after day.

This was no different.

When Kiyani had returned to the hollow, there'd been so much that she'd wanted to ask, to tell him, to prove to him. But she'd been too scared to speak. Scared of what she would do if he attacked her again. She still hardly even remembered picking up that dagger. Though she'd held it in her hand, she doubted she would have been able to use it. Even if necessary.

Kiyani hadn't appeared worried. In fact, as soon as she'd dropped the weapon to the floor, he hadn't taken any time in turning away from her and going to sleep.

Not knowing what else to do, she'd attempted to do the same. Instead, she'd cried for what felt like hours, feeling alone despite the two others in the room. Even if he'd been awake the entire time, her sobs had been lost on him. She was certain, despite her efforts, that they'd been loud enough for him to hear over the howling winds outside.

The man that'd helped ease her fear during the Werebeast attacks, that had cradled her in his arms when she'd discovered her life was a lie, was gone.

Even Kiedo had eventually abandoned her to return to his master's side.

Rubbing her wrists, Fura rolled up her sleeves to reveal the pale skin that had already started to change color from where Kiyani had grasped her wrists. The sickly yellow green of the bruises that were starting to form paralleled how she felt inside.

Kiyani had had outbursts before, but nothing to that degree. Fura had never been doubtful that he could be prone to mean streaks, but what she had witnessed the previous night had been the worst she'd seen him.

Though the physical nature of Kiyani's attack left Fura shaking as she recalled the events, it was the intensity of the rage that had clouded his eyes that truly scared her. Even now, she could still see it all too vividly.

Yet, the one image that stuck in Fura's head, amongst the blinding hate, and the verbal and physical abuse that had been dealt, was of Kiyani on his knees in the snow afterwards and the blank stare that had been present on his face.

It was strange witnessing such polar opposites from one person in such a short period of time.

In fact, she had almost missed it. Fura didn't know what it was that had made her turn around to witness that fleeting moment before she'd ducked into the hollow, and even now she couldn't pinpoint exactly what it was that she'd seen in him.

Disappointment?

Fear?

Fear was what had ravaged her mind during the night, recreating the scene over and over, each time adding new delusions and exaggerating details.

At one point she had woken in the middle of the night, the intense feeling of being alone weighing on her like a brick. The hollow had been dark and empty.

Empty.

In the light of a new day the thought hit with new meaning, the pieces of the puzzle connecting like they hadn't before.

Fura looked around in panic, the fog in her mind clearing as it made way for a sudden fit of clarity.

The hollow was cleared out. The unusual ball of purple light that had become a staple in the small room the past few days had disappeared from existence, and Kiyani's meager belongings were gone. He was nowhere in sight, nor was Kiedo. The only thing that remained was the second bed of pine branches that matched her own, looking withered and lonely.

It *had* been just a dream, hadn't it?

Fura frantically tried to reason with herself, but what more proof did she need? She was alone, the heavy sense of abandonment weighing her down.

She still didn't even know what it was that she'd done to push him over the edge, but now Kiyani was gone. He had finally fulfilled his earlier promise, that threat that had continuously nagged her since he'd spoken the words.

"One of these days you might just wake up and I'll be gone."

He wouldn't really do it though, would he?

The man that had screamed at her, with fire burning in his eyes, a lofty contradiction to the peaceful snow that had been falling about them, just might.

No... would.

The man that'd had her pinned to the tree in full fledged fear, with no knowledge or care that he was hurting her would leave her without a second thought.

But the man that he'd been reduced to in the aftermath wouldn't.

Fura held on to that image of Kiyani, withered in the snow and angry at himself, as she forced herself to stand on shaky limbs and push forward with a new perspective.

Slipping on the leather boots she'd discarded at some point in the middle of the night, she moved into the next room. Though she knew it was probably too much to ask, she held on to the notion that maybe Kiyani had just decided to sleep in the adjacent room. Feeling stifled, residing in the same space as him and the wolf, Fura had entertained the idea herself.

Entering the actual Reln hollow dashed her hopes. The room was just as empty as the one where she'd slept. The only new fixture in the space was the drift of fluffy snow that had accumulated on the floor in front of the entrance.

Fura's heart sank as she took in the sight.

Wiping a tear from her eye, she could see that, despite her sinking spirits, warm sunlight streamed through the opening, extending a welcome to return to the outside world.

The storm had finally broken.

Telling herself that maybe this was for the best, Fura took a deep breath and walked over to the hole, peering outside. Regardless of the nightmare of the day before, it was still a new day.

Taking a moment to determine that there was no immediate need for caution, Fura heaved herself up and out of the hollow and emerged into the daylight.

The scene that greeted her was a complete turnaround from the winter horror land that she had escaped from the night before.

A welcome reprieve after the numerous nights of being forced to listen to the wailing snow storm, it now looked almost spring-like.

The sun's rays glinted off the snow, creating specks of gold that sparkled fancifully as the smallest movement of the trees above shifted the light. Much of the snow had already melted away, revealing patches of green grass that had managed not to wilt with the onset of the sudden frost. A light, gentle breeze had replaced the biting winds. Though she could see her breath in the brisk morning air, a hint of warmth was beginning to seep back into the atmosphere. A welcome reminder that it wasn't winter quite yet.

As gorgeous as it was, Fura hardly noticed the natural beauty. Nor was she distracted by the warm rays of the sun that should have been a comfort after days of being pounded by the chill of the wintery storm. Distracted by something else entirely, she found she didn't even care about the weather.

A few yards to her right Kiyani stood with his back to her, leaning against the trunk of a tree, his arms crossed in front of him as he stared off into the distance.

His black hair and dark dress made him appear as a mere silhouette in the bright light. He looked run down and tired, like he hadn't slept at all, but Fura couldn't think of a more welcome sight.

Her heart was racing as she fought the urge to run forward and hug him, to make sure he was real and not just some vivid reproduction of her imagination.

As scared as she'd been the night before, Fura knew that without him, she really was alone, with no chance in the world. At least, not in this world.

Instead of surging toward Kiyani, Fura took a moment to steady herself before calmly walking up behind him.

She tried to remain quiet but the crunch of snow gave her away before she could find any words to say.

Pulled out of his reverie, Kiyani turned to look at her.

"I thought you left," Fura quietly confessed. She couldn't bring herself to look at him as she moved a bit closer, already blushing. She hadn't meant to let that fear be known, but it was the first thing that came to mind.

Kiyani looked away hesitantly, but not before Fura caught the smallest hint of what appeared to be guilt on his face.

Yet, when he turned again it was gone.

Fura blinked, wondering if she'd merely imagined it. She wouldn't put it past herself to create the illusion of missing emotions, especially after the night she'd had.

As if sensing the need for distraction, Kiedo came bounding towards her from where Kiyani had been looking earlier. The wolf trotted over, his tongue lolling. Bending down to run a hand through his sun-warmed fur, Fura welcomed the small break in the tension. Even if Kiyani was still here with her, it didn't change what had happened between them. The rest of this journey, however long it might be, was bound to be tense and awkward.

It made her realize that she had no idea how to approach the subject of their recent fight. She could feel Kiyani's eyes on her, expectant, but when he finally spoke it was all business.

"Are you ready to go?" he asked.

There was no mention of Fura's first words. No mention of the incident the night before.

It was almost as if nothing had happened. As much as Fura wished that were true, she knew it wasn't. Eventually, they'd have to talk about it, but if Kiyani was willing to pretend that nothing had changed, then Fura was right there with him. At least for a little while.

Fura nodded in reply. She didn't know where they were headed, but she knew there was no reason to stay here. Though she'd vowed to forget him only a few moments before, she couldn't keep the grin off her face, "Just give me a few minutes."

He hadn't left.

The night had been terrifying, but in the light of day, she couldn't believe that she'd allowed her mind to play such cruel tricks on her. She didn't want to know what it would be like if Kiyani left for good, and she told herself that she'd never find out.

"The sooner the better," Kiyani said, turning his attention away. "We should have left days ago."

58

♦♦◇♦♦

DO WHAT YOU WANT

The days that followed felt very much like those that had preceded their run in with Skirvynmire. Only now, the rift between her and Kiyani was much deeper. Leaving Fae Rue behind, Fura had been certain that Kiyani's dour mood had been the Fae Queen's doing. Now there was no denying that his silence stemmed from having her at his side. It would take a lot more than a few carefully crafted kind words to smooth over the jagged walls of their wounded emotions.

Though the whole situation remained a mystery to her, Fura found it easier to remain silent. Even if she'd wanted to talk to Kiyani, she couldn't find the right words to say.

He may have still been present in her life, walking ahead of her and paving the way to new adventures, but Fura was certain that, in his mind, he'd already left her behind.

He'd never declared after leaving the last hollow that they were no longer on speaking terms, but, even so, Fura no longer knew how to talk to him. Every attempt at even menial conversation left her stammering like a fan suddenly meeting their idol. And every raised brow of his in response left her falling back into the silence that had become her security blanket.

She had less of a chance at angering him if she simply followed him without a word. Just as she'd expected, it was tense and uncomfortable, but the situation, though far from ideal, was workable.

All she knew was that she was incredibly lucky that Kiyani hadn't actually carried out his threat.

She could still hear that haunting declaration of his.

One of these days you just might wake up and I'll be gone...

Though she wanted nothing more than to put that day out of her mind for good, she found herself reflecting on that morning again. Though she'd been dazed and still half asleep when she'd woken that first time in the hazy hours of dawn, she still couldn't shake that unnerving feeling of being completely alone. It made her wonder if, just maybe, it hadn't been a trick of her mind at all.

Shuddering at the possibility, she told herself that it was in the past.

What she needed to focus on now was the present... and a future that was looking to be filled with numerous days of lonely silence.

As much as Fura strived for something to break the unbearable silence that had fallen between her and Kiyani, she knew that any attempt at conversation would likely only dig her deeper into that unknown void.

Every little thing she said seemed to offend him, every action driving him into a rage, and it only seemed that the further they went on this journey, the worse it got. Every mishap, every ill-fated incident they went through, only added to the number of notches on the only nerve Kiyani seemed to have reserved for her: a nerve that was dangerously close to snapping.

Then again, they'd never been on good terms.

Fura was kidding herself if she thought otherwise.

She doesn't belong here...

Though the first words he'd spoken to her hadn't been in ill terms, instead joking about the color of the spring in Frielana, that hate-filled statement in Fireswell had been directed towards her before they'd even met.

Watching Kiyani walk ahead, not once glancing back to see if she was still following, it was apparent that he still harbored those initial feelings.

You wouldn't make it three days...

Almost everything he'd ever said to her had been negative and condescending.

Though this whole journey still felt like some fantasy dream, of all the things she'd been through and witnessed thus far, Kiyani still remained the biggest enigma of all. How was it that he could be so calm and reassuring one moment – diplomatically ending arguments with high-ranking officials – and then so quickly fly off the handle the next with something as simple as her walking outside? Even with that question up in the air, she faithfully followed him.

What choice did she really have?

She may have done her best to keep a smile on her face, but she found herself living in a constant state of fear, wavering between the uncertainties of when they'd next run into danger, and when he'd go into another fit of rage at the drop of a hat.

Thinking of all that'd happened so far, Fura wondered briefly if she would have embarked on this journey had she known more about him.

Probably not.

Yet, she had a feeling that wasn't true.

Trying to convince herself against her conflicted emotions, she reasoned that Kiyani's constant anger could've simply been brought on by the stress of the journey.

Whether that was true or not, there was no use in questioning it now. Fura was too far involved to turn back, even if she'd wanted to. Which only left moving forward, no matter how harrowing the road might prove to be. The sad thing was that the further they went, the more Fura found that she had to cling closer to Kiyani, despite him pushing her away. To retain her sanity and keep her head on straight. Everyone that she knew, every single person, the few and far between, that she could lay claim to as friends were back in Barandor. A world where she no longer resided.

She could still barely wrap her head around that fact.

The soil beneath her feet felt the same. The sky was the same color blue. Yet, there was a lingering feeling in her chest that told her something was amiss. It was as if there was a light charge in the air that she could just barely sense, akin to the feeling of standing beneath a high voltage power line. It was that tiny sense of awareness, that strange sensation that grew if she focused on it long enough, that told her things really were different.

There were things here that Fura had a feeling she could never even begin to understand. She had a feeling that that wash of energy she sensed every now and then was from the magic that coursed through this world.

Though she was dying to ask, she refrained from doing so. Eventually, if she could catch him in a good mood, Fura would bring it up to Kiyani.

Yet, it wasn't just the strange surroundings that made her feel as if she didn't belong in this Izandüre.

She was beginning to wonder if she would ever be able to move about on her own, knowing instinctively where she was going without needing the help of a reluctant guide. Would she ever be able to pass as a resident of this world? One that didn't need to be labeled as slow?

It wasn't just that she knew so little about Izandüre. The people were difficult to get along with. From what she'd witness so far, the ones she'd met here were nothing like the friendly people she'd run across almost daily in Barandor. No, the occupants of this world came across as crude and unfriendly, full of distrust, and intent on finding ulterior motives in any action.

At least most of them.

Fura thought of Saiva, and the bubbly personality the bright-haired Fae had possessed. If she missed anyone in this place besides her father so far, Saiva was it. The time spent with her had made Fura think of all the sleepovers and girl time she'd missed out on in school for lack of having such friends to share the time with. Those few hours before that feast Tybithera had prepared for them had been the most fun she'd had since arriving in Izandüre. Thinking back on it, Fura vowed to return to Fae Rue Keep, even if she had to go by herself.

She didn't even have to bring it to Kiyani's attention to know that he would refuse to go back. It had dawned on her not long after the mountain had fallen out of sight that he'd only claimed they might return to make her feel better. His hatred of the Fae Queen left Fura to believe that if he could help it, he'd never go out of his way to make his way back there again.

Smiling as she thought of Saiva, Fura reconciled that there were good people in this world. She just had to find them.

This world.

Though she still had difficulty grasping that reality, it wasn't simply the fact that she was on foreign soil, it was that she belonged here in some strange way.

Not only was she born in Izandüre – or so she assumed – she was a Fireheir. Probably what was considered royalty in this land.

Pausing for a moment as the term came to her, recalling what little Kiyani had told her of her inheritance, Fura wondered what made her so special. What made her any better than the man that walked ahead of her? The one who'd been appointed the guide on this journey due to his knowing this world inside and out. Even if he claimed that he wasn't practiced in fire magic, he deserved such a title far more than she did. It almost made her feel guilty.

Looking down at her hands, she wondered if it was even right for her to carry the title. It didn't matter that she hadn't owned up to it once since stepping foot in Izandüre. As far as she knew, Kiyani was the only one who even knew. Yet, the thought made her sick.

She hadn't even thought of fire since it'd consumed her home. Now she was supposed to pretend to be its master?

This is ridiculous… Fura thought.

"We're stopping here," Kiyani suddenly declared, his voice cutting through her thoughts.

"What?" Fura asked, still lost in the confines of her mind.

Kiyani threw a quick glance her way. "We're stopping here for the night," he said again, clarifying the matter. His gaze lingered briefly as if he was worried about her state of mind. Yet, the moment was short-lived. Without waiting for a reply, he moved ahead, busying himself with making a temporary camp and leaving her to her own devices.

Standing in the middle of the small clearing, Fura looked around as if seeing it for the first time. She'd been so lost in the muddled realm of her thoughts that she'd barely taken notice of the passage of time. Though she could have sworn that the sun was still high in the sky the last time she'd looked, it now floated just above the horizon, presenting itself as a large, hazy sphere of vivid orange, cut by the dark silhouette of the trees. The clouds that hung in the sky were lined with gold, slowly fading into the night in shades of light pinks and dark purples.

There was just enough daylight left to gather a few things before hunkering down for the night. The light fading, the warmth began to dissipate as well, leaving Fura to hug her cloak tighter about her thin frame.

Dreading facing another night of shivering and restless sleep, she wondered what they would do when it really started getting cold out. Were they really going to continue dodging all signs of society, fleeing those that were after them, as they bounced between one Reln hollow and the next?

There had to be a better way.

Of course, having a goal in mind would be a good start.

Watching Kiyani avoid her by keeping busy, gathering fallen pine boughs, Fura wondered again if he actually had a plan or not. She had to assume so. He didn't strike her as the type to simply wander off into the woods without some idea of where he was going. Yet, if he did have a destination in mind, he had yet to share it with her.

Realizing that she was proving to be useless yet again, standing in the middle of the clearing and doing nothing, Fura sighed. Looking down, she saw that Kiedo had come to sit beside her for a few moments before taking off for his nightly prowl, patrolling the area and searching for his own meal. Since the night of Kiyani's last outburst, the wolf had proven to be her only ally. At least he seemed to keep an eye on her, walking faithfully by Kiyani's side, but always looking behind as if checking to see how she fared. It might have been nothing more than wishful thinking, but it made Fura feel a bit better, at the least.

Looking around, she realized that they'd left the trails they'd been following and had moved deeper into the forest. The ground underfoot was spongy with decaying matter, and though the trees surrounding them had begun to cast off their leaves, the foliage was thicker. Even the undergrowth was much denser than what lie alongside the traveling trails they'd been following.

If they could even be considered as such. Though she hadn't brought it to his attention, Fura still found it strange that in all the distance they'd covered so far, that they'd hardly seen a soul besides the people that resided in Skirvynmire and the faeries in Tybithera's Keep.

She wondered if it was simply the time of year that kept people closer to home, or if Kiyani was purposely taking them on the, all too literal, road less traveled.

All she knew was that they couldn't keep going like this, avoiding society forever. Eventually they'd have to make themselves known.

✧ ⌘ ✧

Fura woke later that night with a sense of urgency in her bladder. Sitting up, she looked around, taking in their newest surroundings. Blanketed in shadow, there wasn't much to see. Only the shifting branches in the night.

Kiyani had been right about the frequency of the Reln hollows. The trees were still present, but only in sparse proportions compared to the overall number of trees in the forest they moved through. The hollows, however, had all but disappeared.

They had settled, to Kiyani's discretion, in a cove of pine branches. Outside, it looked like a dense overhang of pine, littered with fallen brush, leaving it barely noticeable to anyone who might have passed by. Yet, inside it was far more spacious than Fura had initially thought. Though it definitely wasn't as sturdy as any of their previous dwellings, nor did it keep out all of the elements, the weave of branches above at least gave the illusion of having a roof over their heads.

Though, after weeks of camping in various Reln hollows, surrounded by solid walls of dirt, and hidden in complete obscurity, Fura felt exposed as she peered through the branches to the outside world. Would anybody wandering by really not be able to see them?

Fidgeting, Fura looked over at Kiyani. He lay a few feet away, his head buried in his arms, facing away from her. She hated to wake him up, but he'd made himself clear the last time she'd left in the middle of the night to never think about going out on her own again. She felt more like a child that needed permission from a parent rather than an equal.

Ever since that night, she'd been on pins and needles, afraid to say much of anything to him, less she set him off again. The silence that hung like a suffocating cloud between them was uncomfortable to say the least, but she didn't question it. His moods moved like the ocean waves, the anger crashing in full force, and taking a few hours to a few days to completely ebb and fade away. Though, just like the waves, it was merely inevitable that no matter how good it got at times, the anger would only come back, again and again.

Moving hesitantly, Fura drew herself up into a crouch. She was almost too scared to bring herself any closer to him. Kiedo raised his head and looked at her from his chosen resting spot between them at their feet.

Looking through the branches, Fura wondered if she could just go and return quickly enough that Kiyani would never even know she'd left. But she knew better. He seemed to have some strange extra sensory perception of his surroundings that worked even in the subconscious dwellings of his sleep.

If he was even sleeping.

Raising an arm to roust him awake, Fura decided against it, remembering all the times he'd tensed and pulled away at her touch.

"Kiyani?" she whispered instead.

Stretching, he silently propped himself up on an elbow and peered over his shoulder at her.

"I have to go to the bathroom," Fura said, getting straight to the point, knowing that he probably wouldn't speak first, and that he definitely wouldn't be in the mood for the small talk that would lead up to it.

He raised a brow in question. "Then go."

"But... you said –"

"I don't care if you go out at night," he said, a bit defensively, seeming to know what she was going to say to justify her intrusion. "Just let me know, and don't stay out there long. And for Star's sake, be quiet."

"You said not to leave, though," Fura said, confused. Did he even realize that he was contradicting his previous statement?

"Because you never tell me where you're going. I wake up to find that you're missing, and I don't know where the hell you are, or even how long you've been gone. You could wander off and get lost or killed, and I would never know because you don't have the courtesy to let me know when you want to go on some damn midnight adventure."

Fura cringed. She'd never thought that he'd actually cared. "I don't like waking you."

"It doesn't matter," Kiyani claimed. Though there was an edge of irritation creeping into his voice, he quickly changed the subject. "I thought you had to go."

"I..." Lost in confusion, Fura had nearly forgotten. "I do."

Kiyani settled back down. "Then go, before I change my mind. If you're not back in ten minutes, I'm coming after you. And take Kiedo."

59

••◇••

WHAT LIES AHEAD

"I don't care what you do..."

The words swam in Fura's mind as she sat on a small rock outcropping that jutted out from the damp earth alongside one of the pines. Curled up in her cloak against the morning chill, she nearly blended in with the bark of the surrounding trees as she watched the shifting fog that hung hazily a few inches from the ground.

It would slowly melt away as the sun rose higher in the sky, a new day in wait, but for now light was only starting to break on the horizon. It was early yet, but Fura couldn't bring herself to sleep any longer. Not with the scare of abandonment still fresh in her mind.

From what she could recall, this was the only time she'd been the first one awake. Almost always, Kiyani was up and roving about long before she first opened her eyes in the morning.

Though she should have woken Kiyani to inform him that she was leaving, Fura didn't feel guilty for once about not telling him. It wasn't nighttime, when the danger they faced generally seemed to materialize. And, technically, she was only a few feet away. A quick glance over her shoulder would give her a glimpse of his sleeping form through the molting branches that made up their shelter.

Even if she'd wanted to, she couldn't find it in herself to wake him.

It was one of the few times she'd actually seen Kiyani sleeping, rather than in the throes of restlessness or faking it. It almost pained her to see that even in sleep he wasn't at peace. There was none of that calm demeanor that overcame one when they fell into unconsciousness. Instead, he was as fitful as ever, as if, even in that state of mind, he was fighting inner demons.

Fura was almost too afraid to ask what exactly those monsters were for him.

She had her own demons, of course, but only recently. The nightmares that she'd had before seemed childish now compared to what haunted her dreams as of late; horrid creatures, ghost towns, and flames that raged out of control, engulfing the entire world.

Fireheir.

Fura sighed as the word crept into her head.

How could she possibly claim heirship to an element that she couldn't even control in her own dreams? She didn't know what was worse; that dawning realization, or the reoccurring visions of the horrid things she'd already seen in person and the new ones that her rampant mind created out of thin air.

The monsters that lurked in the dark where all too real now. It was no longer as easy as waking up in the morning and simply telling herself it had been a dream. Not when the creatures that thrived in the shadows walked in the daylight as well.

Yet, as she peered at Kiyani again, she realized that even her darkest dreams were probably tame compared to what was going through his head.

What plagued him seemed far deeper and much darker. And there was no telling if he was winning the battle.

As the sun rose higher, bringing with it an orange haze of light that washed over the land, Fura was brought out of her reverie by a dark shadow at the edge of her vision.

Kiedo sauntered up from their shelter and came to her side. Slowly he stretched out, loosening the stiffness in his limbs from sleeping before sitting next to her. He didn't look her way, or even take notice of Fura. Instead he seemed to focus on the sun as well, sharing with her the quiet peace of the morning.

It was a silence that was short lived. As dawn finally broke, sunlight streaming through the trees, a chorus of birds steadily rose through the air. Fura smiled as she listened. As noisy as it was, it was a pleasant reminder that the world continued to turn, despite the tragedy and hardships she'd faced. Not to mention, it was good to know that, even if it wasn't always present, there was still other life around.

Too often she felt completely alone. Especially on the days when Kiyani was mad at her, something that was becoming more and more frequent as the days passed.

She let out a breath, trying to tell herself that none of it bothered her.

But Fura knew that was a lie.

Kiedo looked her way as if even though he hadn't acknowledged her presence he'd been fully aware of it, as well as her inner feelings, and was now wondering what could possibly be wrong on such a fine morning.

Expecting confusion in his eyes to go with the questioning cock of his head, Fura was surprised to see a playful air reflected back in the wolf's gaze. The stick she'd picked off the ground earlier, mindlessly sketching lines in the dirt, now seemed to have gained his attention.

Fiddling with the stick as she'd played over her thoughts, Fura had nearly forgotten about it.

Raising it into the air, she grinned as Kiedo's eyes followed it. Rising to stand, he titled his head, waiting. In the moment, he reminded her more of a regular dog than the wild animal he really was.

"Will you go get it if I throw it?" Fura asked. She had to laugh at herself, knowing all too well that he wouldn't answer her.

Yet, in this world, she couldn't be certain. She'd seen a lot in this past month, but talking animals hadn't yet made an appearance. At least it wouldn't be the worst or the strangest thing she had encountered.

She'd never played fetch with a wolf before and had no idea if he would even understand the concept. Her own dog, Barry, had never taken to it no matter how hard she'd tried. After years, Fura had finally just given up. Despite the popular saying, some old dogs just weren't up to new tricks.

Casually tossing the stick, Fura watched the wolf, wondering what he would do, if anything.

Kiedo watched as it sailed through the air, landing a few feet away in the grass, his ears perked. Looking back at her, he seemed to question why she'd so carelessly discarded it. Rather than chase after it excitedly like most dogs, Kiedo took his time walking over to where it'd landed. Sniffing at it with caution, he took it up in his jaws, and sauntered back to where Fura sat.

Dumbfounded, Fura watched as he dropped it at her feet. His eyes moving from her to the stick, it was clear he wanted to continue the game.

Bending to get the stick, Fura threw it again, laughing as Kiedo bounded after it this time, apparently enjoying this small change of pace.

"He must like you."

Fura shot up, startled by the voice. "What?" she asked, turning to face its owner.

Kiyani leaned against one of the pines that had provided their shelter, looking like sleep didn't want to give up its hold over him as he stifled a yawn.

"He doesn't play like that too often," he said, nodding towards Kiedo who, seeing that Fura was distracted, was now laying in the grass chewing the bark off the branch.

"Oh," Fura glancing over towards Kiedo then shyly back to Kiyani.

She hadn't even heard him get up, let alone leave the little shelter or sneak up on her. Fura wondered if he frequently did that on purpose, but she doubted it. In all honesty, from what she'd been able to gather about him, she was beginning to realize that it was just how he was... quiet and sneaky, built from years of experience hunting, or hiding from god knew what.

She could hear the crunching of the slender piece of wood behind her as Kiedo devoted his attention to it, leaving them on their own. Leaving her on her own.

Even with the few words they'd exchanged, Fura could feel her cheeks redden. After all that had transpired between them in the past weeks, she still didn't know how to act around him. Most days felt like an emotional roller coaster. Between the frequent history lessons, though fewer than she would have liked, and Kiyani's mood swings, Fura felt like she was in a never ending fog. A wild fantasy dream with just a hint of nightmare lingering in the background.

"I see you didn't get lost last night," Kiyani commented. There was little emotion in his voice as he moved over to Kiedo.

It had been strange to wander out in the darkness after that conversation.

I don't care what you do.

That phrase still lingered. She'd managed just fine on her own, and had apparently remained within his time constraints. For once, there'd been no danger lurking in the night. No deadly creatures. No bands of men that worked for dark lords after them. Only the silent company of the stars that twinkled in the sky. It should have been calming, but Fura had only found herself on edge. Each little sound leaving her paranoid. If anything, she'd been overly cautious, though she could almost hear Kiyani claim that there was no such thing.

As much as she'd wanted to return to gloat, reminding him that danger didn't follow them every minute of the day, she'd refrained. One night of peace didn't mean they wouldn't run into trouble again. In the next few days. On this morning. There was no telling.

Not knowing what else to say or do, she watched Kiyani. Kneeling down in front of the wolf, he playfully ruffled the gray fur before prying the stick out of his jaws to continue the game that he'd inadvertently halted.

Though Fura could tell that their exchanged words were the last thing on his mind, she couldn't help but wonder if maybe he'd hoped she would get lost in the night.

Always, he came after her, but would there be a time when he simply gave up, deciding she wasn't worth the trouble?

Resuming her place on the outcropping of stone, Fura wrapped her cloak around herself to fend off the brisk fall air and watched the two before her interact as if she wasn't there. A mysterious man that she was afraid of, yet spent all her time with, and a wild beast with the demeanor of a protective saint.

She shook her head as she reflected on that thought. At least Kiyani was talking to her today.

✧ ⌘ ✧

"So, where are we going anyway?" Fura asked later that afternoon, finally dredging up the courage to initiate a conversation consisting of more than a few words.

She didn't know what it was, but Kiyani appeared more approachable today. Maybe it was the fact that he'd slept longer than usual, giving her the idea that they weren't in any immediate danger. If they were, he would have had them back on the road at the crack of dawn, continuing to distance themselves from where they'd started. Or, maybe it'd been the sight of him playing with Kiedo, seeming to loosen up from his usual tense nature.

Though the morning had already waned away, they had yet to leave their camp. It was unusual of Kiyani to have them stick around for so long in one place, but Fura hadn't bothered to question it. At least not this time.

Nor did she question his motives when he'd told her to stay put. She'd kept her inane fears of him leaving and not coming back to herself and had promised not to go anywhere, instead lingering within the shelter of pine branches and indulging in a light nap. He'd taken Kiedo with him, but left his belongings behind. That was enough to take the edge off her worries.

An hour later he had strolled back into camp with a rabbit and what she assumed were edible roots.

Kiyani glanced at her before returning his focus to the pile of sticks he'd gathered. "I thought I told you already."

Fura watched him fervently try to light a fire the old fashioned way. She shook her head. "Trust me, I'm trying to remember everything."

Too busy with the task at hand, he seemed only slightly aware of her presence, or his involvement in the conversation. There was none of the irritable edge that generally accompanied his voice when she began to ask questions.

"I don't think you ever said," Fura added when he didn't reply. She was sure that was the truth, though at this point she couldn't even remember that much. For once his indifference could play to her advantage.

"No?" he answered. Forgetting his task for a moment, he looked at her as if he didn't believe her.

Fura shook her head. "Pretty sure the last you said was just that we were going east."

"Oh." Seeming to remember something, he returned his attention to the task at hand. "Du Reizlan," he answered a few moments later as he fiddled with the pile.

"Do what?" Fura asked. She had no idea what or where this place was, but it sounded like a disease. Not only that, but now she was certain that this was the first Kiyani had mentioned it. How long had he had a destination in mind without telling her?

"Du Reizlan," he said again. "I guess you could say it's the equivalent of our school here," Kiyani added. He must have anticipated the coming questions.

"There are schools here?"

Kiyani raised a brow as if it should have been obvious. "Izandüre's not that far off the map."

"School..." Fura repeated, a sinking feeling in forming in her gut.

True, she hadn't finished high school, though she had been so close, but did she really have to go here? Education was currently the last thing on her mind. Though, if she thought about it, she was sure that whatever was taught in Izandüre was a lot more interesting than the classes in her school in Barandor.

A spark flashed in the kindling Kiyani had piled, then instantly sputtered out. Fura could hear him swear under his breath.

"It's not like Barandor," Kiyani said, as if trying to convince her of something. "It's more magic focused, and the history is way different, if you haven't gathered that already. It could be of use to you."

Taking a break, he leaned back and scratched his head as if willing himself to dig up a different approach to his task.

"But why are we going?"

Good for her. What was that supposed to mean? Kiyani had made no mention of himself in that statement.

"The Witneis Reln."

Fura's head shot up. "It's there?"

How could he have found out? When had he found out, and why was he just telling her now?

Leaning forward, Kiyani began to tackle the fire again. "I doubt it."

"Oh..." she could feel the instant adrenaline of hope fizzle away.

"But they have one of the largest libraries around. If there's any information about the Witneis..."

"It'd be there," Fura finished, understanding.

"Right."

Fura nodded thoughtfully as she watched him work. She didn't feel as if they had time for side trips, but if they could find something, anything, about this strange tree, then it could definitely be worth their time.

"So, this public library would have something about it?"

Kiyani's eyes met hers, a hint of trepidation in the unnatural blue depth of his gaze. "It's not public."

"What?"

"Only students and scholars are allowed access," Kiyani clarified.

So much for thinking they finally had a heading. "How are we going to get in, then?"

"That's yet to be determined."

"Are we going to sneak in?" Fura asked, hoping he wouldn't answer yes to that. He had to know by now that she was no good at such things.

"I'd rather not," he answered to her relief. "I have a feeling we'll have to end up taking classes."

Though it was better than trying to sneak in, Fura wasn't sure she liked the idea of that, either. Eventually, it would probably be fun. But right now, all she could think about was what would be happening to her father as she sat in a classroom listening to Izandüre's history.

"Have you been planning to go there all along?" Fura asked, avoiding that thought.

"No," Kiyani confirmed. "It actually never crossed my mind until I talked to Rowan."

"Rowan?" She'd never heard the name before. When had he had the time to talk to people and come up with ideas?

Kiyani looked up at her with a raised brow as if she should've known who she was speaking of. "Your bard you forced me to talk to?"

"Oh," Fura said. She'd never gotten the man's name, but it made sense now. "So he did have information?"

Kiyani snorted. "Not much. Just useless riddles… the knowledge lies within the words of knowledge… It took me a few days, but Du Reizlan seemed like a good bet. It couldn't hurt to search the library. Plus, it gives me the chance to dig for facts without having to actually bring up to anyone what we're searching for."

Another spark lit momentarily, dying seconds later.

It was easy to see that Kiyani was getting frustrated.

The image of the darkfire he'd created came to her mind, leaving Fura to wonder why he didn't just use magic. But the image of his burnt hands reminded her of his previous answer.

She looked down at her own hands. Did she really have this pyropheric power? And if she did, how could Kiyani be so sure that it wouldn't have the same unwanted effects on her as it did him?

The flickering glow of a flame caught Fura's attention. Looking up she found that Kiyani had turned to her, his task finally accomplished.

His gaze shifted from her hands to her eyes as if reading her thoughts. Uncomfortable, she dropped her hands and averted her eyes.

"Maybe after some schooling you can finally make yourself useful around here."

Offended, Fura went to say something but Kiyani had already gotten up.

As much as she wanted to chase after him and demand an apology for such a rude comment, Fura knew it would be futile. An apology for the brash nature of his words would be the last thing she would ever get from him.

Out of the corner of her eye she could see him busy himself with other things. Whether he had left so abruptly because he had just wanted out of the conversation, or because he actually had other things to do, Fura would never know.

Focusing on what was in front of her, she found that the fire Kiyani had left was now building and feeding upon itself. In a matter of minutes it would fully engulf the pile of wood, charring it until it left nothing but a pile of black ash. It almost reminded her of the fires that had consumed her home, but her actual thoughts were elsewhere.

Gazing into the flames, she wondered if this unsteady, rocky ground that her and Kiyani continually walked on would one day solidify or just eventually crumble out from beneath them.

60

♦♦◇♦♦

A CHANGE IN MOOD

Having eaten her fill of fresh meat, rather than the dried strips left over from Tybithera's supplies, Fura wandered along the path behind Kiyani with more energy than she'd possessed in days. Though she'd felt bad for the rabbit that had become their lunch, Fura hadn't asked where it had come from, or how Kiyani had acquired it. She figured that either he had hunting and trapping on his list of skills that she didn't know about or Kiedo had acquired the prize for them, a loyal gift to his master. Once the smell of meat roasting over an open fire had hit her nose, Fura hadn't cared.

She'd never had rabbit before, nothing any more exotic than the occasional fish dinner here and there, but it had been worth the wait. It couldn't have come at a better time, either. She didn't think she could have handled another loaf of stale bread and the few measly portions of dried meat that she assumed was beef that had been the staple of their diet since they'd departed Skirvynmire. Both of which had been leftover from the rations the Fae Queen had supplied them with upon leaving Fae Rue Keep. Though he hadn't voiced it, apparently Kiyani had felt the same. Both of them had left what little remained of their bread out of the meal entirely.

They'd lingered around their camp for about another hour afterwards. Little had been said and done in that time. And though Fura could have returned to the shelter for another nap, she hadn't dared mention it to Kiyani. Instead, when he'd begun to pack up, Fura had wordlessly followed suit. Minutes later, they'd been back on the figurative road.

Though she still didn't have much of a heading, or even a faint image of their destination, for once Fura had a name. And the validation that they were actually en route to somewhere in particular. She didn't know how she felt about seeking out a school in this strange land, but it made her feel better to know that Kiyani wasn't just leading them blindly.

That she knew of.

Even if he had been leading her astray, Fura would never know. She hadn't grown up in Izandüre. She had no general idea of the layout of the land, of its landmarks. She'd never even glimpsed a map, though she knew they must exist. Every tree, every hill that they passed all looked the same to her. If they were going in circles Fura wouldn't be able to rightfully claim so.

But she had faith in Kiyani, even if he claimed she shouldn't. Fura trusted that he wouldn't lead her off course. She had the feeling that even if he wasn't under the pressure of acting as a guide, that if he was going it alone, he would still find his way. The way he glided effortlessly through the maze of trees gave her the impression that he knew this place inside and out. And even if that wasn't truth, he sure knew how to make others believe so.

Thinking on this Du Reizlan, she wondered how he even knew where it was. He'd said he'd never been there, yet he seemed confident in his direction. Not bothering to question him, her thoughts side-tracked to the worry that they couldn't afford to spend time at this school. If they could simply peruse the library for a few days for any useful articles, and then be on their way, it would be a different story. But even Kiyani had admitted that they might be forced to take classes in order to be admitted. How long would that sidetrack them?

Kiyani had said that the information the library might hold was the draw Du Reizlan held, yet she had a feeling that he was leaving something out. As if he had other ideas that he'd failed to make mention of.

Beyond that nagging feeling, images of Apallo edged into her mind. Knowing now that he was her father, Fura had the desperate urge to see him again, to talk to him in the light of that discovery. How long had she worked within the gates of the Fireswell festival by his side, taking tutelage from him in the art of firedancing? All that time and he'd never said a word to her about it. Not so much as a brief mention. As much as it hurt to think about, she knew that he must've had a good reason for it.

At least she hoped so.

Until she heard Apallo's side of the story, Fura wouldn't pass judgment.

She only hoped that Kiyani would be able to find what he was looking for in Du Reizlan's library so they could continue on. Though she hated not knowing how Apallo was currently doing, she knew he had to have been worse off than they currently were. She shuddered as she recalled the last dream she'd had, depicting him in captivity, bloodied and bruised. She just hoped that the next time she saw him, he'd still be alive.

Clearing the morbid thoughts and images from her mind, Fura tried to focus on the day ahead of her. It was easier said than done. The thrill of being in the woods had worn off long ago, the excitement of being surrounded by nature long gone. Even the initial rush of traveling alone with Kiyani had lost its general appeal. More than not, Fura found it increasingly easy to get lost in her own thoughts, some of which she was glad Kiyani had no knowledge of.

The past few days had been quiet. Kiyani's last mood swing had left her wary of being around him, afraid to spark up conversation. Yet, despite her vow that she'd give up, her feelings for him hadn't subsided in the least. Even so, spurred onward by that unexpected kiss in Skirvynmire, that was one of the last things she'd ever bring up to him.

Yet, curiosity had always gotten the best of her. Knowing that she'd bring it up to him someday, Fura set it aside, currently distracted by the fact that she was alone with Kiyani again.

It was the first time since that dark night that Kiedo had left them for any considerable amount of time. Seeming to sense the change in Kiyani, appearing livelier today, Kiedo had bounded off into the woods not long after they'd left their campsite. Assuming that he'd gone to find himself something to eat, Fura continually kept watch, wondering when he'd return. With the wolf gone, she'd been left to her own devices.

Though she knew there was no conversation to be had with the creature, he still added a sense of entertainment to the long days. She enjoyed watching the wolf bound along playfully at Kiyani's side. If anything, he seemed to take the rough edge away from the wall that'd formed between her and Kiyani.

Despite not having Kiedo with them, the air was awash with a new energy.

Since early that morning, Fura had noticed something different in Kiyani. It was such a meager change that at first Fura had thought she was imagining things, but as the day progressed, she became more confident in her observation.

He seemed more spirited today, despite looking like he hadn't been able to shake sleep earlier. Walking faster than usual, which Fura couldn't say she was all too happy about, Kiyani looked more alert, as if anticipation had him in its grasp. He stood taller and was more focused than he had been in awhile. In his own way, Fura would almost say he was giddy, like how one got when they knew the end of a long car ride was just around the corner.

"We're getting close, aren't we?" Fura asked, taking a stab in the dark. In was her best guess, but she had a feeling she was right.

Though he didn't let up on the pace at all, Kiyani turned his head just slightly at her voice, as if in the thralls of excitement, or the mere fact that she'd been so quiet, he had forgotten that she was even there.

"Closer," he answered. "If not tomorrow, we should run into it in the next few days."

Fura paused for a moment as the realization hit her.

"Already?" When he'd given her the name of their destination she'd simply assumed that it was still a ways away. Maybe a week or more. Not a day.

She had been joking with herself when she'd thought that the impending run in with this Du Reizlan had been the cause of Kiyani's turnaround. The implication of the truth hit her harder than she'd expected.

As much as she wouldn't mind, needed really, a change of pace, Fura wasn't sure if she was ready for that drastic of a change. She had no idea what to expect. As mundane as the days had become, she had fallen quite easily into the groove of mindlessly following Kiyani through the forest. Even the pain of being on her feet for so long and all this newfound exercise that she was so unaccustomed to, had worn off.

"Getting cold feet?" Kiyani asked as if she were auditioning for a big play. There was a hint of sarcasm in his question.

She shook her head. "No." How could she? She hadn't even been given enough time to have cold feet.

Kiyani glanced back at her with a raised eyebrow, but said nothing further.

Fura couldn't justify the defensive edge that resonated in her voice. Though she had nothing to be afraid of, was it possible that he was right again? Why was she so hesitant to come face to face with this school?

She wanted to claim that she didn't know, but the answer was on the tip of her tongue.

Abandonment.

She was afraid of feeling that sense of abandonment again.

What exactly were they going to do there? Did Kiyani really plan on getting them into classes? Would they even find anything useful? Would they be separated?

That last question was what bothered Fura the most. There was no denying it. As awkward as she felt around Kiyani most of the time, she didn't want to be completely void of his presence. Not in this strange world. She felt like he was the only one who could get her through this in one piece, both physically and mentally. What she'd already encountered was enough to fray the edges of her sanity.

Even during Kiyani's worst moments, Fura had never wanted him gone from her life completely.

The first few days spent in Tybithera's dwelling had been the longest consecutive period of time she'd spent away from Kiyani, and the entire time she'd been in a state of panic, afraid that she would never see him again, never be able to make it out of that predicament on her own.

What would she have done if she'd actually been able to plan and execute an escape?

Fura knew the answer and the outcome would have been dim.

Their time in Skirvynmire hadn't necessarily been spent together, but they hadn't been completely separated either. Mostly Fura had only seen Kiyani at night, but at least she'd had a sense of where he was.

No, Fae Rue Keep had been worse.

That was the root of her fear.

Fura didn't want to feel that loss again, that unyielding sense of hopelessness that had plagued her since the fire. Kiyani may have been stubborn, obstinate, and at times scary, but he was a known companion, her protector, and, most of all, her lifeline.

✧ ⌘ ✧

It was later that night as Fura lay in the dark, chasing the tendrils of sleep, that she was shocked into consciousness as a sharp crack drew her attention into the woods surrounding them. She wasn't sure what direction it had come from.

Trying to remain calm, she moved slowly onto her stomach and looked over at Kiyani. He was fast asleep, and completely unaware of the impending danger.

Fura's heart raced as she heard the noise again. It rang through the stillness of night, followed by the rustling of foliage and another dead branch breaking.

Something was out there.

Forced into another lean to of pine branches for the night, she felt overly exposed.

Unable to take it any longer, Fura hesitantly jarred Kiyani out of unconsciousness.

"Kiyani?" she whispered.

He rolled over to look at her, his features murky in the dim light, though his face was a mixture of irritation and the fog of sleep. "What?"

She pointed to the darkness before them. "There's something out there."

Again, the noise resounded through the trees.

Kiyani shifted to look down at his feet where Kiedo lay, his head up and ears perked as he listened to the disturbance. There was no blaming it on him.

Listening and waiting, they lay still and silent. Moments later, just on the edge of their peripheral vision a tawny mass came into view.

Fura closed her eyes and ducked her head, trying to keep her fear under control. She hadn't caught a good glimpse of it, yet her mind was racing out of control with images of what it could be.

"I hate to tell you this," Kiyani said softly, "but you need to stay very still. A very vicious beast, it can smell fear."

She couldn't help it, but a low whine escaped her throat as she shivered. Was this going to end up as another unfortunate lesson in the discovery of the creatures that inhabited this world?

Forcing herself to open her eyes, but not wanting to look out to where she knew the creature was, Fura looked over at Kiyani instead, hoping to see that look in his eyes that would claim everything was going to be okay.

"What is it?" she asked shakily.

His attention was on whatever lay in wait for them out there, but as he turned at her voice, Fura found herself confused. A perfect mirror of contrast to her own rampant emotions, a smile tugged at the corner of Kiyani's mouth.

"It's a deer."

She was silent, taking in what he'd just said. As it dawned on her, Fura had to fight the urge to hit him.

"You're mean," Fura hissed as she swatted at him anyways.

Kiyani artfully dodged her hand, laughing.

Fura's heart skipped a beat at the sound and she turned away, afraid that he would see the effect it'd had on her. It wasn't often that she saw that side of Kiyani, but every time she did it caught her off guard.

"Not everything you come across is dangerous," he said, a playful glimmer in his eye.

We must be close, Fura thought. The past week, his demeanor and actions had been steadily growing darker. Now he was joking with her.

"You can feign ignorance, but don't actually ignore your surroundings."

She nearly sighed in relief. Now, that sounded more like him.

"Now, go back to sleep," Kiyani said, oblivious to her thoughts. "And get some rest, we should be there tomorrow."

He didn't allow her the benefit of replying before he turned and lay back down, though she was sure that she could see him shaking his head in amusement.

Shifting so that she was sitting, Fura looked out into the darkness, wondering if the deer was still out there listening to them, or if they'd scared it away.

Turning to look at Kiyani, he appeared to have already returned to sleep. Bringing her knees up to her chest, she laid her head on them. He'd said they should arrive at Du Reizlan tomorrow, yet Fura didn't know if she was ready for that.

Just thinking about Kiyani's smile quickened her heartbeat, and she looked over at him wishing she could see it again. She was glad to see him happy for once, but Fura couldn't help but wonder if he was so giddy because they were one step closer to hopefully finding information about the Witneis Reln, or if it was because he was one day closer to getting rid of her.

61

•• ◇ ••

DU REIZLAN

"Welcome to Du Reizlan."

Ripped from her train of thought, Fura paused in her step and looked up. "What?"

Spurred on by the possibilities that lay ahead, Kiyani had woken her before dawn that morning, rearing to go. Bleary-eyed, she stumbled out of the shelter, quickly dressing and gobbling down what was left of their dried meat rations. Still fighting the haze of sleep, they'd packed up and were out on the road just as the sun was breaking on the horizon.

A sunny start to a long day of travel.

Miles had disappeared beneath their feet as Fura had slowly come into consciousness as the crystallized dew on the silent grasses melted and evaporated away. Lacking Kiedo's presence, she'd taken to acutely studying the ground.

Though there was still little in the way of conversation between her and Kiyani, the air between them wasn't nearly as brittle as it had been.

Something had taken his edge away and Fura was sure that she knew its name: Du Reizlan. She still had nothing but a name to go on and a faint idea of what exactly it was.

Now, Kiyani stood in front of her on the edge of a stone paved road, holding a hand in the air like a model presenting a prize on a TV show. Behind him, a short distance away, sitting upon a hill surrounded by thick forest, rose a huge building of dark stone.

"Du Reizlan," he repeated again.

Though Kiyani had stopped on the most solid looking path they had seen in their entire journey, Fura held back.

Du Reizlan.

So, this was it.

The place that had been causing her agony since he'd first mentioned it only the day before. The place that had kept her awake half the night without ever laying an eye on it.

Now it stood before her, looking like the grand centerpiece in a museum painting.

Fura stood in the tree line, gawking at the vastness of the building before them as awe, among other emotions, overtook her. Though it was indeed grand, it had the appearance of not belonging, the structure appearing far too big for this world, too large a piece of civilization. Though Fura knew that Kiyani had been purposely keeping them from large towns, she'd had a hard time until now even imagining anything larger than the village of Skirvynmire.

What towered before them now was the largest building they'd encountered yet. Tybithera's dwelling had been vast and ornate, but the Keep had mainly consisted of a sprawling network of cavernous tunnels throughout the mountain. With most of Fae Rue underground, it was hard to compare it with the monolithic gothic structure of Du Reizlan.

Casting her initial reaction aside and looking at the school from afar, Fura realized that it did belong. In fact, the moment she'd learned that this land was full of myth and magic, this was what she'd found herself hoping for. With its peaks and turrets crafted from dark, aged and weathered granite, it looked like a grand castle from the medieval ages.

A brief image of knights in full armor, perched atop massive, decorated horses filled Fura's mind, and she wondered if such a thing existed in this land. Was there a town somewhere, similar to the build of this school, where knights in shining armor adorned princesses with lavish gifts? Where there were daily bouts of jousting and other royal games?

It was a fanciful vision, but Fura doubted the reality of it.

The games of the renaissance, Fura didn't question. This whole world had the feel of being dropped in some movie set from a medieval era film. The knights in shining armor, however, were sure to be in short supply. If they even existed. If they did, she had yet to run across one. As much as she was attracted to him, Kiyani didn't quite fit the bill.

Every day that they moved further ahead, every little thing that Fura added to her repertoire of knowledge on the world of Izandüre lowered her expectations. She wasn't having a terrible time, but it definitely wasn't the fantasy escape from her life that she had found herself hoping for.

This was no different.

What currently towered before them made Fura want to run the other way, back into the arms of the Streig or any of the other nasties they'd had the displeasure of meeting. School itself had never proven to be a problem for her back in Barandor, but it didn't mean she wanted to return to some semblance of it. She may not have had a hard time with the studies, but the social aspect had been hell.

A month and a half had passed since Fura had fled Barandor with no notice. Not that she'd had anyone to notify.

"Haven't you ever wondered why you have no other family?"

Kiyani's words from the night he'd revealed her true heritage drifted through her mind.

It terrified her that she'd never once thought to question what he had so bluntly stated. No family. She knew of no aunts, no uncles, or grandparents, and now she knew the reason why.

Revisiting that revelation made her wonder if there was anyone back in that old life that even knew she was missing.

Would the local television station be running ads with her picture, asking if anyone knew where she was?

Probably not.

If there was anyone who'd taken notice of her absence it would have been those that she'd worked with in Fireswell; Tiyano or Kieli. Apallo might've counted her as missing, but not for the same reason. She wondered if he was as worried about her as she was him. He'd been deeply concerned about her before the siege. She could only imagine what was on his mind now.

Barandor.

Frielana.

That all seemed so long ago.

Throwing caution to the wind for once in her life, Fura took in a deep breath.

None of that matters, she told herself. *This is the here and now.*

"So," Fura finally asked, not sounding nearly as confident as she'd hoped. "This is Du Reizlan?"

Despite the effort at newfound courage, Fura still found herself unable to move, her feet frozen to the ground, acting out what her subconscious willed: refusing to step foot into unknown territory.

Kiyani looked back at her with a faint smile, unaware of her inner struggle. He had yet to move forward himself, but he looked more excited than she felt.

As if sizing up the next leg of their journey, they both quietly stood on the side of the road, looking down the path of stones to the building that lay at its end.

"You were expecting something different, I assume?"

She couldn't say for sure what she'd been expecting. "Maybe a bit smaller?" she said unconvincingly.

"I know you didn't grow up here," Kiyani said. "Haven't been exposed to anything really, but I will warn you, this world isn't nearly as desolate as it's probably come across. I tend to skirt around the large towns and cities, but people really do live here."

Kiyani smiled as he looked back at Fura, as if he were revealing something incredibly important for the first time.

Though her curiosity threatened to get the best of her, Fura just couldn't find the motivation to start the journey forward. She wasn't sure what it was that they were moving towards in the first place, but this hadn't been in her thoughts.

Now that they were here, now that Du Reizlan had proven to be real, Fura didn't quite know what to think.

Without notice Kiyani stepped out onto the road and began the walk down the winding road towards the school.

Fura watched him go, still rooted in place. She wanted to be excited, but fear filled her instead.

What would this mean for their journey? How long would they be here? What would she encounter, and who would she meet? Would Kiyani actually be able to find anything here, or would they find out weeks, maybe even months later, that it had all been a waste of time?

She couldn't help but think that nothing but uncertainty lie ahead in the form of this stone structure, full of people she didn't know and wasn't sure she wanted to meet. A building dedicated to all the things she probably should have known, having been born in Izandüre. What lie before her was a vast tomb of intelligence about a world that she'd only recently heard of.

Kiyani made constant note of her naïve nature enough as it was. Fura could only hope that the people she was bound to meet here wouldn't pick up on it quite so easily. She was becoming increasingly tired of being the follower, the one that didn't know anything. Unfortunately, she had the feeling that here, in Izandüre, that's all she would ever be able to amount to.

Watching Kiyani stroll forward without any hint of hesitation Fura wondered if it had begun already. Would he so easily be consumed with other things that he would forget about her entirely? He was yards down the road already and he hadn't once stopped to see if she was obediently following.

"Hey!" Fura shouted, taking the leap of faith and jumping out onto the path. "Wait for me!"

As soon as her feet hit the solid ground, Fura could feel the large presence behind her.

Turning to see what it was, she let out a scream as the image of a huge chestnut horse filled her vision. Rearing up on his hind legs, her sudden existence startling him, he whinnied in fright. The sight only made Fura's heart pound harder as she quickly sidestepped to get out of the creature's way just in time, the horse's hooves thundering back to the ground in the exact spot Fura had been only seconds before.

"Whoa girl, calm yourself," a man said firmly from the beast's back.

The fear she had seen reflected in the mare's eyes had kept her from noticing her rider.

"I'm sorry," Fura stammered as she bowed clumsily before the man. "I'm so sorry."

Not allowing herself make eye contact with the rider, for fear of having to further explain her stupidity, Fura turned away and rushed forward to where Kiyani stood yards ahead, quietly watching her antics.

Fura halted next to him, out of breath.

He remained where he was for a moment, one eyebrow raised questioningly.

"We're not even in the building yet and you're already causing trouble?" Kiyani shook his head and moved on.

This time she was quick to follow.

"Hasn't anyone ever told you to look both ways before crossing the street?"

Fura could feel the heat rise in her cheeks. "In my defense, I wasn't technically crossing the street."

"Look before you leap?" Kiyani tried again.

"I'm not going to hear the end of this, am I?" Fura sighed. Though the incident had only just occurred, she felt like she'd just given Kiyani something to tease her about for the next few weeks.

"I'm only pointing out the obvious."

"So I made a mistake," Fura huffed. "Excuse me."

His reply was solemn. "Mistakes can cost lives."

"I'm fine. Like you've never made a mistake before?" *Mister perfection,* Fura added in her mind.

"I'm not saying that. But... then again, I've never been nearly trampled by a horse before."

Regaining the normal rhythm of her breathing, Fura looked at the building ahead of them. From this angle on the road it seemed to tower even more menacingly before them. As if to further verify its superiority, the sun had begun setting behind it, casting the background into rich hues of dark orange and making a mere silhouette of the grand structure.

Where she once would've been excited by the prospect of seeing the inside of such a stately structure, now the thought of entering its doors made Fura anxious. After weeks of treading on grass and dirt that softened the sound of their travels, she was all too aware of her echoing footfalls on the stone below. It was as if her conscience were following close behind her, telling her to turn around before it was too late.

Too late for what? she wondered.

Though the road wound further ahead, winding and trailing up the towering hill, Fura stopped next to Kiyani in the middle of the trail, peering at the ornate wrought iron arch that bore the name of the school in pointed gothic lettering.

Du Reizlan

The statement was simple. Just the school's name. No 'welcome to', no 'turn back now', just the name. There was nothing to even give the indication that it was a place of learning.

Fura supposed that it didn't need any of that, that if she had grown up in Izandüre that mere reputation would precede it.

The lettering was accented with an intricate weave of filigreed scrollwork of the same deep black metal. What looked to be the remnants of gold leafing was flaking off from years of abuse by the elements. Anchoring the whole piece were tall rods, reminiscent of huge metal spears, of descending height on either side of the arch that disappeared into the foliage surrounding the structure.

As interesting as it was in architectural standards, she didn't know if it particularly screamed a healthy welcome. If anything it only gave her the chills. She already felt as if she were on the path to entering some abandoned fortress laden with the undead. This was just the rusty gate she needed as a final touch to complete the picture.

Standing in silence, taking in the wonder of this piece of art in the middle of the wilds, Fura became aware of the sound of someone approaching.

It wasn't the softer echoes of another set of feet, but a louder, more metallic *clip-clop*.

Fura already knew who it was before the voice pierced the air.

"Your lady sure gave my Betsy a scare."

Kiyani turned to the man's attention before Fura did.

Only after he'd nodded his head in a silent welcome did he glance over at Fura. As if she weren't embarrassed enough over the incident, she could see the trace of an amused smile on Kiyani's face.

"I'm really sorry about that," Fura apologized again, ignoring Kiyani as he stifled a chuckle. She faced the man, hoping to come across as more sincere this time.

Holding up a hand, the man shook his head. "No need to apologize, my dear. Things happen. The name's Durman, by the way." He leaned forward on his horse, low enough so that he could shake both their hands.

Fura did so reluctantly, not sure if she liked this man or not. She looked to Kiyani for reassurance, but he wasn't paying her much attention, seeming to be relatively at ease with their new acquaintance.

With no discussion of the matter, the group began to move forward.

"A little late for students to be outside, isn't it?" the man inquired as they passed beneath the arch.

"Not students yet," Kiyani answered casually.

Fura listened to him with confusion. He talked with this man like it was someone he'd met before and they were merely catching up. With anyone else he would be guarded, his words equally measured.

The man threw a smile back at Fura who, out of habit, had fallen behind and assumed the position of the rear. She didn't want to get in that horse's way again if she could help it.

"New students, then?"

Kiyani nodded. "So we're hoping."

"Creslin's not fond of late comers, you know."

"I'm aware."

"Don't worry. I'm here to see the master myself. I'll put in a good word for you."

Kiyani bowed his head in appreciation for Durman's sudden generosity. "Do you think you could lead us to his quarters?" he asked as more of an afterthought.

Durman nodded in return. "Of course."

Having been forgotten, Fura followed in the background, wondering why she had mixed feelings about this man when Kiyani seemed to readily trust him.

62

•••◇•••

LATE ENTRY

The stretch of road that lay between the gate of Du Reizlan and the school itself was longer than Fura had initially estimated. By the time the small group arrived at the famed building's large rounded doors the sun had already set, plunging the surrounding forest into deep shadow. Looking up at the mass of stone that towered above them, now blanketed in the shroud of night, only darkened Fura's over-imaginative image of the embankment of stone.

Around them, the air was eerily silent. A faint whisper of a breeze created voices from the valley of foliage below and Fura swore she could hear a twig snap somewhere close. In the skyline a fully rounded moon had begun to cast its moorish glow over the land.

Fura gulped.

This was the place in the horror movie where she would enter the building that would never allow her to leave.

Next to her the two men were still in the midst of a conversation that she had long since fallen out of.

As they'd reached the walkway before the school's entrance, Durman had dismounted and taken to walking alongside her and Kiyani instead, leading Betsy down the road with them.

He tied the mare's reins to a looped bend of metal in an offset of grassy area and strode to the large door.

Raising a fist, he rapped the wood forcefully three times and then took a step back, waiting as the echoes died away in the darkness.

Almost immediately a panel in the door slid away at eye level and the eyes of an unknown person stared back at them.

"State your business," the person claimed in a gravelly voice that Fura couldn't determine was male or female.

"I'm here to discuss some business with Master Creslin," Durman stated professionally, a friendly smile adorning his face.

There was silence on the receiving end of the door as the eyes wandered past Durman and settled on Kiyani and Fura.

The focus returned to Durman. "What business do they have?" the person asked, bringing the question to him, rather than interacting with Kiyani or Fura.

Durman remained unfazed and was quick to answer. "Youths looking for an education."

"The school year has already begun," the voice claimed, as if, because of the short passage of time since the semester's beginning, they could only be seen as a mere bother now.

Were they considered a lost cause now because they were late, Fura wondered. She knew it would have been better for them if they had filtered themselves in with the rush of new students at the beginning of the year. More convenient, really. Whenever that was. Kiyani had failed to mention that particular piece of information, though she doubted, in this case, that it would be any different than regular school in Barandor. The late comers were always the focus of unwanted attention and criticism. The aptly named *new kids* – a title that stuck no matter how long you were around, unless you were lucky enough to have someone transfer in after you, in which case, the name was then transferred as well.

Fura cringed at the thought.

"They are well aware."

As if that was all that was needed, the panel slid shut, leaving the group in the darkness.

Not quite knowing what had happened, Fura wondered if they'd just been shunned. The owner of the voice had neither granted them an audience with the school master, nor told them to leave.

Confused, she looked to Kiyani for an answer. However, his focus was on Durman who still stood before the door, not having taken the hint that they were unwanted.

A moment later, Fura was proven wrong. The sound of metal scraping against metal sounded in the night as the locks on the door were forced open, followed by a drawn out creak as the door was opened.

Once inside, Fura's grand illusions of a theatrical haunted attraction were immediately laid to rest.

It wasn't dark and dusty as she'd expected. The ceilings were firmly in place, far from caving in, and no draping spider webs adorned the corners of the room. The walls were lacking moth-eaten tapestries, and though it was apparent the building was of a well-to-do ancient era, the masonry had yet to begin crumbling around them.

All in all, for however old the school was, it was in excellent condition with years of teaching in its rooms still ahead.

With that her fears eased a bit, but only in the slightest. Where the fears of disturbing sleeping evil had eroded into a fine powder, there was still her initial disinterest of being back in school.

The entrance room was huge, with two grand staircases spiraling up to the second of who knew how many floors. A massive chandelier of triple stacked rings of wrought iron hung from high, vaulted ceilings and lit the entranceway in a flood of warm, inviting light. Behind either staircase darker lit hallways led in opposite directions. Directly in front of them gaped a wide, triple archway encased in stone and decorated with eloquent carvings.

This was the direction in which they were led. The one who had peered through the heavy door to the outside world to ask the reasoning behind their late night appearance had turned out to be a large heavyset woman in her late fifties.

Plain in both dress and appearance, the woman, who had declined to give her name, paved the way effortlessly through the castle as if she had been there her whole life.

Fura wondered if that wasn't too far from the truth. If she had taken classes and merely forgotten that she could leave once her schooling was completed. As if, rather than breaking away and finding her own place in life, she'd been too afraid to leave, and instead had found a job and permanent home within the castle's walls.

The thought of staying that long made Fura shudder. Already she felt like she was in a prison and she'd barely set foot in Du Reizlan.

All she knew was that the hall they were currently traversing was bound to be only one of the many that she would most likely have to remember here in the next few days. Every new hall they passed increased her anxiety as she glanced down the corridors that faded into shadow beyond the light that the torches threw out.

There was no doubt in her mind that she was going to get hopelessly lost in this grand maze of education.

If I even manage to get an education. I'll be too busy getting lost in the halls to even find my classes.

The hall felt like it went on forever, but just when Fura thought she couldn't possibly go another step, it ended in a large circular foyer. Opposite of where they stood was a half circular set of stairs stacked in descending width like a birthday cake that led to a small porch-like rising. An arched double door stood in the middle. Above it two polished bronze signs hung, one above the other.

GRAND MASTER
Markaelo Creslin

Without so much as a glance at her following audience, the woman ascended the stairs in a few swift steps and rapped on the door without a hint of hesitation. As soon as the echoes of her intrusion faded she took one of the round iron knockers and cracked the door open. Just wide enough to squeeze herself through, the woman slid into the darkness beyond the door, not bothering to wait for beckons from inside.

A few drawn out minutes later the woman reappeared.

"Durman," she addressed the man she and Kiyani had just met with her gravelly tone, "Master Creslin will see you now."

Durman bowed his head in thanks and turned to shoot a smile at Kiyani and Fura before heading up the steps to meet with the school's master.

The door clicked shut, swallowing both Durman and the woman, leaving Kiyani and Fura alone in the cavernous hall.

Fura found herself fidgeting in the silence. She assumed that during normal hours these halls must be teeming with students hurrying to get to their next class on time, but at this late night hour they were barren of life. Ever since they had left the mask of night in favor of the fire-lit hallways, Fura hadn't seen another soul beyond that of their small group.

It was just too quiet.

"Have you been here before?" Fura finally asked.

She couldn't help but notice that Kiyani was clearly unfazed by their new surroundings. Unlike herself, who'd been noticeably gawping at the school's architecture, Kiyani had barely moved his head to look around.

Kiyani shook his head.

Not a word had been traded between them since they had met up with Durman.

Unsure of what was going to happen, time seemed to elapse at a dreadfully slow rate.

Determining that Kiyani was, as usual, not in the mood to converse about the menial, or anything otherwise, Fura took to pacing the circular confines of the small room. Kiyani, on the other hand, leaned against the stone that rose to make what could be defined as a small porch in front of the Master's study.

Fura had no idea how much time had passed when the door opened again and Durman came out, looking pleased with himself. She waited for the woman who had led them through the halls to this very spot to make another appearance, but the door closed behind Durman and stayed shut.

Had this Master Creslin flat out declined to see them at this hour, at this point in the school year, Fura asked herself. Had that woman, who had almost instantly taken what appeared to have been a dislike to them, even bothered to announce their presence? That would be the final icing on the cake, wouldn't it... to be led through the school in some late night grand procession with no audience, only to find out after the fact that they'd been left high and dry with no real shot at the prize they had come for.

Durman bounded down the stairs, coming to a halt beside Fura. Kiyani peeled himself away from the porch and silently stalked over, waiting to hear what the man had to say.

"I can't say Creslin is in the best mood ever," Durman spoke. "But I've definitely seen him worse. I've accomplished what I've come for. Now, I only hope that the two of you have the same success." Smoothing his tunic, Durman firmly shook both of their hands. "He will see you now." Waving as he turned to go back down the stone hall, he added, "Good luck."

Waving back, Fura wondered if he would be just another figure that came and went with little consequence. Lately there seemed to be a good number of those, and she knew that there would only be countless more to add to the same ranks as time went on. It felt strange, almost wrong to her in a way, to come across all these good people that she would, in time, never meet again.

What's the point? Fura wondered.

She'd heard once that everyone who came into your life, no matter how small a part they played, did so for a reason. Fura tried to tell herself that that was true. But, only time could tell in the long run.

"Come on," Kiyani said, his eyes on the hall where Durman had already disappeared. "Might as well get this over with."

Fura could only nod. This was one instance where she had no problem with him taking the reins. She had no real idea why they were here and even less knowledge of how to make their stay semi-permanent.

Walking up the steps, Fura felt an increasing sense of dread, as if this was the defining moment, that if there was any time to turn back and run, this would be it. Yet, she knew that wasn't an option.

When the door shut behind them and Fura turned around, she found that the inside of the room wasn't nearly what she had expected. For being the study of the school's Grand Master, the one who took it upon himself the tedious task of playing role model to all the students that he presided over, it was rather plain. Plain, but tidy.

It was one of those rooms that made you wonder if you were clean enough to even be within its walls. Fura wondered if she should have left her shoes at the door and she fought the need to look down to make sure her boots weren't muddy with the roads of long travel.

A large mahogany desk filled the main expanse of the room. Surrounding it, the wall was lined with shelves filled with books and other knick knacks. Yet, for such a grand collection, everything on the shelves seemed to have its place in neat and tidy little rows. A precise puzzle. A lifetime in the making that anyone would be a fool to mess with.

The man behind the desk seemed to carry the same air. His dark gray tunic was neatly pressed, and his albino blond hair was neatly combed back into a ponytail that trailed down his back, revealing striking green eyes that peered out from a sharply boned face that seemed cold and calculating.

Kiyani was the first to speak, clearly not fearing the man as Fura did. Stepping forward he nodded to the man. "Master Creslin."

Creslin leaned forward in his chair and folded his hands beneath his chin. "You know that the semester has already begun," he said as he studied the two of them, his voice just as cold as his appearance. Barely giving a cursory glance at Fura, Creslin took Kiyani in with narrowed eyes.

Fura looked down at the ground. The school's master acted as if he didn't even want to deal with them. She had no idea how Kiyani was going to pull this one through, yet somehow she didn't doubt that he would find a way. Just like he always did.

With his hands flat at his side, Kiyani looked the man straight on, unfaltering in his task. "We are well aware that if we'd shown up on time, like the rest of the students, that it would've been more beneficial for both sides. However, our unfortunate timing was unavoidable, and we ask that you still give us the chance to receive an education here at Du Reizlan."

Listening to him, Fura wondered where this side of Kiyani resided on a daily basis. He was far more kind and diplomatic when speaking to others than he'd ever been to her. At least most people. Tybithera's status had never seemed to change his manner.

"Do you think, Mr. Enderline," Creslin declared coldly, "that due to your father's status you can just waltz in here at whatever moment you see fit and everyone will bow to your whim?"

The man's crude nature stopped Kiyani short. Fura could see him tense at the name. It was the second time she had heard someone they'd only just met refer to him as another, leaving her to wonder if she really knew who she was traveling with. Even Aldam had seemed uncertain, though he'd never spoken as darkly as this man.

Taking a deep breath, Kiyani corrected the man. "My name is Kiyani Ridanthu," he said, putting a particular emphasis on his last name.

The man behind the desk regarded Kiyani for a moment before moving on to Fura, ignoring Kiyani's remark altogether. "And your name, miss?"

Shocked into reality, Fura looked up into the man's eyes. "I –" she stammered as she tried to find the courage to speak. "Fura Feuer."

"Is it now?" Creslin said. There was a hint of amusement in his eyes as he looked from one to the other. "An unlikely pair."

Silence fell over the room like an illness as Kiyani and Fura stood and waited for judgment. Silently, Creslin leaned to one side and pulled open a drawer that was out of their line of sight. Fura could hear papers rustling and she wondered what it was that he was doing, fighting the urge to nonchalantly stand on her tip toes to get a look.

After what felt like eons, the man had assembled two identical piles of papers on the desktop. Another quick search brought forth a quill and a vial of ink. Ignoring the two of them, Creslin flitted between the two documents, scribbling marks here and there.

A few minutes later he set the quill to the side and laid his hands flat on the desk, as if trying to keep the precious documents safe from some invisible wind. "Now, Mr. Enderline, I take it that the two of you are both candidates for the beginner classes."

Kiyani stepped forward, fire in his eyes. "I *told* you my name is Ridanthu."

"Go by whatever you wish," Creslin said, taking up the quill again and nonchalantly scribbling on the papers in front of him. He looked up. "Just know that I will not acknowledge you as such."

His fists balled at his side, Kiyani tried to keep his composure. It would do neither him nor Fura any good if he got them kicked out of Du Reizlan for good. They had to get in.

"Fura," Kiyani said, glaring at the Head Master, "Go wait in the hall."

"I –" Fura looked at him questioningly. She couldn't tell if she should really do as she was told. At the rate the conversation was going between the two men it could easily escalate from harshly spoken words to something more physical. "Okay," she finally spoke, nodding, though neither of them were paying attention.

Kiyani waited until Fura did as he'd asked, listening for the door to click back into place, before he continued.

As soon as the door slid back into place, Fura turned and pressed her ear against the rough grain of the wood. There was no reason why Kiyani had to kick her out. She had done just as he'd instructed, only speaking when spoken to, and still he'd made her leave.

It took only a moment to realize that trying to make heads or tails of the conversation flowing inside was beyond useless. The wood was too thick, making the words that she could hear faint and hard to differentiate from one another. Unless she blatantly barged back into the school master's office, something she could guess neither man would appreciate, there would be no following the conversation.

Fura waited a few more minutes before letting out a sigh and turning to study the circular room again. She would just have to trust that Kiyani would tell her what had happened.

Right, she told herself. He had wanted a private audience with the Grand Master for a reason. *What is it that he's trying to hide from me?*

It wasn't fair that he knew all about her, yet in return, she knew next to nothing about him.

Maybe it will be better to be separated for awhile...

With nothing to hold her interest in the room and not enough courage to attempt to wander back down the hall to see what secrets it held, Fura settled herself onto the edge of the stone porch outside of the office, looking like a delinquent waiting to see if detention was in the future.

Nearly half an hour later Kiyani cracked the door open and looked down at her, sitting on the ledge of the rise with her eyes closed. "Get back in here."

Fura opened an eye and looked at him. She wondered what had happened in the time that had elapsed. It was hard to guess, but she could tell by the tone of Kiyani's voice that he wasn't all that enthused about whatever it was that had transpired.

Reentering the room behind Kiyani, Fura stood silently next to him as they faced Creslin together once more.

Looking up from his papers, Creslin paused, acknowledging them only momentarily before continuing to shuffle through his writing as if looking for something that would condemn them to exile. Apparently coming up short, the man finally looked up at them. If he was unsure of how to handle the situation, he didn't show it.

"Before I give either of you your schedules, I want you to know how rare of me this is. Now, some ground rules that I urge you to follow, less you fancy facing expulsion: Curfew is ten-thirty during the week and midnight on the weekend. Those found out of their dorms after hours will be punished accordingly. You are not to leave the school grounds at anytime. Such is only permitted during winter and summer breaks.

"Don't think that you're getting off easy. You will likely have to attend extended class sessions in order to come up to date with all that you've missed already. Any rules that are broken in your name will be brought to my attention immediately. Do not test my patience. I will not condone trouble-makers. Do I make myself clear?"

Fura and Kiyani both nodded silently to Creslin's satisfaction.

"Good. Now, as you may or may not be aware, students here take a test of abilities at the completion of their first year so as to decide a course of study. This will not be needed due to certain factors. Both of you will find that your predetermined course has already been written on the top right corner of your schedules."

Turning away, Creslin motioned with a hand. A moment later, the woman who had more or less greeted them at the main door emerged from the shadows. Though Fura couldn't recall the woman being there beforehand, she couldn't be sure.

"Marna, please go inform Talia and Thayna, as well as Nylan to clear space for new additions."

"Nylan?" Kiyani asked wearily, perking up at the name.

"Yes," Creslin nodded, his fingers steepling before him. "You didn't think you would be given your own room did you?"

Kiyani was thankful that that was what Creslin had taken from his hesitation and nothing else. "Of course not."

He was only hopeful that it would be a different Nylan than the one that came to mind. If not, this would be a dreadfully long semester.

Marna led the two of them wordlessly through the darkened hallways. Only the flickering of the torches set into the walls in their wrought-iron cages indicated their passing. The dancing firelight painted shadowed pictures on the stone around them. As they walked, Fura didn't dare attempt to add to the stories that had already formed in her mind. She could only hope that the dawn would chase most of her self-induced fantasies away and replace them with a better sense of reality.

Though Fura hadn't noticed any real change in the structure, the woman named Marna stopped in front of a wall in the midst of a wide hallway. As her eyes adjusted to the darkness, she realized why they had stopped. Two large doors stood along the wall, but it was something else that caught her attention.

On the opposite wall was a string of identical sized windows that met with the ceiling and overlooked a courtyard below. Where the windows started, a few feet from the ground, a ledge ran along the wall, just wide enough to sit on and look out. A grand fountain, shaped like a prancing unicorn, created a focal point, the water cascading down and giving off a blue-ish glow in the moonlight. A circle of stone surrounded the fountain and branched off into a multitude of pathways, lined with a well thought out array of flowers and plants. Differing sizes of benches dotted the darkness among the hills of lush grass.

"Boys on the right," Marna said, pointing indifferently to the large door on the right. "Girls on the left."

Fura turned to the sound of the woman's voice and looked at the wall across from the windows.

In between the two doors was an alcove set into the wall that boasted a long wooden bench. Fura guessed, based on this sitting area and the ledge on the opposite wall that this was a kind of meeting place, though it hardly seemed adequate for the number of students that she could only guess attended Du Reizlan.

Crossing her arms, Marna looked down at them sternly. "Now, just so you know, we here at the Manor are here for the lot of you to learn. Foolishness is not allowed and the same goes for any chicanery between you boys and girls. Don't be fooled into thinking you can just slip into each other's dorms unnoticed. If you try, you'll find that each doorway is spelled to stop the opposite sex from entering."

Kiyani shifted uncomfortably from one foot to the other.

Fura blushed, understanding the implied meaning behind the woman's words. She praised the dark, glad that the sudden color in her cheeks would go unnoticed.

"If you need to meet, there are countless other places such as the library," Marna continued, ignoring their restlessness. "Now, Kiyani," she said, her gaze falling on him. "Master Creslin has roomed you with Nylan Rune. If you go up the stairs you will find that his quarters are located within the second door in the fourth hallway you will come to. Fura, you will come with me and I will show you to the room you will be sharing with Talia and Thayna Torske."

Before Fura could follow Marna through the doorway and up the stairs Kiyani caught her shoulder. "I'll meet you here tomorrow morning."

Without waiting for a reply he turned and went through the other door, leaving her alone for the night.

A sudden wave of nausea hit Fura and she had to fight to swallow it back down. None of this was to her liking. Cold school masters, and unfriendly hall dwellers. Being separated from Kiyani. Her fears were already becoming reality. She didn't even want to think what fresh horrors the morning would bring once classes were added to the mix.

✧⌘✧

Kiyani took his time traversing the winding staircase that led to the boy's half of the dormitories. Even after a long day he wasn't all too eager to fall into bed in the company of strangers.

Or, maybe he was.

Nylan Rune.

Rolling the name on his tongue didn't make it any more agreeable. Did the Grand Master know of their previous relationship? He doubted it, but if he did, he had a mighty fine way of welcoming them to the school.

Coming level with a new hallway, Kiyani moved forward slowly, giving himself as much time as possible. At Marna's instructions, he turned down the fourth hall. The corridor was littered with doorways on both sides as if it were designed to frustrate him even further. Upon closer scrutiny he found that each door bore a small plaque with the names of those inside inscribed on its shiny surface.

Names of all those I would probably rather be roomed with.

It didn't take Kiyani nearly long enough to find the name of his new roommate. Staring at the nameplate, he wondered how long it would take anyone to notice if he simply found some random alcove to sleep in. Shaking his head against the thought, he reached for the round brass knocker. His hand lingered on the smooth metal for a moment before he decided against it.

This was Nylan he was talking about. He wasn't about to show any sense of formality.

Taking the door knob in his hand he turned it and barged into the room with no warning.

Though the space within was dark, Kiyani didn't have to wait for his eyes to adjust. An oil lamp flickered on a small table in front of the window, the orange flame mingling with the moonlight to cast a strange glow about the room. As if built for unity, the layout was a mirror of itself with identical twin sized beds, framed by a small bedside table and a dresser on either side of the room. One of the beds was neatly made, declaring it empty and unused. On the other lay a figure he already knew all too well.

Nylan Rune lounged lengthwise on the bed, his ankles crossed, his hands behind his head, an arrogant grin painting his face. "Took you long enough."

It'd been years since he'd seen the man, but he recognized him all the same. His wavy blond hair was longer than he remembered, but the haughty, know-it-all grin was the same.

"Nice to see you again, too," Kiyani managed to choke out. He wondered just how long it would be before they resolved to rip each other's throats out.

"The prodigal son has finally made his appearance at Du Reizlan. How touching. I was beginning to think that you thought you were too advanced for all this."

Instead of lashing out at the words, Kiyani took a deep breath and tried to let it pass. These conversations where what had always gotten him and Nylan in trouble in the first place. Too tired to even put the effort into fighting tonight, he moved towards the empty bed and threw down his belongings.

In an instant Nylan had leapt off his bed and was breathing down Kiyani's neck. "And just what do you think you're doing?" he malevolently hissed in Kiyani's ear.

Kiyani turned to Nylan and stared him down. "Creslin roomed us together," he growled in reply. "Don't think that this was my idea. I'd rather sleep in a pit of vipers."

"Why don't we see if we can arrange that?" Throwing himself on the empty bed, Nylan pointed to the door. "I don't care what Creslin says." As if to illustrate his meaning, he shoved Kiyani's belongings onto the floor. "The room you want is across the hall."

In every aspect, Kiyani didn't care what Creslin said either. Anything had to be better than having to deal with this every day. Taking his chances he threw an angry look at Nylan. "Fine," he declared. As he knelt to retrieve his things off the floor he was grateful that everything had stayed contained within his bag. The last thing he wanted to do was kneel at Nylan's feet for any extended period of time.

Grabbing his things, Kiyani went to the door. He wouldn't bow down to Nylan, but this he had to do or he wouldn't find anything about the Witneis before shooting himself.

The Witneis Reln. That's what we're here for. The sooner we find it, the sooner we can leave.

"Don't worry," Nylan crowed from the darkness. "You'll still be seeing plenty of me."

The caustic sarcasm left a bitter taste in Kiyani's mouth. If it hadn't been so late he would have slammed the door. He stormed across the hall to the room Nylan had so ungraciously sequestered him to and looked at it half heartedly before opening it. There was a single name on the plaque but Kiyani didn't bother to read it.

"Hi," a voice answered him from the confines of the space.

The room that welcomed Kiyani was practically identical to the one he'd just left, except maybe messier. An oil lamp brightly danced in the corner.

Kiyani looked at the owner of the voice skeptically.

"I was expecting you," the boy shrugged sheepishly. "I heard you and Nylan fighting. Don't worry, he picks on me frequently, too," he admitted. "I didn't know he had such a dislike of newcomers, though."

"Nylan and I have had the displeasure of meeting previously," Kiyani offered.

A good foot shorter than Kiyani, this boy was admittedly younger. A mess of short blond hair graced his head and his eyes were wide, bright, and expectant. He reminded Kiyani in brief of Fura, young and looking to be full of too many questions for one person to answer.

"What are you, ten?" Kiyani asked, looking the boy over.

Putting his hands on his hips defiantly, he declared, "Fifteen!"

"Congratulations," Kiyani said mockingly.

To be roomed with Nylan Rune or a little kid. Kiyani took this as the lesser of two evils.

With little hesitation, Kiyani strolled across the room to the bed that was blatantly empty and set his things down. At least this time he wouldn't have to worry about its contents being strewn across the floor.

As much as he just wanted to crawl beneath the sheets and call it a day, Kiyani knew the chances of that were nil. He could feel the boy's eyes upon him, boring into his back, studying him.

"Are you —"

Before the boy could spit out the full question, Kiyani replied with a forceful, "No." He already knew the intent of what he was going to ask, especially if the kid had managed to catch sight of his tattoo.

"Oh." Holding his hand out, he tried again. "My name's Tibben. Tibben Monterey."

Kiyani couldn't help himself. "Your last name's a cheese?"

"Monterey jack is a cheese," Tibben corrected, "it's just Monterey."

"If you say so." Once the hand fell, he methodically offered his name. "Kiyani Ridanthu."

Satisfied for a short spurt, Tibben hustled over to his own bed and jumped in. "Wow," he declared, far from tired, "it'll be nice to have a roommate, finally. I was starting to feel left out."

Turning away from the boy in hope that his lack of interest would quiet him, Kiyani began to sift through his bag and rearrange the bed. He took a quick glance at the paper Creslin had given him before placing it safely among his other belongings.

"So," the boy continued. "Where are you from? How come you're late?"

"Tibben, please," Kiyani said exasperated by the boy's tireless energy. "I really just want to sleep right now."

"Oh, right," Tibben said bashfully. "Sorry. Tomorrow, then."

With that the room fell silent.

✧⌘✧

The walk up the twisting staircase had been a long and tiresome expenditure of what little energy Fura had left. Not only had it been grueling, but it had been unnervingly quiet as well. Marna made no move for conversation and though there was no reason for it, Fura found herself afraid of the woman.

Leading her through a maze of darkly lit hallways, Marna finally stopped in front of one of the doors set into the wall. Fura looked around, wondering how the woman could tell this was the right one. They all looked identical to her.

Pointing to the door, the woman spoke. "Here you go." No sooner had the words left her mouth, she turned and began the trek back down the corridor, leaving Fura to her own devices.

"Thanks," Fura said shyly. The words were so faint, she didn't know if she had actually spoken them aloud. Not that it mattered. Marna was already gone.

Looking around the empty hall, she wondered if she would ever feel like she wasn't a bother to the people in this world. It was as if everyone inherently knew she wasn't from Izandüre, and purposely shunned her because of it.

Though this whole night had left her unsettled, Fura took in a deep breath and turned to the door Marna had indicated. As scared as she was, she had the feeling that this was a turning point in her journey. She couldn't rely on Kiyani forever. This was just her first trial in finding her independence in this land.

Squinting in the darkness, Fura could see now the names etched in a brass plate on the door. Just below it, a round door knocker sat.

Surveying the hall once more, Fura indecisively raised her hand and grabbed the cool metal. Quietly ramming the wood three times, Fura stepped back and waited, hoping she wasn't waking anyone.

Beyond the door, she could hear whisperings and the excited squeals of its inhabitants. Seconds later, the door flew open and two faces greeted her, their smiles filling their whole faces.

"You must be Fura," one of the girls claimed.

Fura nodded shyly before the second of the girls grabbed her wrist and drug her into the room.

The door slid back into place behind her, leaving Fura with a dreaded sense of permanency. There was no escaping now. It suddenly occurred to her that without Kiyani she felt naked and exposed. She'd anticipated this the moment he'd mentioned Du Reizlan and had been dreading it ever since it had come to mind. Though she couldn't say that this was exactly how it had played out in her imagination.

The time had come to step up. Forcing a smile on her face, Fura let the two girls show her the unoccupied bed in the corner that would be hers for however long they remained here.

This is mine, Fura told herself. After the long days of travel, something as simple as a permanent bed was almost unimaginable.

All Fura wanted to do was flop herself onto the spongy mattress and sleep, but the two girls seemed to have a different idea. They sat on either side of her, looking as if rest was some novelty that they didn't need. It was now that, what she hadn't noticed before about the two, came to her attention.

The two faces that stared back at her were nearly identical. Glancing to either side the same set of small hazel eyes stared back at her with casual interest. The only thing that set the two apart was the hair.

"My name is Talia," one of the girls claimed. Her shoulder length hair looked as if it had been neatly pressed into a fountain of glossy brunette waves.

On Fura's opposite side, the other girl offered her own name. "Mine is Thayna." The same color hair framed her face, though it was straight and cut into a short messy bob with bangs that fanned across her eyes.

"You may not be our blood sister," Thayna said, grabbing Fura's hand from her lap, "but we're going to be the best of friends!"

Not sure about that, Fura put a smile on her face and nodded. No longer used to being the center of attention, she found herself sandwiched between the two girls, mainly listening as they bantered on about how much she would love it in Du Reizlan. Only when they actually asked her a question was she able to add her voice to the conversation. Despite the late hour, the two were tireless.

Even after they'd finally given her space, allowing her to change clothes before lying down to attempt to get some sleep before the morning, they continued talking. Though she couldn't make out most of what they were saying, Fura could hear their hushed whispers and giggles from across the room.

Though she wasn't sure how she felt about the girls, she had to admit that she might have overreacted.

Du Reizlan was definitely a change of pace, but it wasn't so bad.

Yet, Fura knew that the next day was when she would learn for certain whether this place would be a dream or a nightmare.

63
♦♦◇♦♦

A NEW HELL

Despite the late night and the few hours of sleep she'd managed to get, Fura woke early the next morning feeling rested and rejuvenated. Her mind was still in tangles, and she couldn't quite shake the apprehension of beginning classes, but her body was thankful for the change of pace. Sleeping on a mattress again, protected from the elements by an actual brick and mortar building had done her good. Rather than spending half an hour or more trying to find a comfortable spot, shivering against the cold the entire time as she'd done night after night while on the road, Fura had fallen asleep almost as soon as her head had hit the pillow.

Pulled from her thoughts by the sound of laughter, Fura yawned and rolled over. Across the room, Talia and Thayna were already awake and dressed. Sitting beside one another on a cushioned window seat that overlooked a green valley below, they giggled again as they shared some sister secret. Wild hand movements further illustrated their conversation as they talked excitedly.

Thayna brightened. "You're up!"

"You better get going," Talia said. Motioning to the sun filtering through the window as if that clearly indicated the time, she added, "Classes start soon."

Throwing the covers off haphazardly, Fura shivered as the air hit her. It wasn't cold, but it was enough to shock her into awareness. Her hand drifted over the blankets, wanting desperately to dive back into their warmth and stay there a few days.

Instead, she swung her legs over the side of the bed and planted her feet on the decorated rug.

I wouldn't be making a very good impression if I was late on my first day.

Even as she dressed, Fura contemplated simply wasting the day away, lazing in bed. Something that she hadn't been able to do in ages. Though she would have thought that there'd be plenty of time for such a thing while on the road, Kiyani had been consistent with their schedule. Despite not being driven by a watch, he always seemed to be awake at dawn, milling about and doing something. As long as it took her to wake up in the morning, he almost always had them out of their camp and walking again not long after the sun rose.

As she struggled with deciding what to wear, Fura's eyes looked at the bed. As tempting as it was, she had a feeling that even if Kiyani couldn't physically come and get her, he'd still find a way to make sure she attended classes. Shuddering, she realized he could simply get Marna to retrieve her if necessary. Not wanting to face the woman's cold scowl again, Fura put the thought of relaxation out of her mind.

Focusing on the day ahead, she finally threw on a dress she hadn't yet worn and dug through her bag.

Sidling over to Fura's side, Thayna threw a slender arm over her shoulder. "So," she said, biding time. "What classes do you have?"

"Um, let me see," Fura said, anxiously pulling away from the girl. They'd only met the night before, yet these sisters acted as if they'd known each her for years.

We're going to be the best of friends.

Though she didn't know why, Fura shuddered at the thought as she continued to dig through her bag. Only when she pulled out the schedule Creslin had hastily written out for her the night before did she realize she hadn't even looked at it herself. Her old, curious self would have studied it immediately. Instead, exhaustion and trepidation had left her unwilling to know just then what the severe-looking school master had in store for her.

Talia removed herself from the window and stalked over, grabbing the paper out of Fura's hands before she could so much as glance at it. With their backs turned to her, the two sisters studied the paper together, pointing and whispering amongst themselves.

It was a rather rude gesture on the second day of knowing someone, but Fura took the free time to gather her things. The invasion of personal space was what friends did. Though that was exactly what the two girls had claimed they were, Fura couldn't find it in herself to believe it. Even with all the questionable characters she'd met at the festival, she didn't quite know what to think of these two. Briefly adopting Kiyani's stance on the world, she wondered what they wanted from her.

A few minutes later, the twins turned back to her, their motions nearly synchronized. As they handed the paper back to her, Fura took it wordlessly.

"Well, two out of four isn't bad," Thayna said with a wry smile.

Bursting through the door that led to the main hall, Fura found herself immediately assaulted by the crowd of people on the other side.

Walking right into the mass, she was pushed around helplessly in the current. Frantically sifting herself out of the exodus of bodies, Fura flattened herself against the wall, breathing heavily.

She could hear Talia and Thayna snicker as they exited the dormitories and came to her side.

Some friends, Fura thought. They knew she was new here. They could have at least warned her.

Trying to ignore the thought, Fura looked at the scene before her. Compared to the ghostly emptiness of the hall the night before, this was pure chaos.

"You get used to it quickly," Talia offered.

Thayna flipped her hair. "You have to." She laid a firm hand on Fura's shoulder like a predator staking its claim.

Fura didn't like the sound of her words. She may have been at school, but she felt like she had been thrown into a den of ravenous wolves. She wasn't one of them. Instead, she was fresh meat. The worst part was that she hadn't even gone to a class yet.

Doing her best not to be so negative this early in the morning, Fura could only begin to imagine what the rest of the day would bring.

At least I'm not in this alone.

The thought that Kiyani was here somewhere as well served as her only consolation in this menagerie of mixed feelings.

She wondered why it was that nothing ever seemed to faze him. The numerous attacks. The long days in the woods. School. Nothing ever came close to breaking that cool shell of his, as if despite his general love for solitude, he was made to withstand chaos. The only thing that ever seemed to bother him was people. He'd immediately butted heads with almost everyone they'd met.

Using the wall as a solid reminder of reality, Fura followed it to the alcove that sat between the doors and positioned herself on the bench, waiting.

Talia and Thayna followed. Standing before her, Talia announced, "Come on, we'll show you to your first class."

Politely holding up a hand, Fura shook her head. "It's okay. Go on ahead. I'm waiting for someone."

In a way, she was glad she wouldn't have to rely on Talia and Thayna. She liked them well enough, but she wasn't sure if they would really wind up as close as the two girls claimed they would be.

The girls' eyes widened, their lips pulling into unison malicious grins.

"A boyfriend already?" Thayna gasped, her reaction implying scandal.

Talia laughed. "Aren't we fast?"

Fura felt her face flush. "No," she claimed. "Just a friend." She could only imagine how Kiyani would react to that inference. Then

543

again, who knew? He was the one that'd claimed they were married in Skirvynmire.

"If you say so," Talia drawled, a wicked smile on her face declaring that she wasn't convinced.

"Come on Tal," Thayna said, grabbing her sister by the arm. "We'll see you later." Waving, the two melded effortlessly into the hoard.

Leaning against the alcove wall, she watched the girls blend into the wave of students that passed by. Only a few people glanced her way, seeming to make a mental note of the new girl as if the term was stamped on her forehead. At least no one had made it a point to tell her what she already knew. Then again, she hadn't yet been to class. Right now she was just another face in the crowd. No one knew quite yet if she was new or had always been there.

All of it was overwhelming.

Barandor was the only town that Fura had ever known until now. For as long as she could remember her home had been the two-story house on East Wixley. She'd had two loving parents and two brothers, and had attended the same school system since she had been old enough to start schooling.

She'd never had the unique experience of being the new kid, but she had watched plenty of others go through the grueling initiation. Twelve years. Fura thought that she had been lucky enough to have escaped all of that, but now it was her turn.

"Who were they?"

Breathing a sigh of relief at the familiar voice, Fura turned to Kiyani. "My roommates."

Avoiding the bench nestled in the alcove as well, he leaned against the wall, looking through the sea of people and gazing out the window, clearly unperturbed by the morning chaos.

The finding of the Witneis Reln was first and foremost above everything else. That much Fura knew. She just wished that it didn't have to involve all this. The crowd of people made her anxious. Graduation had been so close Fura had almost been able to taste it. Now it felt like she was starting all over again, all those previous years put in for nothing.

"How's your roommate?" Fura asked, not knowing what else to say. Like the shadows he seemed to blend into with ease, he'd appeared out of nowhere.

Kiyani shrugged indifferently. "Okay, I guess."

It was his typical reply. When he wasn't lost in the throes of anger, he generally spoke in as few words as was possible. Though it wasn't quite what she'd wanted to hear, at least she could see that his mood was leveled out today.

He may not have been overly excited about ingratiating himself into

Du Reizlan's sub-culture, or nauseous like she currently felt, but Fura could see that he was taking all of this far better than she was.

Down the corridor, Fura could see that Talia and Thayna lingered on the edges of the crowd. She'd thought they'd be long gone by now, but they only seemed to be studying her from afar, staring intently and evaluating what they saw. Huddled together and pointing her way, it only took Fura a moment to realize that it was Kiyani they were frantically discussing. Suddenly fixing her with a wicked gaze, Thayna pulled her sister along, disappearing for good this time. Fura didn't know what had just happened, but she didn't like it.

"Are you okay?" Kiyani asked mildly, seeming to pick up on her distress.

Fura looked over at him. Tampering her emotions, she nodded. "Yeah."

Inside, she wasn't so sure.

Needing something to distract her, Fura shakily pulled her schedule out of her bag again. She hadn't wanted to look at it the night before, and Talia and Thayna had stolen it out of her grasp this morning. She was minutes from starting class and she didn't even know what she was taking.

Now, she studied it with a fierce clarity.

Scanning it morosely, Fura groaned as she read the titles. It was only four courses, but she knew it would be torture. These were probably what were considered elementary courses, yet even those would be a struggle for her. Where were you supposed to start anyways when you didn't even have a foundation to build on?

No matter how many times her eyes flitted over the strange words, Fura just couldn't come to terms with all this. Everything was so new to her, so foreign. What made it even worse was the sheer fact that she felt as if it should've all been second nature to her. This was her world, wasn't it?

Glancing at the map of Du Reizlan provided on the back of the paper did nothing to lessen her anxiety. The lines representing rooms and their corresponding numbers looked like a giant twisting labyrinth.

I would be less likely to get lost going through a corn maze blind.

From what she could tell from the map, the school was four stories high and who knew just how wide, with numerous turrets and towers to add dimension and extra rooms. The grand entranceway and the main hall that Marna had taken them through the night before would hardly put a scratch on a full tour of the Manor. Curious, Fura wondered if she would ever see the school in its entirety.

"What's this?" Fura asked, pointing to a hastily scribbled name and time at the bottom of the paper.

Kiyani glanced at it. "I had Creslin set you up with a tutor."

"Was that necessary?" Fura balked.

It was bad enough that she was suddenly being bombarded by all these odd classes on subjects she didn't know the first thing about. Now, Kiyani had to add a private tutor to that workload. Not only was it degrading, it was downright embarrassing.

"More than you know."

Fura let out an exasperated breath. "Fine." If word of this got out to Talia and Thayna she would never hear the end of it.

What if they had already seen it?

Despite spending the whole night apart, something that had occurred rarely since the start of their journey, Fura found that conversation was lacking.

She doubted that Kiyani was nervous about this like she was, and if he was, he hid it well. Rather, he seemed subdued in his own thoughts, mentally preparing for the day ahead in his own way.

"What's your schedule look like?" she asked with trepidation, breaking the silence. The image of that lonely new girl in the back corner struck her.

"The same," he said to her relief. "I had Creslin give us the same classes. I only switched out one."

Fura looked at the paper in her hand again, wondering which one he had opted out of and why. Voicing her concern, she waited for his reply.

"I decided on *Forge and Arms*, instead."

"Why?"

"Because I wanted to take it."

"Why didn't you have him put me in that one as well?" It couldn't have been any worse than what was already planned out for her in lieu of her own decisions.

"You wouldn't even take the dagger I offered you as protection for fear that you would hurt yourself," Kiyani reminded her. "The last place you need to be is in a shop full of weapons. Your time would be better spent in a class that actually attended to your interests and what you're capable of, like your pyropheric tendencies."

"What?" Fura asked in confusion. Kiyani had mentioned that word once before, but in the madness, she'd forgotten what it meant again. Kiyani sighed.

"Do you still think you don't need this?"

64

✦✧✦

THE POISON IN LIES

If it wasn't for Kiyani's help and his calm demeanor as they wandered through the halls, trying to decipher how classrooms and their corresponding numbers were set up, Fura knew she would have gotten hopelessly lost before ever making it to her first class.

Even with Kiyani at her side, they just barely slid in the door before class started, earning them both a stern look from the teacher at the front of the room.

Not wanting anything to do with the limelight, Fura scanned the room, searching for an empty seat to escape to. As if waiting for them, two sat free just to their right. Barely taking a step to fill them, Kiyani grabbed her arm, holding her back as the teacher addressed them directly.

"Now, now," the man whistled. "You don't think you can get away that easily, do you?" Sitting on the corner of his desk, he beckoned them forward with a hand. "I was told to be expecting the two of you. Come on down and recite your names as I get you the textbooks you'll be needing for your studies."

The room was dimly lit by iron chandeliers that hung above their heads, the candles ensconced within casting a flickering orange glow over the surrounding stone walls. Five long rows of tables sat in a half circle, facing the desk at the front of the room. A path of elongated stairs ran down the center of the room, separating the rows.

Fura felt her cheeks redden as she followed Kiyani down the center aisle. Though she didn't dare look, she was aware of the curious stares from those who waited eagerly in their seats, looking upon the newest spectacle in the classroom. In front of her, Kiyani took no notice.

"Kiyani Ridanthu," Kiyani said dispassionately as soon as he approached the teacher. Taking the book the man held out wordlessly, he didn't go out of his way to offer any additional information regarding himself.

Handing an identical title to Fura, the teacher turned his attention to her, "And your name, my dear?"

547

"Fura Feuer..." she mumbled, reaching for the book.

"Is it now?" the man said, far more interested in her than he was Kiyani. Snatching the text away from her reach, he asked, "Feuer... as in Apallo Feuer?"

Fura nodded silently, not knowing if she should pursue the topic or not. Kiyani had already revealed that her father was *the* Firelord, but she hadn't been aware that his name would be relevant in their travels, recognized by people she'd never met. It made her wonder if she should have given a false name. Then again, it was already written on her schedule. Though, now that she thought about it, she wondered why Master Creslin had made no mention of her relation to the Firelord.

Even though she didn't offer any further detail to continue the conversation, the teacher didn't appear ready to let her go. "I never knew Apallo had a daughter," the professor muttered excitedly as if he were standing before a celebrity. Fura shrunk from his gaze when it fell upon her once more, asking, "You must be brilliant with fire, then!"

"I..." she shook her head, embarrassed. "Not really."

The light in the man's eyes died as if water had doused the flames of interest. As if not knowing what to say in lieu of that piece of information, he finally handed her the book. "Pity." Silence filled the room as the students watched their professor circle the desk, leaving Fura and Kiyani front and center. "My name is Master Gruevaind, and this is *The Beginning History of Izandüre*. You may sit now. I can see two empty seats in the rear of the classroom that will suit the two of you. Those who are last to attend my class are last to reap the benefit of close seats. I will be needing the both of you to remain after class so I can inform you of the topics we've already covered. I expect you have the drive to go over them on your own. However, I will always be here if you need help. Now, hurry on so we can start."

Desperate to blend in with the shadows, Fura rushed to take her seat. Kiyani followed suit, moseying up the stairs as if he had all the time in the world at his disposal.

Once seated, Fura placed the book Master Gruevaind had given her on the table, hastily opening it to the page number he'd scrawled on the chalkboard behind him. Rousing parchment and a quill from her bag, she readied herself to take notes, knowing she'd need all the help she could get.

Settling into the chair beside her, Kiyani left his own textbook closed, his section of the table free from clutter. Crossing his arms over his chest, he leaned back and looked straight ahead, seeming content to merely listen.

Motion at the front of the classroom caught Fura's eye, and she found herself momentarily distracted. Three rows down, Talia and

Thayna sat nestled together at a table in the far corner. Thayna waved. Raising a hand in a feeble reply, Fura found herself glad that she wasn't sitting within speaking distance of the two girls.

With a sigh, Fura returned her focus to the front of the room where she watched Master Gruevaind pace the room as he spoke in a listless drawl.

Already this was going just as she had imagined it.

✧ ⌘ ✧

The following classes, *Lure of the Land* and *Novice Magic* were no more eventful than the first had been. The only thing that stood out between the monotonous drawl of lectures was the fact that they were separated by an hour period for lunch.

In a perverse way, Kiyani was the only thing that made the day tolerable. Even with his last angered outburst lingering in her mind, Fura found his presence comforting. Strangely enough, something about being in Du Reizlan, surrounded by people, seemed to have tamed his generally brash mood. At least for the time being. He may not have been inclined to speak to her any more than usual, but he was still a familiar face in an otherwise alien territory.

The *only* thing familiar.

Everything, from the massive rooms down to the quill she attempted to write with was foreign to her. Though she'd been in Izandüre for almost two months now, she still felt that at any moment someone would suddenly race through the door and tell her this had all been a joke, that she was on candid camera.

In every class, Fura sat awkwardly in her chair, listening to the teachers talk about strange things as she struggled to take legible notes with shaking hands. Histories of towns she'd never heard of. The life cycles of fearsome beasts she hoped to never meet. Terms from a system of magic that she'd never even thought had existed. It was all so much to take in. Her fingers cramping from the jumble of writing, she eventually gave up. Instead, she took a page from Kiyani's book, deciding to simply sit and listen, resigning that she would read the assigned sections later and take better notes then. Trying to memorize every little tidbit of new information, she was left wondering at the end of every session, as she followed students out the door, if she'd retained anything at all.

Kiyani, on the other hand, didn't seem to fight against the same jitters Fura did. No matter the subject, no matter where they were seated, he sat, stoically gazing ahead, almost always appearing ready to take a nap. Fura wanted to ask if he was getting any of this, but kept the question to herself. She had a feeling he wouldn't answer. Though she

549

couldn't help but wonder if he was even listening in the first place. Either he knew most of what was flying over her head, or he didn't care about his studies, instead mulling over the reason they were here in the first place. So far, nothing at all had been mentioned that might so much as relate to the Witneis Reln.

When it came time for her last class of the day, *Apothecary & Herbology: A Mixture of Studies*, Fura was reluctant to let Kiyani leave. She knew he'd been correct in his assumption that she would have felt even more awkward in *Forge & Arms* than she had in any of the previous classes. However, that realization didn't help to ease her anxiety. Had she actually been given a choice in the matter, she probably would've subjected herself to it if it meant keeping Kiyani within her line of sight.

Why is this bothering me so much? Fura chastised herself as she discovered what it was she was telling herself.

All throughout school in Barandor she'd never had any trouble. She hadn't been popular, yet she hadn't been at the bottom of the pack, either. Mostly, she'd ridden somewhere in the middle. One of those people that others knew of but couldn't tell you much about. It hadn't been her ideal position, but it had never caused her this much grief.

What makes this any different? I shouldn't have to rely on Kiyani like a crutch.

"You can find the library by yourself, right?" Kiyani asked belatedly, unaware of her inner turmoil. They stood outside the door that boasted the corresponding numbers of Fura's last class. He looked as collected as ever, silently watching the people pass by as he waited for her answer.

Taking out her schedule and flipping it so the map faced upward, Fura studied the inked sketch of the school. Kiyani had claimed that the Du Reizlan library was one of the most coveted collections of knowledge about the world of Izandüre available to man. Previously, Fura thought that he'd been exaggerating for her benefit. Now, it looked as if he'd been right.

The lines and numbers showed the library as a vast room, larger, and most likely, grander, than even the hall that they'd occupied earlier for lunch. From what Fura could tell, it consisted of four floors and spanned nearly a whole third of the main building.

More than anything, Fura wanted to forget this next class and move ahead to the library. It had been a long time since she'd visited the branch in Barandor, and even though she had yet to explore the one here, she had no doubt that the small, single level building she used to visit once a week would easily be put to shame. Where she'd been filled with trepidation since entering the sprawling monolith, now she was simply curious. This was what she'd wanted since they had gone on the run; to learn anything and everything about this world. The world that she had been a part of for so long without knowing it.

Glancing forlornly at the door next to her, one that would most likely boast another lecture that she wouldn't understand, Fura turned to Kiyani. "Why can't we just go there now?" It didn't matter how large the library was, Fura had no desire to go trekking through the halls by herself in order to find it. Even if it was the only room the building housed, she had a feeling she'd still find a way to get lost.

"Because," Kiyani said, "it doesn't work that way." Nodding at the door, he added, "It's only two more hours."

"Only," Fura muttered.

Ignoring her apprehension, Kiyani raised his hand in a slight wave before turning away. "I'll see you later."

A hard lump formed in the pit of her stomach as she watched him so calmly walk away, heading to his next class. One that he would probably actually enjoy. Not only because it had to do with weaponry, but because he'd be free of her for a few hours. In his eyes, this was likely going to be the best part of the day. To her, it felt as if her lifeline was walking into the void. For the first time since that morning, she would have to face the adversity of being the new kid completely alone.

Steadying herself with a deep breath, Fura opened the door to her class. Knowing that she still had a good ten minutes before the lesson was due to start, she hoped that she could meet the teacher and get her supplies before everyone filtered in.

Only two hours.

Kiyani made it seem like it was no big deal at all.

Walking alone through the halls, Fura could feel a small smile tug at her lips. Finally, she was free for the rest of the day. Just as she'd expected, the last two hours had proven to be the least exciting of the day, and for that Fura was actually thankful. It had been just what she'd needed after the hectic morning.

Having glanced at her schedule between attempting to take notes again, she'd been just as grateful to see that she wasn't set to meet with the tutor Kiyani had set her up with. Not until the next day. At least she could put that off for one more day.

Not only that, but the library proved to be easier to find than Fura had thought.

Feeling proud of herself for accomplishing that small task on her own, Fura entered the room. Inside, she stood just inside the doorway, gawping at what lie before her. She'd never seen anything like it.

Looking around, she felt as if she'd entered yet another dimension. From where she stood, the ceiling was open to reveal every level of the library, each boasting a balcony that looked down to the main floor.

A massive staircase branched from either side of the center of the room and twisted upwards with a flourish of dark gold leafing to the floors above. The second floor was visible from a balcony that hung in the darkness, the intricately carved banisters blending in with the sweep of the stairs. Dark mahogany bookshelves lined the walls, gorged with endless books of differing sizes and colors. From floor to ceiling they filled the room, covering the walls, and stretching into the shadows. A grand, multi-tiered chandelier of iron rings, much like the one Fura had seen in the main hall the night before, hung from the ceiling.

The floor was littered with multi-colored rugs, and chairs of differing sizes were scattered about. Though dark and cozy, light filtered in from a multitude of sources - from the sconces on the wall to a number of fireplaces decorating the walls.

Just standing in the room, Fura wanted to forget her classes completely and stay here forever.

This is what we need, Fura thought excitedly. *If we can't find anything about the Witneis here, then there's nothing to be found.*

Stepping softly across the ornate carpet beneath her feet, Fura glided across the room, wondering how she was supposed to find Kiyani in the midst of all this. He'd told her to meet her in the library. It'd sounded simple enough, but now Fura realized that he might as well have told her to find a needle in a haystack.

"Do you need any help finding something?"

To her right, Fura saw that a long desk ran alongside the wall, boasting a pile of books to be returned to their rightful places, as well as numerous cups of writing utensils, and a few piles of parchment next to a large ledger that she assumed was used in the checking out of materials. Behind the desk sat a woman who gave Fura a welcoming smile, as if she could tell this was Fura's first time entering the grand establishment.

"Not right now," Fura said, shaking her head. "Thanks."

Taking a few more timid steps, Fura turned back around and strolled over to the desk, hoping she didn't look too lost. "Actually, I'm meeting someone –"

As if anticipating the nature of her question the woman spoke in a soft voice. "If you follow those stairs," she said with a point of finger, "you'll find a study area on the second floor where people like to gather. You might want to start there."

Bowing her head, Fura graciously thanked the woman. Ascending the sweeping staircase, she couldn't get over the fact that this was all real.

Curiosity getting the best of her, Fura followed the rail until she stood in the center of the overhang. Looking below, she was awestruck by the quiet beauty of it all, at least until her acute fear of heights took over. Carefully stepping back, Fura turned to study the library's second level.

Much of it looked the same as the preceding story, the same dark colors weaving an intricate air that spoke of the ages. Not too far from where she stood, Fura saw what the librarian had spoken of. A large fireplace was situated along the back wall, the light from its embers dancing across the foiled titles pressed into the spines of countless books. It gave the room an odd ethereal feel, the words sparkling as she moved forward. In front of the large mantle where the flames crackled and popped, was an array of mismatched tables and chairs. Each one bore an oil lamp in the center of its marred surface, revealing not only the words that current students read, but also the marks of usage born with age.

Not every table boasted a full complement of chairs, nor was every table full. Here and there students grouped together in small masses, bent over books and curling pieces of parchment, studying and doing homework. A few briefly gazed at her curiously before returning to their studies. Somehow, it didn't bother Fura here as much as it had in the classrooms.

A small square table to the right of the fireplace caught her eye. Bearing a set of three chairs, Kiyani occupied one of them.

Skirting the tables altogether, Fura wandered over to the table and sat opposite him. "I found it," she announced quietly.

Trudging up the stairs that led to the dormitory a few hours later, Fura found that each step sent a resounding stab of pain throughout her tired body. After a day spent running up and down halls and stairways trying to get to class on time, the only thing she wanted to do was sleep. The barrage of new information she'd received had done no less damage to her mind than the strenuous activity had on her body. The only thing she knew for certain was that if one of the professors suddenly decided that the next day was deserving of a pop quiz, she would fail.

Though she'd looked forward to it, the time in the library had been spent in further frustration. As much as Fura had wanted to get right down to it and begin the search for anything to do with the Witneis Reln, Kiyani had immediately reprimanded her into doing more schoolwork. As if she hadn't had her fill for the day.

Had it been any other day, Fura knew she would have accumulated a whole new slew of questions to ask him. Yet, the sheer amount of information thrown at her since early that morning had simply left her numb. Though she could have questioned Kiyani about any number of things, her mind had gone blank as soon as she'd had the opportunity.

To her surprise, Kiyani had insisted that they spend the first week actually playing student so they didn't end up prematurely kicked out. It wasn't what she wanted to hear, knowing that that meant they would be further removed from the road of their travels. Her father's life was potentially on the line. Though she knew she could definitely pick up some useful information here, it didn't keep her from thinking that they were wasting time that could be better spent elsewhere. Too tired to argue with Kiyani about it, she'd quickly caved, though she was sure, when she looked every now and then, that what he had before him had suspiciously nothing to do with their classes.

Twice, Fura had nearly fallen asleep. The fire before them, its flames dancing lazily and sending out waves of steady heat, lulled her into a haze of neither rest nor awareness. The only sound in the large room was the occasional whisper of pages being turned. When they found the school's ten-thirty curfew looming before them, Kiyani and Fura had silently packed their things and left the comfort of the room.

Not quite looking forward to leaving Kiyani's side again, Fura found that the distance from the library to their dorms was shorter than she'd anticipated. Unwilling to admit to him that she didn't want to return to her room, and knowing that the curfew was minutes away, Fura quietly waved as they parted ways, watching him go before heading through her own door. In the library they had decided that they would meet in the alcove every morning, leaving her with nothing left to say for the night.

Letting out a heavy breath of exhaustion as the door to her room came into view, Fura wondered what the chances of going right to sleep were. The sight that welcomed her as she pushed open the door caused a shiver to run down her spine.

Just inside the room, Talia and Thayna stood, as if they'd been waiting to ambush her. A mirror image of one another, their stance was firm, their arms crossed, the fire in their eyes far from inviting.

Before Fura could escape, Talia grabbed her by the arm and dragged her into the candle-lit area, her sister closing the door and blocking the way to salvation.

Standing in the flickering light, Fura waited for one of the twins to speak, unsure of what other option she had. She felt exposed beneath their intense scrutiny, as if what they wanted to know was written on her face plain as day.

"Spill it, sister," Thayna demanded abruptly. The words were sharp and biting. Lost were all the niceties of the night before.

Fura cringed. "What?" She had no idea what this sudden interrogation was about. They may have had two classes together, but she hadn't spoken to either of them in that time. With no indication of what it was she had done in those hours, Fura waited for a reply.

Talia laughed. "As if you don't know!" she half squealed. Her eyes burned into Fura maniacally.

Still not understanding, Fura shook her head. She wondered if it was too late to try to get a new room assignment.

Thayna took a step forward, making Fura realize that she had unintentionally moved away from the two. "Meeting a *friend*, huh?"

Is that what this is about? They're jealous because I wanted to spend the day with Kiyani and not them?

"You're with, what did he call himself, Kiyani?"

"He *is* my friend," Fura announced, her voice weaker than she had hoped. Was it so weird that she had friends already?

"From what I hear, he's friends with no one," Talia said.

Thayna nodded. "Everyone here has been waiting for his arrival, and he comes here with a little mouse like you in tow?"

Cringing at the cruel meaning behind their comment, Fura wondered how things could have changed so dramatically in such a short period of time. Only the night before they'd claimed they looked forward to being friends. Now they were reprimanding her for something she hadn't even done.

"I tried to talk to him," whined Talia, "and he wouldn't even give me the time of day."

"He blatantly ignores everyone else," Thayna nodded in agreement with her sister's plight. "What makes you so special?"

"I – we're just friends," Fura said. She didn't know what the big deal was. These two had hardly met the man that even she knew little about, and they were already so quick to severely judge him. Proffering one more snippet of information, Fura added, "We've been traveling together."

No sooner had the phrase left her lips, Fura knew she should have kept it to herself. Where she had thought it might help her case, the actions of the girls told otherwise. The twin's mouths dropped in synchronized motion and they turned to discuss it amongst themselves.

Breaking away from their huddle, Thayna commented. "Fire and shadow... how cute." She shook her head as if she mourned Fura's sanity. "You really shouldn't be with him, you know," she said, the conversation striking a sour note.

"He's the son of evil," Talia nodded. "Darkness runs in his veins like cute runs in a puppy. I can't believe he hasn't torn you apart already. You should consider yourself lucky."

Fura could see Thayna's other half in her sister's shadow agreeing with a jerky nod. Ignoring it, she asked defensively, "Why do you care?"

Shrinking away from the conversation, Fura tried to weasel her way to the safety of her bed. If she could just distract them long enough to dive under the covers, maybe she would be safe from their lies. Sleep could take her and she could wake up the next morning, fresh and new, able to escape from this sudden nightmare.

"We're only trying to protect you," they responded in unison.

65

♦♦◇♦♦

THE TWO-HEADED SNAKE

Fura woke with a clouded mind the next morning. Fighting irritably with the sheets, she untangled herself and sat up. Surveying the room, she found that, to her relief, Talia and Thayna had already left.

"Good riddance," Fura muttered.

Their nonsensical rumors had taken root and festered in her thoughts all night like an open sore in dire need of medical attention. No matter how hard she'd tried, their poisonous words had flitted through her mind, trailing their inherent meanings along with them, keeping her awake as she tossed and turned. The sound of the girls' giggling, echoing throughout the room, had only made it worse.

She had gone to bed angry with them, yet it had been tears that'd stained her pillow.

Now Fura understood her initial hesitation when she had first met Talia and Thayna. They had been so quick to welcome her as a friend when in fact it was actually new prey they were sniffing out. The two were a conniving set, and now she was on the wrong side of the wall. She was nothing more to them than a helpless animal stuck in a trap, scrambling to get out when there was no means of escape. Fura knew that if she let them get to her she would be reduced to a sniveling mass in the psych ward in a matter of days.

Grinning, Fura secretly wondered if there actually was a psych ward here. She had no doubt that it would serve its purpose if it did exist.

Casting thoughts of insanity aside, she looked to the window, covering a yawn with her hand.

Even without someone to wake her up on time, Fura found that it was still early. Though she didn't know where the girls had gone, she was glad that Talia and Thayna hadn't taken it upon themselves to continue their verbal torture session into the morning hours. Fura had the unnerving feeling that she wouldn't be lucky enough to be free of their larcenous influence for the whole of the day, but for the time being she was alone.

Taking her time, Fura dressed and underwent the menial task of straightening her meager belongings, attempting to build up what little sanity she could spare. Quickly losing interest, she returned to the window. This was the first time she'd been alone in the room, giving her the opportunity to take in the view below. From what Fura had seen, when the twins weren't hounding her, they were huddled in the window seat, giggling amongst themselves at private jokes that only they could find the humor in.

Wishing that she could lay claim to the window, she looked out across the vast expanse of green forest surrounding the school.

She had no idea what was out there in those trees, hidden in this world, but Fura wished that she and Kiyani could forget this venture and return to their travels. They still didn't have any information on the Witneis, but they shouldn't have had to subject themselves to this torture in order to find it.

The truth of the matter was that they could potentially spend a month here and still not find anything. That was the worst case scenario.

The second was that they would come to find that the Witneis was hundreds of miles in the opposite direction.

Thinking about that devastating possibility, Fura wondered if maybe Apallo hadn't actually sent them on a long, harrowing journey. What if the Witneis had been just outside Frielana this whole time?

I've never even seen a map of Izandüre, Fura realized, thinking that even if that had been the case, she still wouldn't have known which way to go.

Outside the window she watched a set of sparrows flit through the tree tops, feeling envious of them. Unlike her, they were free without a care in the world.

Get a hold of yourself, Fura chastised. *Not even two days here and I already want to leave. What kind of coward am I?* It was no wonder Kiyani never wanted to deal with her. Taking in a deep breath, Fura squared her shoulders. *I can do this,* she told herself.

Knowing that the day wasn't getting any younger, and fearing that Talia and Thayna would return at any moment, Fura grabbed what she needed for her classes.

The moment she moved out of her room and into the hallway, it felt as if the air were cleaner, breathing new life into the day. Closing the door behind her, Fura hoped to do the same with that moment in her life. Strolling down the hallway, she glanced at the other names etched into brass metal on each entranceway. Each plaque bearing the names of other girls whom Fura could have just as easily been paired with.

With every step she took, Fura repeated in her mind, *I can make it through this.*

✧ ⌘ ✧

The slow and resonant creak of a door opening nudged Kiyani into waking. Rolling over, he did his best to ignore it. Though the sun that streamed through the window had already given him fair warning that morning was upon them, the bed was too comfortable to give any real notice. He knew he had to get up, but it didn't keep him from taking a few moments of much needed rest.

Telling himself that he'd only lie there for a few more minutes, he dug himself deeper into the blankets.

It was only moments later when a torrent of icy needles drenched the world around him, followed by a chorus of laughter. An involuntary yelp of surprise fell from Kiyani's lips as he shot up, shocked into awareness by the cold water, searching for the culprits.

In the doorway a group of boys stood, four wide. Cackling like a flock of trouble-making blue jays, their beady eyes focused on the recipient of their prank. Nylan stood front and center, his green eyes boring into Kiyani as the grin on his face widened.

In his hands he held the cold metal pail that had resulted in the icy assailant of water. Nylan crossed his arms. "Don't think that your father's name is going to get you anywhere here. I rule this school. Remember that, or else you'll get far worse." The boys behind him snickered. "Welcome to Du Reizlan." Throwing the bucket at Kiyani, Nylan turned. His cronies parted as they let him through, each one casting a look of distaste at Kiyani before following their leader into the hallway and out of sight.

"Get back here!" Kiyani roared, throwing off the sheets to take after the raucous group. A small hand held him back.

Tibben shook his head. "Don't even try. You'll only get yourself in trouble."

"Once I take it to –"

"Creslin doesn't listen." Staring at the empty doorway, Tibben marched forward to close the gaping hole before any of the other boys in the dorm became privy to the morning's events. "I'm surprised they left me out of it for once."

"They've done this to you before?" Kiyani asked as he shivered in the morning air.

"Plenty of times, along with other things I'd rather not mention."

Grimacing at his meaning, Kiyani sighed and flopped back onto the bed. Landing with a resounding *squish*, he groaned and stood up, forgoing the mattress altogether. The clothes he'd been sleeping in, as well as the sheets, were soaked through. Not to mention, the cold water had forced him into a state of aggravated awareness.

Kicking the bucket in anger, Kiyani went about readying himself for another day. It had been so long since he'd walked the hallways of a school he had almost forgotten what it was like. Du Reizlan may have reigned primitive and grand at the same time over the school that he'd attended before, but it was all the same. Now, the memories of before flooded back to him, stinging him like a horde of angry bees. The quicker they found something about this tree, the better.

Though the bright sunshine that filtered through the tall glass windows overlooking the courtyard hurt Fura's eyes, she ignored it. Morosely, she wished that the morning would have proven to be rain-filled and dreary. Like her own mood.

Thankfully, the hallway outside the dorms didn't appear nearly as crowded as the day before. Whether it was that alone, or the fact that this wasn't as unfamiliar to her, Fura found that she wasn't quite as jumpy as she had been the previous day. Paying no heed to the wave of people that passed by, too absorbed in their own daily worries and conversations, Fura took a seat on the bench. A quick glance around proved that she'd beat Kiyani to their meeting place. Undisturbed by the fact, she realized that, if anything, it gave her a few more minutes to regroup herself.

She didn't want to start the day on such a sour note.

The good thing, Fura noticed, was that the terror twins were still nowhere in sight.

Even though she knew they shared two classes, Fura still hoped that she wouldn't see them during the day. Fortunately for her, those two intersecting hours were among the ones she shared with Kiyani. If they stuck to the same seating arrangements, the girls wouldn't even be within distance to throw a scathing note. The way that Talia and Thayna had been talking about Kiyani the night before gave her an indication that just his presence might be enough to keep them away.

She could only hope.

Curling her feet under her, Fura rummaged in her bag. Bringing forth her schedule, she flipped it over so the map of the school showed. She knew where her classes where now. In a matter of days, Fura hoped to be able to traverse the halls, at least the ones that led to her classrooms, without its guidance. Still, following the lines on the map with her finger, tracing the steps she'd taken the day before, gave her something to do. She hadn't realized in the flurry of activity and confusion the day before just how much of Du Reizlan she'd covered.

Out of the corner of her eye, Fura could see the door to her left open as a group of boys emerged from the dormitory. Focused on the map, she didn't even bother to look over to see if Kiyani was among them. If he was, he would make it known.

Stopping on the other side of the archway, the group quickly convened before one of them broke away. Sidling over, he paused next to Fura, throwing a shadow over the paper that she was studying.

"Hey there, gorgeous."

Fura tensed at the pet name. Not recognizing the voice, she cautiously looked up to see who it belonged to. Not even in Barandor had someone spoken to her as such. "Um, hi?"

The man that looked back at her was no older than Kiyani, though maybe a little taller. A mess of sandy blond hair fell to his shoulders in waves. The affectionate smile that grazed his lips made Fura blush and turn away, knowing that he had to be talking to someone else. However, her eyes confirmed that she was the only one that occupied the bench.

As Fura glanced back at the man, he held out his hand courteously. "You must be the new one everyone's talking about."

Everyone's talking about me? Fura wasn't sure she liked the sound of that.

He said it matter-of-factly, not needing affirmation, as if there was no doubt at all about her status as a student within the walls of Du Reizlan.

Warily, Fura took his hand. Bright green eyes stared back at her as he brought her hand to his lips, lightly kissing it. "Nylan," he said, introducing himself.

"Fura..." she replied, barely able to whisper her own name, flustered by this sudden display of attraction.

Backing away and leaning against the wall, Nylan silently studied her, a slight grin on his face. Hoping that her cheeks weren't too noticeably red, Fura knew she couldn't be so lucky. He watched her without any further words, until a new round of commotion sounded from behind him. Released from his unnerving gaze, Fura looked to the ground and steadied her breathing. Sticking her shaking hands beneath her legs, she looked past Nylan to see what had caused the fray.

A chorus of laughter from the group of boys that Nylan had broken off from sounded as Kiyani strode through the door. Though there was an icy fire in his eyes, he ignored them completely, not giving them the satisfaction of a brief glance their way.

Squinting her eyes, Fura wondered if her mind was playing tricks on her. Kiyani's hair hung around his face in wet strands as if he'd just went swimming, reminding her of that first morning in Frielana when she'd spoken to him by the spring. Fura didn't even know where the baths were, let alone when he would've found the time to have visited one.

Nylan turned to Fura and nodded. "I'll be talking to you later." Bumping into Kiyani, seemingly on purpose, as he went to move, Nylan

561

patted him on the shoulder. "Hey there, buddy. Impromptu shower this morning?" The boys that waited on the fringes of the conversation howled in laughter again as if they were all in on some private joke. Watching Kiyani's reaction to their snickers, Fura wondered if that was the case.

Kiyani glared incredulously at Nylan as he walked away, the man's shoulders held high and proud as his gang pressed in around him, following him down the hall and around the corner. Raising a brow, Kiyani turned to Fura. "What the hell was that about?" he asked darkly.

Fura could only shrug. "I have no idea."

Yet, she could tell he didn't believe her.

"What did he say to you?"

"I –" Fura faltered. What *had* he really said to her? She still wasn't entirely sure. "I think he said I was pretty." She didn't dare repeat the words he'd actually used.

A low growl emanated from Kiyani's throat. His hand balling into a fist at his side, he stared down the hallway as if fighting the urge to go confront Nylan. Fura could see him searching, but they both knew Nylan was already long gone.

"I'll be seeing you later?" Kiyani asked, repeating Nylan's words. "Did you agree to meet him somewhere?"

"No," Fura replied, shaking her head. She hadn't been aware that he'd even heard Nylan's parting words to her. It almost made her feel as if their entire short-lived conversation had been eavesdropped on. In a way, Fura wasn't sure if she should be jealous or thankful that Kiyani had intervened when he had. Their time traveling together, meeting very few people along the way, had made her wary of others, especially those who were so forthright with their words.

"I want you to stay away from him."

"He doesn't seem *that* bad," Fura tried to reason, though she fought the chill that ran down her spine as she recounted the strange meeting. "He's kind of charming in a way..."

"He's as charming as your average python," Kiyani huffed. "Don't be fooled by his sugar-coated words. The only reason he ever introduces himself to someone is when he wants something from them."

Not knowing how to respond, Fura let the remainder of the conversation fall flat as she thought about what had been said, from both Kiyani and Nylan. Kiyani added nothing more, instead watching the passing students with a wary eye as if to ask, *why am I here?*

Fura didn't blame him. The same thought had been present in her own mind since she'd woken, though she didn't voice it aloud. She knew that if she did he would have some scathing answer to give her.

Though Fura knew they should start heading to class soon, neither made a move, none too eager to further the progression of the day other than to merely get it over with. They remained stationary, until a fiber of connected thought hit Fura.

"Nylan..." she whispered. "*That's* your roommate?" she asked. The name had sounded vaguely familiar when it had been given to her, but now Fura knew why.

Kiyani barely looked at her. "Yes and no." Staring tensely down the hallway, it was clear that he was still seething over what had just occurred.

What a great way to start the day, Fura thought. It was bad enough that her morning still held ruminations of the miserable night before, but now Kiyani was just as irritable. The phrase 'getting up on the wrong side of the bed' hit her, and Fura wondered if going back to bed would actually solve anything.

"I don't understand," she finally said, trying to work out the correct way to go about the conversation without sending it into an instant tailspin. "Isn't that who Creslin roomed you with?"

"It is," Kiyani said, "but it's not who I'm with now."

"When did you talk to Creslin about it?" Fura asked, wondering if she could do the same. She would do just about anything to rid herself of that evil set of girls.

"I didn't. Nylan told me to leave and I did."

"You just let him push you around like that?" Fura was astonished. She couldn't imagine Kiyani taking flack from anyone, yet he acted like it was no big deal.

"No," Kiyani said, throwing a heated glance her way. "But I would rather not have to deal with him every morning." Attempting to direct the conversation in a different direction, Kiyani asked, "How are your roommates?"

"Fine," Fura lied. She didn't care to talk about her own problems any more than he seemed willing to talk about his. The last thing she was going to do was tell him about this preconceived reputation he seemed to have.

Plenty more questions stormed her mind, but only one remained front and center. "What happened to your hair?"

"Don't ask," Kiyani growled. The fierce undertone in his voice dared her to inquire any further.

Taking heed of his implied warning, Fura didn't bother to kindle the conversation. Instead, she took leave of the situation entirely and refocused her attentions on the paper in front of her. The map of Du Reizlan had been forgotten completely in all the hubbub. Where before it had given her a certain level of anxiety, it now offered a bit of solace. At least the twisting lines and boxes she understood. This was reality, and it needed nothing more than to be read and interpreted, something that was much easier than the current route of muddled conversations.

The door to the boys' dormitory flew open again, nearly slamming against the wall, breaking Fura's concentration once more. A boy of maybe thirteen or fourteen skidded into the hallway, his breathing labored as if he'd just ran the entire length of the stairway. Looking their way, his eyes lit up.

"Sorry, I couldn't make it down earlier," he said, halting next to Kiyani.

Kiyani let out an exasperated sigh. "It's fine."

The boy nodded as if he'd been given a compliment. "Do you want to walk with me to class?"

"No."

Deflated, the boy muttered, "Oh, okay. Are you sure? We're going to the same place."

"Tibben," Kiyani said shortly as if by way of warning.

Fura remained silent though she cocked her head in amusement.

Taking notice, Kiyani dipped his head toward the youth. "*This* is my roommate."

Understanding, Fura nodded to the boy. "Hi." She remembered seeing him the morning before in their history class, though he'd been seated halfway across the room.

Tibben's eyes widened as he noticed Fura in the alcove. "Wow," he said, "You're hair is pretty."

Letting out a small laugh, Fura thanked him. She didn't know how many more compliments she could handle today, but at least his was genuine.

As if resigning himself to the fact that he wasn't getting rid of either of them, Kiyani heaved a tired sigh. Pushing himself off the wall he stepped into the thinning stream of students. "Come on, let's go."

66
♦♦◇♦♦
LESSONS

A growing sense of apprehension followed Fura like a stale odor as she wandered through the hallways alone. Each meandering branch of the building felt the same to her. Every wall was made of the same dark granite. Every door the same aged wood. The only noticeable variance amongst the torch-lit corridors were the ornate tapestries that hung at regular intervals throughout the building.

Despite her feeble arguments, Kiyani had insisted that she take initiative and find the room where she would be tutored on her own. Though she knew he was right, it didn't leave her feeling any more empowered. Rather, Fura felt dumb traversing the winding passages, continually consulting the map in her hands that had become her lifeline for finding her way in this wretched school.

If she was honest with herself, she was still angry with Kiyani for having set this up in the first place. If he thought she was in such desperate need of tutoring, why didn't he do it himself? It wasn't as if he'd never had to the time to tell her a thing or two about this world. Instead, he'd squandered days seething in silence, pretending that she didn't exist.

Grumbling to herself as she thought about it, Fura consulted the map again as she turned down another hall.

Aside from the events of that morning, the sessions in the classrooms had been rather uneventful. Fura had gotten a few snide looks from Talia and Thayna in the two classes they shared, but no words had been exchanged. Though she was glad for that, Fura still didn't look forward to retiring to her dorm that evening.

Even the fourth class of the day, the only time that she had to split from Kiyani for any real amount of time, had gone off without a hitch. If anything, it had spawned a mixture of feelings ranging from loneliness to boredom. However, it was nothing different than what Fura had frequently experienced within the Barandor school district. The only difference was that in Barandor she had known the names of those who had chosen to ignore her.

Meeting with Kiyani after their classes, they had traveled in measured silence to the dining hall for a light dinner before heading back to the library.

The hours spent in the library, Fura found, was the only time during the day in which she actually felt they were accomplishing anything. The night before they had stumbled upon the grand school, Kiyani had made sure to remind her that under no circumstances was she to outright ask about the Witneis. He had claimed that they'd be under suspicion if it became common knowledge that they were looking for the tree, possibly even putting them in danger.

Fura hadn't understood why, nor had she asked him to explain any further. And though it ate at her, she did as was asked. Questions still lingered though, and plenty of times she had fallen just short of shouting them out loud. Did he have any idea how much quicker this would all go if they had someone helping them? Someone with a higher level of knowledge than the two of them combined. She didn't see why they couldn't enlist the help of some quirky teacher. Maybe Dairnyg from *Herbology* or even Gruevaind from *History*. One of them had to have at least heard something.

Briefly, Fura had brought up the thought, but no sooner had it left her mouth, Kiyani had already shot it down. He was content, it seemed, to try and wrest the information out of one of the millions of surrounding books. Without her help.

Every time she entered the library, Fura felt overwhelmed by the countless subject matter that surrounded her. Even so, she would have felt more useful if she was allowed to assist in the search in some way. But Kiyani had claimed that he didn't need the help. Instead, he made sure that she focused on her schoolwork, deliberately forcing even more facts on her if they coincided with what was being taught in the lecture rooms.

As if thoughtfully deciding that she would get lost no matter what, Kiyani had rousted her out of her seat at a half hour to seven. Fura had wasted five of those minutes arguing with him as to why she had to go alone, and why she needed this in the first place. As usual, Kiyani had masterfully dodged her questions with ease and had eventually succeeded in shooing her out of the library.

She wasn't sure what there was to gain by meeting with this tutor, other than a deeper feeling of incompetence and a new level of frustration. To Fura this was just another form of mental torture, another person to tell her how futile their efforts were, trying to teach over seventeen years worth of knowledge that she should have already known.

Like I don't get enough of that during the regular school day.

It was another few minutes before Fura finally found her bearings and got her directions straight. Entirely of her own accord, an accomplishment she was rather proud of, Fura stood in front of a set of rather unremarkable pine doors.

There was nothing extraordinary about them, unlike most of the other arches that led into the various classrooms. Then again, very little about this venture had felt normal. The further Fura traipsed into the grand school, the more disoriented she became, certain that she was going in the wrong direction. Her destination was on the fourth floor, down a wing of the school that felt as if it had been abandoned for centuries. Walking the dusty corridors, Fura hadn't been sure that wasn't the case.

The room number that had been scrawled on her schedule matched the digits that were engraved on the tarnished brass plate on the door. Still uncertain, Fura put her doubts behind her and pushed the doors open, not knowing what she would find beyond.

What greeted her did little to change Fura's aspect of this wing of the building. The darkly lit stone room was void of any life, save for a lone woman who stood at the far window. Her hands clasped behind her back, she stared out the world beyond the glass. Whether she was unaware of her presence or merely ignoring her, Fura couldn't tell.

Closing the door softly behind her so as to not make a grand entrance, Fura sidled forward. The room felt just as dead as the halls that'd led to it. A thin layer of dust covered most of the surfaces, and even the flames of the torches on the wall were near motionless in the stale air. Fura's apprehension about this personal one-on-one lesson only grew as she approached the stranger. The only thing that made her feel better was that her tutor was a woman.

"Um," Fura began. Realizing how weak her voice sounded, she took in a deep breath and cleared her throat before continuing. "I'm here for my lessons."

"You're late," the woman announced.

Fura recognized the gravelly voice before she saw the woman's face. Turning, the woman's dark eyes bored into her own. A nest of gray curls framed her face and fell down her back in frizzy cascade. And her thin, bony hands were embellished with a network of raised veins.

"Sorry," Fura bowed clumsily to the woman who had let her and Kiyani into the school only a few nights prior.

"As well you should be," the woman declared. "My name is Marna. I already know you, and from what Kiyani was telling Creslin and I, I have my work cut out for me."

It occurred to Fura that the elderly woman had never left the confines of the Grand Master's office when she'd been escorted out to the hallway. It only made her wonder all the more what Kiyani had revealed to the two that she didn't know about. Just how much of their trip was now common knowledge to people Fura wasn't sure she could trust?

"Um," Fura tried to read the hastily inked name on her schedule in the dim light. Though she didn't particularly care who her tutor was, she was sure that the names didn't match up. "My schedule says my tutor is supposed to be a..." she faltered, still trying to make out the name.

"Sabrahé. Yes, but Grand Master Creslin and I decided otherwise."

Marna motioned with her hand as she turned back to the window.

Following orders, Fura covered the short distance in a few strides. Standing next to the woman, she remained silent as she looked out the pane to the landscape below.

"Tell me, miss Feuer, what do you see?"

Unaware if this was her first test or merely a prelude to actual conversation, Fura paused before answering with the obvious. "Trees in a deep valley?"

"Do not answer a question with another question," Marna chided. "And, wrong. What lies before you is the northern edge of the Tempus Grove, on which the opposite side the Sand Straits stretch for miles down the south-eastern coast. Northwest of here is the coastal town of Saibon. I've been told that you've never even laid eyes on a map of Izandüre before."

Fura shook her head, her face flushing with heat. She found herself embarrassed that it had never once crossed her mind to seek out the simplest form of information of this world; a map. The thought had crossed her mind once or twice, but she'd never thought to actually pursue it further. Where did you even find a map in this place? It wasn't as if she could pick one up at the corner gas station. It occurred to her that although she knew that she and Kiyani had traveled a vast distance, she didn't know how far, nor in what direction. She knew the names of the few places they'd been, but none of them held any relevance to her.

"Do you know what the term pyropheric means?" Marna continued.

Fura brightened at the mention of the term. "Kiyani told me that it's the proper name for the powers of the Firelord and his sect of followers."

Marna nodded in approval and Fura felt a hint of elation at not being labeled completely inept. At least she knew something, no matter how small.

However, her satisfaction was short lived as Marna next asked, "Can you conjure flame?"

Feeling like a balloon that had been popped, Fura answered flatly. "No."

"Then we have a lot of work to do."

The old woman relinquished her place at the window and shuffled over to a high shelf on the wall. Shifting a stack of musty books, and digging through multiple piles of paper, a cloud of dust momentarily filled the air before settling again. From the flurry, Marna produced a cracked and yellowed tube of paper.

Showing Fura to a small table in the middle of the room, she gently laid it down. Letting the parchment unroll itself halfway, Marna smoothed out the rest with a hand and weighted the corners with various objects, including a vial of dark green liquid and an odd-shaped paperweight. As interesting as they were, Fura knew that it was what they were holding down that was supposed to be the focus of her attention.

Leaning over the document, it took Fura a moment to realize that she was looking at a large map of Izandüre. Allowing her fingers to lightly brush over the paper, Fura studied it inquisitively, doing her best to allow the strange names to take root in her mind. When Kiyani had said that the world of Izandüre was parallel to her own earth, Fura had assumed that it would look the same on a map. Now, she saw that she was wrong. Nothing about the penciled continents and islands resembled that which she was used to.

"You would do well to learn each and every hill, valley, and mountain peak on that," Marna said, motioning to the paper in front of Fura.

Her head shot up in alarm as the woman spoke the words. Was it possible that she knew all about the quest her and Kiyani were on? She looked to the woman for confirmation, but Marna had already turned away from her and was shifting through objects on another shelf.

It's only a coincidence.

Shooting down her fears, Fura nodded in silent agreement, though she knew the woman couldn't see her. At least this wouldn't be useless information.

Returning to her study, Fura was able to pick up a few of the names that she recognized; Frielana, where they'd started their journey, Tybithera's dwelling, and even the city of Naquaelin that Kiyani had told her to mention to anyone in Skirvynmire who wanted to ask questions of where they were headed.

So, that wasn't just something he made up... Despite his telling her so, Fura had still wondered.

"I do believe that Master Creslin has already told you what Sect you were filtered into?"

Startled, Fura looked up to find that Marna's attention had settled on her again. She nodded. "Fire."

Bowing her head in accord, Marna's face twisted into a half smile. "I'm quite sure you've already ascertained the reasoning behind that decision?"

"Of course." Fura couldn't see, given her supposed heritage, how she could've been placed any differently. Though she knew it had little to do with what she would be learning in the next few hours, Fura couldn't help but voicing a request. "If you don't mind my asking, could you tell me what Sect Kiyani was placed in?"

"It is not our place to disclose that information, nor does it hold any purpose in these lessons," Marna said, her countenance markedly darkening. "If you wish to know, you will have to ask him yourself. Now, rid yourself of such thoughts. We have a lot to accomplish in a short amount of time if you are to go through classes here and not persistently fail."

67
♦♦✦♦♦
CHASING SHADOWS

Sitting in the library, Fura fiddled with the quill in her hand as she stared over Kiyani's shoulder at the flames dancing in the fireplace.

The lessons with Marna the night before had left her exceedingly tired and surprisingly sore, leaving her with little energy to focus on the work laid out before her on the table. In addition to studying the map and memorizing more bits of what Fura considered possibly useless information – at least for what her and Kiyani would be doing – Marna had insisted upon having her at least attempt to summon fire, among other things. Though nothing had gone horribly wrong, nothing had gone all that right either.

For as much as Fura knew about her family and her relation to the current Firelord, and what Kiyani had mentioned about the pyropheric powers she was meant to have, she'd thought that it would've been easier. She couldn't have been more wrong. Nearly half an hour had gone by, tirelessly trying to do what Marna had claimed should have come as second nature to her: creating a small flame in the palm of her hand.

Hardly anything had come of that time, except for Fura's growing resentment of Izandüre and the uneasy feeling that she would forever be labeled useless to everyone, including her own Sect, if she ever saw them again. She'd no sooner lost count of how many times she had tried, ready to call it quits, for the night or for forever, when she finally managed to strike up a spark. Elation had filled her, at least until the pitiful display had fizzled out in mere seconds.

She'd had no idea that delving into magic would be so painfully trying. There was no reason she should've been sore, yet she was. It was almost as if she had spent her life on the couch and had one day decided to run a marathon. There were lingering consequences.

To her dismay, Marna had continued to prove her worthlessness by extending their allotted time. Drilling Fura on this, that, and the other, she'd felt as if her head would explode from all the knowledge she was expected to retain in the frame of a single day. When Marna had finally released her from the torture, Fura had barely had time to scurry back to the dorm before the night's curfew set in.

Fighting a sigh of contempt, Fura glanced back at the parchment before her, the words blending into an incomprehensible blur. She had a feeling nothing would get done tonight.

Peering over at Kiyani, deep in contemplation, she still found it surprising that he hadn't made any hint of wondering how her tutoring had gone the night before, or what had taken her so long. She had a feeling that he'd probably relished the time to himself, sitting amongst these same books, while she'd been trying to learn something useful. Yet, she'd expected him to at least ask how she'd done. Especially since he'd been the one to sign her up for the extra work in the first place.

Resigning to doodling on the page, Fura was just glad that another day was nearly over. From that morning, onwards through classes, and into their nightly library routine, the day had moved at a relatively steady pace. One that Fura knew she'd become accustomed to, whether she liked it or not. Despite her initial hesitation, she found it amazing just how quickly one could fall into a familiar routine.

The only thing that had plagued her throughout the day was the incredulous worry that'd settled into the back of her mind. Dark, and poisonous thoughts that just wouldn't let her be, no matter how hard she tried to focus on her studies instead.

For all that she'd expected to happen the previous night, Fura knew she should have known better than to think that Talia and Thayna would give her a night of uninterrupted rest just because she'd wandered in late.

Instead, they'd been just as vindictive as ever.

Her eyes wandering to the fire again, Fura cringed as she thought about it. She could still see the scene in her head, clear as day, as if she had merely been a witness and not the center of the verbal attack.

It had been dark when she'd traversed the winding stairs to the dorms, but the light that had flickered beneath the door should have been warning enough that the twins were still awake, lying in wait for her.

As soon as she'd entered the room, closing the door softly behind her to avoid waking any who had decided to go to sleep early, Thayna had looked up at her from her place on the window seat. The gleam in her eyes had been wicked.

"Oh, it's back," she'd sneered, addressing Fura not only in third person, but as a mere object.

All she'd wanted was to was fall into bed and sleep. Maybe, if rest didn't come right away, attempt to digest what had happened that day. In retrospect, Fura knew she should have known better.

From her bed in the far corner, Talia had dropped the book she was reading into her lap. "Late night with Kiyani?" It hadn't been a mere question but an accusation.

"There are rules against that kind of thing here, you know." Thayna had snickered.

Fura had wondered if they would go and try to report it, hoping to get her in trouble. Yet, it'd meant nothing to her. They wouldn't get anywhere with the accusations. Even Creslin would've known that she'd been with Marna most of the evening. No, what had bothered her the most was that she was viciously being attacked, and for no reason. And, what'd made it all the worse was the way they'd smiled as they said such hateful things, acting like they were her friends. Like they were only trying to take care of her, as if she didn't know any better and they felt sorry for her.

She still had no idea what it was they had against Kiyani, but they had taken her into the equation simply through association. Fura wondered how tight her 'friendship' with the twins would be if they'd never seen her and Kiyani together. Even as she thought it, Fura knew it was nigh on impossible. She hardly ever left Kiyani's side, and she was aware of it. He was her only friend in this pit.

It was a dangerous reckoning, but Fura just couldn't muster up the courage, nor the want, to find friends. What was the point, anyways? Even if she did manage to chalk up a few buddies she would only end up leaving them behind sooner or later, not knowing if she would ever see them again. It seemed like such a pointless venture when she put her mind to it, especially with all that she was already burdened with. Who had time for the formality of making friends?

Besides, hadn't she tried that once before in the Barandor school system... and look where that had left her. All the more haggard for trying. Not to mention being labeled the firefreak by more than one of her classmates. Sure, a few had thought it was cool that she worked as a firedancer in Fireswell, but even though a couple had come to watch her perform once in awhile they had never taken the initiative to befriend her.

Fura let out a sigh of frustration. She didn't have time for this.

The twins' conversation had traveled further into darker territory, down winding and twisted paths, but even now Fura didn't care to recall much more of it. She'd done her best to ignore them, changing into her sleep attire and sliding under the covers even as they'd continued talking. They had quickly taken her actions into consideration, but instead of ceasing their discussion, they had simply resorted to talking about her instead of to her.

Though Fura had tried to sleep, she hadn't been able to keep herself from listening to what they were saying.

"Poor girl, she really thinks that he's her friend."

"He's no one's friend. He walks alone like a shadow in the night. That's what he's known for, what his family is known for. No one like that just freely attaches to someone else for the sake of goodwill."

"It's a dangerous path she's taking. If only she would listen to us."

"She'll learn soon enough."

Their conversation had gone on deep into the night, eventually ending up in the twisting caverns of Fura's dreams. Even waking to sunshine again that morning, Fura had found it difficult to correctly distinguish just what had been actual conversation and what her mind had felt free to add.

Leaving her unsettled throughout the day, Fura had wanted to talk to Kiyani about it. Yet, every time she'd thought to make an attempt she'd either felt it wasn't the right moment, or he'd been preoccupied.

Glancing at him now, hunched over a book, his eyes scanning the page, it didn't appear any different.

Fura knew that what the twins had said wasn't true, their only motive instilling fear as she ate up their lies, but she had to hear it from someone beside herself.

Even with the few terrifying outbursts she'd witnessed, Kiyani had never done anything to hurt her. Instead, and she hated herself for the thought, he seemed to be the one to consistently keep her out of trouble. The words that Talia and Thayna used to describe him painted a much different, much darker picture than Fura had come to see in their time together. Kiyani might have been a lot of things, but whoever this man was that the twins were so insistent on warning her about, it wasn't him.

He was never one for talking, as Fura had discovered early on, but who better to sort out the twins' fabricated stories than Kiyani himself?

As desperate as she was to have things answered, Fura allowed another hour to go by first. In that time she did what she could to focus on the actual work at hand so that she wouldn't so blatantly fail in her studies. For the most part, she succeeded, but in the back of her mind she was fleshing out just how to go about the conversation she knew was looming. If she could find the courage to pursue it.

When she'd finally finished the homework for both *Izandüre: A History* and *Lure of the Land* Fura carefully closed the book she was using and pushed it aside. Even if she didn't return back to her studies right away, it was the last day of the school week. She would have the entirety of the following day to complete what she'd left untouched. Kiyani made no notice of the change as he absently flipped through a large novel. Fura took the time to assemble her starting line as she did what she could to make it seem like she was merely taking a break.

"How was your class?" Fura asked, stoically. With all that had been happening, she realized she'd never gotten to around to asking him how his *Forge & Arms* class was going. For having opted into the class out of interest, he'd said next to nothing about it. Though she was using it as a platform to other questions, Fura realized that she actually was curious.

"Fine."

Fura could feel her hand clench into a ball, though she refrained from looking at it. He couldn't make this easy on her, could he? Trying to strike an actual conversation with him made conversing with a rock sound easy.

He barely looked at her, engrossed in whatever it was he was reading. Though this was one of the last places Fura had ever imagined seeing him, he appeared to be right at home. It occurred to her that she hadn't even assumed he could read. She felt guilty for the thought, as if just because he hadn't attended school with her in Barandor she naturally viewed him as uneducated. Most days it felt like just the opposite.

Fura couldn't help but ask, "Are you sure you've never been here before?"

"Why are you so insistent that I've been here?"

Fura shrugged. "It just seems like you have." It was true. The way he walked through the halls without a care, and how he currently came across, so easily diving into research in the library, just seemed like second nature to him. She waited a moment before adding, "And people act like they know you."

This got Kiyani's attention. "Really? Like who?"

"No one in particular." She really didn't care for him to be aware that he was the target of a number of Talia and Thayna's conversations. A second person crossed her mind and Fura took a stab at it. "Nylan, maybe?"

"I met Nylan years ago, but not here," he explained curtly.

"He seems to have a vendetta against you." Fura didn't know the extent of the animosity between the two, but Kiyani had already claimed once that they didn't get along, for reasons unknown to her. Even without being privy to that information, any outsider could easily see that there were ill-feelings between the two.

Kiyani shrugged indifferently, letting his eyes drift back to the page. "I've never claimed to be his friend and he's never claimed to be mine."

"I don't suppose I get to hear the rest of that story?"

"It's not pertinent to what we're doing here."

Letting out a breath of frustration, Fura returned to her work. In his fanciful, elaborate language that simply meant 'no'. It wasn't something she was hell-bent on learning, but it still would have been entertaining. Fura would have taken anything that revealed his life previous to meeting her.

"Would you just ask, already?" Kiyani said, the sigh not lost on him.

"What?" Fura asked, confused.

"You're searching for something. What is it?"

"Nothing," Fura huffed.

Though it'd been the perfect opportunity for her, the fact that Kiyani had actually been paying that much attention to her had thrown her off track.

Just as Fura was trying to muster up the courage to ask *the* question, Kiyani cut back in to her surprise. He was generally the last one to keep conversations going. It seemed to be his knack in life to be able to end any conversation with a few short words and be done with it.

"You know, there's actually a girl in my *Forge and Arms* class," he said, as if they'd been speaking of it in the first place. "I was surprised, really, but she's turning out to be a lot better than any of us initially expected. She almost even managed to best Nylan today. I don't think I've ever seen him look more frustrated. Of course, I was just as surprised to find that Creslin is the one that teaches that class." Kiyani stared at the wall opposite Fura as he spoke, as if reliving the events of the class. As if it was an afterthought, he murmured, "Bekka, I think her name was."

Jealously flared up in Fura's gut and she had to fight not to voice it aloud. It would get nothing but negative anger from him in return, but she didn't like the way that he talked about this girl with such ease. Fura had never met this Bekka, knew she wouldn't have been able to pick her out of the crowd of students in the morning rush, but she already detested her.

Shaking her head, Fura attempted to get her thoughts back on track. This wasn't what she'd planned on talking to him about, but he had thrown her off so easily with mention of this girl.

Just as effortlessly as Kiyani had resurrected the conversation he let it fall into remiss, resuming his place in the book opened in front of him. It took Fura another few minutes of pretending to be consumed in her own reading to think of how to bring up her next subject.

"Kiyani?" Fura said shyly, prodding to see exactly what kind of mood he was in before she began. He seemed friendly enough today, but she could never be completely sure.

He only grunted, already lost in the pages.

Surveying the room, Fura made sure the library was completely empty before voicing her concerns. It was one of the reasons she had waited so long to confront him. In the off chance that Kiyani let his rage flare up again without warning, Fura didn't want spectators. "Why would someone say you're the son of evil?" She let the sentence fall as if were a mere side-thought and not something that'd been festering in her mind since Talia and Thayna had made the claim.

Kiyani tensed as the question hung in the air between them. He looked up with deeply furrowed eyebrows. "Who in the hell said that?"

Fura shook her head, not sure if she wanted to reveal actual names. He didn't strike her as the violent type, but she had no idea what he would do if he decided to follow up on the matter and confront the accusers. "Just something I heard in the hall. I don't even know who said it."

Pushing the book to the side, Kiyani crossed his arms, staring as if he didn't believe her. "Who said that, Fura?" he asked again.

Cringing, Fura replied. "Talia and Thayna."

"I thought so. Just ignore them," Kiyani said, as if he could read the fact that it bothered her. His quiet answer surprised her. "It's just like any other school you find. They'll find your weakness and then work incessantly to inflame it. Before you know it, they have you in their grasp, and you don't know who you are or which way is up."

Fura studied him as he spoke. "You sound like you've been there before."

"Don't worry about it."

It wasn't until they'd packed their things and were approaching the dorms, about to part for the night, that Fura asked the other question that'd been on her mind. One that'd been lingering even before she'd had to deal with Talia and Thayna the night before.

Though Fura knew she'd asked enough of him for the day, she knew she couldn't wait another day for the answer.

"Kiyani..." Fura whispered. "What Sect were you placed in?"

His hand on the door to his dorm, Kiyani paused, seeming to dissect the question, rolling it around in his mind. Just before he disappeared behind the door, she could hear his faint reply. "Shadow."

68

♦♦◇♦♦

SIDE-TRACKED

Shadow.

That one word had haunted Fura all night. She'd held no illusions that Kiyani would have been placed in the same Sect as her – he'd been the one to claim that he was no master of fire beforehand – but Shadow?

Fura shivered as the word assaulted her senses again. She had a long way to go in her studies, but from what she'd heard thus far, of all the seven possible routes, Shadow was the darkest and the most dangerous. Shadow was chosen for those with a deeper side that they kept to themselves, for those that had the potential for darker things in life. Shadows changed people.

She wondered how the school's Grand Master had even come to that conclusion. He'd mentioned something about most students undergoing a test to determine their place after taking a semester or more of classes. Fura could see how that process would have been overridden for her, she was Apallo's daughter after all, but how had Kiyani received the same treatment? Was this merely some sick joke that Creslin was playing on them, angry because they'd shown up so late?

Shadow.

It can't be, Fura told herself.

Yet, in a perverse way, thinking back to everything she'd picked up since she'd met Kiyani, it fit. He was quiet. Always keeping to himself. Wary of people. A mere shadow wandering through life as he saw fit. No one could capture him, like he was a mere mist that people tried without success to contain, and regular rules never seemed to apply to him.

As much as she hated to admit it, Creslin might have been right. And a shadow Kiyani played throughout the entirety of that day, for she barely saw him.

✧⌘✧

In his own room, Kiyani sat curled in the window seat that overlooked a portion of the forest below. The sun was making its way over the horizon, brightening the tree tops and casting anything beyond its reach into momentary deep shadow. The sky surrounding was crystal clear and free from clouds, a promise of a good day.

As picturesque as the day was looking to be, Kiyani's thoughts were troubled. He and Fura had only been in Du Reizlan for less than a week, but already things seemed to be headed on a downward spiral.

The two girls that Creslin had placed Fura with were nothing more than trouble makers, planting seeds of doubt and question in her already fragile mind. Kiyani had hoped that, of all the places they had been, that this would be the place that she would find something resembling a friend so that she would leave him alone. That hope had all but backfired. The bullying from her roommates had done nothing but push her in the opposite direction, giving her reason to cling even closer to him than before. She scampered around like a frightened rabbit most days, still bombarding him with questions when there were so many other sources she could consult. Even Kiedo had never bothered him as much when he was a mere pup.

Yet, it wasn't just Fura's troubles that kept him occupied. He had problems of his own to deal with.

The Grand Master had made it clear upon their arrival that he didn't welcome their sudden presence, and had only made matters worse by placing him in a room with one of the people he hated the most in this life. Creslin might as well have sent him back home and locked him in a closet with his father. But, at least he had gotten out of the potential debacle with Nylan.

Kiyani hadn't planned on being so easily recognized, though. Numerous people had come up to him, claiming to know him, while others still merely resorted to talking behind his back. He'd heard the rumors that had begun to float throughout the school day after their arrival. Of course, he should have known better than to think that he could just walk into Du Reizlan and easily blend in with the crowd. Things would never come that easily for him.

As if all that wasn't bad enough, then there was the accursed tree that had brought them here in the first place. The minimal amount of time that he'd found to peruse the library had gotten him nowhere. He knew that it'd only been a few days, but he had yet to make any progress regarding the Witneis Reln. Kiyani had already searched numerous titles and had found no mention of the thing, as if it had never even existed. He had doubted that it would have presented itself as an easy task, but he didn't know just how long they could spare looking for such a thing. Not that having all these classes were of any help to the matter. All they accomplished was adding more to the workload.

Yet, it was an unwanted necessity. Access to the sweeping library was what they had come for, and they would have to unfortunately continue to play the part of students if they wanted to retain their permission to use it.

"So, what are we doing today?"

Startled, Kiyani turned to the source of the voice. Even having traveled with Fura for the past few months, he still found himself not used to being roomed with someone else.

Tibben stood in the middle of the room. Stifling a yawn, the boy rubbed sleep from his eyes, giving him the impression that he'd just woken up.

"When did I ever claim that *we* were doing anything?" Kiyani asked. As if he had time to scamper around with his roommate. He already felt like he was in charge of one child, he didn't need another one.

Tibben shrugged, his face falling as if he'd been punched in the gut. "I just thought that… you know," he faltered, unable to find the words he was searching for. "Maybe we could do something. It is our day off."

Kiyani couldn't help but recognize the sadness in his voice. "Don't you have any friends?" he sighed. He had things to do, but Kiyani could already see where this was heading.

What is it with people and not having friends around here?

It didn't seem to matter where he went, all the loners seemed to attach to him and stick like flies on tape.

"Nylan won't let me," Tibben said, shaking his head.

"He won't *let* you?" Kiyani asked incredulously. He'd never heard such a pitiful musing. "Do you know how pathetic that sounds?"

The excitement gone from his voice, Tibben continued in a slow monotone, "People tend to shun me because of his influence. I guess they figure if they throw in their lot with me, then Nylan will take out his anger on them as well." He let his eyes fall to the floor as if recalling the reasoning had hit him with a whole new clarity. "I don't really blame them."

Scratching his head absently, Kiyani looked out the window. As much as he hated it, he couldn't help but relate to this kid in some way. Turning, he stood up and stretched.

"Fine." If it would get him away from Fura for a bit, then he couldn't really argue. He could afford a few hours, at least.

Instantly the elation in Tibben's face returned. "Really?"

Kiyani nodded. "It just can't take all day. I do have other things to do."

With no real plans in mind, and not knowing what else to do, they ventured outside. It wasn't until he found himself breathing in the fresh air that Kiyani realized just how cramped he'd felt, trapped inside the walls of the school. Unable to leave the grounds, though he fancied a walk in the surrounding woods, they walked side by side through the courtyard he'd glimpsed the night he and Fura had arrived.

Grimacing, as he thought about Fura, Kiyani had to remind himself again that he'd never promised he'd always be free for her pleasure. He'd almost expected her to be waiting in the alcove between the dorms when he and Tibben took to the hallway. To his relief, she'd been nowhere in sight, leaving him to thank his lucky stars. She had to figure out how to function on her own eventually.

Returning his thoughts to the present, he looked around.

Outside, it felt like a completely different world than what they were secluded to within the thick stone of the school. Though the sun above shone in its full brilliance, the air was crisp, threatening to dump more snow on top of the few inches that already graced the ground.

With no real destination in mind, Kiyani settled in a step behind Tibben, letting him lead the way. He had little to add in way of conversation, so Kiyani half-heartedly listened to the boy recount various stories of his life, both inside the school and back at home, as he intently studied the stone path laid before them.

A light dusting of snow had fallen the night before and had settled on the surroundings like a thin layer of dust, as if winter had already taken its claim on the land. Here and there, the sun had melted small patches, leaving splotches of green on the landscape and revealing mounds of expertly placed shrubbery that lined the paths.

Kiyani had only caught a glimpse of the winding maze from above, its paths teeming with small groups of students taking a reprieve from their schoolwork. From that view, height playing to his advantage, the courtyard had never appealed to him. It had always seemed too busy, the bodies that scurried about looking like hordes of ants emerging to scrounge for food. Now that he was level with it all, Kiyani found that the outdoors and the serene landscape that had been created to surround Du Reizlan offered a welcome sense of peace. He knew that the weather had a lot to do with the ghostly solitude of it, and for that he thanked the impending cold. This was how it was meant to be, beautiful in the simplicity of it, not overrun with overworked students seeking refuge.

Coming to a large circular paved area, Kiyani and Tibben traversed the open space. Forgoing the elegantly carved benches that were placed at regular intervals, they walked up to the large fountain that graced the center of the area. Rising a good fifteen to twenty feet in the air was a twisting unicorn rearing its slender legs high in the air, its glossy mane fanning out behind it as it tossed its head. A knee-high wall of polished ivory blocks of stone shone in the sunlight as they circled the great animal. It was the grand splendor of the entire courtyard and it left little to be desired.

The sight of the piece had left even Tibben momentarily speechless. Kiyani took the time to follow the curves of the statue with his eyes, enjoying the masterful work that had been put into it. It wasn't just the artful sweep of the creature that left him feeling at peace, but the water that cascaded down its structure. There was little that could put him at ease like the sound of falling water.

Yet, his tranquility was short-lived.

Despite the wintery chill, they weren't the only ones taking advantage of the day off from classes to venture outdoors. Up until that point, Kiyani had avoided eye contact with others, pretending instead that he and Tibben were the only adventurers. However, a sudden ruckus made Kiyani's stomach drop. He didn't even have to see the group to know that they were trouble.

Kiyani could hear the unmistakable laughter before the insults started flying. "Hey, Tidbit!" a familiar voice crowed. "Think fast."

The two turned just as a Nylan whipped a projectile that was more ice than snow. Whistling through the air, it smacked Tibben in the face, sending him sprawling onto the ground, his head coming just short of connecting with the brick wall of the fountain that loomed next to them. Kiyani cringed as he heard the breath knocked out of the boy.

Ignoring the whistles and hoots of success, Kiyani bent to give Tibben a hand as pushed himself off the ground, struggling to sit up. His nose was bleeding where the chunk of ice had hit, and a welt was beginning to form above his eye where he'd struck the ground.

"I'm fine," Tibben said, waving him away. He winced as the movement of speaking pulled on his injuries.

"Look at him," one of the boys laughed. "He's like a cockroach on his back."

"And just like all bugs, made for stepping on," another added.

"The crunch they make is so satisfying," a third snorted.

"Back off, Nylan," Kiyani said, rising to face Tibben's tormenter.

Nylan broke off from the group that surrounded him and strolled forward, stopping just before Kiyani. His eyes narrowed. "And just like all bugs," he said to those coming in behind him as he looked Kiyani in the eye, "there's always more to replace them."

Kiyani could feel Tibben pull at his pant leg from where he still sat, but he didn't take his eyes off Nylan. He knew to do so would give him the upper hand, no matter the length of time. "Kiyani," Tibben pleaded, "don't bother."

"Oh, look," Nylan crooned. "Kiyani found himself a boyfriend!"

Breathing slowly to keep his cool, Kiyani glared at him. "Why don't you stick to picking on people your own size?"

Nylan raised an eyebrow. "Like you?" he laughed. "I'll keep that in mind." Motioning to those surrounding him, Nylan said, "Come on. Let's leave the lovers to lick their wounds."

Kiyani watched in frustration as Nylan and the group of lemmings he led walked away before turning to check on his roommate.

Tibben had moved to sit on the edge of the fountain, and was wiping the blood from his nose with his sleeve. "You didn't have to do that for me."

"Am I just supposed to stand back and watch?"

Tibben just shrugged. His usual excitement seemed to have been beaten out of him, though from the ice that had been thrown or Nylan's words, Kiyani wasn't sure.

"I'm not going to join them, if that's what you think."

Tibben smiled at the gesture. Holding out his hand to help the boy up, Kiyani said, "Come on, I'll take you to the nurse."

There had been a number of awkward stares directed at him as he'd led Tibben to the medical wing of the building, but Kiyani had ignored them all. He didn't care what these people thought. Of him, or of the kid at his side. He may not have counted many people as friends, but he tried to make it a point to keep those that didn't immediately turn away from him on his side.

Chewing on a fingernail, Kiyani waited by the bed as one of the school's healers attended to Tibben's injuries. He stood in front of the window, aware of Nylan's small group picking on more students. Apparently, Tibben wasn't the only one they preyed on. Watching with furrowed brows as Nylan continued his raid, he listened to the nurse assure Tibben that his injuries appeared worse than they really were.

When the woman left, Kiyani turned to the boy. With the smears of blood wiped away and the rest of the bleeding staunched, he already looked better. Though his usual jovial nature was still dampened.

"You okay?" Kiyani asked.

Tibben nodded and Kiyani continued. "Do you mind if I take off? I still have some things I need to do." He had never had any solid plans for the day, but this was the last place Kiyani figured he would end up.

"It's okay," Tibben assured him. "I'll see you later."

Kiyani nodded. "I doubt they'll keep you overnight."

"Kiyani?" Tibben said before Kiyani made it to the door, his voice containing a nasally whine due to the bag of ice he held to his face to tame the swelling. "Thanks for being my friend."

The unusual voice was what amused him, but Kiyani couldn't help but smile at the kid's words. Nodding in acceptance, he walked out of the room, leaving the boy to rest in the peace and quiet.

Peace and quiet.

It was what he hoped to attain in the remaining hours of the day. The library called to him, yet he couldn't even make it that far before running into more trouble makers.

Turning the corner into the hallway that led past the dorms, Kiyani could see two girls just ahead. One of them sat on the ledge before the windows that looked over the courtyard below. The other leaned against the wall.

If it had been anyone else he would have simply walked by without so much as a cursory glance in their direction. Yet, though he'd never spoken to them, he knew these two girls.

This was the first time he'd seen Fura's roommates beyond catching a glimpse of them in the classes they shared.

Gritting his teeth, he made to walk past anyways, not wanting to deal with the frustration of speaking to them. There were so many things he could say to the two, but he held his tongue.

"Look who's finally paying us a visit!" the girl sitting squealed, nudging her sister who'd been intently sizing up the boys below in the courtyard.

Turning and leaning against the wall seductively, the second ran a hand through her short hair, fluffing it up. "Well now, look who's seeking friendship."

Though he'd been intent to pass, Kiyani paused, giving the girl a brief glance. Looking like the leader of the two, he was certain that this was Thayna.

"Don't flatter yourself," Kiyani huffed.

"And just where do you think you're going?" Thayna asked as he made to continue on.

"I have nothing to say to you," Kiyani replied, moving on, trying to keep himself out of trouble. Even so, he only made it a few steps before turning and facing the girls. "No, actually... what in the hell have you been telling Fura?"

Fura may not have had the guts to stand up to these girls, but he did. Where he knew he should have committed himself to walking away, witnessing Nylan's violence against Tibben earlier had only riled him up. All of this harassment against the few he considered friends was striking a nerve.

But it wasn't only that. They were giving rise to doubts in Fura's mind. Not only about herself, but about him as well.

"Only the truth," Talia sneered.

Kiyani's eyes narrowed. He didn't like these venomous twins. *Of all the people Creslin could have paired her with...* "And what exactly does that mean?"

Thayna clucked her tongue. "Tsk, tsk. Is Fura bringing up questions you don't want to answer? If so, we'd be more than happy to do it for you."

Kiyani strode forward, pinning her to the wall, his face inches from hers. "Don't you dare."

"Or what?" Talia snickered, unfazed by his close proximity and the fire in his eyes.

"Don't think that I can't find anything on you to take to Creslin," Kiyani warned as he backed away, letting Thayna free. Despite his words, he had no idea what he'd be able to do. It was already apparent with Nylan that the Head Master didn't care.

Brushing at her blouse as if his touch had gotten her dirty, Thayna replied nonchalantly, "Oh, trust me, you'll self-annihilate long before that."

Letting the words fly past his ears, Kiyani took a step back and evaluated the two. It was easy to see that this was nothing more than another game for them. And one that they intended to win.

As if Kiyani's presence was a mere annoyance, Thayna sat on the ledge of the windowsill and looked out at the courtyard below. "It's rude for you to lead her on like you are."

"Not to mention, cruel," Talia butted in.

Kiyani's eyes narrowed as he crossed his arms. "Is that what you think I'm doing?" He had a feeling that he already knew where this was going.

"Are you not?" Thayna asked as she pulled a leg up to her chest and turned her head.

"The two of you don't belong together," Talia intersected wanly.

"You deserve someone better, someone more like yourself," Thayna grinned, ignoring her sister.

"Like you?"

Talia's face lit up at the proposition, but Thayna kept her cool, merely letting her face curl into a wicked half smile that matched the merciless light in her eyes. "Thought you would never ask."

"Don't even think about it," Kiyani growled. He couldn't think of a more repulsive situation. He'd rather actually explore a relationship with Fura, as people seemed apt to assume.

The more these two spun their toxic words, the more Kiyani found he hated them. They were both despicable, but it was easy to see that Talia was the follower, merely agreeing with her sister as she added rambling bits of conversation here and there.

If ever there was a perfect match for Nylan, Kiyani thought, *it would be Thayna.*

In fact, Thayna reminded him a lot of Nylan. Condescending and rude, acting as if the world revolved around her.

"You would rather have that little mouse? It's so cute how she follows you like a lost puppy. Or is that it? You just want someone to follow you without question, your own personal slave, if you will?"

"Whatever relationship that is between Fura and I is none of your business."

Thayna's mouth dropped and she let out a laugh. "So, there *is* something!"

"I'm not telling you one way or the other." Kiyani retorted, hating that it had come across that way. "Why would I give you the benefit?"

"We could help you with whatever it is that you're trying to find."

They couldn't possibly know, could they? He'd blatantly told Fura to keep what they were doing a secret. As talkative as she could be, he doubted that she would've revealed anything to these two, but he still had to ask. "What has Fura told you?"

"Nothing," Talia claimed with a cock of her head as she broke into the conversation.

Pushing her sister away, Thayna continued, "But that's why you're here, isn't it? You're searching for something. You wouldn't be otherwise. Why else would you just now show up?"

Ignoring their probing, Kiyani stepped forward. "Just leave Fura alone and stop hounding her with your vindictive words."

"Or what?"

Leaning in so that he was inches from Thayna's face, Kiyani replied, "Trust me, I'll find some way to kick you off that pedestal of yours. I might even get you kicked out."

Thayna laughed. "I'd like to see that," she urged. "Are you going to go to daddy?"

"Don't tempt me," Kiyani spat. Though he would never bring the man into this, didn't care to talk to him anyways, they didn't need to know that. These two were worse than he'd feared.

Done with the conversation, Kiyani stalked away, though he was still within earshot when Thayna threw her last insult.

"You'll get kicked out of here for something. Mark my words. It's only a matter of time."

69

◆◆◇◆◆

FINDING FRIENDS

As soon as class was dismissed for the midday lunch break the following day, Fura hurried out the door. Halfway through the lecture her stomach had started growling angrily, demanding food or else. She'd sat silently in her seat, hoping that no one else had heard its desperate pleas. A few heads had turned, including Kiyani's, but all in all, Fura figured she was safe.

Fidgeting, she stood outside the lecture room door and watched the people pour out. As usual, Kiyani was taking his time. Since he sat next to her she could never understand why it took him so much longer to exit the room. She could've sworn he'd been right behind her.

As relieved as she'd been that morning when she had found Kiyani waiting for her in the alcove, it had proven to be a relatively awkward reunion. He had done his part well, playing the shadow the day before. Not once had Fura run across him, although she'd made a point to try and find him. Down hallways. Out into the courtyard. The dining hall. Even searching the library more than once had proven to be a fruitless affair. Knowing she'd probably looked the part of a new student, Fura had continued to meander the halls, wondering if she was just missing him in each place she looked, or if he'd decided to sleep the day away in his room. Though it didn't sound like him, Fura couldn't deny the possibility. If he wanted to stay away from her, that would've been the easiest option. She probably would have done the same had it not been for the distinct possibility of Talia and Thayna returning.

Halfway through the day, Fura had finally given up her attempts to find Kiyani and had found a corner in the library to finish her leftover homework. She hadn't been sure if her questioning him on his placement had upset him or if he just didn't want to be found for reasons unknown to her. Either way, she'd decided to leave it alone, resolving instead to work on the lesson plans she'd left unfinished the night before.

Though Fura was still positive that Kiyani had just wanted a day free of her influence, she'd refrained from asking that morning, in the off chance that her worries would wind up becoming reality.

Through the sea of people, Fura spotted Kiyani's dark hair and took off after him, squirming her way through a few confused individuals. She hadn't even seen him leave the room, nor had he bothered to wait for her, and now he was going in the wrong direction.

"Kiyani," Fura shouted, knowing very well that he could hear her. "Kiyani!"

Breaking free of the swarm, Fura fell in next to him as he walked. "You're going the wrong way," she stated plainly. It wasn't like him to forget such menial things. If either of them lacked a sense of direction, it was her.

Kiyani briefly gave her a stern look, silently reprimanding her claim. "I'm going to the library," he said, as if that one statement would clear up any and all questions.

"But, I'm hungry." Fura knew it was a pathetic thing to say, but she hadn't been able to stop it before it fell from her lips. Now she only hoped that Kiyani wouldn't hear it as so needy, so dependent on his every action.

He shrugged indifferently. "Then go eat."

"You know I'll get lost." Fura knew that wasn't entirely true. She had made it through the previous day with little help, but she still hoped the flaccid excuse would give him reason to change his mind.

Grunting what sounded like a curse, Kiyani replied, "You have to learn the layout at some point."

"Are you really going to forgo lunch again to spend time amongst all those books?" Fura asked. He'd cut his lunch short only the other day to spend the remaining half an hour continuing his search for anything involving the Witneis. She knew why they were here, what he was looking for, but she didn't think that it restituted giving up everything else in favor of that one and only task. Especially something as necessary as eating.

Whipping around, Kiyani came face to face with her. "We're here for a reason," he snarled.

Shrinking away, Fura looked at the ground. "It's not like any information in there is just going to move on you. It'll still be there after we eat."

"The sooner we find the location of the Witneis, the sooner we can leave."

Then why won't you let me help? Fura yelled at him in her mind, though she didn't dare let the words slip into the open. She knew this would all go faster if Kiyani would allow her to help, but he had been insistent so far that she leave it to him while she learned all that she could about the workings of Izandüre.

"Can't you take ten minutes to come eat?" Fura asked instead.

"I'm not hungry."

Visions of lonely lunches at the cafeteria in Barandor came to mind. "Am I just supposed to eat by myself?"

"Go find Talia or Thayna."

She loved how he'd added the *or*. As if the two of them were ever separated. Fura cringed at the thought. Though the two of them had instantly claimed friendship, it seemed as if they'd turned on her the minute they had learned she was with Kiyani. They still put on an affable front once in awhile, but Fura could easily see through it.

It almost made her nauseous to think that Kiyani would even suggest such a vile thing, until Fura realized that she hadn't yet brought the full account of what was going on with her and the twins to his attention. Nor did she plan to. He already thought she couldn't take care of herself. She didn't want to prove him right.

He paused a moment, his face twisting as if even he were repulsed by what he'd just suggested. "On second thought, don't go searching for them."

The way Kiyani took back his previous comment made Fura wonder if he somehow knew more about her plight than he let on, but she let it slide. Throwing a sidelong glance down the hall that she knew led to sustenance, Fura sighed. "Never mind," she whispered. Falling in stride next to him, she began to follow Kiyani on his trek to the library.

Stopping, Kiyani looked at her, annoyed. "What are you doing?"

"I thought we were going to the library?"

"So the growls of your stomach can accost the silence?"

Fura flushed. "You heard that?" She'd been well aware of her stomach's consistent pleading with her during the extended class, but she didn't know it had been so apparent.

"Who didn't?" Kiyani said. "And how many times do I have to tell you? There's no *we*."

"What do you want me to do?" Fura asked, confused.

"This is a school with hundreds of people," he said, swinging a hand as if to emphasize the vast appeal. "Go find some friends."

Before she could think to reply Kiyani had turned on his heels.

Though she knew he was right, it didn't lessen the sting.

Taking his words to heart, she turned around, feeling deflated, and began the trek to the dining hall. Though she managed to make it there with no detours, it didn't make her feel any better. Kiyani's words reeled in her mind, buzzing around like a horde of angry bees, his accusation making her feel even more alone in the world.

Standing in the majestic arching doorway to the grand hall for a few minutes, Fura surveyed the area inside. Generally spending the time trying to get useful information out of Kiyani while they ate, this was the first time she'd actually taken a real look at the room.

High, vaulted ceilings, and stone that was somehow lighter than the rest of the building made the space look even bigger than it really was. People milled about, both standing and huddled around tables in groups, their voices filling the air.

Though she was reluctant to enter without someone to stand by her side in friendship, the ache in her stomach finally encouraged her to move forward.

No sooner had she entered the room, the self-doubt began to filter in.

Walking through the aisles between the rows of long tables, Fura kept her eyes to the ground, not wanting to look at anybody as they watched her pass.

They're all looking at me. What a nerd, they're whispering.

In reality, Fura could see out of the corner of her eye that only a couple people threw a curious glance her way before returning to their own worries. The long rows of extended tables were far from full. Here and there, small groups of students straddled the benches, conversing between one another, gossiping, doing homework, and taking in their meal before they were off to another class.

Clinging to the shadows, Fura felt like a wallflower as she made her way across the hall and got her food.

Standing before the vast space where no one paid attention to one lonely body, Fura scanned the tables, her tray in hand. There were a few people scattered about who occupied the ends of tables by themselves.

At least I won't be the only one. However, these few seemed to exude a certain confidence that Fura felt she lacked. These were the ones whom the pull of desolate solitude didn't touch. *People like Kiyani.*

Searching the faces, Fura hoped to find someone she knew. She recognized a few people from her classes, but none of them were people that she'd actually taken the time to talk to. The thought of walking up to them now and trying to introduce herself just seemed ludicrous. And though Fura might've chanced the encounter, even Talia and Thayna were absent from the setting.

Giving up, Fura took her tray and found a table end. Settling down, she tried to do her best impression of those who didn't mind eating in seclusion.

They would call it peace, Fura realized.

The vast room was brightly lit, and the walls were adorned with ornate gold filigree where colorful tapestries weren't present, though Fura noticed none of it. She found it hard to enjoy the splendor of the hall when she had no one to share it with.

Picking at her food, Fura found that her hunger had weakened with the onslaught of emotions.

Is this how it's going to be from now on?

"You look like you could use a friend."

Startled, Fura looked up. The face that went with the voice was one that she recognized from more than one of her classes, though she didn't know the name that was attached to it.

Seeming to sense this, the man put out his hand in warm greeting. "Rhyne Mirren," he introduced himself brightly. "We have a few classes together."

Nodding absently, Fura took his hand and shook it. "I know." She didn't know what else to say. The whole time they had been at Du Reizlan, this was the first time anyone had shown any real interest in talking to her, let alone being nice about it, even with her father's status. She no longer counted the sudden advance of the twins the night her and Kiyani had drifted in. Fura wondered briefly if maybe the fact that her father was the Firelord was why people stayed away, likely intimidated by such a thing.

"May I sit here?" Rhyne asked.

Fura hadn't even realized he was still standing, awaiting her permission to invade her space as her mind raced with questions. She couldn't fathom what it was that had so suddenly drawn all this attention to her. "Of course."

In a way, Fura was relaxed. Upon first glance, the blond hair the only thing in her line of vision, she'd thought that maybe Nylan had come to talk to her again. As mildly interested as she was in that aspect, Fura wasn't sure what she would've done had that been the case. The brief interaction that'd occurred with him before hadn't been enough to truly judge him. Yet, after learning that he picked on Kiyani, she wasn't sure she wanted a second chance to make an opinion. Kiyani had warned her against such meetings, and Fura knew that, if anything, he knew more about Nylan than she did.

"There are plenty of people who choose to sit alone," Rhyne said as he sat and rearranged the food on his plate. Fura looked up, brought out of her reverie. She knew it was rude to have such thoughts on her mind when someone she barely even knew had taken time out of their day to talk to her. "But, you didn't seem to be enjoying it."

"Was it that obvious?" Fura asked, embarrassed by how easily people seemed to be able to read her.

That's something I have to work on, she reminded herself.

Rhyne smiled. "Not necessarily. I can't say that I've ever seen you by yourself, though."

"Oh."

Maybe Kiyani was right. Fura knew she needed to branch away from him eventually, but to do so felt blasphemous. Kiyani was her one link back to her home. Without him, Fura knew that she would never be able to make it back on her own.

Of course, Fura thought, *is that even home anymore?*

"No Kiyani?" Rhyne asked, as if to prove his point. It was almost unnerving how everyone grouped the two of them together so readily.

"Not today," Fura said. That was really all she could say about the matter. Even she didn't know what had come over him. It was possible that all of this still had something to do with their last conversation in the library, but Fura couldn't pinpoint, for the life of her, what she might have said.

Stop thinking about it, she chastised herself.

Focusing on Rhyne instead, she vowed to ignore thoughts of Kiyani for at least a moment and try to get to know him instead. "What about you?" Fura asked. "Where are your friends at?"

"Maybe I don't have any."

The statement hit Fura like a ton of bricks. How could that be? One look at his face though, adorned with a grin that made her heart jump, and Fura could tell that he was joking with her. She could feel her own face curl into a smile. "I don't believe that."

Rhyne's nose wrinkled. "Yeah, I didn't think you would. No, they're around. Though most of the time I prefer to sit alone."

Was he joking? Fura couldn't understand why anyone would want to isolate themselves. "Why?"

"Easier to focus on class work, I suppose."

Fura couldn't believe this guy. "You do homework during your lunch?"

"It's better than doing it late at night," Rhyne answered. "Wouldn't you agree?"

Nodding, Fura had to admit she couldn't argue with his logic. Plenty of times she'd wished that she hadn't waited so long to dive into her studies. It just felt like there was never any reprieve from the work. Students only had one day out of the week to catch up and get some rest or do something fun. What school did that? Fura couldn't believe she was already thinking that way. Officially, this was her first full week. She would have to wait until the following Sunday to see if she had survived the full extent of the grueling regimen.

"So, you're new around here, aren't you?" Rhyne inquired.

Fura nodded shyly. She hated people mentioning it like she was the new fish in the sea to poke fun at, but the way he asked made it feel less invasive. His words weren't an attack like everyone else's, but more of a friendly gesture, a means of conversation. She was startled to find a warmth in his eyes when she looked up to meet his gaze. There was something familiar about them, but Fura couldn't recall why.

"How do you like your classes?"

Looking at her food before her, Fura pushed some of it around with her fork. "Okay, I guess." She let out a sigh. "I'm kind of confused, actually."

"Really? But aren't they —"

"Beginner classes?" Fura said, cutting him off. "Yes," she continued before Rhyne could say anything more about it. Kiyani had made her promise not to reveal anything to people they didn't know, but Fura found that she couldn't help it. "I'm not from Izandüre."

Rhyne looked puzzled for a moment before a light entered his eyes. "Really?" Fura was surprised to find that he understood the meaning of her words. She wasn't sure how many people knew of the other world, the one that she had called home for years. "Where exactly are you from, then?"

"Barandor," Fura answered. Knowing that he'd probably never heard of it, she added, "I guess it's by Frielana."

"I know where that's at. All the way over there then... What's it like there?"

"Um, I'm not really sure how to explain it." Fura smiled, remembering Saiva using the same words when she'd asked what it was like to be Fae. Now she knew how Saiva had felt. How *did* you make someone understand what you had known your whole life? "I guess it would be just as confusing for you there as it is for me here." Fura sighed. "That doesn't even make sense, does it?" she asked. She was already well aware that she failed at describing most things.

Rhyne shook his head. "No, I understand what you're trying to say. That must be hard."

Fura smiled, thankful that even if he didn't get her meaning he would claim otherwise, just to make her feel better. "It is. I feel so lost with all this."

"You'll get it eventually," Rhyne reassured.

It felt good to hear that from someone, almost as if she were being praised for something she had yet to do. It was more than Fura had come to expect from Kiyani. "You think so?"

"Of course. Once it all starts setting in, everything else will fall into place right behind it. It just takes some time."

"Thanks," Fura said, unable to look him directly in the eye. This all felt too dreamlike. She was scared that if she closed her eyes for too long, it would all just disappear.

Rhyne laid a hand on hers on the table, allowing her senses to confirm the evidence of reality. "No problem. If you ever need any help with anything, just let me know. I'd be more than happy to give you a hand."

Fura let a smile grace her face. Placing that thought safely in the back of her mind, she vowed to take him up on that offer some time. She didn't know where this man had come from all of a sudden, but if anyone was going to get her through Du Reizlan in one piece, it would be him.

Maybe things wouldn't be so lonely after all.

She wasn't about to let Kiyani off the hook, but at least she had someone else she could count on, who was possibly more reliable than he was currently being.

Continuing to talk, Fura lost all awareness of time as she and Rhyne laughed throughout the lunch hour. It wasn't until the warning bell rang throughout the stone chamber that it hit her just how long she'd been enthralled as she'd sat, listening to him. For a minute, Fura had the distinct feeling that she hated the sound and what it stood for. If she could, she would ignore it and spend the rest of the day sitting here with Rhyne, discussing this and that. But, she knew she couldn't do that, nor did she feel that he was one to decide that skipping class was a good idea.

Standing, Rhyne walked a few paces before stopping and turning to her. "Come on, we have the same class, might as well walk together."

"Do we?" Fura brightened at his words.

"Second and third hours."

70

◆◆◇◆◆

LIKE A WOUNDED BUTTERFLY

Like wet paint trailing down a wall, Fura found that, against her better wishes, the days had begun to blend into one another with little to separate them. Monotony slowly taking hold.

Over a week had passed, and to her utmost surprise, she had survived with little to no damage to her physical self. Though she couldn't say the same for her overworked mind. There was so much knowledge stuffed into her head that she felt like a balloon ready to pop, and when it did, the air surrounding would be filled with snippets of information on this, that, and the other that would descend to the ground like feathers wafting through space.

Most of the time, Fura didn't even know what particular day it was. The only thing that she knew she had to keep honest, and precise, track of was whether or not she was meeting with Marna that day. The woman had taken no time in scolding her when she'd been late for her first tutoring session. She didn't want to discover the consequences of missing a lesson altogether.

As much as Fura yearned to spend the rest of the night in the quiet, dim-lit library, staring at a book in attempt to make it appear as if she were doing homework, this was one of her nights with Marna. Though she would rather sit across from Kiyani in silence, while he continued to search for any information at all on the Witneis, than continue to be battered with the lessons Marna had concocted for their time together, Fura found herself angered with Kiyani as of late.

That day when he had left her to go eat lunch on her own had been the start of it all. She still wasn't sure if he had attended his *Forge & Arms* class that day, but he had skipped out on the class directly following lunch. Not that Fura could have claimed so. She'd been so fascinated with Rhyne, excited that he'd even chosen to sit next to her in their *Novice Magic* class that over half the hour had passed before Fura had realized that Kiyani wasn't there. When she had asked later in the library he'd shrugged her off like it was no big deal, claiming that he'd had better things to do.

As the days slowly passed, Fura began to notice a pattern developing. Here and there he would skip random classes, until it became apparent that he was just going to forgo lectures altogether. Fura still found it hard to believe that he would do such a thing, but the evidence claimed nothing less. He'd been the one that had insisted that they sidetrack from their journey to nowhere to come here, and now he was disregarding everything that had to do with the school. There was no doubt that Fura liked books too, but she couldn't imagine spending the whole day locked away in the library not even knowing what, in particular, to look for.

Location.

That's what Kiyani had claimed when asked.

Again, Fura wondered why it was that Apallo had sent them in search of something that barely anyone had heard of. At first, she had figured that it was a well-known place, a landmark of great importance. But that had quickly proven to be false.

She hated the implications of Kiyani's continued absence, but she kept the anger to herself whenever she met with him after classes in the library. Though it ate at her, she knew better than to bring it up. As argumentative as she felt some days, she didn't feel like trying to reason with him to the point of losing him altogether.

Every day, Fura would go to the library following classes and find him at the same table. They had fallen into such an easy ritual where they would casually greet each other, ask how the day was going – which was always answered by a simple *fine* on both ends – and then work on separate things until they quietly parted ways that night. Not once had Fura questioned Kiyani's absences and, in turn, he never made to answer the 'whys' of the matter.

However, Fura couldn't help but grit her teeth every time she entered a lecture hall to find his seat empty. No one sitting around her asked where he was, nor did the teachers seem to care. Du Reizlan, Fura had discovered, was one of those schools that could care less if you attended classes or not. If a student wasn't going to come to class and do the work, they weren't going to make them. Fura figured that the only thing that mattered to the school was how one did on the finals, but she had yet to figure out if they would even still be around when that time came. Or if Kiyani would even take part in that, either.

What angered Fura the most was that Kiyani had slowly stopped meeting her in the mornings as well. The first time she'd been left waiting in the alcove, Fura had thought that maybe he was sick, but it hadn't taken her long to glean otherwise. She had confronted Tibben only once about Kiyani's actions, but even he couldn't garner what was going on with him.

Every night when she faithfully showed up at the library, always finding him at the same table, though not always surrounded by the same books, Fura had to fight the urge to bring up the subject. She wanted to scream at him, to throw things, to ask him how any of this was helping them. If he was going to decide that this whole thing was a waste of time, then why should she feel any different?

Fura wasn't sure if Kiyani had confronted Talia and Thayna at some point, for he refused to say, but they had seemed to back off at least slightly. Mind boggling conversations still filled the late night hours, but the twins had refrained from including her. Fura was fine with it, though she still hated what they spoke of. Even if she'd been excluded, Fura found that she was still just as much a topic of discussion. They never seemed to tire of using Kiyani and herself as the main subject of ridicule. Every morning when Fura woke, she found that thankfully the girls were gone, and when she retired at night, she walked by them without a glance and went straight to her bed to sleep. If anything, the twins had begun to shun her.

Though it hurt, Fura knew it was far better than the contention she'd dealt with the first few days spent in Du Reizlan.

The only thing that kept Fura going was Rhyne. Faithfully keeping his word, he routinely spent his lunch hours sitting beside her, helping her with class work and answering any questions she thought to pose. And when it had become apparent that Kiyani was going to continue skipping class periods, Rhyne had taken the initiative to move his own seat and sit by her, filling the void Kiyani had left.

"Focus, Fura."

Fura jumped at the sound of the voice. She had done it again, letting her thoughts overrun her mind when she should have been concentrating on the task at hand. It was hard to do when the tiny spark that she could call to her presence refused to turn into anything more than a miniscule pinprick of light. The events of days gone by, wrestling in her mind for a moment of her attention, didn't help her focus.

"You have the attention span of a butterfly," Marna scoffed. She waved her hands in the air in frustration. "Pretty, but constantly flitting off here and there in your own world. Magic takes hard work, but overall it takes concentration. If you lack at least that, then you might as well not even pursue it. Not only is it a fruitless endeavor, it only takes the smallest amount of hesitation for things to go terribly wrong. Only pure luck can take you through that which you're unprepared for."

Fura had already lost track of how many times she'd been scolded in this room, wasn't even aware of how many sessions had gone by already. All she knew for certain was that it felt like she was getting nowhere fast. These one-on-one lessons with Marna were supposed to help her, but Fura only felt as if they were slowing her down instead.

"Try it again," Marna insisted. "*Feirneis reen.* Concentrate on those words and those words only. You can't let anything else get in the way of the natural flow of the magic. Let the words envelope you, let it sink in and feel the wave of energy from within."

Taking a deep breath, Fura muttered the words that roughly translated to *rise fire*, and focused on the palm of her hand where Marna had promised a small flame would form if she did the spell correctly. As usual, a tiny speck of white light pulsed an inch above the flat of her palm, but, try as she might, it refused to do anything else. It didn't grow in size. It didn't get brighter. It simply sat there, stagnant and stubborn.

At first, Fura had been thrilled to learn that she would be able to attain such magic. Now, nearly two weeks later, the sight angered her. All the time that she had spent in this room, trying to perfect this one thing was all for naught.

Marna shook her head, that obvious look of disappointment hitting Fura hard. "You of all people should be able to do this."

Clenching her hand in frustration, the spark that had been trying to form there dissipated, leaving the room all that much darker. "Maybe I'm not all people," she responded irritably.

"Now, now," Marna said sternly. "Don't get testy with me, miss."

The growing sense of aggravation would get her nowhere, but it was hard to ignore when everything was amassed against your wishes. Fura didn't understand why Marna wouldn't just let her move past this and onto something. Anything else.

Feeling suddenly drained of energy, Fura pulled a rickety chair away from the table in the center of the room and sat. "Why is this so hard for me?"

"I've had people placed into other Sects pick up on this faster than you," Marna said, not making Fura feel any better about her situation.

"Give me something easier to do, then." It was a fetid statement, but Fura couldn't help it. She just wanted to try something different that would get her mind off of what she couldn't do. They could always come back to this later, but for just one minute, she would've liked to feel the exhilaration of finding something she was good at.

Marna walked over to the table and smacked her hands flat on the surface. The legs creaked under the sudden exertion of pressure. "If you're the direct descendent of the Firelord, as you so claim, then summoning fire *should* be the easiest thing there is."

Was Kiyani wrong about who I am? Fura wondered. Instantly, Fura pushed the thought aside. Kiyani had never had reason to lie to her, especially not about something as touchy as family relations. What more proof did she need anyways? She carried the same last name and many of the same features as her supposed father.

Fura couldn't bring herself to look at the woman who was taking valuable time out of her day to try and teach her what she would probably never learn. Marna had already left her side anyway, and was now across the room digging through scrolls on a shelf.

Holding her palm out before her, Fura cleared her mind and muttered the words to bring about the speck of light. Knowing that it probably wasn't far from the truth, Fura vowed that she would do this if it took a lifetime to achieve.

"Save it for later," Marna said, breaking Fura's concentration. "For some reason you're holding yourself back. Until you can figure out why, I can do little to help, nor can you progress any further."

Slapping a roll of parchment on the table, Marna unrolled it to reveal a map much like the one she had brought out the first day of her tutelage. To Fura's dismay, this particular map had none of the locations labeled.

"For now, we'll forgo magic altogether and focus on other things." Pointing to a lone mountain range, Marna asked, "What is this?"

Fura scrunched her eyes, trying to remember what name had gone there. "Saibon?" she guessed.

"Wrong," Marna said. "There are no mountain ranges by that name."

Groaning, Fura cradled her head in her hands. She was tired. Tired of being told she was worthless. Tired of not being trusted to do anything on her own. Tired of being the subject of ridicule.

"I've had it," Fura shouted, ramming into the corner of the table as she stood. Grabbing the paper from the table, she threw the parchment across the room. "I can't do this! I'm tired of you treating me like some insolent child."

Marna leaned on the windowsill with her arms crossed. "I will treat you as such until you start acting otherwise."

Moving across the cluttered space, Fura grabbed her bag and the few scattered books she'd accumulated. She could feel the tears welling behind her eyes, but she fought to keep them back, at least until she was in the lone safety of the hall. This was all just too much frustration with too little success.

Kiyani would frown upon her walking out on the tutoring sessions that he'd been so quick to set up for her, but at the moment Fura didn't care. He spent his days holed up in the library in peace. He had no idea the stress she was being put through.

"Think long and hard," Marna said stoically, Fura's outburst not causing so much as a rise from her.

Fura paused in front of the door, her hand hovering dangerously close to the handle that would lead her to freedom.

"If you walk out that door, don't think that you can just come back tomorrow."

Frozen in place, Fura considered the woman's words. Was it really worth it? She could hear the warning in Marna's voice. In no way was it a plea to stay and learn, but there was a sense of finality in her decision.

"Don't make the mistake of thinking that I care what you decide. There are definitely better uses of my time to be found. Just know that if you leave now, we're done. You'll be on your own, because you won't be able to persuade me to reevaluate your teaching. Yet, we both know that you need this."

It was an admission of failure, but Fura knew Marna was right. As it was, she was just skating by in classes and only because of the help she was receiving from Rhyne and the woman waiting for her answer in the dusty shadows behind her. Some days fared better than others, but if she was going to get anywhere in this world, Fura was aware that she had to learn all she could, and fast. She wouldn't have the privilege of staying here for years like the other students.

Turning around and admitting defeat, Fura walked back to the center of the room and set her things back on the table.

"That's what I thought," Marna grunted, pushing away from the stone ledge. "And for that act of insolence, you get to stay here for an additional hour." Refusing to retrieve it herself, she pointed to the roll of parchment Fura had tossed to the floor. "And, in that time, you will study this map until you can draw it with your eyes closed."

71

♦♦◇♦♦

SWORDS AND SHARP WORDS

"Come on," the voice crooned. *"Just one date."*
A chorus of raucous laughter followed.
"Go to hell."
"Oh, honey, I've been there and back. It won't kill you."
Forge & Arms. The name had peaked Kiyani's interest when he'd first set eyes on it on the list of classes that had been presented to him in Creslin's office. Even now, it remained one of his favorite parts of the day. The only thing that would have made it better was if he hadn't discovered on the first day that Nylan was in the course as well. He couldn't have cared less, save for the fact that they'd been stuck into the same class, in the same time slot. If Kiyani never laid eyes on Nylan again, it would be a godsend.

Yet, stuck in this school, he knew there was little chance of that.

"One date… trust me, I'll show you the night of your life."

Kiyani found himself grating his teeth as pieces of the conversation between Nylan and Bekka, the only girl to have opted into this testosterone filled madness, assaulted his ears. He generally did his best to ignore Nylan's ramblings, but some days it was just so damn hard to do. Nylan's voice was just too recognizable to him, and every word that fell from his mouth ground on his last nerve. And, if that didn't do it, then the cackling chorus of Nylan's mindless followers, like a pack of attention-starved hyenas, was never too far behind to fill the silence.

However, this was just going too far, Nylan now targeting Bekka. And Kiyani knew why. Because she was a girl, Nylan saw her as an easy target. As a prize to win over and then dump to the curb like trash once the game was over. It was the same reason he had told Fura the other morning to turn the other cheek, to not even deal with the man. She was unaware of his ways and, therefore, completely unsuspecting of the consequences of attempting to tango with him.

Deciding that he couldn't listen to the conversation anymore without intervening, for Bekka's sake, and his own, Kiyani broke formation with his sparring partner. Sheathing his practice sword, he bowed his head to the man across from him who in turn did the same. The formal act of resignation from the impending fight completed, Kiyani watched the man, whose name he couldn't recall, walk away to pick another opponent. He doubted he would be attacked from behind, but it was second nature to make sure before moving forward.

Across the dirt-floored outdoor area where the class was held, Kiyani could see Master Creslin trying to teach another boy the proper methods of swinging a blade. His attentions held elsewhere, it was easy to see that their teacher wouldn't be the one breaking up Nylan's egotistical raid.

Walking over to where the isolated disturbance was at an angle, Kiyani came to a halt just behind Nylan. "Leave her alone," he warned.

He wasn't sure what exactly it was that he planned to do, but Kiyani held his ground. This was really the first time he'd even spoken in the class. Full of beginners that had barely even seen a sword, let alone wielded one, Kiyani was already ahead of most of the class. However, he kept it to himself, preferring to silently let it become known in the practices. He was probably one of the only ones that actually owned a blade and knew how to properly use and care for it. Yet, if anything, it was an easy recreational class to pass the time and ease some of his pent up frustrations.

Nylan was the thorn in his foot though. And if no one stood up to him eventually, he would just continue teasing those that he considered below him, which, from what Kiyani had already witnessed, seemed to be everyone.

The group of boys that frequently accompanied Nylan were the first to take notice of him, their beady eyes fixing on him as he stood there, waiting for their unpronounced leader to face him on his own. They stood in a semi-circle around Bekka, blocking any chance of escape and forcing her to talk to Nylan, though the fire in her eyes declared that she had better ideas.

Looking around the area, Kiyani could see that Nylan's advancement had already caused a number of stares and frenzied whispers. A few people paused in the middle of practice fights, trying to ascertain what was going on.

Ignoring them, Kiyani waited for Nylan to answer, knowing that the man would never back down from an argument.

One of the first to take notice of his actions, Bekka glared at him as if to claim that she could handle Nylan's rude commentary and actions on her own.

Kiyani didn't doubt it.

This girl had been laughed at and criticized from the moment she had first walked into the class, but she'd proven herself more than equal to, if not better, than most of the others on the first day. If there was ever anyone to ask for his help, Kiyani knew, for a fact, that she would have been one of the last.

However, something in him made him want to defend her, no matter how pointless and contrived it was. Whether it was because he actually had some inkling of feeling for this girl, or just because it was a way for him to get back at Nylan, he couldn't say for certain. Nor did he care. This was the opportunity he had been waiting for, and halfway dreading, since entering the school and learning that one of his least favorite acquaintances was attending classes as well.

It wasn't just Bekka, either. Kiyani was tired of playing witness to how Nylan treated people, plowing down anyone and everyone who stood in his path on his narcissistic raid to lay claim to the entire school. Whether it was through actual friendship, or out of fear, Nylan didn't care. Only as long as the end result was the same.

Nylan only smiled as he turned to face his accuser, as if Kiyani were playing into a plan he had spent hours devising. "Or what, Kiyani?" he sneered as he said the name, a vicious grin playing across his lips.

Kiyani could feel his blood begin to boil as he unconsciously tightened his hand around the sword sheathed at his side. He'd thought he would have been over all this by now, years having passed by with no incident, but he had been wrong. Just the sight of Nylan angered him; the way he acted, and the smug attitude that he consistently carried. The time that had gone by only seemed to have increased his haughtiness, earning him not a good whipping, but rather a devoted band of cronies to follow him in his wicked acts.

Nylan had released Bekka no sooner than Kiyani had challenged him, decidedly taking this as a better worth of his time. They stood in the middle of the trodden dirt arena, staring each other down like two feral cats in a battle over territorial rights.

Grasping the hilt of the sword, Kiyani let it slide a few inches free of its sheath. It wasn't Betrayal, only a chipped and dulled practice sword, but it would do.

"Now, now, boys," Creslin said from afar, clapping his hands as if to make sure he was heard, bringing to attention that he was aware of what was going on not too far behind him. "Break it up."

Starting at the interruption, Kiyani turned his head in the direction of the voice. Taking a deep breath to calm himself, he jammed the sword back into place and turned away.

This wasn't the time.

If they'd met under the same circumstances in a wooded area, void of any life save their own, Kiyani would have attacked without qualm, but as it was he knew he couldn't afford the consequences of those actions. Not here. Here it was a much different story.

Showing such conviction in front of not only his teacher, but a teacher that doubled as the Grand Master of the entire school, would get him nowhere. The only thing that could come of such a display would be the all too real possibility of getting kicked out before he was ready to leave of his own accord. What would Fura think about him then? Creslin had already made it clear upon their first meeting that he would not tolerate anything other than the best behavior from them.

Had he known of our sordid history would Creslin have ever placed me and Nylan in the same room together? Kiyani wondered. *Especially in a class such as this, surrounded by a store-house of weapons we could mangle each other with?*

As much as Kiyani relished the idea, he held himself at bay. That was exactly what Nylan wanted from him; a reaction to his incessant bullying. It stung him to the core, but he wouldn't let his grievance show. He was the better man in all this and he was bound and determined to let it be known. Deciding to quit while he was ahead, Kiyani dropped his hand from the sword and began to walk away.

"Coward," Nylan snarled behind him. "I challenge you, Kiyani." There was a chorus of *oooo's* that resounded through the area at the issued ultimatum. "You think that you're so much better than me? Then prove it."

Kiyani tensed at Nylan's words. He wanted more than anything to turn and tackle him to the ground in what most would have considered an unfair fight. He could see Bekka a few yards away shaking her head, telling him it wasn't worth it. Even she had to know by now that it was no longer about her.

Despite the few muffled cries of *"Fight! Fight!"* the room was completely silent, awaiting his answer.

Just as he squared his shoulders and continued walking the other way, distancing himself from the confrontation, Kiyani heard the unmistakable hiss of a sword cleaving the air.

Pulling his own sword free in a split second reaction, Kiyani whirled around just in time to catch Nylan's sword on his own in a shriek of metal against metal.

He could see the shock on his own face in the blurred reflection of the silver of the blade in front of him. Kiyani couldn't believe that, of all people, Nylan would be the one to so blatantly ignore warning and go against Creslin's direct orders. The polar opposite of his own features, Nylan's face was twisted into a blood-thirsty rage. It was clear that nothing would stop him now that he had tasted the proverbial blood of the fight.

Before Kiyani could even think to talk him down, Nylan spun away. Thinking to confuse his opponent, he feigned a few blows before coming at Kiyani full blast.

Kiyani had never been placed against Nylan in their daily practice duels, and for good reason, but he'd witnessed how he liked to fight;

pushing ahead with such persistence that his unlucky opponent usually tired before they could so much as touch Nylan, or else issuing so many hard hits that his opponent ultimately surrendered before they were turned completely black and blue. Take no prisoners. That was his fighting style. Taking that into account, Kiyani moved forward, meeting each and every blow with the same amount of force and intensity that Nylan threw into it.

It had been a long time since Kiyani had found himself placed against a worthy opponent who didn't fall before him in a short time, but this was no practice match. If not death, or at least a permanent maiming, Nylan had something equally befitting for Kiyani in mind. The violence of their previous encounters would welcome nothing less.

Both dodged and parried multiple attacks meant to draw blood, each time the driving force behind the blows edging ever closer towards threateningly dangerous levels. Each brandished their weapons like aged professionals, though Kiyani could tell that his own returns were more elegant, his mind not so easily clouded by the heat of the fight. If anything, the world abound seemed to have gained a new level of clarity as he precisely calculated each counter attack. Always, he let Nylan attack first, letting him think that he had the upper hand and hoping that he would wear himself out before Kiyani was forced to do any real damage to anything other than Nylan's selfish pride.

For nigh on ten minutes they circled each other, completely unaware of the number of spectators who had gathered around them, watching in awe and placing hurried bets.

His heart beating rapidly with excitement, Kiyani briefly wondered how he fared in the gambling. The thought was short-lived as Nylan dove at him again. As good as he was doing, Kiyani knew he couldn't go much longer. Collectively, the class had yet to do endurance training, so the sparring matches that frequently took place as practice barely lasted a few minutes. And none were nearly as intensive as this. In contrast, Nylan seemed to have an endless supply of energy, making Kiyani wonder where exactly he was storing it.

In a move to end the fight quicker, Kiyani pretended to trip as Nylan came at him again. Throwing his sword a few feet in front of him, Kiyani could hear it hit the ground with a muffled thud as he dove at Nylan's legs. Caught unawares, Nylan toppled to the ground throwing up a cloud of dust. Kiyani took Nylan's moment of confusion as an opportunity and rolled across the field. Quickly taking up his sword, he rose to a crouch, the blade point coming to rest inches from Nylan's throat. His own sword lost in the fray, Nylan instinctively held his hands up in surrender.

The moment that it was apparent Kiyani had won the match a burst of applause rose from the crowd that circled them. Yet, with the blood pounding in his ears, Kiyani only heard it as muffled din. The look of disbelief on Nylan's face, mixed with an outrage that was far more deadly than what had graced his countenance during the fight was a prize enough for Kiyani.

"Everyone clear out!" Creslin shouted as he finally broke through the last line of students. "Nothing to see here!" Grabbing a handful of coins from one student, he threw them to the ground. "How many times do I have to tell you? If I catch any of you gambling, you'll be joining me in my office later! Now, scat!"

Nylan rolled into a crouch while Creslin was busy scattering the audience they'd accumulated. As soon as the Grand Master had come into the picture, Kiyani had let his sword fall lax, leaving Nylan free to stalk away. Brushing the dirt off his clothes, he grabbed his sword from the ground and stuffed it back into the sheath at his side. "This isn't over," Nylan hissed as he purposely rammed into Kiyani's shoulder on his way past.

Kiyani wanted to race after him and finish this whole thing for good, but he restrained himself. This battle, no matter how small, had been won and he would leave it at that. He knew it wouldn't be long before Nylan would try to regain the upper hand. Thinking on that, Kiyani made a mental note to find a way to lock the door to his and Tibben's room before they went to sleep that night.

"I must say, you're a lot better than I had expected," Creslin said as he strolled over. He stroked his chin as he watched Nylan walk away in disgust, his ego temporarily bruised. The spectators had been dismantled, but small groups still remained, watching from afar. A few even continued to sneak coins to one another, paying up on their bets.

Kiyani looked over at the Grand Master abashedly. "Thank you," he muttered. The last thing he had expected from him after that display was praise.

"Not everything you hear in the form of good words is a compliment," Creslin said, fixing him with a stern look.

As Creslin let the words sink in, Kiyani could see Nylan surrounded by his buddies by the wall of the arena. No doubt he was recounting his own exaggerated version of the fight.

"As eloquent of a display as that was," Creslin cut in after a moment, "it was still out of line, and you will be reprimanded for your actions."

"What?" Kiyani spat. "Nylan was the one that started the whole fiasco!"

Creslin shook his head remorsefully. "Resorting to blaming higher class students will not help your case. I act now, not only as your teacher, but as the Grand Master of this school. I will not have students who refuse to abide by my orders. From this moment forward you are temporarily expelled from this class until further notice."

Astonished, Kiyani was silent as he watched Creslin glide away before he could detest the measure. Though he was at a loss for words, inside he was outraged. The regular class activity disrupted, small groups of his peers stood on the outer perimeters of the field. A few of them chattered excitedly amongst themselves, the fight between him and Nylan worthy of gossip. Though most remained silent, everyone's eyes were on him.

Glaring at Nylan through a sheet of his tousled hair, Kiyani saw that he had turned at Creslin's mention of his name, and was watching him with a look of smug satisfaction. Even if he had been the one that had ended up on the ground, flat on his back, Nylan had still won the fight. And he knew it.

Kiyani could feel his lip twist into a sneer as he took in the haughty grin that'd returned to Nylan's face. He couldn't believe this was happening. Not only had Nylan been able to ruin his day, he'd gotten him kicked out of the one class he actually enjoyed. This was what he got for standing up to him. And it wasn't as if he could take it to the Head Master for consideration, as it'd been the man himself that had made the call. Tibben's words echoed in his mind. *Creslin won't do anything*... Though Kiyani hadn't wanted to believe it, the kid had been right.

Tearing at the belt that attached the blade to his side, he flung his sword in the dirt with such force that it let up a cloud of dust as it hit the ground, spreading above it like an angry storm. Before he could do any more damage to the room or his reputation, Kiyani turned and marched out of the arena.

He'd barely made it to the end of the hall when he heard the pounding footsteps of someone running after him. To angry to speak to anyone, he ignored it and continued walking. With his luck it was Nylan honing in for the last word, anyway.

"Kiyani!"

Mildly confused, Kiyani stopped. The voice was unmistakably female. Looking over his shoulder, he was surprised to see Bekka trotting down the hall after him.

Not knowing what she could possibly want, Kiyani remained stationary. As she walked the remaining few feet to his side, Kiyani waited for her to speak. With his blood still boiling from his encounter with Nylan, and Creslin's punishment, he didn't trust himself to keep his thoughts in order.

"You shouldn't have risked your place in Du Reizlan for me."

Kiyani shrugged. "It's no big deal. Nylan would have picked a fight with me eventually. Didn't matter what it was over."

Leaning closer, Bekka stood on her toes and gave him a peck on the cheek before leaving. "Thanks anyway."

Her long blonde hair that she kept wrapped up in a high ponytail swung down to her waist as she walked away. Unsure of what had just happened, Kiyani watched as she strode down the hall and back into the class. It didn't make up for the fact that he'd just been forced out of the one class he was still attending by his sworn enemy, but it sure didn't hurt either.

✧⌘✧

A pile of opened books, all in varying stages of research, told Fura that Kiyani had already been sequestered in the library for some time. The seat where he should have been was vacant, but that wasn't what worried her. Quietly, she strode up and down the rows until she spotted him in a desolate corner.

"What the heck happened?" Fura asked, keeping her voice down as she approached him. She had wanted to race after him when everything had calmed down, but Dairnyg had refused to let the class get out of order, let alone leave. So, she had waited. The fight, from her vantage point, had been quite spectacular, but Fura wanted to know all about it, from Kiyani, not from the rumor mill that had quickly raged out of control in the few hours since the incident.

"Nothing," Kiyani replied, ignoring her presence. Not even bothering to turn his head, he remained where he was, leaning against a shelf, a book in his hands and his back to her. Though he nonchalantly flipped another page, Fura could hear the warning tone in his voice.

Though Fura knew she should leave it alone, she grabbed his arm, repositioning him to face her. "The Herbology class met outside today. I saw the whole thing."

"I *told* you, it was *nothing*," Kiyani hissed.

Backing off a bit, Fura shook her head. If it really was nothing, then he wouldn't be so defensive about it. "Rumor has it that you were banned from the class for the rest of the semester."

"Don't believe everything you hear."

"Is it true?" she prodded. She already knew from experience that everything said in Du Reizlan's halls wasn't always based on truth. Yet, she'd been a partial witness. If she hadn't, then she might have been more inclined to believe him.

"Don't fucking worry about it," Kiyani snapped, surprising her with the intensity of his anger. "It's none of your damn business." Forcefully shoving the book back onto the shelf, he moved around Fura, ignoring her wide-eyed gaze and began walking away.

Though Fura could feel the angered heat coming off him, she couldn't let it go. Over the course of the last few weeks he had changed considerably. His generally calm demeanor had been replaced by an antsy irritation. Though prone to rage in the past, that anger now seemed to continually linger just below the surface, the smallest thing capable of setting it off. Now he was swearing at her for asking a simple question that any one of their fellow students could have approached him with.

Against her better judgment, she stalked after him, intent on discovering the truth of the matter.

"Kiyani," she grouched. "What the hell is going on with you? You started skipping out on classes weeks ago. Now, you don't even go at all. It's like you don't care. And now you've been kicked out of the only class you do go to for fighting? Why are you giving up so easily?"

Kiyani wheeled on her just as they broke through the rows and emerged into the common area before the fireplace. "Don't you fucking talk to me like that! I'm the one spending countless hours holed up in here looking for shit that probably doesn't even exist, while you're off gossiping with those two whores you call your roommates!" It was still early in the day, which meant the tables scattered throughout the area were filled. Distracted from their work in the usually quiet room, eyes looked up at them in interest, wondering what the commotion was about. It was enough to make Fura shirk away from the attention. Kiyani, on the other hand, took no notice, continuing to rage on. "Don't begin to think that you know what the hell is going on in my life. You don't know a damn thing about me, and I doubt you ever will. You're not the one ignoring everyone, every minute of every hellish day, as they talk behind your back about shit you haven't even done!"

Stalking over to the table and feverishly grabbing the parchment that he had been scribbling on, Kiyani stormed out of the room, leaving Fura in the aftermath of the fray. She watched in anguish as he disappeared. Once he was out of sight, she became all too aware of the eyes that were now focused on her and her alone. Despite the sign on the wall declaring the library a place of silence, hushed whispers broke out instantaneously.

Knowing that standing there only brought attention to herself, Fura looked around, wondering what to do. At a loss, she slowly trailed over to their usual table. Forgoing the seat she routinely claimed, she sat in the chair Kiyani generally occupied instead. Fighting the onset of tears, Fura looked at the books Kiyani had left scattered on the table with blurred vision. Though she tried to take in the information on the open pages, wondering just what he'd been reading, she found it impossible to concentrate. Never once allowing her to help in his search, she was unable to even begin to decipher the passages he'd been scanning.

With a shaking hand, she closed the closest tome, and stared at the scratches in the table. She was afraid to look up, not knowing just how many eyes were still focused on her in the aftermath, waiting to see what she'd do.

Knowing that she still had a load of homework to complete before the day's end didn't help in the least.

Blankly staring at the pile of books before her, Fura revisited the conversation, wondering if it would have been for the best if she had just left it alone. The words Kiyani had so harshly used had fallen from his tongue with such ease that she wondered if she really knew him at all.

Sticks and stones may break my bones, but words will never hurt me.
Right.

Fura had heard the saying so many times in the past, but after that display she felt like she had been stabbed repeatedly with a dull knife and left to bleed profusely. Glancing at her hand resting on the table, she saw that she was still shaking. Putting her hands in her lap, she subconsciously wrung them as she tried to focus on her own work. But it was no use.

For the next two hours, she spent her time, slowly and methodically replacing the books that Kiyani had borrowed back onto the shelves. When she had finished that task, Fura wandered through the rows until she found a dark corner where she would be hidden from view.

And it was there she remained until the library emptied.

72

♦♦◇♦♦

IN THE FIRELIGHT

The night was still young, or at least it would have been if they were still out on the road, moving along with who knew what in store.

But they were inside the walls of the famed Du Reizlan, and here life moved at a different pace.

Anger.

Abandonment.

Self-loathing.

For the last week and a half, Fura had been filled with conflicting emotions following her incident with Kiyani.

Anger, not only with herself for inciting Kiyani's rage, but with Kiyani for always thinking that he had to do things on his own. What was wrong with allowing her to help? And just how hard was it for him to admit that he was dealing with problems of his own? They could have shared in their hardships. Instead, he was so damn intent on facing the world alone that he shut her out instead.

And then there was the feeling of loss, of being abandoned. She knew she shouldn't have expected anything less, but Kiyani practically pulling a disappearing act in the days that followed took more of a toll on her than she was willing to admit. Without his presence, she'd felt even more alone in the world. Lost, as she moved methodically through the halls to classes. Neglected, as she did homework alone, often finding herself staring off into the distance. Though, by the third day she'd realized that he wasn't going to make an appearance, Fura had still found it disheartening to come down in the mornings and find the alcove empty of his presence. It didn't matter that he'd stopped meeting her there days before. Every morning as she'd descended the stairs, she'd hoped that maybe that would be the day he'd change his mind, deciding that he was simply being childish in the matter.

On top of that, self-loathing. It didn't matter that she knew Kiyani was the one that was in the wrong in the situation. Fura still felt as if she'd had something to do with the final stage of his turnaround, thinking that if only she hadn't been so insistent in getting him to talk,

611

then he'd still be around.

It had been a trying time, to say the least.

One that she didn't care to repeat any time soon.

Her only saving grace in that period had been Rhyne. She didn't know what she would have done without him by her side, offering a comfort and a friendship that Kiyani could hardly compete with. Not only did he continue to share the majority of his lunch periods with her, he'd taken up the habit of meeting with her again after classes to study and do homework. Though he wasn't available every day, it had made the week far better than it could have been. Not only that, but when class work wasn't their main focus, she'd taken solace in revealing her worries to him. Unlike Kiyani, Rhyne actually listened intently, mulling over her every word and offering useful advice in turn.

If it hadn't been for him, Fura knew she'd probably still be stuck in a downward spiral. Rhyne had been the one after all to suggest that she apologize to Kiyani. Even when she'd flat out refused, he'd continued to encourage the matter. It didn't matter that even he agreed that she hadn't necessarily been in the wrong in the first place. In fact, he'd told her it was best to apologize early on, rather than regret not rekindling a friendship.

It'd been hard, but she'd finally taken his advice. Though she'd still been angry with him, Fura found that she missed Kiyani regardless. Not to mention, without him she'd felt lost and directionless, wondering what would happen with their quest, with her father and the others in Frielana, if they didn't reconcile.

The conversation had been nothing short of awkward, but they'd made amends. And in the days that followed, things had gradually fallen back into a semblance of the routine they'd once shared.

Though Kiyani still refused to attend classes, they'd begun to resume meeting in the library in the evenings. At least that's when Fura would arrive. She'd never been able to muster the courage to ask, but she was certain that he holed up there on the second floor for most of the day. Every time she arrived, she could count on finding him at the same table. Though the books that surrounded him changed frequently, the table, scattered with parchment and ink, gave the appearance that he lived there, slowly becoming a regular fixture amongst the wallpaper of books.

While he researched, Fura searched the endless floor to ceiling shelves in search of help for her homework and the never-ending information on this world, trying to stockpile as much of it as possible in her brain before they decided to move out again. Quite the opposite, Kiyani, who had little to no homework, due to his lack of time actually invested in the classrooms, spent his time delving into one subject and one subject alone: the Witneis Reln.

Yet, despite her reconciliation with Kiyani, the droll of the school day still wore on her.

Tired and frustrated, Fura slammed the book she was currently scanning shut. Closing her eyes, she tried to drown out the countless amount of information that was left spinning in her head after another long day. Though she had been enticed by this world and all that she could learn in the beginning, Fura was quickly coming to terms with the fact that she would never be able to store and understand all of this. It would take her a lifetime, and right now, she didn't have that.

She had never thought it possible, but she missed the mundane days of wandering through the forest, the times that had bordered very closely upon boredom. She missed the lure of the forest that always looked the same to her. The open space. The fresh air. And, she missed Kiedo and his boundless energy.

"You have no confidence in yourself, do you?"

Fura opened one eye to find that Kiyani had briefly barred focus from his own studies to look at her.

"I – " she wanted to tell him that he was wrong, that she didn't know what he was talking about, to strike back with some remark, but Fura was spent. Trying to defend herself was the last thing on her mind.

"I can't do this," she sighed, trying to keep her voice from bordering on whiney. "There's just too much. I'm never going to remember this all!" It was all the fears and tribulations that had been haunting her since the moment they had stepped foot into Du Reizlan. That first night. That first class. Once she let the first sentences loose, Fura found that she couldn't control it. "I've been trod on and humiliated. I can't remember half of this stuff," she claimed, slamming a hand on the book she'd closed in front of her, "let alone do anything resembling magic. People pick on me for being so far behind, for being the Fireheir and not being able to own up to it. I don't deserve that title. Do you know how many people claim I'm lying about it? They don't say it to my face, but I hear it whispered behind my back...

"I hate this place, and this world... I don't even know if we plan on staying here the full semester, but it doesn't really matter, does it, because I'm going to fail anyways. There's no way I'm ever going to be the Fireheir."

Against her will the tears had begun to flow. Frantically wiping at them Fura turned away from Kiyani, embarrassed by the stream of words she'd let spew forth, documenting her fears and troubles.

She was supposed to be making Kiyani think she was becoming stronger. Instead, she was doing quite the opposite. She'd only just gotten him back, and now she felt as if she were on the verge of throwing that away again.

"You can't be doing this now, Fura," Kiyani said.

Fura could hear him close the book he was engrossed in. "I gave you the chance to go back to Barandor, multiple times, I'll remind you, and you flouted it. You made the decision. Now, you have to live with the consequences of it."

Though his words were almost exactly what she'd expected to hear, she was surprised to hear no hint of anger in his reply.

"I'm supposed to be from this world," Fura sniffed, unable to help herself. "I thought it would get easier. Instead I'm just proving how incompetent I can be. Maybe you were right to deem me slow."

Dragging a sleeve across her face, Fura pulled her feet up on the chair and rested her head on her knees, careful not to make eye contact with Kiyani. She could only imagine what he was thinking.

The scrape of the chair on the floor opposite her was followed by the shuffling of papers.

Great, now he's going to leave me here.

Alone amongst tomes of knowledge.

To her surprise, Kiyani came around the table and halted in front of her.

Looking up with watery eyes, Fura found that he had his hand extended to her.

"Come here," Kiyani said quietly.

Cautiously, Fura took his hand.

She didn't know what he was doing, but she let Kiyani lead her over towards the fireplace without debate.

If he wasn't going to outright leave her then she would take the moment in stride. It wasn't too often that his actions bordered on that of good will, at least not where she was concerned.

Stopping in front of the grand stone mantle Kiyani released her hand and turned to her. "Walk in front of the fire and watch it," he instructed.

Not willing to argue at this point, though she had no idea what he was trying to prove, Fura did as she was told. She was glad that there was no one else here to witness her meltdown or this craziness. With curfew approaching, the library had begun to clear out until they'd been the last ones left.

The flames in the fireplace before her danced lazily in the darkness, throwing a warm cast over the room. Fura marched slowly in front of them, losing herself in the warm colors and the heat that emanated. It had been a long time since she had really paid attention to the way they moved, had felt that urge in her body to resume what she did best, had listened to their call.

A feeling of warmth washed over her as she recalled the crowds of adoring fans that had come to watch her night after night in Fireswell. There, she had been somebody that others looked up to. There she had come across as a strong person. Nothing stood in the way of that girl. The fire had been her best friend, never letting her down, allowing her to become its master. What she wouldn't give to return to that. Reflecting back on it, it felt like a much simpler time.

But that time was long gone now.

There's no reason I can't be that here, Fura realized.

In fact, she should have been even more so. She was the Fireheir, after all.

Noticing something out of the ordinary, Fura stopped. Pulled out of her reverie, she looked over at Kiyani as if asking for confirmation. He only smiled.

Not sure that what she'd seen wasn't just a trick of her tired and overworked mind, Fura backtracked along the metal grate that was supposed to hold the fire at bay.

She could swear that the flames were moving with her.

"It follows you for a reason, Fear."

Looking over her shoulder, Fura found that Kiyani was leaning against the wall just on the other side of the stone, his arms crossed as he watched her intently. She could see by the look on his face that he had known prior to this display how the fire would react to her.

So lost in this strange display, she'd nearly missed what sounded like a nickname from him. Though she wanted to pursue it, she was too amazed by what he was saying.

There were no words to describe how she was feeling.

Fura was astonished by what she was seeing, yet, deep down, it felt right. "Why?" she asked.

"It knows that fire runs through your veins," Kiyani explained. "It waits for a command."

"Command? But... no one can control the elements. If anything, they control us, don't they?" Or at least, that's what Fura had been able to garner through her rushed studies.

"There was a time when the two worlds were connected when it was possible. Yes, the elements are not to be controlled, for they won't listen. You are correct that, in most instances, they prefer to maintain control over us. But, over a millennia ago, there were a few who the elements would listen to, and those were the Lords and their heirs. That is still true today in Izandüre."

The implications of what he was saying was extraordinary. "You mean... I can talk to fire?" If that was true, then Fura found herself able to look at her studies, including those with Marna that involved magic, with a profound lucidity.

Kiyani cocked his head thoughtfully. "In a way. Of course, there are rules, which I'm sure Marna is in the process of teaching you."

Fura couldn't bring herself to admit to him that Marna had yet to resume her pursuit of such things. After her little outburst of frustration, they had spent their time focusing on basically everything but the magic-driven side of life in Izandüre.

"Why can't you just teach me all this?" she asked. It sounded like a perfect plan to her, not to mention, that, for some reason she found it easier to remember whatever Kiyani told her. She didn't know if it was her general interest in him in the first place, or just the fact that when he explained things unknown to her he did it in a calm manner, trying to make sure she understood before moving on to more complicated things.

Kiyani shook his head no. "Because that would be an insult to Marna's talents, and because I'm busy looking for this damn tree."

Fura nodded, understanding. She'd already known the answer, yet had thought it couldn't hurt to ask, anyways. "Nothing yet?"

"No," Kiyani said, averting his eyes and running a hand through his hair. Fura could see that the pursuit of it was wearing him thin.

In fact, unable to bring herself to look him straight in the eye since he'd yelled at her right here in this library, she only now saw how ragged he looked from the endless pursuit.

The sooner they found this thing, the sooner they could leave. It would be better for both of them after that, Fura knew. The school itself, not to mention the people within it, with minimal exceptions, was driving them toward actions they wouldn't normally consider. Even Fura knew she had been more on edge as of late.

A comfortable silence fell between them as Fura left Kiyani to his own devices. She moved back and forth before the fire, watching as it danced along with her. A sense of elation filled her and Fura could feel herself smile. All of a sudden, everything seemed to have fallen in place. For once, it all felt so right.

Unbidden, a snippet of song came to her, and as if uncovering a long buried memory, Fura sat on the floor before the flames and began to sing softly:

In the firelight, dancing in the night
Watch it flicker, watch it move
Dancing like the open tomb
Of yesterday's past

In the firelight, dancing so bright
Watch it flicker, watch it flame
Dancing in the night rain
Just for me
That is what you'll see

It felt like such a haunting melody as Fura let the last words fall from her lips. She looked up to see Kiyani glancing at her in question. Unexpectedly, he looked like he had seen a ghost, his face appearing paler than usual in the orange light.

"Where did that come from?" he asked.

She didn't really know what to say.

"I've heard it before," Fura said, her eyes blurring as she looked vacantly across the room. "In my dreams. All these years I thought it was just something I had made up, but I think now that Apallo used to sing that to me." She let the words trail off, knowing how far-fetched it sounded.

"It sounds familiar," Kiyani said, coming over and sitting next to her.

The time slipped away soundlessly as they both stared into the flames, succumbing to the silence. Though, this time it was a comfortable calm that had settled between them.

"You may not believe in yourself," Kiyani began suddenly a little while later, "but the fire still recognizes you as one of its own. The power is there, you just have to harness it. If it helps at all, I believe that you're just over thinking it."

Glancing over at him, a smile still lingering on her face, Fura wondered from under what rock this side of Kiyani had emerged from.

"Are you saying that you believe in me?"

Kiyani's lip twisted into a smile as he turned to her, the light of the fire reflected in his eyes. "I might be."

73

••◇••

IN PLAIN SIGHT

Kiyani pointed to a mass on the map, trying to explain it. "And this is..." his voice trailed off as he looked up at Fura. "Are you getting any of this?"

Things at the school had gotten progressively better in the days after Kiyani had forced her to see what had been there all along – the fire's inherent response to her – but Fura still found that some information just wouldn't stick no matter how hard she tried. Despite Marna's deliberate focus on it, the map detailing the whole of Izandüre was one of those things.

"I'm not stupid," Fura shot back, irritably.

She should have known better than to try and have Kiyani help. His methods of teaching were far from what she was accustomed to in the classroom. The instruction he provided was more than helpful, but he had a brusque manner about it. He refused to let her get up until she'd memorized what she had come to him for, and even afterwards he would continually drill her to make sure that she actually remembered what he was taking his time to teach her. Fura wished that she had known beforehand that if she was going to enlist him into helping with her studies that he was going to be fully committed to the task, and that there would be no weaseling her way out of it later.

If anything, it was her own fault. She had asked him after all. But she'd expected him to outright deny her. In fact, he had, only to surprise her a few days later by rescinding his initial response.

"What's wrong?" Kiyani asked, eying Fura thoughtfully.

Fura looked up, startled at his question, at the actual look of worry on his face. Rarely did she witness such emotion from him. Even if he was right in his accusation, she'd been certain she'd been putting on an acceptable front for once.

She shook her head. "Nothing."

Kiyani leaned back in his chair and crossed his arms, shooting her a look that dared her to keep the lie going. "You expect me to believe that? You've been on the verge of tears for the past week."

Turning away, Fura remained silent. She didn't want to talk about it, not with him. It awed her that he had even taken notice. Kiyani was generally so wrapped up in his own search for the Witneis that he often disregarded anything and everything that didn't apply to it, much less pay her any attention besides the general greetings.

"See, I'm right," Kiyani claimed when Fura refused to elaborate on his observations. "You're not even going to defend yourself."

Still not getting a response, the room fell into silence.

Fura couldn't look him in the eye. Instead, she fought the tears that'd been welling day after day, the pressure of everything building and taking its toll on her. Her willingness to learn and the ability to retain all the information that was thrown at her in the lecture halls had taken a new turn in the last week. The teachers had certainly taken notice. Even Marna had applauded her a few times when Fura had easily answered what were considered higher level questions. Every little compliment raised Fura's spirits exponentially until she felt like she was going to overflow with pride.

However, every night, that bubble burst when she returned to her dorm. Though Fura had thought that her roommates had finally resolved to leave her alone, the twins had also taken notice of her sudden change, and in turn had increased their nightly commentary to include even more hateful things than usual. Fura was sick of it, but she didn't know what she could do.

She had initially thought to take the matter to the Grand Master, until she had learned that it was Creslin who'd expelled Kiyani for fighting, taking Nylan's side over his when it was obvious who had started the brawl. Even Marna didn't seem like a likely candidate to voice her troubles to. Fura could just hear the woman's gravelly voice drawling in her head. *You just have to buck up.*

And though she knew Rhyne would thoughtfully listen, Fura refrained from speaking of it to him, feeling as if all she did was rant when they were together.

"Don't listen to them," Kiyani said, as if he could read her mind. For once, he was the one who wouldn't let the conversation fall short.

"What —" Fura looked at him, still in shock. *Am I really that easy to read?* "How did you know?"

Kiyani shrugged. "Things get around."

"Oh," was all Fura could muster. She highly doubted that he was privy to half the things she was forced to listen to in the dark when the girls thought she was sleeping.

"You're better than they are, remember that."

"You really think so?" Fura asked. She wouldn't put it past him at times to just say things to try and make her feel better.

Nodding, Kiyani picked up the book in front of him and reopened it, flipping through pages to find where he'd left off.

Though out of the ordinary, Fura would take anything that even remotely sounded like a compliment from Kiyani. It was definitely a lot better than having him completely ignore her. Yet, she still couldn't believe that he'd paid enough attention to her throughout the days to come to the realization that something was amiss.

Fura hated to interrupt him, but it was Sunday and they could spend all day in the library if they saw fit. "How much longer do you think we'll be here?"

"It's hard to tell," Kiyani answered. "Until we find something, I guess."

"What if there's nothing to find?" Fura didn't like the sound of the thought coming out of her mouth, but it wasn't the first time it had crossed her mind.

"I'm trying not to think about that at the moment."

"We can't stay here forever."

Flipping a page, Kiyani answered, "I know."

Fura sat back in her chair, ignoring the work that she'd been trying to figure out with little success before Kiyani had gotten the bright idea to quiz her on locations of towns.

"You know, it's not fair," she said, exasperated. It wasn't often that Fura found she was able to talk to Kiyani so freely. "I sit in classes for seven hours a day while you sit in here with all these books. I have like ten minutes to eat, and then I have to go to the tutor that you so ungraciously set me up with for another two long and frustrating hours. And then to top it off, I have homework for days. You. You never even attend classes anymore. You don't join me for lunch and rarely for dinner. What the heck have you been doing?"

Kiyani raised an eyebrow as if to ask where all that had suddenly come from. Fura half expected him to get angry with her again, but when he replied his tone was even, almost bordering on boredom. "What do you think I've been doing? Knitting sweaters? Have you seen the amount of literature in here?"

Fura let out a sigh. "I know."

She was about to ask something else when Kiyani looked past her, something catching his eye.

"Hey, Cheese," Kiyani said flatly before burying himself back into the current tome he was searching through as quickly as his attention had been wrested from it.

Intrigued and confused, Fura turned to see who he was talking to. Walking towards them was the young boy that she had seen Kiyani with here and there. From what she remembered, this was Kiyani's impromptu roommate.

"God, Kiyani," Fura said, flashing him a scowl that he ignored.

"You are so rude!" She knew that Cheese wasn't this kid's name.

The boy held up a hand in amusement as he came to her side. "It's okay." He laughed. "I really don't mind it. It's his nickname for me, because of my last name."

Fura could hear Kiyani chuckle, though he barely lifted his eyes from his book.

She couldn't help but feel mildly sorry for this kid, and she had thought that she was the only victim of Kiyani's incessant teasing. Fura had had enough of that to last her a lifetime, but at least he wasn't cruel about it like the others. Instead, Kiyani had a way of going about it that made it come across as friendly, often leaving the target laughing as well. "I know I've heard your real name before, but you'll have to refresh my memory," Fura said, turning to the boy.

"Tibben," the boy smiled. "Hey, Kiyani, do you think you could help me with the homework from history?"

Kiyani shook his head. "You know I haven't been to class in weeks."

"Oh, okay," Tibben replied, looking and sounding defeated. "I guess I'll see you later, then."

Watching him walk away, shoulders slumped, Fura found that she felt sorry for the kid. Looking down at the papers scattered before her, she stood. "Hey, Tibben," she called, holding up a textbook. "I'm stuck on homework, too."

Turning, Tibben faced her with a smile, his mood brightening. "We're in the same class, right?"

Fura nodded. "We are," she confirmed. "Come on, let's go see what we can find."

✧⌘✧

Though Fura knew that, with little else to do on Sundays, they could spend the whole day in the library, she hadn't actually expected to do so. Yet, as the afternoon rolled into early evening, she discovered that that was exactly how it was turning out.

If someone had told her that morning that the library was where she'd spend the better part of the day, she'd have balked at the idea. To her surprise, she found that the hours had flown by, instead.

Where she'd been content to sit across from Kiyani, struggling with her homework that was due the next day, Fura found that the time spent with his roommate had been quite enjoyable.

Moving into the labyrinth of shelves, they'd sought out extra books to help with their homework for *Izandüre: A History*. It wasn't until Tibben had mentioned the name that she remembered they shared the class. Thinking to the days when Kiyani had abandoned her to figure out the world on her own, she wished she'd realized that fact earlier. Though Rhyne was apt to help her on any topic, she'd felt awkward asking for his assistance on work from classes they didn't share.

She couldn't remember if Tibben had mentioned how much younger he was than her, but it didn't matter to Fura. If anything, that time had been a welcome break from Kiyani's quiet and reserved nature. They'd made plenty of headway with the work, finishing it in what Fura considered record time. Not only had Fura been relieved to know that it was done, but they had actually had fun doing it, sitting on the floor and laughing about nothing.

This is what Sunday's are for, Fura remembered thinking, *a time to rest and rejuvenate.*

When Tibben had finally left, Fura could have sworn that a bit of that newfound happiness had retired with him. It was sad to watch him go, Fura thought. For once, she was beginning to realize what it was like to have friends. Once that occurred to her, she'd made a note to invite Tibben to eat with her if she ever saw that he was alone during lunch. She knew that Rhyne wouldn't mind. In fact, he would probably welcome the added company and the extra voice in their conversations.

Feeling satisfied, Fura meandered through the long, narrow aisles, filled from floor to ceiling with incredulous looking tomes of all shapes and sizes, on all matter of subjects. She didn't even know what she was looking for, only that she didn't want to return to the table with Kiyani, sitting in the hard-backed wooden chairs.

Buzzing with happiness, she didn't even think she could sit still.

Her homework was done anyways, leaving her free to explore. So, what else was there to do in such a large library, besides browse?

There was no use in trying to converse with Kiyani at the moment. Returning momentarily to drop her history book off on the table, Fura found Kiyani still sitting where she'd left him. When she'd made to wander off again, he hadn't even bothered to ask where she was going.

He was still deeply immersed in his own research and becoming increasingly frustrated with anything to do with the matter. Whereas Fura was just starting to find her stride in the school, her spirit lightening, Kiyani seemed to be heading in the opposite direction. Days upon endless days he had sat in that very spot, had scoured these very shelves, and still nothing. It was as if the tree had never existed.

A brief thought ran through Fura's mind that maybe the tree had been cut down and used as the parchment for the books they were currently searching through. She shook the thought from her head immediately after it came to her. If this tree was as special as she assumed it was, then nobody would cut it down. No, it was hidden for some reason. Maybe that was the whole test – not only being able to solve the riddle of its whereabouts, but having the patience to do so.

Aimlessly, Fura walked on, pausing here and there to run her fingers along the colorful spines of the carefully arranged books.

In the middle of aisle four, third shelf from the floor, an expansive heft of a novel caught her eye. Squatting down to bring herself within eye level, Fura let her fingers drift over it and brush the dark green spine. In gold, foiled letters that had begun to fade with use and age the title read: *From Seed to Trunk: A Guide to the Plants of Izandüre.*

With no specific subject matter on her mind to search for and even less desire to go sit next to the fuming Kiyani, Fura pulled the book from the shelf and sat cross-legged on the floor. Leaning against the shelf, she opened the heavy book in her lap.

Not knowing where to start or why this particular volume had even caught her eye in the first place, Fura began to flip through mindlessly. Stopping every now and then she would read a passage about plants she'd never heard of, things with weird names like *tumaeris velcan (the common vine), and storif fein (the giant fern).*

For being a 'common' vine, Fura was sure she had yet to encounter it, looking at the given picture to verify her thoughts.

Storif fein (the giant fern):

The storif fein, or more commonly known as the giant fern is atypical of shuervin fein, low peddlers fern, common in most forest regions, in that if left unattended can grow to heights of ten feet tall...

Fura shuddered as she flipped the page, none all too eager to learn anymore about the giant fern, in case it also came across as carnivorous and intelligent. She couldn't truthfully say that she would appreciate coming across a plant, other than a tree, that was fervently larger than herself. Nor did she want to try and imagine what creatures it could possibly hide in its leafy encasement.

Continuing to scan the passages, Fura could only imagine what the other students would think of her if they caught wind of this. Scared of plants in a book. What the hell was wrong with her? It was a good thing she hadn't come across the volume that listed all the creatures of this world. She'd already had her fair share of encounters with them.

Just as she was about to place the book back where it belonged on the shelf, the gaping dark hole where it had sat waiting to swallow it again, a word caught Fura's attention.

Reln.

This was nothing new to her. The Reln was basically the first oddity she'd been exposed to in this world. Over time it had become a welcome relief to catch sight of one of the grand trees, knowing that they had found refuge from the elements and wandering eyes.

Boredom and a slightly peaked interest kept the book in her hands.

Settling back down, Fura read the passage.

Reln maetificae is the fourth most common tree found in the numerous forested lands of Izandüre, coming close to a tie with the North American timber pine. This stately tree can grow hundreds of feet tall and is generally impervious to pests of the insect variety due to its bitter bark and hard wood. With an average lifespan of a century these trees heartily thrive with age and can greatly exceed those numbers. The Reln, though massly overpopulated by the other three common tree varieties is the oldest on record in Izandüre's history. It is rumored that the oldest of this variety is the Witneis Reln (see Plants with Magical Properties, pg. 497), thought to have been created at the dawn of time...

Her mouth falling open in awe, Fura let her hand drift over the passage. Though there was still another half a page of information in the same flowing script, the rest of it had fallen into a blur. Only one fragment retained her focus:

The Witneis Reln.

One hand firmly in place to mark the passage detailing the Reln in general, Fura hastily flipped through the pages until she reached 497.

The Witneis Reln:

The Witneis, also deemed the Tree of Knowledge by scholars over the centuries, has long been the pinnacle of much debate. This large tree, in the family of reln maetificae, is thought to be not only the oldest tree, but the first tree in creation, its ever-growing rings containing the knowledge of every year of life in Izandürian history.

This is it, Fura thought. *This is what we need, what Kiyani's been searching for since we got here, since Apallo gave us that cryptic message.*

Kiyani.

Fura looked down the empty row and wondered just how much time had elapsed since she'd found this book. There was no real way to tell, but she knew that Kiyani would have come to find her if it was that late already, if he planned on leaving.

Picking herself up off the floor, careful to keep her finger carefully wedged in the page, Fura fought the urge to run back to their table with her newfound prize. All this time he'd refused her help, all these weeks he'd been searching through countless books, and Fura had found it by accident.

Back in the main sitting area, Fura carefully wound her way through the maze of now vacant tables and couches as she made her way back towards Kiyani.

He was exactly as she had left him, hunched over a pile of books, a few of them laying open to random passages that might have something to do with anything. From behind he looked like he was resting, possibly having fallen asleep in the myriad depths of homework, but Fura knew better. It was a stance he took when he didn't feel like delving any further but he continued on regardless.

For both of them, this was one step out of this newfound hell.

Skirting the table, Fura opened the book to the passage on the Witneis Reln and dropped it, face up, right into the midst of the pile that surrounded Kiyani.

"Can I help you?" Kiyani asked rudely, glaring up at her with bloodshot eyes.

Despite his behavior, Fura could hardly keep the grin off her face. "I found it," she beamed. She couldn't remember the last time her efforts had proven anything but fruitless.

Kiyani arched an eyebrow. "What?"

Fura shook her and head and sighed. As if he didn't know. "The Witneis!" Pointing to the page the book lay open to in front of him, she rambled on, not letting him add any of his harsh words to the conversation until she was done. "We were looking in all the wrong places this whole time. The Witneis Reln is just that, a Reln."

Holding the place in the book, Fura flipped it shut, letting Kiyani read the title embossed on its front cover. She could see him scanning it, taking it in.

"A book on trees..." he mumbled as if trying to convince himself. "Are you kidding me?"

Shooing Fura's hand away, Kiyani opened back to the page detailing the Witneis and read it silently to himself.

74

•◆•

A MEANS TO AN END

The following the week was filled with hushed preparations for the impending trip. Each day that passed, following her discovery in the library, left Fura all the more excited. Not only because their journey was on the verge of resuming where they had left off, but also because it meant that, sooner rather than later, they could put this school behind them for good. For as valued as Du Reizlan was, Fura knew she wouldn't be all that sad to see it fade from memory.

She could barely contain herself as she walked through the halls with a newfound confidence. The only thing that kept her from skipping excitedly throughout the rest of the week was the impending frustration of exams. Even after Fura had broken the doldrums that she and Kiyani had found themselves in, Kiyani had insisted that she complete the remaining days of her courses. Fura had been intent on arguing her case on the matter, at least until Kiyani had assured her that he would be sitting right next to her.

The route of that conversation had surprised her. The last thing Fura expected from Kiyani was for him to make a fool out of himself by trying to pass a class on the last day when he'd really only attended for about a week. She had wanted to ask him more about it, but Fura had kept her thoughts to herself. If he was nervous about what his promise entailed, Kiyani didn't show it. It burned Fura as she had a sudden inkling of premonition that, even considering the circumstances, he would somehow do better than her.

He claimed to have never been to Du Reizlan, but his education, from what Fura had witnessed here and there, was far from lacking. The way he carried himself, along with his habit of answering questions with ease, led Fura to believe that he knew more than he led on. Every answer that came from him, involving anything to do with Izandüre, came across like it was read from a textbook, making Fura think that no matter how hard she tried, she would never amass the vast store of knowledge that Kiyani had picked up from unknown sources.

In the end, Kiyani had followed through on his promise, and Fura had been elated to find that exams were nowhere near as hard as she had feared. She doubted that she'd passed any of them with flying colors, but she didn't feel like she had outright bombed any of them, either. Fura was dying to ask Kiyani how he thought he had done, but once they walked out of the last class, neither made any mention of how they thought they had done. Instead, they fell into a comfortable silence as they walked side by side down the hall.

To Fura, it felt as if she were walking through a slow-motion dreamscape, one that mimicked, very vividly, the world that they had been secluded to for the past month and a half. Lights seemed brighter, and the edges of her vision retained a certain haze that she couldn't shake. A great weight had been lifted off her shoulders, but Fura knew that even with their studies completed there would be no long period of rest.

She didn't know where this journey of theirs would take them, or how long it would last, but Fura felt like they had barely made a dent in its side. She only hoped that this time spent side-tracked would actually prove useful in the end.

Sitting with one leg tucked beneath her, Fura looked around the library. It was hard to sit still and, though he didn't say anything, she was sure that Kiyani was well aware of her fidgeting.

Fura had woken at first light that morning and had been anxious to leave soon after. It was the first full day of Du Reizlan's winter break – one of only a handful of times that students were allowed to leave the school's grounds – and Fura couldn't see any reason to prolong their stay any further. But, as usual, Kiyani had already secured different plans without consulting her.

So, here they sat, the only residents in the massive expanse of the library. As if sensing the sudden lack of movement to breathe life into it, the towering levels of the library seemed to have taken on a ghostly aura. Specks of dust floated slowly in the air as if moving through a thick gel. The flames in the fireplace were lower than usual, threatening to die out with every flicker. Even the librarian was absent from her post, having taken advantage of the holiday as well.

Fura and Kiyani were the only souls around. There were a select number of students who had opted to stick around for the holidays, but they were few and far between, almost as if they were ghosts themselves.

Scratching an itch that had presented itself on her arm, Fura shifted in her seat and looked at the map laid out before her, trying again to search out the route that Kiyani had pointed out to her earlier in the day.

"Where did you say we were going again?" Fura found herself asking. Though she knew she'd inquired about the same thing only minutes before, she couldn't help it. She just wanted out of the oppressive, monolithic building.

Kiyani let out an aggravated sigh. "I just told you." He flipped a page of the book Fura had found and scribbled another note on the parchment in front of him. "We're going to take the road back out of Du Reizlan and angle south once we leave the gate."

Fura was actually surprised that he'd chosen to answer, though this time he had refrained from leaning over the table and tracing out the path with his finger like he had done the first two times she'd asked. Looking at the map before her, Fura let her eyes wander over the mysterious names. Marna had stayed true to her word and made Fura memorize every last square inch of the parchment, but to her, they were still only scribbled lines on paper. Nothing about it would be real until she witnessed it firsthand. Just as the only path so far that made sense was the one they'd already traveled.

"All the way to the Far Reach?" Fura questioned.

"I doubt it will be that far away."

In the days after Fura had come across the passage about the Witneis, both her and Kiyani had gone to painstaking lengths to copy and memorize the information it contained. "Shouldn't we be looking for a lake or something?" Of course, just like anything else they happened to encounter, it was wrapped in a multitude of riddles.

"Why?"

Fura shrugged. "The book said to *tread carefully the dangerous waters surrounding.*' Wouldn't that be a lake, or maybe the ocean?"

Flipping the page again, Kiyani answered flatly, "That large a body of water would be too obvious. Besides, living things flock to water like fleas gather on a wild dog. Something as notorious as the Witneis wouldn't be that easy to find."

Confusion reigned supreme. Basically, with those few compacted sentences, he'd just contradicted everything that she had previously thought. "Okay," Fura said. "So, where do *you* think it is?"

Scratching his chin, Kiyani leaned over and tapped a finger lightly on the map. She didn't like what was beneath it. The mass he indicated looked to be nothing more than a dark scribble of trees, yet somehow it came across as sinister, and insignificant to their quest.

The Mire of Mithrim, she read. "Isn't it just a stretch of trees?"

"The Mire is swampland."

Fura couldn't help but wrinkle her nose at the prospect of trudging through a swamp. However, she still didn't see how Kiyani had come to that conclusion. "What's so dangerous about a swamp?"

Kiyani looked at her as if the answer was obvious, though he didn't claim as much. "It's not so much about the land itself as what inhabits it."

"Oh." Fura didn't like the sound of that. Was it necessary for them to run into trouble wherever they went? It was starting to feel like just another part of their routine. It wasn't a full day until they'd found themselves in some kind of mess. It was just an extra special day if it included fighting for their lives.

"I've never been there myself to verify the stories, but it's said that the Mire is where all the outlaws of the land like to gather... your thieves and whatnot."

Not caring for what he said, Fura remained silent as she let his words sink in.

Human thieves? she wanted to ask, though she told herself that he was simply joking. Or, maybe playing another card in his hand as he tried to get her to return to Barandor. Though, even she knew that at this point that wasn't the case. A few weeks ago, she'd finally caved, had told him she wanted to go back, and he'd denied her.

No, she was in this for the long run now, and nothing would stop her.

They had finally found what they needed. Fura wasn't about to scare herself into remission. Apallo himself had declared that what they needed was to be found with this tree and she wasn't about to question her father's wishes. Though she still had to wonder why he'd sent them this far into the void.

"Do you think we'll be coming back here?" Fura asked, attempting to steer the conversation in a more pleasant direction.

She wasn't quite sure how she would have answered if she were in Kiyani's place. Ever since they'd entered Du Reizlan, Fura had longed to escape the walls and run free. However, the long days had become a rather routine existence, complete with hot meals and a solid roof over their heads. The last thing Fura missed was scrounging around at night for an acceptable shelter, wondering when their next meal would be. The possibility of still being attacked by lord knew what, and huddled next to a measly fire made up of a few twigs held no appeal. If she never again went camping in her life, she couldn't say she would be sorry. About the only thing Fura could honestly say she desired were the late night talks with Kiyani, but even those had been exceedingly rare.

Carefully closing the book before him, Kiyani pushed it to the side. "I don't know," he said. "It depends on what we find."

✧ ⌘ ✧

The following morning greeted them in lively spirits. The sun shone brightly in a nearly cloudless expanse of blue sky, and the air was unseasonably warm for the time of year. A few patches of white from the last snowfall remained. Where the ice had melted, blades of grass that remained green poked through, searching for warmth. Even a few birds twittered greetings from their treetop perches. To any unknowing bystander, it appeared that spring was on its way.

Though Fura knew that wasn't the case, it didn't keep her from hoping that they could somehow skip the frosty winter months.

Telling herself that it didn't matter, that they were on the road again, Fura sped along the plowed stone path in the courtyard, feeling the crisp air bite at her cheeks, turning them red. Her heart raced at the sudden exertion of running. It had been too long of a time to accurately compare, but she felt like an excited child who'd just found out that school was closed for a snow day. The possibilities that reigned for such an unexpected turn of events were endless.

Not to mention – besides the night before, when Fura had finally coerced Kiyani into taking a walk outside – this was the first time, other than having to go to class, that she'd really been outside the school. Fura had wanted to see the courtyard in person. Not just through the glimpses she'd seen out the window. Now, she found that the grand fountain and the surrounding area were just as gorgeous in the light of morning as it had been at dusk.

Skipping along, Fura was entranced by the glitter of the sun on the icy water falling from the fountain. Even the masterfully sculpted unicorn, made of ivory colored stone, sparkled brilliantly, making it look like it was dancing in the sunlight.

As if she'd forgotten nearly everything useful from their previous travels while stuck inside Du Reizlan, it didn't take long for Fura to make a fool of herself. Kiyani's lessons of *be wary of your surroundings*, and *watch where you're going*, didn't set until she found herself splayed out on the ground, having slipped on a clear patch of ice.

But, even that couldn't darken her mood. She quickly picked herself up and brushed off her clothes before Kiyani, who was trailing slowly behind, could catch up to her. When he came to the spot where she stood waiting, he merely shook his head.

"Sorry," Fura said with a shrug. "I'm a little excited."

"You think?"

Any other day, Fura knew he probably would have scolded her for being irresponsible, but she could see the slight grin on his face that told her he was merely amused. The sight of him nearly cracking a smile left her feeling all the better about this trip. The change in pace would be good for both of them. She could already tell that it was having a positive effect on Kiyani.

He looked better than he had in days, as if the night before had been the first time he'd slept in weeks. Every day, he had become increasingly haggard, looking like a hermit stuffed away amongst all the books in the library. Fura had worried about him, but had said little involving her observations, knowing that he'd only claim that it was a necessity. His health nowhere near as important as finding the single scrap of information needed to continue on their way. Yet, she'd only hoped that he wasn't taking the common-place *you can sleep when you're dead* to heart. It was a good thing that Du Reizlan had a curfew, or else she knew Kiyani would have never left the library.

The walk from the courtyard, all the way down the stretch of path that led to and away from Du Reizlan felt like a shorter distance than when they had first traversed its winding length. When they came to the iron gate boasting the school's name, Fura turned to look at the building that had been her impromptu home for almost two months. Standing tall and proud on top of the grassy knoll, bathed in sunlight that accented its features like liquid gold, Fura found that it looked much more inviting during the day.

If I never have the chance to come back, Fura thought, *this is how I want to remember it.*

It was far better than the Halloween-esque image that had presented itself the night they'd arrived in the setting darkness.

Yet, even now it looked just as desolate.

Where the day before the school had been bustling with life, with students packing their belongings and rushing down the halls and out the doors, today Du Reizlan looked abandoned. In the long corridors, only every other torch had been lit, leaving the halls darker than usual. The stone underfoot had echoed with the steps of the few who had chosen to remain behind for their own personal reasons.

As strange as it might have felt, all Fura had cared about was that she was finally free. They too were leaving the ghost town of the school behind. Her and Kiyani weren't going back home to family, like all the others, but they were still escaping.

No more classes.

No more ornery tutors.

No more vindictive roommates.

Just freedom.

Taking in a deep breath of fresh air, Fura looked around. The surrounding trees, though already having shed their fall colors, felt welcoming, as if, all this time, something had been missing.

Not too far off the man-made path, a mass of gray crouched among the greenery. Fura stepped back, startled at first, until recognition hit her.

"Kiedo!"

631

Twisting his head at the sound of his name, the wolf rose from his resting place and trotted over. He let Fura hug him and ruffle his fur with a few excited pats, before shaking as if he'd just received a bath and strolling over to sit beside to Kiyani.

"Good boy," Kiyani said, laying a hand on Kiedo's head.

Every time the wolf rejoined them, Fura found herself even more amazed. For being a wild animal, Kiedo was better trained than her own dog had ever been. "How did he know?" she asked.

Kiyani stepped off the road and began walking towards the towering trees before answering. "He didn't."

"But –"

"He just tends to stick around."

"Oh," Fura mumbled to herself.

She remained in front of Du Reizlan's gate, taking in the image of Kiyani and the wolf that so loyally followed him as they drew closer to the woods. It wasn't until Kiedo paused in his step to look back at her, as if to question why she was still standing there, that Fura moved to follow.

It all just felt so right.

This is how it's supposed to be, Fura thought. *We're back on track.*

75

◆◆✧◆◆

SECRETS REVEALED

"What?" Apallo asked irritably, fighting the urge to push a greasy and tangled strand of hair from his face, as he looked upon the image of the Shadowlord standing in the doorway of his cell. "Did you come to gloat some more?"

So few times Zariah had entered the room where he'd been residing, left like some old toy in storage. Only taken out and looked upon one in a while when the fancy struck.

Zariah grinned deviously. "I can't simply visit an old friend?" he asked.

There might have been a time when that question had been genuine. Now it was only laced with mocking intentions. Though Apallo hated to find himself drawn into the man's games, routinely telling himself in the darkness of his solitude that he would remain silent when the Shadowlord came to him, he always found himself caving. As snide as the man was, as wicked and cunning, he was Apallo's only link to the outside world.

Though he had to question if he should actually believe anything the man said. Yet, the truth of the matter was that as twisted as his views were, he'd never been one to lie. Not when he knew that the honest truth could cut deeper than anything he could devise in false words.

Yet, there was something about the friendly illusion on the man's face that Apallo didn't trust. Zariah's moments of glee always depicted something far worse than when he was encased in silent rage.

"What's happened to her?" Apallo asked, unable to keep the blatant worry from his voice.

Where Zariah had been intently studying the low-burning sconce on the wall, he turned his head, a new glee present in his eyes. "So quick to assume," he declared. "What makes you think that I have any news?"

"Why else would you be here?"

The Shadowlord snickered blithely. "I have no reason to reveal that to you." Turning, he made for the door.

Unsure of what the man's intent had been, Apallo found himself suddenly needing to know why Zariah had taken a moment out of his day to supposedly visit. Yet, before he could say anything to draw the man back in, the Shadowlord turned of his own accord, the grin still present. The man was far too jovial today, frightening Apallo.

"Though," Zariah drawled. "Now that you mention it… I may actually have some news of the daughter you cast aside."

Apallo cringed at the accusation, though he couldn't deny that the man was right. He'd never allowed himself to think about it in those terms, but that was exactly what he'd done to the girl. The years spent teaching her the arts of working with fire on the stage could never atone for the fact that he'd abandoned her. And for what reason? Had it really been because of the terror that had raged through Izandüre at that time? Or had it simply been because he hadn't thought himself fit for the job of a father?

Casting the thoughts aside, Apallo looked up at the man. What could he possibly have to tell him that would leave him in such a mood?

"What did Kiyani do to her?"

This only earned a wider grin from the man. "Testy today…" He shook his head in amusement. "So quick to decide that something bad has happened."

Fixing him with a narrowed gaze, Apallo tried to decipher the man's riddle. "It had to have."

"Actually," Zariah said, quick to correct him. "They're almost to the Witneis."

"What?" Apallo gawped. How could that be? They'd really been able to find it? He still didn't like the thought that Fura was traveling with Kiyani, but he was astonished that they'd made it so far. Only in the time he'd been given, sitting alone in the darkness with his own thoughts to haunt him, had he realized just how ridiculous of a message that'd been. So few people knew of the Witneis that lived in Izandüre. Yet, he'd sent his daughter that knew absolutely nothing of this realm to find what many considered a myth. Though he didn't know how much of it had been Kiyani's doing, he was proud of Fura. He shook his head in disbelief. "How…"

"I'll admit, I was just as surprised. However, find it or not, just what do you expect them to do when they get there? What do you expect them to find? There's nothing there to help them."

Avoiding the man's gaze, Apallo didn't want to evaluate the truth in that.

"Amazing, really," Zariah continued. "That despite hating the boy, you sent your daughter on a journey where she needed his help. Did you really think that she could have found it on her own? So terribly naïve… or does that simply run in the Feuer family?"

Gritting his teeth, Apallo spat, "As darkness does in the Enderline family?"

Though Apallo expected the Shadowlord to deny his accusation, Zariah only looked at him with amusement. "Do you really expect anything less?"

It was a far cry from the man he'd once known way back in the day. The Zariah he'd been friends with would have adamantly defended himself against such words, not snickered in agreement. It was times like this that, despite his wishes, Apallo truly knew that any semblance of the friendship they'd once shared was gone.

"How did you do it?" Apallo asked sullenly. He didn't want to think about how easily Zariah had been able to lay Frielana to waste. Not just because it was heresy against the Draimaele that had given rise to the Sect of Seven centuries ago, but because it had been a blatant display of just how weak he'd let himself become. He'd known for the longest time that he was slipping as Firelord, but that had only brought the full extent of it to the light of day.

"You think I'd give away all my secrets?"

Apallo shook his head, both answering, but also still lost in disbelief. "It shouldn't have been that easy."

To his surprise, Zariah strolled over closer, his cloak dragging across the cold stone. "You don't give yourself nearly enough credit," he said, crouching to look Apallo in the eye. "Weak minds are easily broken." Standing, he turned and made his way back towards the door, looking intent on leaving this time. "Though," he said over his shoulder. "It's amazing what a little mobizane in the water will do."

Mobizane, Apallo thought incredulously. That illusive drug that temporarily stripped magic users of their powers. So, there had been trickery involved.

As the door opened, Apallo spoke again, surprising even himself. "Last time... you said you had a proposition for me?"

Letting the door shut behind him, Zariah smiled wickedly. "Are you saying you're interested?"

76

••◇••

THROUGH THE MIRE

The Mire of Mithrim was even more sinister in person, Fura decided as she walked alongside Kiyani through the dark stretch of twisting trees. The first six days of traveling had presented forests and winding rivers that looked the same to Fura as what they'd already trekked. On the seventh day, however, the Mire had made no question of its presence. Even from afar, it had presented itself as a hazy black mass that looked like it didn't belong on the landscape. A void that was meant to be bypassed, not traveled through.

Even before the trees, stripped of any vegetation and black as night, came into clear sight, the ground below their feet had announced the change. Gradually the compacted dirt had given way to soft loam, and then to a stinking mix of decaying matter and water that sunk and gave way with every step.

An eerie twilight swept over them as soon as they stepped foot into the dense mass of dead forest. Though the trees were bare, they found a way to intertwine their branches that resembled skeletal hands, into a vine-like canopy high above. The knot of wood let in strange and subdued triangles of light that scattered amongst the forest floor, but did little to brighten the shadows that followed them.

Blackened trees that looked like they had been victims of a fire long past twisted in an odd array of shapes. The air was musty and filled with a rank odor that fell somewhere between wet and decaying vegetation, and other things that Fura knew she'd rather not identify. As they trudged forward, she found it increasingly difficult to walk, her boots continually getting sucked into the muck and slime. Only the edges of the pools of dark and stagnant sludge were rimmed with ice that cracked underfoot as she and Kiyani skirted the water's edge. The rest seemed to have escaped the onset of winter, as if it refused to play to the tune of nature's will.

Dried and brittle vines hung limply from the bare arms of the trees like ancient cobwebs that no one had bothered to brush away as the years slowly passed by. The only thing that appeared to be living in the

Mire was the moss that clung to the sides of some trees and hung in clumps among the watery graves that Fura could swear boasted the bones of unfortunate animals. Yet, even that miniscule show of life seemed darkened by age, as if it weren't allowed to let its true colors be seen.

Prehistoric, Fura thought. *This place is downright prehistoric.*

The only thing it was missing was dinosaurs. That would have completed the picture, making it look closer to those textbook drawings of the days when the giant reptiles had roamed the land freely than Fura ever would have liked.

Rubbing her arm, Fura found that goose bumps had formed on her skin. She wanted to let out a laugh as she thought back to her first encounter with Du Reizlan and how she had compared it, in her mind, to a haunted house. The old, weathered school came across as a carnival attraction now compared to this. Even if she wanted to chuckle about it, Fura felt like she couldn't, like the surroundings would forbid any such display of emotion, the twisting hands of the trees reaching out to grab her if she dared make fun of them.

Kiyani strolled forward with caution as he restlessly kept watch. He had made them stop and make camp the night before, cautioning Fura that they not go through the Mire unless it was full daylight. Now she understood his reasoning. It didn't matter if they had run across other life yet or not, this was not a place to be spending the night if you could help it. Not if you wanted any sleep.

She had no idea how large this swamp was – Kiyani had claimed that they were only going through the eastern edge of it – but she hoped that they would breach the other side before darkness fell again. Even Kiedo walked closely beside them with his fur bristled, as if just the foreboding nature of the landscape was enough reason to be on edge.

Kiyani had bid her to be quiet as they traveled through the Mire, but Fura felt she had to say something before the fear rooted even further in her mind.

"So, why have I never heard of this place?" she asked. It was true. In all her classes the Mire had never once been mentioned. To her, it had remained as nothing more than a speck on the map that Marna had forced her to memorize with no questions asked. Before, that hadn't been a problem. Only now did the name and the place it dictated spark her interest. Now, Fura wanted to know more. She wanted to know everything about this morbid place. All the places that she had seen thus far in Izandüre had been bright with life, even if the people living there hadn't given the same impression. In contrast, the Mire felt like nothing more than a deep scar on the landscape.

Kiyani surveyed the shadows, as if searching for anything or anyone who might be listening before answering. "That doesn't surprise me. I doubt they teach the lore of it at Du Reizlan, let alone in first year classes."

"Why is that?" Fura had seen pictures of swamplands before, had read about them in Barandor, but this was no regular marshy landscape. Swamps were supposed to be alive with an abundance of wildlife, strange and mystical. The chittering of crickets and the sounds of frogs. Filled with creatures. It was for that reason that they were generally protected.

But this, this was nowhere near normal. Here, everything was dead. It was as if someone, long ago had declared the spot unfit for life of any kind. Fura wondered, as they passed, if the blackened trees were still alive, or if they were just skeletons of former life, anchored in the ground for all eternity.

Carefully pushing a decrepit vine aside, Kiyani let Fura pass before him. "It might be sparingly mentioned, but for them to go any deeper than that would likely raise questions the professors wouldn't want to answer, for fear of enticing students to come here on dares."

"This isn't some ordinary marsh, is it?"

Kiyani shook his head. "There's a legend that declares that a wizard by the name of Andoris Mithrim fell subject to the lure of dark magic. Yet, no one took notice until he vowed to use his newfound powers to lay siege to a number of the bigger cities. Fortunately, he didn't get far. He had planned on uprooting the trees and using them as a demented kind of army. But in his inexperience the spell he was using backfired. He ended up killing himself in the process, but it also left a permanent mark on the land. It's said that nothing has grown here since."

"Wouldn't that be beneficial to teach, though?" Fura questioned. "It's a lesson in the use of magic."

"For one thing, it's guesstimated that there's no one still alive who knows the truth about this place. So, it's left to question whether the stories are true or just myths made up to scare us away."

Fura shivered. "If anyone ever actually visited this place I don't think they would question it."

"You think it's true, then?" Kiyani asked contritely.

"Don't you?"

"It's a dark energy that lurks here, that's for sure," Kiyani remarked. "If there's any other explanation for why everything, save the moss, refuses to grow here, then I don't know what it is." He fell silent, before adding a few moments later, "By the way, seeing as the moss seems to thrive here, I wouldn't touch it."

Looking at the moss in a new light, Fura decided to follow Kiyani's advice. "So, this place is named after the wizard, himself?"

"It would appear that way."

"Well, isn't that proof enough that events of legend are true?"

Kiyani shrugged. "It's hard to tell what exactly people need in order to believe such things."

It wasn't until the trees started thinning and the sun came back into view that Fura realized she had barely been breathing the whole time. As if letting out a breath would disturb the sleeping malice that filled the strange forest. Knowing that they were close to the end, Fura felt as if a great weight had been lifted, each step closer to the edge leaving her lighter.

Crossing through the Mire was something Fura vowed she never wanted to attempt again. The only thing that she was thankful for was that the stories Kiyani had spoken of that were interwoven with the name had been verified as false. Or, at the least, winter just wasn't a time for thieves and criminals to inhabit the swampy land.

"Wow, we got through it," Fura said as the sunlight increased.

Kiyani glanced back at her. "Don't speak too soon," he said. "We're still on the outer edges."

After the briefing on the legend of the Mire, barely a word had been exchanged in the murky forest, for fear of their voices echoing with little foliage to absorb the sounds.

"Please tell me we don't have to go through that again on the way back."

"Shush!" There was a hint of worry in his tone of voice, foreboding in its forced command.

Just as Fura tried to make sense of it, she heard the snap of dead wood underfoot. Next to her, Kiyani tensed at the sound, knowing that it hadn't been them. Slowly, he turned to face what he had hoped, beyond reason, they would be able to avoid.

Turning with him, Fura knew that advantage was not on their side this time as it might have fleetingly been in previous situations. There was nowhere to hide, no diving into the shadows and hoping that they hadn't been seen, nor did they have the go-to excuse that they were just passing by and had gotten lost. No. Whatever lay behind them, they were on their territory.

Fura stifled a yelp the moment she opened her eyes and got a good look at their captors.

Not ten feet away stood a group of fifteen to twenty rough and tumble men. They were haggard and unshaven. Streaks of mud caked the tattered clothing they wore and the bare limbs that showed beneath. Black tattoos of unrecognizable glyphs, etched into the dark and weathered skin, were visible through the cloth. Corded muscle rippled beneath the skin of various arms as they flexed their hands, readying for attack.

This was worse than Fura had expected. She'd thought, hoped even, that maybe it'd been a pack of wolves. She hadn't expected a group of humans, devious and cunning. Though, from what little she'd experienced in this world, what little she knew, Fura already had the sinking feeling that they weren't simply dealing with members of the human race.

They don't look like the kind to talk things out, Fura thought, wishing she could sink into the soft dirt. Human or not, these weren't the kind that were simply willing to diplomatically discuss matters.

No, these were the kind of men who attacked without qualm, and hoped that no one asked questions later.

Paralyzed by fear, she surreptitiously eyed the metal length of the sword, Betrayal, that hung at Kiyani's side, wondering just how many of them it could take down before they were wrested to the ground.

Forcing herself to glance back at the men before them, Fura found that none of them carried any substantial weaponry. A few had short hunting knives tucked into the belts at their waist, but she could see nothing else. Not that they needed it. She could easily tell, even from a distance, that most, if not all of them, stood taller than both her and Kiyani. Their lithe, but thickly muscled bodies holding far more strength.

The word *Streig* flashed through her mind, but somehow it didn't quite fit them, like it was an inaccurate term for their description. There was something in their eyes that seemed more feral than the Streig had come across as. It was almost familiar in a way, though Fura couldn't think, for the life of her, why that would be.

A few of the men leered, while others dug their feet into the earth, anxiously waiting for a command.

In the center of the group, one man strode forward with an air of confidence that surpassed that of the rest. Long blond hair fell in greasy waves just beyond his shoulders, and an unearthly set of copper eyes stared back at them.

"You don't know the mess you've found yourselves in," he claimed. Though there was nothing to rightfully claim as much, it was apparent that he was the leader of this rag tag group.

When Fura looked past the man, she found that limp hair clung to emaciated faces in a tangled frame, but all of them had the same unnerving copper eyes. She didn't know who these people were, if they were even human, but they looked like they had been in a battle months ago, and had been wandering the land like ghosts ever since.

"That was a lovely story you spun back there," the man sneered, making Fura realize that they hadn't been alone in the forest for some time. Maybe, they never had been. "You have some nerve, boy, to go wandering the Mire," the man continued. "And to bring your little girlfriend with you to boot. I betcha didn't think you would run into the beasts of the land though, did ya?" The man laughed, leaning on a twisted staff that Fura couldn't recall when it had presented itself in the picture. "It's too bad, really. But, you see, it's been awhile since the Hunt, and we're starving. The Pact may prevent us from hunting outright, but it says nothing against partaking of a meal that runs into us, on our territory."

The Hunt.

Pact.

Months.

The words ran through Fura's mind, until it all came together at once. *Werebeasts,* she realized.

She'd never gotten a good look at their animal forms the night of the Hunt, but, seeing what stood before her now, in human form, Fura knew she didn't want to. What little she had glimpsed had been more than enough to incite nightmares.

Kiyani held an arm out, his opposite hand falling on the sword at his side, and stepped in front of Fura, putting himself in the Werebeasts' path. Weaponless and defenseless, Fura clutched at the metal clasp of her cloak and cringed behind him. She had no idea how this was going to go, but she knew for certain it probably wouldn't be good. Right now, nothing was in their favor.

She could feel Kiedo's tail brush against her leg as he moved around behind her, never having left their side. The wolf crouched low to the ground and bore his teeth, snarling at the group in front of them.

The leader of the beasts let out a vindictive chuckle. "A metal stick and a little dog won't protect you," he declared, directing his words at Kiyani.

Procuring a small dagger from the unraveling cloth at his waist, the Werebeast leader let his eyes drift away from them as he proceeded to dig dirt out from under his ragged fingernails with the tarnished blade. Seemingly satisfied, he held his hand out and inspected it before flashing them a wicked smile that revealed a set of pointed canines.

As if by some unseen signal, the men moved forward until they circled Kiyani and Fura completely. The blond man followed suit, never breaking eye contact as he walked slowly around his two captives as if sizing up his prey. Fura shied away as he grabbed a lock of her hair and let it slide between his fingers. "Go ahead," he whispered, leaning in close to her ear. "Run. I doubt you'll get very far, but, then again, the chase is half the fun."

She could feel his fetid breath on the back of her neck as he spoke the words. Fura looked to Kiyani for help, but his eyes were focused on the man alone.

This is the end, Fura thought. She'd had that thought plenty of times throughout their journey, but this was the closest she'd felt to knocking on death's door. *There's no way we're escaping this alive.*

"Man!" one of the men behind them suddenly exclaimed. "He's a *gold*."

A wave of sound raced through the group. "But, that means we can't do anything to him!" another of the group protested.

Their leader remained quiet, though he glared at the man who had broken the silence, before fixing his eyes on Kiyani.

"You know who that is, don't you?" another added, as if he had to remind the man to keep to whatever twisted code they lived by.

The leader turned back to Kiyani, cocking his head as his eyes turned to slits, examining him, contemplating.

"I thought you looked familiar," he said after a moment's consideration. "A lucky break, wouldn't you say?"

Kiyani shook his head. "I don't know what you're talking about," he said, finally speaking. He could feel Fura's eyes on him, wondering what was going on.

"Are you not Zariyick?" The leader asked with a smirk, as his eyes flitted to Fura. It wasn't so much a question to be answered, as a comment that dared to be spoken against.

Kiyani shook his head again, not sure if he should play it or not.

"It's definitely him!" someone shouted from the back of the group.

"You know," the pack leader said as he brought the knife in his hand closer to his face, examining its sharp edges. "You may be trying to run from it, but right about now would be a good time to lay claim to that title. It would certainly be in your favor."

"He's got the mark!" The man in the back spouted again. "I saw it! He's not just a *gold*, he's Enderline."

"That means we can't do anything to him," another repeated.

It was clear that the lot of them were disappointed, but there was also a level of hesitation in their words, as if they couldn't wait to leave the scene.

"What does that matter?" another voice spoke out brusquely, adding his word to the conversation. "He's the runaway, the fake, the family outcast…"

Their leader ran a gnarled finger along the chipped blade of the dagger. "It doesn't matter."

The man continued to argue. "You really think he would be missed?"

"It would be violating the Pact," their master said calmly.

"As if we follow that anymore!"

"Come along."

"What about her?" The man said, pointing at Fura.

"She is under his protection."

"I won't have this!" he snarled.

The pack's leader whirled around, smacking the man across the face. He waited until the troublemaker began to pick himself off the ground before speaking again. "If you go against my orders," he growled, "we'll be having *you* for lunch."

With that display of command, the men under the blond's control began to file back into the dark trees. A few threw heated glances toward Kiyani and Fura. One even growled at them. But the others, knowing that the prospect of food was long gone, hustled out of the clearing without contest, the fight gone from their eyes, dulling them to a strange brown.

When he was sure everyone was following through on his orders, the pack leader turned. Ignoring Fura, the man's eyes fell on Kiyani, as he dipped his head in parting. "Until we meet again."

77

♦♦◇♦♦

GHOSTS OF THE MIST

The mood remained somber as they continued on. Fura could still feel her heart hammering in her chest hours after the strange encounter with the Werebeasts. They had been certified dog meat. There was no other way to view it, yet, here they were, somehow still alive. With not even a scratch. They hadn't even had to run for their lives like times before.

Gold.

With that one strange term, they'd been set free as if it had all been a simple misunderstanding. She had no idea what the term meant to the Werebeasts, yet, as unsettling as that was, what was left to linger in Fura's mind was that that wasn't the first time that Kiyani had been called out as another. And not just from the people they ran across, like Master Creslin back in Du Reizlan. But, from strange, dark creatures. Why would the leader of the Werebeast pack think that he knew Kiyani? Even Tybithera had hinted that Kiyani was keeping something secret.

Overall, Fura found that she couldn't even begin to grasp what had happened back there. Nor did she feel as if she even wanted to know.

In any case, Kiyani was just as reluctant to talk about it as she was to so much as breech the subject.

The rest of the day moved on in relative silence, and both of them were content to let it stay that way.

Even at the insistence of the Werebeast leader that they had immunity from whatever rituals and mutilated rules it was that they followed, Kiyani and Fura had made it a point to get as far away from the Mire as possible before laying out camp. A few of the snaggled trees stood in sparse clumps here and there as they'd continued on, making it known that, despite escaping the swamp unscathed, they weren't completely free of its influence. They had noticed as well that the ground underfoot had grown rocky and unstable, shifting beneath their feet with each carefully placed step. It had made for uncomfortable sleeping arrangements, but after what they had been through that day,

Fura didn't dare complain. Sleeping on stabbing rocks was far better than being torn apart by Werebeasts. Trying not to think on it, she couldn't help but recall the drunk man's savage screams of terror back on the night of the Hunt in Skirvynmire.

No, they had definitely won this round. Even if they still felt as lost as ever.

It wasn't until the next day that things changed substantially.

As if pumped full of life from an unknown source nearby, the landscape had gradually brightened, something that Fura had attributed to the sun that streamed down on them from cloudless skies. That was, until she found she had to squint her eyes to see, the intensity of the light almost too much to bear.

Around mid-afternoon a monotonous roar echoed through the trees. Kiedo had perked his ears in curiosity early on, his acute sense of hearing picking up on the crashing noise long before his human companions. Kiyani and Fura both looked at one another as soon as the sound reached their own ears, wondering, if just maybe this was it.

The book that had detailed the possible reality of the Witneis had warned that it was surrounded by *'dangerous lands'* and a *'watery grave.'* Fura hadn't cared for either description, but if the Mire had been the land half of the equation, she didn't necessarily want to find out what the watery grave entailed. It was bad enough that she was afraid of water on a good day. Throw in the morbidity of the word *grave* next to it and she was out of there, no questions asked.

Unfortunately, Fura knew that wasn't an option. Though it had come to fruition, she was well aware that she would likely come across a time when she'd simply have to suck it up and face her fears. Especially in this land. Izandüre may have been pretty, but she'd quickly learned that it was downright dangerous.

Against her wishes, Fura found that the reality of her fears would catch up to her much sooner than later.

It wasn't long after their ears had been assailed by the dull roar that they came across a wide, gray river. Fura had given it one sidelong glance and had instantly felt the butterflies flare up in the pit of her stomach. If it'd been up to her, she would have chosen a different direction, but Kiyani was the one that seemed to know where they were going. He was the one leading, and it had been his choice to follow the river south.

The river rambled on at a good click, and Fura eyed it nervously as she and Kiyani followed its length. Taking heed of the direction of its flow, they allowed it to guide them along as if they were riding its rippling current. The further they traveled beside the river's edge, the stranger things became. When she'd first seen the swirling banks of mist, she'd thought it was just her imagination playing tricks, the exhaustion of traveling again taking its toll. However, before they knew it, they'd found themselves encased in a thick white fog. Blanketing the landscape in a dense wall of white, it made traveling all the more difficult, cutting off their line of sight and depositing drops of dew on their skin.

Not too far into the bank of moisture, Fura could see the hazy outline of Kiyani's body as he turned to her. "Stay close," he whispered.

Fura nodded. She had no problem following that command.

"If this is what I think it is, then we need to be careful," Kiyani continued.

"And, what do you think this is?" Fura asked, not sure if she wanted the answer. She had a creeping feeling that she already knew.

"The Mist Loch."

Stopping dead in her tracks, Fura let the name sink in, as well as all the stories and questions that had surrounded it when her professor for *Lure of the Land* had spoken of it. "The Mist Loch?" she questioned, making sure she'd heard right. Kiyani wouldn't knowingly lead them into that, would he? "As in the origin of the Ghosts of the Mist stories?"

The Mist Loch. Begrudgingly, Fura found herself trying to recall any of the specific stories the teacher had rattled off. The only image that she could bring to mind was one that the teacher had painted of dead souls floating just out of sight in the monotone sea of fog, waiting with cold hands to bring any unsuspecting victims to the other side with them.

Fura shuddered, the mist suddenly feeling colder, as if the ghosts of the story were breathing down her neck, waiting for the right moment to snatch her away.

Kiyani had stopped, waiting for Fura to catch up with him. "They actually taught you about that?" he asked as she hurried to his side.

"You would know that if you'd attended classes."

Half shrugging to show he didn't really care, Kiyani moved on. "I already knew about it."

"Have you been here before?" Fura asked, repeating a question she had voiced so many times over she knew he must have been bored of it. Yet, she couldn't ignore just how much he seemed to know on such a various array of topics.

"Fura," Kiyani replied with a sigh. "If I had scoured every square inch of Izandüre, as you so believe, I would have known where the Witneis was months ago."

Letting out a silent 'oh' Fura continued on. He made a good point. If he'd known where the Witneis was in the beginning, it would have saved them a hell of a lot of trouble.

It was a few more minutes, that seemed to drag on forever in an eternity of mist, before Fura gathered up enough courage to inquire about the other things on her mind. "These ghosts," she asked. "Are they real?"

"I guess we'll see," was his placid reply.

Fura grew ever more paranoid the farther they entered the haze, all too aware of the fact that, at times, she could barely see the hand in front of her face, let alone Kiyani's form a mere foot in front of her. More than once she had grabbed at his hand in reassurance, receiving a strange glance from him when she found it. She couldn't help her rising panic, wondering what was out there watching them. As if playing along to the tune of her fears, Fura swore she saw glowing eyes every now and then, but when she turned to look, they were always gone. And, seemingly addressing her worries about the storied ghosts of the mist, Fura was aware of undulating shapes in the dense fog. She repeatedly told herself that they were merely dark and bare trees, like those of the Mire, but they still looked too human-esque for her liking.

Just as Fura was about to try and convince Kiyani that they had taken a wrong turn somewhere miles back, the mist began to lift and the steady hum that had grown slowly into white noise turned into a full-fledged roar. Through the dissipating moisture that hung in the air, she saw, just ahead, what looked like a dense mass of strangely shaped bushes. Bits of it were bare, with branches sticking out at strange angles as if in need of an expert gardener to trim back the unruliness. A cacophony of birds suddenly added their chitters to the sounds that already assaulted Fura's ears, and she saw that a number of them flitted in and out of the foliage ahead. She watched them dance in dizzying patterns as they chased one another in fun, unaware of their confused guests.

The closer they got, the larger the shrubs got. Strangely, the air surrounding it turned into a vacant void that shimmered in the sunlight as patches of the mist lazed along.

As if suddenly caught in some magnetic pull, Fura found herself being tugged forward by some unknown force. Wary as she should have been, she wanted nothing more than to get lost in the dramatic change of land.

The lure of it was so strong that Fura had to will herself to stop when she realized that one step more and the ground beneath her would have lost all its green covering, fading into a flat, white shelf of stone.

"No way," Kiyani muttered as he stopped beside her, making Fura wonder when it was that she had pulled ahead of him.

She wanted to ask what had elicited that reaction from him, but before she could think to form any words, he'd moved from her side. Taking his lead, Fura fell in line beside him. Up ahead, Kiedo already sat, unmoving, where it appeared that the landing of weather-flattened rock abruptly ended.

Stopping just behind the wolf, Fura let out a gasp that was mirrored less audibly by Kiyani as they stood and admired the wonder that they had stumbled across.

All thoughts of ghosts disappeared, like dew being burned off by the sun, as they looked over the sight that greeted them below.

What they'd assumed was a sudden shift from grass to full-fledged rock, presented itself as the overhang of a massive cliff. The roar that had lingered in the air all throughout the day belonged to the river they had been following. Coming to the stone's edge, it cascaded over and down with great force, plummeting miles below into a deep valley. And the giant shrub revealed itself to be the very top of what was the biggest Reln that Fura had ever laid eyes upon.

She'd never seen such an imposing tree in her life, and she doubted that there was any other to match its splendor, even in this strange land known as Izandüre.

There was no doubt, in either of their minds, as they looked below, like two gods resting in the clouds, that the massive tree that swayed ever so slightly in the wind was the revered Witneis.

✧ ⌘ ✧

It took Kiyani and Fura the better part of the day to circle the precipice that surrounded the grand Reln, searching for a path that would take them safely down the rock face and into the secluded valley.

Once they'd come to the conclusion that finding a path was their only way into the valley, Fura had looked at the stone's edge with an uneasiness that rivaled even that of facing the Werebeasts again. Water was not her thing, nor were heights. And here, she faced both.

Yet, there was no other way. Though the Witneis soared to heights even above where they'd stood on the cliff's edge, it remained unreachable. It's location made for easy viewing, but kept those that didn't face a dire need to reach it away.

She'd wondered as they'd searched if this was a part of the *dangerous lands surrounding* the book had spoken of.

Short of simply jumping off the waterfall, hoping that the impact at the bottom wouldn't kill you, the only other way was down an equally treacherous and rocky slope. Though nothing had immediately presented itself, both she and Kiyani had agreed that there must be something somewhere

To her relief, they had discovered a small path that slowly wound down into the valley, what felt like hours later. The trail was heavily weeded from lack of use, and so narrow that they had to descend the bank single-file, clinging to the rocks more often than Fura would have liked. The passage was so well hidden that they had nearly missed it altogether. At least from their angle of view. It had been Kiedo in the end who'd sniffed it out, sitting, quite stubbornly, next to the spot until Kiyani relented and went to see what he'd found. It was just another time that Fura found it reassuring that they had the guidance of Kiedo in their travels. There were already times when she didn't know what they would have done without his presence.

To her body's aching relief, the sight of level ground welcomed them again at nightfall. Though it could have still been considered early, the land was nearing the full throes of winter, leaving the sun to set earlier and earlier with each passing day. Yet, even if another half hour of sunlight remained, standing on the edges of the deep bowl the Witneis sat in, they'd been introduced to an early sunset.

Sliding down the last few feet of the rocky embankment, Fura found herself taking in the grand tree from the opposite side from which she had originally viewed it. Getting a glimpse of the Witneis from above, she thought she'd understood the immensity of its nature. But now, standing at ground level with it, Fura sucked in a breath as she craned her neck to look up at the overwhelming tree that towered at least a mile above her.

She had to pinch herself to make sure that she hadn't escaped to dreamland. The pain of the motion was all too real, but what surrounded her still told a different story.

Where she and Kiyani stood, contemplating their next actions, the land was flat and mostly rocky. Here and there, small patches of grass shot forth, claiming what little nutrients it could from the sandy soil it could find purchase in. This rocky rim only protruded a few feet from the wall's edge, varying in width depending on where one stood. Where the ridge abruptly ended, water took over, lapping barely an inch below the stone, as if the bowl were filled to a predetermined level.

The water that filled the basin was a shimmering turquoise blue, its depth reflected in the crystal clear pond. And, in the center of it all, stood the majestic Witneis Reln on a large, grass-covered island.

Though the sun had already set behind the cliff face, the scene that transfixed her had barely lost any of its splendor. Rather, it was still bathed in an eerie ethereal luminescence that almost seemed to be coming from the tree itself, or maybe even the water surrounding.

"So," Fura whispered, afraid that if she spoke too loud it would break the spell that seemed to transfix the scene before her. "How do we get over there?"

Swimming would be the most obvious answer, but even though the glistening water beat out a warm greeting on the ground near her feet, Fura was less than enthusiastic about that particular plan.

Pointing, Kiyani motioned to a spot not too far away where numerous gray mounds rose inches above the crystal clear waterline, forming a rocky path clear to the other side.

"Oh," Fura noted nonchalantly, as if that had been what she was thinking previously.

Unaware of her hesitation, Kiyani strolled over to the nearest stone and strained his neck to get a good glimpse into the depths of the water below. Daintily resting one foot on the rock before him, he tested it before letting it succumb to his full weight.

The minute Kiyani's foot left the embankment things turned sour. As if an unseen switch had been flipped, the surrounding area, once almost too bright to be able to see without the aid of sunglasses, changed dramatically. They were plunged into an overcast darkness that settled over the valley, along with a ghostly mist that closely resembled what they'd traversed through earlier that morning. What was left that was visible of the water below had turned a dark gray, while clouds of debris swirled in its depths, as if something sinister were growing from the lakebed.

It was all a far cry from the picture perfect paradise it had been only a moment before.

Sensing the viable danger with the change, Kiyani stepped back onto the rocky ledge, taking care to avoid the water below.

As soon as he was back on the same ground as she was, Fura scurried over to Kiyani's side, aware that Kiedo, who stood a few feet away, had his fur bristled and his teeth bared.

Following the wolf's gaze, Fura looked across the valley and let out a shriek.

Through the dancing gray mist, she could see a dark silhouetted form make its way out of a black hole in the cliff face.

Quicker than she could blink, the apparition stood only a few feet before them, revealing himself to be a withered old man. Though ancient and friendly, he looked anything but. The way he had glided effortlessly across the valley with little to no noise made Fura uneasy. But, the fact that he stood solidly in the middle of the mist that coated the once turquoise pool, a few clicks over from where the stone path lay, with no sound of water splashing, made Fura's heart stop cold.

So, the ghosts of the mist were real.

The man looked both Kiyani and Fura over stoically. A halo of frizzy white hair floated about his head, and deep lines creased his weather-beaten face. A long scar drew itself along his left cheek, cutting through the wrinkles of age.

"I am the watcher and the protector, the friend and the guide," the man chanted in deep gravel of a voice, breaking the silence. "But, only if you have nothing sinister to hide. Nurtier you may call me, but only if your intentions are pure. Anything less and the ghosts of the mist you shall learn to fear."

Fura inched further behind Kiyani as if she could escape from the man's white-eyed gaze by doing so.

Before either her or Kiyani could think to speak, the man called Nurtier continued. "I give you this one chance to think these things through," he said, rhyming his words with a precise accuracy, though he appeared to give little thought to it. "If you have no evil dwelling then you shall be free to pass, no trials, fair and true. So stop now, think and decide, this is your own time to bide. But beware, for waiting below you, in the waters deep, are those who came before you, those who thought of nothing but themselves and in doing so, they died."

As if enchanted by the old man's words, the fog that drifted along the edges of the island housing the great Reln rose up as if commanded. Forming dark columns of mist, it transformed into the hazy spirits of a line of numerous men. Fura couldn't tell exactly how many there were, though she didn't dare count. All she could tell from this distance was that none of them seemed overly inviting. Rather, they all look weather-beaten and worn, as if life had gotten the best of them.

Further stating his point, the mist dissipated momentarily above the water and a white flash revealed the bleached bones that had settled at the bottom of the ravine. A few of the carcasses retained bits of flesh that floated in the grimy water, drifting in various states of decay.

"Here they rest, and behind me they stand, waiting to put you to the test. So, what sayeth you? Will you stay here and face an early demise, try your fate, proving yourself little wise, or," the man flashed a grin at them, "will you stay and fight. To lose such youths would surely be an unworthy plight."

Fura kept her eyes on the man, afraid to let him out of her sight for even the briefest of moments. She wondered if, what they had seen before, the brilliantly lit paradise, dotted with colorful birds and vivid colors, was nothing more than a well-executed illusion. "Let's go," she whispered to Kiyani, tugging at his sleeve.

She trusted him most of the time, but she also trusted the wolf who stayed by his side. And, right now, Kiedo didn't seem to care for the situation any more than she did. Fura could hear him growl intermittently. As usual, Kiyani remained unreadable. Where she was clearly trembling with fear, he was stoic, contemplating.

"No," Kiyani stated, loud enough for Nurtier and the spirits that resided behind him to hear. His answer echoed through the mist, bouncing off the surrounding stone and echoing back to them. "We were sent here for answers and we're not leaving until we get them."

"Kiyani," Fura whimpered. She didn't like how this was going, and already during this trip they had been too close to probable death for her comfort. Even in the face of continued death, Kiyani refused to drop that defiant air of his. "Is this really worth it?"

Kiyani turned his head to reply, "Apallo sent us here. He had to have known about this." The words were hissed through clenched teeth, the tone implying that she had better trust her father's words, because he didn't.

"But," the sudden thought hit her like a brick wall. She'd thought it once before, but now it felt like the only possibility. "What if the Shadowlord *made* him say all that about the Witneis?" Fura couldn't believe that she had never gotten around to revealing her theory to Kiyani before they'd left. The siege had been so quick, and apparently well thought out. It wasn't out of the question. "What if this whole thing is a trap?"

Pulling away from her frantic grasp, Kiyani stepped forward. His foot hovered above the stone he had stepped on before, the rock that seemed to have been the trigger for this whole display. Hopping onto the stone with all the elegance of a dancer, Kiyani stood tall and faced the man who stood amongst the mist in the middle of the lake. "I guess we'll find out," Kiyani stated, answering Fura's question.

Nurtier steepled his hands before him, an amused grin on his face. "Very well." His palm facing down, he waved an arm over the water and the fog overlying the stones dissipated, leaving it as the only visible path. Sliding backwards, he stood on the edge of the island before the Witneis, the head of his ghostly charges, and waited for the two teens to try their luck on the now cleared pass-way. "Go ahead and try your luck, but don't say you weren't warned. If you pass unperturbed this will be nothing more than a nightmare scorned."

Kiyani took a second step forward, and then another, becoming more confident with each move. He was already halfway across, still keeping an eye on Nurtier and his ghostly crew, and nothing had happened. No arrows had shot out of the sky, no leviathans had leapt out of the water. There seemed to be no traps of any kind. Only dead silence.

Fura swallowed the lump in her throat. Water was not her specialty – of course, neither were ghosts – but she decided to just go ahead and go through with it, before Kiyani turned to her with that look that so easily asked 'what are you waiting for.' He had already taken the first step into this destined madness, and according to Nurtier, once that move was made, there was no going back.

It was too late for that now, so the only way left was forward.

Taking a deep breath, she lolled by the water's edge before taking the all too literal leap. Putting herself on auto-pilot mode and setting the all too real fear of drowning aside, Fura bounded across the stones in one breath, though she stopped just behind Kiyani. Just over halfway, he'd paused as the line of ghosts approached him. Floating over the bone-filled waters, they surrounded him on all sides, their faces twisted in uncertainty.

Teetering on her stone, Fura watched the display, wondering if they would make it through this. Though a few drifted over to give her the same disapproving looks, the ones that hovered beside Kiyani lifted their hands.

Shirking away from the ones that were unnervingly close enough to her to feel their cold breaths on her skin, she could see that Kiyani's hands were shaking, as if he'd only now realized the immensity of the situation.

Before she could scream at him to watch out, one of the ghosts had taken a stand before him before plunging a translucent hand straight into Kiyani's chest. Though he made no sound, Kiyani tensed, feeling the man's cold hand wrapped around his heart.

Just as quickly as it'd occurred, the ghost released his hold, drew his hand back, and moved around him before dashing straight through Fura.

Screaming, she barely had the time to throw her arms over her face, in a fated attempt to protect herself, before she could feel the pull of the cold winds of death as they passed straight through her.

She didn't know how long she stood like that, wondering if she was dead, before she dropped her arms and opened her eyes. Around her, the ghosts had all fallen back to clear the path, though they still stood within an arm's length away beside the stones. Across the way, though visibly shaken, Kiyani stood on the edge of the opposite shore, appearing to still be alive as well.

As soon as she figured she was in the clear, Fura raced across the remaining stones, nearly ramming into Kiyani when she reached the other side. Once she was on dry land again, Fura bent over, her hands on her knees as she fought against the urge to vomit. Though the ghosts hadn't left any physical sign of trauma, she could still feel their cold aura.

Registering the look on Kiyani's face as that of question and concern, she held a hand up in a gesture that said she was okay. Shaking his head, visibly shaken himself, Kiyani stood his ground and faced Nurtier.

"Well met," the man congratulated. "The trial's come and gone, so now there's nothing left but to go ahead and move on."

The fact that nothing had happened, coupled with the fact that the ghostly man had congratulated them, led Fura to believe that the worst was over. Whatever the valley had wanted of them, they must have given it, though Fura didn't feel any different for it. Proving her assumptions correct, the dank mist around them began to lift and the bright light slowly returned to the valley. The band of ghosts behind Nurtier burned away and evaporated into the air, leaving only their leader behind.

"Don't dawdle, but take this time," Nurtier said, "to explore as you will. For now, I am done with my rhyme."

Giving a slight, respective nod, Kiyani took off, as if that was all the permission he needed.

Any other time, Fura would have been hesitant to let him wander, afraid that she would lose him, especially after what'd just happened, but she doubted the possibility. Now that the fog had lifted, she found that the island the Witneis rested upon wasn't all that big, and the shape of the basin in which it grew allowed for nearly everything to remain in her peripheral vision, a fact that Fura was fond of.

Straightening as her breathing regained its normalcy, Fura craned her head to look up at the Witneis and found that, standing amongst its roots, she felt insignificant. She had a feeling that if one were to compare them from above, from the cliff upon which her and Kiyani had stood only that morning, that she would look like nothing more than an ant compared to the behemoth of a tree.

She was unnervingly aware of Nurtier's continued presence, but she said nothing more, afraid to so much as look his way, let alone ask questions. Though, on one occasion, when she'd inadvertently drawn too close, she'd found that the old man's eyes were a milky white, though she knew from the way he maneuvered that he most likely wasn't blind.

Ignoring the feeling of worthlessness, and the unease brought about by Nurtier, Fura strode forward to get a better look at the Witneis, taking notice of Kiedo who must have just as easily come across the stones as they had, and was now curiously sniffing at the ground. The wolf looked to be at ease with the change of scenery and Fura felt better for it. If this place was of any further danger to them, Kiedo would be the first to let them know.

Upon closer inspection, Fura could see that, aside from the Witneis's massive size, it indeed showed its age. An age that would indefinitely remain a mystery, if what little information they had found on it thus far was anything to go by. She thought to ask Nurtier, but doubted that even he knew. All Fura knew was that it was a number much higher than that which she could easily comprehend. The thought of all the wisdom it contained sent a shiver down Fura's spine, and she wondered briefly just how they were supposed to go about extracting such a thing.

The tree itself was hard to pin down to an exact size, but the diameter of the base had to have been at least fifty yards across, if not more, and over a mile tall. The bark was peeling in places, and deep gashes ran along the surface here and there where it looked as if some sort of beast with huge claws had attacked it in a fury. Where most trees reached straight up into the air, this one grew and twisted at strange angles. As grotesque as it would have appeared in any other setting, here it looked grand and majestic, as if it had survived years of misfortune and still stood proud, a masterpiece and testament of the ages.

Surrounding the base of the tree were odd convoluted arches consisting of a few of the massive roots that anchored the Witneis. They seemed to have tired of the ground, breaking free and rising year after year, until they stood taller than Fura. They looked like the knobby elbows of decrepit arms trying to push themselves into the dirt to hide. Mounds of vivid green moss clung to the wood, and a tangled system of vines grew amongst the natural architecture.

Pulling herself away from the awe-inspiring sight, Fura moved to what she assumed was the front of the tree. Like many of the other Relns that her and Kiyani had happened across, this one stood atop a hollow. However, everything about this one was grand in size, and far from hidden. Though it looked like a natural play of the shadows, a doorway of sorts greeted them. The interior was dark and not nearly as inviting as Fura would have liked, but she set that thought aside. Even the customary ferns that generally grew with vigor around the Relns of the forest were more than double in size here, their feathery stalks towering far above her.

Before Fura realized it, Kiyani was standing next to her and she wondered briefly if his thoughts were the same as hers.

"Do we go in?" Fura asked, voicing the only plausible question in such a situation.

Glancing back at her, Kiyani only nodded.

78

◆◆◇◆◆

TESTIMONY FROM A WITNEIS

As if sensing their trepidation about actually entering the towering tree, Nurtier joined Kiyani and Fura at the Reln's grand entrance.

"It's up to you now, to determine what you came for, whether it be the search for lost information, answers to questions, or merely to settle a score. Go 'neath the tangled root and find, hopefully that which will settle your mind. The only advice I give here freely, don't touch the heart or you will pay dearly."

Nodding in agreement, Kiyani went to move forward, eager to get this all over and done with.

Before he could get a step further, Nurtier blocked the way with an outstretched arm. "No weapons beneath the Witneis," he declared, breaking his pattern of rhyme. His eyes flickered to the sword at Kiyani's side.

Kiyani's brows furrowed at the request, as if he still refused to fully trust the man. However, he silently did as he was told. Unstrapping the belt from his waist, he placed it, and the sword in its sheath, on the ground next to his feet. "That better still be here when we come back," he warned, with little regard that they were not the ones to be placing orders.

"Go," Nurtier chuckled. "I have little use for your ancient weapons of torture."

Though still wary of the man's request, Kiyani bowed his head before moving on into the shadow of the hollow.

Just before Fura entered the archway, she turned and asked, "Aren't you coming with us?"

Shaking his head, Nurtier replied, "No, my duties end here. You have already been found fit to enter the tree of knowledge, and only you, and you alone, know of the nature of your business. The rest is for you to figure out on your own."

"Will you be here when we get back?"

Nurtier only smiled, and backed into the light, disappearing in a haze of mist that drifted away on the wind.

✧⌘✧

It would have been romantic, Fura thought briefly, if Kiyani had taken her hand and they'd both entered the hollow together. Not to mention, it definitely would have helped to calm her nerves. However, she knew better. And she chastised herself for even thinking such a thing at the moment. That wasn't what they were there for.

Watching Kiyani stroll ahead of her with little contemplation, Fura kept her hapless thoughts to herself as she followed after him, Kiedo not far behind. Of all the people she had met in Izandüre, she couldn't have felt safer than with these two.

As soon as they entered the hollow, the darkness descended, tearing away every last scrap of brightness that had assailed them just outside. Fura blinked her eyes, but found that it did little to bring relief.

"Kiyani?" she whispered, wondering if maybe they should have thought this through first. Maybe asked Nurtier more about the Witneis before just diving under it. Or at least asked for a lamp. This could all very well still be part of a trap.

"Just keep walking," came his reply.

Fura could tell that he was just in front of her, though it would have been a lot more comforting if she could actually see him. Or anything at all, for that matter.

As if reading her thoughts, Kiyani reminded her, "This is what we've been searching for. You can't back out now."

Though she knew it was a useless gesture, Fura nodded in the darkness, knowing the truth of his words. They had to assume that the worst was already over. They had passed this so-called test. What other trouble could they possibly get into? Yet, from what they'd been through, she didn't want to know the possible answer to that question.

Reaching out, she used the wall as a guide and continued on without further comment. The sooner this was all over with, the better.

The floor sloped beneath them, leading them deeper into the earth. Walking for what seemed like miles, though, in reality was probably only a few meters, Fura spotted a speck of light ahead. She focused on the brightness to keep her feet moving, following Kiyani's silhouette. Gradually, the light grew bigger and brighter, eventually filling the whole space and chasing away the darkness behind them.

The moment she and Kiyani came forth from the tunnel, all of Fura's previous apprehension melted away.

Just when she thought this place they had stumbled upon couldn't get any more spectacular – when it wasn't filled with ghosts and foreboding mist – Fura was proven wrong. Where she'd been tentatively debating the intelligence of diving head-first, figuratively speaking, into a darkness unexplored, once they entered the space beneath the grand tree, all Fura wanted to do was look around, suddenly transfixed by her curiosity.

The dark and corroded tunnel that had led them here opened up into the biggest hollow that Fura had ever seen. It definitely put the last that Kiyani had found, the one with the extra room in it, to shame.

The walls surrounding were a gorgeous honey-oak color that shone as if it had been polished with wax. Moving closer to get a better look, Fura found that she could see her reflection in its surface. Deep grooves were carved into the walls, making it look as if they were on the inside of a screw, and creating a multitude of interesting shelves. Stored away into the crevices were little odds and ends that Fura had no doubt were magical, as well as ancient-looking texts in both book and parchment form.

As intriguing as the items were, Fura found herself drawn to the middle of the room. Resting on an alter of twisted branches was a large, delicately cut crystal the size of her head.

Kiyani already stood in front of it, quietly studying the piece. Moving to join him, she found herself mysteriously drawn to the gem. Though it was clear, as any stone of its like should have been, she could see, in its depths, a milky opalescence that swirled like an undulating mist within it. Leaning forward to get a better look, Fura could see her face reflected many times over in the multi-faceted gem.

Only inches from the glassy surface, Fura jumped back in surprise. She could have sworn that she'd heard... voices.

A hand grabbed Fura's arm to steady her, and she turned to see Kiyani scowling at her. Keeping a firm hold on her arm, Kiyani shook his head, as if to keep her from doing anything stupid, like actually touching the crystal. Neither of them knew what it was capable of.

The gem shone with an eerie brilliance that almost rivaled that of the valley of the Mist Loch. At her sudden intrusion the light that emanated from the stone began to pulse, sending waves of white ambience scattering across the walls. Only now did Fura come to the conclusion that the gem before her was the light source for the hollow, though she doubted that that was all it was.

"I assume that's the heart that Nurtier was talking about," Fura claimed.

When Kiyani finally let his hand fall from her arm, Fura asked, "What do we do now?"

"Speak your business clear and well, and the Witneis may just decide to tell..." Kiyani said, his voice monotonous as he recited a piece of the passage from the only book that had detailed the ancient Reln.

Speak your business clear and well... Fura mulled over the words in her mind, trying to think of a response to Kiyani's cryptic reply. She'd wondered about the meaning of the phrase ever since her eyes had read it in *From Seed to Trunk*, and even more so when Nurtier had repeated it.

What exactly *was* their business?

Fura couldn't honestly say. Was Apallo sending them a cryptic message on a whim really considered business, or did he actually have something set up for them here? The possibility that this could all still be a trap floated through her mind, and Fura restlessly pushed it back to the recesses it'd come from.

"Well," Fura began a few moments later, sneaking a glance at Kiyani who stood waiting. "Are you going to say something?"

Kiyani pulled his eyes away from the gem and looked at her. "It's not my business, it's yours," he said. "*The Witneis will lead the way...*' Apallo's words were meant for you, not me. If anything, he probably thought I had something to do with the siege."

She didn't know what he meant by that, but she kept her thoughts on the matter silent. Instead, Fura's heart sank as she understood what Kiyani was saying. "He had to have known you would be here as well. Apallo didn't expect me to find this on my own did he?"

It made no sense. Apallo had to have known, even then, just how little she knew of Izandüre. The fact that she hadn't even known the name Izandüre at the time must have been apparent to everyone save herself.

"I don't know what, exactly, he was thinking," Kiyani shrugged, making it known that he wasn't withholding the truth from her. "All I know is that he wouldn't have helped me alone."

"Maybe we shouldn't have come," Fura mumbled. She turned away from the crystal with the dancing light, intending to head back to the tunnel they had come in from.

Before she could make her getaway, Kiyani's hand fell upon her arm, holding her back. "We're doing this, Fura," he said, staring at her intensely. "We came all this way. We're not leaving without answers of some kind." Pushing her back towards the heart of the Witneis, he continued, "Go ahead."

"I don't know what to say!" Fura replied frantically. She'd been fearing this moment ever since she had read those accursed words, but, for some reason, she had assumed that, just like any other time, Kiyani would be the one doing the talking. The one taking the lead, the one with the initiative to puzzle this all out. If it'd been clear before that this would end up on her shoulders, she never would have come.

"Just say why we're here," Kiyani assured, as if it were no big deal. "I'll leave if you want."

"No. Stay." Sucking in a breath to calm herself, Fura took one step towards the gem. She stared at it, wondering what to say, where to even start. "Um... hi, Witneis."

Cringing at how childish her voice and her words came across, Fura looked away, hoping that Kiyani couldn't see her face and the tears that were welling in her eyes, threatening to break loose.

When Kiyani broke away from her side and wandered off a few feet behind her to give her some room, Fura hesitantly continued. "My name is Fura, and we were sent here by Apallo Feuer. The Firelord." Stopping, Fura tried to gather her thoughts better, knowing that what she was trying to say was coming across as nothing more than a string of broken sentences. "There's trouble in Frielana, and he told us to come here, that the Witneis would lead the way." A tear streaked down her face as some of what she'd gone through came rushing back to her, but she refused to wipe it away. "So," she continued, trailing off. "If you could help. In any way. It would be appreciated."

The tears fell freely now as she let her words fade away. Nothing was going to happen. They had come all this way for nothing, and it was all her fault.

Closing her eyes, Fura willed the whole scene away. She just wanted to be back in her bed. In Du Reizlan. In Barandor. Anywhere but here.

Forcing her eyes open, telling herself that she would just streak past Kiyani and back through the tunnel before he could catch her, Fura found that the gem before her had begun pulsing more rapidly. With each beat, almost as if it were the heartbeat of the tree itself, the light grew brighter. Just when she thought she couldn't stand to look at it anymore, her eyes watering from the intensity, a stream of pure white light shot out of the top of the crystal and fanned out, forcing Fura to clench her eyes shut to keep from being permanently blinded by the luminosity that drenched them.

And, just like that, the light disappeared.

When Fura felt a set of hands fall upon her shoulders, indicating that Kiyani had rejoined her, she cautiously reopened her eyes.

An array of colored mist now swirled above the Witneis's heart, twisting and convulsing with the beat of the gem itself. Dancing about merrily for a few moments, it began to arrange itself until the form of a familiar person stood before them.

Fura stumbled backwards at the sight, forgetting that Kiyani was there and running into him. "Apallo?" she choked.

Though the image before them was a picture perfect representation of the Firelord, Fura knew, though she wished she could declare otherwise, that he wasn't real. Just like the ghosts of the mist who had come between them and the tree, what now seemed ages ago, this was an imposter. Just a shimmering image through which you could see the wall on the other side. However, that didn't keep Fura's heart from hammering in her chest, or the tears from continuing to seep from her eyes.

"Dad?" she whimpered, feeling strange at having used the term for the first time with him.

"It's a holographic image," Kiyani concluded, echoing Fura's initial thoughts.

"So, he's here?" Fura asked, hopeful. She found that she wanted, more than ever, to actually speak to him.

Kiyani shook his head. "It's prerecorded. The only thing you will hear from him is the message he was trying to give at the time."

"Fura?" the replica of the Firelord spoke anxiously, coming to life.

Starting at the sound of her name, Fura replied, "I'm here," despite the fact that Kiyani had just told her that there would be no real communication between them and this hologram.

Fura's skin tingled as she recognized that it was magic that drove this place. Old magic. But what made her stomach flutter even more was the sight of her father. Not just the singular fact that his image was standing before her, but what it entailed. She assumed, from Kiyani's words, that this was how he had looked when his words had been recorded.

"Fura," the shimmering image of Apallo started again. "I'm so sorry to have to talk to you like this." His voice was a strained hush, his breathing labored, as if he were in hiding, and a smear of mud ran across his face as if he'd already been attacked at the time.

This was directly before the siege, Fura realized. *Or, maybe even during.*

"There's so much that we never had a chance to talk about. So much that I should have taken the time to discuss with you." The image turned its head as if making sure he was still alone. "However, if you're listening to this, then that means you made it to the Witneis and that all is not lost.

"I don't know if you are alone, or not. Maybe Kiyani has accompanied you."

Fura could swear that she could hear him mumble *'I hope not'* under his breath. She told herself she was hearing things, but the way that Kiyani tensed next to her at the mention of his name made her think otherwise.

"I stick to my previous word when I say that I don't want you around him." Kiyani let his hands fall from Fura's shoulders at the proclamation. "But that point may be null and void by now, not to mention of little importance if this is the only time I'll be able to talk to you.

"I regret the years that I sequestered you in Barandor, making you think that the Keeple's were your family, but it was so busy here, what with the Augden murders, the Werebeast's running rampant, and everything else at the time. Busy, and dangerous. I never dreamed that you would come to me in Fireswell, but I guess you just can't keep fire contained, now, can you?" He laughed nervously before continuing. "You may or may not know by now that I am indeed your biological father.

"I only wish that I had been able to tell you all of this in person. However, with that being said, it's easy to see that times are still dangerous here in Izandüre. I don't know what will become of me, but I only hope that you do not befall the same fate. As much as I want to see you in person one more time..." Apallo trailed off, looking frantically at the door again. It was apparent, even watching the message, months later, that he was running out of time and that his words would be cut short. Turning back towards them, he continued, "There is nothing that can be done at this time, not with what little training you have. As much as I want you to go back to Barandor and forget about all of this, I know that is no longer an option. I want you to go to the school of Du Reizlan and complete your training, for you are the Fireheir, and if anything happens to me, it is up to you to take my place." A crash sounded and Apallo fell silent again. "No matter what you do, do *not* come looking for me!" He shouted the last words as a set of hands fell upon his shoulders, dragging him down before the message and his image broke up and fell silent.

Fura could feel the hot tears stream down her cheeks as the translucent figure of her father shimmered hazily and began to fade away. It was more difficult than she had expected to see his image now, not knowing what had become of him, or if he were even still alive at the moment. What hurt more though, were his words. How could she *not* try to find him? Especially after all that she had discovered in these last few months.

"This is bullshit!" Kiyani growled.

Before Fura could turn to him to ask what he meant, though she already knew all too well, he had stormed out of the hollow.

✧⌘✧

Standing before the heart of the Witneis in the cavernous hollow, Fura stared at the holographic image of the father she'd never really known, chipped and faded like it was from centuries ago. She didn't know how long she'd been in the underground room, nor did she know for certain how long it had been since Kiyani had abruptly left. It had taken her awhile to get her body to stop shaking, not only from seeing Apallo again, but also the words that had filtered through the air. Would she ever be able to see him again, to talk to him in person at least once more?

It was all just more questions that she didn't know the answers to. And though she wished otherwise, she knew that watching the message over and over again wouldn't change its contents.

Fighting the tears again, Fura sighed and waved a hand across the image, finally letting it fade into obscurity. She'd already had her cry. Now, it was time to get up.

It would do no good to sit and reminisce on the few times they had shared. And it wouldn't bring him back any faster. No. That was up to her.

She didn't care what his wishes were. If she really did have the same fiery attitude as everyone claimed that Apallo had, then did he truly expect her to follow his expectations and just let him fall to dust in her memories? Already she and Kiyani had been through far too much on the quest to return him to power. Fura wasn't about to stop now. Even if they didn't reach that ultimate goal, all she really wanted was to see him again. To be wrapped in his warm, fatherly embrace. Thinking back to the hug he'd encapsulated her in outside her burning house the night of the fires in Barandor, Fura told herself that she'd be able to relive that moment again.

Somehow.

Some way.

Though, looking around the desolate hollow, Fura knew she had to find Kiyani first.

He'd left right after the message had reached its end, swearing up a storm during his departure. He could have been halfway back to Du Reizlan already, but Fura couldn't get herself to move just yet.

This had all the elements of just another dream sequence gone wrong, yet something in the back of her mind told her it was completely real. The glossy walls of the age-polished Reln wood beckoned to her, asking for her to run her fingers ever so gently along it, but Fura held back. It felt as if to do so would disturb time.

Wrenching herself away from the scene in which she'd last seen her father, Fura turned away from the alter and took one last look at the surrounding hollow and all its preserved glory. She had no idea if she would ever see it again. Even as gorgeous as it was, the room seemed to have lost all its luster after listening to the Firelord's disheartening message so many times over.

Outside Fura had to shade her eyes with a hand as the bright light of the misty valley stung her eyes.

Standing next to the Witneis, listening to the pristine clear blue water lap the shores of the small island, as colorful birds flitted about the air, it was hard to imagine any troubles.

But reality was far from. It always had been.

Not too far away, Fura spotted Kiyani. He'd taken refuge on the grassy ground, sitting with one leg pulled up to his chest. Staring out into nothing, he periodically whipped stones out into the water, watching the growing ripples they created as they found purchase before sinking in the shallow depths.

"What are we going to do now?" Fura asked, coming to stand just behind him. Though she didn't know if it was a good time to approach him, she followed through, anyways. Was there ever a good time with him?

Kiyani didn't even bother to look up at her. "How the hell am I supposed to know?"

Fura felt the bottom give out on her hopes, the pit of her stomach quickly becoming an empty hole. "You don't know?"

At that, Kiyani stood up abruptly. Pelting the blue waters with the remaining stones in his hand he turned to her. "I was banking on this to give us a direction. Instead, I find that we've come all this way to be told to go back and do *nothing*."

With little else to say, Kiyani stalked away from her.

Not knowing what else to do, Fura watched the circles where the stones had hit the water grow and intertwine with one another.

This couldn't really be the end, could it?

It was only at that moment, as Fura looked around at the stone valley with its mythical dream look, that she realized she'd seen it before. On a tapestry back in Fae Rue Keep.

Remembering that day she'd run from the Fae Queen, fearing what the feast might have meant, she wished that she'd asked about the elegantly crafted pictures on the walls. If she'd been her normal self, the curious girl she'd always been in Barandor, she would have been inquisitive about everything she saw. Asking about every little thing that had been presented to her.

Instead, she'd been afraid.

Of the danger she'd run from.

Of the oddities of this world.

Of the strange, winged woman herself.

Of her own shadow.

But she wasn't the only one to blame.

Clenching her teeth, Fura glanced over her shoulder at Kiyani.

If he hadn't been so stubborn... if he hadn't butted heads with Tybithera, insisting that they leave so early... Why had he been so adamant that they not tell her where they were going? Or more about what had been happening? The woman could have helped them.

Shaking her head in frustration, Fura knew it didn't matter now. Yet, she couldn't help but wonder just how different of a journey they would have had, had they known about the Witneis earlier and where they could find it.

Fura closed her eyes and took in a deep breath of the misty air. It was only more *what ifs*...

79

♦♦◇♦♦

WAVE OF DARKNESS

Standing on the precipice of the balcony, Zariah took in the sight of the changing landscape before him.

Winter's darkness had settled nicely over the land, leaving trees stripped of their colorful leaves, their bare branches reaching to the sky in twisted spires. A blanket of snow had settled over the ground, plunging Izandüre into a colorless sea of white. And the clouds overhead remained overcast, the wisps of hanging gray warning of more snow to come.

As if on cue, flakes began to fall, quickly settling into a stark contrast against his dark hair.

Yet, despite the desolation presented to him and the chill in the air, the Shadowlord had never felt more alive.

This was his kingdom of shadow and ruin.

Closing his eyes and taking a deep breath of the icy air, filled with the promise of the frozen tendrils of death, he could hear Zendel approach.

"M'Lord," he said, lingering in the doorway.

Turning his head to acknowledge his presence, Zariah simply glanced at him before returning his focus to the scene before him.

Knowing he would get little else, Zendel scurried forward to his side. "M'Lord," he said again, performing a quick bow. "They found the Witneis."

"Is that so?" Zariah said with a nefarious grin.

Zendel nodded, peering out over the frozen landscape, as if searching for how to proceed. "Would you like me to dispatch another group to go after them?"

"There is no need for that."

"M'Lord?" Zendel questioned. Was this not what the man had wanted them to avoid?

Turning his head, Zariah took in the confusion on the man's face. "Their travels are the least of my concern. Let the tree tell them whatever it wants. Neither of them know what it is they actually seek."

"Are you telling me to cease watching them?"

"No," Zariah said. "Continue to track their travels. But don't bother me with meddlesome details. Unless they get in my way, what they do is of little importance to me."

Zendel dipped his head in agreement, though he still found it hard to understand the man's words. "And Apallo?" he questioned, wondering just what the man had in plan for his prisoner.

Zariah grinned. "Do not worry. The Firelord is no longer a threat to us."

Cringing, Zendel wondered just what the Shadowlord's words implied. Not wanting to know, he let the subject fall out of favor.

"So, what do we do now?"

"Now," the Shadowlord mused, a wicked smile growing on his face. "We move on to the others."

80

♦♦✧♦♦

LOST BEARINGS

The trip back to Du Reizlan was arduous and painfully silent. As if anything living in the surrounding area could pick up on Kiyani's seething emotions, nothing bothered them. No squirrels chattered above as they passed, no birds chirped out their songs of winter, and even Kiedo bounded alongside them, subdued in his usual nature. The only thing that Fura was thankful for was that the Werebeast pack was non-existent on their return trek.

Though Fura hadn't known what to expect, she'd thought that their journey to the Witneis would give them the answer to where their path led next. Instead, not knowing what else to do, they trailed back to the school. It wasn't what had been on her mind. She hadn't had to ask Kiyani to know that he'd had the same thoughts. Yet, where Fura had steeled herself in preparation for the days of listening to him rage about Apallo's message, he had remained eerily quiet.

The subdued anger actually scared her, but from experience, Fura let him be, hoping that maybe he'd open up in the days to come.

Yet, when they returned to Du Reizlan the silence continued, made all the worse with the school's deserted hallways.

The monstrous building felt like a mausoleum. Just over two weeks they spent on the road, to the Witneis Reln and back, and still it was only half way through winter recess, leaving the halls void of the general commotion. Classrooms were closed. Passageways were deathly calm. And even the dining hall was eerie. As if the school had been abandoned completely.

With little to keep Fura occupied the days dragged on, yet the actual time that elapsed quickly muddled together. To her dismay, Kiyani avoided her most days and, though she'd initially searched for him, Fura eventually returned the favor. Even if she'd wanted to track him down it was nigh on impossible. Just as the days following his outburst after his expulsion, he was nowhere to be found.

The difference now was that she had nothing else to occupy her mind, save for that feeling of abandonment.

They'd found what they had spent months desperately searching for. The hours spent with their noses stuck in books were long behind them. The trepidation of not knowing what each day would bring, what lingered around each corner, was no more. Instead, they'd been left with the empty void of looking forward to something only to find that the actual result was severely disappointing.

Even so, every now and then, out of habit and pure curiosity, Fura peeked into the library, wondering if Kiyani had resumed his scholarly routine, but it was always empty.

The only consolation during the whole period was that Talia and Thayna had gone home for the break. For once, Fura had the room to herself, and for that she was glad. Knowing that the girls wouldn't come in during the days to cut her with harsh words, Fura found sanctuary in the room, and resigned to spend most of her time there. When she wasn't lazing the day away, napping or reading, she curled up in the window seat and watched the winter continue to take hold of the forest below.

It wasn't a bad routine. Just lonely.

Unfortunately, Rhyne had been homeward bound as well when they'd first left. She'd wished him well then, thinking that she probably wouldn't see him again. Now, she wished that he'd remained behind.

Tibben, Kiyani's roommate, was one of the few who had opted to remain in the school. Yet, she didn't even see him often. They would talk when they ran into each other, but they never seemed sure what to say to one another. Nor did he have much to report on Kiyani other than what she already knew.

Fura found it hard to believe that Kiyani would actually take Apallo's advice and continue their classes here, but she had yet to talk to him long enough to find out what he was really thinking. He was upset and not thinking clearly. That much she knew. Beyond that, however, there was little to go on.

If it wasn't for the damn enchantments on the dormitory arches, Fura would have walked right up the stairs to the boys' rooms and confronted Kiyani herself.

Instead, she was stuck with her own meandering thoughts.

Nearly a week later, with only four days remaining until classes began again, Fura found herself wandering through the dark hallways, attempting to stave off the increasing boredom. As desperately as she wanted to leave the school, continue on, do something, anything really, a part of her couldn't wait until Du Reizlan sprung back to life.

Though it meant the return of the evil twins, Fura had been

counting down the days for the past week, anxious for something, even the torture of book work, to get her mind off things. The more Fura thought about it, the more she knew, even if her father hadn't mentioned it in his message, that staying at Du Reizlan and continuing what they'd started was probably the right choice. Everyone was right. Even if they wouldn't say it straight to her face, she had heard mention of her lack of abilities more than once behind her back.

With her current training, which was next to none, there was no way she could succeed as the Firelord if that time ever came. Fura felt a nauseating sense of trepidation at the thought, but pushed it away. Now and then she thought back to what she'd had in Barandor, the life that had been so suddenly uprooted for this one. She knew, for a fact, that it would prove to be so much easier if she returned. She could figure out how to finish out her senior year of high school. Get an apartment. Be an adult. Do what normal people did. Drive a car, and get a job. Pay bills. Not do magic and live on the run. Not tangle with creatures that shouldn't have even existed.

Yet, she couldn't face that reality, could no longer imagine that particular situation.

Just going back and falling into her old life style felt wrong to her. Not to mention, half of her life had revolved around being a member of the firedancers in Fireswell. She had no idea what would become of them if Apallo failed to return.

What she did know was that this was her life now, and she was bound and determined to live it. No matter what it would take.

Despite everything that she'd been through in the last few months, everything here in Izandüre was so much more exciting and brilliant. Fura couldn't think to give that up now. Why would she? In Barandor, she had basically been a loner, a nobody, save for when she was on the stage. But here, if she played her cards right, she could make something of herself. She already had the title of Fireheir attached to her name. She was destined for greatness, if only she could get herself on the right path. And that started with learning.

Vowing to make the most of this next semester and to apply herself more than she had the previous round, Fura walked through the school with her head held high. She watched, with excitement, the way the torches flickered with the onset of her presence as she strolled past.

I can do this.

Marna would've been proud, Fura thought, to have discovered this newfound confidence. Where previously Fura had hated the thought of being tutored privately to fill in all the gaps of her nonexistent education, now she couldn't wait to go back.

The spark that she had been able to call forth from her being under the care of Marna's instruction had been growing steadily during their sessions. With the current high that she was experiencing, Fura felt that she could set the entire hallway ablaze if she put her mind to it.

If they were going to remain here, then this next semester would be the best ever. She would ignore Talia and Thayna, maybe even talk to Master Creslin to see if she could get her room arrangements switched.

Yes, that was what she would do.

Fura smiled.

This new plan of hers was settling nicely into place. She only wished that she'd felt this way the first time she had entered Du Reizlan. It would have made things a lot easier. But, it didn't matter now. That first semester was done and over, and this next one would be a major improvement.

And, Fura thought merrily, *I won't have to waste the majority of my time worrying about finding the Witneis.*

Even though Kiyani had made her work on class related subjects, the Witneis had still been front and center in her mind, often leading her mind to wander when she should have been paying attention to other things.

Down one hall and through another, she traveled on her lonesome. There was no destination in mind. All she had wanted to do was stretch her legs and clear her mind. Glad for the lack of life in the halls for once, Fura found herself stopping frequently on her walk to take in everything that she'd missed before. Taking the opportunity to actually study and appreciate the architecture of the old building, as well as the numerous tapestries that blanketed the walls. Part of her wished that she had someone else tagging along to tell her the stories behind the elegantly woven pictures. However, in the absence of someone to teach her the tales of old, she created her own fantastical myths.

Without realizing where it was she was going, or even how long she had been walking, Fura found herself in the circular room that opened before Grand Master Creslin's office. She followed the curve of the wall, drawing her hand along the waist-high ledge.

Turning to leave, Fura found herself drawn back to the area as she remembered the plan that had begun to form in her head. There was no one else around. What better time would she have to talk to the Grand Master? She would go up to the door, knock, talk to Markaelo, get her room switched to someone she could stand, maybe even actually make friends with, and make this day all the much better for doing so.

Nodding in agreement with herself, Fura strode across the room in a few bold strides and bounded up the stairs. Sucking in a breath of air, she raised her hand to knock and stopped.

She could hear voices inside, indicating that the Grand Master was indeed present, but the second was not Marna, as she would have expected. Fura thought about waiting, but had no idea how long it would take for whoever else was in the room to finish their business. Turning to leave again, Fura told herself that she would certainly come back later. There were still three days left after all. Placing a foot on the top step, Fura paused and looked back at the door.

There was something familiar about that second voice.

Knowing it was wrong, Fura pushed her conscience aside and soundlessly padded up the stairs. Instantly, she recalled the night of her arrival here and how the door had been too thick to eavesdrop.

However, tonight was different. The sounds from within weren't crystal clear but she was able to make out more than the previous time, as if the building felt that no secrets needed to be kept when all the students were gone.

Scanning the corridor, Fura squinted her eyes to look down the hallway, making sure it was clear before placing an ear to the door.

"Are you sure that that is the best option?" she could hear Markaelo ask.

"It's the *only* option," the second voice replied angrily, as if they'd been done with the conversation minutes ago.

A moment later she realized why it was that she'd been so drawn to it.

Kiyani…

Her heart beating in her chest from the sudden comprehension, Fura placed a hand over her heart and leaned against the wall next to the door. She didn't know why overhearing something that clearly wasn't meant for her affected her so much, but she could feel her overwhelming sense of excitement from before fade away into nothing.

Markaelo said something else that Fura couldn't quite make out, but Kiyani's answer was loud and clear, almost echoing in the room outside the office.

"I don't want your opinion on *my* decisions!" he shouted. "All I'm asking is that you make sure Fura doesn't get in trouble."

"Does she know?" the Grand Master asked, unaffected by Kiyani's outburst.

"Of course not."

"And, do you plan to tell her?"

"Are you kidding me? If I did that she would only insist on following me, and I can't have that!"

Fura could almost envision him wearing a line into the carpet, pacing back and forth in the small room while arguing with Markaelo. Sinking down the wall, Fura watched her hands shake. There was no question that she was the topic of conversation between the two men.

"So, why not take her?"

"I don't want her along," Kiyani replied harshly. "She would only be a nuisance."

"Would she?"

"You're not going to change my mind. She would be better off to remain here, anyways. Do you know how difficult it is to travel with someone that doesn't know left from right in this world?"

Fear seeped into Fura and she could feel her body tremble as she began to understand the implications of the words being exchanged.

He's leaving me!

What had she even done? Before their small adventure to uncover the Witneis Reln, Fura had felt that she and Kiyani had actually been getting along better than usual. He'd been talking to her. Actually paying attention to what she was saying and doing. Was this sudden return to his initial views really all to do with Apallo's message, or was there something else at play here?

Hearing a chair scrape inside, Fura bolted off the stone landing and down the hall. Kiyani already didn't want her going with him to wherever he was planning to take off to. The last thing she needed was to have him catch her eavesdropping.

Hastily turning into the nearest corridor off the main stretch of hall, she plastered herself against the wall and tried to slow her breathing.

Taken by the shadows, she watched as Kiyani strode by seconds later, his face set in a stony glare. Luckily he was too wrapped up in his seething thoughts to look around and discover her. For that, Fura was thankful, knowing she was lucky in that aspect. Any other time, Kiyani would have been too observant to pass her by that easily.

What Fura didn't like was the blatant anger plastered on his face and the tense stride of his body as he stormed down the hall, that showed all the signs of a man who had already started on the path he was dead set on. One that declared that no one could change his mind.

✧⌘✧

Fura could feel her eyelids drooping sleepily, but she forced herself to stay awake. Though the warmth of her sheets beckoned to her, she ignored their call. She was on a mission, and she would sit here, in the cold, on this window seat for as long as it took. Even if it didn't prove to be tonight, she would wait, night after night to prove her assumptions.

Goosebumps formed on her arms from the chill as the night steadily grew darker, and silence enveloped her so that the only thing Fura was aware of was her own breathing. The only motion outside was the clouds passing over the silver sliver of the moon in the midnight hour, steadily threatening to lull Fura into sleep.

In a attempt to pass the time, Fura fogged up the window with her breath and proceeded to draw on the pane mindlessly.

She had just finished writing her name in the disappearing moisture when movement from between the letters caught her eye. Wiping away the remaining haze, Fura leaned forward and squinted her eyes.

There, down on the ground, making a cautious run towards the trees under cover of night, with a pack strapped to his back and a sword dangling at his side, was Kiyani.

ABOUT THE AUTHOR

Kendrick von Schiller is a figment of your imagination.
This is a ghost story.

For more about Nyte-Fyre Prophecy visit the following:

♦♦✧♦♦

www.facebook.com/NyteFyreProphecy

https://slythranoirvaere.wordpress.com

www.twitter.com/KendrickvonSchi

Or Email at:

Night-FireDesigns@hotmail.com